MURDER & MAYHEM

THREE THRILLING NOVELS

TESS GERRITSEN

IN THEIR FOOTSTEPS

UNDER THE KNIFE

CALL AFTER MIDNIGHT

Also available by ***Tess Gerritsen***

NEVER SAY DIE

Coming soon

STOLEN

TESS GERRITSEN

MURDER & MAYHEM

MIRA

First published in Great Britain 2007
MIRA Books, Eton House, 18-24 Paradise Road,
Richmond, Surrey, TW9 1SR

MURDER & MAYHEM

ISBN-10: 0 7783 01451
ISBN-13: 978 0 7783 01455

59-0107

Printed in Great Britain
by Clays Ltd, St Ives plc

IN THEIR FOOTSTEPS

To Misty, Mary and the Breakfast Club

Prologue

Paris, 1973

HE WAS LATE. It was not like Madeline, not like her at all.

Bernard Tavistock ordered another café au lait and took his time sipping it, every so often glancing around the outdoor café for a glimpse of his wife. He saw only the usual Left Bank scene: tourists and Parisians, red-checked tablecloths, a riot of summertime colors. But no sign of his raven-haired wife. She was half an hour late now; this was more than a traffic delay. He found himself tapping his foot as the worries began to creep in. In all their years of marriage, Madeline had rarely been late for an appointment, and then only by a few minutes. Other men might moan and roll their eyes in masculine despair over their perennially tardy spouses, but Bernard had no such complaints—he'd been blessed with a punctual wife. A beautiful wife. A woman who, even after fifteen years of marriage, continued to surprise him, fascinate him, tempt him.

Now where the dickens *was* she?

He glanced up and down Boulevard Saint-Germain. His uneasiness grew from a vague toe-tapping anxiety to outright worry. Had there been a traffic accident? A last-minute alert from their

French Intelligence contact, Claude Daumier? Events had been moving at a frantic pace these last two weeks. Those rumors of a NATO intelligence leak—of a mole in their midst—had them all glancing over their shoulders, wondering who among them could not be trusted. For days now, Madeline had been awaiting instructions from MI6 London. Perhaps, at the last minute, word had come through.

Still, she should have let him know.

He rose to his feet and was about to head for the telephone when he spotted his waiter, Mario, waving at him. The young man quickly wove his way past the crowded tables.

"M. Tavistock, there is a telephone message for you. From *madame.*"

Bernard gave a sigh of relief. "Where is she?"

"She says she cannot come for lunch. She wishes you to meet her."

"Where?"

"This address." The waiter handed him a scrap of paper, smudged with what looked like tomato soup. The address was scrawled in pencil: 66, Rue Myrha, #5.

Bernard frowned. "Isn't this in Pigalle? What on earth is she doing in that neighborhood?"

Mario shrugged, a peculiarly Gallic version with tipped head, raised eyebrow. "I do not know. She tells me the address, I write it down."

"Well, thank you." Bernard reached for his wallet and handed the fellow enough francs to pay for his two café au laits, as well as a generous tip.

"*Merci,*" said the waiter, beaming. "You will return for supper, M. Tavistock?"

"If I can track down my wife," muttered Bernard, striding away to his Mercedes.

He drove to Place Pigalle, grumbling all the way. What on earth had possessed her to go there? It was not the safest part of Paris for a woman—or a man, either, for that matter. He took comfort in the knowledge that his beloved Madeline could take care of herself quite well, thank you very much. She was a far better marksman than he was, and that automatic she carried in her purse was always kept fully loaded—a precaution he insisted upon ever since that near-disaster in Berlin. Distressing how one couldn't trust one's own people these days. Incompetents everywhere, in MI6, in NATO, in French Intelligence. And there had been Madeline, trapped in that building with the East Germans, and no one to back her up. *If I hadn't arrived in time…*

No, he wouldn't relive that horror again.

She'd learned her lesson. And a loaded pistol was now a permanent accessory to her wardrobe.

He turned onto Rue de Chapelle and shook his head in disgust at the deteriorating street scene, the tawdry nightclubs, the scantily clad women poised on street corners. They saw his Mercedes and beckoned to him eagerly. Desperately. "Pig Alley" was what the Yanks used to call this neighborhood. The place one came to for quick delights, for guilty pleasures. *Madeline,* he thought, *have you gone completely mad? What could possibly have brought you here?*

He turned onto Boulevard Bayes, then Rue Myrha, and parked in front of number 66. In disbelief, he stared up at the building and saw three stories of chipped plaster and sagging balconies. Did she really expect him to meet her in this firetrap? He locked the Mercedes, thinking, *I'll be lucky if the car's still here when I return.* Reluctantly he entered the building.

Inside there were signs of habitation: children's toys in the stairwell, a radio playing in one of the flats. He climbed the stairs. The smell of frying onions and cigarette smoke seemed to hang permanently in the air. Numbers three and four were on the second floor; he kept climbing, up a narrow staircase to the top floor. Number five was the attic flat; its low door was tucked between the eaves.

He knocked. No answer.

"Madeline?" he called. "Really now, this isn't some sort of practical joke, is it?"

Still there was no answer.

He tried the door; it was unlocked. He pushed inside, into the garret flat. Venetian blinds hung over the windows, casting slats of shadow and light across the room. Against one wall was a large brass bed, its sheets still rumpled from some prior occupant. On a bedside table were two dirty glasses, an empty champagne bottle and various plastic items one might delicately refer to as "marital aids." The whole room smelled of liquor, of sweating passion and bodies in rut.

Bernard's puzzled gaze gradually shifted to the foot of the brass bed, to a woman's high-heeled shoe lying discarded on the floor. Frowning, he took a step toward it and saw that the shoe lay in a glistening puddle of crimson. As he rounded the foot of the bed, he froze in disbelief.

His wife lay on the floor, her ebony hair fanned out like a raven's wings. Her eyes were open. Three sunbursts of blood stained her white blouse.

He dropped to his knees beside her. "No," he said. "*No.*" He touched her face, felt the warmth still lingering in her cheeks. He pressed his ear to her chest, her bloodied chest, and heard no heartbeat, no breath. A sob burst forth from his throat, a disbelieving cry of grief. "*Madeline!*"

As the echo of her name faded, there came another sound behind him—footsteps. Soft, approaching…

Bernard turned. In bewilderment, he stared at the pistol—Madeline's pistol—now pointed at him. He looked up at the face hovering above the barrel. It made no sense—no sense at all!

"Why?" asked Bernard.

The answer he heard was the dull thud of the silenced automatic. The bullet's impact sent him sprawling to the floor beside Madeline. For a few brief seconds, he was aware of her body close beside him, and of her hair, like silk against his fingers. He reached out and feebly cradled her head. *My love,* he thought. *My dearest love.*

And then his hand fell still.

Chapter One

Buckinghamshire, England
Twenty years later

JORDAN TAVISTOCK lounged in Uncle Hugh's easy chair and amusedly regarded, as he had a thousand times before, the portrait of his long-dead ancestor, the hapless Earl of Lovat. Ah, the delicious irony of it all, he thought, that Lord Lovat should stare down from that place of honor above the mantelpiece. It was testimony to the Tavistock family's sense of whimsy that they'd chosen to so publicly display their one relative who'd, literally, lost his head on Tower Hill—the last man to be officially decapitated in England—unofficial decapitations did not count. Jordan raised his glass in a toast to the unfortunate earl and tossed back a gulp of sherry. He was tempted to pour a second glass, but it was already five-thirty, and the guests would soon be arriving for the Bastille Day reception. *I should keep at least a few gray cells in working order,* he thought. *I might need them to hold up my end of the chitchat.* Chitchat being one of Jordan's least favorite activities.

For the most part, he avoided these caviar and black-tie bashes his Uncle Hugh seemed so addicted to throwing. But tonight's event—in honor of their house guests, Sir Reggie and Lady Helena Vane—might prove more interesting than the usual gathering of the horsey set. This was the first big affair since Uncle Hugh's retirement from British Intelligence, and a number of Hugh's former colleagues from MI6 would make an appearance. Throw into the brew a few old chums from Paris—all of them in London for the recent economic summit—and it could prove to be a most intriguing night. Anytime one threw a group of ex-spies and diplomats together in a room, all sorts of surprising secrets tended to surface.

Jordan looked up as his uncle came grumbling into the study. Already dressed in his tuxedo, Hugh was trying, without success, to fix his bow tie; he'd managed, instead, to tie a stubborn square knot.

"Jordan, help me with this blasted thing, will you?" said Hugh.

Jordan rose from the easy chair and loosened the knot. "Where's Davis? He's much better at this sort of thing."

"I sent him to fetch that sister of yours."

"Beryl's gone out again?"

"Naturally. Mention the words 'cocktail party,' and she's flying out the door."

Jordan began to loop his uncle's tie into a bow. "Beryl's never been fond of parties. And just between you and me, I think she's had just a bit too much of the Vanes."

"Hmm? But they've been lovely guests. Fit right in—"

"It's the nasty little barbs flying between them."

"Oh, *that*. They've always been that way. I scarcely notice it anymore."

"And have you seen the way Reggie follows Beryl about, like a puppy dog?"

Hugh laughed. "Around a pretty woman, Reggie *is* a puppy dog."

"Well, it's no wonder Helena's always sniping at him." Jordan stepped back and regarded his uncle's bow tie with a frown.

"How's it look?"

"It'll have to do."

Hugh glanced at the clock. "Better check on the kitchen. See that things are in order. And why aren't the Vanes down yet?"

As if on cue, they heard the sound of querulous voices on the stairway. Lady Helena, as always, was scolding her husband. "*Someone* has to point these things out to you," she said.

"Yes, and it's always you, isn't it?"

Sir Reggie fled into the study, pursued by his wife. It never failed to puzzle Jordan, the obvious mismatch of the pair. Sir Reggie, handsome and silver haired, towered over his drab little mouse of a wife. Perhaps Helena's substantial inheritance explained the pairing; money, after all, was the great equalizer.

As the hour edged toward six o'clock, Hugh poured out glasses of sherry and handed them around to the foursome. "Before the hordes arrive," he said, "a toast, to your safe return to Paris." They sipped. It was a solemn ceremony, this last evening together with old friends.

Now Reggie raised his glass. "And here's to English hospitality. Ever appreciated!"

From the front driveway came the sound of car tires on gravel. They all glanced out the window to see the first limousine roll into view. The chauffeur opened the door and out stepped a fiftyish woman, every ripe curve defined by a green gown ablaze with bugle beads. Then a young man in a shirt of purple silk emerged from the car and took the woman's arm.

"Good heavens, it's Nina Sutherland and her brat," Helena muttered. "What broom did *she* fly in on?"

Outside, the woman in the green gown suddenly spotted them standing in the window. "Hello, Reggie! Helena!" she called in a voice like a bassoon.

Hugh set down his sherry glass. "Time to greet the barbarians," he said, sighing. He and the Vanes headed out the front door to welcome the first arrivals.

Jordan paused a moment to finish his drink, giving himself time to paste on a smile and get the old handshake ready. Bastille Day—what an excuse for a party! He tugged at the coattails of his tuxedo, gave his ruffled shirt one last pat, and resignedly headed out to the front steps. Let the dog and pony show begin.

Now where in blazes was his sister?

AT THAT MOMENT, the subject of Jordan Tavistock's speculation was riding hell-bent for leather across a grassy field. *Poor old Froggie needs the workout,* thought Beryl. *And so do I.* She bent forward into the wind, felt the lash of Froggie's mane against her face, and inhaled that wonderful scent of horseflesh, sweet clover and warm July earth. Froggie was enjoying the sprint just as much as she was, if not more. Beryl could feel those powerful muscles straining for ever more speed. *She's a demon, like me,* thought Beryl, suddenly laughing aloud—the same wild laugh that always made poor Uncle Hughie cringe. But out here, in the open fields, she could laugh like a wanton woman and no one would hear. If only she could keep on riding, forever and ever! But fences and walls seemed to be everywhere in her life. Fences of the mind, of the heart. She urged her mount still faster, as though through speed she could outrun all the devils pursuing her.

Bastille Day. What a desperate excuse for a party.

Uncle Hugh loved a good bash, and the Vanes *were* old family friends; they deserved a decent send-off. But she'd seen the guest list, and it was the same tiresome lot. Shouldn't ex-spies and diplomats lead more interesting lives? She couldn't imagine James Bond, retired, pottering about in his garden.

Yet that's what Uncle Hugh seemed to do all day. The highlight of *his* week had been harvesting the season's first hybrid Nepal tomato—his earliest tomato ever! And as for her uncle's friends, well, she couldn't imagine *them* ever sneaking around the back alleys of Paris or Berlin. Philippe St. Pierre, perhaps—yes, she could picture *him* in his younger days; at sixty-two, he was still charming, a Gallic lady-killer. And Reggie Vane might have cut a dashing figure years ago. But most of Uncle Hugh's old colleagues seemed so, well…used up.

Not me. Never me.

She galloped harder, letting Froggie have free rein.

They raced across the last stretch of field and through a copse of trees. Froggie, winded now, slowed to a trot, then a walk. Beryl pulled her to a halt by the church's stone wall. There she dismounted and let Froggie wander about untethered. The churchyard was deserted and the gravestones cast lengthening shadows across the lawn. Beryl clambered over the low wall and walked among the plots until she came to the spot she'd visited so many times before. A handsome obelisk towered over two graves, resting side by side. There were no curlicues, no fancy angels carved into that marble face. Only words.

Bernard Tavistock, 1930-n1973
Madeline Tavistock, 1934-n1973
On earth, as it is in heaven, we are together.

Beryl knelt on the grass and gazed for a long time at the resting place of her mother and father. *Twenty years ago tomorrow,* she thought. *How I wish I could remember you more clearly! Your faces, your smiles.* What she did remember were odd things, unimportant things. The smell of leather luggage, of Mum's perfume and Dad's pipe. The crackle of paper as she and Jordan would unwrap the gifts Mum and Dad brought home to them. Dolls from France. Music boxes from Italy. And there was laughter. Always lots of laughter…

Beryl sat with her eyes closed and heard that happy sound through the passage of twenty years. Through the evening buzz of insects, the clink of Froggie's bit and bridle, she heard the sounds of her childhood.

The church bell tolled—six chimes.

At once Beryl sat up straight. Oh, no, was it already that late? She glanced around and saw that the shadows had grown, that Froggie was standing by the wall regarding her with frank expectation. *Oh Lord,* she thought, *Uncle Hugh will be royally cross with me.*

She dashed out of the churchyard and climbed onto Froggie's back. At once they were flying across the field, horse and rider blended into a single sleek organism. *Time for the shortcut,* thought Beryl, guiding Froggie toward the trees. It meant a leap over the stone wall, and then a clip along the road, but it would cut a mile off their route. Froggie seemed to understand that time was of the essence. She picked up speed and approached the stone wall with all the eagerness of a seasoned steeplechaser. She took the jump cleanly, with inches to spare. Beryl felt the wind rush past, felt her mount soar, then touch down on the far side of the wall. The biggest hurdle was behind them. Now, just beyond that bend in the road—

She saw a flash of red, heard the squeal of tires across

pavement. Froggie swerved sideways and reared up. The sudden lurch caught Beryl by surprise. She tumbled out of the saddle and landed with a stunning thud on the ground.

Her first reaction, after her head had stopped spinning, was astonishment that she had fallen at all—and for such a stupid reason.

Her next reaction was fear that Froggie might be injured.

Beryl scrambled to her feet and ran to snatch the reins. Froggie was still spooked, nervously trip-trapping about on the pavement. The sound of a car door slamming shut, of someone running toward them, only made the horse edgier.

"Don't come any closer!" hissed Beryl over her shoulder.

"Are you all right?" came the anxious inquiry. It was a man's voice, pleasantly baritone. American?

"I'm fine," snapped Beryl.

"What about your horse?"

Murmuring softly to Froggie, Beryl knelt down and ran her hands along Froggie's foreleg. The delicate bones all seemed to be intact.

"Is he all right?" said the man.

"It's a she," answered Beryl. "And yes, she seems to be just fine."

"I really *can* tell the difference," came the dry response. "When I have a view of the essential parts."

Suppressing a smile, Beryl straightened and turned to look at the man. Dark hair, dark eyes, she noted. And the definite glint of humor—nothing stiff-upper-lip about this one. Forty plus years of laughter had left attractive creases about his eyes. He was dressed in formal black tie, and his broad shoulders filled out the tuxedo jacket quite impressively.

"I'm sorry about the spill," he said. "I guess it *was* my fault."

"This is a country road, you know. Not exactly the place to be speeding. You never can tell what lies around the bend."

"So I've discovered."

Froggie gave her an impatient nudge. Beryl stroked the horse's neck, all the time intensely aware of the man's gaze.

"I do have something of an excuse," he said. "I got turned around in the village back there, and I'm running late. I'm trying to find some place called Chetwynd. Do you know it?"

She cocked her head in surprise. "You're going to Chetwynd? Then you're on the wrong road."

"Am I?"

"You turned off a half mile too soon. Head back to the main road and keep going. You can't miss the turn. It's a private drive, flanked by elms—quite tall ones."

"I'll watch for the elms, then."

She remounted Froggie and gazed down at the man. Even viewed from the saddle, he cut an impressive figure, lean and elegant in his tuxedo. And strikingly confident, not a man to be intimidated by anyone—even a woman sitting astride nine hundred muscular pounds of horseflesh.

"Are you sure you're not hurt?" he asked. "It looked like a pretty bad fall to me."

"Oh, I've fallen before." She smiled. "I have quite a hard head."

The man smiled, too, his teeth straight and white in the twilight. "Then I shouldn't worry about you slipping into a stupor tonight?"

"*You're* the one who'll be slipping into a stupor tonight."

He frowned. "Excuse me?"

"A stupor brought on by dry and endless palaver. It's a distinct possibility, considering where you're headed." Laughing, she turned the horse around. "Good evening," she called. Then, with a farewell wave, she urged Froggie into a trot through the woods.

As she left the road behind, it occurred to her that she would get to Chetwynd before he did. That made her laugh again. Perhaps Bastille Day would turn out more interesting than she'd expected. She gave the horse a nudge of her boot. At once Froggie broke into a gallop.

RICHARD WOLF STOOD BESIDE his rented M.G. and watched the woman ride away, her black hair tumbling like a horse's mane about her shoulders. In seconds she was gone, vanished from sight into the woods. He never even caught her name, he thought. He'd have to ask Lord Lovat about her. *Tell me, Hugh. Are you acquainted with a black-haired witch tearing about your neighborhood?* She was dressed like one of the village girls, in a frayed shirt and grass-stained jodhpurs, but her accent bespoke the finest of schools. A charming contradiction.

He climbed back into the car. It was almost six-thirty now; that drive from London had taken longer than he'd expected. Blast these backcountry lanes! He turned the car around and headed for the main road, taking care this time to slow down for curves. No telling what might be lurking around the bend. A cow or a goat.

Or another witch on horseback.

I have quite a hard head. He smiled. A hard head, indeed. She slips off the saddle—bump—and she's right back on her feet. And cheeky to boot. As if I couldn't tell a mare from a stallion. All I needed was the right view.

Which he certainly had had of her. There was no doubt whatsoever that it was the female of the species he'd been looking at. All that raven hair, those laughing green eyes. *She almost reminds me of…*

He suppressed the thought, shoved it into the quicksand of bad memories. Nightmares, really. Those terrible echoes of his first assignment, his first failure. It had colored his career, had kept him from ever again taking anything for granted. That was the way one *should* operate in this business. Check the facts, never trust your sources, and always, always watch your back.

It was starting to wear him down. *Maybe I should kick back and retire early. Live the quiet country life like Hugh Tavistock.* Of course Tavistock had a title and estate to keep him in comfort, though Richard had to laugh when he thought of the rotund and balding Hugh Tavistock as earl of anything. *Yeah, I should just settle down on those ten acres in Connecticut. Declare myself Earl of Whatever and grow cucumbers.*

But he'd miss the work. Those delicious whiffs of danger, the international chess game of wits. The world was changing so fast, and you didn't know from day to day who your enemies were….

He spotted, at last, the turnoff to Chetwynd. Flanked by majestic elms, it was as the black-haired woman had described it. That impressive driveway was more than matched by the manor house standing at the end of the road. This was no mere country cottage; this was a castle, complete with turrets and ivy-covered stone walls. Formal gardens stretched out for acres, and a brick path led to what looked like a medieval maze. So this was where old Hugh Tavistock had repaired to after those forty years of service to queen and country. Earldom must have its benefits—one certainly didn't acquire this much wealth in government service. And Hugh had struck him as such a down-to-earth fellow! Not at all the country nobleman type. He had no airs, no pretensions; he was more like some absentminded civil servant who'd wandered, quite by accident, into MI6's inner sanctum.

Amused by the grandeur of it all, Richard went up the steps, breezed through the security gauntlet, and walked into the ballroom.

Here he saw a number of familiar faces among the dozens of guests who'd already arrived. The London economic summit had drawn in diplomats and financiers from across the continent. He spotted at once the American ambassador, swaggering and schmoozing like the political appointee he was. Across the room he saw a trio of old acquaintances from Paris. There was Philippe St. Pierre, the French finance minister, deep in conversation with Reggie Vane, head of the Paris Division, Bank of London. Off to the side stood Reggie's wife, Helena, looking ignored and crabby as usual. Had Richard *ever* seen that woman look happy?

A woman's loud and brassy laugh drew Richard's attention to another familiar figure from his Paris days—Nina Sutherland, the ambassador's widow, shimmering from throat to ankle in green silk and bugle beads. Though her husband was long dead, the old gal was still working the crowd like a seasoned diplomat's wife. Beside her was her twenty-year-old son, Anthony, rumored to be an artist. In his purple shirt, he cut just as flashy a figure as his mother did. What a resplendent pair they were, like a couple of peacocks! Young Anthony had obviously inherited his ex-actress mother's gene for flamboyance.

Judiciously avoiding the Sutherland pair, Richard headed to the buffet table, which was graced with an elaborate ice sculpture of the Eiffel Tower. This Bastille Day theme had been carried to ridiculous extremes. *Everything* was French tonight: the music, the champagne, the tricolors hanging from the ceiling.

"Rather makes one want to burst out singing the 'Marseillaise,' doesn't it?" said a voice.

Richard turned and saw a tall blond man standing beside him. Slenderly built, with the stamp of aristocracy on his face, he seemed elegantly at ease in his starched shirt and tuxedo. Smiling, he handed a glass of champagne to Richard. The chandelier light glittered in the pale bubbles. "You're Richard Wolf," the man said.

Richard nodded, accepting the glass. "And you are…?"

"Jordan Tavistock. Uncle Hugh pointed you out as you walked into the room. Thought I'd come by and introduce myself."

The two men shook hands. Jordan's grip was solid and connected, not what Richard expected from such smoothly aristocratic hands.

"So tell me," said Jordan, casually picking up a second glass of champagne for himself, "which category do you fit into? Spy, diplomat or financier?"

Richard laughed. "I'm expected to answer that question?"

"No. But I thought I'd ask, anyway. It gets things off to a flying start." He took a sip and smiled. "It's a mental exercise of mine. Keeps these parties interesting. I try to pick up on the cues, deduce which ones are with Intelligence. And half of these people are. Or were." Jordan gazed around the room. "Think of all the secrets contained in all these heads—all those little synapses snapping with classified data."

"You seem to have more than a passing acquaintance with the business."

"When one grows up in this household, one lives and breathes the game." Jordan regarded Richard for a moment. "Let's see. You're American…."

"Correct."

"And whereas the corporate executives arrived in groups by stretch limousine, you came on your own."

"Right so far."

"And you refer to intelligence work as *the business*."

"You noticed."

"So my guess is…CIA?"

Richard shook his head and smiled. "I'm just a private security consultant. Sakaroff and Wolf, Inc."

Jordan smiled back. "Clever cover."

"It's not a cover. I'm the real thing. All these corporate executives you see here want a safe summit. An IRA bomb could ruin their whole day."

"So they hire you to keep the nasties away," finished Jordan.

"Exactly," said Richard. And he thought, *Yes, this is Madeline and Bernard's son, all right. He resembles Bernard, has got the same sharply observant brown eyes, the same finely wrought features. And he's quick. He notices things—an indispensable talent.*

At that moment, Jordan's attention suddenly shifted to a new arrival. Richard turned to see who had just entered the ballroom. At his first glimpse of the woman, he stiffened in surprise.

It was that black-haired witch, dressed not in old jodhpurs and boots this time, but in a long gown of midnight blue silk. Her hair had been swept up into an elegant mass of waves. Even from this distance, he could feel the magical spell of her attraction—as did every other man in the room.

"It's her," murmured Richard.

"You mean you two have met?" asked Jordan.

"Quite by accident. I spooked her horse on the road. She was none too pleased about the fall."

"You actually unhorsed her?" said Jordan in amazement. "I didn't think it was possible."

The woman glided into the room and swept up a glass of champagne from a tray, her progress cutting a noticeable swath through the crowd.

"She certainly knows how to fill a dress," Richard said under his breath, marveling.

"I'll tell her you said so," Jordan said dryly.

"You wouldn't."

Laughing, Jordan set down his glass. "Come on, Wolf. Let me properly introduce you."

As they approached her, the woman flashed Jordan a smile of greeting. Then her gaze shifted to Richard, and instantly her expression went from easy familiarity to a look of cautious speculation. *Not good,* thought Richard. *She's remembering how I knocked her off that horse. How I almost got her killed.*

"So," she said, civilly enough, "we meet again."

"I hope you've forgiven me."

"Never." Then she smiled. What a smile!

Jordan said, "Darling, this is Richard Wolf."

The woman held out her hand. Richard took it and was surprised by the firm, no-nonsense handshake she returned. As he looked into her eyes, a shock of recognition went through him. *Of course. I should have seen it the very first time we met. That black hair. Those green eyes. She has to be Madeline's daughter.*

"May I introduce Beryl Tavistock," said Jordan. "My sister."

"SO HOW DO YOU HAPPEN to know my Uncle Hugh?" Beryl asked as she and Richard strolled down the garden path. Dusk had fallen, that soft, late dusk of summer, and the flowers had faded into shadow. Their fragrance hung in the air, the scent of sage and roses, lavender and thyme. *He moves like a cat in the darkness,* Beryl thought. *So quiet, so unfathomable.*

"We met years ago in Paris," he said. "We lost touch for a long time. And then, a few years ago, when I set up my consulting firm, your uncle was kind enough to advise me."

"Jordan tells me your company's Sakaroff and Wolf."

"Yes. We're security consultants."

"And is that your real job?"

"Meaning what?"

"Have you a, shall we say, *unofficial* job?"

He threw back his head and laughed. "You and your brother have a knack for cutting straight to the chase."

"We've learned to be direct. It cuts down on the small talk."

"Small talk is society's lubricant."

"No, small talk is how society avoids telling the truth."

"And you want to hear the truth," he said.

"Don't we all?" She looked up at him, trying to see his eyes in the darkness, but they were only shadows in the silhouette of his face.

"The truth," he said, "is that I really am a security consultant. I run the firm with my partner, Niki Sakaroff—"

"Niki? That wouldn't be Nikolai Sakaroff?"

"You've heard the name?" he asked, in a tone that was just a trifle too innocent.

"Former KGB?"

There was a pause. "Yes, at one time," he said evenly. "Niki may have had connections."

"Connections? If I recall correctly, Nikolai Sakaroff was a full colonel. And now he's your business partner?" She laughed. "Capitalism does indeed make strange bedfellows."

They walked a few moments in silence. She asked quietly, "Do you still do business for the CIA?"

"Did I say I did?"

"It's not a difficult conclusion to come to. I'm very discreet, by the way. The truth is safe with me."

"Nevertheless I refuse to be interrogated."

She looked up at him with a smile. "Even under torture, I assume?"

Through the darkness she could see his teeth gleaming in a grin. "That depends on the type of torture. If a beautiful woman nibbles on my ear, well, I might admit to anything."

The brick path ended at the maze. For a while, they stood contemplating that leafy wall of shadow.

"Come on, let's go in," she said.

"Do you know the way out?"

"We'll see."

She led him through the opening and they were quickly swallowed up by hedge walls. In truth, she knew every turn, every blind end, and she moved through the maze with confidence. "I could do this blindfolded," she said.

"Did you grow up at Chetwynd?"

"In between boarding schools. I came to live with Uncle Hugh when I was eight. After Mum and Dad died."

They rustled through the last slot in the hedge and emerged into the center. In a small clearing there was a stone bench and enough moonlight to faintly see each other's face.

"They were in the business, too," she said, circling the grassy clearing slowly. "Or did you already know that?"

"Yes, I've…heard of your parents."

At once she sensed an undertone of caution in his voice and wondered why he'd gone evasive on her. She saw that he was standing by the stone bench, his hands in his pockets. *All these family secrets. I'm sick of it. Why can't anyone ever tell the truth in this house?*

"What have you heard about them?" she asked.

"I know they died in Paris."

"In the line of duty. Uncle Hugh says it was a classified mission and refuses to talk about it, so we never do." She stopped circling and turned to face him. "I seem to be thinking about it a lot these days."

"Why?"

"Because it happened on the fifteenth of July. Twenty years ago tomorrow."

He moved toward her, his face still hidden in shadow. "Who reared you, then? Your uncle?"

She smiled. "'Reared' is a bit of an exaggeration. Uncle Hugh gave us a home, and then he pretty much turned us loose to grow up as we pleased. Jordan's done quite well for himself, I think. Gone to university and all. But then, Jordie's the smart one in the family."

Richard moved closer—so close she thought she could see his eyes glittering above her in the darkness. "And which one are you?"

"I suppose…I suppose I'm the wild one."

"The wild one," he murmured. "Yes, I think I can tell…."

He touched her face. With that one brief contact, he left her skin tingling. She was suddenly aware of her pounding heart, her quickening breath. *Why am I letting this happen?* she wondered. *I thought I'd sworn off romance. But now this man I scarcely know is dragging me back into the game—a game at which I've proved myself a miserable failure. It's stupid, it's impulsive. It's insanity itself.*

And it's leaving me quite hungry for more….

His lips grazed hers; it was the lightest of kisses, but it was heady with the taste of champagne. At once she craved another kiss, a longer kiss. For a moment, they stared at each other, both hovering on the edge of temptation.

Beryl surrendered first. She swayed toward him, against him. His arms went around her, trapping her in their embrace. Eagerly she met his lips, met his kiss with one just as fierce.

"The wild one," he whispered. "Yes, definitely the wild one."

"Demanding, too…"

"I don't doubt it."

"...and *very* difficult."

"I hadn't noticed...."

They kissed again, and by the ragged sound of his breathing, she knew that he, too, was a helpless victim of desire. Suddenly a devilish impulse seized her.

She pulled away. Coyly she asked, "Now will you tell me?"

"Tell you what?" he asked, plainly confused.

"Whom you really work for?"

He paused. "Sakaroff and Wolf, Inc.," he said. "Security consultants."

"Wrong answer," she said. Then, laughing wickedly, she turned and scampered out of the maze.

Paris

AT 8:45, AS WAS HER HABIT, Marie St. Pierre patted on her bee pollen face cream, ran a brush through her stiff gray hair, and then slipped under the covers of her bed. She flicked on the TV remote control and awaited her favorite program of the week—"Dynasty." Though the voices were obviously dubbed and the settings garishly American, the stories were close to her heart. Love and power. Pain and retribution. Yes, Marie knew all about love and pain. It was the retribution part she hadn't quite mastered. Every time the anger bubbled up inside her and those old fantasies of revenge began to play out in her mind, she had only to consider the consequences of such action, and all thoughts of vengeance died. No, she loved Philippe too much. And they had come so far together! From finance minister to prime minister would be such a short, short climb....

She suddenly focused on the TV as a brief news item flashed on the screen—the London economic summit. Would Philippe's face appear? No, just a pan of the conference table, a five-second view of two dozen men in suits and ties. No Philippe. She sat back in disappointment and wondered, for the hundredth time, if she should have accompanied her husband to London. She hated to fly, and he'd warned her the trip would be tiresome. Better to stay home, he'd told her; she would hate London.

Still, it might have been nice to go away with him for a few days. Just the two of them in a hotel room. A change of scenery, a new bed. It might have been the spark their marriage so terribly needed—

A thought suddenly crossed her mind. A thought so painful that it twisted her heart in knots. *Here I am. And there is Philippe, alone in London….*

Or was he alone?

She sat trembling for a moment, considering the possibilities. The images. At last she could resist the impulse no longer. She reached for the telephone and dialed Nina Sutherland's Paris apartment.

The phone rang and rang. She hung up and dialed again. Still it rang unanswered. She stared at the receiver. So Nina has gone to London, too, she thought. And there they would be together, in his hotel room. *While I wait at home in Paris.*

She rose from the bed. "Dynasty" had just come on the TV; she ignored it. Instead she got dressed. *Perhaps I am jumping to conclusions,* she thought. *Perhaps Nina is really home and refuses to answer her telephone.*

She would drive past Nina's apartment in Neuilly. Check the windows to see if her lights were on inside.

And if they were not?

No, she wouldn't think about that, not yet.

Fully dressed now, she hurried downstairs, picked up her purse and keys in the darkened living room, and opened the front door. Just as she felt the night air against her face, her ears were blasted by a deafening roar.

The explosion threw her off her feet, flinging her forward down the front steps. Only her outstretched arms beneath her prevented her head from slamming against the concrete. She was vaguely aware of glass raining down around her and then of the soft crackle of flames. Slowly she managed to roll over onto her back. There she lay, staring upward at the fingers of fire shooting through her bedroom window.

It was meant for her, she thought. The bomb was meant for her.

As fire sirens wailed closer, she lay on her back in the broken glass and thought, *Is this what it's come to, my love?*

And she watched her bedroom burn above her.

Chapter Two

Buckinghamshire, England

THE EIFFEL TOWER was melting. Jordan stood beside the buffet table and watched the water drip, drip from the ice sculpture into the silver platter of oysters below it. So much for Bastille Day, he thought wearily. Another night, another party. And this one's about run its course.

"You have had more than enough oysters for one night, Reggie," said a peevish voice. "Or have you forgotten your gout?"

"Haven't had an attack in months."

"Only because *I've* been watching your diet," said Helena.

"Then tonight, dear," said Reggie, plucking up another oyster, "would you mind looking the other way?" He lifted the shell to his mouth and tipped the oyster. Nirvana was written on his face as the slippery glob slid into his throat.

Helena shuddered. "It's disgusting, eating a live animal." She glanced at Jordan, noting his quietly bemused look. "Don't you agree?"

Jordan gave a diplomatic shrug. "A matter of upbringing, I suppose. In some cultures, they eat termites. Or quivering fish. I've even heard of monkeys, their heads shaved, immobilized—"

"Oh, please," groaned Helena.

Jordan quickly escaped before the marital spat could escalate. It was not a healthy place to be, caught between a feuding husband and wife. Lady Helena, he suspected, normally held the upper hand; money usually did.

He wandered over to join Finance Minister Philippe St. Pierre and found himself trapped in a lecture on world economics. The summit was a failure, Philippe declared. The Americans want trade concessions but refuse to learn fiscal responsibility. And on and on and on. It was almost a relief when bugle-beaded Nina Sutherland swept into the conversation, trailing her peacock son, Anthony.

"It's not as if Americans are the only ones who have to clean up their act," snorted Nina. "We're none of us doing very well these days, even the French. Or don't you agree, Philippe?"

Philippe flushed under her direct gaze. "We are all of us having difficulties, Nina—"

"Some of us more than others."

"It is a worldwide recession. One must be patient."

Nina's jaw shot up. "And what if one cannot afford to wait?" She drained her glass and set it down sharply. "What then, Philippe, darling?"

Conversation suddenly ceased. Jordan noticed that Helena was watching them amusedly, that Philippe was clutching his glass in a white-knuckled fist. What the blazes was going on here? he wondered. Some private feud? Bizarre tensions were weaving through the gathering tonight. Perhaps it's all that free-flowing champagne. Certainly Reggie had had too much. Their portly houseguest had wandered from the oyster tray to the champagne table. With an unsteady hand, he picked up yet another glass and raised it to his lips. No one was acting quite right tonight. Not even Beryl.

Certainly not Beryl.

He spied his sister as she reentered the ballroom. Her cheeks were flushed, her eyes glittering with some unearthly fire. Close on her heels was the American, looking just as flushed and more than a little bothered. Ah, thought Jordan with a smile. A bit of hanky-panky in the garden, was it? Well, good for her. Poor

Beryl could use some fresh romance in her life, anything to make her forget that chronically unfaithful surgeon.

Beryl whisked up a glass of champagne from a passing servant and headed Jordan's way. "Having fun?" she asked him.

"Not as much as you, I suspect." He glanced across at Richard Wolf, who'd just been waylaid by some American businessman. "So," he whispered, "did you wring a confession out of him?"

"Not a thing." She smiled over her champagne glass. "Extremely tight-lipped."

"Really?"

"But I'll have another go at him later. After I let him cool his heels for a while."

Lord, how beautiful his baby sister could be when she was happy, thought Jordan. Which, it seemed, wasn't very often lately. Too much passion in that heart of hers; it made her far more vulnerable than she'd ever admit. For a year now she'd been lying doggo, had dropped out entirely from the old mating game. She'd even given up her charity work at St. Luke's—a job she'd dearly loved. It was too painful, always running into her ex-lover on the hospital grounds.

But tonight the old sparkle was back in her eyes and he was glad to see it. He noticed how it flared even more brightly as Richard Wolf glanced her way. All those flirtatious looks passing back and forth! He could almost feel the crackle of electricity flying between them.

"…a well-deserved honor, of course, but a bit late, don't you think, Jordan?"

Jordan glanced in puzzlement at Reggie Vane's flushed face. The man had been drinking entirely too much. "Excuse me," he said, "I'm afraid I wasn't following."

"The Queen's medal for Leo Sinclair. You remember Leo, don't you? Wonderful chap. Killed a year and a half ago. Or was it two years?" He gave his head a little shake, as though to clear it. "Anyway, they're just getting 'round to giving the widow his medal. I think that's inexcusable."

"Not everyone who was killed in the Gulf got a medal," Nina Sutherland cut in.

"But Leo was Intelligence," said Reggie. "He deserved some sort of honor, considering how he…died."

"Perhaps it was just an oversight," said Jordan. "Papers getting mislaid, that sort of thing. MI6 does try to honor its dead, and Leo sort of fell through the cracks."

"The way Mum and Dad did," said Beryl. "They died in the line of duty. And they never got a medal."

"Line of duty?" said Reggie. "Not exactly." He lifted the champagne glass unsteadily to his lips. Suddenly he paused, aware that the others were staring at him. The silence stretched on, broken only by the clatter of an oyster shell on someone's plate.

"What do you mean by 'not exactly'?" asked Beryl.

Reggie cleared his throat. "Surely…Hugh must have told you…." He looked around and his face blanched. "Oh, no," he murmured, "I've put my foot in it this time."

"Told us what, Reggie?" Jordan persisted.

"But it was public knowledge," said Reggie. "It was in all the Paris newspapers…."

"Reggie," Jordan said slowly. Deliberately. "Our understanding was that my mother and father were shot in Paris. That it was murder. Is that not true?"

"Well, of course there was a murder involved—"

"*A* murder?" Jordan cut in. "As in singular?"

Reggie glanced around, befuddled. "I'm not the only one here who knows about it. You were all in Paris when it happened!"

For a few heartbeats, no one said a thing. Then Helena added, quietly, "It was a very long time ago, Jordan. Twenty years. It hardly makes a difference now."

"It makes a difference to *us*," Jordan insisted. "What happened in Paris?"

Helena sighed. "I told Hugh he should've been honest with you, instead of trying to bury it."

"Bury *what?*" asked Beryl.

Helena's mouth drew tight.

It was Nina who finally spoke the truth. Brazen Nina, who had never bothered with subtleties. She said flatly, "The police said it was a murder. Followed by a suicide."

Beryl stared at Nina. Saw the other woman's gaze meet hers without flinching. "No," she whispered.

Gently Helena touched her shoulder. "You were just a child,

Beryl. Both of you were. And Hugh didn't think it was appropriate—"

Beryl said again, "No," and pulled away from Helena's outstretched hand. Suddenly she whirled and fled in a rustle of blue silk across the ballroom.

"Thank you. All of you," said Jordan coldly. "For your most refreshing candor." Then he, too, turned and headed across the room in pursuit of his sister.

He caught up with her on the staircase. "Beryl?"

"It's not true," she said. "I don't believe it!"

"Of course it's not true."

She halted on the stairs and looked down at him. "Then why are they all saying it?"

"Ugly rumors. What else can it be?"

"Where's Uncle Hugh?"

Jordan shook his head. "He's not in the ballroom."

Beryl looked up toward the second floor. "Come on, Jordie," she said, her voice tight with determination. "We're going to set this thing straight."

Together they climbed the stairs.

Uncle Hugh was in his study; through the closed door, they could hear him speaking in urgent tones. Without knocking, they pushed inside and confronted him.

"Uncle Hugh?" said Beryl.

Hugh cut her off with a sharp motion for silence. He turned his back and said into the telephone, "It *is* definite, Claude? Not a gas leak or anything like that?"

"Uncle Hugh!"

Stubbornly he kept his back turned to her. "Yes, yes," he said into the phone, "I'll tell Philippe at once. God, this is horrid timing, but you're right, he has no choice. He'll have to fly back tonight." Looking stunned, Hugh hung up and stared at the telephone.

"Did you tell us the truth?" asked Beryl. "About Mum and Dad?"

Hugh turned and frowned at her in bewilderment. "What? What are you talking about?"

"You told us they were killed in the line of duty," said Beryl. "You never said anything about a suicide."

"Who told you that?" he snapped.

"Nina Sutherland. But Reggie and Helena knew about it, too. In fact, the whole world seems to know! Everyone except us."

"Blast that Sutherland woman!" roared Hugh. "She had no right."

Beryl and Jordan stared at him in shock. Softly Beryl said, "It *is* a lie. Isn't it?"

Abruptly Hugh started for the door. "We'll discuss it later," he said. "I have to take care of this business—"

"Uncle Hugh!" cried Beryl. "Is it a lie?"

Hugh stopped. Slowly he turned and looked at her. "I never believed it," he said. "Not for a second did I think Bernard would ever hurt her…."

"What are you saying?" asked Jordan. "That it was Dad who killed her?"

Their uncle's silence was the only answer they needed. For a moment, Hugh lingered in the doorway. Quietly he said, "Please, Jordan. We'll talk about it later. After everyone leaves. Now I really must see to this phone call." He turned and left the room.

Beryl and Jordan looked at each other. They each saw, in the other's eyes, the same shock of comprehension.

"Dear God, Jordie," said Beryl. "It must be true."

FROM ACROSS THE BALLROOM, Richard saw Beryl's hasty exit and then, seconds later, the equally rapid departure of a grim-faced Jordan. What the hell was going on? he wondered. He started to follow them out of the room, then spotted Helena, shaking her head as she moved toward him.

"It's a disaster," she muttered. "Too much bloody champagne flowing tonight."

"What happened?"

"They just heard the truth. About Bernard and Madeline."

"Who told them?"

"Nina. But it was Reggie's fault, really. He's so drunk he doesn't know what he's saying."

Richard looked at the doorway through which Jordan had just vanished. "I should talk to them, tell them the whole story."

"I think that's their uncle's responsibility. Don't you? He's the one who kept it from them all these years. Let him do the explaining."

After a pause, Richard nodded. "You're right. Of course you're right. Maybe I'll just go and strangle Nina Sutherland instead."

"Strangle my husband while you're at it. You have my permission."

Richard turned and spotted Hugh Tavistock reentering the ballroom. "Now what?" he muttered as the man hurried toward them.

"Where's Philippe?" snapped Hugh.

"I believe he was headed out to the garden," said Helena. "Is something wrong?"

"This whole evening's turned into a disaster," muttered Hugh. "I just got a call from Paris. A bomb's gone off in Philippe's flat."

Richard and Helena stared at him in horror.

"Oh, my God," whispered Helena. "Is Marie—"

"She's all right. A few minor injuries, but nothing serious. She's in hospital now."

"Assassination attempt?" Richard queried.

Hugh nodded. "So it would seem."

IT WAS LONG PAST MIDNIGHT when Jordan and Uncle Hugh finally found Beryl. She was in her mother's old room, huddled beside Madeline's steamer trunk. The lid had been thrown open, and Madeline's belongings were spilled out across the bed and the floor: silky summer dresses, flowery hats, a beaded evening purse. And there were silly things, too: a branch of sea coral, a pebble, a china frog—items of significance known only to Madeline. Beryl had removed all of these things from the trunk, and now she sat surrounded by them, trying to absorb, through these inanimate objects, the warmth and spirit that had once been Madeline Tavistock.

Uncle Hugh came into the bedroom and sat down in a chair beside her. "Beryl," he said gently, "it's time…it's time I told you the truth."

"The time for the truth was years ago," she said, staring down at the china frog in her hand.

"But you were both so very young. You were only eight, and Jordan was ten. You wouldn't have understood—"

"We could've dealt with the facts! Instead you hid them from us!"

"The facts were painful. The French police concluded—"

"Dad would *never* have hurt her," said Beryl. She looked up at him with a ferocity that made Hugh draw back in surprise. "Don't you remember how they were together, Uncle Hugh? How much in love they were? *I* remember!"

"So do I," said Jordan.

Uncle Hugh took off his spectacles and wearily rubbed his eyes. "The truth," he said, "is even worse than that."

Beryl stared at him incredulously. "How could it be any worse than murder and suicide?"

"Perhaps...perhaps you should see the file." He rose to his feet. "It's upstairs. In my office."

They followed their uncle to the third floor, to a room they seldom visited, a room he always kept locked. He opened the cabinet and pulled a folder from the drawer. It was a classified MI6 file labeled Tavistock, Bernard and Madeline.

"I suppose I...I'd hoped to protect you from this," said Hugh. "The truth is, I myself don't believe it. Bernard didn't have a traitorous bone in his body. But the evidence was there. And I don't know any other way to explain it." He handed the file to Beryl.

In silence she opened the folder. Together she and Jordan paged through the contents. Inside were copies of the Paris police report, including witness statements and photographs of the murder scene. The conclusions were as Nina Sutherland had told them. Bernard had shot his wife three times at close range and had then put the gun to his own head and pulled the trigger. The crime photos were too horrible to dwell on; Beryl flipped quickly past those and found herself staring at another report, this one filed by French Intelligence. In disbelief, she read and reread the conclusions.

"This isn't possible," she said.

"It's what they found. A briefcase with classified NATO files. Allied weapons data. It was in the garret, where their bodies were discovered. Bernard had those files with him when he died—files that shouldn't have been out of the embassy building."

"How do you know *he* took them?"

"He had access, Beryl. He was our Intelligence liaison to NATO. For months, Allied documents were showing up in East

German hands, delivered to them by someone they code-named Delphi. We knew we had a mole, but we couldn't identify him—until those papers were found with Bernard's body."

"And you think Dad was Delphi," said Jordan.

"No, that's what French Intelligence concluded. I couldn't believe it, but I also couldn't dispute the facts."

For a moment, Beryl and Jordan sat in silence, dismayed by the weight of the evidence.

"You don't really believe it, Uncle Hugh?" said Beryl softly. "That Dad was the one?"

"I couldn't argue with the findings. And it *would* explain their deaths. Perhaps they knew they were on the verge of being discovered. Disgraced. So Bernard took the gentleman's way out. He would, you know. Death before dishonor."

Uncle Hugh sank back in the chair and wearily ran his fingers through his gray hair. "I tried to keep the report as quiet as possible," he said. "The search for Delphi was halted. I myself had a few sticky years in MI6. Brother of a traitor and all, can we trust him, that sort of thing. But then, it was forgotten. And I went on with my career. I think...I think it was because no one at MI6 could quite believe the report. That Bernard had gone to the other side."

"I don't believe it, either," said Beryl.

Uncle Hugh looked at her. "Nevertheless—"

"I *won't* believe it. It's a fabrication. Someone at MI6, covering up the truth—"

"Don't be ridiculous, Beryl."

"Mum and Dad can't defend themselves! Who else will speak up for them?"

"Your loyalty's commendable, darling, but—"

"And where's *your* loyalty?" she retorted. "He was your brother!"

"I didn't want to believe it."

"Then did you confirm that evidence? Did you discuss it with French Intelligence?"

"Yes, and I trusted Daumier's report. He's a thorough man."

"Daumier?" queried Jordan. "Claude Daumier? Isn't he chief of their Paris operations?"

"At the time, he was their liaison to MI6. I asked him to review the findings. He came to the same conclusions."

"Then this Daumier fellow is an idiot," said Beryl. She turned to the door. "And I'm going to tell him so myself."

"Where are you going?" asked Jordan.

"To pack my things," she said. "Are you coming, Jordan?"

"Pack?" said Hugh. "Where in blazes are you headed?"

Beryl threw a glance over her shoulder. "Where else," she answered, "but Paris?"

RICHARD WOLF GOT THE CALL at six that morning. "They are booked on a noon flight to Paris," said Claude Daumier. "It seems, my friend, that someone has pried open a rather nasty can of worms."

Still groggy with sleep, Richard sat up in bed and gave his head a shake. "What are you talking about, Claude? Who's flying to Paris?"

"Beryl and Jordan Tavistock. Hugh has just called me. I think this is not a good development."

Richard collapsed back on his pillow. "They're adults, Claude," he said, yawning. "If they want to jet off to Paris—"

"They are coming to find out about Bernard and Madeline."

Richard closed his eyes and groaned. "Oh, wonderful, just what we need."

"My sentiments precisely."

"Can't Hugh talk them out of it?"

"He tried. But this niece of his…" Daumier sighed. "You have met her. So you would understand."

Yes, Richard knew exactly how stubborn Miss Beryl Tavistock could be. Like mother, like daughter. He remembered that Madeline had been just as unswerving, just as unstoppable.

Just as enchanting.

He shook off those haunting memories of a long-dead woman and said, "How much do they know?"

"They have seen my report. They know about Delphi."

"So they'll be digging in all the right places."

"All the dangerous places," amended Daumier.

Richard sat up on the side of the bed and clawed his fingers through his hair as he considered the possibilities. The perils.

"Hugh is concerned for their safety," said Daumier. "So am I. If what we think is true—"

"Then they're walking into quicksand."

"And Paris is dangerous enough as it is," added Daumier, "what with the latest bombing."

"How is Marie St. Pierre, by the way?"

"A few scratches, bruises. She should be released from the hospital tomorrow."

"Ordnance report back?"

"Semtex. The upper apartment was completely demolished. Luckily Marie was downstairs when the bomb went off."

"Who's claiming responsibility?"

"There was a telephone call shortly after the blast. It was a man, said he belonged to some group called Cosmic Solidarity. They claim responsibility."

"Cosmic Solidarity? Never heard of that one."

"Neither have we," said Daumier. "But you know how it is these days."

Yes, Richard knew only too well. Any wacko with the right connections could buy a few ounces of Semtex, build a bomb, and join the revolution—any revolution. No wonder his business was booming. In this brave new world, terrorism was a fact of life. And clients everywhere were willing to pay top dollar for security.

"So you see, my friend," said Daumier, "it is not a good time for Bernard's children to be in Paris. And with all the questions they will ask—"

"Can't you keep an eye on them?"

"Why should they trust me? It was *my* report in that file. No, they need another friend here, Richard. Someone with sharp eyes and unerring instincts."

"You have someone in mind?"

"I hear through the grapevine that you and Miss Tavistock shared a degree of…simpatico?"

"She's way too rich for my blood. And I'm too poor for hers."

"I do not usually ask for favors," said Daumier quietly. "Neither does Hugh."

And you're asking for one now, thought Richard. He sighed. "How can I refuse?"

After he'd hung up, he sat for a moment contemplating the task ahead. This was a baby-sitting job, really—the sort of assignment he despised. But the thought of seeing Beryl Tavistock again, and the memory of that kiss they'd shared in the garden, was enough to make him grin with anticipation. *Way too rich for my blood,* he thought. *But a man can dream, can't he? And I do owe it to Bernard and Madeline.*

Even after all these years, their deaths still haunted him. Perhaps the time had come to close the mystery, to answer all those questions he and Daumier had raised twenty years ago. The same questions MI6 and Central Intelligence had firmly suppressed.

Now Beryl Tavistock was poking her aristocratic nose into the mess. And a most attractive nose it was, he thought. He hoped it didn't get her killed.

He rose from the bed and headed for the shower. So much to do, so many preparations to make before he headed to the airport.

Baby-sitting jobs—how he hated them.

But at least this one would be in Paris.

ANTHONY SUTHERLAND STARED out his airplane window and longed fervently for the flight to be over and done with. Of all the rotten luck to be booked on the same Air France flight as the Vanes! And then to be seated straight across the first-class aisle from them—well, this really was intolerable. He considered Reggie Vane a screaming bore, especially when intoxicated, which at the moment Reggie was well on the way to becoming. Two whiskey sours and the man was starting to babble about how much he missed jolly old England, where food was boiled as it should be, not sautéed in all that ghastly butter, where people lined up in proper queues, where crowds didn't reek of garlic and onions. He'd lived too many years in Paris now—surely it was time to retire from the bank and go home? He'd put in many years at the Bank of London's Paris branch. Now that there were so many clever young V.P.s ready to step into his place, why not let them?

Lady Helena, who appeared to be just as fed up with her husband as Anthony was, simply said, "Shut up, Reggie," and ordered him a third whiskey sour.

Anthony didn't much care for Helena, either. She reminded him of some sort of nasty rodent. Such a contrast to his mother! The two women sat across the aisle from each other, Helena drab and proper in her houndstooth skirt and jacket, Nina so striking in her whitest-white silk pantsuit. Only a woman with true confidence could wear white silk, and his mother was one who could. Even at fifty-three, Nina was stunning, her dark, upswept hair showing scarcely a trace of gray, her figure the envy of any twenty-year-old. *But of course,* thought Anthony, *she's my mother.*

And, as usual, she was getting in her digs at Helena.

"If you and Reggie hate it so much in Paris," sniffed Nina, "why do you stay? If you ask me, people who don't adore the city don't deserve to live there."

"Of course, you *would* love Paris," said Helena.

"It's all in the attitude. If you'd kept an open mind..."

"Oh, no, we're much too stuffy," muttered Helena.

"I didn't say that. But there is a certain British attitude. God is an Englishman, that sort of thing."

"You mean He isn't?" Reggie interjected.

Helena didn't laugh. "I just think," she said, "that a certain amount of order and discipline is needed for the world to function properly."

Nina glanced at Reggie, who was noisily slurping his whiskey. "Yes, I can see you both believe in discipline. No wonder the evening was such a disaster."

"We weren't the ones who blurted out the truth," snapped Helena.

"At least *I* was sober enough to know what I was saying!" Nina declared. "They would have found out in any event. After Reggie there let the cat out of the bag, I just decided it was time to be straight with them about Bernard and Madeline."

"And look at the result," moaned Helena. "Hugh says Beryl and Jordan are flying to Paris this afternoon. Now they'll be mucking around in things."

Nina shrugged. "Well, it was a long time ago."

"I don't see why you're so nonchalant. If anyone could be hurt, it's you," muttered Helena.

Nina frowned at her. "What do you mean by that?"

"Oh, nothing."

"No, really! What do you mean by that?"

"Nothing," Helena snapped.

Their conversation came to an abrupt halt. But Anthony could tell his mother was fuming. She sat with her hands balled up in her lap. She even ordered a second martini. When she rose from her seat and headed down the aisle for a bit of exercise, he followed her. They met at the rear of the plane.

"Are you all right, Mother?" he asked.

Nina glanced in agitation toward first class. "It's all Reggie's bloody fault," she whispered. "And Helena's right, you know. I *am* the one who could be hurt."

"After all these years?"

"They'll be asking questions again. Digging. Lord, what if those Tavistock brats find something?"

Anthony said quietly, "They won't."

Nina's gaze met his. In that one look they saw, in each other's eyes, the bond of twenty years. "You and me against the world," she used to sing to him. And that's how it had felt—just the two of them in their Paris flat. There'd been her lovers, of course, insignificant men, scarcely worth noting. But mother and son—what love could be stronger?

He said, "You've nothing to worry about, darling. Really."

"But the Tavistocks—"

"They're harmless." He took her hand and gave it a reassuring squeeze. "I guarantee it."

Chapter Three

FROM THE WINDOW of her suite at the Paris Ritz, Beryl looked down at the opulence of Place Vendôme, with its Corinthian pilasters and stone arches, and saw the evening parade of well-heeled tourists. It had been eight years since she'd last visited Paris, and then it had been on a lark with her girlfriends—three wild chums from school, who'd preferred the Left Bank bistros and seedy nightlife of Montparnasse to this view of unrepentant luxury. They'd had a grand time of it, too, had drunk countless bottles of wine, danced in the streets, flirted with every Frenchman who'd glanced their way—and there'd been a lot of them.

It seemed a million years ago. A different life, a different age.

Now, standing at the hotel window, she mourned the loss of all those carefree days and knew they would never be back. *I've changed too much,* she thought. *It's more than just the revelations about Mum and Dad. It's me. I feel restless. I'm longing for…I don't know what. Purpose, perhaps? I've gone so long without purpose in my life….*

She heard the door open, and Jordan came in through the connecting door from his suite. "Claude Daumier finally returned my call," he said. "He's tied up with the bomb investigation, but he's agreed to meet us for an early supper."

"When?"

"Half an hour."

Beryl turned from the window and looked at her brother. They'd scarcely slept last night, and it showed in Jordan's face. Though freshly shaved and impeccably dressed, he had that ragged edge of fatigue, the lean and hungry look of a man operating on reserve strength. *Like me.*

"I'm ready to leave anytime," she said.

He frowned at her dress. "Isn't that…Mum's?"

"Yes. I packed a few of her things in my suitcase. I don't know why, really." She gazed down at the watered-silk skirt. "It's eerie, isn't it? How well it fits. As if it were made for me."

"Beryl, are you sure you're up to this?"

"Why do you ask?"

"It's just that—" Jordan shook his head "—you don't seem at all yourself."

"Neither of us is, Jordie. How could we be?" She looked out the window again, at the lengthening shadows in Place Vendôme. The same view her mother must have looked down upon on *her* visits to Paris. The same hotel, perhaps even the same suite. *I'm even wearing her dress.* "It's as if—as if we don't know who we are anymore," she said. "Where we spring from."

"Who you are, who I am, has never been in doubt, Beryl. Whatever we learn about them doesn't change us."

She looked at him. "So you think it might be true."

He paused. "I don't know," he said. "But I'm preparing myself for the worst. And so should you." He went to the closet and took out her wrap. "Come on. It's time to confront the facts, little sister. Whatever they may be."

At seven o'clock, they arrived at Le Petit Zinc, the café where Daumier had arranged to meet them. It was early for the usual Parisian supper hour, and except for a lone couple dining on soup and bread, the café was empty. They took a seat in a booth at the rear and ordered wine and bread and a *remoulade* of mustard and celeriac to stave off their hunger. The lone couple finished their meal and departed. The appointed time came and went. Had Daumier changed his mind about meeting them?

Then, at seven-twenty, the door opened and a trim little Frenchman in suit and tie walked into the dining room. With his graying temples and his briefcase, he could have passed for any distinguished banker or lawyer. But the instant his gaze locked on Beryl, she knew, by his nod of acknowledgment, that this must be Claude Daumier.

But he had not come alone. He glanced over his shoulder as the door opened again, and a second man entered the restaurant. Together they approached the booth where Beryl and Jordan were seated. Beryl stiffened as she found herself staring not at Daumier but at his companion.

"Hello, Richard," she said quietly. "I had no idea you were coming to Paris."

"Neither did I," he said. "Until this morning."

Introductions were made, hands shaken all around. Then the two men slid into the booth. Beryl faced Richard straight across the table. As his gaze met hers, she felt the earlier sparks kindle between them, the memory of their kiss flaring to mind. *Beryl, you idiot,* she thought in irritation, *you're letting him distract you. Confuse you. No man has a right to affect you this way—certainly not a man you've only kissed once in your life. Not to mention one you met only twenty-four hours ago.*

Still, she couldn't seem to shake the memory of those moments in the garden at Chetwynd. Nor could she forget the taste of his lips. She watched him pour himself a glass of wine, watched him raise the glass to sip. Again, their eyes met, this time over the gleam of ruby liquid. She licked her own lips and savored the aftertaste of Burgundy.

"So what brings you to Paris?" she asked, raising her glass.

"Claude, as a matter of fact." He tilted his head at Daumier.

At Beryl's questioning look, Daumier said, "When I heard my old friend Richard was in London, I thought why not consult him? Since he is an authority on the subject."

"The St. Pierre bombing," Richard explained. "Some group no one's ever heard of is claiming responsibility. Claude thought perhaps I'd be able to shed some light on their identity. For years I've been tracking every reported terrorist organization there is."

"And did you shed some light?" asked Jordan.

"Afraid not," he admitted. "Cosmic Solidarity doesn't show up on my computer." He took another sip of wine, and his gaze locked with hers. "But the trip isn't entirely wasted," he added, "since I discover you're in Paris, as well."

"Strictly business," said Beryl. "With no time for pleasure."

"None at all?"

"None," she said flatly. She pointedly turned her attention to Daumier. "My uncle did call you, didn't he? About why we're here?"

The Frenchman nodded. "I understand you have both read the file."

"Cover to cover," said Jordan.

"Then you know the evidence. I myself confirmed the witness statements, the coroner's findings—"

"The coroner could have misinterpreted the facts," Jordan asserted.

"I myself saw their bodies in the garret. It was not something I am likely to forget." Daumier paused as though shaken by the memory. "Your mother died of three bullet wounds to the chest. Lying beside her was Bernard, a single bullet in his head. The gun had his fingerprints. There were no witnesses, no other suspects." Daumier shook his head. "The evidence speaks for itself."

"But where's the motive?" said Beryl. "Why would he kill someone he loved?"

"Perhaps that is the motive," said Daumier. "Love. Or loss of love. She may have found someone else—"

"That's impossible," Beryl objected vehemently. "She loved him."

Daumier looked down at his wineglass. He said quietly, "You have not yet read the police interview with the landlord, M. Rideau?"

Beryl and Jordan looked at him in puzzlement. "Rideau? I don't recall seeing that interview in the file," said Jordan.

"Only because I chose to exclude it when I sent the file to Hugh. It was a…matter of discretion."

Discretion, thought Beryl. Meaning he was trying to hide some embarrassing fact.

"The attic flat where their bodies were found," said Daumier, "was rented out to a Mlle Scarlatti. According to the landlord, Rideau, this Scarlatti woman used the flat once or twice a week. And only for the purpose of…" He paused delicately.

"Meeting a lover?" Jordan said bluntly.

Daumier nodded. "After the shooting, the landlord was asked to identify the bodies. Rideau told the police that the woman he called Mlle Scarlatti was the same one found dead in the garret. Your mother."

Beryl stared at him in shock. "You're saying my mother met a *lover* there?"

"It was the landlord's testimony."

"Then we'll have to talk face-to-face with this landlord."

"Not possible," said Daumier. "The building has been sold several times over. M. Rideau has left the country. I do not know where he is."

Beryl and Jordan sat in stunned silence. So that was Daumier's theory, thought Beryl. That her mother had a lover. Once or twice a week she would meet him in that attic flat on Rue Myrha. And then her father found out. So he killed her. And then he killed himself.

She looked up at Richard and saw the flicker of sympathy in his eyes. He believes it, too, she thought. Suddenly she resented him simply for being here, for hearing the most shameful secret of her family.

They heard a soft beeping. Daumier reached under his jacket and frowned at his pocket pager. "I am afraid I will have to leave," he said.

"What about that classified file?" asked Jordan. "You haven't said anything about Delphi."

"We'll speak of it later. This bombing, you understand—it is a crisis situation." Daumier slid out of the booth and picked up his briefcase. "Perhaps tomorrow? In the meantime, try to enjoy your stay in Paris, all of you. Oh, and if you dine here, I would recommend the duckling. It is excellent." With a nod of farewell, he turned and swiftly walked out of the restaurant.

"We just got the royal runaround," muttered Jordan in frustration. "He drops a bomb in our laps, then he scurries for cover, never answering our questions."

"I think that was his plan from the start," said Beryl. "Tell us something so horrifying, we'll be afraid to pursue it. Then our questions will stop." She looked at Richard. "Am I right?"

He met her gaze without wavering. "Why are you asking me?"

"Because you two obviously know each other well. Is this the way Daumier usually operates?"

"Claude's not one to spill secrets. But he also believes in helping out old friends, and your uncle Hugh's a good friend of his. I'm sure Claude's keeping your best interests at heart."

Old friends, thought Beryl. Daumier and Uncle Hugh and Richard Wolf—all of them linked together by some shadowy past, a past they would not talk about. This was how it had been, growing up at Chetwynd. Mysterious men in limousines dropping in to visit Hugh. Sometimes Beryl would hear snatches of conversation, would pick up whispered names whose significance she could only guess at. Yurchenko. Andropov. Baghdad. Berlin. She had learned long ago not to ask questions, never to expect answers. "Not something to bother your pretty head about," Hugh would tell her.

This time, she wouldn't be put off. This time she demanded answers.

The waiter came to the table with the menus. Beryl shook her head. "We won't be staying," she said.

"You're not interested in supper?" asked Richard. "Claude says it's an excellent restaurant."

"Did Claude ask you to show up?" she demanded. "Keep us well fed and entertained so we won't trouble him?"

"I'm delighted to keep you well fed. And, if you're willing, entertained." He smiled at her then, a smile with just a spark of mischief. Looking into his eyes, she found herself wavering on the edge of temptation. *Have supper with me,* she read in his smile. *And afterward, who knows? Anything's possible.*

Slowly she sat back in the booth. "We'll have supper with you, on one condition."

"What's that?"

"You play it straight with us. No dodging, no games."

"I'll try."

"Why are you in Paris?"

"Claude asked me to consult. As a personal favor. The summit's over now, so my schedule's open. Plus, I was curious."

"About the bombing?"

He nodded. "Cosmic Solidarity is a new one for me. I try to keep up with new terrorist groups. It's my business." He held a menu out to her and smiled. "And that, Miss Tavistock, is the unadulterated truth."

She met his gaze and saw no flicker of avoidance in his eyes. Still, her instincts told her there was something more behind that smile, something yet unsaid.

"You don't believe me," he said.

"How did you guess?"

"Does this mean you're not having supper with me?"

Up until that moment, Jordan had sat watching them, his gaze playing Ping-Pong. Now he cut in impatiently. "We are definitely having supper. Because I'm hungry, Beryl, and I'm not moving from this booth until I've eaten."

With a sigh of resignation, Beryl took the menu. "I guess that answers that. Jordie's stomach has spoken."

AMIEL FOCH'S TELEPHONE rang at precisely seven-fifteen.

"I have a new task for you," said the caller. "It's a matter of some urgency. Perhaps this time around, you'll prove successful."

The criticism stung, and Amiel Foch, with twenty-five years' experience in the business, barely managed to suppress a retort. The caller held the purse strings; he could afford to hurl insults. Foch had his retirement to consider. Requests for his services were few and far between these days. One's reflexes, after all, did not improve with age.

Foch said, with quiet control, "I planted the device as you instructed. It went off at the time specified."

"And all it did was make a lot of bloody noise. The target was scarcely hurt."

"She did the unexpected. One cannot control such things."

"Let's hope this time you keep things under better control."

"What is the name?"

"Two names. A brother and sister, Beryl and Jordan Tavistock. They're staying at the Ritz. I want to know where they go. Who they see."

"Nothing more?"

"For now, just surveillance. But things may change at any time, depending on what they learn. With any luck, they'll simply turn around and run home to England."

"If they do not?"

"Then we'll take further action."

"What about Mme St. Pierre? Do you wish me to try again?"

The caller paused. "No," he said at last, "she can wait. For now, the Tavistocks take priority."

OVER A MEAL OF poached salmon and duck with raspberry sauce, Beryl and Richard thrusted and parried questions and answers. Richard, an accomplished verbal duelist, revealed only the barest sketch of his personal life. He was born and reared in Connecticut. His father, a retired cop, was still living. After leaving Princeton University, Richard joined the U.S. State Department and served as political officer at embassies around the world. Then, five years ago, he left government service to start up business as a security consultant. Sakaroff and Wolf, based in Washington, D.C., was born.

"And that's what brought me to London last week," he said. "Several American firms wanted security for their executives during the summit. I was hired as consultant."

"And that's all you were doing in London?" she asked.

"That's all I was doing in London. Until I got Hugh's invitation to Chetwynd." His gaze met hers across the table.

His directness unsettled her. *Is he telling me the truth, fiction or something in between?* That matter-of-fact recitation of his career had struck her as rehearsed, but then, it would be. People in the intelligence business always had their life histories down pat, the details memorized, fact blending smoothly with fantasy. What did she really know about him? Only that he smiled easily, laughed easily. That his appetite was hearty and he drank his coffee black.

And that she was intensely, insanely, attracted to him.

After supper, he offered to drive them back to the Ritz. Jordan sat in the back seat, Beryl in the front—right next to Richard. She kept glancing sideways at him as they drove up Boulevard Saint-Germain toward the Seine. Even the traffic, outrageously rude and noisy, did not seem to ruffle him. At a stoplight, he turned and looked at her and that one glimpse of his face through the darkness of the car was enough to make her heart do a somersault.

Calmly he shifted his attention back to the road. "It's still early," he said. "Are you sure you want to go back to the hotel?"

"What's my choice?"

"A drive. A walk. Whatever you'd like. After all, you're in Paris. Why not make the most of it?" He reached down to shift gears, and his hand brushed past her knee. A shiver ran through her—a warm, delicious sizzle of anticipation.

He's tempting me. Making me dizzy with all the possibilities. Or is it the wine? What harm can there be in a little stroll, a little fresh air?

She called over her shoulder, "How about it, Jordie? Do you feel like taking a walk?" She was answered by a loud snore.

Beryl turned and saw to her astonishment that her brother was sprawled across the back seat. A sleepless night and two glasses of wine at supper had left him dead to the world. "I guess that's a negative," she said with a laugh.

"What about just you and me?"

That invitation, voiced so softly, sent another shiver of temptation up her spine. After all, she thought, she was in Paris....

"A short walk," she agreed. "But first, let's put Jordan to bed."

"Valet service coming up," Richard said, laughing. "First stop, the Ritz."

Jordan snored all the way back to the hotel.

THEY WALKED IN THE Tuileries, a stroll that took them along a gravel path through formal gardens, past statues glowing a ghostly white under the street lamps.

"And here we are again," said Richard, "walking through another garden. Now if only we could find a maze with a nice little stone bench at the center."

"Why?" she asked with a smile. "Are you hoping for a repeat scenario?"

"With a slightly different ending. You know, after you left me in there, it took me a good five minutes to find my way out."

"I know." She laughed. "I was waiting at the door, counting the minutes. Five minutes wasn't bad, really. But other men have done better."

"So that's how you screen your men. You're the cheese in the maze—"

"And you were the rat."

They both laughed then, and the sound of their voices floated through the night air.

"And my performance was only...adequate?" he said.

"Average."

He moved toward her, his smile gleaming in the shadows. "Better than adequate?"

"For you, I'll make allowances. After all, it was dark...."

"Yes, it was." He moved closer, so close she had to tilt her head up to look at him. So close she could almost feel the heat radiating from his body. "Very dark," he whispered.

"And perhaps you were disoriented?"

"Extremely."

"And it *was* a nasty trick I played...."

"For which you should be soundly punished."

He reached up and took her face in his hands. The taste of his lips on hers sent a shudder of pleasure through her body. *If this is my punishment,* she thought, *oh, let me commit the crime again....* His fingers slid through her hair, tangling in the strands as his kiss pressed ever deeper. She felt her legs wobble and melt away, but she had no need of them; he was there to support them both. She heard his murmur of need and knew that these kisses were dangerous, that he, too, was fast slipping toward the same cliff's edge. She didn't care—she was ready to make the leap.

And then, without warning, he froze.

One moment he was kissing her, and an instant later his hands went rigid against her face. He didn't pull away. Even as she felt his whole body grow tense against her, he kept her firmly in his embrace. His lips glided to her ear.

"Start walking," he whispered. "Toward the Concorde."

"What?"

"Just move. Don't show any alarm. I'll hold your hand."

She focused on his face, and through the shadows she saw his look of feral alertness. Swallowing back the questions, she allowed him to take her hand. They turned and began to walk casually toward the Place de la Concorde. He gave her no explanation, but she knew just by the way he gripped her hand that something was wrong, that this was not a game. Like any other pair of lovers, they strolled through the garden, past flower beds deep in shadow, past statues lined up in ghostly formation. Gradually she became more and more aware of sounds: the distant roar of traffic, the wind in the trees, their shoes crunching across the gravel…

And the footsteps, following somewhere behind them.

Nervously she clutched his hand. His answering squeeze of reassurance was enough to dull the razor edge of fear. *I've known this man only a day,* she thought, *and already I feel that I can count on him.*

Richard picked up his pace—so gradually she almost didn't notice it. The footsteps still pursued them. They veered right and crossed the park toward Rue de Rivoli. The sounds of traffic grew louder, obscuring the footsteps of their pursuer. Now was the greatest danger—as they left the darkness behind them and their pursuer saw his last chance to make a move. Bright lights beckoned from the street ahead. *We can make it if we run,* she thought. *A dash through the trees and we'll be safe, surrounded by other people.* She prepared for the sprint, waiting for Richard's cue.

But he made no sudden moves. Neither did their pursuer. Hand in hand, she and Richard strolled nonchalantly into the naked glare of Rue de Rivoli.

Only as they joined the stream of evening pedestrians did Beryl's pulse begin to slow again. There was no danger here, she thought. Surely no one would dare attack them on a busy street.

Then she glanced at Richard's face and saw that the tension was still there.

They crossed the street and walked another block.

"Stop for a minute," he murmured. "Take a long look in that window."

They paused in front of a chocolate shop. Through the glass they saw a tempting display of confections: raspberry creams and velvety truffles and Turkish delight, all nestled in webs of spun sugar. In the shop, a young woman stood over a vat of melted chocolate, dipping fresh strawberries.

"What are we waiting for?" whispered Beryl.

"To see what happens."

She stared in the window and saw the reflections of people

passing behind them. A couple holding hands. A trio of students in backpacks. A family with four children.

"Let's start walking again," he said.

They headed west on Rue de Rivoli, their pace again leisurely, unhurried. She was caught by surprise when he suddenly pulled her to the right, onto an intersecting street.

"Move it!" he barked.

All at once they were sprinting. They made another sharp right onto Mont Thabor, and ducked under an arch. There, huddled in the shadow of a doorway, he pulled her against him so tightly that she felt his heart pounding against hers, his breath warming her brow. They waited.

Seconds later, running footsteps echoed along the street. The sound moved closer, slowed, stopped. Then there was no sound at all. Almost too terrified to look, Beryl slowly shifted in Richard's arms, just enough to see a shadow slide past their archway. The footsteps moved down the street and faded away.

Richard chanced a quick look up the street, then gave Beryl's hand a tug. "All clear," he whispered. "Let's get out of here."

They turned onto Castiglione Street and didn't stop running until they were back at the hotel. Only when they were safely in her suite and he'd bolted the door behind them, did she find her voice again.

"What happened out there?" she demanded.

He shook his head. "I'm not sure."

"Do you think he meant to rob us?" She moved to the phone. "I should call the police—"

"He wasn't after our money."

"What?" She turned and frowned at him.

"Think about it. Even on Rue de Rivoli, with all those witnesses, he didn't stop following us. Any other thief would've given up and gone back to the park. Found himself another victim. But he didn't. He stayed with us."

"I didn't even see him! How do you know there *was* any—"

"A middle-aged man. Short, stocky. The sort of face most people would forget."

She stared at him, her agitation mounting. "What are you saying, Richard? That he was following us in particular?"

"Yes."

"But why would anyone follow you?"

"I could ask the same question of you."

"I'm of no interest to anyone."

"Think about it. About why you came to Paris."

"It's just a family matter."

"Apparently not. Since you now seem to have strange men following you around town."

"How do I know he wasn't following you? You're the one who works for the CIA!"

"Correction. I work for myself."

"Oh, don't palm off that rubbish on me! I practically grew up in MI6! I can smell you people a mile away!"

"Can you?" His eyebrow shot up. "And the odor didn't scare you off?"

"Maybe it should have."

He was pacing the room now, moving about like a restless animal, locking windows, pulling curtains. "Since I can't seem to deceive your highly perceptive nose, I'll just confess it. My job description is a bit looser than I've admitted to."

"I'm astonished."

"But I'm still convinced the man was following *you*."

"Why would anyone follow me?"

"Because you're digging in a mine field. You don't understand, Beryl. When your parents were killed, there was more involved than just another sex scandal."

"Wait a minute." She crossed toward him, her gaze hard on his face. "What do you know about it?"

"I knew you were coming to Paris."

"Who told you?"

"Claude Daumier. He called me in London. Said that Hugh was worried. That someone had to keep an eye on you and Jordan."

"So you're our nanny?"

He laughed. "In a manner of speaking."

"And how much do you know about my mother and father?"

She knew by his brief silence that he was debating his answer, weighing the consequences of his next words. She fully expected to hear a lie.

Instead he surprised her with the truth. “I knew them both,” he said. “I was here in Paris when it happened.”

The revelation left her stunned. She didn’t doubt for an instant that it was the truth—why would he fabricate such a story?

“It was my very first posting,” he said. “I thought it was incredible luck to draw Paris. Most first-timers get sent to some bug-infested jungle in the middle of nowhere. But I drew Paris. And that’s where I met Madeline and Bernard.” Wearily he sank into a chair. “It’s amazing,” he murmured, studying Beryl’s face, “How very much you look like her. The same green eyes, the same black hair. She used to sweep hers back in this sort of loose chignon. But strands of it were always coming loose, falling about her neck….” He smiled fondly at the memory. “Bernard was crazy about her. So was every man who ever met her.”

“Were you?”

“I was only twenty-two. She was the most enchanting woman I’d ever met.” His gaze met hers. Softly he added, “But then, I hadn’t met her daughter.”

They stared at each other, and Beryl felt those silken threads of desire tugging her toward him. Toward a man whose kisses left her dizzy, whose touch could melt even stone. A man who had not been straight with her from the very start.

I’m so tired of secrets, so tired of trying to tease apart the truths from the half truths. And I’ll never know which is which with this man.

Abruptly she went to the door. “If we can’t be honest with each other,” she said, “there’s no point in being together at all. So why don’t we say good-night. And goodbye.”

“I don’t think so.”

She turned and frowned at him. “Excuse me?”

“I’m not ready to say goodbye. Not when I know you’re being followed.”

“You’re concerned about my welfare, is that it?”

“Shouldn’t I be?”

She shot him a breezy smile. “I’m very good at taking care of myself.”

“You’re in a foreign city. Things could happen—”

“I’m not exactly alone.” She crossed the room to the connecting door leading to Jordan's suite. Yanking it open, she called, "Wake up, Jordie! I'm in need of some brotherly assistance."

There was no answer from the bed.

"Jordie?" she said.

"Your bodyguard stays right on his toes, doesn't he?" said Richard.

Annoyed, Beryl flicked on the wall switch. In the sudden flood of light, she found herself blinking in astonishment.

Jordan's bed was empty.

Chapter Four

THAT WOMAN is staring at me again.

Jordan stirred a teaspoon of sugar into his cappuccino and casually glanced in the direction of the blonde sitting three tables away. At once she averted her gaze. She was attractive enough, he noted. Mid-twenties, with a lean, athletic build. Nothing overripe about that one. Her hair was cut like a boy's, with elfin wisps feathering her forehead. She wore a black sweater, black skirt, black stockings. Fashion or camouflage? He shifted his gaze ahead to the street and the evening parade of pedestrians. Out of the corner of his eye, he spied the woman again looking his way. Ordinarily it would have flattered him to know he was the object of such intense feminine scrutiny. But something about this particular woman made him uneasy. Couldn't a fellow wander the streets of Paris these days without being stalked by carnivorous females?

It had been such a pleasant outing up till now. Minutes after sending Beryl and Richard on their way, he'd slipped out of his hotel room in search of a decent watering hole. A stroll across Place Vendôme, a visit to the Olympia Music Hall, then a midnight snack at Café de la Paix—what better way to spend one's first evening in Paris?

But perhaps it was time to call it a night.

He finished his cappuccino, paid the tab, and began walking toward the Rue de la Paix. It took him only half a block to realize the woman in black was following him.

He had paused at a shop window and was gazing in at a display of men's suits when he spotted a fleeting glimpse of a blond head reflected in the glass. He turned and saw her standing across the street, intently staring into a window. A lingerie shop, he noted. Judging by the rest of her outfit, she'd no doubt choose her knickers in black, as well.

Jordan continued walking in the direction of Place Vendôme. Across the street, the woman was parralleling his route.

This is getting tiresome, he thought. *If she wants to flirt, why doesn't she just come over and bat her eyelashes?* The direct approach, he could appreciate. It was honest and straightforward, and he liked honest women. But this stalking business unnerved him.

He walked another half block. So did she.

He stopped and pretended to study another shop window. She did likewise. *This is ridiculous,* he thought. *I am not going to put up with this nonsense.*

He crossed the street and walked straight up to her. "*Mademoiselle?*" he said.

She turned and regarded him with a startled look. Plainly she had not expected a face-to-face confrontation.

"*Mademoiselle,*" he said, "may I ask why you're following me?"

She opened her mouth and shut it again, all the time staring at him with those big gray eyes. Rather pretty eyes, he observed.

"Perhaps you don't understand me? *Parlez-vous anglais?*"

"Yes," she murmured, "I speak English."

"Then perhaps you can explain why you're following me."

"But I am not following you."

"Yes, you are."

"No, I am not!" She glanced up and down the street. "I am taking a walk. As you are."

"You're dogging my every step. Stopping where I stop. Watching every move I make."

"That is preposterous." She pulled herself up, a spark of

outrage lighting her eyes. Real or manufactured? He couldn't be sure. "I have no interest in you, *Monsieur!* You must be imagining things."

"Am I?"

In answer, she spun around and stalked away up the Rue de la Paix.

"I don't think I am imagining things!" he called after her.

"You English are all alike!" she flung over her shoulder.

Jordan watched her storm off and wondered if he had jumped to conclusions. If so, what a fool he'd made of himself! The woman rounded a corner and vanished, and he felt a moment's regret. After all, she had been rather attractive. Lovely gray eyes, unbeatable legs.

Ah, well.

He turned and continued on his way toward the Place Vendôme and the hotel. Only as he reached the lobby doors of the Ritz did that sixth sense of his begin to tingle again. He paused and glanced back. In a distant archway, he spied a flicker of movement, a glimpse of a blond head just before it ducked into the shadows.

She was still following him.

DAUMIER ANSWERED the phone on the fifth ring. "*Allo?*"

"Claude, it's me," said Richard. "Are you having us tailed?"

There was a pause, then Daumier said, "A precaution, my friend. Nothing more."

"Protection? Or surveillance?"

"Protection, naturally! A favor to Hugh—"

"Well, it scared the living daylights out of us. The least you could've done was warn me." Richard glanced toward Beryl, who was anxiously pacing the hotel room. She hadn't admitted it, but he knew she was shaken, and that for all her bravado, all her attempts to throw him out of her suite, she was relieved he'd stayed. "Another thing," he said to Daumier, "we seem to have misplaced Jordan."

"Misplaced?"

"He's not in his suite. We left him here hours ago. He's since vanished."

There was a silence on the line. "This is worrisome," said Daumier.

"Do your people have any idea where he is?"

"My agent has not yet reported in. I expect to hear from her in another—"

"Her?" Richard cut in.

"Not our most experienced operative, I admit. But quite capable."

"It was a man following us tonight."

Daumier laughed. "Richard, I am disappointed! I thought you, of all people, knew the difference."

"I can bloody well tell the difference!"

"With Colette, there is no question. Twenty-six, rather pretty. Blond hair."

"It was a man, Claude."

"You saw the face?"

"Not clearly. But he was short, stocky—"

"Colette is five foot five, very slender."

"It wasn't her."

Daumier said nothing for a moment. "This is disturbing," he concluded. "If it was not one of our people—"

Richard suddenly pivoted toward the door. Someone was knocking. Beryl stood frozen, staring at him with a look of fear.

"I'll call you back, Claude," Richard whispered into the phone. Quietly he hung up.

There was another knock, louder this time.

"Go ahead," he murmured, "ask who it is."

Shakily she called out, "Who is it?"

"Are you decent?" came the reply. "Or should I try again in the morning?"

"Jordan!" cried a relieved Beryl. She ran to open the door. "Where have you been?"

Her brother sauntered in, his blond hair tousled from the night wind. He saw Richard and halted. "Sorry. If I've interrupted anything—"

"Not a thing," snapped Beryl. She locked the door and turned to face her brother. "We've been worried sick about you."

"I just went for a walk."

"You could have left me a note!"

"Why? I was right in the neighborhood." Jordan flopped lazily into a chair. "Having quite a nice evening, too, until some woman started following me around."

Richard's chin snapped up in surprise. "Woman?"

"Rather nice-looking. But not my type, really. A bit vampirish for my taste."

"Was she blond?" asked Richard. "About five foot five? Mid-twenties?"

Jordan shook his head in amazement. "Next you'll tell me her name."

"Colette."

"Is this a new parlor trick, Richard?" Jordan said with a laugh. "ESP?"

"She's an agent working for French Intelligence," said Richard. "Protective surveillance, that's all."

Beryl gave a sigh of relief. "So that's why we were followed. And you had me scared out of my wits."

"You *should* be scared," said Richard. "The man following us wasn't working for Daumier."

"You just said—"

"Daumier had only one agent assigned to surveillance tonight. That woman, Colette. Apparently she stayed with Jordan."

"Then who was following us?" demanded Beryl.

"I don't know."

There was a silence. Then Jordan asked peevishly, "Have I missed something? Why are we all being followed? And when did Richard join the fun?"

"Richard," said Beryl tightly, "hasn't been completely honest with us."

"About what?"

"He neglected to mention that he was here in Paris in 1973. He knew Mum and Dad."

Jordan's gaze at once shot to Richard's face. "Is that why you're here now?" he asked quietly. "To prevent us from learning the truth?"

"No," said Richard. "I'm here to see that the truth doesn't get you both killed."

"Could the truth really be that dangerous?"

"It's got someone worried enough to have you both followed."

"Then you don't believe it *was* a simple murder and suicide," said Jordan.

"If it was that simple—if it was just a case of Bernard shooting Madeline and then taking his own life—no one would care about it after all these years. But someone obviously does care. And he—or she—is keeping a close watch on your movements."

Beryl, strangely silent, sat down on the bed. Her hair, which she'd gathered back with pins, was starting to loosen, and silky tendrils had drifted down her neck. All at once Richard was struck by her uncanny resemblance to Madeline. It was the hairstyle and the watered-silk dress. He recognized that dress now—it was her mother's. He shook himself to dispel the notion that he was looking at a ghost.

He decided it was time to tell the truth, and nothing but. "I never did believe it," he said. "Not for a second did I think Bernard pulled that trigger."

Slowly Beryl looked up at him. What he saw in her gaze—the wariness, the mistrust—made him want to reach out to her, to make her believe in him. But trust wasn't something she was about to give him, not now. Perhaps not ever.

"If he didn't pull the trigger," she asked, "then who did?"

Richard moved to the bed. Gently he touched her face. "I don't know," he said. "But I'm going to help you find out."

AFTER RICHARD LEFT, Beryl turned to her brother. "I don't trust him," she said. "He's told us too many lies."

"He didn't lie to us exactly," Jordan observed. "He just left out a few facts."

"Oh, right. He conveniently neglects to mention that he knew Mum and Dad. That he was here in Paris when they died. Jordie, for all we know, *he* could've pulled the trigger!"

"He seems quite chummy with Daumier."

"So?"

"Uncle Hugh trusts Daumier."

"Meaning we should trust Richard Wolf?" She shook her head and laughed. "Oh, Jordie, you must be more exhausted than you realize."

"And you must be more smitten than you realize," he said. Yawning, he crossed the floor toward his own suite.

"What's that supposed to mean?" she demanded.

"Only that your feelings for the man obviously run hot and heavy. Because you're fighting them every inch of the way."

She pursued him to the connecting door. "Hot?" she said incredulously. "Heavy?"

"There, you see?" He breathed a few loud pants and grinned. "Sweet dreams, baby sister. I'm glad to see you're back in circulation."

Then he closed the door on her astonished face.

WHEN RICHARD ARRIVED at Daumier's flat, he found the Frenchman still awake but already dressed in his bathrobe and slippers. The latest reports on the bombing of the St. Pierre residence were laid out across his kitchen table, along with a plate of sausage and a glass of milk. Forty years with French Intelligence hadn't altered his preference for working in close proximity to a refrigerator.

Waving at the reports, Daumier said, "It is all a puzzle to me. A Semtex explosive planted under the bed. A timing mechanism set for 9:10—precisely when the St. Pierres would be watching Marie's favorite television program. It has all the signs of an inside operation, except for one glaring mistake—Philippe was in England." He looked at Richard. "Does it not strike you as an inconceivable blunder?"

"Terrorists are usually brighter than that," admitted Richard. "Maybe they intended it only as a warning. A statement of purpose. 'We can reach you if we want to,' that sort of thing."

"I still have no information on this Cosmic Solidarity League." Wearily Daumier ran his hands through his hair. "The investigation, it goes nowhere."

"Then maybe you can turn your attention for a moment to my little problem."

"Problem? Ah, yes. The Tavistocks." Daumier sat back and smiled at him. "Hugh's niece is more than you can handle, Richard?"

"Someone else was definitely tailing us tonight," said Richard. "Not just your agent, Colette. Can you find out who it was?"

"Give me something to work with," said Daumier. "A middle-aged man, short and stocky—that tells me nothing. He could have been hired by anyone."

"It was someone who knew they were coming to Paris."

"I know Hugh told the Vanes. They, in turn, could have mentioned it to others. Who else was at Chetwynd?"

Richard thought back to the night of the reception and the night of Reggie's indiscretion. Blast Reggie Vane and his weakness for booze. That was what had set this off. A few too many glasses of champagne, a wagging tongue. Still, he couldn't bring himself to dislike the man. Poor Reggie was a harmless soul; certainly he'd never meant to hurt Beryl. Rather, it was clear he adored her like a daughter.

Richard said, "There were numbers of people the Vanes might have spoken to. Philippe St. Pierre. Nina and Anthony. Perhaps others."

"So we are talking about any number of people," Daumier said, sighing.

"Not a very short list," Richard had to admit.

"Is this such a wise idea, Richard?" The question was posed quietly. "Once before, if you recall, we were prevented from learning the truth."

How could he not remember? He'd been stunned to read that directive from Washington: "Abort investigation." Claude had received similar orders from his superior at French Intelligence. And so the search for Delphi and the NATO security breach had come to an abrupt halt. There'd been no explanation, no reasons given, but Richard had formed his own suspicions. It was clear that Washington had been clued in to the truth and feared the repercussions of its airing.

A month later, when U.S. Ambassador Stephen Sutherland leaped off a Paris bridge, Richard thought his suspicions confirmed. Sutherland had been a political appointee; his unveiling as an enemy spy would have embarrassed the president himself.

The matter of the mole was never officially resolved.

Instead, Bernard Tavistock had been posthumously implicated as Delphi. Conveniently tried and found guilty, thought Richard. Why not pin the blame on Tavistock? A dead man can't deny the charges.

And now, twenty years later, the ghost of Delphi is back to haunt me.

With new determination, Richard rose from the chair. "This time, Claude," he said, "I'm tracking him down. And no order from Washington is going to stop me."

"Twenty years is a long time. Evidence has vanished. Politics have changed."

"One thing hasn't changed—the guilty party. What if we were wrong? What if Sutherland wasn't the mole? Then Delphi may still be alive. And operational."

To which Daumier added, "And very, very worried."

BERYL WAS AWAKENED the next morning by Richard knocking on her door. She blinked in astonishment as he handed her a paper sack, fragrant with the aroma of freshly baked croissants.

"Breakfast," he announced. "You can eat it in the car. Jordan's already waiting for us downstairs."

"Waiting? For what?"

"For you to get dressed. You'd better hurry. Our appointment's for eight o'clock."

Bewildered, she shoved back a handful of tangled hair. "I don't recall making any appointments for this morning."

"I made it for us. We're lucky to get one, considering the man doesn't see many people these days. His wife won't allow it."

"Whose wife?" she said in exasperation.

"Chief Inspector Broussard. The detective in charge of your parents' murder investigation." Richard paused. "You do want to speak to him, don't you?"

He knows I do, she thought, clutching together the edges of her silk robe. *He's got me at a disadvantage. I'm scarcely awake and he's standing there like Mr. Sunshine himself.* And since when had Jordan turned into an early riser? Her brother almost never rolled out of bed before eight.

"You don't have to come," he said, turning to leave. "Jordan and I can—"

"Give me ten minutes!" she snapped and closed the door on him.

She made it downstairs in nine minutes flat.

Richard drove with the self-assurance of a man long familiar with the streets of Paris. They crossed the Seine and headed south along crowded boulevards. The traffic was as insane as London's, thought Beryl, gazing out at the crush of buses and taxis. *Thank heavens he's behind the wheel.*

She finished her croissant and brushed the crumbs off the file folder lying in her lap. Contained in that folder was the twenty-year-old police report, signed by Inspector Broussard. She wondered how much the man would remember about the case. After all this time, surely the details had blended together with all the other homicide investigations of his career. But there was always the chance that some small unreported detail had stayed with him.

"Have you met Broussard?" she asked Richard.

"We met during the course of the investigation. When I was interviewed by the police."

"They questioned you? Why?"

"He spoke to all your parents' acquaintances."

"I never saw your name in the police file."

"A number of names didn't make it to that file."

"Such as?"

"Philippe St. Pierre. Ambassador Sutherland."

"Nina's husband?"

Richard nodded. "Those were politically sensitive names. St. Pierre was in the Finance Ministry, and he was a close friend of the prime minister's. Sutherland was the American ambassador. Neither were suspects, so their names were kept out of the official report."

"Meaning the good inspector protected the high and mighty?"

"Meaning he was discreet."

"Why did your name escape the report?"

"I was just a bit player asked to comment on your parents' marriage. Whether they ever argued, seemed unhappy, that's all. I was only on the periphery."

She touched the file on her lap. "So tell me," she said, "why are you getting involved now?"

"Because you and Jordan are. Because Claude Daumier asked me to look after you." He glanced at her and added quietly, "And because I owe it to your father. He was…a good man." She thought he would say more, but then he turned and gazed straight ahead at the road.

"Wolf," asked Jordan, who was sitting in the back seat, "are you aware that we're being followed?"

"What?" Beryl turned and scanned the traffic behind them. "Which car?"

"The blue Peugeot. Two cars back."

"I see it," said Richard. "It's been tailing us all the way from the hotel."

"You knew the car was there all the time?" said Beryl. "And you didn't think of mentioning it?"

"I expected it. Take a good look at the driver, Jordan. Blond hair, sunglasses. Definitely a woman."

Jordan laughed. "Why, it's my little vampiress in black. Colette."

Richard nodded. "One of the friendlies."

"How can you be sure?" asked Beryl.

"Because she's Daumier's agent. Which makes her protection, not a threat." Richard turned off Boulevard Raspail. A moment later, he spotted a parking space and pulled up at the curb. "In fact, she can keep an eye on the car while we're inside."

Beryl glanced at the large brick building across the street. Over the entrance archway were displayed the words *Maison de Convalescence.* "What is this place?"

"A nursing home."

"This is where Inspector Broussard lives?"

"He's been here for years," said Richard, as he gazed up at the building with a look of pity. "Ever since his stroke."

JUDGING BY THE PHOTOGRAPH tacked to the wall of his room, ex-Chief Inspector Broussard had once been an impressive man. The picture showed a beefy Frenchman with a handlebar mustache and a lion's mane of hair, posing regally on the steps of a Paris police station.

It bore little resemblance to the shrunken creature now propped up, his body half-paralyzed, in bed.

Mme Broussard bustled about the room, all the time speaking with the precise grammar of a former teacher of English. She fluffed her husband's pillow, combed his hair, wiped the drool from his chin. "He remembers everything," she insisted. "Every case, every name. But he cannot speak, cannot hold a pen. And that is what frustrates him! It is why I do not let him have visitors. He wishes so much to talk, but he cannot form the words. Only a few, here and there. And how it upsets him! Sometimes, after a visit with friends, he will moan for days." She moved to the head of the bed and stood there like a guardian angel. "You ask him only a few questions, do you understand? And if he becomes upset, you must leave immediately."

"We understand," said Richard. He pulled up a chair next to the bedside. As Beryl and Jordan watched, he opened the police file and slowly laid the crime-scene photos on the coverlet for Broussard to see. "I know you can't speak," he said, "but I want you to look at these. Nod if you remember the case."

Mme Broussard translated for her husband. He stared down at the first photo—the gruesome death poses of Madeline and Bernard. They lay like lovers, entwined in a pool of blood. Clumsily Broussard touched the photo, his fingers lingering on Madeline's face. His lips formed a whispered word.

"What did he say?" asked Richard.

"*La belle*. Beautiful woman," said Mme Broussard. "You see? He does remember."

The old man was gazing at the other photos now, his left hand beginning to quiver in agitation. His lips moved helplessly; the effort to speak came out in grunts. Mme Broussard leaned forward, trying to make out what he was saying. She shook her head in bewilderment.

"We've read his report," said Beryl. "The one he filed twenty years ago. He concluded that it was a murder and suicide. Did he truly believe that?"

Again, Mme Broussard translated.

Broussard looked up at Beryl, his gaze focusing for the first time on her black hair. A look of wonder came over his face, almost a look of recognition.

His wife repeated the question. Did he believe it was a murder and suicide?

Slowly Broussard shook his head.

Jordan asked, "Does he understand the question?"

"Of course he does!" snapped Mme Broussard. "I told you, he understands everything."

The man was tapping at one of the photos now, as though trying to point something out. His wife asked a question in French. He only slapped harder at the photo.

"Is he trying to point at something?" asked Beryl.

"Just a corner of the picture," said Richard. "A view of empty floor."

Broussard's whole body seemed to be quivering with the effort to speak. His wife leaned forward again, straining to make out his words. She shook her head. "It makes no sense."

"What did he say?" asked Beryl.

"*Serviette.* It is a napkin or a towel. I do not understand." She snatched up a hand towel from the sink and held it up to her husband. "*Serviette de toilette?*"

He shook his head and angrily batted away the towel.

"I do not know what he means," Mme Broussard said with a sigh.

"Maybe I do," said Richard. He bent close to Broussard. "*Porte documents?*" he asked.

Broussard gave a sigh of relief and collapsed against his pillows. Wearily he nodded.

"That's what he was trying to say," said Richard. "*Serviette porte documents.* A briefcase."

"Briefcase?" echoed Beryl. "Do you think he means the one with the classified file?"

Richard frowned at Broussard. The man was exhausted, his face a sickly gray against the white linen.

Mme Broussard took one look at her husband and moved in to shield him from Richard. "No further questions, Mr. Wolf! Look at him! He is drained—he cannot tell you more. Please, you must leave."

She hurried them out of the room and into the hallway. A nun glided past, carrying a tray of medicines. At the end of the hall, a woman in a wheelchair was singing lullabies to herself in French.

"Mme Broussard," said Beryl, "we have more questions, but your husband can't answer them. There was another detective's name on that report—an Etienne Giguere. How can we get in touch with him?"

"Etienne?" Mme Broussard looked at her in surprise. "You mean you do not know?"

"Know what?"

"He was killed nineteen years ago. Hit by a car while crossing the street." Sadly she shook her head. "They did not find the driver."

Beryl caught Jordan's startled look; she saw in his eyes the same dismay she felt.

"One last question," said Jordan. "When did your husband have his stroke?"

"1974."

"Also nineteen years ago?"

Mme Broussard nodded. "Such a tragedy for the department! First, my husband's stroke. Then three months later, they lose Etienne." Sighing, she turned back to her husband's room. "But that is life, I suppose. And there is nothing we can do to change it...."

Back outside again, the three of them stood for a moment in the sunshine, trying to shake off the gloom of that depressing building.

"A hit and run?" said Jordan. "The driver never caught? I have a bad feeling about this."

Beryl glanced up at the archway. *"Maison de Convalescence,"* she murmured sarcastically. "Hardly a place to recover. More like a place to die." Shivering, she turned to the car. "Please, let's just get out of here."

They drove north, to the Seine. Once again, the blue Peugeot followed them, but none of them paid it much attention; the French agent had become a fact of life—almost a reassuring one.

Suddenly Jordan said, "Hold on, Wolf. Let me off on Boulevard Saint-Germain. In fact, right about here would be fine."

Richard pulled over to the curb. "Why here?"

"We just passed a café—"

"Oh, Jordan," groaned Beryl, "you're not hungry already, are you?"

"I'll meet you back at the hotel," said Jordan, climbing out of the car. "Unless you two care to join me?"

"So we can watch you eat? Thank you, but I'll pass."

Jordan gave his sister an affectionate squeeze of the shoulder and closed the car door. "I'll catch a taxi back. See you later." With a wave, he turned and strolled down the boulevard, his blond hair gleaming in the sunshine.

"Back to the hotel?" asked Richard softly.

She looked at him and thought, *It's always there shimmering between us—the attraction. The temptation. I look in his eyes, and suddenly I remember how safe it feels to be in his arms. How easy it would be to believe in him. And that's where the danger lies.*

"No," she said, looking straight ahead. "Not yet."

"Then where to?"

"Take me to Pigalle. Rue Myrha."

He paused. "Are you certain you want to go there?"

She nodded and stared down at the file in her lap. "I want to see the place where they died."

CAFÉ HUGO. YES, THIS WAS the place, thought Jordan, gazing around at the crowded outdoor tables, the checkered tablecloths, the army of waiters ferrying espresso and cappuccino. Twenty years ago, Bernard had visited this very café. Had sat drinking coffee. And then he had paid the bill and left, to meet his death in a building in Pigalle. All this Jordan had learned from the police interview with the waiter. But it happened a long time ago, thought Jordan. The man had probably moved on to other jobs. Still, it was worth a shot.

To his surprise, he discovered that Mario Cassini was still employed as a waiter. Well into his forties now, his hair a salt-and-pepper gray, his face creased with the lines of twenty years of smiles, Mario nodded and said, "Yes, yes. Of course I remember. The police, they come to talk to me three, four times. And each time I tell them the same thing. M. Tavistock, he comes for café au lait, every morning. Sometimes, *madame* is with him. Ah, beautiful!"

"But she wasn't with him on that particular day?"

Mario shook his head. "He comes alone. Sits at that table there." He pointed to an empty table near the sidewalk, red-checked cloth fluttering in the breeze. "He waits a long time for *madame*."

"And she didn't come?"

"No. Then she calls. Tells him to meet her at another place. In Pigalle. I take the message and give it to M. Tavistock."

"She spoke to you? On the telephone?"

"*Oui.* I write down address, give to him."

"That would be the address in Pigalle?"

Mario nodded.

"My father—M. Tavistock—did he seem at all upset that day? Angry?"

"Not angry. He seems—how do you say?—worried. He does not understand why *madame* goes to Pigalle. He pays for his coffee, then he leaves. Later I read in the newspaper that he is dead. Ah, *horrible!* The police, they are asking for information. So I call, tell them what I know." Mario shook his head at the tragedy of it all. At the loss of such a lovely woman as Mme Tavistock and such a generous man as her husband.

No new information here, thought Jordan. He turned to leave, then stopped and turned back.

"Are you certain it was Mme Tavistock who called to leave the message?" he asked.

"She says it is her," said Mario.

"And you recognized her voice?"

Mario paused. It lasted just the blink of an eye, but it was enough to tell Jordan that the man was not absolutely certain. "Yes," said Mario. "Who else would it be?"

Deep in thought, Jordan left the café and walked a few paces along Boulevard Saint-Germain, intending to return on foot to the hotel. But half a block away, he spotted the blue Peugeot. His little blond vampiress, he thought, still following him about. They were headed in the same direction; why not ask her for a ride?

He went to the Peugeot and pulled open the passenger door. "Mind dropping me off at the Ritz?" he asked brightly.

An outraged Colette stared at him from the driver's seat. "What do you think you are doing?" she demanded. "Get out of my car!"

"Oh, come, now. No need for hysterics—"

"Go away!" she cried, loudly enough to make a passerby stop and stare.

Calmly Jordan slid into the front seat. He noted that she was dressed in black again. What was it with these secret agent types? "It's a long walk to the Ritz. Surely it's not *verboten*, is it? To give me a lift back to my hotel?"

"I do not even know who you are," she insisted.

"I know who *you* are. Your name's Colette, you work for Claude Daumier, and you're supposed to be keeping an eye on me." Jordan smiled at her, the sort of smile that usually got him exactly what he wanted. He said, quite reasonably, "Rather than sneaking around after me all the way up the boulevard, why not be sensible about it? Save us both the inconvenience of this silly cat-and-mouse game."

A spark of laughter flickered in her eyes. She gripped the steering wheel and stared straight ahead, but he could see the smile tugging at her lips. "Shut the door," she snapped. "And use the seat belt. It is regulation."

As they drove up Boulevard Saint-Germain, he kept glancing at her, wondering if she was really as fierce as she appeared. That black leather skirt and the scowl on her face couldn't disguise the fact she was actually quite pretty.

"How long have you worked for Daumier?" he asked.

"Three years."

"And is this your usual sort of assignment? Following strange men about town?"

"I follow instructions. Whatever they are."

"Ah. The obedient type." Jordan sat back, grinning. "What did Daumier tell you about this particular assignment?"

"I am to see you and your sister are not harmed. Since today she is with M. Wolf, I decide to follow you." She paused and added under her breath, "Not as simple as I thought."

"I'm not all that difficult."

"But you do the unexpected. You catch me by surprise." A car was honking at them. Annoyed, Colette glanced up at the rearview mirror. "This traffic, it gets worse every—"

At her sudden silence, Jordan glanced at her. "Is something wrong?"

"No," she said after a pause, "I am just imagining things."

Jordan turned and peered through the rear window. All he saw was a line of cars snaking down the boulevard. He looked back at Colette. "Tell me, what's a nice girl like you doing in French Intelligence?"

She smiled—the first real smile he'd seen. It was like watching the sun come out. "I am earning a living."

"Meeting interesting people?"

"Quite."

"Finding romance?"

"Regrettably, no."

"What a shame. Perhaps you should find a new line of work."

"Such as?"

"We could discuss it over supper."

She shook her head. "It is not allowed to fraternize with a subject."

"So that's all I am," he said with a sigh. "A subject."

She dropped him off on a side street, around the corner from the Ritz. He climbed out, then turned and said, "Why not come in for a drink?"

"I am on duty."

"It must get boring, sitting in that car all day. Waiting for me to make another unexpected move."

"Thank you, but no." She smiled—a charmingly impish grin. It carried just a hint of possibility.

Jordan left the car and walked into the hotel.

Upstairs, he paced for a while, pondering what he'd just learned at Café Hugo. That phone call from Madeline—it just didn't fit in. Why on earth would she arrange to meet Bernard in Pigalle? It clearly didn't go along with the theory of a murder-suicide. Could the waiter be lying? Or was he simply mistaken? With all the ambient noise of a busy café, how could he be certain it was really Madeline Tavistock making that phone call?

I have to go back to the café. Ask Mario, specifically, if the voice was an Englishwoman's.

Once again he left the hotel and stepped into the brightness of midday. A taxi sat idling near the front entrance, but the driver was nowhere to be seen. Perhaps Colette was still parked around the corner; he'd ask her to drive him back to Boulevard Saint-Germain. He turned up the side street and spotted the blue Peugeot still parked there. Colette was sitting inside; through the tinted windshield, he saw her silhouette behind the steering wheel.

He went to the car and tapped on the passenger window. "Colette?" he called. "Could you give me another lift?"

She didn't answer.

Jordan swung open the door and slid in beside her. "Colette?"

She sat perfectly still, her eyes staring rigidly ahead. For a moment, he didn't understand. Then he saw the bright trickle of blood that had traced its way down her hairline and vanished into the black fabric of her turtlenecked shirt. In panic, he reached out to her and gave her shoulder a shake. "*Colette?*"

She slid toward him and toppled into his lap.

He stared at her head, now resting in his arms. In her temple was a single, neat bullet hole.

He scarcely remembered scrambling out of the car. What he did remember were the screams of a woman passerby. Then, moments later, he focused on the shocked faces of people who'd been drawn onto this quiet side street by the screams. They were all pointing at the woman's arm hanging limply out of the car. And they were staring at him.

Numbly, Jordan looked down at his own hands.

They were smeared with blood.

Chapter Five

FROM THE CROWD of onlookers standing on the corner, Amiel Foch watched the police handcuff the Englishman and lead him away. An unintended development, he thought. Not at all what he'd expected to happen.

Then again, he hadn't expected to see Colette LaFarge ever again. Or, even worse, to be seen by her. They'd worked together only once, and that was three years ago in Cyprus. He'd hoped, when he walked past her car, with his head down and his shoulders hunched, that she would not notice him. But as he'd headed away, he'd heard her call out his name in astonishment.

He'd had no alternative, he thought as he watched the attendants load her body into the ambulance. French Intelligence thought he was dead. Colette could have told them otherwise.

It hadn't been an easy thing to do. But as he'd turned to face her, his decision was already made. He had walked slowly back to her car. Through the windshield, he'd seen her look of wonder at a dead colleague come back to life. She'd sat frozen, staring at the apparition. She had not moved as he approached the driver's side. Nor did she move as he thrust his silenced automatic into her car window and fired.

Such a waste of a pretty girl, he thought as the ambulance drove away. But she should have known better.

The crowd was dispersing. It was time to leave.

He edged toward the curb. Quietly he dropped his pistol in the gutter and kicked it down the storm drain. The weapon was stolen, untraceable; better to have it found near the scene of the crime. It would cement the case against Jordan Tavistock.

Several blocks away, he found a telephone. He dialed his client.

"Jordan Tavistock has been arrested for murder," said Foch.

"Whose murder?" came the sharp reply.

"One of Daumier's agents. A woman."

"Did Tavistock do it?"

"No. I did."

There was a sudden burst of laughter from his client. "This is priceless! Absolutely priceless! I ask you to follow Jordan, and you have him framed for murder. I can't wait to see what you do with his sister."

"What do you wish me to do?" asked Foch.

There was a pause. "I think it's time to resolve this mess," he said. "Finish it."

"The woman is no problem. But her brother will be difficult to reach, unless I can find a way into the prison."

"You could always get yourself arrested."

"And when they identify my fingerprints?" Foch shook his head. "I need someone else for that job."

"Then I'll find you someone," came the reply. "For now, let's work on one thing at a time. Beryl Tavistock."

A TURKISH MAN NOW OWNED the building on Rue Myrha. He'd tried to improve it. He'd painted the exterior walls, shored up the crumbling balconies, replaced the missing roof slates, but the building, and the street on which it stood, seemed beyond rehabilitation. It was the fault of the tenants, explained Mr. Zamir, as he led them up two flights of stairs to the attic flat. What could one do with tenants who let their children run wild? By all appearances, Mr. Zamir was a successful businessman, a man whose tailored suit and excellent English bespoke prosperous roots. There were four families in the building, he said, all of them reliable enough with the rent. But no one lived in the attic flat—he'd always had difficulty renting that one out. People had come to inspect the place, of course, but when they heard of the murder, they quickly backed out. These silly superstitions! Oh, people claim they do not believe in ghosts, but when they visit a room where two people have died…

"How long has the flat been empty?" asked Beryl.

"A year now. Ever since I have owned the building. And before that—" he shrugged "—I do not know. It may have been empty for many years." He unlocked the door. "You may look around if you wish."

A puff of stale air greeted them as they pushed open the door—the smell of a room too long shut away from the world. It was not an unpleasant room. Sunshine washed in through a large, dirt-streaked window. The view looked down over Rue Myrha, and Beryl could see children kicking a soccer ball in the street. The flat was completely empty of furniture; there were only bare walls and floor. Through an open door, she glimpsed the bathroom with its chipped sink and tarnished fixtures.

In silence Beryl circled the flat, her gaze moving across the wood floor. Beside the window, she came to a halt. The stain was barely visible, just a faint brown blot in the oak planks. *Whose blood?* she wondered. *Mum's? Dad's? Or is it both of theirs, eternally mingled?*

"I have tried to sand the stain away," said Mr. Zamir. "But it goes very deep into the wood. Even when I think I have erased it, in a few weeks the stain seems to reappear." He sighed. "It frightens them away, you know. The tenants, they do not like to see such reminders on their floor."

Beryl swallowed hard and turned to look out the window. *Why on this street?* she wondered. *In this room? Of all the places in Paris, why did they die here?*

She asked quietly, "Who owned this building, Mr. Zamir? Before you did?"

"There were many owners. Before me, it was a M. Rosenthal. And before him, a M. Dudoit."

"At the time of the murder," said Richard, "the landlord was a man named Jacques Rideau. Did you know him?"

"I am sorry, I do not. That would have been many years ago."

"Twenty."

"Then I would not have met him." Mr. Zamir turned to the door. "I will leave you alone. If you have questions, I will be down in number three for a while."

Beryl heard the man's footsteps creak down the stairs. She looked at Richard and saw that he was standing off in a corner, frowning at the floor. "What are you thinking?" she asked.

"About Inspector Broussard. How he kept trying to point at that photo. The spot he was pointing to would be somewhere around here. Just to the left of the door."

"There's nothing to look at. And there was nothing in the photo, either."

"That's what bothers me. He seemed so troubled by it. And there was something about a briefcase...."

"The NATO file," she said softly.

He looked at her. "How much have you been told about Delphi?"

"I know it wasn't Mum or Dad. They would never have gone to the other side."

"People go over for different reasons."

"But not them. They certainly didn't need the money."

"Communist sympathies?"

"Not the Tavistocks!"

He moved toward her. With every step he took, her pulse seemed to leap faster. He came close enough to make her feel threatened. And tempted. Quietly he said, "There's always blackmail."

"Meaning they had secrets to hide?"

"Everyone does."

"Not everyone turns traitor."

"It depends on the secret, doesn't it? And how much one stands to lose because of it."

In silence they gazed at each other, and she found herself wondering how much he really did know about her parents. How much he wasn't admitting to. She sensed he knew a lot more than he was letting on, and that suspicion loomed like a barrier between them. Those secrets again. Those unspoken truths. She had grown up in a household where certain conversational doors were always kept locked. *I refuse to live my life that way. Ever again.*

She turned away. "They had no reason to be vulnerable to blackmail."

"You were just a child, eight years old. Away at boarding school in England. What did you really know about them? About their marriage, their secrets? What if it was your mother who rented this flat? Met her lover here?"

"I don't believe it. I won't."

"Is it so difficult to accept? That she was human, that she might have had a lover?" He took her by the shoulders, willing her to meet his gaze. "She was a beautiful woman, Beryl. If she'd wanted to, she could have had any number of lovers."

"You're making her out to be a tramp!"

"I'm considering all the possibilities."

"That she sold out Queen and country? To keep some vile little secret from surfacing?" Angrily she wrenched away from him. "Sorry, Richard, but my faith runs a little deeper than that. And if you'd known them, really known them, you'd never consider such a thing." She pivoted away and walked to the door.

"I did know them," he said. "I knew them rather well."

She stopped, turned to face him. "What do you mean by 'rather well'?"

"We...moved in the same circles. Not the same team, exactly. But we worked at similar purposes."

"You never told me."

"I didn't know how much I *should* tell you. How much you should know." He began to slowly circle the room, carefully considering each word before he spoke. "It was my first assignment. I'd just completed my training at Langley—"

"CIA?"

He nodded. "I was recruited straight out of the university. Not exactly my first career choice. But somehow they'd gotten hold of my master's thesis, an analysis of Libyan arms capabilities. It turned out to be amazingly close to the mark. They knew I was fluent in a few languages. And that I had taken out quite a large sum in student loans. That was the carrot, you see—the loan payoff. The foreign travel. And, I have to admit, the idea intrigued me, the chance to work as an Intelligence analyst..."

"Is that how you met my parents?"

He nodded. "NATO knew it had a security leak, originating in Paris. Somehow weapons data were slipping through to the East Germans. I'd just arrived in Paris, so there was no question that I was clean. They assigned me to work with Claude Daumier at French Intelligence. I was asked to compose a dummy weapons report, something close to, but not quite, the truth. It was encoded and transmitted to a few select embassy officials in Paris. The idea was to pinpoint the possible source of the leak."

"How were my parents involved?"

"They were attached to the British embassy. Bernard in Communications, Madeline in Protocol. Both were really working for MI6. Bernard was one of a few who had access to classified files."

"So he was a suspect?"

Richard nodded. "Everyone was. British, American, French. Right up to ambassadorial level." Again he began to pace, carefully measuring his words. "So the dummy file went out to the embassies. And we waited to see if it would turn up, like the others, in East German hands. It didn't. It ended up here, in a briefcase. In this very room." He stopped and looked at her. "With your parents."

"And that closed the file on Delphi," she said. Bitterly she added, "How neat and easy. You had your culprit. Lucky for you he was dead and unable to defend himself."

"I didn't believe it."

"Yet you dropped the matter."

"We had no choice."

"You didn't care enough to learn the truth!"

"No, Beryl. We didn't have the choice. We were instructed to call off the investigation."

She stared at him in astonishment. "By whom?"

"My orders came straight from Washington. Claude's from the French prime minister. The matter was dropped."

"And my parents went on record as traitors," she said. "What a convenient way to close the file." In disgust she turned and left the room.

He followed her down the stairs. "Beryl! I never really believed Bernard was the one!"

"Yet you let him take the blame!"

"I told you, I was ordered to—"

"And of course you always follow orders."

"I was sent back to Washington soon afterward. I couldn't pursue it."

They walked out of the building into the bedlam of Rue Myrha. A soccer ball flew past, pursued by a gaggle of tattered-looking children. Beryl paused on the sidewalk, her eyes temporarily dazzled by the sunshine. The street sounds, the shouts of the children, were disorienting. She turned and looked up at the building, at the attic window. The view suddenly blurred through her tears.

"What a place to die," she whispered. "God, what a horrible place to die…."

She climbed into Richard's car and pulled the door closed. It was a blessed relief to shut out the noise and chaos of Rue Myrha.

Richard slid in behind the driver's seat. For a moment, they sat in silence, staring ahead at the ragamuffins playing street soccer.

"I'll take you back to the hotel," he said.

"I want to see Claude Daumier."

"Why?"

"I want to hear his version of what happened. I want to confirm that you're telling me the truth."

"I am, Beryl."

She turned to him. His gaze was steady, unflinching. *An honest look if ever I've seen one,* she thought. *Which only proves how gullible I am.* She wanted to believe him, and there was the danger. It was that blasted attraction between them—the feverish tug of hormones, the memory of his kisses—that clouded her judgment. *What is it about this man? I take one look at his face, inhale a whiff of his scent, and I'm aching to tear off his clothes. And mine, as well.*

She looked straight ahead, trying to ignore all those heated signals passing between them. "I want to talk to Daumier."

After a pause, he said, "All right. If that's what it'll take for you to believe me."

A phone call revealed that Daumier was not in his office; he'd just left to conduct another interview with Marie St. Pierre. So they drove to Cochin Hospital, where Marie was still a patient.

Even from the far end of the hospital corridor, they could tell which room was Marie's; half a dozen policemen were stationed outside her door. Daumier had not yet arrived. Madame St. Pierre, informed that Lord Lovat's niece had arrived, at once had Beryl and Richard escorted into her room.

They discovered they weren't the only visitors Marie was entertaining that afternoon. Seated in chairs near the patient's bed were Nina Sutherland and Helena Vane. A little tea party was in progress, complete with trays of biscuits and finger sandwiches set on a rolling cart by the window. The patient, however, was not partaking of the refreshments; she sat propped up in bed, a sad and weary-looking French matron dressed in a gray robe to match her gray hair. Her only visible injuries appeared to be a bruised cheek and some scratches on her arms. It was clear from the woman's look of unhappiness that the bomb's most serious damage had been emotional. Any other patient would have been discharged by now; only her status as St. Pierre's wife allowed her such pampering.

Nina poured two cups of tea and handed them to Beryl and Richard. "When did you arrive in Paris?" she said.

"Jordan and I flew in yesterday," said Beryl. "And you?"

"We flew home with Helena and Reggie." Nina sat back down and crossed her silk-stockinged legs. "First thing this morning, I thought to myself, I really should drop in to see how Marie's doing. Poor thing, she does need cheering up."

Judging by the patient's glum face, Nina's visit had not yet achieved the desired result.

"What's the world coming to, I ask you?" said Nina, balancing her cup of tea. "Madness and anarchy! No one's immune, not even the upper class."

"Especially the upper class," said Helena.

"Has there been any progress on the case?" asked Beryl.

Marie St. Pierre sighed. "They insist it is a terrorist attack."

"Well, of course," said Nina. "Who else plants bombs in politicians' houses?"

Marie's gaze quickly dropped to her lap. She looked at her hands, the bony fingers woven together. "I have told Philippe we should leave Paris for a while. Tonight, perhaps, when I am released. We could visit Switzerland...."

"An excellent idea," murmured Helena gently. She reached out to squeeze Marie's hand. "You need to get away, just the two of you."

"But that's turning tail," said Nina. "Letting the criminals know they've won."

"Easy for you to say," muttered Helena. "It wasn't your house that was bombed."

"And if it was my house, I'd stay right in Paris," Nina retorted. "I wouldn't give an inch—"

"You've never had to."

"What?"

Helena looked away. "Nothing."

"What are you muttering about, Helena?"

"I only think," said Helena, "that Marie should do exactly what she wants. Leaving Paris for a while makes perfect sense. Any friend would back her up."

"I *am* her friend."

"Yes," murmured Helena, "of course you are."

"Are you saying I'm not?"

"I didn't say anything of the kind."

"You're muttering again, Helena. Really, it drives me up a wall. Is it so difficult to come right out and say things?"

"Oh, please," moaned Marie.

A knock on the door cut short the argument. Nina's son, Anthony, entered, dressed with his usual offbeat flair in a shirt of electric blue, a leather jacket. "Ready to leave, Mum?" he asked Nina.

At once Nina rose huffily to her feet. "More than ready," she sniffed and followed him to the door. There she stopped and gave Marie one last glance. "I'm only speaking as a friend," she said. "And I, for one, think you should stay in Paris." She took Anthony's arm and walked out of the room.

"Good heavens, Marie," muttered Helena, after a pause. "Why do you put up with the woman?"

Marie, looking small as she huddled in her bed, gave a small shrug. *They are so very much alike,* thought Beryl, comparing Marie St. Pierre and Helena. Neither one blessed with beauty, both on the fading side of middle age, and trapped in marriages to men who no longer adored them.

"I've always thought you were a saint just to let that bitch in your door," said Helena. "If it were up to me…"

"One must keep the peace" was all Marie said.

They tried to carry on a conversation, the four of them, but so many silences intervened. And overshadowing their talk of bomb blasts and ruined furniture, of lost artwork and damaged heirlooms, was the sense that something was being left unsaid. That even beyond the horror of these losses was a deeper loss. One had only to look in Marie St. Pierre's eyes to know that she was reeling from the devastation of her life.

Even when her husband, Philippe, walked into the room, Marie did not perk up. If anything, she seemed to recoil from Philippe's kiss. She averted her face and looked instead at the door, which had just swung open again.

Claude Daumier entered, saw Beryl, and halted in surprise. "You are *here?*"

"We were waiting to see you," said Beryl.

Daumier glanced at Richard, then back at Beryl. "I have been trying to find you both."

"What's wrong?" asked Richard.

"The matter is…delicate." Daumier motioned for them to follow. "It would be best," he said, "to discuss this in private."

They followed him into the hallway, past the nurses' station. In a quiet corner, Daumier stopped and turned to Richard.

"I have just received a call from the police. Colette was found shot to death in her car. Near Place Vendôme."

"Colette?" said Beryl. "The agent who was watching Jordan?"

Grimly Daumier nodded.

"Oh, my God," murmured Beryl. "Jordie—"

"He is safe," Daumier said quickly. "I assure you, he's not in danger."

"But if they killed her, they could—"

"He has been placed under arrest," said Daumier. His gaze, quietly sympathetic, focused on Beryl's shocked face. "For murder."

LONG AFTER EVERYONE ELSE had left the hospital room, Helena remained by Marie's bedside. For a while they said very little; good friends, after all, are comfortable with silence. But then

Helena could not hold it in any longer. "It's intolerable," she said. "You simply can't stand for this, Marie."

Marie sighed. "What else am I to do? She has so many friends, so many people she could turn against me. Against Philippe…."

"But you must do something. Anything. For one, refuse to speak to her!"

"I have no proof. Never do I have proof."

"You don't need proof. Use your eyes! Look at the way they act together. The way she's always around him, smiling at him. He may have told you it was over, but you can see it isn't. And where is he, anyway? You're in the hospital and he scarcely visits you. When he does, it's just a peck on the cheek and he's off again."

"He is preoccupied. The economic summit—"

"Oh, yes," Helena snorted. "Men's business is always so bloody important!"

Marie started to cry, not sobs, but noiseless, pitiful tears. Suffering in silence—that was her way. Never a complaint or a protest, just a heart quietly breaking. *The pain we endure,* thought Helena bitterly, *all for the love of men.*

Marie said in a whisper, "It is even worse than you know."

"How can it possibly be any worse?"

Marie didn't reply. She just looked down at the abrasions on her arms. They were only minor scrapes, the aftermath of flying glass, but she stared at them with what looked like quiet despair.

So that's it, thought Helena, horrified. *She thinks they're trying to kill her. Why doesn't she strike back? Why doesn't she fight?*

But Marie hadn't the will. One could see that, just by the slump of her shoulders.

My poor, dear friend, thought Helena, gazing at Marie with pity, *how very much alike we are. And yet, how very different.*

A MAN SAT ON THE BENCH across from him, silently eyeing Jordan's clothes, his shoes, his watch. A well-pickled fellow by the smell of him, thought Jordan with distaste. Or did that delightful odor, that unmistakable perfume of cheap wine and ripe underarms, emanate from the other occupant of the jail cell? Jordan glanced at the man snoring blissfully in the far corner. Yes, there was the likely source.

The man on the bench was still staring at him. Jordan tried to ignore him, but the man's gaze was so intrusive that Jordan finally snapped, "What are you looking at?"

"C'est en or?" the man asked.

"Pardon?"

"La montre. C'est en or?" The man pointed at Jordan's watch.

"Yes, of course it's gold!" said Jordan.

The man grinned, revealing a mouthful of rotted teeth. He rose and shuffled across the cell to sit beside Jordan. Right beside him. His gaze dropped speculatively to Jordan's shoes. *"C'est italienne?"*

Jordan sighed. "Yes, they're Italian."

The man reached over and fingered Jordan's linen jacket sleeve.

"All right, that's it," said Jordan. "Hands to yourself, chap! *Laissez-moi tranquille!*"

The man simply grinned wider and pointed to his own shoes, a pair of cardboard and plastic creations. "You like?"

"Very nice," groaned Jordan.

The sound of footsteps and clinking keys approached. The man sleeping in the corner suddenly woke up and began to yell, *"Je suis innocent! Je suis innocent!"*

"M. Tavistock?" called the guard.

Jordan jumped at once to his feet. "Yes?"

"You are to come with me."

"Where are we going?"

"You have visitors."

The guard led him down a hall, past holding cells jammed full with prisoners. Good grief, thought Jordan, and he'd thought his cell was bad. He followed the guard through a locked door into the booking area. At once his ears were assaulted with the sounds of bedlam. Everywhere phones seemed to be ringing, voices arguing. A ragtag line of prisoners waited to be processed, and one woman kept yelling that it was a mistake, all a mistake. Through the babble of French, Jordan heard his name called.

"Beryl?" he said in relief.

She ran to him, practically knocking him over with the force of her embrace. "Jordie! Oh, my poor Jordie, are you all right?"

"I'm fine, darling."

"You're really all right?"

"Never better, now that you're here." Glancing over her shoulder, he saw Richard and Daumier standing behind her. The cavalry had arrived. Now this terrible business could be cleared up.

Beryl pulled away and frowned at his face. "You look ghastly."

"I probably smell even worse." Turning to Daumier, he said, "Have they found out anything about Colette?"

Daumier shook his head. "A single bullet, nine millimeters, in the temple. Plainly an execution, with no witnesses."

"What about the gun?" asked Jordan. "How can they accuse me without having a murder weapon?"

"They do have one," said Daumier. "It was found in the storm drain, very near the car."

"And no witnesses?" said Beryl. "In broad daylight?"

"It is a side street. Not many passersby."

"But someone must have seen something."

Daumier gave an unhappy nod. "A woman did report seeing a man force his way into Colette's car. But it was on Boulevard Saint-Germain."

Jordan groaned. "Oh, great. That would've been me."

Beryl frowned. "You?"

"I talked her into giving me a ride back to the hotel. My fingerprints will be all over the inside of that car."

"What happened after you got into the car?" Richard asked.

"She let me off at the Ritz. I went up to the room for a few minutes, then came back down to talk to her. That's when I found…" Groaning, he clutched his head. "Lord, this can't be happening."

"Did you see anything?" Richard pressed him.

"Not a thing. But…" Jordan's head slowly lifted. "Colette may have."

"You're not sure?"

"While we were driving to the hotel, she kept frowning at the mirror. Said something about imagining things. I looked, but all I saw was traffic." Miserable, he turned to Daumier. "I blame myself, really. I keep thinking, if only I'd paid more attention, if I hadn't been so wrapped up—"

"She knew how to protect herself," interrupted Daumier. "She should have been prepared."

"That's what I don't understand," said Jordan. "That she was caught so off guard." He glanced at his watch. "There's still plenty of daylight. We could go back to Boulevard Saint-Germain. Retrace my steps. Something might come back to me."

His suggestion was met with dead silence.

"Jordie," said Beryl, softly, "you can't."

"What do you mean, I can't?"

"They won't release you."

"But they have to release me! I didn't do it!" He looked at Daumier. To his dismay, the Frenchman regretfully shook his head.

Richard said, "We'll do whatever it takes, Jordan. Somehow we'll get you out of here."

"Has anyone called Uncle Hugh?"

"He's not at Chetwynd," said Beryl. "No one knows where he is. It seems he left last night without telling anyone. So we're going to see Reggie and Helena. They've friends in the embassy. Maybe they can pull some strings."

Dismayed by the news, Jordan could only stand there, surrounded by the chaos of milling prisoners and policemen. *I'm in prison and Uncle Hugh's vanished,* he thought. *This nightmare is getting worse by the second.*

"The police think I'm guilty?" he ventured.

"I am afraid so," said Daumier.

"And you, Claude? What do you think?"

"Of course he knows you're innocent!" declared Beryl. "We all do. Just give me time to clear things up."

Jordan turned to his sister, his beautiful, stubborn sister. The one person he cared most about in the world. He took off his watch and firmly pressed it into her hand.

She frowned. "Why are you giving me this?"

"Safekeeping. I may be in here a rather long time. Now, I want you to go home, Beryl. The next plane to London. Do you understand?"

"But I'm not going anywhere."

"Yes, you are. And Richard is damn well going to see to it."

"How?" she retorted. "By dragging me off by the hair?"

"If that's what it takes."

"You need me here!"

"Beryl." He took her by the shoulders and spoke quietly. Sensibly. "A woman's been killed. And she was trained to defend herself."

"It doesn't mean I'm next."

"It means they're frightened. Ready to strike back. You have to go home."

"And leave you in this place?"

"Claude will be here. And Reggie—"

"So I fly home and leave you to rot in prison?" She shook her head in disagreement. "Do you really think I'd do that?"

"If you love me, you will."

Her chin came up. "If I love you," she said, "I'll do no such thing." She threw her arms around him in a fierce, uncompromising embrace. Then, brushing away tears, she turned to Richard. "Let's go. The sooner we talk to Reggie, the sooner we'll clear up this mess."

Jordan watched his sister walk away. It was just like her, he thought, to steer her own straight and stubborn course through that unruly crowd of pickpockets and prostitutes. "Beryl!" he yelled. "Go home! Don't be a bloody idiot!"

She stopped and looked back at him. "But I can't help it, Jordie. It runs in the family." Then she turned and walked out the door.

Chapter Six

"YOUR BROTHER'S RIGHT," said Richard. "You should go home."

"Don't *you* start now," she snapped over her shoulder.

"I'll drive you to the hotel to pack. Then I'm taking you to the airport."

"You and what regiment?"

"For once will you take some advice?" he yelled.

She spun around on the crowded sidewalk and turned to confront him. "Advice, yes. Orders, no."

"Okay, then just listen for a minute. Your coming to Paris was a crazy move to begin with. Sure, I understand why you did it. I understand that you'd want to know the truth about your parents. But things have changed, Beryl. A woman's been killed. It's a whole new ball game now."

"What am I supposed to do about Jordan? Just leave him there?"

"I'll take care of it. I'll talk to Reggie. We'll get him the best lawyer there is—"

"And I run home? Wash my hands of the whole mess?" She looked down at the watch she was holding. Jordan's watch. Quietly she said, "He's my family. Did you see how wretched he looked? It would kill him to stay in that place. If I left him there, I'd never forgive myself."

"And if something happened to you, Jordan would never forgive himself. And neither would I."

"I'm not your responsibility."

"But you are."

"And who decided that?"

He reached for her then, trapping her face in his hands. "I did," he whispered, and pressed his lips to hers. She was so stunned by the ferocity of his kiss that at first she couldn't react; too many glorious sensations were assaulting her at once. She heard his murmurings of need, felt the hot surge of his tongue into her mouth. Her own body responded, every nerve singing with desire. She was oblivious to the traffic, the passersby on the sidewalk. There were only the two of them and the way their bodies and mouths melted together. All day they'd been fighting this, she thought. And all day she knew it was hopeless. She knew it would come to this—one kiss on a Paris street, and she was lost.

Gently he pulled away and gazed down at her. "*That's* why you have to leave Paris," he murmured.

"Because you command it?"

"No. Because it makes sense."

She stepped back, desperate to put space between them, to regain some control—any control—over her emotions. "Sense to you, perhaps," she said softly. "But not to me." Then she turned and climbed into his car.

He slid in beside her and shut the door. Though they sat in silence, she could feel his frustration radiating throughout the car.

"What can I say that would make you change your mind?" he asked.

"*My* mind?" She looked at him and managed a tight, uncompromising smile. "Absolutely nothing."

"IT'S RATHER a sticky situation," said Reggie Vane. "If the charges weren't so serious—theft, perhaps, or even assault—then the embassy might be able to do something. But murder? I'm afraid that's beyond diplomatic intervention."

They were talking in Reggie's private study, a masculine, dark-paneled room very much like her Uncle Hugh's at Chetwynd. The bookshelves were lined with English classics, the walls hung with hunting scenes of foxes and hounds and gentlemen on horseback. The stone fireplace was an exact copy, Reggie had told them, of the hearth in his childhood home in Cornwall. Even the smell of Reggie's pipe tobacco reminded Beryl of home. How comforting to discover that here, on the outskirts of Paris, was a familiar world transplanted straight from England.

"Surely the ambassador can do something?" said Beryl. "This is Jordan we're talking about, not some soccer-club hooligan. Besides, he's innocent."

"Of course he's innocent," said Reggie. "Believe me, if there was anything I could do about it, our Jordan wouldn't stay in that cell a moment longer." He sat down on the couch beside her and clasped her hands, the whole time focusing his mild blue eyes on her face. "Beryl, darling, you have to understand. Even the ambassador himself can't work miracles. I've spoken to him, and he's not optimistic."

"Then there's nothing you or he can do?" Beryl asked miserably.

"I'll arrange for a lawyer—one our embassy recommends. He's an excellent fellow, someone they call in for just this sort of thing. Specializes in English clients."

"And that's all we can hope for? A good attorney?"

Reggie's answer was a regretful nod.

In her disappointment, Beryl didn't hear Richard move to stand close behind her, but she did feel his hands coming to rest protectively on her shoulders. *How I've come to rely on him,* she thought. *A man I shouldn't trust. And yet I do.*

Reggie looked at Richard. "What about the Intelligence angle?" he asked. "Any evidence forthcoming?"

"French Intelligence is working with the police. They'll be running ballistic tests on the gun. No fingerprints were found on it. The fact that he's Lord Lovat's nephew will get him some special consideration. But in the end, it's still a murder charge. And the victim's a Frenchwoman. Once the local papers get hold of the story, it will sound like some spoiled English brat trying to slither out of criminal charges."

"And there's enough ill will toward us British as it is," said Reggie. "After thirty years in this country, I should know. I tell you, as soon as my year's up at the bank, I'm going home." His gaze wandered longingly to the painting over the mantelpiece. It was of a country home, its walls festooned with blue wisteria blossoms. "Helena hated it in Cornwall—thought the house was far too primitive. But it suited my parents. And it suits me." He looked at Beryl. "It's a frightening thing, getting into trouble so far from home. One is always aware that one is vulnerable. And neither class nor money can make things right."

"I've told Beryl she should fly home," said Richard.

Reggie nodded. "My feelings exactly."

"I can't," said Beryl. "I'd feel like a rat jumping ship."

"At least you'd be a live rat," said Richard.

Angrily she shrugged off his touch. "But a rat all the same."

Reggie reached for her hand. "Beryl," he said quietly, "listen to me. I was your mother's oldest friend—we grew up together. So I feel a special responsibility. And you have no idea how painful it is for me to see one of Madeline's children in such a fix. It's awful enough that Jordan's in trouble, but to worry about you, as well…" He gave her hand a squeeze. "Listen to your Mr. Wolf here. He's a sensible fellow. Someone you can trust."

Someone I can trust. Beryl felt Richard's gaze on her back, felt it as acutely as a touch, and her spine stiffened. She focused firmly on Reggie. Dear Reggie, whose shared past with Madeline made him part of her family.

She said, "I know you mean only the best, Reggie, but I can't leave Paris."

The two men looked at each other, exchanging shared expressions of frustration, but not surprise. After all, they had both known Madeline; they could expect nothing less than stubbornness from her daughter.

There was a knock on the study door. Helena poked her head in. "All right for me to come in?"

"Of course," said Beryl.

Helena entered, carrying a tray of tea and biscuits, which she set down on the end table. "I'm always careful to ask first," she said with a smile as she poured out four cups, "before I trespass in Reggie's private abode." She handed Beryl a cup. "Have we made any headway, then?"

From the silence that greeted her question, Helena knew the

answer. She looked at once apologetic. “Oh, Beryl. I’m so sorry. Isn’t there *something* you can do, Reggie?”

“I’m already doing it,” said Reggie, with more than a hint of impatience. Turning his back to her, he took a pipe down from the mantelpiece and lit it. For a moment, there was only the sound of the teacups clinking on saucers and the soft put-put-put of Reggie’s lips on the pipe stem.

“Reggie?” ventured Helena again. “It seems to me that calling an attorney is merely being reactive. Isn’t there something, well, *active* that could be done?”

“Such as?” asked Richard.

“For instance, the crime itself. We all know Jordan couldn’t have done it. So who did?”

Reggie grunted. “You’re hardly qualified as a detective.”

“Still, it’s a question that will have to be answered. That young woman was killed while watching over Jordan. So this may all stem from the reason Jordan’s in Paris to begin with. Though I can’t quite see how a twenty-year-old case of murder could be so dangerous to someone.”

“It was more than murder,” Beryl observed. “Espionage was involved.”

“That business with the NATO mole,” Reggie said to Helena. “You remember. Hugh told us about it.”

“Oh, yes. Delphi.” Helena glanced at Richard. “MI6 never actually identified him, did they?”

“They had their suspicions,” said Richard.

“I myself always wondered,” said Helena, reaching for a biscuit, “about Ambassador Sutherland. And why he committed suicide so soon after Madeline and Bernard died.”

Richard nodded. “You and I think along the same lines, Lady Helena.”

“Though I can’t say he didn’t have other reasons to jump off that bridge. If I were a man married to Nina, I’d have killed myself long ago.” Helena bit sharply into the biscuit; it was a reminder that even mousy women have teeth.

Reggie tapped his pipe and said, “It’s not right for us to speculate.”

“Still, one can’t help it, can one?”

By the time Reggie walked his guests to the front door, darkness had fallen and the night had taken on a damp, unseasonable chill. Even the high walls surrounding the Vanes' private courtyard couldn't seem to shut out the sense of danger that hung in the air that night.

"I promise you," said Reggie, "I'll do everything I can."

"I don't know how to thank you," Beryl murmured.

"Just give me a smile, dear. Yes, that's it." Reggie took her by the shoulders and planted a kiss on her forehead. "You look more and more like your mother every day. And from me, there is no higher compliment." He turned to Richard. "You'll look out for the girl?"

"I promise," said Richard.

"Good. Because she's all we have left." Sadly he touched Beryl's cheek. "All we have left of Madeline."

"WERE THEY ALWAYS that way together?" asked Beryl. "Reggie and Helena?"

Richard kept his eyes on the road as he drove. "What do you mean?"

"The sniping at each other. The put-downs."

He chuckled. "I'm so used to hearing it, I hardly notice it anymore. Yes, I guess it was that way when I met them twenty years ago. I'm sure part of it's due to his resentment of Helena's money. No man likes to feel, well, kept."

"No," she said quietly, looking straight ahead. "I suppose no man would." *Is that how it would be between us?* she wondered. *Would he hold my money against me? Would his resentment build up over the years, until we ended up like Reggie and Helena, sharing a lifetime of hell together?*

"Part of it, too," said Richard, "is the fact that Reggie never really liked being in Paris, and he never liked being a banker. Helena talked him into taking the post."

"She doesn't seem to like it here much, either."

"No. And so there they are, always sniping at each other. I'd see them at parties with your parents, and I was always struck by the contrast. Bernard and Madeline seemed so much in love. Then again, every man who met your mother couldn't help but fall in love, just a little."

"What was it about her?" asked Beryl. "You said once that she was…enchanting."

"When I met her, she was about forty. Oh, she had a gray hair here and there. A few laugh lines. But she was more fascinating than any twenty-year-old woman I'd ever met. I was surprised to hear that she wasn't born to nobility."

"She was from Cornwall. Old Spanish blood. Dad met her one summer while on holiday." Beryl smiled. "He said she beat him in a footrace. In her bare feet. And that's when he knew she was the one for him."

"They were well matched, in every way. I suppose that's what fascinated me—their happiness. My parents were divorced. It was a pretty nasty split, and it soured me on the whole idea of marriage. But your parents made it look so easy." He shook his head. "I was more shocked than anyone about their deaths. I couldn't believe that Bernard would—"

"He didn't do it. I know he didn't."

After a pause, Richard said, "So do I."

They drove for a moment without speaking, the lights of passing traffic flashing at them through the windshield.

"Is that why you never married?" she asked. "Because of your parents' divorce?"

"It was one reason. The other is that I've never found the right woman." He glanced at her. "Why didn't you marry?"

She shrugged. "Never the right man."

"There must have been someone in your life."

"There was. For a while." She hugged herself and stared out at the darkness rushing past.

"Didn't work out?"

She managed a laugh. "I'm lucky it didn't."

"Do I detect a trace of bitterness?"

"Disillusionment, really. When we first met, I thought he was quite extraordinary. He was a surgeon about to leave on a mercy mission to Nigeria. It's so rare to find a man who really cares about humanity. I visited him, twice, in Africa. He was in his element out there."

"And what happened?"

"We were lovers for a while. And then I came to realize how

he saw himself. The great white savior. He'd swoop into a primitive hospital, save a few lives, then fly home to England for a bracing dose of adulation. Which, it turned out, he could never get enough of. One adoring woman wasn't sufficient. He had to have a dozen." Softly she added, "And I wanted to be the only one." She leaned back against the car seat and stared out at the glow of Paris. The City of Light, she thought. Still, there were those shadows, those dark alleys and even darker secrets.

Back at the Place Vendôme, they sat for a moment in the parked car, not speaking, just sitting side by side in the gloom. *We're both exhausted,* she thought. *And the night isn't over yet. I'll have to pack Jordan's things. A toothbrush, a change of clothes. Bring them back to the prison....*

"Then I can't talk you into leaving," he said.

She looked out at the plaza, at the silhouette of two lovers strolling arm in arm through the darkness. "No. Not until he's free. Not until we see this through to the end."

"I was afraid you'd say that. But I'm not surprised. Just the other day you told me you had a hard head."

She looked at his face, saw the gleam of his smile in the shadows. "This isn't hardheadedness, Richard. This is loyalty. To Jordan. To my parents. We're Tavistocks, you see, and we stand by each other."

"Standing by Jordan, I can see. But your parents are dead."

"It's a matter of honor."

He shook his head. "Bernard and Madeline aren't around to care about honor. It's a medieval concept, to march into battle for something as abstract as the family name."

She climbed out of the car. "Obviously the Wolf family name means nothing to you," she said coldly.

He was out of the car and moving right beside her as she walked through the hotel lobby and stepped into the elevator. "Maybe it's my peculiarly American point of view, but my name is what *I* make of it. I don't wear the family crest tattooed on my forehead."

"You couldn't possibly understand."

"Of course not," he retorted as they stepped out of the elevator. "I'm just a dumb Yank."

"I never called you any such thing!"

He followed her into the suite and shut the door with a thud. "Still, it's clear I'm not up to her Ladyship's standards."

She whirled around and faced him in anger. "You're holding it against me, aren't you? My name. My wealth."

"What's bothering me has nothing to do with your being a Tavistock."

"What *is* bothering you, then?"

"The fact that you won't listen to reason."

"Ah. My hard head."

"Yes, your hard head. And your dumb sense of honor. And your…your…"

She moved right up to him. Tilting up her chin, she stared him straight in the eye. "My what?"

He took her face in his hands and planted a kiss on her mouth, a kiss so long and hard that she had difficulty catching her breath. When at last he pulled back, her legs were wobbly and her pulse was roaring in her ears.

"*That's* what's bothering me," he said. "I can't think straight when you're around. Can't concentrate long enough to tie my own shoelaces. You brush past me, or just look at me, and my mind goes off on certain tangents I'd rather not specify. It's the kind of situation that leads to mistakes. And I don't like to make mistakes."

"You're the one who can't concentrate. And I'm the one who has to fly home?" She turned and started across the room toward the connecting door to Jordan's suite. "Sorry, Richard," she said, moving past the window, "but you'll just have to keep those lusty male hormones under—"

Her words were cut off by the crack of the shattering window.

Reflexes made her pivot away from the sting of flying glass. In the next instant, Richard lunged at her and sent her sprawling to the shard-littered floor.

Another bullet zinged through the window and thudded into the far wall.

"The light!" shouted Richard. "Got to kill the light!" He began to crawl toward the bedside lamp and had almost reached it when the second window shattered. Broken glass rained on top of him.

"Richard!" screamed Beryl.

"Stay down!" He took a deep breath, then rolled across the

floor. He grabbed the lamp cord and yanked the plug from the outlet. Instantly the room was plunged into darkness. The only light came through the windows, shining dimly in from the Place Vendôme. An eerie silence fell over the room, broken only by the hammering of Beryl's heartbeat in her ears.

She started to rise to her knees.

"Don't move!" warned Richard.

"He can't see us."

"He might have an infrared scope. Stay down."

Beryl dropped back to the floor and felt the bite of broken glass through her sleeves. "Where's it coming from?"

"Has to be one of the buildings across the plaza. Long-range rifle."

"What do we do now?"

"We call for reinforcements." She heard him crawling in the darkness, then heard the clang of the telephone hitting the floor. An instant later, he muttered an oath. "Line's dead! Someone's cut the wire."

New panic shot through Beryl. "You mean they've been in the room?"

"Which means—" Suddenly he fell silent.

"Richard?"

"Shh. Listen."

Over her pounding heartbeat, she heard the faint whine of the hotel elevator as it came to a stop at their floor.

"I think we're in trouble," said Richard.

Chapter Seven

"HE CAN'T GET IN," said Beryl. "The door's locked."

"They'll have a passkey. If they managed to get in here earlier…"

"What do we do?"

"Jordan's room. Move!"

At once she was on her knees and crawling toward the connecting door. Only when she'd reached it did she realize Richard wasn't following her.

"Come on!" she whispered.

"You go. I'll hold them off."

She glanced back in disbelief. "What?"

"They'll check this room first to see if we've been hit. I'll slow them down. You get out through Jordan's suite. Head for the stairwell and don't stop running."

Beryl crouched frozen in the connecting doorway. *This is suicide. He has no gun, no weapon at all.* Already he was slipping through the shadows. She could just make out his figure, poised by the door. Waiting for the attack.

The knock on the door made her jerk in panic. "Mlle Tavistock?" called a man's voice. Beryl didn't answer; she didn't dare to. *"Mademoiselle?"* the voice called again.

Richard was gesturing frantically at her through the darkness. *Get out! Now.*

I can't leave him, she thought. *I can't let him fight this alone.*

A key grated in the lock.

There was no time to consider the risks. Beryl grabbed the bedside lamp, scrambled toward Richard, and planted herself right beside him.

"What the hell are you doing?" he whispered.

"Shut up," she hissed back.

They both flattened against the wall as the door swung open in front of them. There was a pause, the span of just a few heartbeats, and then they heard footsteps cross the threshold into the room. The door slowly swung closed, revealing the silhouettes of the intruders—two men, standing in the darkness. Beryl could feel Richard coil up beside her, could almost hear his silent one-two-three countdown. Suddenly he was flying at the nearest man; the force of the impact sent both men slamming to the floor.

Beryl raised the lamp and brought it crashing down on the head of the second intruder. He collapsed at her feet, facedown and groaning. She dropped beside him and began patting his clothes for a gun. Through his jacket, she felt a hard lump under his arm. A holster? She rolled him over onto his back. Only then, as a crack of light through the partially closed door spilled across his face, did she realize their mistake.

"Oh, my God," she said. She glanced at Richard, who'd just grabbed his opponent by the collar and was about to shove him against the wall. "Richard, don't!" she yelled. "Don't hurt him!"

He paused, still clutching the other man's collar in his fists. "Why the hell not?" he muttered.

"Because these are the wrong men, that's why!" She went to the wall switch and flicked on the overhead light.

Richard blinked in the sudden brightness. He stared at the hotel manager, cowering in his grip. Then he turned and looked at the man who lay groaning by the door. It was Claude Daumier.

At once Richard released the manager, who promptly shrank away in terror. "Sorry," said Richard. "My mistake."

"If I'd known it was you," said Beryl, pressing a bag of ice to Daumier's head, "I wouldn't have whacked you so hard."

"If you had known it was me," muttered Daumier, "I would

hope you wouldn't have whacked me at all." He sat up on the couch and caught the bag of ice before it could slide off. "*Zut alors,* what did you use, *chérie?* A brick?"

"A lamp. And not a very big one, either." She glanced at Richard and the hotel manager. Both men were looking slightly the worse for wear—especially the manager. That black eye of his was colorful testimony to the damaging potential of Richard's fist. Now that the crisis was over, and they were safely barricaded in the manager's office, the situation struck Beryl as more than a little hilarious. A senior French Intelligence agent, beaned by a lamp? Richard, still nursing his bruised knuckles. And the poor hotel manager, assiduously maintaining a safe distance from those same knuckles. She could have laughed—if the whole affair hadn't been so frightening.

There was a knock on the door. Instantly Beryl tensed, only to relax again when she saw that it was a policeman. *I'm still high on adrenaline,* she thought as she watched Daumier and the cop converse in French. *Still expecting the worst.*

The policeman withdrew, closing the door behind him.

"What did he say?" Beryl asked.

"The shots were fired from across the plaza," said Daumier. "They have found bullet casings on the rooftop."

"And the gunman?" asked Richard.

Regretfully Daumier shook his head. "Vanished."

"Then he's still on the loose," said Richard. "And we don't know when he'll strike again." He looked at the manager. "What about that telephone wire? Who could've cut it?"

The man shrank back a step, as though expecting another blow. "I do not know, *monsieur!* One of the maids, she says her passkey was misplaced for a few hours today."

"So anyone could have gotten in."

"No one from our staff! They are thoroughly checked. You see, we have many important guests."

"I want your employees revetted. Every last one of them."

The manager nodded meekly. Then, still wincing in pain from the black eye, he left the office.

Richard began to pace, carelessly yanking his tie loose as he moved. "We have an intruder who cuts the phone line. A marksman stationed across the plaza. A high-powered rifle positioned for a shot straight into Beryl's room. Claude, this is sounding worse by the minute."

"Why would they try to kill me?" asked Beryl. "What have I done?"

"You've asked too many questions, that's what." Richard turned to Daumier. "You had it right, Claude. The matter's not dead, not by a long shot."

"We were both in that room, Richard," said Beryl. "How do you know he was aiming at me?"

"I wasn't the one walking past that window."

"You're the one who's CIA."

"The qualifying prefix is *ex*, as in, no longer with the Company. I'm not a threat to anyone."

"And I am?"

"Yes. By virtue of your name—not to mention your curiosity." He glanced at Daumier. "We need a safe house, Claude. Can you arrange it?"

"We keep a flat in Passy for protection of witnesses. It will serve your purpose."

"Who else knows about it?"

"My people. A few ministry officials."

"That's too many."

"It is the best I can offer. It has an alarm system. And I will assign guards."

Richard paused, thinking, weighing the risks. At last he nodded. "It will have to do for tonight. Tomorrow, we'll come up with something else. Maybe a plane ticket." He looked at Beryl.

This time she didn't protest. Already she could feel the adrenaline fading away. A moment ago, every nerve felt wired for action; now a plane home was beginning to sound sensible. All it took was a short flight across the Channel, and she'd be safe in the refuge of Chetwynd. It was all so easy, so tempting.

And she was so very, very tired.

With a numb sense of detachment, Beryl listened as Daumier made the necessary phone calls. He hung up and said, "I will have a car and escort brought around. Beryl's clothes will be delivered to the flat later. Oh, and Richard, you will no doubt want this." He reached under his suit jacket and withdrew a semiautomatic pistol from his shoulder holster. He handed it to Richard. "A loan. Just between us, of course."

"Are you sure you want to part with it?"

"I have another." Daumier slid off his holster, which he also gave to Richard. "You remember how to use one?"

Richard checked the ammunition clip and nodded grimly. "I think it'll come back."

A policeman knocked on the door. The car was waiting.

Richard took Beryl's arm and helped her to her feet. "Time to drop out of sight for a while. Are you ready?"

She looked at the gun he was holding, noted how easily he handled it, how comfortably he slid it into the holster. A professional, she thought. The transformation was almost frightening. *How well do I really know you, Richard Wolf?*

For now, the question was irrelevant. He was the one man she could count on, the one man she had to trust.

She followed him out the door.

"WE SHOULD BE SAFE HERE. For tonight, at least." Richard double-bolted the apartment door and turned to look at her.

She was standing in the center of the living room, her arms wrapped around her shoulders, a dazed look in her eyes. This was not the brash and stubborn Beryl he knew, he thought. This was a woman who'd faced sheer terror and knew the worst wasn't over yet. He wanted to go to her, to take her in his arms and promise her that nothing would ever hurt her while he was around, but they both knew it was a promise he might not be able to keep. In silence, he circled the flat, checking to see that the windows were secure, the drapes closed. A glance outside told him there were two guards watching the building, one at the front entrance, one at the rear. A safety net, he thought. For when I let my attention slip. And it *would* slip. Sooner or later, he would have to sleep.

Satisfied that all was locked up tight, he went back to the living room. He found Beryl sitting on the couch, very quiet, very still. Almost…defeated.

"Are you all right?" he asked.

She gave a shrug, as though the question was irrelevant—as though they had far more important things to consider.

He took off his jacket and tossed it over a chair. "You haven't eaten. There's some food in the kitchen."

Her gaze focused on his shoulder holster. "Why did you quit the business?" she asked.

"You mean the Company?"

She nodded. "When I saw you holding that gun, it…it suddenly struck me. What you used to be."

He sat down beside her. "I've never killed anyone. If that makes a difference."

"But you're trained to do it."

"Only in self-defense. That's not the same thing as murder."

She nodded, as though trying very hard to agree with him.

He took the Glock from the holster and held it out to her. She regarded it with undisguised abhorrence.

"Yes, I understand how you feel," he said. "This gun's a semi-automatic. Nine millimeter bullets, sixteen cartridges to the magazine. Some people consider it a work of art. I think of it as a tool of last resort. Something I hope to God I never have to use." He set it on the coffee table, where it lay like an evil reminder of violence. "Pick it up if you want to. It's not very heavy."

"I'd rather not." She shuddered and looked away. "I'm not afraid of guns. I mean, I've handled rifles before. I used to go shooting with Uncle Hugh. But those were only clay pigeons."

"Not quite the same thing."

"No. Not quite."

"You asked why I quit the Company." He pointed to the Glock. "That was one of the reasons. I've never killed anyone, and I'm not itching to. For me, the intelligence business was a game. A challenge. The enemy was well-defined—the Russians, the East Germans. But now…" He picked up the gun and held it thoughtfully in his palm. "The world's turned into a crazy place. I can't tell who the enemy is anymore. And I knew that sooner or later, I'd lose my edge. I could already feel it happening."

"Your edge?"

"It's my age, you know. You hit forty and you don't react the way you did as a twenty-year-old. I like to think I've grown smarter, instead, but what I really am is more cautious. And a lot less willing to take risks." He looked at her. "With anyone's life."

She met his gaze. Looking into her eyes, he suddenly found himself wanting to babble all sorts of crazy things. To tell her that the one life he didn't want to risk was hers. When had this stopped being a mere baby-sitting job? he wondered. When had it become something much more? A mission. An obsession.

"You frighten me, Richard," she said.

"It's the gun."

"No, it's you. All the things I don't know about you. All the secrets you're keeping from me."

"From now on, I promise I'll be absolutely honest with you."

"But it started out as half truths. Not telling me you knew my parents. Or how they died. Don't you see, it's my childhood all over again! Uncle Hugh with his head full of classified secrets." She let out a breath of frustration and looked away. "Then I see you with that…thing."

He touched her face and gently turned it toward him. "It's just a temporary evil," he murmured. "Until this is over." She kept looking at him, her eyes bright and moist, her hair tumbling about her shoulders. *She wants to trust me,* he thought. *But she's afraid.*

He couldn't help himself. He kissed her. Once. Twice. The second time, he felt her lips yield under his, felt her whole body seem to turn liquid at his touch. He kissed her a third time and found his hands sliding through her hair, his fingers hopelessly becoming tangled in all that raven silk. She sighed, a delicious sound of surrender, invitation, and she sagged backward onto the couch.

Suddenly he, too, was falling, tumbling on top of her. Their lips met in a touch that instantly turned electric. She reached around his neck and pulled him down hard against her—

And flinched. That blasted gun again. The holster had pushed into her breast, had served as an ugly reminder of all the things that had happened today. All the things that could still happen.

He looked at her face, at her hair flung across the cushions, at the mingling of fear and desire he saw in her eyes. *Not now,* he thought. *Not this way.*

Slowly he pulled away and they both sat up. For a moment, they remained side by side on the couch, not touching, not speaking.

She said, "I'm not ready for this. I'll put my life in your hands, Richard. But my heart, that's a different matter."

"I understand."

"Then you'll also understand that I'm not a fan of James Bond, or anyone remotely like him. I'm not impressed by guns, or by the men who use them." She rose to her feet and moved pointedly away from the couch. Away from him.

"So what does impress you?" he asked. "If not a man's gun?"

She turned to him and he saw a flicker of humor cross her face. *The old Beryl,* he thought. *Thank God she's still there, somewhere.*

"Straight talk," she said. "That's what impresses me."

"Then that's what you'll get. I promise."

She turned and walked to the bedroom. "We'll see."

JORDAN WAS NOT IMPRESSED by this lawyer, no, he was not impressed at all.

The man had greasy hair and a greasy little mustache, and he spoke English with the exaggerated accent of a second-rate actor playing a stereotypical Frenchman. All those "eets" and "zees" and "*Mon Dieus.*" Still, Jordan reasoned, since Beryl had hired the man, he must be one of the best attorneys in Paris.

You could have fooled me, thought Jordan, gazing across the prison interview table at the smarmy M. Jarre.

"Not to worry," said the man. "Everything will be taken care of. I am reviewing the papers now, and I believe we will soon reach an agreement to have you released."

"What about the investigation?" asked Jordan. "Any progress?"

"Very slow. You know how it is, M. Tavistock. In a city as large as Paris, the police, they are overworked. You cannot be impatient."

"And my uncle? Have you been able to reach him?"

"He is in complete agreement with my planned course of action."

"Is he coming to Paris?"

"He is detained. Business keeps him at home, I am afraid."

"At home? But I thought..." Jordan paused. Didn't Beryl say Uncle Hugh had left Chetwynd?

M. Jarre rose from the table. "Rest assured that all that can be done, will be done. I have instructed the police to transfer you to a more comfortable cell."

"Thank you," said Jordan, still puzzling over the reference to Uncle Hugh. As the attorney was leaving the room, Jordan called out, "M. Jarre? Did my uncle happen to mention how his…negotiations went in London?"

The attorney glanced back. "They are still in progress, I understand. But I am sure he will tell you himself." He gave a nod of farewell. "Good evening, M. Tavistock. I hope you find your new cell more agreeable." He walked out.

What the dickens is going on? thought Jordan. He wondered about this all the way to his cell—his new cell. One look at the pair of shady characters seated inside and his suspicions about M. Jarre deepened. *This* was more agreeable quarters?

Reluctantly Jordan stepped inside and flinched at the clang of the door shutting behind him. The jailer walked away, his footsteps echoing down the hall.

The two prisoners were staring at his fine Italian shoes, which contrasted dreadfully with the regulation prison garb he was wearing.

"Hello," said Jordan, for want of anything else to say.

"Anglais?" asked one of the men.

Jordan swallowed. *"Oui. Anglais."*

The man grunted and pointed to an empty bunk. "Yours."

Jordan went to the bunk, set his bundle of street clothes on the foot of the bed, and stretched out on the mattress. As the two prisoners babbled away in French, Jordan kept wondering about that greasy attorney and why he had lied about Uncle Hugh. If only he could get in touch with Beryl, ask her what was going on…

He sat up at the sound of footsteps approaching the cell. It was the guard, escorting yet another prisoner—this one a balding, round-cheeked man with a definite waddle and a pleasant enough face. The sort of fellow you'd expect to see standing behind a bakery counter. *Not your typical criminal,* thought Jordan. *But then, neither am I.*

The man entered the cell and was directed to the fourth and last bunk. He sat down, looking stunned by the circumstances in which he found himself. François was his name, and from what Jordan could gather using his elementary command of French, the man's crime had something to do with the fair sex.

Solicitation, perhaps? François was not eager to talk about it. He simply sat on his bed and stared at the floor. *We're both new to this,* thought Jordan.

The other two cellmates were still watching him. Sullen young men, obviously sociopathic. He'd have to keep his eye on them.

Supper came—an atrocious goulash accompanied by French bread. Jordan stared at the muddy brown gravy and thought wistfully of his supper the night before—poached salmon and roast duckling. Ah, well. One had to eat regardless of one's circumstances. What a shame there wasn't a bottle of wine to wash down the meal. A nice Beaujolais, perhaps, or just a common Burgundy. He took a bite of goulash and decided that even a bad bottle of wine would be welcome—anything to dull the taste of this gravy. He forced himself to eat it and made a silent vow that when he got out of here—*if* he got out of here—the first place he'd head for was a decent restaurant.

At midnight, the lights were turned off. Jordan stretched out on the blanket and made every effort to sleep, but found he couldn't. For one thing, his cellmates were snoring to wake the dead. For another, the day's events kept playing and replaying in his mind. That drive with Colette from Boulevard Saint-Germain. The way she had glanced at the rearview mirror. If only he had paid more attention to who might be following them back to the hotel. And then, against his will, he remembered the horror of finding her body in the car, remembered the stickiness of her blood on his hands.

Rage bubbled up inside him—an impotent sense of fury about her death. *It's my fault,* he thought. If she hadn't been watching over him, protecting him.

But that's not why she died, Jordan thought suddenly. He was nowhere nearby when it happened. So why did they kill her? Did she know something, see something…

… or someone?

His thoughts veered in a new direction. Colette must have spotted a face in her rearview mirror, a face in the car that was following them. After she'd dropped Jordan off at the Ritz, maybe she'd seen that someone again. Or he'd seen her and knew she could identify him.

Which made the killer someone Colette knew. Someone she recognized.

He was so intent on piecing together the puzzle, he didn't pay much attention to the creak of the bunk springs somewhere in the cell. Only when he heard the soft rustle of movement did he realize that one of his cellmates was approaching his bed.

It was dark; he could make out only faintly a shadowy figure moving toward him. One of those young hoods, he thought, come to rifle his jacket.

Jordan lay perfectly still and willed his breathing to remain deep and even. *Let the coward think I'm still asleep. When he moves close enough, I'll surprise him.*

The shadow slipped quietly through the darkness. Six feet away, now five. Jordan's heart was pounding, his muscles already tensed for action. *Just a little closer. A little closer. He'll be reaching for the jacket hanging at the foot of the bed....*

But the man moved instead to Jordan's head. There was a faint arc of shadow—an arm being raised to deliver a blow. Jordan's hand shot out just as his assailant attacked.

He caught the other man's wrist and heard a grunt of surprise. His attacker came at him with his free hand. Jordan deflected the blow and scrambled off the bunk. Still gripping his attacker's wrist, he gave it a vicious twist, eliciting a yelp of pain. The man was thrashing to get free now, but Jordan held on. He was not going to get away. Not without learning a lesson. He shoved the man backward and heard the satisfying thud of his opponent's body hitting the cinder-block wall. The man groaned and tried to pull free. Again, Jordan shoved. This time they both toppled over onto a cot, landing on its sleeping occupant. The man in Jordan's grasp began to writhe, to jerk. At once Jordan realized this was no longer a man fighting to free himself. This was a man in the throes of a convulsion.

He heard the sound of footsteps and then the cell lights flashed on. A guard yelled at him in French.

Jordan released his assailant and backed away in surprise. It was the moon-faced François. The man lay sprawled on the bed, his limbs twitching, his eyes rolled back. The young hood on whom François had landed frantically rolled away from beneath the body and stared in horror at the bizarre display.

François gave a last grunt of agony and fell still.

For a few seconds, everyone watched him, expecting him to move again. He didn't.

The guard gave a shout for assistance. Another guard came running. Yelling at the prisoners to stand back, they rushed into the cell and examined the motionless François. Slowly they straightened and looked at Jordan.

"Est mort," one of them murmured.

"That-that's impossible!" said Jordan. "How can he be dead? I didn't hit him that hard!"

The guards merely stared at him. The other two prisoners regarded Jordan with new respect and backed away to the far side of the cell.

"Let me look at him!" demanded Jordan. He pushed past the guards and knelt by François. One glance at the body and he knew they were right. François was dead.

Jordan shook his head. "I don't understand...."

"*Monsieur,* you come with us," said one of the guards.

"I couldn't have killed him!"

"But you see for yourself he is dead."

Jordan suddenly focused on a fine line of blood trickling down François's cheek. He bent closer. Only then did he spot the needle-thin dart impaled in the dead man's scalp. It was almost invisible among the salt-and-pepper hairs of his temple.

"What in blazes...?" muttered Jordan. Swiftly he glanced around the floor for a syringe, a dart gun—whatever might have injected that needle point. He saw nothing on the floor or on the bed. Then he looked down at the dead man's hand and saw something clutched in his left fist. He pried open the frozen fingers and the object slid out and landed on the bedcovers.

A ballpoint pen.

At once he was hauled back and shoved toward the cell door. "Go," said the guard. "Walk!"

"Where?"

"Where you can hurt no one." The guard directed Jordan into the corridor and locked the cell door. Jordan caught a fleeting glimpse of his cellmates, watching him in awe, and then he was hustled down the hallway and into a private cell, this one obviously reserved for the most dangerous prisoners. Double-barred, no windows, no furniture, only a concrete slab on which to lie. And a light blazing down relentlessly from the ceiling.

Jordan sank onto the slab and waited. For what? he wondered. Another attack? Another crisis? How could this nightmare possibly get any worse?

An hour passed. He couldn't sleep, not with that light shining overhead. Footsteps and the clank of keys alerted him to a visitor. He looked up to see a guard and a well-dressed gentleman with a briefcase.

"M. Tavistock?" said the gentleman.

"Since there's no one else here," muttered Jordan, rising to his feet, "I'm afraid that must be me."

The door was unlocked, and the man with the briefcase entered. He glanced around in dismay at the Spartan cell. "These conditions… Outrageous," he said.

"Yes. And I owe it all to my wonderful attorney," said Jordan.

"But *I* am your attorney." The man held out his hand in greeting. "Henri Laurent. I would have come sooner, but I was attending the opera. I received M. Vane's message only an hour ago. He said it was an emergency."

Jordan shook his head in confusion. "Vane? Reggie Vane sent you?"

"Yes. Your sister requested my immediate services. And M. Vane—"

"Beryl hired you? Then who the hell was…" Jordan paused as the bizarre events suddenly made sense. Horrifying sense. "M. Laurent," said Jordan, "a few hours ago, there was a lawyer here to see me. A M. Jarre."

Laurent frowned. "But I was not told of another attorney."

"He claimed my sister hired him."

"But I spoke to M. Vane. He told me Mlle Tavistock requested *my* services. What did you say was the other attorney's name?"

"Jarre."

Laurent shook his head. "I am not familiar with any such criminal attorney."

Jordan sat for a moment in stunned silence. Slowly he raised his head and looked at Laurent. "I think you'd better contact Reggie Vane. At once."

"But why?"

"They've already tried to kill me once tonight." Jordan shook his head. "If this keeps up, M. Laurent, by morning I may be quite dead."

Chapter Eight

THEY WERE FOLLOWING her again. Black hounds, trotting across the dead leaves of the forest. She heard them rustle through the underbrush and knew they were moving closer.

She gripped Froggie's bridle, struggled to calm her, but the mare panicked. Suddenly Froggie yanked free of Beryl's grasp and reared up.

The hounds attacked.

Instantly they were at the horse's throat, ripping, tearing with their razor teeth. Froggie screamed, a human scream, shrill with terror. *Have to save her,* thought Beryl. *Have to beat them away.* But her feet seemed rooted to the ground. She could only stand and watch in horror as Froggie dropped to her knees and collapsed to the forest floor.

The hounds, mouths bloodied, turned and looked at Beryl.

She awakened, gasping for breath, her hands clawing at the darkness. Only as her panic faded did she hear Richard calling her name.

She turned and saw him standing in the doorway. A lamp was shining in the room behind him, and the light gleamed faintly on his bare shoulders.

"Beryl?" he said again.

She took a deep breath, still trying to shake off the last threads of the nightmare. "I'm awake," she said.

"I think you'd better get up."

"What time is it?"

"Four a.m. Claude just phoned."

"Why?"

"He wants us to meet him at the police station. As soon as possible."

"The police station?" She sat up sharply as a terrible thought came to mind. "Is it Jordan? Has something happened to him?"

Through the shadows, she saw Richard nod. "Someone tried to kill him."

"AN INGENIOUS DEVICE," said Claude Daumier, gingerly laying the ballpoint pen on the table. "A hypodermic needle, a pressurized syringe. One stab, and the drug would be injected into the victim."

"Which drug?" asked Beryl.

"It is still being analyzed. The autopsy will be performed in the morning. But it seems clear that this drug, whatever it was, was the cause of death. There is not enough trauma on the body to explain otherwise."

"Then Jordan won't be blamed for this?" said Beryl in relief.

"Hardly. He will be placed in isolation, no other prisoners, a double guard. There should be no further incidents."

The conference room door opened. Jordan appeared, escorted by two guards. *Dear Lord, he looks terrible,* thought Beryl as she rose from her chair and went to hug him. Never had she seen her brother so disheveled. The beginnings of a thick blond beard had sprouted on his jaw, and his prison clothes were mapped with wrinkles. But as they pulled apart, she gazed in his eyes and saw that the old Jordan was still there, good-humored and ironic as ever.

"You're not hurt?" she asked.

"Not a scratch," he answered. "Well, perhaps a few," he amended, frowning down at his bruised fist. "It's murder on the old manicure."

"Jordan, I swear I never hired any lawyer named Jarre. The man was a fraud."

"I suspected as much."

"The man I did hire, M. Laurent, Reggie swears he's the best there is."

"I'm afraid even the best won't get me out of this fix," Jordan observed disconsolately. "I seem destined to be a long-term resident of this fine establishment. Unless the food kills me first."

"Will you be serious for once?"

"Oh, but you haven't tasted the goulash."

Beryl turned in exasperation to Daumier. "What about the dead man? Who was he?"

"According to the arrest record," said Daumier, "his name was François Parmentier, a janitor. He was charged with disorderly conduct."

"How did he end up in Jordan's cell?" asked Richard.

"It seems that his attorney, Jarre, made a special request for both his clients to be housed in the same cell."

"Not just a request," amended Richard. "It must've been a bribe. Jarre and the dead man were a team."

"Working on whose behalf?" asked Jordan.

"The same party who tried to kill Beryl," said Richard.

"*What?*"

"A few hours ago. It was a high-powered rifle, fired at her hotel window."

"And she's still in Paris?" Jordan turned to his sister. "That's it. You're going home, Beryl. And you're leaving at once."

"I've been trying to tell her the same thing," said Richard. "She won't listen."

"Of course she won't. My darling little sister never does!" Jordan scowled at Beryl. "This time, though, you don't have a choice."

"You're right, Jordie," said Beryl. "I don't have a choice. That's why I'm staying."

"You could get yourself killed."

"So could you."

They stood facing each other, neither one willing to give ground. *Deadlock,* thought Beryl. *He's worried about me, and I'm worried about him. And we're both Tavistocks, which means neither of us will ever concede defeat.*

But I have the upper hand on this one. He's in jail. I'm not.

In disgust, Jordan turned and flopped into a chair. "For Pete's sake, work on her, Wolf!" he muttered.

"I'm trying to," said Richard. "Meanwhile, we still haven't answered a basic question—who wants you both dead?"

They fell silent for a moment. Through a cloud of fatigue, Beryl looked at her brother, thinking that he was supposed to be the clever one in the family. If he couldn't figure it out, who could?

"The key to all this," said Jordan, "is François, the dead man." He looked at Daumier. "What else do you know about him? Friends, family?"

"Only a sister," said Daumier. "Living in Paris."

"Have your people spoken to her yet?"

"There is no point to it."

"Why not?"

"She is, how do you say…?" Daumier tapped his forehead. "*Retardataire*. She lives at the Sacred Heart Nursing Home. The nuns say she cannot speak, and she is in very poor health."

"What about his job?" said Richard. "You said he worked as a janitor."

"At Galerie Annika. An art gallery, in Auteuil. It is a reputable establishment. Known for its collection of works by contemporary artists."

"What does the gallery say about him?"

"I spoke only briefly to Annika. She says he was a quiet man, very reliable. She will be in later this morning to answer questions." He glanced at his watch. "In the meantime, I suggest we all try to catch some sleep. For a few hours, at least."

"What about Jordan?" asked Beryl. "How do I know he'll be safe here?"

"As I said, he will be kept in a private cell. Strict isolation—"

"That might be a mistake," said Richard. "There'd be no witnesses."

If anything happens to him… Beryl shivered.

Jordan nodded. "Wolf's right. I'd feel a whole lot safer sharing a cell with someone."

"But they could lock you up with another hired killer," said Beryl.

"I know just the fellows to share my cell," said Jordan. "A pair of harmless enough chaps. I hope."

Daumier nodded. "I will arrange it."

It was wrenching to see Jordan marched away. In the doorway, he paused and gave her a farewell wave. That's when Beryl realized she was taking this far harder than he was. But that's old Jordie for you, she mused. Never one to lose his good humor.

Outside, the first streaks of daylight had appeared in the sky, and the sound of traffic had already begun its morning crescendo. Beryl, Richard and Daumier stood on the sidewalk, all of them tottering on the edge of collapse.

"Jordan will be safe," said Daumier. "I will see to it."

"I want him to be more than safe," said Beryl. "I want him out of there."

"For that, we must prove him innocent."

"Then that's exactly what we'll do," she said.

Daumier looked at her with bloodshot eyes. He seemed far older tonight, this kindly Frenchman in whose face the years had etched deep furrows. He said, "What you must do, *chérie,* is stay alert. And out of sight." He turned toward his car. "Tonight, we talk again."

By the time Beryl and Richard had returned to the flat in Passy, Beryl could feel herself nodding off. The latest jolt of tension had worn off, and her energy was on a fast downhill slide. Thank God Richard still seemed to be operating on all cylinders, she thought as they climbed out of the car. If she collapsed, he could drag her up those steps.

He practically did. He put his arm around her and walked her through the door, up the hall and into the bedroom. There, he sat her down on the bed.

"Sleep," he said, "as long as you need to."

"A week should about do it," she murmured.

He smiled. And though sleep was blurring her vision, she saw his face clearly enough to register, once again, that flicker of attraction between them. It was always there, ready to leap into full flame. Even now, exhausted as she was, images of desire were weaving into shape in her mind. She remembered how he'd stood, shirtless, in the bedroom doorway, the lamplight gleaming on his shoulders. She thought how easy it would be to invite him into her bed, to ask for a hug, a kiss. And then, much, much more. *Too much bloody chemistry between us,* she pondered. *It addles my brain, keeps me from concentrating on the important issues. I take one look at him, I inhale one whiff of his scent, and all I can think about is pulling him down on top of me.*

Gently he kissed her forehead. "I'll be right next door," he said, and left the room.

Too tired to undress, she lay down fully clothed on the bed. Daylight brightened outside the window, and the sounds of traffic drifted up from the street. If this nightmare was ever over, she thought, she'd have to stay away from him for a while. Just to get her bearings again. Yes, that's what she'd do. She'd hide out at Chetwynd. Wait for that crazy attraction between them to fade.

But as she closed her eyes, the images returned, more vivid and tempting than ever. They pursued her, right into her dreams.

RICHARD SLEPT FIVE HOURS and rose just before noon. A shower, a quick meal of eggs and toast, and he felt the old engines fire up again. There were too few hours in the day, too many matters to attend to; sleep would have to assume a lower priority.

He peeked in on Beryl and saw that she was still asleep. Good. By the time she woke up, he should be back from making his rounds. Just in case he wasn't, though, he left a note on the nightstand. "Gone out. Back around three. R." Then, as an afterthought, he laid the gun beside the note. If she needed it, he figured, it'd be there for her.

After confirming that the two guards were still on duty, he left the flat, locking the door behind him.

His first stop was 66 Rue Myrha, the building where Madeline and Bernard died.

He had gone over the Paris police report again, had read and reread the landlord's statement. M. Rideau claimed he'd discovered the bodies on the afternoon of July 15, 1973, and had at once notified the police. Upon being questioned, he'd told them that the attic was rented to a Mlle Scarlatti, who used the place only infrequently and paid her rent in cash. On occasion, he had heard moans, whimpers, and a man's voice emanating from the flat. But the only person he ever saw face-to-face was Mlle Scarlatti, whose head scarves and sunglasses made it difficult for him to be specific about her appearance. Nevertheless, M. Rideau was certain that the dead woman in the flat was indeed the lusty Scarlatti woman. And the dead man? The landlord had never seen him before.

Three months after this testimony, M. Rideau had sold the building, packed up his family, and left the country.

That last detail had garnered only a footnote in the police report: "Landlord no longer available for statements. Has left France."

Richard had a hunch that the landlord's departure from the country just might be the most important clue they had. If he could locate Rideau's current whereabouts and question him about those events of twenty years before…

He knocked at each flat in the building, but came up with no leads. Twenty years was a long time; people moved in, moved out. No one remembered any M. Rideau.

Richard went outside and stood for a moment on the sidewalk. A ball hurtled past, pursued by a pack of scruffy kids. The endless soccer match, he mused, watching the tangle of dirty arms and legs.

Over the children's heads, he spotted an elderly woman sitting on her stoop. At least seventy years old, he guessed. Perhaps she'd lived here long enough to know the former residents of this street.

He went over to the woman and spoke to her in French. "Good afternoon."

She smiled a sweet, toothless grin.

"I am trying to find someone who remembers M. Jacques Rideau. The man who used to own that building over there." He pointed to number 66.

Also in French, she answered: "He moved away."

"You knew him, then?"

"His son was all the time visiting in my house."

"I understand the whole family left France."

She nodded. "They went to Greece. And how do you suppose he managed that, eh? Him, with that old car! And the clothes their children wore! But off they go to their villa." She sighed. "And I am here, where I'll always be."

Richard frowned. "Villa?"

"I hear they have a villa, near the sea. Of course, it may not be true—the boy was always making up stories. Why should he start telling the truth? But he claimed it was a villa, with flowers growing up the posts." She laughed. "They must all be dead by now."

"The family?"

"The flowers. They could not even remember to water their pots of geraniums."

"Do you know where in Greece they moved to?"

The woman shrugged. "Somewhere near the sea. But then, isn't all of Greece near the sea?"

"The name of the village?"

"Why should I remember these things? He was not *my* boyfriend."

Frustrated, Richard was about to turn away when he suddenly registered what the woman had just said. "You mean, the landlord's son—he was your daughter's boyfriend?"

"My granddaughter."

"Did he call her? Write her any letters?"

"A few. Then he stopped." She shook her head. "That is how it is with young people. No devotion."

"Did she keep any of those letters?"

The woman laughed. "All of them. To remind her husband what a fine catch he made."

It took a bit of persuasion for Richard to be invited inside the old woman's apartment. It was a dark, cramped flat. Two small children sat at the kitchen table, gnawing fistfuls of bread. Another woman—most likely in her mid-thirties, but with much older eyes—sat spooning cereal into an infant's mouth.

"He wants to see your letters from Gerard," said the grandmother.

The younger woman eyed Richard with suspicion.

"It's important I speak with his father," explained Richard.

"His father doesn't want to be found," she said, and resumed feeding the baby.

"Why not?"

"How should I know? Gerard didn't tell me."

"Does it have to do with the murders? The two English people?"

She paused, the spoon halfway to the baby's mouth. "You are English?"

"No, American." He sat down across from her. "Do you remember the murders?"

"It was a long time ago." She wiped the baby's face. "I was only fifteen."

"Gerard wrote you letters, then stopped. Why?"

The woman gave a bitter laugh. "He lost interest. Men always do."

"Or something could have happened to him. Maybe he couldn't write to you. And he wanted to, very much."

Again, she paused.

"If I go to Greece, I can inquire on your behalf. I only need to know the name of the village."

She sat for a moment, thinking. Wiping up the baby's mess. She looked at her two children, both of them runny nosed and whining. *She's longing to escape,* he imagined. *Wishing her life had turned out some other way. Any other way. And she's thinking about this long-lost boyfriend, and how things might have been, for the two of them, in a villa by the sea....*

She stood up and went into another room. A moment later, she returned and laid a thin bundle of letters down on the table.

There were only four—not exactly a record of devotion. All were still tucked in their envelopes. Richard skimmed their contents, noting an outpouring of adolescent yearnings. "I will come back for you. I will love you always. Do not forget me...." By the fourth letter, the passion was clearly cooling.

There was no return address, either on the letters or on the envelopes. The family's whereabouts were obviously meant to be kept secret. But on one of the envelopes, a postmark was clearly printed: Paros, Greece.

Richard handed the letters back to the woman. She cradled them for a moment, as though savoring the memories. *So many years ago, a lifetime ago, and see what has become of me....*

"If you find Gerard...if he is still alive," she said, "ask him..."

"Yes?" Richard said gently.

She sighed. "Ask him if he remembers me."

"I will."

She held the letters a moment longer. And then, with a sigh, she laid them aside and picked up the spoon. In silence, she began to feed the baby.

HE MADE ONE MORE STOP before returning to the flat, this time at the Sacred Heart Nursing Home.

It was a far grimmer institution than the one Richard had visited the day before. No private rooms here, no sweet-faced nuns gliding down the halls. This was one step above a prison, and a crowded one at that, with three or four patients to a room, many of them restrained in their beds. Julee Parmentier, François's retarded sister, occupied one of the grimmest rooms of all. Barely clothed, she lay on top of a plastic-lined mattress. Protective mitts covered her hands; around her waist was a wide belt, its ends secured to the bed with just enough slack for her to shift from side to side, but not sit up. She barely seemed to register Richard's presence; instead she moaned and stared relentlessly at the ceiling.

"She has been like this for many years," said the nurse. "An accident, when she was twelve. She fell from a tree and hit her head on some stones."

"She can't speak at all? Can't communicate?"

"When her brother François would visit, he said she would smile. He insisted he saw it. But..." The nurse shrugged. "I saw nothing."

"Did he visit often?"

"Every day. The same time, nine o'clock in the morning. He would stay until lunch, then he would go to his work at the gallery."

"He did this every day?"

"Yes. And on Sunday he would stay later—until four o'clock."

Richard gazed at the woman in the bed and tried to imagine what it must have been like for François to sit for hours in this room with its noise and its smells. To devote every free hour of his life to a sister who could not even recognize his face.

"It is a tragedy," said the nurse. "He was a good man, François."

They left the room and walked away from the sight of that pitiful creature lying on her plastic sheet.

"What will happen to her now?" asked Richard. "Will someone see that she's cared for?"

"It hardly matters now."

"Why do you say that?"

"Her kidneys are failing." The nurse glanced up the hall, toward Julee Parmentier's room, and shook her head sadly. "Another month, two months, and she will be dead."

"BUT YOU MUST KNOW where he went," insisted Beryl.

The French agent merely shrugged. "He did not say, *Mademoiselle.* He only instructed me to watch over the flat. And see that you came to no harm."

"And that's all he said? And then he drove off?"

The man nodded.

In frustration, Beryl turned and went back into the flat, where she reread Richard's note: "Gone out. Back around three." No explanations, no apologies. She crumpled it up and threw it at the rubbish can. And what was she supposed to do now? Wait around all day for him to return? What about Jordan? What about the investigation?

What about lunch?

Her hunger pangs could no longer be ignored. She went to the kitchen and opened the refrigerator. She stared in dismay at the contents: a carton of eggs, a loaf of bread and a shriveled sausage. No fruit, no vegetables, not even a puny carrot. Stocked, no doubt, by a man.

I'm not going to eat that, she determined, closing the refrigerator door. *But I'm not going to starve, either. I'm going to have a proper meal—with or without him.*

Daumier's men had delivered her belongings to the flat the night before. From the closet, she chose her most nondescript black dress, pinned up her hair under a wide-brimmed hat, and slid on a pair of dark glasses. *Not too hideous,* she decided, glancing at herself in the mirror.

She walked out of the flat into the sunshine.

The guard stationed at the front door confronted her at once. "*Mademoiselle,* you are not allowed to leave."

"But you let *him* leave," she countered.

"Mr. Wolf specifically instructed—"

"I'm hungry," she said. "I get quite cranky when I'm hungry. And I'm not about to live on eggs and toast. So if you can just direct me to the nearest Métro station…"

"You are going *alone*?" he asked in horror.

"Unless you'd care to escort me."

The man glanced uneasily up and down the street. "I have no instructions in this matter."

"Then I'll go alone," she said, and breezily started to walk away.

"Come back!"

She kept walking.

"*Mademoiselle!*" he called. "I will get the car!"

She turned and flashed him her most brilliant smile. "My treat."

Both guards accompanied her to a restaurant in the nearby neighborhood of Auteuil. She suspected they chose the place not for the quality of its food, but for the intimate dining room and the easily surveyed front entrance. The meal itself was just a shade above mediocre: bland vichyssoise and a cut of lamb that could have doubled for leather. But Beryl was hungry enough to savor every morsel and still have an appetite for the *tarte aux pommes*.

By the time the meal was over, her two companions were in a much more jovial mood. Perhaps this bodyguard business was not such a bad thing, if the lady was willing to spring for a meal every day. They even relented when Beryl asked them to make a stop on the drive back to the flat. It would only take a minute, she said, to look over the latest art exhibit. After all, she might find something to strike her fancy.

And so the men accompanied her to Galerie Annika.

The exhibit area was one vast, soaring gallery—three stories, connected by open walkways and spiral staircases. Sunlight shone down through a skylit dome, illuminating a collection of bronze sculptures displayed on the first floor.

A young woman, her spiky hair a startling shade of red, came forward to greet them. Was there something in particular *Mademoiselle* wished to see?

"May I just look around a bit?" asked Beryl. "Or perhaps you could direct me to some paintings. Nothing too modern—I prefer classical artists."

"But of course," said the woman, and guided Beryl and her escorts up the spiral stairs.

Most of what she saw hanging on the walls was hideous. Landscapes populated by deformed animals. Birds with dog heads. City scenes with starkly cubist buildings. The young woman stopped at one painting and said, "Perhaps this is to your liking?"

Beryl took one look at the nude huntress holding aloft a dead rabbit and said, "I don't think so." She moved on, taking in the eccentric collection of paintings, fabric hangings and clay masks. "Who chooses the work to be displayed here?" she asked.

"Annika does. The gallery owner."

Beryl stopped at a particularly grotesque mask—a man with a forked tongue. "She has a…unique eye for art."

"Quite daring, don't you think? She prefers artists who take risks."

"Is she here today? I'd very much like to meet her."

"Not at the moment." The woman shook her head sadly. "One of our employees died last night, you see. Annika had to speak to the police."

"I'm sorry to hear that."

"Our janitor." The woman sighed. "It was quite unexpected."

They returned to the first-floor gallery. Only then did Beryl spot a work she'd consider purchasing. It was one of the bronze sculptures, a variation on the Madonna-and-child theme. But as she moved closer to inspect it, she realized it wasn't a human infant nursing at the woman's breast. It was a jackal.

"Quite intriguing, don't you think?"

Beryl shuddered and looked at her spiky-haired guide. "What brilliant mind dreamed *this* one up?"

"A new artist. A young man, just building his reputation here in Paris. We are hosting a reception in his honor tonight. Perhaps you will attend?"

"If I can."

The woman reached into a basket and plucked out an elegantly embossed invitation. This she handed to Beryl. "If you are free tonight, please drop in."

Beryl was about to slip the card carelessly into her purse when she suddenly focused on the artist's name. A name she recognized.

Galerie Annika presente:
Les sculptures de Anthony Sutherland
17 juillet 7-n9 du soir.

Chapter Nine

"THIS IS CRAZY," said Richard. "An unacceptable risk."

To his annoyance, Beryl simply waltzed over to the closet and stood surveying her wardrobe. "What do you think would be appropriate tonight? Formal or semi?"

"You'll be out in the open," said Richard. "An art reception! I can't think of a more public place."

Beryl took out a black silk sheath, turned to the mirror, and calmly held the dress to her body. "A public place is the safest place to be," she observed.

"You were supposed to stay here! Instead you go running around town—"

"So did you."

"I had business…."

She turned and walked into the bedroom. "I did, too," she called back cheerfully.

He started to follow her, but halted in the doorway when he saw that she was undressing. At once he turned around and stood with his back pressed against the doorjamb. "A craving for a three-star meal doesn't constitute necessity!" he snapped over his shoulder.

"It wasn't a three-star meal. It wasn't even a half star. But it was better than eggs and moldy bread."

"You're like some finicky kitten, you know that? You'd rather starve than deign to eat canned food like every other cat."

"You're quite right. I'm a spoiled Persian and I want my cream and chicken livers."

"I would've brought you back a meal. Catnip included."

"You weren't here."

And that was his mistake, he realized. He couldn't leave this woman alone for a second. She was too damn unpredictable.

No, actually she *was* predictable. She'd do whatever he *didn't* want her to do.

And what he didn't want her to do was leave the flat tonight.

But he could already hear her stepping into the black dress, could hear the whisper of silk sliding over stockings, the hiss of the zipper closing over her back. He fought to suppress the images those sounds brought to mind—the long legs, the curve of her hips… He found himself clenching his jaw in frustration, at her, at himself, at the way events and passions were spinning out of his control.

"Do me up, will you?" she asked.

He turned and saw that she'd moved right beside him. Her back was turned and the nape of her neck was practically within kissing distance.

"The hook," she said, tossing her hair over one shoulder. He inhaled the flowery scent of shampoo. "I can't seem to fasten it."

He attached the hook and eye and found his gaze lingering on her bare shoulders. "Where did you get that dress?" he asked.

"I brought it from Chetwynd." She breezed over to the dresser and began to slip on earrings. The silk sheath seemed to mold itself to every luscious curve of her body. "Why do you ask?"

"It's Madeline's dress. Isn't it?"

She turned to look at him. "Yes, it is," she said quietly. "Does that bother you?"

"It's just—" he let out a breath "—it's a perfect fit. Curve for curve."

"And you think you're seeing a ghost."

"I remember that dress. I saw her wear it at an embassy reception." He paused. "God, it's really eerie, how that dress seems made for you."

Slowly she moved toward him, her gaze never wavering from his face. "I'm not her, Richard."

"I know."

"No matter how much you may want her back—"

"Her?" He took her wrists and pulled her close to him. "When I look at you, I see only Beryl. Of course, I notice the resemblance. The hair, the eyes. But *you're* the one I'm looking at. The one I want." He bent toward her and gently grazed her lips with a kiss. "That's why I want you to stay here tonight."

"Your prisoner?" she murmured.

"If need be." He kissed her again and heard an answering purr of contentment from her throat. She tilted her head back, and his lips slid to her neck, so smooth, so deliciously perfumed.

"Then you'll have to tie me up…" she whispered.

"Whatever you want."

"…because there's no other way you're going to keep me here tonight." With a maddening laugh, she wriggled free and walked into the bathroom.

Richard suppressed a groan of frustration. From the doorway, he watched as she pinned up her hair. "Exactly what do you expect to get out of this event, anyway?" he demanded.

"One never knows. That's the joy of intelligence gathering, isn't it? Keep your ears and eyes open and see what turns up. I think we've learned quite a lot already about François. We know he has a sister who's ill. Which means François needed money. Working as a janitor in an art gallery couldn't possibly pay for all the care she needed. Perhaps he was desperate, willing to do anything for money. Even work as a hired assassin."

"Your logic is unassailable."

"Thank you."

"But your plan of action is insane. You don't need to take this risk—"

"But I do." She turned to him, her hair now regally swept into a chignon. "Someone wants me and Jordan dead. And there I'll be tonight. A perfectly convenient target."

What a magnificent creature she is, he thought. *It's that unbeatable bloodline, those Bernard and Madeline genes. She thinks she's invincible.*

"That's the plan, is it?" he said. "Tempt the killer into making a move?"

"If that's what it takes to save Jordan."

"And what's to stop the killer from carrying it out?"

"My two bodyguards. And you."

"I'm not infallible, Beryl."

"You're close enough."

"I could make a mistake. Let my attention slip."

"I trust you."

"But I don't trust myself!" Agitated, he began to pace the bedroom floor. "I've been out of the business for years, I'm out of practice, out of condition. I'm forty-two, Beryl, and my reflexes aren't what they used to be."

"Last night they seemed quick enough to me."

"Walk out that door, Beryl, and I can't guarantee your safety."

She came toward him, looking him coolly in the eye. "The fact is, Richard, you can't guarantee my safety anywhere. In here, out on the streets, at an artist's reception. Wherever I am, there's a chance things could go wrong. If I stay in this flat, if I stare at these walls any longer, thinking of all the things that could happen, I'll go insane. It's better to be out *there.* Doing something. Jordan isn't able to, so I have to be the one."

"The one to set yourself up as bait?"

"Our only lead is a dead man—François. Someone hired him, Richard. Someone who may have connections to Galerie Annika."

For a moment Richard stood gazing at her, thinking, *She's right, of course. It's the same conclusion I came to. She's clever enough to know exactly what needs to be done. And reckless enough to do it.*

He went to the nightstand and picked up the Glock. A pound and a half of steel and plastic, that's all he had to protect her with. It felt flimsy, insubstantial, against all the dangers lurking beyond the front door.

"You're coming with me?" she said.

He turned and looked at her. "You think I'd let you go alone?"

She smiled, so full of confidence it frightened him. It was Madeline's old smile. Madeline, who'd been every bit as confident.

He slid the Glock into his shoulder holster. "I'll be right beside you, Beryl," he said. "Every step of the way."

Anthony Sutherland stood posing like a little emperor beside his bronze cast of the Madonna with jackal. He was wearing a pirate shirt of purple silk, black leather pants and snakeskin boots, and he seemed not in the least bit fazed by all the photographers' flashbulbs that kept popping around him. The art critics were in vapors over the show. "Frightening." "Disturbing." "Images that twist convention." These were some of the comments Beryl overheard being murmured as she wandered through the gallery.

She and Richard stopped to look at another of Anthony's bronzes. At first glance, it had looked like two nude figures entwined in a loving embrace. Closer inspection, however, revealed it to be a man and woman in the process of devouring each other alive.

"Do you suppose that's an allegory for marriage?" said a familiar voice. It was Reggie Vane, balancing a glass of champagne in one hand and two dainty plates of canapés in the other.

He bent forward and gave Beryl an affectionate kiss on the cheek. "You're absolutely stunning tonight, dear. Your mother would be proud of you."

"Reggie, I had no idea you were interested in modern art," said Beryl.

"I'm not. Helena dragged me here." In disgust, he glanced around at the crowd. "Lord, I hate these things. But the St. Pierres were coming, and of course Marie always insists Helena show up as well, just to keep her company." He set his empty champagne glass on top of the bronze couple and laughed at the whimsical effect. "An improvement, wouldn't you say? As long as these two are going to eat each other, they might as well have some bubbly to wash each other down."

An elegantly attired woman swooped in and snatched away the glass. "Please, be more respectful of the work, Mr. Vane," she scolded.

"Oh, I wasn't being disrespectful, Annika," said Reggie. "I just thought it needed a touch of humor."

"It is absolutely perfect as it is." Annika gave the bronze heads a swipe of her napkin and stood back to admire the interwoven figures. "Whimsy would ruin its message."

"What message is that?" asked Richard.

The woman turned to look at him, and her head of boyishly cropped hair suddenly tilted up with interest. "The message," she said, gazing intently at Richard, "is that monogamy is a destructive institution."

"That's marriage, all right," grunted Reggie.

"But free love," the woman continued, "love that has no constraints and is open to all pleasures—that is a positive force."

"Is that Anthony's interpretation of this piece?" asked Beryl.

"It's how *I* interpret it." Annika shifted her gaze to Beryl. "You are a friend of Anthony's?"

"An acquaintance. I know his mother, Nina."

"Where is Nina, by the way?" asked Reggie. "You'd think she'd be front-and-center stage for *darling* Anthony's night of *glory*."

Beryl had to laugh at Reggie's imitation of Nina. Yes, when Queen Nina wanted an audience, all she had to do was throw one of these stylish bashes, and an audience would invariably turn up. Even poor Marie St. Pierre, just out of the hospital, had put in an appearance. Marie stood off in a corner with Helena Vane, the two women huddled together like sparrows in a gathering of peacocks. It was easy to see why they'd be such close friends; both of them were painfully plain, neither one was happily married. That their marriages were not happy was only too clear tonight. The Vanes were avoiding each other, Helena off in her corner darting irritated looks, Reggie standing as far away as possible. And as for Marie St. Pierre—her husband wasn't even in the room at the moment.

"So this is in praise of free love, is it?" said Reggie, eyeing the bronze with new appreciation.

"That is how I see it," said Annika. "How a man and a woman should love."

"I quite agree," said Reggie with a sudden burst of enthusiasm. "Banish marriage entirely."

The woman looked provocatively at Richard. "What do you think, Mr....?"

"Wolf," said Richard. "I'm afraid I don't agree." He took Beryl's arm. "Excuse us, will you? We still have to see the rest of the collection."

As he led Beryl away toward the spiral staircase, she whispered, "There's nothing to see upstairs."

"I want to check out the upper floors."

"Anthony's work is all on the first floor."

"I saw Nina slink up the stairs a few minutes ago. I want to see what she's up to."

They climbed the stairs to the second-floor gallery. From the open walkway, they paused to look over the railing at the crowd on the first floor. It was a flashy gathering, a sea of well-coiffed heads and multicolored silks. Annika had moved into the limelight with Anthony, and as a new round of flashbulbs went off, they embraced and kissed to the sound of applause.

"Ah, free love," sighed Beryl. "She obviously has samples to pass around."

"So I can see."

Beryl gave him a sly smile. "Poor Richard. On duty tonight and can't indulge."

"*Afraid* to indulge. She'd eat me up alive. Like that bronze statue."

"Aren't you tempted? Just a little?"

He looked at her with amusement. "You're baiting me, Beryl."

"Am I?"

"Yes, you are. I know exactly what you're up to. Putting me to the test. Making me prove I'm not like your friend the surgeon. Who, as you implied, also believed in free love."

Beryl's smile faded. "Is that what I'm doing?" she asked softly.

"You have a right to." He gave her hand a squeeze and glanced down again at the crowd. *He's always alert, always watching out for me,* she thought. *I'd trust him with my life. But my heart? I still don't know....*

In the downstairs gallery, a pair of musicians began to play. As the sweet sounds of flute and guitar floated through the building, Beryl suddenly sensed a pair of eyes watching her. She looked down at the cluster of bronze statues and spotted Anthony Sutherland, standing by his Madonna with jackal. He was gazing right at her. And the expression in his eyes was one of cold calculation.

Instinctively she shrank away from the railing.

"What is it?" asked Richard.

"Anthony. It's the way he looks at me."

But by then Anthony had already turned away and was shaking Reggie Vane's hand. An odd young man, thought Beryl. What sort of mind dreams up these nightmarish visions? Women nursing jackals. Couples devouring each other. Had it been so difficult, growing up as Nina Sutherland's son?

She and Richard wandered through the second-floor gallery, but found no sign of Nina.

"Why are you so interested in finding her?" asked Beryl.

"It's not her so much as the way she went up those stairs. Obviously trying not to be noticed."

"And you noticed her."

"It was the dress. Those trademark bugle beads of hers."

They finished their circuit of the second floor and headed up the staircase to the third. Again, no sign of Nina. But as they moved along the walkway, the musicians in the first-floor gallery suddenly ceased playing. In the abrupt silence that followed, Beryl heard Nina's voice—a few loud syllables—just before it dropped to a whisper. Another voice answered—a man's, speaking softly in reply.

The voices came from an alcove, just ahead.

"It's not as if I haven't been patient," said Nina. "Not as if I haven't *tried* to be understanding."

"I know. I know—"

"Do you know what it's been *like* for me? For Anthony? Have you any *idea?* All those years, waiting for you to make up your mind."

"I never let you want for anything."

"Oh, how *fortunate* for us! My goodness, how generous of you!"

"The boy has had the best—everything he's ever wanted. Now he's twenty-one. My responsibility ends."

"Your responsibility," said Nina, "has only just *begun.*"

Richard yanked Beryl around the corner just as Nina emerged from the alcove. She stormed right past them, too angry to notice her audience. They could hear her high heels tapping down the staircase to the lower galleries.

A moment later, a second figure emerged from the alcove, moving like an old man.

It was Philippe St. Pierre.

He went over to the railing and stared down at the crowd in the gallery below. He seemed to be considering the temptation of that two-story drop. Then, sighing deeply, he walked away and followed Nina down the stairs.

Down in the first-floor gallery, the crowd was starting to thin out. Anthony had already left; so had the Vanes. But Marie St. Pierre was still standing in her corner, the abandoned wife waiting to be reclaimed. A full room's length away stood her husband Philippe, nursing a glass of champagne. And standing between them was that macabre sculpture, the bronze man and woman devouring each other alive.

Beryl thought that perhaps Anthony had hit upon the truth with his art. That if people weren't careful, love would consume them, destroy them. As it had destroyed Marie.

The image of Marie St. Pierre, standing alone and forlorn in the corner, stayed with Beryl all the way back to the flat. She thought how hard it must be to play the politician's wife—forever poised and pleasant, always supportive, never the shrew. And all the time knowing that your husband was in love with another woman.

"She must have known about it. For years," said Beryl softly.

Richard kept his gaze on the road as he navigated the streets back to Passy. "Who?" he asked.

"Marie St. Pierre. She must have known about her husband and Nina. Every time she looks at young Anthony, she'd see the resemblance. And how it must hurt her. Yet all these years, she's put up with him."

"And with Nina," said Richard.

Beryl sat back, puzzled. *Yes, she does put up with Nina. And that's the part I don't understand. How she can be so civil, so gracious, to her husband's mistress. To her husband's bastard son....*

"You think Philippe is Anthony's father?"

"That's what Nina meant, of course. All that talk about Philippe's responsibilities. She meant Anthony." She paused. "Art school must be very expensive."

"And Philippe must've paid a pretty bundle over the years, supporting the boy. Not to mention Nina, whose tastes are extravagant, to say the least. Her widow's pension couldn't have been enough to—"

"What is it?" asked Beryl.

"I just had a flash of insight about her husband, Stephen Sutherland. He committed suicide a month after your parents died—jumped off a bridge."

"Yes, you told me that."

"All these years, I've thought his death was related to the Delphi case. I suspected he was the mole, that he killed himself when he thought he was about to be discovered. But what if his reasons for jumping off that bridge were entirely personal?"

"His marriage."

"And young Anthony. The boy he discovered wasn't his son at all."

"But if Stephen Sutherland wasn't Delphi…"

"Then we're back to a person or persons unknown."

Persons unknown. Meaning someone who could still be alive. And afraid of discovery.

Instinctively she glanced over her shoulder, checking to see if they were being followed. Just behind them was the Peugeot with the two French agents; beyond that she saw only a stream of anonymous headlights. Richard was right, she thought. She should have stayed in the flat. She should have kept her head low, her face out of sight. Anyone could have spotted her this afternoon. Or they could be following her right this moment, could be watching her from somewhere in that sea of headlights.

Suddenly she longed to be back in the flat, safely surrounded by four walls. It began to seem endless, this drive to Passy, a journey through a darkness full of perils.

When at last they pulled up in front of the building, she was so anxious to get inside that she quickly started to climb out of the car. Richard pulled her back in.

"Don't get out yet," he said. "Let the men check it first."

"You don't really think—"

"It's a precaution. Standard operating procedure."

Beryl watched the two French agents climb the steps and unlock the front door. While one man stood watch on the steps, the other vanished inside.

"But how could anyone find out about the flat?" she asked.

"Payoffs. Leaks."

"You don't think Claude Daumier—"

"I'm not trying to scare you, Beryl. I just believe in being careful."

She watched as the lights came on inside the flat. First the living room, then the bedroom. At last, the man on the steps gave them the all-clear signal.

"Okay, it must be clean," said Richard, climbing out of the car. "Let's go."

Beryl stepped out onto the curb. She turned toward the building and took one step up the sidewalk—

—and was slammed backward against the car as an explosion rocked the earth. Shattered glass flew from the building and rained onto the street. Seconds later, the sky lit up with the hellish glow of flames shooting through the broken windows. Beryl sank to the ground, her ears still ringing from the blast. She stared numbly as tongues of flame slashed the darkness.

She couldn't hear Richard's shouts, didn't realize he was crouched right beside her until she felt his hands on her face. "Are you all right?" he cried. "Beryl, look at me!"

Weakly she nodded. Then her gaze traveled to the front walkway, to the body of the French agent lying sprawled near the steps.

"Stay put!" yelled Richard as he pivoted away from her. He dashed over to the fallen man and knelt beside him just long enough to feel for a pulse. At once he was back at Beryl's side. "Get in the car," he said.

"But what about the men?"

"That one's dead. The other one didn't stand a chance."

"You don't know that!"

"Just get in the car!" ordered Richard. He opened the door and practically shoved her inside. Then he scrambled around to the driver's side and slid behind the wheel.

"We can't just leave them there!" cried Beryl.

"We'll have to." He started the engine and sent the car screeching away from the curb.

Beryl watched as a succession of streets blurred past. Richard drove like a madman, but she was too stunned to feel afraid, too bewildered to focus on anything but the river of red taillights stretching ahead of them.

"Jordan," she whispered. "What about Jordan?"

"Right now I have to think about you."

"They found the flat. They can get to him!"

"I'll take care of it later. First we get you to a safe place."

"Where?"

He swerved across two lanes and shot onto an off ramp. "I'll come up with one. Somewhere."

Somewhere. She stared out at the night glow of Paris. A sprawling city, an ocean of light. A million different places to hide.

To die.

She shivered and shrank deep into the seat. "And then what?" she whispered. "What happens next?"

He looked at her. "We get out of Paris. Out of the country."

"You mean—go home?"

"No. It won't be safe in England, either." He turned his gaze back to the road. The car seemed to leap through the darkness. "We're going to Greece."

DAUMIER ANSWERED the phone on the second ring. *"Allo?"*

A familiar voice growled at him from the receiver. *"What the hell is going on?"*

"Richard?" said Daumier. "Where are you?"

"A safe place. You'll understand if I don't reveal it to you."

"And Beryl?"

"She's unhurt. Though I can't say the same for your two men. Who knew about the flat, Claude?"

"Only my people."

"Who else?"

"I told no one else. It should have been a safe enough place."

"Apparently you were wrong. Someone found out."

"You were both out of the flat earlier today. One of you could have been followed."

"It wasn't me."

"Beryl, then. You should not have allowed her out of the building. She could've been spotted at Galerie Annika this afternoon and followed back to the flat."

"My mistake. You're right, I shouldn't have left her alone. I can't afford to make any more mistakes."

Daumier sighed. "You and I, Richard, we have known each other too long. This is not the time to stop trusting each other."

There was a brief silence on the other end. Then Richard said, "I'm sorry, but I have no choice, Claude. We're going under."

"Then I will not be able to help you."

"We'll go it alone. Without your help."

"Wait, Richard—"

But the line had already gone dead. Daumier stared at the receiver, then slowly laid it back in the cradle. There was no point in trying to trace the call; Richard would have used a pay phone—and it would be in a different neighborhood from where he'd be staying. The man was once a professional; he knew the tricks of the trade.

Maybe—just maybe—it would keep them both alive.

"Good luck, my friend," murmured Daumier. "I am afraid you will need it."

RICHARD RISKED one more call from the pay phone, this one to Washington, D.C.

His business partner answered with his usual charmless growl. "Sakaroff here."

"Niki, it's me."

"Richard? How is beautiful Paris? Having a good time?"

"A lousy time. Look, I can't talk long. I'm in trouble."

Niki sighed. "Why am I not surprised?"

"It's the old Delphi case. You remember? Paris, '73. The NATO mole."

"Ah, yes."

"Delphi's come back to life. I need your help to identify him."

"I was KGB, Richard. Not Stasi."

"But you had connections to the East Germans."

"Not directly. I had little contact with Stasi agents. The East Germans, you know…they preferred to operate independently."

"Then who *would* know about Delphi? There must be some old contact you can pump for information."

There was a pause. "Perhaps…"

"Yes?"

"Heinrich Leitner," said Sakaroff. "He is the one who could tell you. He oversaw Stasi's Paris operations. Not a field man—he never left East Berlin. But he would be familiar with Delphi's work."

"Okay, he's the man I'll talk to. So how do I get to him?"

"That is the difficult part. He is in Berlin—"

"No problem. We'll go there."

"—in a high-security prison."

Richard groaned. "That *is* a problem." In frustration, he turned and stared through the phone-booth door at the subway platform. "I've got to get in to see him, Niki."

"You'll need approval. That will take days. Papers, signatures..."

"Then that's what I'll have to get. If you could make a few calls, speed things up."

"No guarantees."

"Understood. Oh, and one more thing," said Richard. "We've been trying to get ahold of Hugh Tavistock. It seems he's vanished. Have you heard anything about it?"

"No. But I will check my sources. Anything else?"

"I'll let you know."

Sakaroff grunted. "I was afraid you would say that."

Richard hung up. Stepping away from the pay phone, he glanced around at the subway platform. He saw nothing suspicious, only the usual stream of nighttime commuters—couples holding hands, students with backpacks.

The train for Creteil-Préfecture rolled into the station. Richard stepped onto it, rode it for three stops, then got off. He lingered on the next platform for a few minutes, surveying the faces. No one looked familiar. Satisfied that he hadn't been followed, he boarded the Bobigny-Picasso train and rode it to Gare de l'Est. There he stepped off, walked out of the station, and headed briskly back to the *pension*.

He found Beryl still awake and sitting in an armchair by the window. She'd turned off all the lights, and in the darkness she was little more than a silhouette against the glow of the night sky. He shut and bolted the door. "Beryl?" he said. "Everything all right?"

He thought he saw her nod. Or was it just the quivering of her chin as she took a breath and let out a soft, slow sigh?

"We'll be safe here," he said. "For tonight, at least."

"And tomorrow?" came the murmured question.

"We'll worry about that when the time comes."

She leaned back against the chair cushions and stared straight ahead. "Is this how it was for you, Richard? Working for Intelligence? Living day to day, not daring to think about tomorrows?"

He moved slowly to her chair. "Sometimes it was like this. Sometimes I wasn't sure there'd be a tomorrow for me."

"Do you miss that life?" She looked at him. He couldn't see her face, but he felt her watching him.

"I left that life behind."

"But do you miss it? The excitement? That lovely promise of violence?"

"Beryl. Beryl, please." He reached for her hand; it was like a lump of ice in his grasp.

"Didn't you enjoy it, just a little?"

"No." He paused. Then softly he said, "Yes. For a short time. When I was very young. Before it turned all too real."

"The way it did tonight. Tonight, it was real for me. When I saw that man lying there..." She swallowed. "This afternoon, you see, we had lunch together, the three of us. They had the veal. And a bottle of wine, and ice cream. And I got them to laugh...." She looked away.

"It seems like a game, at first," said Richard. "A make-believe war. But then you realize that the bullets are real. So are the people." He held her hand in his and wished he could warm it, warm her. "That's what happened to me. All of a sudden, it got too real. And there was a woman...."

She sat very still, waiting, listening. "Someone you loved?" she asked softly.

"No, not someone I loved. But someone I liked, very much. It was in Berlin, before the Wall came down. We were trying to bring over a defector to the West. And my partner, she got trapped on the wrong side. The guard spotted her. Fired." He lifted Beryl's hand to his lips and kissed it, held it.

"She...didn't make it?"

He shook his head. "And it wasn't a game of make-believe any longer. I could see her body lying in the no-man's-zone. And I couldn't reach her. So I had to leave her there, for the other side...." He released her hand. He moved to the window and looked out at the lights twinkling over Paris. "That's when I left the business. I didn't want another death on my conscience. I didn't want to feel...responsible." He turned to her. In the faint glow from the city, her face looked pale, almost luminous. "That's what makes this so hard for me, Beryl. Knowing what could happen if I make a mistake. Knowing that your life depends on what I do next."

For a long time, Beryl sat very still, watching him. Feeling his gaze through the darkness. That spark of attraction crackled like fire between them as it always did. But tonight there was something more, something that went beyond desire.

She rose from the chair. Though he didn't move, she could feel the fever of his gaze as she glided toward him, could hear the sharp intake of his breath as she reached up and touched his beard-roughened face. "Richard," she whispered, "I want you."

At once she was swept into his arms. No other embrace, no other kiss, had ever stolen her breath the way this one did. *We are like that couple in bronze,* she thought. *Starved for each other. Devouring each other.*

But this was a feast of love, not destruction.

She whimpered and her head fell back as his mouth slid to her throat. She could feel every stroke of his hands through the silky fabric of her dress. Oh Lord, if he could do this to her with her clothes on, what lovely torment would he unleash on her naked flesh? Already her breasts were tingling under his touch, her nipples turned to tight buds.

He unzipped her dress and slowly eased it off her shoulders.

It hissed past her hips and slid into a silken ripple on the floor. He, too, traced the length of her torso, his lips moving slowly down her throat, her breasts, her belly. Shuddering with pleasure, she gripped his hair and moaned, "No fair..."

"All's fair," he murmured, easing her stockings down her thighs. "In love and war...."

By the time he had her fully undressed, by the time he'd shed his own clothes, she was beyond words, beyond protest. She'd lost all sense of time and space; there was only the darkness, and the warmth of his touch, and the hunger shuddering deep inside her. She scarcely realized how they found their way to the bed. Eagerly she sank backward onto the mattress, and heard the squeak of the springs, the quickening duet of their breathing. Then she pulled him down against her, drew him onto and into her.

Starved for each other, she thought as he captured her mouth under his, invaded it, explored it. *Devouring each other.*

And like two who were famished, they feasted.

He reached for her hands, and their fingers entwined in a tighter and tighter knot as their bodies joined, thrusted, exulted. Even as her last shudders of desire faded away, he was still gripping her hands.

Slowly he released them and cradled her face instead. He pressed gentle kisses to her lips, her eyelids. "Next time," he whispered, "we'll take it slower. I won't be in such a hurry, I promise."

She smiled at him. "I have no complaints."

"None?"

"None at all. But next time…"

"Yes?"

She twisted her body beneath him, and they tumbled across the sheets until her body was lying atop his. "Next time," she murmured, lowering her lips to his chest, "it's my turn to do the tormenting."

He groaned as her mouth slid hotly down to his belly. "We're taking turns?"

"You're the one who said it. All's fair…"

"…in love and war." He laughed. And he buried his hands in her hair.

THEY MET IN THE usual place, the warehouse behind Galerie Annika. Against the walls were stacked dozens of crates containing the paintings and sculptures of would-be artists, most of them no doubt talentless amateurs hoping for a spot on a gallery wall. *But who can really say which is art and which is rubbish?* thought Amiel Foch, gazing around at the room full of crated dreams. *To me, it is all the same. Pigment and canvas.*

Foch turned as the warehouse door swung open. "The bomb went off as planned," he said. "The job is done."

"The job is *not* done," came the reply. Anthony Sutherland emerged from the night and stepped into the warehouse. The thud of the door shutting behind him echoed across the bare concrete floor. "I wanted the woman neutralized. She is still alive. So is Richard Wolf."

Foch stared at Anthony. "It was a delayed fuse, set off two minutes after entry! It could not have ignited on its own."

"Nevertheless, they are still alive. Thus far, your record of success is abysmal. You could not finish off even that stupid creature, Marie St. Pierre."

"I will see to Mme St. Pierre—"

"Forget her! It's the Tavistocks I want dead! Lord, they're like cats! Nine bloody lives."

"Jordan Tavistock is still in custody. I can arrange—"

"Jordan will keep for a while. He's harmless where he is. But Beryl has to be taken care of soon. My guess is that she and Wolf are leaving Paris. Find them."

"How?"

"You're the professional."

"So is Richard Wolf," said Foch. "He will be difficult to trace. I cannot perform miracles."

There was a long silence. Foch watched the other man pace among the crates, and he thought, *This boy is nothing like his mother. This one has the ruthlessness to see things through. And the nerve not to flinch at the consequences.*

"I cannot search blindly," said Foch. "I must have a lead. Will they go to England, perhaps?"

"No, not England." Anthony suddenly stopped pacing. "Greece. The island of Paros."

"You mean…the Rideau family?"

"Wolf will try to contact him. I'm sure of it." Anthony let out a snort of disgust. "My mother should have taken care of Rideau years ago. Well, there's still time to do it."

Foch nodded. "I leave for Paros."

AFTER FOCH HAD LEFT, Anthony Sutherland stood alone in the warehouse, gazing about at the crates. *So many hopes and dreams locked away in here,* he reflected. *But not mine. Mine are on display for all to see and admire. The work of these poor slobs may molder into eternity. But I am the toast of Paris.*

It took more than talent, more than luck. It took the help of Philippe St. Pierre's cold hard cash. Cash that would instantly dry up if his mother was ever exposed.

My father Philippe, thought Anthony with a laugh. *Still unsuspecting after all these years. I have to hand it to my lovely mother—she knows how to keep them under her spell.*

But feminine wiles could take one only so far.

If only Nina had cleaned up this matter years ago. Instead, she'd left a live witness, had even paid the man to leave the country. And as long as that witness lived, he was like a time bomb, ticking away on some lonely Greek island.

Anthony left the warehouse, walked down the alley, and climbed into his car. It was time to go home. Mustn't keep his mother awake; Nina did worry about him so. He tried never to distress her. She was, after all, the only person in this world who really loved him. Understood him.

Like peas in a pod, Mother and I, he thought with a smile. He started his car and roared off into the night.

THEY CAME TO ESCORT HIM from his cell at 9:00 a.m. No explanations, just the clink of keys in the door, and a gruff command in French.

Now what? wondered Jordan as he followed the guard up the corridor to the visitation room. He stepped inside, blinking at the glare of overhead fluorescent lights.

Reggie Vane was waiting in the room. At once he waved Jordan to a chair. "Sit down. You look bloody awful, my boy."

"I feel bloody awful," said Jordan, and sank into the chair.

Reggie sat down, too. Leaning forward, he whispered conspiratorially, "I brought what you asked for. There's a nice little *charcuterie* around the corner. Lovely duckling terrine. And a few *baguettes.*" He shoved a paper bag under the table. *"Bon appétit."*

Jordan glanced in the bag and gave a sigh of pleasure. "Reggie, old man, you're a saint."

"Had some nice leek tarts to go with it, but the cop at the front desk insisted on helping himself."

"What about wine? Did you manage a decent bottle or two?"

Reggie shoved a second bag under the table, eliciting a musical clink from the contents. "But of course. A Beaujolais and a rather nice Pinot noir. Screw-top caps, I'm afraid—they wouldn't allow a corkscrew. And you'll have to hand over the bottles as soon as they're empty. Glass, you know."

Jordan regarded the Beaujolais with a look of sheer contentment. "How on earth did you manage it, Reggie?"

"Just scratched a few itchy palms. Oh, and those books you wanted—Helena will bring them by this afternoon."

"Capital!" Jordan folded the bag over the bottles. "If one must be in prison, one might as well make it a civilized experience." He looked up at Reggie. "Now, what's the latest news? I've had no word from Beryl since yesterday."

Reggie sighed. "I was dreading that question."

"What's happened?"

"I think she and Wolf have left Paris. After the explosion last night—"

"What?"

"I heard it from Daumier this morning. The flat where Beryl was staying was bombed last night. Two French agents killed. Wolf and your sister are fine, but they're dropping out for a while, leaving the country."

Jordan gave a sigh of relief. Thank God Beryl was out of the picture. It was one less problem to worry about. "What about the explosion?" he asked. "What does Daumier say about it?"

"His people feel there are similarities."

"To what?"

"The bombing of the St. Pierre residence."

Jordan stared at him. "But that was a terrorist attack. Cosmic Solidarity or some crazy group—"

"Apparently bombs are sort of like fingerprints. The way they're put together identifies their maker. And both bombs had identical wiring patterns. Something like that."

Jordan shook his head. "Why would terrorists attack Beryl? Or me? We're civilians."

"Perhaps they think otherwise."

"Or perhaps it wasn't terrorists in the first place," said Jordan, suddenly pushing out of his chair. He paced the room, pumping fresh blood to his legs, his brain. Too many hours in that cell had turned his body to mush; he needed a stiff walk, a slap of fresh air. "What if," he suggested, "that bombing of the St. Pierre place wasn't a terrorist attack at all? What if that Cosmic Solidarity nonsense was just a cover story to hide the real motive?"

"You mean it wasn't a political attack?"

"No."

"But who would want to kill Philippe St. Pierre?"

Jordan suddenly stopped dead as the realization hit him. "Not Philippe," he said softly. "His wife. Marie."

"*Marie* planted the bomb?"

"No! Marie was the *target!* She was the only one home when the bomb went off. Everyone assumes it was a mistake, an error in timing. But the bomber knew exactly what he was doing. He was trying to kill Marie, not her husband." Jordan looked at Reggie with new urgency. "You have to reach Wolf. Tell him what I just said."

"I don't know where he is."

"Ask Daumier."

"He doesn't know, either."

"Then find out where my uncle's gone off to. If ever I needed a family connection, it's right now."

After Reggie had left, the guard escorted Jordan back to his cell. The instant he stepped inside, the familiar smells assaulted him—the odor of sour wine and ripe bodies. Back with old friends, he thought, looking at the two Frenchmen snoring in their cots, the same two men whose cell he'd shared when he was first arrested. A drunk, a thief and him. What a happy little trio they made. He went to his cot and set down the two paper bags with the food and wine. At least he wouldn't have to gag on any more goulash.

Lying down, he stared at the cobwebs in the corner. So many leads to follow, to run down. *A killer's on the loose and here I am, locked up and useless. Unable to test my theories. If I could just get the help of someone I trust, someone I know beyond a doubt is on my side…*

Where the hell is Beryl?

THE GREEK TAVERN KEEPER slid two glasses of retsina onto their table. "Summertime, we have many tourists," he said with a shrug. "I cannot keep track of foreigners."

"But this man, Rideau, isn't a tourist," said Richard. "He's been living on this island twenty years. A Frenchman."

The tavern keeper laughed. "Frenchmen, Dutchmen, they are all the same to me," he grunted and went back into the kitchen.

"Another dead end," muttered Beryl. She took a sip of retsina and grimaced. "People actually *drink* this brew?"

"And some of them even enjoy it," said Richard. "It's an acquired taste."

"Then perhaps I'll acquire it another time." She pushed the glass away and looked around the gloomy taverna. It was midday, and passengers from the latest cruise ship had started trickling in from the heat, their shopping bags filled with the usual tourist purchases: Grecian urns, fishermen's caps, peasant dresses. Immersed in the babble of half a dozen languages, it was easy for Beryl to understand why the locals might not bother to distinguish a Frenchman from any other outsider. Foreigners came, they spent money, they left. What more did one need to know about them?

The tavern keeper reemerged from the kitchen carrying a sizzling platter of calamari. He set it on a table occupied by a German family and was about to head back to the kitchen when Richard asked, "Who might know about this Frenchman?"

"You waste your time," said the tavern keeper. "I tell you, there is no one on this island named Rideau."

"He brought his family with him," said Richard. "A wife and a son. The boy would be in his thirties now. His name is Gerard."

A dish suddenly clattered to the floor behind the counter of the bar. The dark-eyed young woman standing at the tap was frowning at Richard. "Gerard?" she said.

"Gerard Rideau," said Richard. "Do you know him?"

"She doesn't know anything," the tavern keeper insisted, and waved the young woman toward the kitchen.

"But I can see she does," said Richard.

The woman stood staring at him, as though not certain what to do, what to say.

"We've come from Paris," said Beryl. "It's very important we speak to Gerard's father."

"You are not French," said the woman.

"No, I'm English." Beryl nodded toward Richard. "He's American."

"He said…he said it was a Frenchman I should be careful of."

"Who did?"

"Gerard."

"He's right to be careful," said Richard. "But he should know things have gotten even more dangerous. There may be others coming to Paros, looking for his family. He has to talk to us, *now*." He pointed to the tavern keeper. "He'll be your witness. If anything goes wrong."

The woman hesitated, then went into the kitchen. A moment later, she reemerged. "He does not answer the telephone," she said. "I will have to drive you there."

It was a bumpy ride down a lonely stretch of road to Logaras beach. Clouds of dust flew in the open window and coated the jet black hair of their driver. Sofia was her name, and she had been born on the island. Her father managed the hotel near the harbor; now her three brothers ran the business. She could do a better job of it, she thought, but of course no one valued a woman's opinion, so she worked instead at Theo's tavern, frying calamari, rolling dolmas. She spoke four languages; one must, she explained, if one wished to live off the tourist trade.

"How do you know Gerard?" asked Beryl.

"We are friends" was the answer.

Lovers, guessed Beryl, seeing the other woman's cheeks redden.

"His family is French," said Sofia. "His mother died five years ago, but his father is still alive. But their name is not Rideau. Perhaps—" she looked at them hopefully "—it is a different family you are looking for?"

"They might have changed their name," said Beryl.

They parked near the beach and strode out across the rocks and sand. "There," said Sofia, pointing to a distant sailboard skimming the water. "That is Gerard." She waved and called to him in Greek.

At once the board spun around, the multicolored sail snapping about in a neat jibe. With the wind at his back, Gerard surfed to the beach like a bronzed Adonis and dragged the board onto the sand.

"Gerard," said Sofia, "these people are looking for a man named Rideau. Is that your father?"

Instantly Gerard dropped his sailboard. "Our name is not Rideau," he said curtly. Then he turned and walked away.

"Gerard?" called Sofia.

"Let me talk to him," said Richard, and he followed the other man up the beach.

Beryl stood by Sofia and watched the two men confront each other. Gerard was shaking his head, denying any knowledge of any Rideau family. Through the whistle of the wind, Beryl heard Richard's voice and the words "bomb" and "murder." She saw Gerard glance around nervously and knew that he was afraid.

"I hope I have done the right thing," murmured Sofia. "He is worried."

"He should be worried."

"What has his father done?"

"It's not what he's done. It's what he knows."

At the other end of the beach, Gerard was looking more and more agitated. Abruptly he turned and walked back to Sofia. Richard was right behind him.

"What is it?" asked Sofia.

"We go," snapped Gerard. "My father's house."

This time the drive took them along the coast, past groves of struggling olive trees on their left, and the gray-green Aegean on their right. The smell of Gerard's suntan lotion permeated the car. Such a dry and barren land, Beryl observed, looking out across the scrub grass. But to a man from a French slum, this would have seemed like a paradise.

"My father," said Gerard as he drove, "speaks no English. I will have to explain to him what you are asking. He may not remember."

"I'm sure he does remember," said Richard. "It's the reason you left Paris."

"That was twenty years ago. A long time…"

"Do *you* remember anything?" asked Beryl from the back seat. "You were…what? Fifteen, sixteen?"

"Fifteen," said Gerard.

"Then you must remember 66 Rue Myrha. The building where you lived."

Gerard gripped the steering wheel tightly as they bounced onto a dirt road. "I remember the police coming to see the attic. Asking my father questions. Every day, for a week."

"What about the woman who rented the attic?" asked Richard. "Her name was Scarlatti. Do you remember her?"

"Yes. She had a man," said Gerard. "I used to listen to them through the door. Every Wednesday. All the sounds they made!" Gerard shook his head in amusement. "Very exciting for a boy my age."

"So this Mlle Scarlatti, she used the attic only as a love nest?" asked Beryl.

"She was never there except to make love."

"What did they look like, these two lovers?"

"The man was tall—that's all I remember. The woman, she had dark hair. Always wore a scarf and sunglasses. I do not remember her face very well, but I remember she was quite beautiful."

Like her mother, thought Beryl. Could she be wrong? Had it really been her, meeting her lover in that run-down flat in Pigalle?

She asked softly, "Was the woman English?"

Gerard paused. "She could have been."

"Meaning you're not certain."

"I was young. I thought she was foreign, but I did not know from where. Then, after the murders, I heard she was English."

"Did you see their bodies?"

Gerard shook his head. "My father, he would not allow it."

"So your father was the first to see them?" asked Richard.

"No. It was the man."

Richard glanced at Gerard in surprise. "Which man?"

"Mlle Scarlatti's lover. We saw him climb the steps to the attic. Then he came running back down, quite frantic. That's when we knew something was wrong and called the police."

"What happened to that man?"

"He drove away. I never saw him again. I assumed he was afraid of being accused. And that was why he sent us the money."

"The payoff," said Richard. "I guessed as much."

"For silence?" asked Beryl.

"Or false testimony." He asked Gerard, "How was the money delivered?"

"A man came with a briefcase only hours after the bodies were found. I'd never seen him before—a short, rather stocky Frenchman. He came to our flat, took my father into a back room. I did not hear what they said. Then the short man left."

"Your father never spoke to you about it?"

"No. And he told us we were not to speak of it to the police."

"You're certain that the briefcase contained money?"

"It must have."

"How do you know?"

"Because suddenly we had things. New clothes, a television. And then, soon afterward, we came to Greece. And we bought the house. There, you see?" He pointed. In the distance was a sprawling villa with a red-tiled roof. As they drove closer, Beryl saw bougainvillea trailing up the whitewashed walls and spilling over a covered veranda. Just below the house, waves lapped at a lonely beach.

They parked next to a dusty Citroën and climbed out. The wind whistled in from the sea, stinging their faces with sand. There was no other house in sight, only this solitary building, tucked into the crags of a barren hill.

"Papa?" called Gerard, climbing the stone steps. He swung open the wrought-iron gate. "Papa?"

No one answered.

Gerard pushed through the front door and stepped across the threshold, Beryl and Richard right behind him. Their footsteps echoed through silent rooms.

"I called here from the tavern," said Sofia. "There was no answer."

"His car is outside," said Gerard. "He must be here." He crossed the living room and started toward the dining room. "Papa?" he said, and halted in the doorway. An anguished cry was suddenly wrenched from his throat. He took a step forward and seemed to stumble to his knees. Over his shoulder, Beryl caught a view into the formal dining room beyond.

A wood table stretched the length of the room. At the far end of the table, a gray-haired man had slumped onto his dinner plate, scattering chick-peas and rice across the table's surface.

Richard pushed past Gerard and went to the fallen man. Gently he grasped the head and lifted the face from its pillow of mashed rice.

In the man's forehead was punched a single bullet-hole.

Chapter Ten

AMIEL FOCH sat at an outdoor café table, sipping espresso and watching the tourists stroll past. Not the usual dentures-and-bifocals crowd, he observed as a shapely redhead wandered by. This must be the week for honeymooners. It was five o'clock, and the last public ferry to Piraeus would be sailing in half an hour. If the Tavistock woman planned to leave the island tonight, she'd have to board that ferry. He'd keep an eye on the gangplank.

He polished off his snack of stuffed grape leaves and started in on dessert, a walnut pastry steeped in syrup. Curious, how the completion of a job always left him ravenous. For other men, the spilling of blood resulted in a surge of libido, a sudden craving for hot, fast sex. Amiel Foch craved food instead; no wonder his weight was such a problem.

Dispatching the old Frenchman Rideau had been easy; killing Wolf and the woman would not be so simple. Earlier today he had considered an ambush, but Rideau's house stood on an empty stretch of shoreline, the only access a five-mile-long dirt road, and there was nowhere to conceal his car. Nowhere to lie in wait without being detected. Foch had a rule he never broke: always leave an escape route. The Rideau house, set in the midst of barren scrub, was too exposed for any such retreat. Richard Wolf was armed and would be watching for danger signs.

Amiel Foch was not a coward. But he was not a fool, either.

Far wiser to wait for another opportunity—perhaps in Piraeus, with its crowded streets and chaotic traffic. Pedestrians were killed all the time. An accident, two dead tourists—it would raise hardly a stir of interest.

Foch's gaze sharpened as the afternoon ferry pulled into port. There was only a brief unloading of passengers; the island of Paros was not, after all, on the usual Mykonos-Rhodes-Crete circuit made by tourists. At the bottom of the gangplank, a few dozen people had already gathered to board. Quickly Foch surveyed the crowd. To his consternation, he saw neither the woman nor Wolf. He knew they'd been on the island today; his contact had spotted the pair in a tavern this morning. Had they slipped away by some other route?

Then he noticed the man in the tattered Windbreaker and black fisherman's cap. Though his shoulders were hunched, there was no disguising the man's height—six feet tall, at least, with a tautly athletic build. The man turned sideways, and Foch caught a glimpse of his face, partly obscured by a few days' worth of stubble. It was, indeed, Richard Wolf. But he appeared to be traveling alone. Where was the woman?

Foch paid his café bill and wandered over to the landing. He mingled with the waiting passengers and studied their faces. There were a number of women, tanned tourists, Greek housewives clad modestly in black, a few hippies in blue jeans. Beryl Tavistock was not among them.

He felt a brief spurt of panic. Had the woman and Wolf separated? If so, he might never find her. He was tempted to stay on the island, to search her out....

The passengers were moving up the gangplank.

He weighed his choices and decided to follow Wolf. Better to stick with a flesh-and-blood quarry. Sooner or later, Wolf would reunite with the woman. Until then, Foch would have to bide his time, make no moves.

The man in the fisherman's cap walked up the gangplank and into the cabin. After a moment, Foch followed him inside and took a seat two rows behind him, next to an old man with a box of salted fish. It wasn't long before the engines growled to life and the ferry slid away from the dock.

Foch settled back for the ride, his gaze focused on the back of Wolf's head. The smell of fuel and dried fish soon became nauseating. The ferry pitched and heaved on the water, and his lunch of dolmas and espresso was threatening to come back up. Foch rose from his seat and scrambled outside. Standing at the rail, he gulped in a few breaths of fresh air and waited for the nausea to pass. At last it eased, and he reluctantly turned to go back into the cabin. He headed up the aisle, past Wolf—

Or the man he'd *thought* was Wolf.

He was wearing the same ratty Windbreaker, the same black fisherman's cap. But this man was clean shaven, younger. Definitely not the same man!

Foch glanced around the cabin. No Wolf. He hurried outside to the deck. No Wolf. He climbed the stairs to the upper level. Again, no Wolf.

He turned and saw the island of Paros receding behind them, and he let out a strangled curse. It was all a feint! They were still on the island—they had to be.

And I'm trapped on this boat to Piraeus.

Foch slapped the railing and cursed himself for his own stupidity. Wolf had outsmarted him—again. The old professional using his bag of tricks. There was no point interrogating the man in the cabin; he was probably just some local dupe hired to switch places with Wolf for the ferry ride.

He looked at his watch and calculated how many hours it would take him to get back to the island via a hired boat. With any luck, he could be stalking them tonight. If they were still there. He'd find them, he vowed. Wolf might be a professional. But then, so was he.

FROM INSIDE A NEARBY CAFÉ, Richard watched the ferry glide out of the harbor and heaved a sigh of relief. The old bait and switch had worked; no one had followed him off the boat. He'd been suspicious of one man in particular—a balding fellow in nondescript tourist clothes. Richard had noticed how the man had scanned the boarding passengers, how his gaze had paused momentarily on Richard's face.

Yes, he was the one. The bait was laid out for him.

The switch was a snap.

Once inside the ferry cabin, Richard had tossed his cap and jacket on a seat, walked up the aisle, and exited out the other door. By prior arrangement, Sofia's brother—six foot one and with black hair—had slid into that same seat, donned the cap and jacket, and promptly cradled his face in his arms, as though to sleep.

Richard had waited behind some crates on deck just long enough for all the passengers to board. Then he'd simply walked off the boat.

No one had followed him.

He left the café and climbed into Sofia's car.

It was a six-mile drive to the cove. Sofia and her brothers had *Melina,* the family fishing boat, ready to go, her engine running, her anchor line set to hoist. Richard scrambled out of the rowboat and up the rope ladder to *Melina*'s deck.

Beryl was waiting for him. He took her in his arms, hugged her, kissed her. "It's all right," he murmured. "I lost him."

"I was afraid I'd lose *you.*"

"Not a chance." He pulled back and smiled at her. With her black hair whipping in the wind, and her eyes the same crystalline green as the Aegean, she reminded him of some Greek goddess. Circe, Aphrodite. A woman who could hold a man forever bewitched.

The anchor thudded on deck. Sofia's brothers guided *Melina*'s bow around to face the open sea.

It started out a rough passage, the summer winds fierce and constant, the sea a rolling carpet of swells. But at sunset, as the sky deepened to a glorious shade of red, the wind suddenly died and the water turned glassy. Beryl and Richard stood on deck and gazed at the darkening silhouettes of the islands.

Sofia said, "We arrive late tonight."

"Piraeus?" asked Richard.

"No. Too busy. We pull in at Monemvassia where no one will see us."

"And then?"

"You go your way. We go ours. It is safer, for all of us." Sofia glanced toward the stern at her two brothers, who were laughing and clapping each other on the back. "Look at them! They think this is a nice little adventure! If they had seen Gerard's father…"

"Will you be all right?" asked Beryl.

Sofia looked at her. "I worry more about Gerard. They may be looking for him."

"I don't think so," said Richard. "He was only a boy when he left Paris. His testimony can't hurt them."

"He remembered enough to tell *you*," countered Sofia.

Richard shook his head. "But I'm not sure what any of it meant."

"Perhaps the killer knows. And he will be looking for Gerard next." Sofia glanced back across the stern, toward the island. Toward Gerard, who had refused to flee. "His stubbornness. It will get him killed," she muttered, and wandered away into the cabin.

"What do you think it meant?" asked Beryl. "That business about the short man with the briefcase? Was it just a payoff to Rideau, to keep him silent?"

"Partly."

"You think there was something else in that briefcase," she said. "Something besides money."

He turned and saw the glow of the sunset on her face, the intensity of her gaze. *She's quick*, he thought. *She knows exactly what I'm thinking*. He said, "I'm sure there was. I think the lover of our mysterious Mlle Scarlatti found himself in a very sticky situation. Two dead bodies in his garret, the police certain to be notified. He sees a way to extricate himself from two crises at once. He sends his man to pay off Rideau, asks him not to identify him to police."

"And the second crisis?"

"His status as a mole."

"Delphi?"

"Maybe he knew Intelligence was about to close in. So he places the NATO documents in a briefcase…"

"And has his hired man plant the briefcase in the garret," finished Beryl. "Near my father's body."

Richard nodded. "*That's* what Inspector Broussard was trying to tell us—something about a briefcase. Remember that police photo of the murder scene? He kept pointing to an empty spot near the door. What if the briefcase was planted *after* that initial crime photo was taken? The inspector would have realized it was done postmortem."

"But he couldn't pursue the matter, because French Intelligence confiscated the briefcase."

"Exactly."

"They assumed my father was the one who brought the documents into the garret." She looked at him, her eyes glittering with determination. "How do we prove it? Any of it?"

"We identify Mlle Scarlatti's lover."

"But our only witness was Rideau. And Gerard was just a boy. He scarcely remembers what the man looked like."

"So we go to another source. A man who would know Delphi's true identity—his East German spymaster. Heinrich Leitner."

She stared at him in surprise. "Do you know how to reach him?"

"He's in a high-security prison in Berlin. Trouble is, German Intelligence won't exactly allow us free access to their prisoners."

"As a diplomatic favor?"

His laugh was plainly skeptical. "An ex-CIA agent isn't exactly on their most-favored list. Besides, Leitner might not want to see me. Still, it's a chance we'll take." He turned to gaze over the bow at the darkening sea.

He felt her move close beside him, felt her nearness as acutely as the warmth of the setting sun. It was enough to drive him crazy, having her so close and being unable to make love to her. He found himself counting the hours until they would be alone again, until he could undress her, make love to her. *And I once considered her too rich for my blood. Maybe she is. Maybe this is just a fever that'll burn itself out, leaving us both sadder and wiser. But for now she's all I think about, all I crave.*

"So that's where we're headed next," she whispered. "Berlin."

"There'll be risks." Their gazes met through the velvet dusk. "Things could go wrong…."

"Not while you're around," she said softly.

I hope you're right, he thought as he pulled her into his arms. *I hope to God you're right.*

THE DICE CLATTERED against the cell wall and came to rest with a five and a six showing.

"Ah-hah!" crowed Jordan, raising a fist in triumph. "What does that make it? Ten thousand francs? *Dix mille*?"

His cellmates, Leroi and Fofo, nodded resignedly.

Jordan held out his hand. “Pay up, gentlemen.” Two grubby slips of paper were slapped into his palm. On each was written the number ten thousand. Jordan grinned. “Another round?”

Fofo shook the dice, threw them against the wall, and groaned. A three and a five. Leroi threw a pair of twos.

Jordan threw another five and six. His cellmates handed over two more grubby slips of paper. *Why, I’ll be a millionaire by tomorrow,* Jordan rejoiced, looking down at the growing pile of IOUs. On paper, anyway. He picked up the dice and was about to make another toss when he heard footsteps approach.

Reggie Vane was standing outside the cell, holding a basket of smoked salmon and crackers. “Helena sent these over,” he said as he slid the basket through the small opening at the bottom of the cell door. “Oh, and there’s fresh linen, napkins and such. One can’t dine properly on paper, can one?”

“Certainly not,” agreed Jordan, gratefully accepting the basket of goodies. “You are a true friend, indeed, Reggie.”

“Yes, well…” Reggie grinned and cleared his throat. “Anything for a child of Madeline’s.”

“Any word from Uncle Hugh?”

“Still unreachable, according to your people at Chetwynd.”

Jordan set the basket down in frustration. “This is most bizarre! I’m in prison. Beryl’s vanished. And Uncle Hugh’s probably off on some classified mission for MI6.” He began to pace the cell, oblivious to the fact that Fofo and Leroi were hungrily raiding the contents of the basket. “What about that bomb investigation? Anything new?”

“The two bombings are definitely linked. The devices were manufactured by the same hand. It appears someone’s targeted both Beryl and the St. Pierres.”

“I think the target was Marie St. Pierre, in particular.” Jordan stopped and looked at Reggie. “Let’s say Marie *was* the target. What’s the motive?”

Reggie shrugged. “She’s not the sort of woman to pick up enemies.”

“You should be able to come up with an answer. She and your

wife are best chums, after all. Helena must know who'd want to kill Marie."

Reggie gave him a troubled look. "It's not as if there's any, well…proof."

Jordan moved toward him. "What are you thinking?"

"Just rumors. Things Helena might have mentioned."

"Was it about Philippe?"

Reggie looked down. "I feel a bit…well, ungentlemanly, bringing it up. You see, it happened years ago."

"What did?"

"The affair. Between Philippe and Nina."

Jordan stared at him through the bars. *There it is,* he thought. *There's the motive.* "How long have you known about this?" he asked.

"I heard about it fifteen, twenty years ago. You see, I couldn't understand why Helena disliked Nina so much. It was almost a…a hatred. You know how it is sometimes with females, all those catty looks. I assumed it was jealousy. My Helena's never been comfortable with more…well, attractive women. As a matter of fact, if I so much as glance at a pretty face, she gets downright nasty about it."

"How did she learn about Philippe and Nina?"

"Marie told her."

"Who else knew about it?"

"I doubt there were many. Poor Marie's not one to advertise her humiliation. To have one's husband dallying with a…a piece of baggage like Nina!"

"Yet she stayed married to Philippe all these years."

"Yes, she's loyal that way. And what good would it do to make a public stink of it? Ruin his career? Now he's finance minister. Chances are, he'll go to the top. And Marie will be with him. So in the long run, it was worth it."

"If she lives to see it."

"You're not saying Philippe would kill his own wife? And why now, at this late date?"

"Perhaps she issued an ultimatum. Think about it, Reggie! Here he is, inches away from being prime minister. And Marie says, 'It's your mistress or me. Choose.'"

Reggie looked thoughtful. "If he chooses Nina, he'd have to get rid of his wife."

"Ah, but what if he chooses Marie? And Nina's the one left out in the cold?"

They frowned at each other through the bars.

"Call Daumier," said Jordan. "Tell him what you just told me, about the affair. And ask him to put a tail on Nina."

"You don't really think—"

"I think," said Jordan, "that we've been looking at this from the wrong angle entirely. The bombing wasn't a political act. All that Cosmic Solidarity rubbish was merely a smoke screen, to cover up the real reason for the attack."

"You mean it was personal?"

Jordan nodded. "Murder usually is."

THE FLIGHT TO BERLIN was half-empty, so the only logical reason that disheveled pair of passengers in row two should be sitting in first class was that they must have actually paid the fare, a fact the flight attendant found difficult to believe, considering their appearance. Both wore dark sunglasses, wrinkled clothes and unmistakable expressions of exhaustion. The man had a week's worth of dark stubble on his jaw. The woman was deeply sunburned and her black hair was tangled and powdered with dust. Their only carryon was the woman's purse, a battered straw affair coated with sand. The attendant glanced at the couple's ticket stubs. Athens—Rome—Berlin. With a forced smile, she asked them if they wished to order cocktails.

"Bloody Mary," said the woman in the Queen's perfect English.

"A Rob Roy," said the man. "Hold the bitters."

The woman went to fetch their drinks. When she returned, the man and woman were holding hands and looking at each other with the weary smiles of fellow survivors. They took their drinks from the tray.

"To our health?" the man asked.

"Definitely," the woman answered.

And, grinning, they both tipped back their glasses in a toast.

The meal cart was wheeled out and on it were lobster patties, crown roast of lamb, wild rice and mushroom caps. The couple ate double servings of everything and topped their dinner off with a split of wine. Then, like a pair of exhausted puppies, they curled up against each other and fell asleep.

They slept all the way to Berlin. Only when the plane rolled to a stop at the terminal did they jerk awake, both of them instantly alert and on guard. As the passengers filed out, the flight attendant kept her gaze on that rumpled pair from Athens. There was no telling who they were or what they might be up to. First-class passengers did not usually travel the world dressed like bums.

The couple was the last to disembark.

The attendant followed the pair onto the passenger ramp and stood watching as they walked toward a small crowd of greeters. They made it as far as the waiting area.

Two men stepped into their path. At once the couple halted and pivoted as though to flee back toward the plane. Three more men magically appeared, blocking off their escape. The couple was trapped.

The attendant caught a glimpse of the woman's panicked face, the man's grim expression of defeat. She had been sure there was something wrong about them. They were terrorists, perhaps, or international thieves. And there were the police to make the arrest. She watched as the pair was led away through the murmuring crowd. Definitely not first class, she thought with a sniff of satisfaction. Oh, yes, one could always tell.

RICHARD AND BERYL were shoved forward into a windowless room. "Stay here!" came the barked command, then the door was slammed shut behind them.

"They were waiting for us," said Beryl. "How did they know?"

Richard went to the door and tested the knob. "Dead bolt," he muttered. "We're locked in tight." In frustration, he began to circle the room, searching for another way out. "Somehow they knew we were coming to Berlin…."

"We paid for the tickets in cash. There was no way they could have known. And those were airport guards, Richard. If they want us dead, why bother to arrest us?"

"To keep you from getting your heads shot off," said a familiar voice. "That's why."

Beryl wheeled around in astonishment at the portly man who'd just opened the door. "Uncle *Hugh?*"

Lord Lovat scowled at his niece's wrinkled clothes and tangled hair. "You're a fine mess. Since when did you adopt the gypsy look?"

"Since we hitchhiked halfway across Greece. Credit cards, by the way, are *not* the preferred method of payment in small Greek towns."

"Well, you made it to Berlin." He glanced at Richard. "Good work, Wolf."

"I could've used some assistance," growled Richard.

"And we would've happily provided it. But we had no idea where to find you, until I spoke with your man, Sakaroff. He said you'd be headed for Berlin. We only just found out you'd gone via Athens."

"What are *you* doing in Berlin, Uncle Hugh?" demanded Beryl. "I thought you were off on another one of your secret missions."

"I'm fishing."

"Not for fish, obviously."

"For answers. Which I'm hoping Heinrich Leitner will provide." He took another look at Beryl's clothes and sighed. "Let's get to the hotel and clean you both up. Then we'll pay a visit to Herr Leitner's prison cell."

"You have clearance to speak to him?" said Richard in surprise.

"What do you think I've been doing here these last few days? Wining and dining the necessary officials." He waved them out of the room. "The car's waiting."

In Uncle Hugh's hotel suite, they showered off three days' worth of Greek dust and sand. A fresh set of clothes was delivered to the room, courtesy of the concierge—sober business attire, outfits appropriate for a visit to a high-security prison.

"How do we know Leitner will tell us the truth?" asked Richard as they rode in the limousine to the prison.

"We don't," said Hugh. "We don't even know how much he *can* tell us. He oversaw Paris operations from East Berlin, so he'd be acquainted with code names, but not faces."

"Then we may come away with nothing."

"As I said, Wolf, it's a fishing expedition. Sometimes you reel in an old tire. Sometimes a salmon."

"Or, in this case, a mole."

"If he's cooperative."

"Are you prepared to hear the truth?" asked Richard. The question was directed at Hugh, but his gaze was on Beryl. Delphi could still be Bernard or Madeline, his eyes said.

"Right now, I'd say ignorance is far more dangerous," Hugh observed. "And there's Jordan to consider. I have people watching out for him. But there's always the chance things could go wrong."

Things have already gone wrong, thought Beryl, looking out the car window at the drab and dreary buildings of East Berlin.

The prison was even more forbidding—a massive concrete fortress surrounded by electrified fences. The very best of security, she noted, as they moved through the gauntlet of checkpoints and metal detectors. Uncle Hugh had obviously been expected, and he was greeted with the chilling disdain of an old Cold War enemy. Only when they'd arrived at the commandant's office was any courtesy extended to them. Glasses of hot tea were passed around, cigars offered to the men. Hugh accepted; Richard declined.

"Up until recently, Leitner was most uncooperative," said the commandant, lighting a cigar. "At first, he denied his role entirely. But our files on him are proof positive. He *was* in charge of Paris operations."

"Has Leitner provided any names?" asked Richard.

The commandant peered at Richard through the drifting cloud of cigar smoke. "You were CIA, were you not, Mr. Wolf?"

Richard gave only the briefest nod of acknowledgment. "It was years ago. I've left the business."

"But you understand how it is, to be dogged by one's past associations."

"Yes, I understand."

The commandant rose and went to look out his window at the barbed-wire fence enclosing his prison kingdom. "Berlin is filled with people running from their shadows. Their old lives. Whether it was for money or for ideology, they served a master. And now the master is dead and they hide from the past."

"Leitner's already in prison. He has nothing to lose by talking to us."

"But the people who worked for him—the ones not yet exposed—they have everything to lose. Now the East German files are open. And every day, some curious citizen opens one of those files and discovers the truth. Realizes that a friend or husband or lover was working for the enemy." The commandant turned, his pale blue eyes focused on Richard. "That's why Leitner has been reluctant to give names—to protect his old agents."

"But you say he's more cooperative these days?"

"In recent weeks, yes."

"Why?"

The commandant paused. "A bad heart, the doctors say. It fails, little by little. In two months, three..." He shrugged. "Leitner sees the end coming. And in exchange for a few last comforts, he's sometimes willing to talk."

"Then he may give us answers."

"If he is in the mood." The commandant turned to the door. "So, let us see what sort of mood Herr Leitner is in today."

They followed him down secured corridors, past mounted cameras and grim-faced guards, into the very core of the complex. Here there were no windows; the air itself seemed hermetically sealed from the outside world. *From here there is no escape,* thought Beryl. *Except through death.*

They stopped at cell number five. Two guards, each with his own key, opened separate locks. The door swung open.

Inside, on a wooden chair, sat an old man. Oxygen tubing snaked from his nostrils. His regulation prison garb—tan shirt and pants, no belt—hung loosely on his shrunken frame. The fluorescent lights gave his face a yellowish cast. Beside the man's chair stood an oxygen tank; except for the hiss of the gas flowing through his nasal prongs, the room was silent.

The commandant said, "*Guten Tag,* Heinrich."

Leitner said nothing. Only by a brief flicker of his eyes did he acknowledge the greeting.

"I have brought with me today, Lord Lovat, from England. You are familiar with the name?"

Again, a flicker in the old man's blue eyes. And a whisper, barely audible, "MI6."

"That's right," said Hugh. "Since retired."

"So am I," was the reply, not without a trace of humor. Leitner's gaze shifted to Beryl and Richard.

"My niece," said Hugh. "And a former associate. Richard Wolf."

"CIA?" said Leitner.

Richard nodded. "Also retired."

Leitner managed a faint smile. "How differently we enjoy our retirements." He looked once again at Hugh. "A social call on an old enemy? How thoughtful."

"Not a social call, exactly," said Hugh.

Leitner began to cough, and the effort seemed almost too much for him; when at last he settled back into his chair, his face had a distinctly blue tinge. "What is it you wish to know?"

"The identity of your double agent in Paris. Code name Delphi."

Leitner didn't speak.

"Surely the name is familiar, Herr Leitner. Over the years, Delphi must have passed on invaluable documents. He was your link to NATO operations. Don't you remember?"

"That was twenty years ago," murmured Leitner. "The world has changed."

"We want only his name. That's all."

"So you may put Delphi in a cage like this? Shut away from the sun and air?"

"So we can stop the killing," said Richard.

Leitner frowned. "What killing?"

"It's going on right now. A French agent, murdered in Paris. A man, shot to death in Greece. It's all linked to Delphi."

"That cannot be possible," said Leitner.

"Why?"

"Delphi has been put to sleep."

Hugh frowned at him. "Are you saying he's dead?"

"But that makes no sense," said Richard. "If Delphi's dead, why is the killing still going on?"

"Perhaps," said Leitner, "it has nothing at all to do with Delphi."

"Perhaps you are lying," said Richard.

Leitner smiled. "Always a possibility." Suddenly he began to cough again; it had the gurgling sound of a man drowning in his own secretions. When at last he could speak, it was only between gasps for oxygen. "Delphi was a paid recruit," he said. "Not a true believer. We preferred the believers, you see. They did not cost as much."

“So he did it for money?” asked Richard.

“A rather generous sum, over the years.”

“When did it stop?”

“When it became a risk to all involved. So Delphi ended the association. Covered all tracks before your counterintelligence could close in.”

“Is that why my parents were killed?” asked Beryl. “Because Delphi had to cover his tracks?”

Leitner frowned. “Your parents?”

“Bernard and Madeline Tavistock. They were shot to death in a garret in Pigalle.”

“But that was a murder and suicide. I saw the report.”

“Or were they both murdered? By Delphi?”

Leitner looked at Hugh. “I gave no such order. And that is the truth.”

“Meaning some of what you told us is *not* the truth?” Richard probed.

Leitner took a deep breath of oxygen and painfully wheezed it out. “Truth, lies,” he whispered. “What does it matter now?” He sank back in his chair and looked at the commandant. “I wish to rest. Take these people away.”

“Herr Leitner,” said Richard, “I’ll ask this one last time. Is Delphi really dead?”

Leitner met his gaze with one so steady, so unflinching, it seemed that surely he was about to tell the truth. But the answer he gave was puzzling at best.

“Dormant,” he said. “That is the word I would use.”

“So he’s not dead.”

“For your purposes,” Leitner said with a smile, “he is.”

Chapter Eleven

"A SLEEPER. That's what Delphi must be," said Richard. They had not dared discuss the matter in the limousine—no telling whom their driver really worked for. But here, in a noisy restaurant, with waiters whisking back and forth, Richard could finally spell out his theories. "I'm sure that's what he meant."

"A sleeper?" asked Beryl.

"Someone they recruit years in advance," said her uncle. "As a young adult. The person may be kept inactive for years. They live a normal life, try to gain influence in some trusted position. And then the signal's sent. And the sleeper's activated."

"So that's what he meant by dormant," said Beryl. "Not dead. But not active, either."

"Precisely."

"For this sleeper to be of any use to them, he'd have to be in a position of influence. Or close to it," said Beryl thoughtfully.

"Which describes Stephen Sutherland to a T," said Richard. "American ambassador. Access to all security data."

"It also describes Philippe St. Pierre," said Hugh. "Minister of Finance. In line for French prime minister—"

"And extremely vulnerable to blackmail," added Beryl, thinking of Nina and Philippe. And of Anthony, the son born of their illicit affair.

"I'll contact Daumier," said Hugh. "Have St. Pierre vetted again."

"While he's at it," said Richard, "ask him to vet Nina."

"Nina?"

"Talk about positions of influence! An ambassador's wife. Mistress to St. Pierre. She could've heard secrets from both sides of the bed."

Hugh shook his head. "Considering her double digit IQ, Nina Sutherland's the last person I'd expect to work for Intelligence."

"And the one person who'd get away with it."

Hugh glanced around impatiently for the waiter. "We have to leave for Paris at once," he said, and slapped enough marks on the table to pay for their coffees. "There's no telling what's happening to Jordan."

"If it is Nina, do you think she could get at Jordan?" asked Beryl.

"All these years, I've overlooked Nina Sutherland," said Hugh. "I'm not about to make the same mistake now."

DAUMIER MET THEM at Orly Airport. "I have reexamined the security files on Philippe and Nina," he said as they rode together in his limousine. "St. Pierre is clean. His record is unblemished. If he is the sleeper, we have no evidence of it."

"And Nina?"

Daumier gave a deep sigh. "Our dear Nina presents a problem. There was an item that was not addressed in her earlier vetting. She was eighteen when she first appeared on the London stage. A small part, quite insignificant, but it launched her acting career. At that time, she had an affair with one of her fellow actors—an East German by the name of Berte Klausner. He claimed he was a defector. But three years later, he vanished from England and was never heard from again."

"A recruiter?" asked Richard.

"Possibly."

"How on earth did this little affair make it past Nina's vetting?" asked Beryl.

Daumier shrugged. "It was noted when Nina and Sutherland were married. By then she'd retired from the theater to become a diplomat's wife. She didn't serve in any official capacity. As a rule, security checks on wives—especially if they are American—are not as demanding. So Nina slipped through."

"Then you have evidence of possible recruitment," said Beryl. "And she could have had access to NATO secrets by way of her husband. But you can't prove she's Delphi. Nor can you prove she's a murderer."

"True," admitted Daumier.

"I doubt you'll get her to confess, either," said Richard. "Nina was once an actress. She could probably brazen her way through anything."

"That is why I suggest the following action," said Daumier. "A trap. Tempt her into making a move."

"With what bait?" asked Richard.

"Jordan."

"That's out of the question!" said Beryl.

"He has already agreed to it. This afternoon, he will be released from prison. We move him to a hotel where he will attempt to be conspicuous."

Hugh laughed. "Not much of a stretch for our Jordan."

"My men will be stationed at strategic points in the hotel. If—and when—an attack occurs, we will be prepared."

"Things could go wrong," said Beryl. "He could be hurt—"

"He could be hurt in prison, as well," said Daumier. "At least this may provide us with answers."

"And possibly a dead body."

"Have you a better suggestion?"

Beryl glanced at Richard, then at her uncle. They were both silent. *I can't believe they're agreeing to this,* she thought.

She looked at Daumier. "What do you want *me* to do?"

"You'd complicate things, Beryl," said Hugh. "It's better for you to stay out of the picture."

"The Vanes' house has excellent security," said Daumier. "Reggie and Helena have already agreed that you should stay with them."

"But I haven't agreed," said Beryl.

"Beryl." It was Richard. He spoke quietly. Unbendingly. "Jordan will be protected from all angles. They'll be ready for the attack. This time, nothing will go wrong."

"Can you guarantee it? Can any of you?"

There was silence.

"Nothing can be guaranteed, Beryl," said Daumier quietly. "We have to take this chance. It may be the only way to catch Delphi."

In frustration, she looked out the window, thinking of the options. Realizing there were none—not if any of this was to be resolved—she said softly, "I'll agree to it on one condition."

"What's that?"

She looked at Richard. "I want you to be with him. I trust you, Richard. If you're watching Jordan, I know he'll be all right."

Richard nodded. "I'll be right by his side."

"Who else knows about this plan?" asked Hugh.

"Just a few of my people," said Daumier. "I was careful not to let any of this leak out to Philippe St. Pierre."

"What do Reggie and Helena know?" asked Beryl.

"Only that you need a safe place to stay. They are doing this as a favor to old friends."

As an old friend was exactly the way Beryl was greeted upon arrival at the Vanes' residence. As soon as the gates closed behind the limousine, and they were inside the high walls of the compound, she was swept into the comfort of their home. It all seemed so safe, so familiar: the English wallpaper, the tray of tea and biscuits on the end table, the vases of flowers perfuming the rooms. Surely nothing could hurt her here....

There was scarcely time to say goodbye to Richard. While Daumier and Hugh waited outside in the car, Richard pulled Beryl into his arms. They shared a last embrace, a last kiss.

"You'll be perfectly safe here," he whispered. "Don't leave the compound for any reason."

"*You're* the one I worry about. You and Jordan."

"I won't let anything happen to him." He tipped up her chin and pressed his lips to hers. "And that," he murmured, "is a promise." He touched her face and grinned, a confident grin that made her believe anything was possible.

Then he walked away.

She stood on the doorstep and watched the car drive out of the compound, saw the iron gates close shut behind it. *I'm with you,* she thought. *Whatever happens, Richard, I'm right there beside you.*

"Come, Beryl," said Reggie, affectionately draping his arm around her shoulders. "I have an instinct about these things. And I'm positive everything will turn out just fine."

She looked up at Reggie's smiling face. *Thank God for old friends,* she thought. And she let him lead her back into the house.

JORDAN WAS DOWN on all fours in his jail cell, rattling a pair of dice in his hand. His cellmates, the two shaggy, ripe-smelling ruffians—or could that odor be Jordan's?—hovered behind him, stamping their feet and yelling. Jordan threw the dice; they tumbled across the floor and clattered against the wall. Two fives.

"Zut alors!" groaned the cellmates.

Jordan raised his fist in triumph. *"Oh, là là!"* Only then did he see his visitors staring at him through the bars. "Uncle Hugh!" he said, jumping to his feet. "Am I glad to see you!"

Hugh's disbelieving gaze scanned the interior of the cell. Over the cot was draped a red-checked tablecloth, laid out with platters of sliced beef, poached salmon, a bowl of grapes. A bottle of wine sat chilling in a plastic bucket. And on a chair beside the bed was neatly stacked a half dozen leather-bound books and a vase of roses. "This is a prison?" quipped Hugh.

"Oh, I've spruced it up a bit," said Jordan. "The food was wretched, so I had some delivered. Brought in the reading material, as well. But," he said with a sigh, "I'm afraid it's still very much a prison." He tapped the bars. "As you can see." He looked at Daumier. "So, are we ready?"

"If you are still willing."

"Haven't much of a choice, have I? Considering the alternative."

The guard unlocked the door and Jordan stepped out, carrying his bundle of street clothes. But he couldn't walk away without a proper goodbye to his cellmates. He turned and found Fofo and Leroi staring at him mournfully. "Afraid this is it, fellows," he said. "It's been—" he thought a moment, struggling to come up with the right adjective "—a uniquely fragrant experience." On impulse, he tossed his tailored linen jacket to the disbelieving Fofo. "I think that might fit you," he said. "Wear it in good health." Then, with a farewell wave, he followed his companions out of the building and into Daumier's limousine.

They drove him to the Ritz—same floor, different room. A fashionably appropriate place for an assassination, he thought wryly as he came out of the shower and dressed in a fresh suit.

"Bulletproof windows," said Daumier. "Microphones in the front room. And there'll be two men, stationed across the hall. Also, you should have this." Daumier reached into his briefcase and pulled out an automatic pistol. He handed it to Jordan, who regarded the weapon with a raised eyebrow.

"Worst-case scenario? I'll actually have to defend myself?"

"A precaution. You know how to use one?"

"I suppose I can muddle through," said Jordan, expertly sliding in the ammunition clip. He looked at Richard. "Now what happens?"

"Have a meal in the restaurant downstairs," said Richard. "Take your time, make sure you're seen by as many employees as possible. Leave a big tip, be conspicuous. And return to your room."

"And then?"

"We wait and see who comes knocking."

"What if no one does?"

"They will," said Daumier grimly. "I guarantee it."

AMIEL FOCH RECEIVED the call a mere thirty minutes later. It was the hotel maid—the same woman who'd been so useful a week before, when he'd needed access to the Tavistocks' suites.

"He is back," she said. "The Englishman."

"Jordan Tavistock? But he's in prison—"

"I have just seen him in the hotel. Room 315. He seems to be alone."

Foch grimaced in amazement. Perhaps those Tavistock family connections had come through. Now he was a free man—and a vulnerable target. "I need to get into his room," said Foch. "Tonight."

"I cannot do it."

"You did it before. I'll pay double."

The maid gave a snort of disgust. "It's still not enough. I could lose my job."

"I'll pay more than enough. Just get me the passkey again."

There was a silence. Then the woman said, "First, you leave the envelope. Then, I get you the key."

"Agreed," said Foch, and hung up.

He immediately made a call to Anthony Sutherland. "Jordan Tavistock is out of prison," he said. "He's taken a room at the Ritz. Do you still wish me to proceed?"

"This time, I want it done right. Even if I have to supervise it myself. When do we move?"

"I do not think it is wise—"

"When do we move?"

Foch swallowed his angry response. It was a mistake letting Sutherland take part. The boy was just a voyeur, eager to experience the ultimate power—the taking of a life. Foch had sensed it years ago, from the day they'd first met. He'd known just by looking at him that he'd be addicted to thrills, to intensity, be it sexual or otherwise.

Now the young man wished to experience something novel. Murder. This was a mistake, surely, a mistake....

"Remember who's paying your fees, M. Foch," said Sutherland. "And outrageous fees, too. I'm the one who makes the decisions, not you."

Even if they are stupid, dangerous decisions? wondered Foch. At last he said, "It will be tonight. We wait for him to sleep."

"Tonight," agreed Sutherland. "I'll be there."

AT ELEVEN-THIRTY, JORDAN turned off the lights in his hotel room, stuffed three pillows under the bedspread, and fluffed it all up so that it vaguely resembled a human shape. Then he took his position by the door, next to Richard. In the darkness they sat and waited for something to happen. Anything to happen. So far, the evening had been a screaming bore. Daumier had made him a prisoner of his own hotel room. He'd watched two hours of telly, glanced through *Paris Match,* and completed five crossword puzzles. *What must I do to attract this assassin?* he wondered. *Send him an engraved invitation?*

Sighing, he leaned back against the wall. "Is this the sort of thing you used to do, Wolf?" he murmured.

"A lot of waiting around. A lot of boredom," said Richard. "And every so often, a moment of abject terror."

"What made you leave the business? The boredom or the terror?"

Richard paused. "The rootlessness."

"Ah. The man longs for home and hearth." Jordan smiled. "So tell me, does my sister figure into the equation?"

"Beryl is...one of a kind."

"You didn't answer the question."

"The answer is, I don't know," Richard admitted. He squared his shoulders to ease the tension in his muscles. "Sometimes, it seems like the world's worst possible match. Sure, I can put on a tuxedo, stand around swirling a snifter of brandy. But I don't fool anyone, least of all myself. And certainly not Beryl."

"You really think that's what she needs? A fop in black tie?"

"I don't know what she needs. Or what she wants. I know she probably thinks she's in love. But how the devil can anyone know for certain, when things are so crazy?"

"You wait till things *aren't* so crazy. Then you decide."

"And live with the consequences."

"You're already lovers, aren't you?"

Richard looked at him in surprise. "Are you always so inquisitive about your sister's love life?"

"I'm her closest male relative. And therefore responsible for defending her honor." Jordan laughed softly. "Someday, Wolf, I may have to shoot you. That is, if I survive the night."

They both laughed. And they settled back to wait.

At 1:00 a.m., they heard the faint click of a door closing in the hallway. Had someone just stepped out of the stairwell? Instantly Jordan snapped fully alert, his adrenaline kicking into overdrive. He whispered, "Did you hear—"

Richard was already rising to a crouch. Through the darkness, Jordan could sense the other man tensing for action. Where were Daumier's agents? he wondered frantically. Were the two of them on their own?

A key grated slowly in the lock. Jordan froze, heart thundering, the sweat breaking out on his palms. The gun felt slippery in his grasp.

The door swung open; two figures slowly edged into the room. The first took aim at the bed. A single bullet was all the gunman managed to squeeze off before Richard flew at him sideways. The force of his assault sent both men thudding to the floor.

Jordan shoved his gun into the ribs of the second intruder and barked, "Freeze!"

To Jordan's astonishment, the man didn't freeze, but turned and fled from the room.

Jordan dashed after him into the hall, just in time to see the two French agents tackle the fugitive to the floor. They yanked him, kicking and squirming, back to his feet. In amazement, Jordan stared at the man. *"Anthony?"*

"I'm bleeding!" spat Anthony Sutherland. "They broke my nose! I think they broke my nose!"

"Keep squealing, and they'll break a lot more," growled Richard.

Jordan turned and saw Richard haul the gunman out of the room. He yanked his head back, so Jordan could see his face. "Take a good look. Recognize him?"

"Why, it's my bogus attorney," said Jordan. "M. Jarre."

Richard nodded and forced the balding Frenchman to the floor. "Now let's find out his real name."

"IT'S EXTRAORDINARY," mused Reggie, "how very much you look like your mother."

The butler had long since cleared away the coffee cups, and Helena had vanished upstairs to see to the guest room. Beryl and Reggie sat alone together, enjoying a nip of brandy in his wood-paneled library. A fire crackled in the hearth—not for warmth on this July night, but for reassurance, the ancestral comfort of flames against the night, against the world's evils.

Beryl cradled the brandy snifter in her hands and watched the reflection of firelight in the golden liquid. She said, "When I remember her, it's from a child's point of view. So I remember only the things a child finds important. Her smile. The softness of her hands."

"Yes, yes. That was Madeline."

"I've been told she was quite enchanting."

"She was," said Reggie softly. "She was the loveliest, most extraordinary woman I've ever known…."

Beryl looked up and saw that he was staring at the fire as though seeing, in its flames, the faces of old ghosts. She gave him a fond look. "Mother told me once that you were her oldest and dearest friend."

"Did she?" Reggie smiled. "Yes, I suppose that's true. Did you know we played together, as children. In Cornwall…" He blinked and she thought she saw the faint gleam of tears on his lashes. "I was the first, you know," he murmured. "Before Bernard. Before…" Sighing, he sank back in his chair. "But that was a long time ago."

"You still think of her a great deal."

"It's difficult not to." He drained his brandy glass. Unsteadily he poured another—his third. "Every time I look at you, I think, 'There's Madeline, come back to life.' And I remember how much, how very much I miss her—" Suddenly he stiffened and glanced at the doorway. Helena was standing there, wearily shaking her head. "You've had more than enough for tonight, Reggie."

"It's only my third."

"And how many more will come after that one?"

"Bloody few, if you have your way."

Helena came into the room and took his arm. "Come, darling. You've kept Beryl up long enough. It's time for bed."

"It's only one o'clock."

"Beryl's tired. And you should be considerate."

Reggie looked at their guest. "Oh. Oh, yes, perhaps you're right." He rose to his feet and moved on unsteady legs toward Beryl. She turned her face as he bent over to plant a kiss on her cheek. It was a wet, sloppy kiss, heavy with the smell of brandy, and she had to suppress the urge to pull away. He straightened, and once again she saw the sheen of tears in his eyes. "Good night, dear," he murmured. "You'll be perfectly safe with us."

With a sense of pity, Beryl watched the old man shuffle out of the library.

"He's simply not able to tolerate spirits the way he used to," said Helena, sighing. "The years pass, you know, and he forgets that things change. Including his capacity for liquor." She gave Beryl a rueful smile. "I do hope he didn't bore you too much."

"Not at all. We talked about Mother. He said I remind him of her."

Helena nodded. "Yes, you do resemble her. Of course, I didn't know her nearly as well as Reggie did." She sat down on the armrest of a chair. "I remember the first time I met her. It was at my wedding. Madeline and Bernard were there, practically newlyweds themselves. You could see it, just by the way they looked at each other. Quite a lovely couple…" Helena picked up Reggie's brandy snifter, tidied the table. "When we met again in Paris, it was fifteen years later, and she hadn't aged a bit. It was eerie how unchanged she was. When all the rest of us felt so acutely the passage of time."

There was a long pause. Then Beryl asked, "Did she have a lover?" The question was asked softly, so softly it was almost swallowed in the gloom of that library.

The silence that followed stretched on so long, she thought perhaps her words had gone unnoticed. But then Helena said, "It shouldn't surprise you, should it? Madeline had that magic about her. That certain something the rest of us seem to lack. It's a matter of luck, you know. It's not something one achieves through effort or study. It's in one's genes. An inheritance, like a silver spoon in one's mouth."

"My mother wasn't born with a silver spoon."

"She didn't need one. She had that magic, instead." Abruptly Helena turned to leave. But in the doorway she caught herself and looked back at Beryl with a smile. "I'll see you in the morning. Good night."

Beryl nodded. "Good night, Helena."

For a long time, Beryl frowned at the empty doorway and listened to Helena ascend the stairs. She went to the hearth and stared at the dying embers. She thought of her mother, wondered if Madeline had ever stood here, in this library, in this house. Yes, of course she would have. Reggie was her oldest friend. They would have visited back and forth, the two couples, as they had in England years before….

Before Helena had insisted Reggie accept the Paris post.

The question suddenly came to her: *Why?* Was there some unspoken reason the Vanes had suddenly left England? Helena had grown up in Buckinghamshire; her ancestral home was a mere two miles from Chetwynd. Surely it must have been difficult to pack up her household, to leave behind all that was familiar, and move to a city where she couldn't even speak the language. One didn't blithely make such a move.

Unless one was fleeing *from* something.

Beryl's head lifted. She found herself staring at a ridiculous statuette on the mantelpiece—a fat little man holding a rifle. It had the inscription: "Reggie Vane—most likely to shoot his own foot. Tremont Gun Club." Lined up beside it were various knick-knacks from Reggie's past—a soccer medal, an old photo of a cricket team, a petrified frog. Judging by the items on display, this must be Reggie's private abode, the room to which he retreated from the world. The room that would hold his secrets.

She scanned the photos, and nowhere did she see a picture of Helena. Nor was there one on the desk or on the bookshelves a fact she thought odd, for she remembered her father's library and all the snapshots of Madeline he kept so conspicuously in view. She moved to Reggie's cherry desk and quietly began to open the drawers. The first revealed the expected clutter of pens and paper clips. She opened the second and saw only a sheaf of cream-colored stationery and an address book. She closed the drawers and began to circle the room, thinking, *This is where you keep your most private treasures. The memories you hide, even from your wife….*

Her gaze came to rest on the leather footstool. It appeared to be a matched set with the easy chair, but it had been moved out of position, and instead sat at the side of the chair where it served no purpose…except to stand on.

She glanced directly up at the mahogany breakfront that stood against the wall. The shelves were filled with antique books, protected behind glass doors. The cabinet was at least eight feet tall, and on top was a matched pair of china bowls.

Beryl pushed the footstool over to the breakfront, climbed onto the stool, and reached up to retrieve the first bowl. It was empty and coated in dust. So was the second bowl. But as she slid the bowl back onto the cabinet, she met resistance. She reached back as far as she could, and her fingers met something flat and leathery. She grasped the edge and pulled it off the cabinet.

It was a photo album.

She took it over to the hearth and sat down by the dying fire. There she opened the cover to the first picture in the album. It was of a laughing, black-haired girl. The girl was twelve years old perhaps, and sitting on a swing, her skirt bunched up hoydenishly around her thighs, her bare legs dangling. On the next page was another photo—the same girl, a bit older now, dressed in May Day finery, flowers woven into her tangled hair. More photos, all of the black-haired girl: clad in waders and fishing in a stream, waving from a car, hanging upside down from a tree branch. And last—a wedding photo. It had been torn jaggedly in two, so that the groom was missing, and only the bride remained.

For an eternity, Beryl stared at the face she knew from her childhood—the face so very much like her own. She touched the smiling lips, traced the upswept tendrils of black hair. She thought about how it must be for a man to so desperately love a woman. To lose her to another man. To flee from those memories of her to a foreign city, only to have her reappear in that same city. And to find that, even fifteen years later, the feelings remain, and there is nothing you can do to ease your anguish, nothing at all…so long as she is alive.

Beryl shut the album and went to the telephone. She didn't know how to reach Richard, so she dialed Daumier's number instead and was greeted by a recorded message, intoned in businesslike French.

After the beep, she said, "Claude, it's Beryl. I have to speak to you at once. I think I've found some new evidence. Please, come get me! As soon as you—" She stopped, her hand suddenly frozen on the receiver. What was that click on the line?

She listened for other sounds, but heard only the pounding of her own heart—and silence. She hung up. The extension, she thought. Someone had been listening on the extension.

Quickly she rose to her feet. *I can't stay here, not in this house. Not under this roof. Not when I know he could have been the one.*

Clutching the album firmly in her arms, she left Reggie's library and hurried across the foyer. After disarming the security system, she stepped out the front door.

Outside, it was a cool night, the sky clear, the stars faintly twinkling against the distant haze of city light. She looked across the stone courtyard and saw that the iron gates were closed—no doubt locked, as well. As a bank executive in Paris, Reggie was a prime target for terrorists; he would install the very best security for his home.

I have to get out of here, she determined. *Without anyone knowing.*

And then what? Thumb a ride to the nearest police station? Daumier's flat? *Anywhere but here.*

She traced the perimeter of the courtyard, searching the high wall for a doorway, an exit. She spotted another gate, but it, too, was locked. No way around it, she thought. She'd have to climb over. Quickly she scanned the trees and spotted an apple tree with a branch overhanging the wall. Clutching the photo album in one hand, she scrambled up onto the lowest branch. It was an easy climb to the next branch, and the next, but every movement made the tree sway and sent apples thudding noisily to the ground. At the top of the wall, she tossed the album down on the other side and dropped to the ground beside it. At once she scooped up the album and turned toward the road.

The blinding beam of a flashlight made her freeze.

"So it's not a burglar after all," said a voice. "What on earth are you doing, Beryl?"

Squinting against the light, Beryl could barely make out Helena's silhouette standing before her. "I…I wanted to take a walk. But the gate was locked."

"I would have opened it for you."

"I didn't want to wake you." She turned her gaze from the flashlight. "Please, could you drop the torch? It hurts my eyes."

The beam slowly fell, and stopped at the photo album in Beryl's arms. Beryl had clasped the album to her chest, hoping Helena hadn't recognized it, but it was too late. She had already seen it.

"Where was it?" asked Helena softly. "Where did you find it?"

"The library," said Beryl. No point in lying now; the evidence was there, plainly in her grasp.

"All these years," murmured Helena. "He kept it all these years. And he swore to me—"

"What, Helena? What did he swear to?"

There was silence. "That he no longer loved her," came the whispered answer. Then a laugh, full of self-mockery. "I've lost out to a ghost. It was hopeless enough when she was alive. But now she's dead, and I can't fight back. The dead, you see, don't grow old. They stay young and beautiful. And perfect."

Beryl took a step forward, her arms extended in sympathy. "They weren't lovers, Helena. I know they weren't."

"I was never perfect enough."

"But he married you. There must have been love involved—"

Helena stepped away, angrily brushing off Beryl's offer of comfort. "Not love! It was spite. Some stupid, masculine gesture to show her he couldn't be hurt. We were married a month after she was. I was his consolation prize, you see. I gave him all the right connections. And the money. He happily accepted those. But he never really wanted my love."

Again, Beryl tried to reach out to her; again, Helena rebuffed the gesture. Beryl said softly, "It's time to move on, Helena. Make your own life, without him. While you're still young…"

"He *is* my life."

"But all these years, you must have known! You must have suspected that Reggie was the one who—"

"Not Reggie."

"Helena, please think about it!"

"Not Reggie."

"He was obsessed, unable to let her go! To let another man have her—"

"It was me."

Those three words, uttered so quietly, chilled Beryl's blood to ice. She stared at the silhouette standing before her, her thoughts instantly shifting to ones of escape. She could flee down the road, pound at the nearest door…. She shifted onto the balls of her feet and was about to make a dash past Helena, when she heard the click of the pistol hammer.

"You look so very much like her," whispered Helena. "When I first saw you, years ago at Chetwynd, it was almost as if she'd come back. And now, I have to kill her all over again."

"But I'm not Madeline—"

"It makes no difference now who you are. Because you know." Helena raised her arm and Beryl saw, through the shadows, the faint gleam of the gun in her hand. "The garage, Beryl," she said. "We're going for a drive."

Chapter Twelve

"AMIEL FOCH," said Daumier, flipping through a file folder. "Age forty-six, formerly with French Intelligence. Presumed dead three years ago, after a helicopter crash off Cyprus—"

"He faked his own death?" asked Richard.

Daumier nodded. "It is not an easy matter to resign from Intelligence and simply start work as a mercenary. One would be subject to constraints."

"But if one is declared dead—"

"Precisely." Daumier skimmed the next page and stopped. "Here it is," he said. "The link we have been searching for. In 1972, M. Foch served as our liaison to the American mission. It seems there was a telephone threat against Ambassador Sutherland's family. For several years, Amiel Foch remained in contact with the Sutherland household. He was later reassigned to other duties, until his… death."

"When he became available for private clients. To perform any service," said Hugh.

"Including assassination." Daumier closed the folder and said to his assistant, "Bring in Mrs. Sutherland."

The woman who walked through the door was the same brash and confident Nina Sutherland that Richard had always known.

She swept into the room, glanced around with disdain at her audience, then gracefully settled into a chair. "A bit late in the day for a command performance, don't you think?" she asked.

And a performance was just what they were going to get, thought Richard. Unless they shook her up. He pulled up a chair and sat down, facing her. "You know that Anthony's been taken into custody?"

A flicker of fear—just a flicker—rippled through her eyes. "It's a mistake, of course. He's never done anything wrong in his life."

"Murder through hire? Contracts with assassins?" Richard raised an eyebrow. "Ironclad charges, multiple witnesses. I'd say this is serious enough to warrant a very long stay behind bars."

"But he's only a boy and not—"

"He's of age. And fully responsible for his crimes." Richard glanced at Daumier. "Claude and I were just discussing what a shame it was. To be locked up so young. He'll be, how old when he's released, Claude? Fifty, do you think?"

"I would guess closer to sixty," said Daumier.

"Sixty." Richard shook his head and sighed. "His whole life behind him. No wife. No children." Richard looked Nina sympathetically in the eyes. "No grandchildren…"

Nina's face had turned ashen. She said in a whisper, "What do you want from me?"

"Cooperation."

"And what's my payback?"

"We can be lenient," said Daumier. "After all, he *is* just a boy."

Swallowing hard, Nina looked away. "It's not his fault. He doesn't deserve to be—"

"He's responsible for the deaths of two French agents. And the attempted murders of Marie St. Pierre and Jordan."

"He didn't do anything!"

"But he hired Amiel Foch to do his dirty work. What kind of a monster did you raise, Nina?"

"He was only trying to protect *me!*"

"From what?"

Nina's head drooped. "The past," she whispered. "It never goes away. Everything else changes, but the past…"

The past, thought Richard, remembering Heinrich Leitner's

words. *We're always in its shadow.* "You were Delphi," he said. "Weren't you?"

Nina said nothing.

He leaned forward, and his voice dropped to a quiet, almost intimate murmur. "Perhaps it started out as a bit of a lark," he suggested. "An amusing game of spies and counterspies. Perhaps you liked the excitement. Or was it the money that tempted you? Whatever the reason, you passed a secret or two to the other side. Then it was classified documents. And suddenly you were in their pocket."

"It was only for a short time!"

"But by then it was too late. NATO intelligence got wind of it. And they were closing in. So you worked out a way to shift the blame. Somehow you lured Bernard and Madeline to your little love nest in Rue Myrha. There you shot them both."

"No."

"You planted the documents near Bernard's body."

"No."

Richard grabbed Nina by the shoulders and forced her to look at him. "And then you walked away and went on with your merry life. Isn't that how it went?"

Nina gave a pitiful sob. "I didn't kill them!"

"Isn't it?"

"I swear I didn't kill them! They were already dead!"

Richard released her. Nina sank back into the chair, her whole body shuddering with sobs.

"Who killed them?" demanded Richard. "Amiel Foch?"

"No, I never asked him to."

"Philippe?"

She looked up sharply. "No! He was the one who *found* them. He was frantic when he called me. Afraid he'd be accused of it. That's when I called in Foch. Asked him to make arrangements with Rideau, the landlord. A cash payment to change his testimony."

"And the documents? Who planted them?"

"Foch did. By then, the police had already been called. Foch had to slip the briefcase into the garret."

Jordan cut in, "She's just admitted she's Delphi. Now we're supposed to believe some other mysterious culprit did the killing?"

"It's the truth!" insisted Nina.

"Oh, right!" sneered Jordan. "And the killer just happened to choose the very flat where you and Philippe met every week?"

Nina shook her head in bewilderment. "I don't know why he chose our flat."

"It had to be you. Or Philippe," said Jordan.

"I would never...he would never..."

"Who else knew about the garret?" asked Richard.

"No one."

"Marie St. Pierre?"

"No." She paused, then whispered, "Yes, perhaps..."

"So Philippe's wife knew."

Nina nodded miserably. "But no one else."

"Wait," Jordan suddenly interjected. "Someone else *did* know about it."

Everyone looked at him.

"What?" said Richard.

"I heard it from Reggie. Helena knew about the affair—Marie told her. And if Marie knew about the garret on Rue Myrha, then—"

"So did Helena." Richard stared at Jordan. With that one look, they both knew what the other was thinking.

Beryl.

Instantly they both turned to leave. "Get us some backup!" Richard snapped to Daumier. "Have them meet us there!"

"The Vanes' residence?"

Richard didn't answer; he was already running out the door.

"GET IN THE CAR," said Helena.

Beryl halted, her hand frozen on the door handle of the Mercedes. "There'll be questions, Helena."

"And I'll have the answers. I was asleep, you see. I slept all night. And when I woke up, you were gone. Left the compound on your own, never to be seen again."

"Reggie will remember—"

"Reggie won't remember a thing. He's stone drunk. As far as he knows, I never left the bed."

"They'll suspect you—"

"It's been twenty years, Beryl. And they still don't suspect." She raised the gun. "Get in. The driver's seat. Or do I have to change my story? Tell them I thought I was shooting a burglar?"

Beryl stared at the gun barrel pointed squarely at her chest. She had no choice. Helena really would shoot her. She climbed into the car.

Helena slid in beside her and tossed the keys into Beryl's lap. "Start the engine."

Beryl turned the key; the Mercedes purred to life like a contented cat. "My mother never meant to hurt you," said Beryl softly. "She was never interested in Reggie. She never wanted him."

"But he wanted *her.* Oh, I saw how he used to look at her! Do you know, he used to say her name in his sleep. There I'd be, lying next to him, and he'd be thinking of her. I never knew, I never really knew, if they were…" She swallowed. "Drive."

"Where?"

"Just go out the gate. Go!"

Beryl eased the Mercedes out of the garage and across the cobblestoned courtyard. Helena pressed a remote control and the iron gate automatically swung open. It closed again behind them as they drove through. Ahead stretched the tree-lined road. No other cars, no other witnesses.

The steering wheel felt slick with her sweat. Beryl gripped it tightly, just to keep her hands from shaking. "My father never hurt you," she whispered. "Why did you have to kill him?"

"Someone had to be blamed. Why not make it a dead man? And the fact it was Nina's secret flat—that made it all the more convenient." She laughed. "You should have seen how Nina and Philippe scrambled to cover things up."

"And Delphi?"

Helena shook her head in bewilderment. "What about Delphi?"

So she knows nothing about it, thought Beryl. *All this time, we've been chasing the wrong clues. Richard will never know—will never suspect—what really happened.*

The road began to curve and wind through the trees. They were headed into the depths of the Bois de Boulogne. *Is this where they'll find me?* she wondered, dismayed. *In some lonely copse of trees? At the muddy bottom of a pond?*

She peered ahead to the road beyond their headlights. They were approaching another curve.

It may be my only chance. I can let her shoot me. Or I can go down fighting. She pointed the car on a straight course. Then she hit the accelerator pedal. The engine roared and tires screamed. Beryl was thrust back against the seat as the Mercedes lurched forward.

Helena cried out, "No!" and clawed for control of the wheel. A split-second before they hit the trees, Helena managed to swerve them sideways. Suddenly they were tumbling like helpless riders in an out-of-control carnival ride. The Mercedes toppled over and over, windows shattered, and the two passengers were flung against the dashboard.

The car came to rest on its roof.

It was the blare of the horn that dragged Beryl back to consciousness. And the pain. Excruciating pain, tearing at her leg. She tried to move and realized that her chest was wedged against the steering wheel, and that her head was somehow cradled in the small space between the windshield and the upside-down dashboard. She pushed away from the steering wheel. The effort made her cry out in pain, but she managed to slide her body a few precious inches across the crumpled roof. For a moment, she rested, gasping for breath, waiting for the pain in her leg to ease. Then, gritting her teeth, she pushed again and managed to slide through into a larger pocket of space. The front seat? Everything seemed so mangled, so confusing in the darkness. The tumble had left her disoriented.

But she was not so dazed that she didn't smell the odor of gasoline growing stronger every second. *I have to get to a window—have to squeeze through before it explodes.* Blindly she reached out to feel her surroundings, and her hand shoved up against something warm. Something wet. She twisted her head around and came face-to-face with Helena's corpse.

Beryl screamed. Suddenly frantic to get out, to escape those sightless eyes, she squirmed away, clawing for the window. New pain, even more excruciating, ripped through her shattered leg and flooded her eyes with tears. She touched window frame, bits of glass and then…a branch! *I'm almost there. Almost there.*

Half crawling, half dragging herself, she managed to squeeze through the opening. Just as her body rolled onto the ground, the dirt beneath her seemed to give way and she began to slide down a leafy embankment. She landed in a ditch near some trees.

A burst of light suddenly shot into the sky. Through eyes blurred with agony, she looked up and saw the first flicker of the inferno. Seconds later, she heard the popping of glass, then a terrifying whoosh as a fountain of flames engulfed the vehicle.

Why, Helena? Why? The flames blurred, faded into a gathering darkness. She closed her eyes and shivered among the fallen leaves.

THREE MILES FROM the Vanes' residence, they spotted the fire. It was a car, upended, stretched diagonally across the road. A Mercedes.

"It's Helena's," shouted Richard. "My God, it's Helena's!" He leaped out and ran toward the burning car. He almost tripped over a shoe lying in the road. To his horror he saw it was a woman's pump. *"Beryl!"* he screamed. He was about to make a desperate lunge for the car door when the flames suddenly shot higher. A window burst out, scattering glass across the pavement. The searing heat sent him stumbling backward, his nostrils stinging with the stench of his own singed hair. He recovered his balance and was about to make another lunge through the flames when Jordan grabbed his arm.

"Wait!" cried Jordan.

Richard wrenched away. "Have to get her out!"

"No, *listen!*"

That's when he heard it—a moan, almost inaudible. It came not from the car, but from somewhere in the trees.

At once he and Jordan were scrambling along the roadside, yelling Beryl's name. Again, Richard heard the moan, closer now, coming from the shadows just below the road. He clambered down the dirt bank and stumbled into a drainage ditch.

That's where he found her, sprawled among the leaves. Barely conscious.

He gathered her up and was terrified by how limp, how cold her body felt in his arms. *She's in shock,* he realized. *We have precious little time....*

"Have to get her to a hospital!" he yelled.

Jordan ran ahead and yanked open the car door. Richard, clutching Beryl in his arms, slid into the back seat.

"Go!" he barked.

"Hang on," muttered Jordan, scrambling into the driver's seat. "It's going to be a wild ride."

With a screech of tires, their car shot off down the road. *Stay with me, Beryl,* Richard begged silently as he cradled her body in his arms. *Please, darling. Stay with me....*

But as the car sped through the darkness, she seemed to grow ever colder to his touch.

THROUGH THE HAZE of anesthesia, she heard him call her name, but the sound of his voice seemed so very far away, seemed to come from a distant place she could not possibly reach. Then she felt his hand close tightly over hers, and she knew he was right beside her. She could not see his face; she could not muster enough strength to open her eyes. Yet she knew he was there, that he would still be there when she awoke the next morning.

But it was Jordan whom she saw sitting by her bed. The late-morning sunlight streamed over his fair hair and a leather-bound book of poetry lay in his lap. He was reading Milton. *Dear Jordan,* she thought. *Ever reliable, ever serene. If only I had inherited such peace of mind.*

Jordan glanced up from the page and saw that she was awake. "Welcome back to the world, little sister," he said with a smile.

She groaned. "I'm not so sure I want to be back."

"The leg?"

"Killing me."

He reached for the call button. "Time to indulge in the miracle of morphine."

But even miracles take time. After the nurse delivered the injection, Beryl closed her eyes and waited for the pain to ease, for the blessed numbness to descend.

"Better?" asked Jordan.

"Not yet." She took a deep breath. "God, I hate being an invalid. Talk to me. Please."

"About what?"

Richard, she thought. *Please tell me about Richard. Why he isn't here. Why he's not the one sitting in that chair….*

Jordan said, quietly, "You know, he was here. Earlier this morning. But then Daumier called."

She lay still, not speaking. Waiting to hear more.

"He cares about you, Beryl. I'm sure he does." Jordan closed his book and set it on the bedside table. "Really, he seems an agreeable fellow. Quite capable."

"Capable," she murmured. "Yes, he is that."

"He didn't turn tail and run. He did look after you."

"As a favor," she amended. "To Uncle Hugh."

He didn't answer. And she thought that Jordie, too, had his doubts about their odds for happiness. And so did she. From the very beginning.

The morphine began to take effect. Little by little, she felt herself drift toward sleep. Only vaguely did she hear Richard enter the room and speak softly to Jordan. They murmured something about Helena and her body being burned beyond recognition. As the drug swept her brain toward unconsciousness, a memory suddenly flashed with horrifying vividness into her mind—the flames engulfing the car, engulfing Helena.

For loving too deeply, too fiercely, this was Helena's punishment.

She felt Richard take her hand and press it to his lips.

And what punishment, she wondered, would be hers?

Epilogue

Buckinghamshire, England
Six weeks later

FROGGIE WAS RESTLESS, stamping about in her stall, whinnying for escape.

"Look at her, the poor thing," Beryl said and sighed. "She hasn't been run nearly enough, and I think she's going quite insane. You'll have to exercise her for me."

"Me? On the back of that…that maniac?" Jordan snorted. "I'm much too fond of my own neck."

Beryl hobbled over to the stall on her crutches. At once Froggie poked her head over the door and gave Beryl an insistent want-to-go-running nudge. "Oh, but she's such a pussycat."

"A pussycat with a foul temper."

"And she so badly needs a good, hard gallop."

Jordan looked at his sister, who was wobbling unsteadily on leg cast and crutches. She seemed so pale and thin these days. As if those long weeks in the hospital had drained something vital from her spirit. A bit of pallor was to be expected, of course, considering all the blood she'd lost, all the days of pain she'd suffered after the operation to pin her shattered femur. Now the leg was healing well, and the pain was only a memory, but she still seemed only a ghost of herself.

It was Richard Wolf's fault.

At least the fellow had been decent enough to hang around during Beryl's hospitalization. In fact, he'd practically haunted her room, spending every daylight hour by her bed. And all the flowers! Every morning, a fresh bouquet.

Then, one day, he was gone. Jordan hadn't heard the explanation. He'd walked into his sister's hospital room that morning and found her staring out the window, all packed and ready to go home to Chetwynd.

Three weeks ago, they'd flown back. And she's been brooding ever since, he thought, looking at her wan face.

"Go on, Jordie," she said. "Give her a bit of a run. It'll be another month before I can ride her again."

Resignedly, Jordan swung open the stall door and led Froggie out to be saddled. "You'd better behave, young lady," he muttered to the beast. "No rearing. No bucking. And definitely no trampling your poor, defenseless rider."

Froggie gave him a look that could only be interpreted as the equine equivalent of *we'll see about that.*

Jordan mounted and gave Beryl a wave.

"Take care of her!" Beryl called out. "See she doesn't hurt herself!"

"Your concern is most touching!" he managed to blurt out just before Froggie took off at a mad gallop for the fields. Jordan managed a last backward glance at Beryl standing forlornly by the stable. How small she looked, how fragile. Not at all the Beryl he knew. Would she ever be herself again?

Froggie was bearing him toward the woods. He concentrated on hanging on for dear life as the beast made a beeline for the stone wall. "You just have to take that bloody hurdle, don't you?" he muttered as Froggie's mane whipped his face. "Which means *I* have to take the bloody hurdle—"

Together they flew over the wall, clearing it neatly. *Still in the saddle,* thought Jordan with a grin of triumph. *Not so easy to get rid of me, is it?*

It was the last thought in his head before Froggie tossed him off her back.

Jordan landed, fortunately enough, on a large clump of moss. As he sprawled beneath the wildly spinning treetops, he was vaguely aware of the sound of tires grinding across the dirt road, and then he heard someone call his name. Groggily he sat up.

Froggie was standing over him, looking not in the least bit apologetic. And behind her, climbing out of a red M.G., was Richard Wolf.

"Are you all right?" Richard called out, running toward him.

"Tell me, Wolf," Jordan groaned. "Are you out to kill all the Tavistocks? Or are you after one of us in particular?"

Laughing, Richard helped him to his feet. "I'd lay the blame where it belongs. On the horse."

Both men looked at Froggie. She answered with what sounded suspiciously like a laugh.

Richard asked quietly, "How's Beryl doing these days?"

Jordan began to clap the dirt from his trousers. "Her leg's healing fine."

"Besides the leg?"

"Not so fine." Jordan straightened and looked the other man in the eye. "Why did you walk out?"

Sighing, Richard looked off in the direction of Chetwynd. "She asked me to."

"What?" Jordan stared at him in bewilderment. "She never told me—"

"She's a Tavistock, like you. Doesn't believe in whining or complaining. Or losing face. It's that pride of hers."

"Ah, so it was like that, was it?" Jordan said. "An argument?"

"Not even that. It just seemed, with all those differences between us…" He shook his head and laughed. "Face it, Jordan. She's tea and crumpets, I'm coffee and doughnuts. She'd hate it in Washington. And I'm not sure I could adjust to…this." He gestured to the rolling fields of Chetwynd.

But you will adjust, foresaw Jordan. *And so will she. Because it's plain for any idiot to see that you two belong together.*

"Anyway," said Richard, "when Niki called and reminded me we had a job in New Delhi, Beryl told me to go. She thought it would be a good test for us to be apart for a while. Said the Royal Family does it that way. To see if absence makes the heart—and hormones—forget."

"And does it?"

Richard grinned. "Not a chance," he said, and climbed back into his car. "I may be signing up with your wild and crazy family, after all. Any objections?"

"None," said Jordan. "But I *will* offer a bit of advice. That is, if you two expect to share a long and healthy life together."

"What's the advice?"

"Shoot the horse."

Laughing, Richard let out the brake and sped away toward Chetwynd.

Toward Beryl.

As Jordan watched the M.G. vanish around the bend, he thought, *Good luck to you, little sister. I'm glad one of us has finally found someone to love. Now if only I could be so fortunate...*

He turned to Froggie. "And as for you," he said aloud, "I am about to teach you exactly who's boss around here."

Froggie gave a snort. Then, with a triumphant toss of her mane, she turned and galloped away, riderless, toward Chetwynd.

"IT'S QUITE UNLIKE YOU to be brooding this way," said Uncle Hugh as he picked another tomato and set it in his basket. He looked faintly ridiculous in his floppy gardening hat. More like the groundskeeper than the lord of the manor. Crouching on his knees, he uncovered another bright red globe and carefully plucked the treasure. "Don't know why you're so gloomy these days. After all, the leg's almost healed."

"It's not the leg," said Beryl.

"One would think you were permanently crippled."

"It's not the leg."

"Well, what is it, then?" asked Hugh, moving on to the row of pole beans. Suddenly he stopped and glanced back at her. "Oh, it's him, isn't it?"

Sighing, Beryl reached for her crutches and rose from the garden bench. "I don't wish to discuss it."

"You never do."

"I still don't," she said, and stubbornly headed down the brick path toward the maze. She brushed past the edging of lavender, stirring the scents of the late summer garden. Once they'd walked this path together, she thought. And now she was walking it alone.

She entered the maze and, using her crutches, maneuvered around all the secret twists and turns. At last she emerged at the center and sat down on the stone bench. *Yes, I'm brooding again,* she realized. *Uncle Hugh's right. Have to stop this and get on with my life.*

But first, she would have to stop thinking of him. Had he stopped thinking of her? All the doubts, the fears, came back to assail her. She'd put him to the test, she thought. And he'd failed it.

From a distance, she heard someone call her name. It was so faint at first, she thought she might have imagined it. But there it was again—moving closer now!

She lurched to her feet, wobbling on the crutches. *"Richard?"*

"Beryl?" came the answering shout. "Where are you?"

"In the maze!"

His footsteps moved closer along the path. "Where?"

"The center!"

Through the high hedge walls, she heard his sheepish laughter. "And now I'm expected to find my way to the cheese?"

"Just think of it," she challenged him, "as a test of true love."

"Or true insanity," he muttered, rustling into the maze.

"I'm quite annoyed with you, you know," she called.

"I think I've noticed."

"You didn't write. You didn't call, not once!"

"I was too busy trying to catch planes back to London. And besides, I wanted you to miss me. Did you?"

"No, I didn't."

"You didn't?"

"Not at all." She bit her lip. "Oh, perhaps a bit…"

"Ah, so you *did* miss me—"

"But not much."

"I missed *you.*"

She paused. "Did you?" she asked softly.

"So much, in fact, that if I don't find the bloody center of this bloody maze pretty damn quick, I'm going to—"

"Going to what?" she asked breathlessly.

A rustle of branches made her turn. Suddenly he was there beside her, pulling her into his arms, covering her mouth with a kiss so deep, so insistent, she felt herself swaying dizzily. The crutches slipped away and fell to the ground. She didn't need them—not when he was there to hold her.

He drew away and smiled at her. "Hello again, Miss Tavistock," he whispered.

"You came back," she murmured. "You really came back."

"Did you think I wouldn't?"

"Does that mean you've thought about it? About us?"

He laughed. "I could scarcely concentrate on anything else. On the job, the client. Finally I had to call in Niki to pinch-hit for me, while I straighten out this mess with you."

She asked softly, "You think it *can* be straightened out?"

Gently he framed her face with his hands. "I don't know. Some folks would probably call us a long shot."

"And they'd be right. There are so many things that could pull us apart...."

"And just as many things that will keep us together." He lowered his face to hers, gently brushed her lips with his. "I confess, I'll never make a proper gentleman. Cricket's not my bag. And you'll have to put a gun to my head to get me up on a horse. But if you're willing to overlook those terrible flaws..."

She threw her arms around his neck. "What flaws?" she whispered, and their lips met again.

From the distance came the peal of the ancient church bells. Six o'clock. The coming of twilight and shadows, sweetly scented. *And love,* thought Beryl as he pulled her, laughing, into his arms.

Quite definitely, love.

UNDER THE KNIFE

To my mother and father

Prologue

DEAR GOD, HOW THE PAST COMES *back to haunt us.*

From his office window, Dr. Henry Tanaka stared out at the rain battering the parking lot and wondered why, after all these years, the death of one poor soul had come back to destroy him.

Outside, a nurse, her uniform spotty with rain, dashed to her car. Another one caught without an umbrella, he thought. That morning, like most Honolulu mornings, had dawned bright and sunny. But at three o'clock the clouds had slithered over the Koolau range and now, as the last clinic employees headed for home, the rain became a torrent, flooding the streets with a river of dirty water.

Tanaka turned and stared down at the letter on his desk. It had been mailed a week ago; but like so much of his correspondence, it had been lost in the piles of obstetrical journals and supply catalogs that always littered his office. When his receptionist had finally called it to his attention this morning, he'd been alarmed by the name on the return address: Joseph Kahanu, Attorney at Law.

He had opened it immediately.

Now he sank into his chair and read the letter once again.

Dear Dr. Tanaka,

As the attorney representing Mr. Charles Decker, I hereby request any and all medical records pertaining to the obstetrical care of Ms. Jennifer Brook, who was your patient at the time of her death....

Jennifer Brook. A name he'd hoped to forget.

A profound weariness came over him—the exhaustion of a man who has discovered he cannot outrun his own shadow. He tried to muster the energy to go home, to slog outside and climb into his car, but he could only sit and stare at the four walls of his office. His sanctuary. His gaze traveled past the framed diplomas, the medical certificates, the photographs. Everywhere there were snapshots of wrinkled newborns, of beaming mothers and fathers. How many babies had he brought into the world? He'd lost count years ago....

It was a sound in the outer office that finally drew him out of his chair: the click of a door shutting. He rose and went to peer out at the reception area. "Peggy? Are you still here?"

The waiting room was deserted. Slowly his gaze moved past the flowered couch and chairs, past the magazines neatly stacked on the coffee table, and finally settled on the outer door. It was unlocked.

Through the silence, he heard the muted clang of metal. It came from one of the exam rooms.

"Peggy?" Tanaka moved down the hall and glanced into the first room. Flicking on the light, he saw the hard gleam of the stainless-steel sink, the gynecologic table, the supply cabinet. He turned off the light and went to the next room. Again, everything was as it should be: the instruments lined up neatly on the counter, the sink wiped dry, the table stirrups folded up for the night.

Crossing the hall, he moved toward the third and last exam room. But just as he reached for the light switch, some instinct made him freeze: a sudden awareness of a presence—something malevolent—waiting for him in the darkness.

In terror, he backed out of the room. Only as he spun around to flee did he realize that the intruder was standing behind him.

A blade slashed across his neck.

Tanaka staggered backward into the exam room and toppled an instrument stand. Stumbling to the floor, he found the linoleum was already slick with his blood. Even as he felt his life drain away, a coldly rational pocket of his brain forced him to assess his own wound, to analyze his own chances. *Severed artery. Exsanguination within minutes. Have to stop the bleeding....* Numbness was already creeping up his legs.

So little time. On his hands and knees, he crawled toward the cabinet where the gauze was stored. To his half-senseless mind, the feeble light reflecting off those glass doors became his guiding beacon, his only hope of survival.

A shadow blotted out the glow from the hall. He knew the intruder was standing in the doorway, watching him. Still he kept moving.

In his last seconds of consciousness, Tanaka managed to drag himself to his feet and wrench open the cabinet door. Sterile packets rained down from the shelf. Blindly he ripped one apart, withdrew a wad of gauze and clamped it against his neck.

He didn't see the attacker's blade trace its final arc.

As it plunged deep into his back, Tanaka tried to scream but the only sound that issued from his throat was a sigh. It was the last breath he took before he slid quietly to the floor.

CHARLIE DECKER LAY NAKED in his small hard bed and he was afraid.

Through the window he saw the blood-red glow of a neon sign: *The Victory Hotel*. Except the *t* was missing from *Hotel*. And what was left made him think of *Hole*, which is what the place really was: *The Victory Hole*, where every triumph, every joy, sank into some dark pit of no return.

He shut his eyes but the neon seemed to burrow its way through his lids. He turned away from the window and pulled the pillow over his head. The smell of the filthy linen was suffocating. Tossing the pillow aside, he rose and paced over to the window. There he stared down at the street. On the sidewalk below, a stringy-haired blonde in a miniskirt was dickering with a man in a Chevy. Somewhere in the night people laughed and a jukebox was playing "It Don't Matter Anymore." A stench rose from the alley, a peculiar mingling of rotting trash and frangipani: the smell of the back streets of paradise. It made him nauseated. But it was too hot to close the window, too hot to sleep, too hot even to breathe.

He went over to the card table and switched on the lamp. The same newspaper headline stared up at him.

Honolulu Physician Found Slain.

He felt the sweat trickle down his chest. He threw the newspaper on the floor. Then he sat down and let his head fall into his hands.

The music from the distant jukebox faded; the next song started, a thrusting of guitars and drums. A singer growled out: "I want it bad, oh yeah, baby, so bad, so bad…."

Slowly he raised his head and his gaze settled on the photograph of Jenny. She was smiling; as always, she was smiling. He touched the picture, trying to remember how her face had felt; but the years had dimmed his memory.

At last he opened his notebook. He turned to a blank page. He began to write.

This is what they told me:
"It takes time…
Time to heal, time to forget."
This is what I told them:
That healing lies not in forgetfulness
But in remembrance
Of you.
The smell of the sea on your skin;
The small and perfect footprints you leave in the sand.
In remembrance there are no endings.
And so you lie there, now and always, by the sea.
You open your eyes. You touch me.
The sun is in your fingertips.
And I am healed.
I am healed.

Chapter One

WITH A STEADY HAND, Dr. Kate Chesne injected two hundred milligrams of sodium Pentothal into her patient's intravenous line. As the column of pale yellow liquid drifted lazily through the plastic tubing, Kate murmured, "You should start to feel sleepy soon, Ellen. Close your eyes. Let go…."

"I don't feel anything yet."

"It will take a minute or so." Kate squeezed Ellen's shoulder in a silent gesture of reassurance. The small things were what made a patient feel safe. A touch. A quiet voice. "Let yourself float," Kate whispered. "Think of the sky… clouds…."

Ellen gave her a calm and drowsy smile. Beneath the harsh operating-room lights, every freckle, every flaw stood out cruelly on her face. No one, not even Ellen O'Brien, was beautiful on the operating table. "Funny," she murmured. "I'm not afraid. Not in the least…."

"You don't have to be. I'll take care of everything."

"I know. I know you will." Ellen reached out for Kate's hand. It was only a touch, a brief mingling of fingers. The warmth of Ellen's skin against hers was one more reminder that not just a body, but a woman, a friend, was lying on this table.

The door swung open and the surgeon walked in. Dr. Guy

Santini was as big as a bear and he looked faintly ridiculous in his flowered paper cap. "How we doing in here, Kate?"

"Pentothal's going in now."

Guy moved to the table and squeezed the patient's hand. "Still with us, Ellen?"

She smiled. "For better or worse. But on the whole, I'd rather be in Philadelphia."

Guy laughed. "You'll get there. But minus your gallbladder."

"I don't know.... I was getting kinda...fond of the thing...." Ellen's eyelids sagged. "Remember, Guy," she whispered. "You promised. No scar...."

"Did I?"

"Yes...you did....."

Guy winked at Kate. "Didn't I tell you? Nurses make the worst patients. Demanding broads!"

"Watch it, Doc!" one of the O.R. nurses snapped. "One of these days we'll get *you* up on that table."

"Now *that's* a terrifying thought," remarked Guy.

Kate watched as her patient's jaw at last fell slack. She called softly: "Ellen?" She brushed her finger across Ellen's eyelashes. There was no response. Kate nodded at Guy. "She's under."

"Ah, Katie, my darlin'," he said, "you do such good work for a—"

"For a *girl*. Yeah, yeah. I know."

"Well, let's get this show on the road," he said, heading out to scrub. "All her labs look okay?"

"Blood work's perfect."

"EKG?"

"I ran it last night. Normal."

Guy gave her an admiring salute from the doorway. "With you around, Kate, a man doesn't even have to think. Oh, and ladies?" He called to the two O.R. nurses who were laying out the instruments. "A word of warning. Our intern's a lefty."

The scrub nurse glanced up with sudden interest. "Is he cute?"

Guy winked. "A real dreamboat, Cindy. I'll tell him you asked." Laughing, he vanished out the door.

Cindy sighed. "How does his wife stand him, anyway?"

For the next ten minutes, everything proceeded like clockwork. Kate went about her tasks with her usual efficiency. She inserted the endotracheal tube and connected the respirator. She adjusted the flow of oxygen and added the proper proportions of forane and nitrous oxide. She was Ellen's lifeline. Each step, though automatic, required double-checking, even triple-checking. When the patient was someone she knew and liked, being sure of all her moves took on even more urgency. An anesthesiologist's job is often called ninety-nine percent boredom and one percent sheer terror; it was that one percent that Kate was always anticipating, always guarding against. When complications arose, they could happen in the blink of an eye.

But today she fully expected everything to go smoothly. Ellen O'Brien was only forty-one. Except for a gallstone, she was in perfect health.

Guy returned to the O.R., his freshly scrubbed arms dripping wet. He was followed by the "dreamboat" lefty intern, who appeared to be a staggering five-feet-six in his elevator shoes. They proceeded on to the ritual donning of sterile gowns and gloves, a ceremony punctuated by the brisk snap of latex.

As the team took its place around the operating table, Kate's gaze traveled the circle of masked faces. Except for the intern, they were all comfortably familiar. There was the circulating nurse, Ann Richter, with her ash blond hair tucked neatly beneath a blue surgical cap. She was a coolheaded professional who never mixed business with pleasure. Crack a joke in the O.R. and she was likely to flash you a look of disapproval.

Next there was Guy, homely and affable, his brown eyes distorted by thick bottle-lens glasses. It was hard to believe anyone so clumsy could be a surgeon. But put a scalpel in his hand and he could work miracles.

Opposite Guy stood the intern with the woeful misfortune of having been born left-handed.

And last there was Cindy, the scrub nurse, a dark-eyed nymph with an easy laugh. Today she was sporting a brilliant new eye shadow called Oriental Malachite, which gave her a look reminiscent of a tropical fish.

"Nice eye shadow, Cindy," noted Guy as he held his hand out for a scalpel.

"Why thank you, Dr. Santini," she replied, slapping the instrument into his palm.

"I like it a lot better than that other one, Spanish Slime."

"Spanish *Moss*."

"This one's really, really striking, don't you think?" he asked the intern who, wisely, said nothing. "Yeah," Guy continued. "Reminds me of my favorite color. I think it's called Comet cleanser."

The intern giggled. Cindy flashed him a dirty look. So much for the dreamboat's chances.

Guy made the first incision. As a line of scarlet oozed to the surface of the abdominal wall, the intern automatically dabbed away the blood with a sponge. Their hands worked automatically and in concert, like pianists playing a duet.

From her position at the patient's head, Kate followed their progress, her ear tuned the whole time to Ellen's heart rhythm. Everything was going well, with no crises on the horizon. This was when she enjoyed her work most—when she knew she had everything under control. In the midst of all this stainless steel, she felt right at home. For her, the whooshes of the ventilator and the beeps of the cardiac monitor were soothing background music to the performance now unfolding on the table.

Guy made a deeper incision, exposing the glistening layer of fat. "Muscles seem a little tight, Kate," he observed. "We're going to have trouble retracting."

"I'll see what I can do." Turning to her medication cart, she reached for the tiny drawer labeled Succinylcholine. Given intravenously, the drug would relax the muscles, allowing Guy easier access to the abdominal cavity. Glancing in the drawer, she frowned. "Ann? I'm down to one vial of Succinylcholine. Hunt me down some more, will you?"

"That's funny," said Cindy. "I'm sure I stocked that cart yesterday afternoon."

"Well, there's only one vial left." Kate drew up 5 cc's of the crystal-clear solution and injected it into Ellen's IV line. It would take a minute to work. She sat back and waited.

Guy's scalpel cleared the fat layer and he began to expose the abdominal muscle sheath. "Still pretty tight, Kate," he remarked.

She glanced up at the wall clock. "It's been three minutes. You should notice some effect by now."

"Not a thing."

"Okay. I'll push a little more." Kate drew up another 3 cc's and injected it into the IV line. "I'll need another vial soon, Ann," she warned. "This one's just about—"

A buzzer went off on the cardiac monitor. Kate glanced up sharply. What she saw on the screen made her jump to her feet in horror.

Ellen O'Brien's heart had stopped.

In the next instant the room was in a frenzy. Orders were shouted out, instrument trays shoved aside. The intern clambered onto a footstool and thrust his weight again and again on Ellen's chest.

This was the proverbial one percent, the moment of terror every anesthesiologist dreads.

It was also the worst moment in Kate Chesne's life.

As panic swirled around her, she fought to stay in control. She injected vial after vial of adrenaline, first into the IV lines and then directly into Ellen's heart. *I'm losing her,* she thought. *Dear God, I'm losing her.* Then she saw one brief fluttering across the oscilloscope. It was the only hint that some trace of life lingered.

"Let's cardiovert!" she called out. She glanced at Ann, who was standing by the defibrillator. "Two hundred watt seconds!"

Ann didn't move. She remained frozen, her face as white as alabaster.

"Ann?" Kate yelled. "*Two hundred watt seconds!*"

It was Cindy who darted around to the machine and hit the charge button. The needle shot up to two hundred. Guy grabbed the defibrillator paddles, slapped them on Ellen's chest and released the electrical charge.

Ellen's body jerked like a puppet whose strings have all been tugged at once.

The fluttering slowed to a ripple. It was the pattern of a dying heart.

Kate tried another drug, then still another in a desperate attempt to flog some life back into the heart. Nothing worked. Through a film of tears, she watched the tracing fade to a line meandering aimlessly across the oscilloscope.

"That's it," Guy said softly. He gave the signal to stop cardiac massage. The intern, his face dripping with sweat, backed away from the table.

"No," Kate insisted, planting her hands on Ellen's chest. "It's not over." She began to pump—fiercely, desperately. *"It's not over."* She threw herself against Ellen, pitting her weight against the stubborn shield of rib and muscles. The heart had to be massaged, the brain nourished. She had to keep Ellen alive. Again and again she pumped, until her arms were weak and trembling. *Live, Ellen,* she commanded silently. *You have to live….*

"Kate." Guy touched her arm.

"We're not giving up. Not yet…."

"Kate." Gently, Guy tugged her away from the table. "It's over," he whispered.

Someone turned off the sound on the heart monitor. The whine of the alarm gave way to an eerie silence. Slowly, Kate turned and saw that everyone was watching her. She looked up at the oscilloscope.

The line was flat.

KATE FLINCHED AS AN ORDERLY zipped the shroud over Ellen O'Brien's body. There was a cruel finality to that sound; it struck her as obscene, this convenient packaging of what had once been a living, breathing woman. As the body was wheeled off to the morgue, Kate turned away. Long after the squeak of the gurney wheels had faded down the hall, she was still standing there, alone in the O.R.

Fighting tears, she gazed around at the bloodied gauze and empty vials littering the floor. It was the same sad debris that lingered after every hospital death. Soon it would be swept up and incinerated and there'd be no clue to the tragedy that had just been played out. Nothing except a body in the morgue.

And questions. Oh, yes, there'd be questions. From Ellen's parents. From the hospital. Questions Kate didn't know how to answer.

Wearily she tugged off her surgical cap and felt a vague sense of relief as her brown hair tumbled free to her shoulders. She needed time alone—to think, to understand. She turned to leave.

Guy was standing in the doorway. The instant she saw his face, Kate knew something was wrong.

Silently he handed her Ellen O'Brien's chart.

"The electrocardiogram," he said. "You told me it was normal."

"It was."

"You'd better take another look."

Puzzled, she opened the chart to the EKG, the electrical tracing of Ellen's heart. The first detail she noted was her own initials, written at the top, signifying that she'd seen the page. Next she scanned the tracing. For a solid minute she stared at the series of twelve black squiggles, unable to believe what she was seeing. The pattern was unmistakable. Even a third-year medical student could have made the diagnosis.

"That's why she died, Kate," Guy said.

"But— This is impossible!" she blurted. "I couldn't have made a mistake like this!"

Guy didn't answer. He simply looked away—an act more telling than anything he could have said.

"Guy, you *know* me," she protested. "You know I wouldn't miss something like—"

"It's right there in black and white. For God's sake, your *initials* are on the damn thing!"

They stared at each other, both of them shocked by the harshness of his voice.

"I'm sorry," he apologized at last. Suddenly agitated, he turned and clawed his fingers through his hair. "Dear God. She'd had a heart attack. A *heart attack*. And we took her to surgery." He gave Kate a look of utter misery. "I guess that means we killed her."

"IT'S AN OBVIOUS CASE OF malpractice."

Attorney David Ransom closed the file labeled O'Brien, Ellen, and looked across the broad teak desk at his clients. If he had to choose one word to describe Patrick and Mary O'Brien, it would be *gray*. Gray hair, gray faces, gray clothes. Patrick was wearing a dull tweed jacket that had long ago sagged into shapelessness. Mary wore a dress in a black-and-white print that seemed to blend together into a drab monochrome.

Patrick kept shaking his head. "She was our only girl, Mr. Ransom. Our only child. She was always so good, you know? Never complained. Even when she was a baby. She'd just lie there in her crib and smile. Like a little angel. Just like a darling little—" He suddenly stopped, his face crumpling.

"Mr. O'Brien," David said gently, "I know it's not much of a comfort to you now, but I promise you, I'll do everything I can."

Patrick shook his head. "It's not the money we're after. Sure, I can't work. My back, you know. But Ellie, she had a life insurance policy, and—"

"How much was the policy?"

"Fifty thousand," answered Mary. "That's the kind of girl she was. Always thinking of us." Her profile, caught in the window's light, had an edge of steel. Unlike her husband, Mary O'Brien was done with her crying. She sat very straight, her whole body a rigid testament to grief. David knew exactly what she was feeling. The pain. The anger. Especially the anger. It was there, burning coldly in her eyes.

Patrick was sniffling.

David took a box of tissues from his drawer and quietly placed it in front of his client. "Perhaps we should discuss the case some other time," he suggested. "When you both feel ready…."

Mary's chin lifted sharply. "We're ready, Mr. Ransom. Ask your questions."

David glanced at Patrick, who managed a feeble nod. "I'm afraid this may strike you as…cold-blooded, the things I have to ask. I'm sorry."

"Go on," prompted Mary.

"I'll proceed immediately to filing suit. But I'll need more information before we can make an estimate of damages. Part of that is lost wages—what your daughter would have earned had she lived. You say she was a nurse?"

"In obstetrics. Labor and delivery."

"Do you know her salary?"

"I'll have to check her pay stubs."

"What about dependants? Did she have any?"

"None."

"She was never married?"

Mary shook her head and sighed. "She was the perfect daughter, Mr. Ransom, in almost every way. Beautiful. And brilliant. But when it came to men, she made…mistakes."

He frowned. "Mistakes?"

Mary shrugged. "Oh, I suppose it's just the way things are these days. And when a woman gets to be a—a certain age, she feels, well, *lucky* to have any man at all…." She looked down at her tightly knotted hands and fell silent.

David sensed they'd strayed into hazardous waters. He wasn't interested in Ellen O'Brien's love life, anyway. It was irrelevant to the case.

"Let's turn to your daughter's medical history," he said smoothly, opening the medical chart. "The record states she was forty-one years old and in excellent health. To your knowledge, did she ever have any problems with her heart?"

"Never."

"She never complained of chest pain? Shortness of breath?"

"Ellie was a long-distance swimmer, Mr. Ransom. She could go all day and never get out of breath. That's why I don't believe this story about a—a heart attack."

"But the EKG was strongly diagnostic, Mrs. O'Brien. If there'd been an autopsy, we could have proved it. But I guess it's a bit late for that."

Mary glanced at her husband. "It's Patrick. He just couldn't stand the idea—"

"Haven't they cut her up enough already?" Patrick blurted out.

There was a long silence. Mary said softly, "We'll be taking her ashes out to sea. She loved the sea. Ever since she was a baby…"

It was a solemn parting. A few last words of condolence, and then the handshakes, the sealing of a pact. The O'Briens turned to leave. But in the doorway, Mary stopped.

"I want you to know it's not the money," she declared. "The truth is, I don't care if we see a dime. But they've ruined our lives, Mr. Ransom. They've taken our only baby away. And I hope to God they never forget it."

David nodded. "I'll see they never do."

After his clients had left, David turned to the window. He took a deep breath and slowly let it out, willing the emotions to drain from his body. But a hard knot seemed to linger in his stomach. All that sadness, all that rage; it clouded his thinking.

Six days ago, a doctor had made a terrible mistake. Now, at the age of forty-one, Ellen O'Brien was dead.

She was only three years older than me.

He sat down at his desk and opened the O'Brien file. Skipping past the hospital record, he turned to the curricula vitae of the two physicians.

Dr. Guy Santini's record was outstanding. Forty-eight years old, a Harvard-trained surgeon, he was at the peak of his career. His list of publications went on for five pages. Most of his research dealt with hepatic physiology. He'd been sued once, eight years ago; he'd won. Bully for him. Santini wasn't the target anyway. David had his crosshairs on the anesthesiologist.

He flipped to the three-page summary of Dr. Katharine Chesne's career.

Her background was impressive. A B.Sc in chemistry from U.C., Berkeley, an M.D. from Johns Hopkins, anesthesia residency and intensive-care fellowship at U.C., San Francisco. Now only thirty years old, she'd already compiled a respectable list of published articles. She'd joined Mid Pac Hospital as a staff anesthesiologist less than a year ago. There was no photograph, but he had no trouble conjuring up a mental picture of the stereotypical female physician: frumpy hair, no figure, and a face like a horse—albeit an extremely intelligent horse.

David sat back, frowning. This was too good a record; it didn't match the profile of an incompetent physician. How could she have made such an elementary mistake?

He closed the file. Whatever her excuses, the facts were indisputable: Dr. Katharine Chesne had condemned her patient to die under the surgeon's knife. Now she'd have to face the consequences.

He'd make damn sure she did.

GEORGE BETTENCOURT DESPISED DOCTORS. It was a personal opinion that made his job as CEO of Mid Pac Hospital all the more difficult, since he had to work so closely with the medical staff. He had both an M.B.A. and a Masters in public health. In his ten years as CEO, he'd achieved what the old doctor-led administration had been unable to do: he'd turned Mid Pac from a comatose institution into a profitable business. Yet all he ever heard from those stupid little surrogate gods in their white coats was criticism. They turned their superior noses up at the very idea that their saintly work could be dictated by profit-and-loss graphs. The cold reality was that saving lives, like selling linoleum, was a business. Bettencourt knew it. The doctors didn't. They were fools, and fools gave him headaches.

And the two sitting across from him now were giving him a migraine headache the likes of which he hadn't felt in years.

Dr. Clarence Avery, the white-haired chief of anesthesia, wasn't the problem. The old man was too timid to stand up to his own shadow, much less to a controversial issue. Ever since his wife's stroke, Avery had shuffled through his duties like a sleepwalker. Yes, he could be persuaded to cooperate. Especially when the hospital's reputation was at stake.

No, it was the other one who worried Bettencourt: the woman. She was new to the staff and he didn't know her very well. But the minute she'd walked into his office, he'd smelled trouble. She had that look in her eye, that crusader's set of the jaw. She was a pretty enough woman, though her brown hair was in a wild state of anarchy and she probably hadn't held a tube of lipstick in months. But those intense green eyes of hers were enough to make a man overlook all the flaws of that face. She was, in fact, quite attractive.

Too bad she'd blown it. Now she was a liability. He hoped she wouldn't make things worse by being a bitch, as well.

KATE FLINCHED AS BETTENCOURT dropped the papers on the desk in front of her. "The letter arrived in our attorney's office this morning, Dr. Chesne," he said. "Hand delivered by personal messenger. I think you'd better read it."

She took one look at the letterhead and felt her stomach drop away: *Uehara and Ransom, Attorneys at Law*.

"One of the best firms in town," explained Bettencourt. Seeing her stunned expression, he went on impatiently, "You and the hospital are being sued, Dr. Chesne. For malpractice. And David Ransom is personally taking on the case."

Her throat had gone dry. Slowly she looked up. "But how—how can they—"

"All it takes is a lawyer. And a dead patient."

"I've explained what happened!" She turned to Avery. "Remember last week—I told you—"

"Clarence has gone over it with me," cut in Bettencourt. "That isn't the issue we're discussing here."

"What *is* the issue?"

He seemed startled by her directness. He let out a sharp breath. "The issue is this: we have what looks like a million-dollar lawsuit on our hands. As your employer, we're responsible for the damages. But it's not just the money that concerns us." He paused. "There's our reputation."

The tone of his voice struck her as ominous. She knew what was coming and found herself utterly voiceless. She could only sit there, her stomach roiling, her hands clenched in her lap, and wait for the blow to fall.

"This lawsuit reflects badly on the whole hospital," he said. "If the case goes to trial, there'll be publicity. People—patients—will read those newspapers and it'll scare them." He looked down at his desk. "I realize your record up till now has been acceptable—"

Her chin shot up. "Acceptable?" she repeated incredulously. She glanced at Avery. The chief of anesthesia knew her record. And it was flawless.

Avery squirmed in his chair, his watery blue eyes avoiding hers. "Well, actually," he mumbled, "Dr. Chesne's record has been—up till now, anyway—uh, more than acceptable. That is…"

For God's sake, man! she wanted to scream. *Stand up for me!*

"There've never been any complaints," Avery finished lamely.

"Nevertheless," continued Bettencourt, "you've put us in a touchy situation, Dr. Chesne. That's why we think it'd be best if your name was no longer associated with the hospital."

There was a long silence, punctuated only by the sound of Dr. Avery's nervous cough.

"We're asking for your resignation," stated Bettencourt.

So there it was. The blow. It washed over her like a giant wave, leaving her limp and exhausted. Quietly she asked, "And if I refuse to resign?"

"Believe me, Doctor, a resignation will look a lot better on your record than a—"

"Dismissal?"

He cocked his head. "We understand each other."

"No." She raised her head. Something about his eyes, their cold self-assurance, made her stiffen. She'd never liked Bettencourt. She liked him even less now. "You don't understand me at all."

"You're a bright woman. You can see the options. In any event, we can't let you back in the O.R."

"It's not right," Avery objected.

"Excuse me?" Bettencourt frowned at the old man.

"You can't just fire her. She's a physician. There are channels you have to go through. Committees—"

"I'm well acquainted with the proper channels, Clarence! I was hoping Dr. Chesne would grasp the situation and act appropriately." He looked at her. "It really is easier, you know. There'd be no blot on your record. Just a notation that you resigned. I can have a letter typed up within the hour. All it takes is your..." His voice trailed off as he saw the look in her eyes.

Kate seldom got angry. She usually managed to keep her emotions under tight control. So the fury she now felt churning to the surface was something new and unfamiliar and almost frightening. With deadly calm she said, "Save yourself the paper, Mr. Bettencourt."

His jaw clicked shut. "If that's your decision..." He glanced at Avery. "When is the next Quality Assurance meeting?"

"It's—uh, next Tuesday, but—"

"Put the O'Brien case on the agenda. We'll let Dr. Chesne present her record to committee." He looked at Kate. "A judgment by your peers. I'd say that's fair. Wouldn't you?"

She managed to swallow her retort. If she said anything else, if she let fly what she really thought of George Bettencourt, she'd ruin her chances of ever again working at Mid Pac. Or anywhere else, for that matter. All he had to do was slap her with the label Troublemaker; it would blacken her record for the rest of her life.

They parted civilly. For a woman who'd just had her career ripped to shreds, she managed a grand performance. She gave Bettencourt a level look, a cool handshake. She kept her composure all the way out the door and on the long walk down the carpeted hall. But as she rode the elevator down, something inside her seemed to snap. By the time the doors slid open again, she was shaking violently. As she walked blindly through the noise and bustle of the lobby, the realization hit her full force.

Dear God, I'm being sued. Less than a year in practice and I'm being sued....

She'd always thought that lawsuits, like all life's catastrophes, happened to other people. She'd never dreamed she'd be the one charged with incompetence. *Incompetence.*

Suddenly feeling sick, she swayed against the lobby telephones. As she struggled to calm her stomach, her gaze fell on the local directory, hanging by a chain from the shelf. *If only they knew the facts,* she thought. *If I could explain to them...*

It took only seconds to find the listing: *Uehara and Ransom, Attorneys at Law.* Their office was on Bishop Street.

She wrenched out the page. Then, driven by a new and desperate hope, she hurried out the door.

Chapter Two

"MR. RANSOM IS UNAVAILABLE."

The gray-haired receptionist had eyes of pure cast iron and a face straight out of *American Gothic*. All she needed was the pitchfork. Crossing her arms, she silently dared the intruder to try—just try—to talk her way in.

"But I have to see him!" Kate insisted. "It's about the case—"

"Of course it is," the woman said dryly.

"I only want to explain to him—"

"I've just told you, Doctor. He's in a meeting with the associates. He can't see you."

Kate's impatience was simmering close to the danger point. She leaned forward on the woman's desk and managed to say with polite fury, "Meetings don't last forever."

The receptionist smiled. "This one will."

Kate smiled back. "Then so can I."

"Doctor, you're wasting your time! Mr. Ransom *never* meets with defendants. Now, if you need an escort to find your way out, I'll be happy to—" She glanced around in annoyance as the telephone rang. Grabbing the receiver, she snapped, "Uehara and Ransom! Yes? Oh, yes, Mr. Matheson!" She pointedly turned her back on Kate. "Let's see, I have those files right here…"

In frustration, Kate glanced around at the waiting room, noting the leather couch, the Ikebana of willow and proteus, the Murashige print hanging on the wall. All exquisitely tasteful and undoubtedly expensive. Obviously, Uehara and Ransom was doing a booming business. All off the blood and sweat of doctors, she thought in disgust.

The sound of voices suddenly drew Kate's attention. She turned and saw, just down the hall, a small army of young men and women emerging from a conference room. Which one was Ransom? She scanned the faces but none of the men looked old enough to be a senior partner in the firm. She glanced back at the desk and saw that the receptionist still had her back turned. It was now or never.

It took Kate only a split-second to make her decision. Swiftly, deliberately, she moved toward the conference room. But in the doorway she came to a halt, her eyes suddenly dazzled by the light.

A long teak table stretched out before her. Along either side, a row of leather chairs stood like soldiers at attention. Blinding sunshine poured in through the southerly windows, spilling across the head and shoulders of a lone man seated at the far end of the table. The light streaked his fair hair with gold. He didn't notice her; all his attention was focused on a sheaf of papers lying in front of him. Except for the rustle of a page being turned, the room was absolutely silent.

Kate swallowed hard and drew herself up straight. "Mr. Ransom?"

The man looked up and regarded her with a neutral expression. "Yes? Who are you?"

"I'm—"

"I'm so sorry, Mr. Ransom!" cut in the receptionist's outraged voice. Hauling Kate by the arm, the woman muttered through her teeth, "I *told* you he was unavailable. Now if you'll come with me—"

"I only want to talk to him!"

"Do you want me to call security and have you thrown out?"

Kate wrenched her arm free. "Go ahead."

"Don't tempt me, you—"

"What the hell is going on here?" The roar of Ransom's voice echoed in the vast room, shocking both women into silence. He aimed a long and withering look at Kate. "Just who *are* you?"

"Kate—" She paused and dropped her voice to what she hoped was a more dignified tone. "*Doctor* Kate Chesne."

A pause. "I see." he looked right back down at his papers and said flatly, "Show her out, Mrs. Pierce."

"I just want to tell you the facts!" Kate persisted. She tried to hold her ground but the receptionist herded her toward the door with all the skill of a sheepdog. "Or would you rather *not* hear the facts, is that it? Is that how you lawyers operate?" He studiously ignored her. "You don't give a damn about the truth, do you? You don't want to hear what really happened to Ellen O'Brien!"

That made him look up sharply. His gaze fastened long and hard on her face. "Hold on, Mrs. Pierce. I've just changed my mind. Let Dr. Chesne stay."

Mrs. Pierce was incredulous. "But—she could be violent!"

David's gaze lingered a moment longer on Kate's flushed face. "I think I can handle her. You can leave us, Mrs. Pierce."

Mrs. Pierce muttered as she walked out. The door closed behind her. There was a very long silence.

"Well, Dr. Chesne," David said. "Now that you've managed the rather miraculous feat of getting past Mrs. Pierce, are you just going to stand there?" He gestured to a chair. "Have a seat. Unless you'd rather scream at me from across the room."

His cold flippancy, rather than easing her tension, made him seem all the more unapproachable. She forced herself to move toward him, feeling his gaze every step of the way. For a man with his highly regarded reputation, he was younger than she'd expected, not yet in his forties. *Establishment* was stamped all over his clothes, from his gray pinstripe suit to his Yale tie clip. But a tan that deep and hair that sun-streaked didn't go along with an Ivy League type. *He's just a surfer boy, grown up*, she thought derisively. He certainly had a surfer's build, with those long, ropy limbs and shoulders that were just broad enough to be called impressive. A slab of a nose and a blunt chin saved him from being pretty. But it was his eyes she found herself focusing on. They were a frigid, penetrating blue; the sort of eyes that missed absolutely nothing. Right now those eyes were boring straight through her and she felt an almost irresistible urge to cross her arms protectively across her chest.

"I'm here to tell you the facts, Mr. Ransom," she said.

"The facts as you see them?"

"The facts as they *are.*"

"Don't bother." Reaching into his briefcase, he pulled out Ellen O'Brien's file and slapped it down conclusively on the table. "I have all the facts right here. Everything I need." *Everything I need to hang you,* was what he meant.

"Not everything."

"And now *you're* going to supply me with the missing details. Right?" He smiled and she recognized immediately the unmistakable threat in his expression. He had such perfect, sharp white teeth. She had the distinct feeling she was staring into the jaws of a shark.

She leaned forward, planting her hands squarely on the table. "What I'm going to supply you with is the truth."

"Oh, naturally." He slouched back in his chair and regarded her with a look of terminal boredom. "Tell me something," he asked offhandedly. "Does your attorney know you're here?"

"Attorney? I—I haven't talked to any attorney—"

"Then you'd better get one on the phone. Fast. Because, Doctor, you're damn well going to need one."

"Not necessarily. This is nothing but a big misunderstanding, Mr. Ransom. If you'll just listen to the facts, I'm sure—"

"Hold on." He reached into his briefcase and pulled out a cassette recorder.

"Just what do you think you're doing?" she demanded.

He turned on the recorder and slid it in front of her. "I wouldn't want to miss some vital detail. Go on with your story. I'm all ears."

Furious, she reached over and flicked the Off button. "This isn't a deposition! Put the damn thing away!"

For a few tense seconds they sized each other up. She felt a distinct sense of triumph when he put the recorder back in his briefcase.

"Now, where were we?" he asked with extravagant politeness. "Oh, yes. You were about to tell me what *really* happened." He settled back, obviously expecting some grand entertainment.

She hesitated. Now that she finally had his full attention, she didn't know quite how to start.

"I'm a very...careful person, Mr. Ransom," she said at last. "I take my time with things. I may not be brilliant, but I'm thorough. And I don't make stupid mistakes."

His raised eyebrow told her exactly what he thought of that statement. She ignored his look and went on.

"The night Ellen O'Brien came into the hospital, Guy Santini admitted her. But I wrote the anesthesia orders. I checked the lab results. And I read her EKG. It was a Sunday night and the technician was busy somewhere so I even ran the strip myself. I wasn't rushed. I took all the time I needed. In fact, more than I needed, because Ellen was a member of our staff. She was one of *us*. She was also a friend. I remember sitting in her room, going over her lab tests. She wanted to know if everything was normal."

"And you told her everything was."

"Yes. Including the EKG."

"Then you obviously made a mistake."

"I just told you, Mr. Ransom. I don't make stupid mistakes. And I didn't make one that night."

"But the record shows—"

"The record's wrong."

"I have the tracing right here in black and white. And it plainly shows a heart attack."

"That's *not* the EKG I saw!"

He looked as if he hadn't heard her quite right.

"The EKG I saw that night was normal," she insisted.

"Then how did this abnormal one pop into the chart?"

"Someone put it there, of course."

"Who?"

"I don't know."

"I see." Turning away, he said under his breath: "I can't wait to see how this plays in court."

"Mr. Ransom, if I made a mistake, I'd be the first to admit it!"

"Then you'd be amazingly honest."

"Do you really think I'd make up a story as—as *stupid* as this?"

His response was an immediate burst of laughter that left her cheeks burning. "No," he answered. "I'm sure you'd come up with something much more believable." He gave her an inviting nod. In a voice thick with sarcasm, he jeered, "Please, I'm *dying* to know how this extraordinary mix-up happened. How did the wrong EKG get in the chart?"

"How should I know?"

"You must have a theory."

"I don't."

"Come on, Doctor, don't disappoint me."

"I said I don't."

"Then make a guess!"

"Maybe someone beamed it there from the *Starship Enterprise*!" she yelled in frustration.

"Nice theory," he said, deadpan. "But let's get back to reality. Which, in this case, happens to be a particular sheet of wood by-product, otherwise known as paper." He flipped the chart open to the damning EKG. "Explain *that* away."

"I told you, I can't! I've gone crazy trying to figure it out! We do dozens of EKGs every day at Mid Pac. It could have been a clerical error. A mislabeled tracing. Somehow, that page was filed in the wrong chart."

"But you've written your initials on this page."

"No, I didn't."

"Is there some other K.C., M.D.?"

"Those are my initials. But I didn't write them."

"What are you saying? That this is a forgery?"

"It—it has to be. I mean, yes, I guess it is...." Suddenly confused, she shoved back a rebellious strand of hair off her face. His utterly calm expression rattled her. Why didn't the man react, for God's sake? Why did he just sit there, regarding her with that infuriatingly bland expression?

"Well," he said at last.

"Well what?"

"How long have you had this little problem with people forging your name?"

"Don't make me sound paranoid!"

"I don't have to. You're doing fine on your own."

Now he was silently laughing at her; she could see it in his eyes. The worst part was that she couldn't blame him. Her story *did* sound like a lunatic's ravings.

"All right," he relented. "Let's assume for the moment you're telling the truth."

"Yes!" she snapped. "Please do!"

"I can think of only two explanations for why the EKG would be intentionally switched. Either someone's trying to destroy your career—"

"That's absurd. I don't have any enemies."

"Or someone's trying to cover up a murder."

At her stunned expression, he gave her a maddeningly superior smile. "Since the second explanation obviously strikes both of us as equally absurd, I have no choice but to conclude you're lying." He leaned forward and his voice was suddenly soft, almost intimate. The shark was getting chummy; that had to be dangerous. "Come on, Doctor," he prodded. "Level with me. Tell me what really happened in the O.R. Was there a slip of the knife? A mistake in anesthesia?"

"There was nothing of the kind!"

"Too much laughing gas and not enough oxygen?"

"I told you, there were *no* mistakes!"

"Then why is Ellen O'Brien dead?"

She stared at him, stunned by the violence in his voice. And the blueness of his eyes. A spark seemed to fly between them, ignited by something entirely unexpected. With a shock, she realized he was an attractive man. Too attractive. And that her response to him was dangerous. She could already feel the blush creeping into her face, could feel a flood of heat rising inside her.

"No answer?" he challenged smoothly. He settled back, obviously enjoying the advantage he held over her. "Then why don't I tell *you* what happened? On April 2, a Sunday night, Ellen O'Brien checked into Mid Pac Hospital for routine gallbladder surgery. As her anesthesiologist, you ordered routine pre-op tests, including an EKG, which you checked before leaving the hospital that night. Maybe you were rushed. Maybe you had a hot date waiting. Whatever the reason, you got careless and you made a fatal error. You missed those vital clues in the EKG: the elevated ST waves, the inverted T waves. You pronounced it normal and signed your initials. Then you left for the night—never realizing your patient had just had a heart attack."

"She never had any symptoms! No chest pain—"

"But it says right here in the nurses' notes—let me quote—" he flipped through the chart "—'Patient complaining of abdominal discomfort.'"

"That was her gallstone—"

"Or was it her heart? Anyway, the next events are indisputable. You and Dr. Santini took Ms. O'Brien to surgery. A few whiffs of anesthesia and the stress was too much for her weakened heart. So it stopped. And you couldn't restart it." He paused dramatically, his eyes as hard as diamonds. "There, Dr. Chesne. You've just lost your patient."

"That's not how it happened! I remember that EKG. It was *normal*!"

"Maybe you'd better review your textbook on EKGs."

"I don't need a textbook. I *know* what's normal!" She scarcely recognized her own voice, echoing shrilly through the vast room.

He looked unimpressed. Bored, even. "Really—" he sighed "—wouldn't it be easier just to admit you made a mistake?"

"Easier for whom?"

"For everyone involved. Consider an out-of-court settlement. It'd be fast, easy and relatively painless."

"A settlement? But that's admitting a mistake I never made!"

What little patience he had left finally snapped. "You want to go to trial?" he shot back. "Fine. But let me tell you something about the way I work. When I try a case, I don't do it halfway. If I have to tear you apart in court, I'll do it. And when I'm finished, you'll wish you'd never turned this into some ridiculous fight for your honor. Because let's face it, Doctor. You don't have a snowball's chance in hell."

She wanted to grab him by those pinstriped lapels. She wanted to scream out that in all this talk about settlements and courtrooms, her own anguish over Ellen O'Brien's death had been ignored. But suddenly all her rage, all her strength, seemed to drain away, leaving her exhausted. Wearily she slumped back in her chair. "I wish I *could* admit I made a mistake," she said quietly. "I wish I could just say, 'I know I'm guilty and I'll pay for it.' I wish to God I could say that. I've spent the last week wondering about my memory. Wondering how this could have happened. Ellen trusted me and I let her die. It makes me wish I'd never become a doctor, that I'd been a clerk or a waitress—anything else. I love my work. You have no idea how hard it's been—how much I've given up—just to get to where I am. And now it looks as if I'll lose my job...." She swallowed and her head drooped in defeat. "And I wonder if I'll ever be able to work again...."

David regarded her bowed head in silence and fought to ignore the emotions stirring inside him. He'd always considered himself a good judge of character. He could usually look a man in the eyes and tell if he was lying. All during Kate Chesne's little speech, he'd been watching her eyes, searching for some inconsistent blip, some betraying flicker that would tell him she was lying through her teeth.

But her eyes had been absolutely steady and forthright and as beautiful as a pair of emeralds.

The last thought startled him, popping out as it did, almost against his will. As much as he might try to suppress it, he was all at once aware that she *was* a beautiful woman. She was wearing a simple green dress, gathered loosely at the waist, and it took just one glance to see that there were feminine curves beneath that silky fabric. The face that went along with those very nice curves had its flaws. She had a prizefighter's square jaw. Her shoulder-length mahogany hair was a riot of waves, obviously untamable. The curly bangs softened a forehead that was far too prominent. No, it wasn't a classically beautiful face. But then he'd never been attracted to classically beautiful women.

Suddenly he was annoyed not only at himself but at her, at her effect on him. He wasn't a dumb kid fresh out of law school. He was too old and too smart to be entertaining the peculiarly male thoughts now dancing in his head.

In a deliberately rude gesture, he looked down at his watch. Then, snapping his briefcase shut, he stood up. "I have a deposition to take and I'm already late. So if you'll excuse me..."

He was halfway across the room when her voice called out to him softly: "Mr. Ransom?"

He glanced back at her in irritation. "What?"

"I know my story sounds crazy. And I guess there's no reason on earth you should believe me. But I swear to you: it's the truth."

He sensed her desperate need for validation. She was searching for a sign that she'd gotten through to him; that she'd penetrated his hard shell of skepticism. The fact was, he didn't *know* if he believed her, and it bothered the hell out of him that his usual instinct for the truth had gone haywire, and all because of a pair of emerald-green eyes.

"Whether I believe you or not is irrelevant," he said. "So don't waste your time on me, Doctor. Save it for the jury." The words came out colder than he'd intended and he saw, from the quick flinch of her head, that she'd been stung.

"Then there's nothing I can do, nothing I can say—"

"Not a thing."

"I thought you'd listen. I thought somehow I could change your mind—"

"Then you've got a lot to learn about lawyers. Good-day, Dr. Chesne." Turning, he headed briskly for the door. "I'll see you in court."

Chapter Three

You don't have a snowball's chance in hell.

That was the phrase Kate kept hearing over and over as she sat alone at a table in the hospital cafeteria. And just how long did it take for a snowball to melt, anyway? Or would it simply disintegrate in the heat of the flames?

How much heat could she take before she fell apart on the witness stand?

She'd always been so adept at dealing with matters of life and death. When a medical crisis arose, she didn't wring her hands over what needed to be done; she just did it, automatically. Inside the safe and sterile walls of the operating room, she was in control.

But a courtroom was a different world entirely. That was David Ransom's territory. He'd be the one in control; she'd be as vulnerable as a patient on the operating table. How could she possibly fend off an attack by the very man who'd built his reputation on the scorched careers of doctors?

She'd never felt threatened by men before. After all, she'd trained with them, worked with them. David Ransom was the first man who'd ever intimidated her, and he'd done it effortlessly. If only he was short or fat or bald. If only she could think of him as human and therefore vulnerable. But just the thought of facing those cold blue eyes in court made her stomach do a panicky flip-flop.

"Looks like you could use some company," said a familiar voice.

Glancing up, she saw Guy Santini, rumpled as always, peering down at her through those ridiculously thick glasses.

She gave him a listless nod. "Hi."

Clucking, he pulled up a chair and sat down. "How're you doing, Kate?"

"You mean except for being unemployed?" She managed a sour laugh. "Just terrific."

"I heard the old man pulled you out of the O.R. I'm sorry."

"I can't really blame it on old Avery. He was just following orders."

"Bettencourt's?"

"Who else? He's labeled me a financial *liability*."

Guy snorted. "That's what happens when the damned M.B.A.'s take over. All they can talk about is profits and losses! I swear, if George Bettencourt could make a buck selling the gold out of patients' teeth, he'd be roaming the wards with pliers."

"And then he'd send them a bill for oral surgery," Kate added morosely.

Neither of them laughed. The joke was too close to the truth to be funny.

"If it makes you feel any better, Kate, you'll have some company in the courtroom. I've been named, too."

She looked up sharply. "Oh, Guy! I'm sorry…."

He shrugged. "It's no big deal. I've been sued before. Believe me, it's that first time that really hurts."

"What happened?"

"Trauma case. Man came in with a ruptured spleen and I couldn't save him." He shook his head. "When I saw that letter from the attorney, I was so depressed I wanted to leap out the nearest window. Susan was ready to drag me off to the psych ward. But you know what? I survived. So will you, as long as you remember they're not attacking *you*. They're attacking the job you did."

"I don't see the difference."

"And *that's* your problem, Kate. You haven't learned to separate yourself from the job. We both know the hours you put in. Hell, sometimes I think you practically live here. I'm not saying dedication's a character flaw. But you can overdo it."

What really hurt was that she knew it was true. She did work long hours. Maybe she needed to; it kept her mind off the wasteland of her personal life.

"I'm not completely buried in my job," she said. "I've started dating again."

"It's about time. Who's the man?"

"Last week I went out with Elliot."

"That guy from computer programming?" He sighed. Elliot was six-foot-two and one hundred and twenty pounds, and he bore a distinct resemblance to Pee-Wee Herman. "I bet that was a barrel of laughs."

"Well it was sort of…fun. He asked me up to his apartment."

"He did?"

"So I went."

"You *did*?"

"He wanted to show me his latest electronic gear."

Guy leaned forward eagerly. "What happened?"

"We listened to his new CDs. Played a few computer games."

"And?"

She sighed. "After eight rounds of Zork I went home."

Groaning, Guy sank back in his chair. "Elliot Lafferty, last of the red-hot lovers. Kate, what you need is one of these dating services. Hey, I'll even write the ad for you. 'Bright, attractive female seeks—'"

"Daddy!" The happy squeal cut straight through the cafeteria's hubbub.

Guy turned as running feet pattered toward him. "There's my Will!" Laughing, he rose to his feet and scooped up his son. It took only a sweep of his arms to send the spindly five-year-old boy flying into the air. Little Will was so light he seemed to float for a moment like a frail bird. He fell to a very soft, very safe landing in his father's arms. "I've been waiting for you, kid," Guy said. "What took you so long?"

"Mommy came home late."

"Again?"

Will leaned forward and whispered confidentially. "Adele was *really* mad. Her boyfriend was s'posed to take her to the movies."

"Uh-oh. We *certainly* don't want Adele to be mad at us, do we?" Guy flashed an inquiring look at his wife Susan, who was threading her way toward them. "Hey, are we wearing out the nanny already?"

"I swear, it's that full moon!" Susan laughed and shoved back a frizzy strand of red hair. "All my patients have gone absolutely loony. I couldn't get them out of my office."

Guy muttered grumpily to Kate, "And she swore it'd be a part-time practice. Ha! Guess who gets called to the E.R. practically every night?"

"Oh, you just miss having your shirts ironed!" Susan reached up and gave her husband an affectionate pat on the cheek. It was the sort of maternal gesture one expected of Susan Santini. "My mother hen," Guy had once called his wife. He'd meant it as a term of endearment and it had fit. Susan's beauty wasn't in her face, which was plain and freckled, or in her figure, which was as stout as a farm wife's. Her beauty lay in that serenely patient smile that she was now beaming at her son.

"Daddy!" William was prancing like an elf around Guy's legs. "Make me fly again!"

"What am I, a launching pad?"

"Up! One more time!"

"Later, Will," said Susan. "We have to pick up Daddy's car before the garage closes."

"Please!"

"Did you hear that?" Guy gasped. "He said the magic word." With a lion's roar, Guy pounced on the shrieking boy and threw him into the air.

Susan gave Kate a long-suffering look. "Two children. That's what I have. And one of them weighs two hundred and forty pounds."

"I heard that." Guy reached over and slung a possessive arm around his wife. "Just for that, lady, you have to drive me home."

"Big bully. Feel like McDonald's?"

"Humph. I know someone who doesn't want to cook tonight."

Guy gave Kate a wave as he nudged his family toward the

door. “So what’ll it be, kid?” Kate heard him say to William. “Cheeseburger?”

“Ice cream.”

“Ice cream. Now that’s an alternative I hadn’t thought of….”

Wistfully Kate watched the Santinis make their way across the cafeteria. She could picture how the rest of their evening would go. She imagined them sitting in McDonald’s, the two parents teasing, coaxing another bite of food into Will’s reluctant mouth. Then there’d be the drive home, the pajamas, the bedtime story. And finally, there’d be those skinny arms, curling around Daddy’s neck for a kiss.

What do I have to go home to? she thought.

Guy turned and gave her one last wave. Then he and his family vanished out the door. Kate sighed enviously. *Lucky man.*

AFTER HE LEFT HIS OFFICE THAT afternoon, David drove up Nuuanu Avenue and turned onto the dirt lane that wound through the old cemetery. He parked his car in the shade of a banyan tree and walked across the freshly mown lawn, past the marble headstones with their grotesque angels, past the final resting places of the Doles and the Binghams and the Cookes. He came to a section where there were only bronze plaques set flush in the ground, a sad concession to modern graveskeeping. Beneath a monkeypod tree, he stopped and gazed down at the marker by his feet.

Noah Ransom
Seven Years Old

It was a fine spot, gently sloping, with a view of the city. Here a breeze was always blowing, sometimes from the sea, sometimes from the valley. If he closed his eyes, he could tell where the wind was coming from, just by its smell.

David hadn’t chosen this spot. He couldn’t remember who had decided the grave should be here. Perhaps it had simply been a matter of which plot was available at the time. When your only child dies, who cares about views or breezes or monkeypod trees?

Bending down, he gently brushed the leaves that had fallen on the plaque. Then, slowly, he rose to his feet and stood in silence beside his son. He scarcely registered the rustle of the long skirt or the sound of the cane thumping across the grass.

"So here you are, David," called a voice.

Turning, he saw the tall, silver-haired woman hobbling toward him. "You shouldn't be out here, Mother. Not with that sprained foot."

She pointed her cane at the white clapboard house sitting near the edge of the cemetery. "I saw you through my kitchen window. Thought I'd better come out and say hello. Can't wait around forever for you to come visit me."

He kissed her on the cheek. "Sorry. I've been busy. But I really *was* on my way to see you."

"Oh, naturally." Her blue eyes shifted and focused on the grave. It was one of the many things Jinx Ransom shared with her son, that peculiar shade of blue of her eyes. Even at sixty-eight, her gaze was piercing. "Some anniversaries are better left forgotten," she said softly.

He didn't answer.

"You know, David, Noah always wanted a brother. Maybe it's time you gave him one."

David smiled faintly. "What are you suggesting, Mother?"

"Only what comes naturally to us all."

"Maybe I should get married first?"

"Oh, of course, of course." She paused, then asked hopefully: "Anyone in mind?"

"Not a soul."

Sighing, she laced her arm through his. "That's what I thought. Well, come along. Since there's no gorgeous female waiting for you, you might as well have a cup of coffee with your old mother."

Together they crossed the lawn toward the house. The grass was uneven and Jinx moved slowly, stubbornly refusing to lean on her son's shoulder. She wasn't supposed to be on her feet at all, but she'd never been one to follow doctors' orders. A woman who'd sprained her ankle in a savage game of tennis certainly wouldn't sit around twiddling her thumbs.

They passed through a gap in the mock-orange hedge and climbed the steps to the kitchen porch. Gracie, Jinx's middle-aged companion, met them at the screen door.

"There you are!" Gracie sighed. She turned her mouse-brown eyes to David. "I have absolutely *no* control over this woman. None at all."

He shrugged. "Who does?"

Jinx and David settled down at the breakfast table. The kitchen was a dense jungle of hanging plants: asparagus fern and baby's tears and wandering Jew. Valley breezes swept in from the porch, and through the large window, there was a view of the cemetery.

"What a shame they've trimmed back the monkeypod," Jinx remarked, gazing out.

"They had to," said Gracie as she poured coffee. "Grass can't grow right in the shade."

"But the view's just not the same."

David batted away a stray fern. "I never cared for that view anyway. I don't see how you can look at a cemetery all day."

"I like my view," Jinx declared. "When I look out, I see my old friends. Mrs. Goto, buried there by the hedge. Mr. Carvalho, by the shower tree. And on the slope, there's our Noah. I think of them all as sleeping."

"Good Lord, Mother."

"Your problem, David, is that you haven't resolved your fear of death. Until you do, you'll never come to terms with life."

"What do you suggest?"

"Take another stab at immortality. Have another child."

"I'm not getting married again, Mother. So let's just drop the subject."

Jinx responded as she always did when her son made a ridiculous request. She ignored it. "There was that young woman you met in Maui last year. Whatever happened to her?"

"She got married. To someone else."

"What a shame."

"Yeah, the poor guy."

"Oh, David!" cried Jinx, exasperated. "When are you going to grow up?"

David smiled and took a sip of Gracie's tar-black coffee, on which he promptly gagged. Another reason he avoided these visits to his mother. Not only did Jinx stir up a lot of bad memories, she also forced him to drink Gracie's god-awful coffee.

"So how was *your* day, Mother?" he asked politely.

"Getting worse by the minute."

"More coffee, David?" urged Gracie, tipping the pot threateningly toward his cup.

"No!" David gasped, clapping his hand protectively over the cup. The women stared at him in surprise. "I mean, er, no, thank you, Gracie."

"So touchy," observed Jinx. "Is something wrong? I mean, besides your sex life."

"I'm just a little busier than usual. Hiro's still laid up with that bad back."

"Humph. Well, you don't seem to like your work much anymore. I think you were much happier in the prosecutor's office. Now you take the job so damned seriously."

"It's a serious business."

"Suing doctors? Ha! It's just another way to make a fast buck."

"My doctor was sued once," Gracie remarked. "I thought it was terrible, all those things they said about him. Such a saint..."

"Nobody's a saint, Gracie," David said darkly. "Least of all, doctors." His gaze wandered out the window and he suddenly thought of the O'Brien case. It had been on his mind all afternoon. Or rather, *she'd* been on his mind, that green-eyed, perjuring Kate Chesne. He'd finally decided she was lying. This case was going to be even easier than he'd thought. She'd be a sitting duck on that witness stand and he knew just how he'd handle her in court. First the easy questions: name, education, postgraduate training. He had a habit of pacing in the courtroom, stalking circles around the defendant. The tougher the questions, the tighter the circles. By the time he came in for the kill, they'd be face-to-face. He felt an unexpected thump of dread in his chest, knowing what he'd have to do to finish it. Expose her. Destroy her. That was his job, and he'd always prided himself on a job well done.

He forced down a last sip of coffee and rose to his feet. "I have to be going," he announced, ducking past a lethally placed hanging fern. "I'll call you later, Mother."

Jinx snorted. "When? Next year?"

He gave Gracie a sympathetic pat on the shoulder and muttered in her ear, "Good luck. Don't let her drive you nuts."

"*I*? Drive *her* nuts?" Jinx snorted. "Ha!"

Gracie followed him to the porch door where she stood and waved. "Goodbye, David!" she called sweetly.

FOR A MOMENT, GRACIE PAUSED in the doorway and watched David walk through the cemetery to his car. Then she turned sadly to Jinx.

"He's *so* unhappy!" she said. "If only he could forget."

"He won't forget." Jinx sighed. "David's just like his father that way. He'll carry it around inside him till the day he dies."

Chapter Four

TEN-KNOT WINDS WERE BLOWING in from the northeast as the launch bearing Ellen O'Brien's last remains headed out to sea. It was such a clean, such a natural resolution to life: the strewing of ashes into the sunset waters, the rejoining of flesh and blood with their elements. The minister tossed a lei of yellow flowers off the old pier. The blossoms drifted away on the current, a slow and symbolic parting that brought Patrick O'Brien to tears.

The sound of his crying floated on the wind, over the crowded dock, to the distant spot where Kate was standing. Alone and ignored, she lingered by the row of tethered fishing boats and wondered why she was here. Was it some cruel and self-imposed form of penance? A feeble attempt to tell the world she was sorry? She only knew that some inner voice, begging for forgiveness, had compelled her to come.

There were others here from the hospital: a group of nurses, huddled in a quiet sisterhood of mourning; a pair of obstetricians, looking stiffly uneasy in their street clothes; Clarence Avery, his white hair blowing like dandelion fuzz in the wind. Even George Bettencourt had made an appearance. He stood apart, his face arranged in an impenetrable mask. For these people, a hospital was more than just a place of work; it was another home, another family.

Doctors and nurses delivered each other's babies, presided over each other's deaths. Ellen O'Brien had helped bring many of their children into the world; now they were here to usher her out of it.

The far-off glint of sunlight on fair hair made Kate focus on the end of the pier where David Ransom stood, towering above the others. Carelessly he pushed a lock of windblown hair into place. He was dressed in appropriately mournful attire—a charcoal suit, a somber tie—but in the midst of all this grief, he displayed the emotions of a stone wall. She wondered if there was anything human about him. *Do you ever laugh or cry? Do you ever hurt? Do you ever make love?*

That last thought had careened into her mind without warning. Love? Yes, she could imagine how it would be to make love with David Ransom: not a sharing but a claiming. He'd demand total surrender, the way he demanded surrender in the courtroom. The fading sunlight seemed to knight him with a mantle of unconquerability. What chance did she stand against such a man?

Wind gusted in from the sea, whipping sailboat halyards against masts, drowning out the minister's final words. When at last it was over, Kate found she didn't have the strength to move. She watched the other mourners pass by. Clarence Avery stopped, started to say something, then awkwardly moved on. Mary and Patrick O'Brien didn't even look at her. As David approached, his eyes registered a flicker of recognition, which was just as quickly suppressed. Without breaking stride, he continued past her. She might have been invisible.

By the time she finally found the energy to move, the pier was empty. Sailboat masts stood out like a row of dead trees against the sunset. Her foosteps sounded hollow against the wooden planks. When she finally reached her car, she felt utterly weary, as though her legs had carried her for miles. She fumbled for her keys and felt a strange sense of inevitability as her purse slipped out of her grasp, scattering its contents across the pavement. She could only stand there, paralyzed by defeat, as the wind blew her tissues across the ground. She had the absurd image of herself standing here all night, all week, frozen to this spot. She wondered if anyone would notice.

David noticed. Even as he waved goodbye and watched his clients drive away, he was intensely aware that Kate Chesne was somewhere on the pier behind him. He'd been startled to see her here. He'd thought it a rather clever move on her part, this public display of penitence, obviously designed to impress the O'Briens. But as he turned and watched her solitary walk along the pier, he noticed the droop of her shoulders, the downcast face, and he realized how much courage it had taken for her to show up today.

Then he reminded himself that some doctors would do anything to head off a lawsuit.

Suddenly disinterested, he started toward his car. Halfway across the parking lot, he heard something clatter against the pavement and he saw that Kate had dropped her purse. For what seemed like forever, she just stood there, the car keys dangling from her hand, looking for all the world like a bewildered child. Then, slowly, wearily, she bent down and began to gather her belongings.

Almost against his will, he was drawn toward her. She didn't notice his approach. He crouched beside her, scooped a few errant pennies from the ground, and held them out to her. Suddenly she focused on his face and then froze.

"Looks like you need some help," he said.

"Oh."

"I think you've got everything now."

They both rose to their feet. He was still holding out the loose change, of which she seemed oblivious. Only after he'd deposited the money in her hand did she finally manage a weak "Thank you."

For a moment they stared at each other.

"I didn't expect to see you here," he remarked. "Why did you come?"

"It was—" she shrugged "—a mistake, I think."

"Did your lawyer suggest it?"

She looked puzzled. "Why would he?"

"To show the O'Briens you care."

Her cheeks suddenly flushed with anger. "Is that what you think? That this is some sort of—of *strategy*?"

"It's not unheard of."

"Why are *you* here, Mr. Ransom? Is this part of *your* strategy? To prove to your clients you care?"

"I do care."

"And you think I don't."

"I didn't say that."

"You implied it."

"Don't take everything I say personally."

"I take everything you say personally."

"You shouldn't. It's just a job to me."

Angrily, she shoved back a tangled lock of hair. "And what *is* your job? Hatchet man?"

"I don't attack people. I attack their mistakes. And even the best doctors make mistakes."

"You don't need to tell me that!" Turning, she looked off to sea, where Ellen O'Brien's ashes were newly drifting. "I live with it, Mr. Ransom. Every day in that O.R. I know that if I reach for the wrong vial or flip the wrong lever, it's someone's life. Oh, we find ways to deal with it. We have our black jokes, our gallows humor. It's terrible, the things we laugh about, and all in the name of survival. Emotional survival. You have no idea, you lawyers. You and your whole damned profession. You don't know what it's like when everything goes wrong. When we lose someone."

"I know what it's like for the family. Every time you make a mistake, someone suffers."

"I suppose *you* never make mistakes."

"Everyone does. The difference is, you bury yours."

"You'll never let me forget it, will you?"

She turned to him. Sunset had painted the sky orange, and the glow seemed to burn in her hair and in her cheeks. Suddenly he wondered how it would feel to run his fingers through those wind-tumbled strands, wondered what that face would feel like against his lips. The thought had popped out of nowhere and now that it was out, he couldn't get rid of it. Certainly it was the last thing he ought to be thinking. But she was standing so dangerously close that he'd either have to back away or kiss her.

He managed to hold his ground. Barely. "As I said, Dr. Chesne, I'm only doing my job."

She shook her head and her hair, that sun-streaked, mahogany hair, flew violently in the wind. "No, it's more than that. I think you have some sort of vendetta. You're out to hang the whole medical profession. Aren't you?"

David was taken aback by her accusation. Even as he started to deny it, he knew she'd hit too close to home. Somehow she'd found his old wound, had reopened it with the verbal equivalent of a surgeon's scalpel. "Out to hang the whole profession, am I?" he managed to say. "Well, let me tell you something, Doctor. It's incompetents like you that make my job so easy."

Rage flared in her eyes, as sudden and brilliant as two coals igniting. For an instant he thought she was going to slap him. Instead she whirled around, slid into her car and slammed the door. The Audi screeched out of the stall so sharply he had to flinch aside.

As he watched her car roar away, he couldn't help regretting those unnecessarily brutal words. But he'd said them in self-defense. That perverse attraction he'd felt to her had grown too compelling; he knew it had to be severed, right there and then.

As he turned to leave, something caught his eye, a thin shaft of reflected light. Glittering on the pavement was a silver pen; it had rolled under her car when she'd dropped her purse. He picked it up and studied the engraved name: Katharine Chesne, M.D.

For a moment he stood there, weighing the pen, thinking about its owner. Wondering if she, too, had no one to go home to. And it suddenly struck him, as he stood alone on the windy pier, just how empty he felt.

Once, he'd been grateful for the emptiness. It had meant the blessed absence of pain. Now he longed to feel something—anything—if only to reassure himself that he was alive. He knew the emotions were still there, locked up somewhere inside him. He'd felt them stirring faintly when he'd looked into Kate Chesne's burning eyes. Not a full-blown emotion, perhaps, but a flicker. A blip on the tracing of a terminally ill heart.

The patient wasn't dead. Not yet.

He felt himself smiling. He tossed the pen up in the air and caught it smartly. Then he slipped it into his breast pocket and walked to his car.

THE DOG WAS DEEPLY ANESTHETIZED, its legs spread-eagled, its belly shaved and prepped with iodine. It was a German shepherd, obviously well-bred and just as obviously unloved.

Guy Santini hated to see such a handsome creature end up on his research table, but lab animals were scarce these days and he had to use whatever the supplier sent him. He consoled himself with the knowledge that the animals suffered no pain. They slept blissfully through the entire surgical procedure and when it was over, the ventilator was turned off and they were injected with a lethal dose of Pentothal. Death came peacefully; it was a far better end than the animals would have faced on the streets. And each sacrifice yielded data for his research, a few more dots on a graph, a few more clues to the mysteries of hepatic physiology.

He glanced at the instruments neatly laid out on the tray: the scalpel, the clamps, the catheters. Above the table, a pressure monitor awaited final hookup. Everything was ready. He reached for the scalpel.

The whine of the door swinging closed made him pause. Footsteps clipped toward him across the polished lab floor. Glancing across the table, he saw Ann Richter standing there. They looked at each other in silence.

"I see you didn't go to Ellen's services, either," he said.

"I wanted to. But I was afraid."

"Afraid?" He frowned. "Of what?"

"I'm sorry, Guy. I no longer have a choice." Silently, she held out a letter. "It's from Charlie Decker's lawyer. They're asking questions about Jenny Brook."

"*What?*" Guy stripped off his gloves and snatched the paper from her hand. What he read there made him look up at her in alarm. "You're not going to tell them, are you? Ann, you can't—"

"It's a subpoena, Guy."

"Lie to them, for God's sake!"

"Decker's out, Guy. You didn't know that, did you? He was released from the state hospital a month ago. He's been calling me. Leaving little notes at my apartment. Sometimes I even think he's following me…."

"He can't hurt you."

"Can't he?" She nodded at the paper he was holding. "Henry got one, just like it. So did Ellen. Just before she…" Ann stopped, as if voicing her worst fears somehow would turn them to reality. Only now did Guy notice how haggard she was. Dark circles shadowed her eyes, and the ash-blond hair, of which she'd always been so proud, looked as if it hadn't been combed in days. "It has to end, Guy," she said softly. "I can't spend the rest of my life looking over my shoulder for Charlie Decker."

He crumpled the paper in his fist. He began to pace back and forth, his agitation escalating to panic. "You could leave the islands—you could go away for a while—"

"How long, Guy? A month? A year?"

"As long as it takes for this to settle down. Look, I'll give you the money—" He fumbled for his wallet and took out fifty dollars, all the cash he had. "Here. I promise I'll send you more—"

"I'm not asking for your money."

"Go on, take it."

"I told you, I—"

"For God's sake, *take it*!" His voice, harsh with desperation, echoed off the stark white walls. "Please, Ann," he urged quietly. "I'm asking you, as a friend. Please."

She looked down at the money he was holding. Slowly, she reached out and took it. As her fingers closed around the bills she announced, "I'm leaving tonight. For San Francisco. I have a brother—"

"Call me when you get there. I'll send you all the money you need." She didn't seem to hear him. "Ann? You'll do this for me. Won't you?"

She looked off blankly at the far wall. He longed to reassure her, to tell her that nothing could possibly go wrong; but they'd both know it was a lie. He watched as she walked slowly to the door. Just before she left, he said, "Thank you, Ann."

She didn't turn around. She simply paused in the doorway. Then she gave a little shrug, just before she vanished out the door.

AS ANN HEADED FOR THE bus stop, she was still clutching the money Guy had given her. Fifty dollars! As if that was enough! A thousand, a million dollars wouldn't be enough.

She boarded the bus for Waikiki. From her window seat she stared out at a numbing succession of city blocks. At Kalakaua, she got off and began to walk quickly toward her apartment building. Buses roared past, choking her with fumes. Her hands turned clammy in the heat. Concrete buildings seemed to press in on all sides and tourists clotted the sidewalks. As she wove her way through them, she felt a growing sense of uneasiness.

She began to walk faster.

Two blocks north of Kalakaua, the crowd thinned out and she found herself at a corner, waiting for a stoplight to change. In that instant, as she stood alone and exposed in the fading sunlight, the feeling suddenly seized her: *someone is following me.*

She swung around and scanned the street behind her. An old man was shuffling down the sidewalk. A couple was pushing a baby in a stroller. Gaudy shirts fluttered on an outdoor clothing rack. Nothing out of the ordinary. Or so it seemed….

The light changed to green. She dashed across the street and didn't stop running until she'd reached her apartment.

She began to pack. As she threw her belongings into a suitcase, she was still debating her next move. The plane to San Francisco would take off at midnight; her brother would put her up for a while, no questions asked. He was good that way. He understood that everyone had a secret, everyone was running away from something.

It doesn't have to be this way, a stray voice whispered in her head. *You could go to the police….*

And tell them what? The truth about Jenny Brook? Do I tear apart an innocent life?

She began to pace the apartment, thinking, fretting. As she walked past the living-room mirror, she caught sight of her own reflection, her blond hair in disarray, her eyes smudged with mascara. She hardly recognized herself; fear had transformed her face into a stranger's.

It only takes a single phone call, a confession. A secret, once revealed, is no longer dangerous….

She reached for the telephone. With unsteady hands she dialed Kate Chesne's home phone number. Her heart sank when, after four rings, a recording answered, followed by the message beep.

She cleared the fear from her throat. "This is Ann Richter," she said. "Please, I have to talk to you. It's about Ellen. I know why she died."

Then she hung up and waited for the phone to ring.

IT WAS HOURS BEFORE KATE HEARD the message.

After she left the pier that afternoon, she drove aimlessly for a while, avoiding the inevitable return to her empty house. It was Friday night. T.G.I.F. She decided to treat herself to an evening out. So she had supper alone at a trendy little seaside grill where everyone but her seemed to be having a grand old time. The steak she ordered was utterly tasteless and the chocolate mousse so cloying she could barely force it down her throat. She left an extravagant tip, almost as an apology for her lack of appetite.

Next she tried a movie. She found herself wedged between a fidgety eight-year-old boy on one side and a young couple passionately making out on the other.

She walked out halfway through the film. She never did remember the title—only that it was a comedy, and she hadn't laughed once.

By the time she got home, it was ten o'clock. She was half undressed and sitting listlessly on her bed when she noticed that the telephone message light was blinking. She let the messages play back as she wandered over to the closet.

"Hello, Dr. Chesne, this is Four East calling to tell you Mr. Berg's blood sugar is ninety-eight.... Hello, this is June from Dr. Avery's office. Don't forget the Quality Assurance meeting on Tuesday at four.... Hi, this is Windward Realty. Give us a call back. We have a listing we think you'd like to see...."

She was hanging up her skirt when the last message played back.

"This is Ann Richter. Please, I have to talk to you. It's about Ellen. I know why she died...."

There was the click of the phone hanging up, and then a soft whir as the tape automatically rewound. Kate scrambled back to the recorder and pressed the replay button. Her heart was racing as she listened again to the agonizingly slow sequence of messages.

"It's about Ellen. I know why she died...."

Kate grabbed the phone book from her nightstand. Ann's address and phone number were listed; her line was busy. Again and again Kate dialed but she heard only the drone of the busy signal.

She slammed down the receiver and knew immediately what she had to do next.

She hurried back to the closet and yanked the skirt from its hanger. Quickly, feverishly, she began to dress.

THE TRAFFIC HEADING INTO WAIKIKI was bumper-to-bumper.

As usual, the streets were crowded with a bizarre mix of tourists and off-duty soldiers and street people, all of them moving in the surreal glow of city lights. Palm trees cast their spindly shadows against the buildings. An otherwise distinguished-looking gentleman was flaunting his white legs and Bermuda shorts. Waikiki was where one came to see the ridiculous, the outrageous. But tonight, Kate found the view through her car window frightening—all those faces, drained of color under the glow of streetlamps, and the soldiers, lounging drunkenly in nightclub doorways. A wild-eyed evangelist stood on the corner, waving a Bible as he shouted "The end of the world is near!"

As she pulled up at a red light, he turned and stared at her and for an instant she thought she saw, in his burning eyes, a message meant only for her. The light turned green. She sent the car lurching through the intersection. His shout faded away.

She was still jittery ten minutes later when she climbed the steps to Ann's apartment building. As she reached the door, a young couple exited, allowing Kate to slip into the lobby.

It took a moment for the elevator to arrive. Leaning back against the wall, she forced herself to breathe deeply and let the silence of the building calm her nerves. By the time she finally stepped into the elevator, her heart had stopped its wild hammering. The doors slid closed. The elevator whined upward. She felt a strange sense of unreality as she watched the lights flash in succession: three, four, five. Except for a faint hydraulic hum, the ride was silent.

On the seventh floor, the doors slid open.

The corridor was deserted. A dull green carpet stretched out before her. As she walked toward number 710, she had the strange sensation that she was moving in a dream, that none of this was real—not the flocked wallpaper or the door looming at the end of the corridor. Only as she reached it did she see it was slightly ajar. "Ann?" she called out.

There was no answer.

She gave the door a little shove. Slowly it swung open and she froze, taking in, but not immediately comprehending, the scene before her: the toppled chair, the scattered magazines, the bright red splatters on the wall. Then her gaze followed the trail of crimson as it zigzagged across the beige carpet, leading inexorably toward its source: Ann's body, lying facedown in a lake of blood.

Beeps issued faintly from a telephone receiver dangling off an end table. The cold, electronic tone was like an alarm, screaming at her to move, to take action. But she remained paralyzed; her whole body seemed stricken by some merciful numbness.

The first wave of dizziness swept over her. She crouched down, clutching the doorframe for support. All her medical training, all those years of working around blood, couldn't prevent this totally visceral response. Through the drumbeat of her own heart she became aware of another sound, harsh and irregular. Breathing. But it wasn't hers.

Someone else was in the room.

A flicker of movement drew her gaze across to the living room mirror. Only then did she see the man's reflection. He was cowering behind a cabinet, not ten feet away.

They spotted each other in the mirror at the same instant. In that split second, as the reflection of his eyes met hers, she imagined she saw, in those hollows, the darkness beckoning to her. An abyss from which there was no escape.

He opened his mouth as if to speak but no words came out, only an unearthly hiss, like a viper's warning just before it strikes.

She lurched wildly to her feet. The room spun past her eyes with excruciating slowness as she turned to flee. The corridor stretched out endlessly before her. She heard her own scream echo off the walls; the sound was as unreal as the image of the hallway flying past.

The stairwell door lay at the other end. It was her only feasible escape route. There was no time to wait for elevators.

She hit the opening bar at a run and shoved the door into the concrete stairwell. One flight into her descent, she heard the door above spring open again and slam against the wall. Again she heard the hiss, as terrifying as a demon's whisper in her ear.

She stumbled to the sixth-floor landing and grappled at the door. It was locked tight. She screamed and pounded. Surely someone would hear her! Someone would answer her cry for help!

Footsteps thudded relentlessly down the stairs. She couldn't wait; she had to keep running.

She dashed down the next flight and hit the fifth floor landing too hard. Pain shot through her ankle. In tears, she wrenched and pounded at the door. It was locked.

He was right behind her.

She flew down the next flight and the next. Her purse flew off her shoulder but she couldn't stop to retrieve it. Her ankle was screaming with pain as she hurtled toward the third-floor landing. Was it locked, as well? Were they all locked? Her mind flew ahead to the ground floor, to what lay outside. A parking lot? An alley? Is that where they'd find her body in the morning?

Sheer panic made her wrench with superhuman strength at the next door. To her disbelief, it was unlocked. Stumbling through, she found herself in the parking garage. There was no time to think about her next move; she tore off blindly into the shadows. Just as the stairwell door flew open again, she ducked behind a van.

Crouching by the front wheel, she listened for footsteps but heard nothing except the torrent of her own blood racing in her ears. Seconds passed, then minutes. Where was he? Had he abandoned the chase? Her body was pressed so tightly against the van, the steel bit into her thigh. She felt no pain; every ounce of concentration was focused on survival.

A pebble clattered across the ground, echoing like a pistol shot in the concrete garage.

She tried in vain to locate the source but the explosions seemed to come from a dozen different directions at once. *Go away!* she wanted to scream. *Dear God, make him go away....*

The echoes faded, leaving total silence. But she sensed his presence, closing in. She could almost hear his voice whispering to her *I'm coming for you. I'm coming....*

She had to know where he was, if he was drawing close.

Clinging to the tire, she slowly inched her head around and peered beneath the van. What she saw made her reel back in horror.

He was on the other side of the van and moving toward the rear. Toward her.

She sprang to her feet and took off like a rabbit. Parked cars melted into one continuous blur. She plunged toward the exit ramp. Her legs, stiff from crouching, refused to move fast enough. She could hear the man right behind her. The ramp seemed endless, spiraling around and around, every curve threatening to send her sprawling to the pavement. His footsteps were gaining. Air rushed in and out of her lungs, burning her throat.

In a last, desperate burst of speed, she tore around the final curve. Too late, she saw the headlights of a car coming up the ramp toward her.

She caught a glimpse of two faces behind the windshield, a man and a woman, their mouths open wide. As she slammed into the hood, there was a brilliant flash of light, like stars exploding in her eyes. Then the light vanished and she saw nothing at all. Not even darkness.

Chapter Five

"MANGO SEASON," SERGEANT BROPHY said as he sneezed into a soggy handkerchief. "Worst time of year for my allergies." He blew his nose, then sniffed experimentally, as if checking for some new, as yet undetected obstruction to his nasal passages. He seemed completely unaware of his gruesome surroundings, as though dead bodies and blood-spattered walls and an army of crime-lab techs were always hanging about. When Brophy got into one of his sneezing jags, he was oblivious of everything but the sad state of his sinuses.

Lieutenant Francis "Pokie" Ah Ching had grown used to hearing the sniffles of his junior partner. At times, the habit was useful. He could always tell which room Brophy was in; all he had to do was follow the man's nose.

That nose, still bundled in a handkerchief, vanished into the dead woman's bedroom. Pokie refocused his attention on his spiral notebook, in which he was recording the data. He wrote quickly, in the peculiar shorthand he'd evolved over his twenty-six years as a cop, seventeen of them with homicide. Eight pages were filled with sketches of the various rooms in the apartment, four pages of the living room alone. His art was crude but to the point. Body there. Toppled furniture here. Blood all over.

The medical examiner, a boyish, freckle-faced woman known to everyone simply as M.J., was making her walkaround before she examined the body. She was wearing her usual blue jeans and tennis shoes—sloppy dress for a doctor, but in her specialty, the patients never complained. As she circled the room, she dictated into a cassette recorder.

"Arterial spray on three walls, pattern height about four to five feet.... Heavy pooling at east end of living room where body is located.... Victim is female, blond, age thirty to forty, found in prone position, right arm flexed under head, left arm extended.... No hand or arm lacerations noted." M.J. crouched down. "Marked dependent mottling. Hmm." Frowning, she touched the victim's bare arm. "Significant body cooling. Time is now 12:15 a.m." She flicked off the cassette and was silent for a moment.

"Somethin' wrong, M.J.?" Pokie asked.

"What?" She looked up. "Oh, just thinking."

"What's your prelim?"

"Let's see. Looks like a single deep slash to the left carotid, very sharp blade. And very fast work. The victim never got a chance to raise her arms in defense. I'll get a better look when we wash her down at the morgue." She stood up and Pokie saw her tennis shoes were smeared with blood. How many crime scenes had those shoes tramped through?

Not as many as mine, he thought.

"Slashed carotid," he said thoughtfully. "Does that remind you of somethin'?"

"First thing I thought of. What was that guy's name a few weeks back?"

"Tanaka. He had a slash to the left carotid."

"That's him. Just as bloody a mess as this one, too."

Pokie thought a moment. "Tanaka was a doctor," he remarked. "And this one..." He glanced down at the body. "This one's a nurse."

"Was a nurse."

"Makes you wonder."

M.J. snapped her lab kit closed. "There's lots of doctors and nurses in this town. Just because these two end up on my slab doesn't mean they knew each other."

A loud sneeze announced Brophy's emergence from the

bedroom. "Found a plane ticket to San Francisco on her dresser. Midnight flight." He glanced at his watch. "Which she just missed."

A plane ticket. A packed suitcase. So Ann Richter was about to skip town. Why?

Mulling over that question, Pokie made another circuit of the apartment, going through the rooms one by one. In the bathroom, he found a lab tech microscopically peering down at the sink.

"Traces of blood in here, sir. Looks like your killer washed his hands."

"Yeah? Cool cat. Any prints?"

"A few here and there. Most of 'em old, probably the victim's. Plus one fresh set off the front doorknob. Could belong to your witness."

Pokie nodded and went back to the living room. That was their ace in the hole. The witness. Though dazed and in pain, she'd managed to alert the ambulance crew to the horrifying scene in apartment 710.

Thereby ruining a good night's sleep for Pokie.

He glanced at Brophy. "Have you found Dr. Chesne's purse yet?"

"It's not in the stairwell where she dropped it. Someone must've picked it up."

Pokie was silent a moment. He thought of all the things women carried in their purses: wallets, driver's licenses, house keys.

He slapped his notebook closed. "Sergeant?"

"Sir?"

"I want a twenty-four-hour guard placed on Dr. Chesne's hospital room. Effective immediately. I want a man in the lobby. And I want you to trace every call that comes in asking about her."

Brophy looked dubious. "All that? For how long?"

"Just as long as she's in the hospital. Right now she's a sitting duck."

"You really think this guy'd go after her in the hospital?"

"I don't know." Pokie sighed. "I don't know what we're dealing with. But I've got two identical murders." Grimly he slid the notebook into his pocket. "And she's our only witness."

PHIL GLICKMAN WAS MAKING a pest of himself as usual.

It was Saturday morning, the one day of the week David could work undisturbed, the one day he could catch up on all the paperwork that perpetually threatened to bury his desk. But today, instead of solitude, he'd found Glickman. While his young associate was smart, aggressive and witty, he was also utterly incapable of silence. David suspected the man talked in his sleep.

"So I said, 'Doctor, do you mean to tell me the posterior auricular artery comes off *before* the superficial temporal?' And the guy gets all flustered and says, 'Oh, did I say that? No, of course it's the other way around.' Which blew it right there for him." Glickman slammed his fist triumphantly into his palm. "Wham! He's dead meat and he knows it. We just got the offer to settle. Not bad, huh?" At David's lackluster nod, Glickman looked profoundly disappointed. Then he brightened and asked, "How's it going with the O'Brien case? They ready to yell uncle?"

David shook his head. "Not if I know Kate Chesne."

"What, is she dumb?"

"Stubborn. Self-righteous."

"So it goes with the white coat."

David tiredly dragged his fingers through his hair. "I hope this doesn't go to trial."

"It'll be like shooting rabbits in a cage. Easy."

"Too easy."

Glickman laughed as he turned to leave. "Never seemed to bother you before."

Why the hell does it bother me now? David wondered.

The O'Brien case was like an apple falling into his lap. All he had to do was file a few papers, issue a few threatening statements, and hold his hand out for the check. He should be breaking out the champagne. Instead, he was moping around on a gorgeous Saturday morning, feeling sleazy about the whole affair.

Yawning, he leaned back and rubbed his eyes. It'd been a lousy night, spent tossing and turning in bed. He'd been plagued by dreams—disturbing dreams; the kind he hadn't had in years.

There had been a woman. She'd stood very still, very quiet in the shadows, her face silhouetted against a window of hazy light. At first he'd thought she was his ex-wife, Linda. But there were things about her that weren't right, things that confused him. She'd stood motionless, like a deer pausing in the forest. Eagerly he'd reached out to undress her, but his hands had been impossibly clumsy and in his haste, he'd torn off one of her buttons. She had laughed, a deliciously throaty sound that reminded him of brandy.

That's when he knew she wasn't Linda. Looking up, he'd stared into the green eyes of Kate Chesne.

There were no words between them, only a look. And a touch: her fingers, sliding gently down his face.

He'd awakened, sweating with desire. He'd tried to fall back to sleep. Again and again the dream had returned. Even now, as he sank back in his chair and closed his eyes, he saw her face again and he felt that familiar ache.

Brutally wrenching his thoughts back to reality, he dragged himself over to the window. He was too old for this nonsense. Too old and too smart to even fantasize about an affair with the opposition.

Hell, attractive women walked into his office all the time. And every so often, one of them would give off the sort of signals any red-blooded man could recognize. It took only a certain tilt of the head, a provocative flash of thigh. He'd always been amused but never tempted; bedding down clients wasn't included in his list of services.

Kate Chesne had sent out no such signals. In fact she plainly despised lawyers as much as he despised doctors. So why, of all the women who'd walked through his door, was she the one he couldn't stop thinking about?

He reached into his breast pocket and pulled out the silver pen. It suddenly occurred to him that this wasn't the sort of item a woman would buy for herself. Was it a gift from a boyfriend? he wondered, and was startled by his instant twinge of jealousy.

He should return it.

The thought set his mind off and racing. Mid Pac Hospital was only a few blocks away. He could drop off the pen on his way home. Most doctors made Saturday-morning rounds, so there was a good chance she'd be there. At the prospect of seeing her again, he felt a strange mixture of anticipation and dread, the same churning in his stomach he used to feel as a teenager scrounging up the courage to ask a girl for a date. It was a very bad sign.

But he couldn't get the idea out of his mind.

The pen felt like a live wire. He shoved it back in his pocket and quickly began to stuff his papers into the briefcase.

Fifteen minutes later he walked into the hospital lobby and went to a house telephone. The operator answered.

"I'm trying to reach Dr. Kate Chesne," David said. "Is she in the building?"

"Dr. Chesne?" There was a pause. "Yes, I believe she's in the hospital. Who's calling?"

He started to give his name, then thought better of it. If Kate knew it was his page, she'd never answer it. "I'm a friend," he replied lamely.

"Please hold."

A recording of some insipid melody came on, the sort of music they probably played on elevators in hell. He caught himself drumming the booth impatiently. That's when it struck him just how eager he was to see her again.

I must be nuts, he thought, abruptly hanging up the phone. Or desperate for female companionship. Maybe both.

Disgusted with himself, he turned to leave, only to find that his exit was blocked by two very impressive-looking cops.

"Mind coming with us?" one of them asked.

"Actually," responded David, "I would."

"Then lemme put it a different way," said the cop, his meaning absolutely clear.

David couldn't help an incredulous laugh. "What did I do, guys? Double-park? Insult your mothers?"

He was grasped firmly by both arms and directed across the lobby, into the administrative wing.

"Is this an arrest or what?" he demanded. They didn't answer. "Hey, I think you're supposed to inform me of my rights." They didn't. "Okay," he amended. "Then maybe it's time *I* informed *you* of my rights." Still no answer. He shot out his weapon of last resort. "I'm an attorney!"

"Goody for you" was the dry response as he was led toward a conference room.

"You know damn well you can't arrest me without charges!"

They threw open the door. "We're just following orders."

"*Whose* orders?"

The answer was boomed out in a familiar voice. "*My* orders."

David turned and confronted a face he hadn't seen since his days with the prosecutor's office. Homicide Detective Pokie Ah Ching's features reflected a typical island mix of bloods: a hint of Chinese around the eyes, some Portuguese in the heavy jowls, a strong dose of dusky Polynesian coloring. Except for a hefty increase in girth, he had changed little in the eight years since they'd last worked together. He was even wearing the same old off-the-rack polyester suit, though it was obvious those front buttons hadn't closed in quite some time.

"If it isn't Davy Ransom," Pokie grunted. "I lay out my nets, and look what comes swimming in."

"Yeah," David muttered, jerking his arm free. "The wrong fish."

Pokie nodded at the two policemen. "This one's okay."

The officers retreated. The instant the door closed, David barked out: "What the hell's going on?"

In answer, Pokie moved forward and gave David a long, appraising look. "Private practice must be bringin' in the bucks. Got yourself a nice new suit. Expensive shoes. Humph. Italian. Doing well, huh, Davy?"

"I can't complain."

Pokie settled down on the edge of the table and crossed his arms. "So how's it, workin' out of a nice new office? Miss the ol' cockroaches?"

"Oh, sure."

"I made lieutenant a month after you left."

"Congratulations."

"But I'm still wearin' the same old suit. Driving the same old car. And the shoes?" He stuck out a foot. "Taiwan."

David's patience was just about shredded. "Are you going to tell me what's going on? Or am I supposed to guess?"

Pokie reached in his jacket for a cigarette, the same cheap brand he'd always smoked, and lit up. "You a friend of Kate Chesne's?"

David was startled by the abrupt shift of subject. "I know her."

"How well?"

"We've spoken a few times. I came to return her pen."

"So you didn't know she was brought to the E.R. last night? Trauma service."

"*What?*"

"Nothing serious," Pokie said quickly. "Mild concussion. Few bruises. She'll be discharged today."

David's throat had suddenly tightened beyond all hope of speech. He watched, stunned, as Pokie took a long, blissful drag on his cigarette.

"It's a funny thing," Pokie remarked, "how a case'll just sit around forever, picking up dust. No clues. No way of closing the file. Then, pow! We get lucky."

"What happened to her?" David asked in a hoarse voice.

"She was in the wrong place at the wrong time." He blew out a lungful of smoke. "Last night she walked in on a very bad scene."

"You mean…she's a witness? To what?"

Pokie's face was impassive through the haze drifting between them. "Murder."

THROUGH THE CLOSED DOOR of her hospital room, Kate could hear the sounds of a busy hospital: the paging system, crackling with static, the ringing telephones. All night long she'd strained to hear those sounds; they had reminded her she wasn't alone. Only now, as the sun spilled in across her bed and a profound exhaustion settled over her, did she finally drift toward sleep. She didn't hear the first knock, or the voice calling to her through the door. It was the gust of air sweeping into the room that warned her the door had swung open. She was vaguely aware that someone was approaching her bed. It took all her strength just to open her eyes. Through a blur of sleep, she saw David's face.

She felt a feeble sense of outrage struggle to the surface. He had no right to invade her privacy when she was so weak, so exposed. She knew what she *ought* to say to him, but exhaustion had sapped her last reserves of emotion and she couldn't dredge up a single word.

Neither could he. It seemed they'd both lost their voices.

"No fair, Mr. Ransom," she whispered. "Kicking a girl when she's down…" Turning away, she gazed down dully at the sheets. "You seem to have forgotten your handy tape recorder. Can't take a deposition without a tape recorder. Or are you hiding it in one of your—"

"Stop it, Kate. Please."

She fell instantly still. He'd called her by her first name. Some unspoken barrier between them had just fallen, and she didn't know why. What she did know was that he was here, that he was standing so close she could smell the scent of his after-shave, could almost feel the heat of his gaze.

"I'm not here to…kick you while you're down." Sighing, he added, "I guess I shouldn't be here at all. But when I heard what happened, all I could think of was…"

She looked up and found him staring at her mutely. For the first time, he didn't seem so forbidding. She had to remind herself that he *was* the enemy; that this visit, whatever its purpose, had changed nothing between them. But at that moment, what she felt wasn't threatened but protected. It was more than just his commanding physical presence, though she was very aware of that, too; he had a quiet aura of strength. Competence. If only he'd been *her* attorney; if only he'd been hired to defend, not prosecute her. She couldn't imagine losing any battle with David Ransom at her side.

"All you could think of was what?" she asked softly.

Shifting, he turned awkwardly toward the door. "I'm sorry. I should let you sleep."

"Why did you come?"

He halted and gave a sheepish laugh. "I almost forgot. I came to return this. You dropped it at the pier."

He placed the pen in her hand. She stared down in wonder, not at the pen, but at his hands. Large, strong hands. How would it feel, to have those fingers tangled in her hair?

"Thank you," she whispered.

"Sentimental value?"

"It was a gift. From a man I used to—" Clearing her throat, she looked away and repeated, "Thank you."

David knew this was his cue to walk out. He'd done his good deed for the day; now he should cut whatever threads of conversation were being spun between them. But some hidden force seemed to guide his hand toward a chair and he pulled it over to the bed and sat down.

Her hair lay tangled on the pillow and a bruise had turned one cheek an ugly shade of blue. He felt an instinctive flood of rage against the man who'd tried to hurt her. The emotion was entirely unexpected; it surprised him by its ferocity.

"How are you feeling?" he asked, for want of anything else to say.

She gave a feeble shrug. "Tired. Sore." She paused and added with a weak laugh, "Lucky to be alive."

His gaze shifted to the bruise on her cheek and she automatically reached up to hide what stood out so plainly on her face. Slowly she let her hand fall back to the bed. He found it a very sad gesture, as if she was ashamed of being the victim, of bearing that brutal mark of violence.

"I'm not exactly at my most stunning today," she said.

"You look fine, Kate. You really do." It was a stupid thing to say but he meant it. She looked beautiful; she was alive. "The bruise will fade. What matters is that you're safe."

"Am I?" She looked at the door. "There's been a guard sitting out there all night. I heard him, laughing with the nurses. I keep wondering why they put him there…."

"I'm sure it's just a precaution. So no one bothers you."

She frowned at him, suddenly puzzled. "How did *you* get past him?"

"I know Lieutenant Ah Ching. We worked together, years ago. When I was with the prosecutor's office."

"You?"

He smiled. "Yeah. I've done my civic duty. Got my education in sleaze. At slave wages."

"Then you've talked to Ah Ching? About what happened?"

"He said you're a witness. That your testimony's vital to his case."

"Did he tell you Ann Richter tried to call me? Just before she was killed. She left a message on my recorder."

"About what?"

"Ellen O'Brien."

He paused. "I didn't hear about this."

"She *knew* something, Mr. Ransom. Something about Ellen's death. Only she never got a chance to tell me."

"What was the message?"

"'I know why she died.' Those were her exact words."

David stared at her. Slowly, reluctantly, he found himself drawn deeper and deeper into the spell of those green eyes. "It may not mean anything. Maybe she just figured out what went wrong in surgery—"

"The word she used was *why*. 'I know *why* she died.' That implies there was a reason, a—a *purpose* for Ellen's death."

"Murder on the operating table?" He shook his head. "Come on."

She turned away. "I should have known you'd be skeptical. It would ruin your precious lawsuit, wouldn't it? To find out the patient was murdered."

"What do the police think?"

"How would I know?" she shot back in frustration. Then, in a tired voice, she said, "Your friend Ah Ching never says much of anything. All he does is scribble in that notebook of his. Maybe he thinks it's irrelevant. Maybe he doesn't want to hear any confusing facts." Her gaze shifted to the door. "But then I think about that guard. And I wonder if there's something else going on. Something he won't tell me…"

There was a knock on the door. A nurse came in with the discharge papers. David watched as Kate sat up and obediently signed each one. The pen trembled in her hand. He could hardly believe this was the same woman who'd stormed into his office. That day he'd been impressed by her iron will, her determination.

Now he was just as impressed by her vulnerability.

The nurse left and Kate sank back against the pillows.

"Do you have somewhere to go?" he asked. "After you leave here?"

"My friends…they have this cottage they hardly ever use. I hear it's on the beach." She sighed and looked wistfully out the window. "I could use a beach right now."

"You'll be staying there alone? Is that safe?"

She didn't answer. She just kept looking out the window. It made him uneasy, thinking of her in that cottage, alone, unprotected. He had to remind himself that she wasn't his concern. That he'd be crazy to get involved with this woman. Let the police take care of her; after all, she was their responsibility.

He stood up to leave. She just sat there, huddled in the bed, her arms crossed over her chest in a pitiful gesture of self-protection. As he walked out of the room, he heard her say, softly, "I don't think I'll ever feel safe again."

Chapter Six

"IT'S JUST A LITTLE PLACE," EXPLAINED Susan Santini as she and Kate drove along the winding North Shore highway. "Nothing fancy. Just a couple of bedrooms. An absolutely ancient kitchen. Prehistoric, really. But it's cozy. And it's so nice to hear the waves…." She turned off the highway onto a dirt road carved through the dense shrubbery of halekoa. Their tires threw up a cloud of rich red dust as they bounced toward the sea. "Seems like we hardly use the place these days, what with one of us always being on call. Sometimes Guy talks about selling. But I'd never dream of it. You just don't find bits of paradise like this anymore."

The tires crunched onto the gravel driveway. Beneath a towering stand of ironwood trees, the small plantation-era cottage looked like nothing more than a neglected dollhouse. Years of sun and wind had faded the planks to a weathered green. The roof seemed to sag beneath its burden of brown ironwood needles.

Kate got out and stood for a moment beneath the trees, listening to the waves hiss onto the sand. Under the midday sun, the sea shone a bright and startling blue.

"There they are," said Susan, pointing down the beach at her son William, who was dancing a joyous little jig in the sand. He moved like an elf, his long arms weaving delicately, his head bobbing back and forth as he laughed. The baggy swim trunks barely clung to his scrawny hips. Framed against the brilliance of the sky, he seemed like nothing more than a collection of twigs among the trees, a mythical creature who might vanish in the blink of an eye. Nearby, a young woman with a sparrowlike face was sitting on a towel and flipping listlessly through a magazine.

"That's Adele," Susan whispered. "It took us half a dozen ads and twenty-one interviews to find her. But I just don't think she's going to work out. What worries me is William's already getting attached to her."

William suddenly spotted them. He stopped in his tracks and waved. "Hi, Mommy!"

"Hello, darling!" Susan called. Then she touched Kate's arm. "We've aired out the cottage for you. And there should be a pot of coffee waiting."

They climbed the wooden steps to the kitchen porch. The screen door squealed open. Inside hung the musty smell of age. Sunlight slanted in through the window and gleamed dully on the yellowed linoleum floor. A small pot of African violets sat on the blue-tiled countertop. Taped haphazardly to the walls was a whimsical collection of drawings: blue and green dinosaurs, red stick men, animals of various colors and unidentifiable species, each labeled with the artist's name: William.

"We keep the line hooked up for emergencies," Susan informed her, pointing to the wall telephone. "I've already stocked the refrigerator. Just the basics, really. Guy said we can pick up your car tomorrow. That'll give you a chance to do some decent grocery shopping." She made a quick circuit of the kitchen, pointing out various cabinets, the pots and pans, the dishes. Then, beckoning to Kate, she led the way to the bedroom. There she went to the window and spread apart the white lace curtains. Her red hair glittered in the stream of sunlight. "Look, Kate. Here's that view I promised you." She gazed out lovingly at the sea. "You know, people wouldn't need psychiatrists if they just had this to look at every day. If they could lie in the sun, hear the waves, the birds." She turned and smiled at Kate. "What do you think?"

"I think..." Kate gazed around at the polished wood floor, the filmy curtains, the dusty gold light shimmering through the window. "I think I never want to leave," she replied with a smile.

Footsteps pattered on the porch. Susan looked around as the screen door slammed. "So endeth the peace and quiet." She sighed.

They returned to the kitchen and found little William singing tunelessly as he laid out a collection of twigs on the kitchen table. Adele, her bare shoulders glistening with suntan oil, was pouring him a cup of apple juice. On the counter lay a copy of *Vogue*, dusty with sand.

"Look, Mommy!" exclaimed William, pointing proudly to his newly gathered treasure.

"My goodness, what a collection," said Susan, appropriately awed. "What are you going to do with all those sticks?"

"They're not sticks. They're swords. To kill monsters."

"Monsters? But, darling, I've told you. There aren't any monsters."

"Yes, there are."

"Daddy put them all in jail, remember?"

"Not all of them." Meticulously, he lay another twig down on the table. "They're hiding in the bushes. I heard one last night."

"William," Susan said quietly. "What monsters?"

"In the bushes. I told you, last night."

"Oh." Susan flashed Kate a knowing smile. "That's why he crawled into our bed at two in the morning."

Adele placed the cup of juice beside the boy. "Here, William. Your…" She frowned. "What's that in your pocket?"

"Nothing."

"I saw it move."

William ignored her and took a slurp of juice. His pocket twitched.

"William Santini, give it to me." Adele held out her hand.

William turned his pleading eyes to the court of last appeals: his mother. She shook her head sadly. Sighing, he reached into his pocket, scooped out the source of the twitching, and dropped it in Adele's hand.

Her shriek was startling, most of all to the lizard, which promptly flung itself to freedom, but only after dropping its writhing tail in Adele's hand.

"He's getting away!" wailed William.

There followed a mad scrambling on hands and knees by everyone in the room. By the time the hapless lizard had been recaptured and jailed in a teacup, they were all breathless and weak from laughter. Susan, her red hair in wild disarray, collapsed onto the kitchen floor, her legs sprawled out in front of her.

"I can't *believe* it," she gasped, falling back against the refrigerator. "Three grown women against one itty-bitty lizard. Are we helpless or what?"

William wandered over to his mother and stared at the sunlight sparkling in her red hair. In silent fascination, he reached for a loose strand and watched it glide sensuously across his fingers. "My mommy," he whispered.

She smiled. Taking his face in her hands, she kissed him tenderly on the mouth. "My baby."

"YOU HAVEN'T TOLD ME THE WHOLE story," said David. "Now I want to know what you've left out."

Pokie Ah Ching took a mammoth bite of his Big Mac and chewed with the fierce concentration of a man too long denied his lunch. Swiping a glob of sauce from his chin, he grunted, "What makes you think I left something out?"

"You've thrown some heavy-duty manpower into this case. That guard outside her room. The lobby stakeout. You're fishing for something big."

"Yeah. A murderer." Pokie took a pickle slice out of his sandwich and tossed it disgustedly on a mound of napkins. "What's with all the questions, anyway? I thought you left the prosecutor's office."

"I didn't leave behind my curiosity."

"Curiosity? Is that all it is?"

"Kate happens to be a friend of mine—"

"Hogwash!" Pokie shot him an accusing look. "You think I don't ask questions? I'm a detective, Davy. And I happen to know she's no friend of yours. She's the defendant in one of your lawsuits." He snorted. "Since when're you getting chummy with the opposition?"

"Since I started believing her story about Ellen O'Brien. Two days ago, she came to me with a story so ridiculous I laughed her out of my office. She had no facts at all, nothing but a disjointed tale that sounded flat-out paranoid. Then this nurse, Ann Richter, gets her throat slashed. Now *I'm* beginning to wonder. Was Ellen O'Brien's death malpractice? Or murder?"

"Murder, huh?" Pokie shrugged and took another bite. "That'd make it my business, not yours."

"Look, I've filed a lawsuit that claims it was malpractice. It's going to be pretty damned embarrassing—not to mention a waste of my time—if this turns out to be murder. So before I get up in front of a jury and make a fool of myself, I want to hear the facts. Level with me, Pokie. For old times' sake."

"Don't pile on the sentimental garbage, Davy. You're the one who walked away from the job. Guess that fat paycheck was too hard to resist. Me? I'm still here." He shoved a drawer closed. "Along with this crap they call furniture."

"Let's get one thing straight. My leaving the job had nothing to do with money."

"So why did you leave?"

"It was personal."

"Yeah. With you it's always *personal*. Still tight as a clam, aren't you?"

"We were talking about the case."

Pokie sat back and studied him for a moment. Through the open door of his office came the sound of bedlam—loud voices and ringing telephones and clattering typewriters. A normal afternoon in the downtown police station. In disgust, Pokie got up and shoved his office door closed. "Okay." He sighed, returning to his chair. "What do you want to know?"

"Details."

"Gotta be specific."

"What's so important about Ann Richter's murder?"

Pokie answered by grabbing a folder from the chaotic pile of papers on his desk. He tossed it to David. "M.J.'s preliminary autopsy report. Take a look."

The report was three pages long and cold-bloodedly graphic. Even though David had served five years as deputy prosecutor, had read dozens of such reports, he couldn't help shuddering at the clinical details of the woman's death.

Left carotid artery severed cleanly...razor-sharp instrument.... Laceration on right temple probably due to incidental impact against coffee table.... Pattern of blood spatter on wall consistent with arterial spray....

"I see M.J. hasn't lost her touch for turning stomachs," David said, flipping to the second page. What he read there made him frown. "Now, this finding doesn't make sense. Is M.J. sure about the time of death?"

"You know M.J. She's always sure. She's backed up by mottling and core body temp."

"Why the hell would the killer cut the woman's throat and then hang around for three hours? To enjoy the scenery?"

"To clean up. To case the apartment."

"Was anything missing?"

Pokie sighed. "No. That's the problem. Money and jewelry were lying right out in the open. Killer didn't touch any of it."

"Sexual assault?"

"No sign of it. Victim's clothes were intact. And the killing was too efficient. If he was out for thrills, you'd think he would've taken his time. Gotten a few more screams out of her."

"So you've got a brutal murder and no motive. What else is new?"

"Take another look at that autopsy report. Read me what M.J. wrote about the wound."

"'Severed left carotid artery. Razor-sharp instrument.'" He looked up. "So?"

"So those are the same words she used in another autopsy report two weeks ago. Except that victim was a man. An obstetrician named Henry Tanaka."

"Ann Richter was a nurse."

"Right. And here's the interesting part. Before she joined the O.R. staff, she used to moonlight in obstetrics. Chances are, she knew Henry Tanaka."

David suddenly went very, very still. He thought of another nurse who'd worked in obstetrics. A nurse who, like Ann Richter, was now dead. "Tell me more about that obstetrician," he said.

Pokie fished out a pack of cigarettes and an ashtray. "Mind?"

"Not if you keep talking."

"Been dying for one all morning," Pokie grunted. "Can't light up when Brophy's around, whining about his damned sinuses." He flicked off the lighter. "Okay." He sighed, gratefully expelling a cloud of smoke. "Here's the story. Henry Tanaka's office was over on Liliha. You know, that god-awful concrete building. Two weeks ago, after the rest of his staff had left, he stayed behind in the office. Said he had to catch up on some paperwork. His wife says he always got home late. But she implied it wasn't paperwork that was keeping him out at night."

"Girlfriend?"

"What else?"

"Wife know any names?"

"No. She figured it was one of the nurses over at the hospital. Anyway, about seven o'clock that night, couple of janitors found the body in one of the exam rooms. At the time we thought it was just a case of some junkie after a fix. There were drugs missing from the cabinet."

"Narcotics?"

"Naw, the good stuff was locked up in a back room. The killer went after worthless stuff, drugs that wouldn't bring you a dime on the streets. We figured he was either stoned or dumb. But he was smart enough not to leave prints. Anyway, with no other evidence, the case sort of hit a wall. The only lead we had was something one of the janitors saw. As he was coming into the building, he spotted a woman running across the parking lot. It was drizzling and almost dark, so he didn't get a good look. But he says she was definitely a blonde."

"Was he positive it was a woman?"

"What, as opposed to a man in a wig?" Pokie laughed. "That's one I didn't think of. I guess it's possible."

"So what came of your lead?"

"Nothing much. We asked around, didn't come up with any names. We were starting to think that mysterious blonde was a red herring. Then Ann Richter got killed." He paused. "She was blond." He snuffed out his cigarette. "Kate Chesne's our first big break. Now at least we know what our man looks like. The artist's sketch'll hit the papers Monday. Maybe we'll start pulling in some names."

"What kind of protection are you giving Kate?"

"She's tucked away on the North Shore. I got a patrol car passing by every few hours."

"That's all?"

"No one'll find her up there."

"A professional could."

"What am I supposed to do? Slap on a permanent guard?" He nodded at the stack of papers on his desk. "Look at those files, Davy! I'm up to my neck in stiffs. I call myself lucky if a night goes by without a corpse rolling in the door."

"Professionals don't leave witnesses."

"I'm not convinced he *is* a pro. Besides, you know how tight things are around here. Look at this junk." He kicked the desk. "Twenty years old and full of termites. Don't even mention that screwy computer. I still gotta send fingerprints to California to get a fast ID!" Frustrated, he flopped back in his twenty-year-old chair. "Look, Davy. I'm reasonably sure she'll be okay. I'd like to guarantee it. But you know how it is."

Yeah, David thought. *I know how it is.* Some things about police work never changed. Too many demands and not enough money in the budget. He tried to tell himself that his only interest in this case was as the plaintiff's attorney; it was his job to ask all these questions. He had to be certain his case wouldn't crumble in the light of new facts. But his thoughts kept returning to Kate, sitting so alone, so vulnerable, in that hospital bed.

David wanted to trust the man's judgment. He'd worked with Pokie Ah Ching long enough to know the man was, for the most part, a competent cop. But he also knew that even the best cops made mistakes. Unfortunately cops and doctors had something in common: they both buried their mistakes.

THE SUN SLANTED DOWN ON Kate's back, its warmth lulling her into an uneasy sleep. She lay with her face nestled in her arms as the waves lapped at her feet and the wind riffled the pages of her paperback book. On this lonely stretch of beach, where the only disturbance was the birds bickering and thrashing in the trees, she had found the perfect place to hide away from the world. To be healed.

She sighed and the scent of coconut oil stirred in her nostrils.

Little by little, she was tugged awake by the wind in her hair, by a vague hunger for food. She hadn't eaten since breakfast and already the afternoon had slipped toward evening.

Then another sensation wrenched her fully awake. It was the feeling that she was no longer alone. That she was being watched. It was so definite that when she rolled over and looked up she was not at all surprised to see David standing there.

He was wearing jeans and an old cotton shirt, the sleeves rolled up in the heat. His hair danced in the wind, sparkling like bits of fire in the late-afternoon sunlight. He didn't say a thing; he simply stood there, his hands thrust in his pockets, his gaze slowly taking her in. Though her swimsuit wasn't particularly revealing, something about his eyes—their boldness, their directness—seemed to strip her against the sand. Sudden warmth flooded her skin, a flush deeper and hotter than any the sun could ever produce.

"You're a hard lady to track down," he said.

"That's the whole idea of going into hiding. People aren't supposed to find you."

He glanced around, his gaze quickly surveying the lonely surroundings. "Doesn't seem like such a bright idea, lying out in the open."

"You're right." Grabbing her towel and book, she rose to her feet. "You never know who might be hanging around out here. Thieves. Murderers." Tossing the towel smartly over her shoulder, she turned and walked away. "Maybe even a lawyer or two."

"I have to talk to you, Kate."

"I have a lawyer. Why don't you talk to him?"

"It's about the O'Brien case—"

"Save it for the courtroom," she snapped over her shoulder. She stalked away, leaving him standing alone on the beach.

"I may not be seeing you in the courtroom," he yelled.

"What a pity."

He caught up to her as she reached the cottage, and was right on her heels as she skipped up the steps. She let the screen door swing shut in his face.

"Did you hear what I said?" he shouted from the porch.

In the middle of the kitchen she halted, suddenly struck by

the implication of his words. Slowly she turned and stared at him through the screen. He'd planted his hands on either side of the doorframe and was watching her intently. "I may not be in court," he said.

"What does that mean?"

"I'm thinking of dropping out."

"Why?"

"Let me in and I'll tell you."

Still staring at him, she pushed the screen door open. "Come inside, Mr. Ransom. I think it's time we talked."

Silently he followed her into the kitchen and stood by the breakfast table, watching her. The fact that she was barefoot only emphasized the difference in their heights. She'd forgotten how tall he was, and how lanky, with legs that seemed to stretch out forever. She'd never seen him out of a suit before. She decided she definitely liked him better in blue jeans. All at once she was acutely aware of her own state of undress. It was unsettling, the way his gaze followed her around the kitchen. Unsettling, and at the same time, undeniably exciting. The way lighting a match next to a powder keg was exciting. Was David Ransom just as explosive?

She swallowed nervously. "I—I have to dress. Excuse me."

She fled into the bedroom and grabbed the first clean dress within reach, a flimsy white import from India. She almost ripped it in her haste to pull it on. Pausing by the door, she forced herself to count to ten but found her hands were still unsteady.

When she finally ventured back into the kitchen, she found him still standing by the table, idly thumbing through her book.

"A war novel," she explained. "It's not very good. But it kills the time. Which I seem to have a lot of these days." She waved vaguely toward a chair. "Sit down, Mr. Ransom. I—I'll make some coffee." It took all her concentration just to fill the kettle and set it on the stove. She found she was having trouble with even the simplest task. First she knocked the box of paper filters into the sink. Then she managed to dump coffee grounds all over the counter.

"Let me take care of that," he said, gently nudging her aside.

She watched, voiceless, as he wiped up the spilled coffee. Her awareness of his body, of its closeness, its strength, was suddenly overwhelming. Just as overwhelming was the unexpected wave of sexual longing. On unsteady legs, she moved to the table and sank into a chair.

"By the way," he asked over his shoulder, "can we cut out the 'Mr. Ransom' bit? My name's David."

"Oh. Yes. I know." She winced, hating the breathless sound of her own voice.

He settled into a chair across from her and their eyes met levelly over the kitchen table.

"Yesterday you wanted to hang me," she stated. "What made you change your mind?"

In answer, he pulled a piece of paper out of his shirt pocket. It was a photocopy of a local news article. "That story appeared about two weeks ago in the *Star-Bulletin*."

She frowned at the headline: Honolulu Physician Found Slashed To Death. "What does this have to do with anything?"

"Did you know the victim, Henry Tanaka?"

"He was on our O.B. staff. But I never worked with him."

"Look at the newspaper's description of his wounds."

Kate focused again on the article. "It says he died of wounds to the neck and back."

"Right. Wounds made by a very sharp instrument. The neck was slashed only once, severing the left carotid artery. Very efficient. Very fatal."

Kate tried to swallow and found her throat was parched. "That's how Ann—"

He nodded. "Same method. Identical results."

"How do you know all this?"

"Lieutenant Ah Ching saw the parallels almost immediately. That's why he slapped a guard on your hospital room. If these murders are connected, there's something systematic about all this, something rational—"

"*Rational?* The killing of a doctor? A nurse? If anything, it sounds more like the work of a psychotic!"

"It's a strange thing, murder. Sometimes it has no rhyme or reason to it. Sometimes the act makes perfect sense."

"There's no such thing as a *sensible* reason to kill someone!"

"It's done every day, by supposedly sane people. And all for the most mundane of reasons. Money. Power." He paused. "Then again," he said softly, "there's the crime of passion. It seems Henry Tanaka was having an affair with one of the nurses."

"Lots of doctors have affairs."

"So do lots of nurses."

"Which nurse are we talking about?"

"I was hoping you could tell me."

"I'm sorry, but I'm not up on the latest hospital gossip."

"Even if it involves your patients?"

"You mean Ellen? I—I wouldn't know. I don't usually delve into my patients' personal lives. Not unless it's relevant to their health."

"Ellen's personal life may have been very relevant to her health."

"Well, she was a beautiful woman. I'm sure there were…men in her life." Kate's gaze fell once again to the article. "What does this have to do with Ann Richter?"

"Maybe nothing. Maybe everything. In the last two weeks, three people on Mid Pac's staff have died. Two were murdered. One had an unexpected cardiac arrest on the operating table. Coincidence?"

"It's a big hospital. A big staff."

"But those three particular people knew each other. They even worked together."

"But Ann was a surgical nurse—"

"Who used to work in obstetrics."

"What?"

"Eight years ago, Ann Richter went through a very messy divorce. She ended up with a mile-high stack of credit-card bills. She needed extra cash, fast. So she did some moonlighting as an O.B. nurse. The night shift. That's the same shift Ellen O'Brien worked. They knew each other, all right. Tanaka, Richter, O'Brien. And now they're all dead."

The scream of the boiling kettle tore through the silence but she was too numb to move. David rose and took the kettle off the stove. She heard him set out the cups and pour the water. The smell of coffee wafted into her awareness.

"It's strange," she remarked. "I saw Ann almost every day in that O.R. We'd talk about books we'd read or movies we'd seen. But we never really talked about *ourselves*. And she was always so private. Almost unapproachable."

"How did she react to Ellen's death?"

Kate was silent for a moment, remembering how, when everything had gone wrong, when Ellen's life had hung in the balance, Ann had stood white-faced and frozen. "She seemed…paralyzed. But we were all upset. Afterward she went home sick. She didn't come back to work. That was the last time I saw her. Alive, I mean…." She looked down, dazed, as he slid a cup of coffee in front of her.

"You said it before. She must have known something. Something dangerous. Maybe they all did."

"But, David, they were just ordinary people who worked in a hospital—"

"All kinds of things can go on in hospitals. Narcotics theft. Insurance fraud. Illicit love affairs. Maybe even murder."

"If Ann knew something dangerous, why didn't she go to the police?"

"Maybe she couldn't. Maybe she was afraid of self-incrimination. Or she was protecting someone else."

A deadly secret, Kate thought. Had all three victims shared it? Softly she ventured, "Then you think Ellen was murdered."

"That's why I'm here. I want you to tell *me*."

She shook her head in bewilderment. "How can I?"

"You have the medical expertise. You were there in the O.R. when it happened. How could it be done?"

"I've already gone over it a thousand times—"

"Then do it again. Come on, Kate, *think*. Convince me it was murder. Convince me I *should* drop out of this case."

His blunt command seemed to leave her no alternative. She felt his eyes goading her to recall every detail, every event leading up to those frantic moments in the O.R. She remembered how everything had gone so smoothly, the induction of anesthesia, the placement of the endotracheal tube. She'd double-checked the tanks and the lines; she knew the oxygen had been properly hooked up.

"Well?" he prodded.

"I can't think of anything."

"Yes, you can."

"It was a completely routine case!"

"What about the surgery itself?"

"Faultless. Guy's the best surgeon on the staff. Anyway, he'd just started the operation. He was barely through the muscle layer when—" She stopped.

"When what?"

"He—he complained about the abdominal muscles being too tight. He was having trouble retracting them."

"So?"

"So I injected a dose of succinylcholine."

"That's pretty routine, isn't it?"

She nodded. "I give it all the time. But in Ellen, it didn't seem to work. I had to draw up a second dose. I remember asking Ann to fetch me another vial."

"You had only one vial?"

"I usually keep a few in my cart. But that morning there was only one in the drawer."

"What happened after you gave the second dose of succinylcholine?"

"A few seconds went by. Maybe it was ten. Fifteen. And then—" Slowly she looked up at him. "Her heart stopped."

They stared at each other. Through the window, the last light of day slanted in, knifelike, across the kitchen. He leaned forward, his eyes hard on hers. "If you could prove it—"

"But I can't! That empty vial went straight to the incinerator, with all the rest of the trash. And there's not even a body left to autopsy." She looked away, miserable. "Oh, he was smart, David. Whoever the killer was, he knew exactly what he was doing."

"Maybe he's too smart for his own good."

"What do you mean?"

"He's obviously sophisticated. He knew exactly which drugs you'd be likely to give in the O.R. And he managed to slip something deadly into one of those vials. Who has access to the anesthesia carts?"

"They're left in the operating rooms. I suppose anyone on the hospital staff could get to them. Doctors. Nurses. Maybe even the janitors. But there were always people around."

"What about nights? Weekends?"

"If there's no surgery scheduled, I guess they just close the suite down. But there's always a surgical nurse on duty for emergencies."

"Does she stay in the O.R. area?"

She shrugged helplessly. "I'm only there if we have a case. I have no idea what happens on a quiet night."

"If the suite's left unguarded, then anyone on the staff could've slipped in."

"It's not someone on the staff. I *saw* the killer, David! That man in Ann's apartment was a stranger."

"Who could have an associate. Someone in the hospital. Maybe even someone you know."

"A conspiracy?"

"Look at the systematic way these murders are being carried out. As if our killer—or killers—has some sort of list. My question is: Who's next?"

The clatter of her cup dropping against the saucer made Kate jump. Glancing down, she saw that her hands were shaking. *I saw his face,* she thought. *If he has a list, then my name's on it.*

The afternoon had slid into dusk. Agitated, she rose and paced to the open doorway. There she stood, staring out at the sea. The wind, so steady just moments before, had died. There was a stillness in the air, as if evening were holding its breath.

"He's out there," she whispered. "Looking for me. And I don't even know his name." The touch of David's hand on her shoulder made her tremble. He was standing behind her, so close she could feel his breath in her hair. "I keep seeing his eyes, staring at me in the mirror. Black and sunken. Like one of those posters of starving children…"

"He can't hurt you, Kate. Not here." David's breath seared her neck. A shudder ran through her body—not one of fear but of arousal. Even without looking at him, she could sense his need, simmering to the surface.

Suddenly it was more than his breath scorching her flesh; it was his lips. His face burrowed through the thick strands of her hair to press hungrily against her neck. His fingers gripped her shoulders, as if he was afraid she'd pull away. But she didn't. She couldn't. Her whole body was aching for him.

His lips left a warm, moist trail as they glided to her shoulder, and then she felt the rasp of his jaw.

He swung her around to face him. The instant she turned, his mouth was on hers.

She felt herself falling under the force of his kiss, falling into some deep and bottomless well, until her back suddenly collided with the kitchen wall. With the whole hard length of his body he pinned her there, belly against belly, thigh against thigh. Her lips parted and his tongue raged in, claiming her mouth as his. There was no doubt in her mind he intended to claim the rest of her, as well.

The match had been struck; the powder keg was about to explode, and her with it. She willingly flung herself into the conflagration.

No words were spoken; there were only the low, aching moans of need. They were both breathing so hard, so fast, that her ears were filled with the sound. She scarcely heard the telephone ringing. Only when it had rung again and again did her feverish brain finally register what it was.

It took all her willpower to swim against the flood of desire. She struggled to pull away. "The—the telephone—"

"Let it ring." His mouth slid down to her throat.

But the sound continued, grating and relentless, nagging her with its sense of urgency.

"David. Please…"

Groaning, he wrenched away and she saw the astonishment in his eyes. For a moment they stared at each other, neither of them able to believe what had just happened between them. The phone rang again. Jarred to her senses at last, she forced herself across the kitchen and picked up the receiver. Clearing her throat, she managed a hoarse "Hello?"

She was so dazed it took her a few seconds to register the silence on the line. "Hello?" she repeated.

"Dr. Chesne?" a voice whispered, barely audible.

"Yes?"

"Are you alone?"

"No, I— Who is this?" Her voice suddenly froze as the first fingers of terror gripped her throat.

There was a pause, so long and empty she could hear her own heart pounding in her ears. *"Hello?"* she screamed. *"Who is this?"*

"Be careful, Kate Chesne. For death is all around us."

Chapter Seven

THE RECEIVER SLIPPED FROM HER grasp and clattered on the linoleum floor. She reeled back in terror against the counter. "It's him," she whispered. Then, in a voice tinged with hysteria she cried out: *"It's him!"*

David instantly scrabbled on the floor for the receiver. "Who is this? Hello? *Hello?*" Cursing, he slammed the receiver back in the cradle and turned to her. "What did he say? Kate!" He took her by the shoulders and gave her a shake. "What did he say?"

"He—he said to be careful—that death was all around...."

"Where's your suitcase?" he snapped.

"What?"

"Your suitcase!"

"In—in the bedroom closet."

He stalked into the bedroom. Automatically she followed him and watched as he dragged her Samsonite down from the shelf. "Get your things together. You can't stay here."

She didn't ask where they were going. She only knew that she had to escape; that every minute she remained in this place just added to the danger.

Suddenly driven by the need to get away, she began to pack. By the time they were ready to leave, her compulsion to escape was so strong she practically flew down the porch steps to his car.

As he thrust the key in the ignition, she was seized by a wild terror that the car wouldn't start; that like some unfortunate victim in a horror movie, she would be stranded here, doomed to meet her death.

But at the first turn of the key, the engine started. The ironwood trees lunged at them as David sent the BMW wheeling around. Branches slashed the windshield. She felt another stab of panic as their tires spun uselessly in the sand. Then the car leaped free. The headlights trembled as they bounced up the dirt lane.

"How did he find me?" she sobbed.

"That's what I'm wondering." David hit the gas pedal as the car swung onto paved road. The BMW responded instantly with a burst of power that sent them hurtling down the highway.

"No one knew I was here. Only the police."

"Then there's been a leak of information. Or—" he shot a quick look at the rearview mirror "—you were followed."

"Followed?" She whipped her head around but saw only a deserted highway, shimmering under the dim glow of street lamps.

"Who took you to the cottage?" he asked.

She turned and focused on his profile, gleaming faintly in the darkness. "My—my friend Susan drove me."

"Did you stop at your house?"

"No. We went straight to the cottage."

"What about your clothes? How'd you get them?"

"My landlady packed a suitcase and brought it to the hospital."

"He might have been watching the lobby entrance. Waiting for you to be discharged."

"But we didn't see anyone follow us."

"Of course you didn't. People almost never do. We normally focus our attention on what's ahead, on where we're going. As for your phone number, he could've looked it up in the book. The Santinis have their name on the mailbox."

"But it doesn't make sense," she cried. "If he wants to kill me, why not just do it and get it over with? Why threaten me with phone calls?"

"Who knows how he thinks? Maybe he gets a thrill out of

scaring his victims. Maybe he just wants to keep you from cooperating with the police."

"I was alone. He could have done it right there…on the beach…." She tried desperately not to think of what could have happened, but she couldn't shut out the image of her own blood seeping into the sand.

High on the hillside, the lights of houses flashed by, each one an unreachable haven of safety. In all that darkness, was there a haven for her? She huddled against the car seat, wishing she never had to leave this small cocoon of safety.

Closing her eyes, she forced herself to concentrate on the hum of the engine, on the rhythm of the highway passing beneath their wheels—anything to banish the bloodstained image. BMW. The ultimate driving machine, she thought inanely. Wasn't that what the ads said? High-tech German engineering. Cool, crisp performance. Just the kind of car she'd expect David to own.

"…and there's plenty of room. So you can stay as long as you need to."

"What?" Bewildered, she turned and looked at him. His profile was a hard, clean shadow against the passing streetlights.

"I said you can stay as long as you need to. It's not the Ritz, but it'll be safer than a hotel."

She shook her head. "I don't understand. Where are we going?"

He glanced at her and the tone of his voice was strangely unemotional. "My house."

"HOME," SAID DAVID, PUSHING open the front door. It was dark inside. Through the huge living-room windows, moonlight spilled in, faintly illuminating a polished wood floor, the dark and hulking silhouettes of furniture. David guided her to a couch and gently sat her down. Then, sensing her desperate need for light, for warmth, he quickly walked around the room, turning on all the lamps. She was vaguely aware of the muted clink of a bottle, the sound of something being poured. Then he returned and put a glass in her hand.

"Drink it," he said.

"What—what is it?"

"Whiskey. Go on. I think you could use a stiff one."

She took a deep and automatic gulp; the fiery sting instantly brought tears to her eyes. "Wonderful stuff." She coughed.

"Yeah. Isn't it?" He turned to leave the room and she felt a sudden, irrational burst of panic that he was abandoning her.

"David?" she called.

He immediately sensed the terror in her voice. Turning back, he spoke quietly: "It's all right, Kate. I won't leave you. I'll be right next door, in the kitchen." He smiled and touched her face. "Finish that drink."

Fearfully she watched him vanish through the doorway. Then she heard his voice, talking to someone on the phone. The police. As if there was anything they could do now. Clutching the glass in both hands, she forced down another sip of whiskey. The room seemed to swim as her eyes flooded with tears. She blinked them away and slowly focused on her surroundings.

It was, somehow, every inch a man's house. The furniture was plain and practical, the oak floor unadorned by even a single throw rug. Huge windows were framed by stark white curtains and she could hear, just outside, waves crashing against the seawall. Nature's violence, so close, so frightening.

But not nearly as frightening as the violence of man.

AFTER DAVID HUNG UP, he paused in the kitchen, trying to scrape together some semblance of composure. The woman was already frightened enough; seeing his agitation would only make things worse. He quickly ran his fingers through his ruffled hair. Then, taking a deep breath, he pushed open the kitchen door and walked back into the living room.

She was still huddled pitifully on the couch, her hands clenched around the half-empty glass of whiskey. At least a trace of color had returned to her face, but it was barely enough to remind him of a frost-covered rose petal. A little more whiskey was what she needed. He took the glass, filled it to the brim and placed it back in her hands. Her skin was icy. She looked so stunned, so vulnerable. If he could just take her hands in his, if he could warm her in his arms, maybe he could coax some life back into those frozen limbs. But he was afraid to give in to the impulse; he knew it could lead to far more compelling urges.

He turned and poured himself a tall one. What she needed from him right now was protection. Reassurance. She needed to know that she would be taken care of and that things were still right with the world, though the truth of the matter was, her world had just gone to hell in a hand basket.

He took a deep gulp of whiskey, then set it down. What she really needed was a sober host.

"I've called the police," he said over his shoulder.

Her response was almost toneless. "What did they say?"

He shrugged. "What could they say? Stay where you are. Don't go out alone." Frowning at his glass, he thought, What the hell, and recklessly downed the rest of the whiskey. Bottle in hand, he returned to the couch and set the whiskey down on the coffee table. They were sitting only a few feet apart but it felt like miles of emptiness between them.

She stirred and looked toward the kitchen. "My—my friends—they won't know where I am. I should call them."

"Don't worry about it. Pokie'll let them know you're safe." He watched her sink back listlessly on the couch. "You should eat something," he said.

"I'm not hungry."

"My housekeeper makes great spaghetti sauce."

She lifted one shoulder—only one, as if she hadn't the energy for a full-blown shrug.

"Yep," he continued with sudden enthusiasm. "Once a week Mrs. Feldman takes pity on a poor starving bachelor and she leaves me a pot of sauce. It's loaded with garlic. Fresh basil. Plus a healthy slug of wine."

There was no response.

"Every woman I've ever served it to swears it's a powerful aphrodisiac."

At last there was a smile, albeit a very small one. "How helpful of Mrs. Feldman," she remarked.

"She thinks I'm not eating right. Though I don't know why. Maybe it's all those frozen-dinner trays she finds in my trash can."

There was another smile. If he kept this up, he just might coax a laugh out of her by next week. Too bad he was such a lousy comedian. Anyway, the situation was too damned grim for jokes.

The clock on the bookshelf ticked loudly—a nagging reminder of how much silence had passed between them. Kate suddenly stiffened as a gust rattled the windows.

"It's just the wind," he said. "You'll get used to it. Sometimes, in a storm, the whole house shudders and it feels like the roof will blow off." He gazed up affectionately at the beams. "It's thirty years old. Probably should have been torn down years ago. But when we bought it, all we could see were the possibilities."

"We?" she asked dully.

"I was married then."

"Oh." She stirred a little, as though trying to show some semblance of interest. "You're divorced."

He nodded. "We lasted a little over seven years—not bad, in this day and age." He gave a short, joyless laugh. "Contrary to the old cliché, it wasn't an itch that finished us. It was more like a…fading out. But—" he sighed "—Linda and I are still friendly. Which is more than most divorced couples can say. I even like her new husband. Great guy. Very devoted, caring. Something I guess I wasn't…." He looked away, uncomfortable. He hated talking about himself. It made him feel exposed. But at least all this small talk was doing the trick. It was bringing her back to life, nudging the fear from her mind. "Linda's in Portland now," he went on quickly. "I hear they've got a baby on the way."

"You didn't have any children?" It was a perfectly natural question. He wished she hadn't asked it.

He nodded shortly. "A son."

"Oh. How old is he?"

"He's dead." How flat his voice sounded. As if Noah's death were as casual a topic as the weather. He could already see the questions forming on her lips. And the words of sympathy. That was the last thing he wanted from her. He'd heard enough well-meaning words of sympathy to last him the rest of his life.

"So anyway," he said, shifting the subject, "I'm what you'd call a born-again bachelor. But I like it this way. Some men just aren't meant to be married, I guess. And it's great for my career. Nothing to distract me from the practice, which seems to be going big guns these days."

Damn. She was still looking at him with those questions in her eyes. He headed them off with another change of topic.

"What about you?" he asked quickly. "Were you ever married?"

"No." She looked down, as if contemplating the benefits of another slug of whiskey. "I lived with a man for a while. In fact, he's the reason I came to Honolulu. To be near him." She gave a bitter laugh. "Guess that'll teach me."

"What?"

"Not to go chasing after some stupid man."

"Sounds like a nasty breakup."

She hiccuped. "It was very—civil, actually. I'm not saying it didn't hurt. Because it did." Shrugging, she surrendered to another gulp of whiskey. "It's hard, you know. Trying to be everything at once. I guess I couldn't give him what he needed: dinner waiting on the table, my undivided attention."

"Is that what he expected?"

"Isn't that what every man expects?" she snorted angrily. "Well, I didn't need all that—that male crap. I had a job that required me to jump at every phone call. Rush in for every emergency. He didn't understand."

"Was it worth it?"

"Was what worth it?"

"Sacrificing your love life for your career?"

She didn't answer for a while. Then her head drooped. "I used to think so," she said quietly. "Now I think of all those hours I put in. All those ruined weekends. I thought I was indispensable to the hospital. And then I find out I'm just as dispensable as anyone else. All it took was a lawsuit. Hell of an eye-opener." She tipped her glass at him bitterly. "Thanks for the revelation, counselor."

"Why blame me? I was just hired to do a job."

"For a nice fat fee, I imagine."

"I took the case on contingency. I won't be seeing a cent."

"You gave up all that money? Just because you think I'm telling the truth?" She shook her head in amazement. "I'm surprised the truth means so much to you."

"You have a nice way of making me sound like scum. But yes, the truth does matter to me. A great deal, in fact."

"A lawyer with principles? I didn't know there was such a thing."

"We're a recognized subspecies." His gaze inadvertently slid to the neckline of her gauze dress. The memory of how that silky skin had felt under his exploring fingers suddenly hit him with such force that he quickly turned and reached for the whiskey. There was no glass handy so he took a swig straight from the bottle. *Right,* he thought. *Get yourself drunk. See how many stupid things you can say before morning.*

Actually, they were both getting thoroughly soused. But he figured she needed it. Twenty minutes ago she'd been in a state of shock. Now, at least, she was talking. In fact she'd just managed to insult him. That had to be a good sign.

She gazed fervently into her glass. "God, I hate whiskey!" she said with sudden passion and gulped down the rest of the drink.

"I can tell. Have some more."

She eyed him suspiciously. "I think you're trying to get me drunk."

"Whatever gave you that idea?" He laughed, shoving the bottle toward her.

She regarded it for a moment. Then, with a look of utter disgust, she refilled her glass. "Good old Jack Daniel's," she sighed. Her hand was unsteady as she recapped the bottle. "What a laugh."

"What's so funny?"

"It was Dad's favorite brand. He used to swear this stuff was medicinal. Absolutely *hated* all my hair-of-the-dog lectures. Boy, would he get a kick out of seeing me now." She took a swallow and winced. "Maybe he's right. Anything that tastes this awful *has* to be medicinal."

"I take it your father wasn't a doctor."

"He wanted to be." She stared down moodily at her drink. "Yeah, that was his dream. He planned on being a country doctor. You know, the kind of guy who'd deliver a baby in exchange for a few dozen eggs. But I guess things didn't work out. I came along and then they needed money and…" She sighed. "He had a repair shop in Sacramento. Oh, he was handy! I used to watch him putter around in that basement. Dad could fix anything you put in his hands. TVs. Washing machines. He even held seventeen patents, none of them worth a damn cent. Except maybe the Handy Dandy apple slicer." She glanced at him hopefully. "Ever heard of it?"

"Sorry. No."

She shrugged. "Neither has anyone else."

"What does it do, exactly?"

"One flick of the wrist and whack! Six perfect slices." At his silence she gave him a rueful smile. "I can see you're terribly impressed."

"But I am. I'm impressed that your father managed to invent you. He must've been happy you became a doctor."

"He was. When I graduated from med school, he told me it was the very best day of his life." She stopped, her smile suddenly fading. "I think that's sad, don't you? That out of all the years of his life, that was the one single day he was happiest…." She cleared her throat. "After he died, Mom sold the shop. She got married to some high-powered banker in San Francisco. What a snooty guy. We can't stand each other." She looked down at her glass and her voice dropped. "I still think about that shop sometimes. I miss the old basement. I miss all those dumb, useless gadgets of his. I miss—"

He saw her lower lip tremble and he thought with sudden panic: *Oh, no. Now she's going to cry.* He could deal with sobbing clients. He knew exactly how to respond to their tears. Pull out the box of Kleenex. Pat them on the back. Tell them he'd do everything he could.

But this was different. This wasn't his office but his living room. And the woman on the verge of tears wasn't a client but someone he happened to like very much.

Just as he thought the dam would burst, she managed to drag herself together. He saw only the briefest glitter of tears in her eyes, then she blinked and they were gone. Thank God. If she started bawling now, he'd be utterly useless.

He took her glass and deliberately set it down on the table. "I think you've had enough for tonight. Come on, doctor lady. It's time for bed. I'll show you the way." He reached for her hand but she reflexively pulled back. "Something wrong?"

"No. It's just…"

"Don't tell me you're worried about how it looks? Your staying here, I mean."

"A little. Not much, actually. I mean, not under the circumstances." She gave an awkward laugh. "Fear does strange things to one's sense of propriety."

"Not to mention one's sense of legal ethics." At her puzzled look, he said, "I've never done this before."

"What? Brought a woman home for the night?"

"Well, I haven't done *that* in a while, either. What I meant was, I make it a point never to get involved with any of my clients. And certainly never with the opposition."

"Then I'm the exception?"

"Yes. You are definitely the exception. Believe it or not, I don't normally paw every female who walks into my office."

"Which ones do you paw?" she asked, a faint smile suddenly tracing her lips.

He moved toward her, drawn by invisible threads of desire. "Only the green-eyed ones," he murmured. Gently he touched her cheek. "Who happen to have a bruise here and there."

"That last part sounds suspiciously kinky," she whispered.

"No, it's not." The intimate tone of his voice made Kate suddenly fall very still. His finger left a scorching trail as it stroked down her face.

She knew the danger of this moment. This was the man who'd once vowed to ruin her. He could still ruin her. *Consorting with the enemy,* she thought in sudden panic as his face drew closer. But she couldn't seem to move. A sense of unreality swept over her; a feeling that none of this could be happening, that it was only some hot, drunken fantasy. Here she was, sharing a couch with the very man she'd once despised, and all she could think of was how much she wanted him to haul her into his arms and kiss her.

His lips were gentle. It was no more than a brushing of mouths, a cautious savoring of what they both knew might follow, but it was enough to touch off a thousand flames inside her. Jack Daniel's had never tasted so good!

"And what will the bar association say to that?" she murmured.

"They'll call it outrageous…."

"Unethical."

"And absolutely insane. Which it is." Drawing away, he studied her for a moment; and his struggle for control showed plainly in his face. To her disappointment, common sense won out. He rose from the couch and tugged her to her feet. "When you file your complaint with the state bar, don't forget to mention how apologetic I was."

"Will it make a difference?"

"Not to them. But I hope it does to you."

They stood before the window, staring at each other. The wind lashed the panes, a sound as relentless as the pounding of her own heartbeat in her ears.

"I think it's time to go to bed," he said hoarsely.

"What?"

He cleared his throat. "I mean it's time you went to your bed. And I went to mine."

"Oh."

"Unless…"

"Unless?"

"You don't want to."

"Want to what?"

"Go to bed."

They looked at each other uneasily. She swallowed. "I think maybe I'd better."

"Yeah." He turned away and agitatedly plowed his fingers through his hair. "I think so, too."

"David?"

He glanced over his shoulder. "Yes?"

"Is it really a violation of legal ethics? Letting me stay here?"

"Under the circumstances?" He shrugged. "I think I'm still on safe ground. Barely. As long as nothing happens between us." He scooped up the whiskey bottle. Matter-of-factly he slid it into the liquor cabinet and shut the door. "And nothing will."

"Of course not," she responded quickly. "I mean, I don't need that kind of complication in my life. Certainly not now."

"Neither do I. But for the moment, we seem to need each other. So I'll provide you with a safe place to stay. And you can help me figure out what really happened in that O.R. A convenient arrangement. I ask only one thing."

"What's that?"

"We keep this discreet. Not just now but also after you leave. This sort of thing can only hurt both our reputations."

"I understand. Perfectly."

They both took a simultaneous breath.

"So…I think I'll say good-night," she said. Turning, she started across the living room. Her whole body felt like rubber. She only prayed she wouldn't fall flat on her face.

"Kate?"

Her heart did a quick somersault as she spun around to face him. "Yes?"

"Your room's the second door on the right."

"Oh. Thanks." Her flip-flopping heart seemed to sink like a stone as she left him standing there in the living room. Her only consolation was that he looked every bit as miserable as she felt.

LONG AFTER KATE HAD GONE to her room, David sat in the living room, thinking. Remembering how she had tasted, how she had trembled in his arms. And wondering how he'd gotten himself into this mess. It was bad enough, letting the woman sleep under his roof, but to practically seduce her on his couch—that was sheer stupidity. Though he'd wanted to. God, how he'd wanted to.

He could tell by the way she'd melted against him that she hadn't been kissed in a very long time. Terrific. Here they were, two normal, healthy, *deprived* adults, sleeping within ten feet of each other. You couldn't ask for a more explosive situation.

He didn't want to think about what his old ethics professor would say to this. Strictly speaking, he couldn't consider himself off the O'Brien case yet. Until he actually handed the file over to another firm, he still had to behave as their attorney and was bound by legal ethics to protect their interests. To think how scrupulous he'd always been about separating his personal from his professional life!

If he'd had his head screwed on straight, he would have avoided the whole mess by taking Kate to a hotel or a friend's house. Anywhere but here. The problem was, he'd been having trouble thinking straight since the day he met her. Tonight, after that phone call, he'd had only one thought in mind: to keep her safe and warm and protected. It was a fiercely primitive instinct over which he had no control; and he resented it. He also resented her for stirring up all these inconvenient male responses.

Annoyed at himself, he rose from the couch and circled the living room, turning off lights. He decided he wasn't interested in being any woman's white knight. Besides, Kate Chesne wasn't the kind of woman who needed a hero. Or any man, for that matter. Not that he didn't like independent women. He did like them.

He also liked *her*. A lot.

Maybe too much.

KATE LAY CURLED UP IN BED, listening to David's restless pacing in the living room. She held her breath as his footsteps creaked up the hall past her door. Was it her imagination or did he pause there for a moment before continuing on to the next room? She could hear him moving around, opening and closing drawers, rattling hangers in the closet. *My God,* she thought. *He's sleeping right next door.*

Now the shower was running. She wondered if it was a cold shower. She tried not to think about what he'd look like, standing under the stream of water, but the image had already formed in her head, the soapsuds sliding down his shoulders, the gold hairs matted and damp on his chest.

Now stop it. Right now.

She bit her lip—bit it so hard the image wavered a little. Damn. So this was lust, pure and unadulterated. Well, maybe slightly adulterated—by whiskey. Here she was, thirty years old, and she'd never wanted any man so badly. She wanted him on a level that was raw and wild and elemental.

She'd certainly never felt this way about Eric. Her relationship with Eric had been excruciatingly civilized; nothing as primitive as this—this animal heat. Even their parting had been civilized. They'd discussed their differences, decided they were irreconcilable, and had gone their separate ways. At the time she'd thought it devastating, but now she realized what had been hurt most by the breakup was her pride. All these months, she'd nursed the faint hope that Eric would come back to her. Now she could barely conjure up a picture of his face. It kept blurring into the image of a man in a shower.

She buried her head in the pillow, an act that made her feel about as brilliant as an ostrich. And she was supposed to be so bright, so levelheaded. Why, it was even official, having been stated in her performance evaluation as a resident: *Dr. Chesne is a superbly competent, levelheaded physician.* Ha! Levelheaded? Try dim-witted. Besotted. Or just plain dumb—for lusting after the man who'd once threatened to ruin her in court.

She had so many important things to worry about; matters, literally, of life and death. She was losing her job. Her career was on the skids. A killer was searching for her.

And she was wondering how much hair David Ransom had on his chest.

SHE WAS RUNNING DOWN HUNDREDS of steps, plunging deeper and deeper into a pit of darkness. She didn't know what lay at the end; all she knew was that something was right behind her, something terrible; she didn't dare look back to see its face. There were no doors, no windows, no other avenue of escape. Her flight was noiseless, like the flickering reel of a movie with no sound. In this silence lay the worst terror of all: no one would hear her scream.

With a sob, Kate wrenched herself awake and found herself staring up wildly at an unfamiliar ceiling. Somewhere a telephone was ringing. Daylight glowed in the window and she heard waves lapping the seawall. The ringing telephone suddenly stopped; David's voice murmured in another room.

I'm safe, she told herself. *No one can hurt me. Not here. Not in this house.*

The knock on the door made her sit up sharply.

"Kate?" David called through the closed door.

"Yes?"

"You'd better get dressed. Pokie wants us down at the station."

"Right now?"

"Right now."

It was his low tone of urgency that alarmed her. She scrambled out of bed and opened the door. "Why? What is it?"

His gaze slid briefly to her nightgown, then focused, utterly neutral, on her face. "The killer. They know his name."

Chapter Eight

POKIE SLID THE BOOK OF MUG shots toward Kate. "See anyone you know, Dr. Chesne?"

Kate scanned the photographs and immediately focused on one face. It was a cruel portrait; every wrinkle, every hollow had been brought into harsh clarity by the camera lights. Yet the man didn't squint. He gazed straight ahead with wide eyes. It was the look of a lost soul. Softly she said, "That's him."

"You positive?"

"I—I remember his eyes." Swallowing hard, she turned away. Both men were watching her intently. They were probably worried she'd faint or get hysterical or do something equally ridiculous. But she wasn't feeling much of anything. It was as if she were detached from her body and were floating somewhere near the ceiling, watching a stock scene from a police procedural: the witness unerringly pointing out the face of the killer.

"That's our man," Pokie said with grim satisfaction.

A wan sergeant in plainclothes brought her a cup of hot coffee. He seemed to have a cold; he was sniffling. Through the glass partition, she saw him return to his desk and take out a bottle of nose spray.

Her gaze returned to the photo. "Who is he?" she asked.

"A nut case," replied Pokie. "The name's Charles Decker. That photo was taken five years ago, right after his arrest."

"On what charge?"

"Assault and battery. He kicked down the door of a medical office. Tried to strangle the doctor right there in front of the whole staff."

"A doctor?" David's head came up. "Which one?"

Pokie sat back, his weight eliciting a squeal of protest from the old chair. "Guess."

"Henry Tanaka."

Pokie's answer was a satisfied display of nicotine-stained teeth. "One and the same. It took us a while, but the name finally popped up on a computer search."

"Arrest records?"

"Yeah. We should've picked it up earlier, but it kind of slipped by during the initial investigation. See, we asked Mrs. Tanaka if her husband had any enemies. You know, routine question. She gave us some names. We followed up on 'em but they all came up clean. Then she mentioned that five years back, some nut had attacked her husband. She didn't remember his name and as far as she knew, the man was still in the state hospital. We went to the files and finally pulled out an arrest report. It was Charlie Decker's. And this morning I got word from the lab. Remember that set of fingerprints on the Richter woman's doorknob?"

"Charlie Decker's?"

Pokie nodded. "And now—" he glanced at Kate "—our witness gives us a positive ID. I'd say we got our man."

"What was his motive?"

"I told you. He's crazy."

"So are thousands of other people. Why did this one turn killer?"

"Hey, I'm not the guy's shrink."

"But you have an answer, don't you?"

Pokie shrugged. "All I got is a theory."

"That man threatened my life, Lieutenant," said Kate. "I think I have the right to know more than just his name."

"She does, Pokie," agreed David quietly. "You won't find it in any of your police manuals. But I think she has the right to know who this Charles Decker is."

Sighing, Pokie fished a spiral notebook out of his desk. "Okay," he grunted, flipping through the pages. "Here's what I got so far. Understand, it's still gotta be confirmed. Decker, Charles Louis, white male born Cleveland thirty-nine years ago. Parents divorced. Brother killed in a gang fight at age fifteen. Great start. One married sister, living in Florida."

"You talked to her?"

"She's the one who gave us most of this info. Let's see. Joined the navy at twenty-two. Based in various ports. San Diego. Bremerton. Got shipped here to Pearl six years ago. Served as corpsman aboard the USS *Cimarron*—"

"Corpsman?" Kate questioned.

"Assistant to the ship's surgeon. According to his superior officers, Decker was kind of a loner. Pretty much kept to himself. No history of emotional problems." Here he let out a snort. "So much for the accuracy of military files." He flipped to the next page. "Had a decent service record, couple of commendations. Seemed to be moving up the ranks okay. And then, five years ago, it seems something snapped."

"Nervous breakdown?" asked David.

"Lot more than that. He went berserk. And it all had to do with a woman."

"You mean a girlfriend?"

"Yeah. Some gal he'd met here in the Islands. He put in for permission to get married. It was granted. But then he and his ship sailed for six months of classified maneuvers off Subic Bay. Sailor in the next bunk remembers Decker spent every spare minute writing poems for that girlfriend. Must've been nuts about her. Just nuts." Pokie shook his head and sighed. "Anyway, when the *Cimarron* returned to Pearl, the girlfriend wasn't waiting on the pier with all the other honeys. Here's the part where things get a little confused. All we know is Decker jumped ship without permission. Guess it didn't take long for him to find out what'd happened."

"She found another guy?" David guessed.

"No. She was dead."

There was a long silence. In the next office, a telephone was ringing and typewriters clattered incessantly.

Kate asked softly, "What happened to her?"

"Complications of childbirth," explained Pokie. "She had some kind of stroke in the delivery room. The baby girl died, too. Decker never even knew she was pregnant."

Slowly, Kate's gaze fell to the photograph of Charlie Decker. She thought of what he must have gone through, that day in Pearl Harbor. The ship pulling into the crowded dock. The smiling families. *How long did he search for her face?* she wondered. *How long before he realized she wasn't there? That she'd never be there?*

"That's when the man lost it," continued Pokie. "Somehow he found out Tanaka was his girlfriend's doctor. The arrest record says he showed up at the clinic and just about strangled the doctor on the spot. After a scuffle, the police were called. A day later, Decker got out on bail. He went and bought himself a Saturday-night special. But he didn't use it on the doctor. He put the barrel in his own mouth. Pulled the trigger." Pokie closed the notebook.

The ultimate act, thought Kate. *Buy a gun and blow your own head off.* He must have loved that woman. And what better way to prove it than to sacrifice himself on her altar?

But he wasn't dead. He was alive. And he was killing people.

Pokie saw her questioning look. "It was a very cheap gun. It misfired. Turned his mouth into bloody pulp. But he survived. After a few months in a rehab facility, he was transferred to the state hospital. The nuthouse. Their records show he regained function of just about everything but his speech."

"He's mute?" asked David.

"Not exactly. Vocal cords were ripped to shreds during the resuscitation. He can mouth words, but his voice is more like a—a hiss."

A hiss, thought Kate. The memory of that unearthly sound, echoing in Ann's stairwell, seemed to reach out from her worst nightmares. *The sound of a viper about to strike.*

Pokie continued. "About a month ago, Decker was discharged from the state hospital. He was supposed to be seeing some shrink by the name of Nemechek. But Decker never showed up for the first appointment."

"Have you talked to Nemechek?" asked Kate.

"Only on the phone. He's at a conference in L.A. Should be back on Tuesday. Swears up and down that his patient was harmless. But he's covering his butt. Looks pretty bad when the patient you just let out starts slashing throats."

"So that's the motive," said David. "Revenge. For a dead woman."

"That's the theory."

"Why was Ann Richter killed?"

"Remember that blond woman the janitors saw running through the parking lot?"

"You think that was her?"

"It seems she and Tanaka were—how do I put it?—very well acquainted."

"Does that mean what I think it means?"

"Let's just say Ann Richter's neighbors had no trouble recognizing Tanaka's photo. He was seen at her apartment more than once. The night he was killed, I think she went to pay her favorite doctor a little social call. Instead she found something that scared the hell out of her. Maybe she saw Decker. And he saw her."

"Then why didn't she go to the police?" asked Kate.

"Maybe she didn't want the world to know she was having an affair with a married man. Or maybe she was afraid she'd be accused of killing her lover. Who knows?"

"So she was just a witness," said Kate. "Like me."

Pokie looked at her. "There's one big difference between you and her. Decker can't get to *you.* Right now no one outside this office knows where you're staying. Let's keep it that way." He glanced at David. "There's no problem, keeping her at your house?"

David's face was unreadable. "She can stay."

"Good. And it's better if she doesn't use her own car."

"My car?" Kate frowned. "Why not?"

"Decker has your purse. And a set of your car keys. So he knows you drive an Audi. He'll be watching for one."

Watching for me, she thought with a shudder. "For how long?" she whispered.

"What?"

"How long before it's all over? Before I have my life back?"

Pokie sighed. "It might take a while to find him. But hang in there, Doc. The man can't hide forever."

Can't he? wondered Kate. She thought of all the places a man could hide on Oahu: the nooks and crannies of Chinatown where no one ever asks questions. The tin-roofed fishing shacks of Sand Island. The concrete alleys of Waikiki. Somewhere, in some secret place, Charlie Decker was quietly mourning for a dead woman.

They rose to leave and a question suddenly came to her mind. "Lieutenant," she asked. "What about Ellen O'Brien?"

Pokie, who was gathering a pile of papers into a folder, glanced up. "What about her?"

"Does she have some connection to all this?"

Pokie looked down one last time at Charlie Decker's photo. Then he shut the folder. "No," he answered. "No connection at all."

"BUT THERE *HAS* TO BE a connection!" Kate blurted as they walked out of the station into the midmorning heat. "Some piece of evidence he hasn't found—"

"Or won't tell us about," finished David.

She frowned at him. "Why wouldn't he? I thought you two were friends."

"I deserted the trenches, remember?"

"You make police work sound like jungle warfare."

"For some cops, the job *is* a war. A holy war. Pokie's got a wife and four kids. But you'd never know it, looking at all the hours he puts in."

"So you do think he's a good cop?"

David shrugged. "He's a plough horse. Solid but not brilliant. I've seen him screw up on occasion. He could be wrong this time, too. But right now I have to agree with him. I don't see how Ellen O'Brien fits into this case."

"But you heard what he said! Decker was a corpsman. Assistant to the ship's surgeon—"

"Decker's profile doesn't fit the pattern, Kate. A psycho who works like Jack the Ripper doesn't bother with drug vials and EKGs. That takes a totally different kind of mind."

She stared down the street in frustration. "The trouble is, I can't see any way to prove Ellen *was* murdered. I can't even be sure it's possible."

David paused on the sidewalk. "Okay." He sighed. "So we can't prove anything. But let's think about the logistics."

"You mean of murder?"

He nodded. "Let's take a man like Decker. An outsider. Someone who knows a little about medicine. And surgery. Tell me, step by step. How would he go about getting into the hospital and killing a patient?"

"I suppose he'd have to…to…" Her gaze wandered up the street. She frowned as her eyes focused on a paperboy, waving the morning edition to passing cars. "Today's Sunday," she said suddenly.

"So?"

"Ellen was admitted on a Sunday. I remember being in her room, talking to her. It was eight o'clock on a Sunday night." She glanced feverishly at her watch. "That's in ten hours. We could go through the steps…."

"Wait a minute. You've lost me. What, exactly, are we doing in ten hours?"

She turned to him. Softly she said, "Murder."

THE VISITOR PARKING LOT was nearly empty when David swung his BMW into the hospital driveway at ten o'clock that night. He parked in a stall near the lobby entrance, turned off the engine and looked at Kate. "This won't prove a thing. You know that, don't you?"

"I want to see if it's possible."

"Possibilities don't hold up in court."

"I don't care how it plays in court, David. As long as *I* know it's possible."

She glanced out at the distant red Emergency sign, glowing like a beacon in the darkness. An ambulance was parked at the loading dock. On a nearby bench, the driver sat idly smoking a cigarette and listening to the crackle of his dispatch radio.

A Sunday night, quiet as usual. Visiting hours were over. And in their rooms, patients would already be settling into the blissful sleep of the drugged.

David's face gleamed faintly in the shadows. "Okay." He sighed, shoving open his door. "Let's do it."

The lobby doors were locked. They walked in the E.R. entrance, through a waiting room where a baby screamed in the lap of its glassy-eyed mother, where an old man coughed noisily into a handkerchief and a teenage boy clutched an ice bag to his swollen face. The triage nurse was talking on the telephone; they walked right past her and headed for the elevators.

"We're in, just like that?" David asked.

"The E.R. nurse knows me."

"But she hardly looked at you."

"That's because she was too busy ogling *you*," Kate said dryly.

"Boy, have you got a wild imagination." He paused, glancing around the empty lobby. "Where's Security? Isn't there a guard around?"

"He's probably making rounds."

"You mean there's only one?"

"Hospitals are really pretty boring places, you know," she replied and punched the elevator button. "Besides, it's Sunday."

They rose up to the fourth floor and stepped off into the antiseptic-white corridor. Freshly waxed linoleum gleamed under bright lights. A row of gurneys sat lined up against the wall, as though awaiting a deluge of the wounded. Kate pointed to the double doors marked No Admittance.

"The O.R.'s through there."

"Can we get in?"

She took a few experimental steps forward. The doors automatically slid open. "No problem."

Inside, only a single dim light shone over the reception area. A cup, half filled with lukewarm coffee, sat abandoned on the front desk awaiting its owner's return. Kate pointed to a huge wallboard where the next day's surgery schedule was posted.

"All tomorrow's cases are listed right there," she explained. "One glance will tell you which O.R. the patient will be in, the procedure, the names of the surgeon and anesthesiologist."

"Where was Ellen?"

"The room's right around the corner."

She led him down an unlit hall and opened the door to O.R. 5. Through the shadows they saw the faint gleam of stainless steel. She flicked on the wall switch; the sudden flood of light was almost painful.

"The anesthesia cart's over there."

He went over to the cart and pulled open one of the steel

drawers. Tiny glass vials tinkled in their compartments. "Are these drugs always left unlocked?"

"They're worthless on the street. No one would bother to steal any of those. As for the narcotics—" she pointed to a wall cabinet "—we keep them locked in there."

His gaze slowly moved around the room. "So this is where you work. Very impressive. Looks like a set for a sci-fi movie."

She grinned. "Funny. I've always felt right at home in here." She circled the room, affectionately patting the equipment as she moved. "I think it's because I'm the daughter of a tinkerer. Gadgets don't scare me. I actually like playing with all these buttons and dials. But I suppose some people do find it all pretty intimidating."

"And you've never been intimidated?"

She turned and found he was staring at her. Something about his gaze, about the intensity of those blue eyes, made her fall very still. "Not by the O.R.," she said softly.

It was so quiet she could almost hear her own heartbeat thudding in that stark chamber. For a long time they stared at each other, as though separated by some wide, unbreachable chasm. Then, abruptly, he shifted his attention to the anesthesia cart.

"How long would it take to tamper with one of these drug vials?" he asked. She had to admire his control. At least he could still speak; she was having trouble finding her own voice.

"He'd—he'd have to empty out the succinylcholine vials. It would probably take less than a minute."

"As easy as that?"

"As easy as that." Her gaze shifted reluctantly to the operating table. "They're so helpless, our patients. We have absolute control over their lives. I never saw it that way before. It's really rather frightening."

"So murder in the O.R. isn't that difficult."

"No," she conceded. "I guess it isn't."

"What about switching the EKG? How would our killer do that?"

"He'd have to get hold of the patient's chart. And they're all kept on the wards."

"That sounds tricky. The wards are crawling with nurses."

"True. But even in this day and age, nurses are still a little intimidated by a white coat. I bet if we put you in uniform, you'd be able to breeze your way right into the nurses' station, no questions asked."

He cocked his head. "Want to try it?"

"You mean right now?"

"Sure. Find me a white coat. I've always wanted to play doctor."

It took only a minute to locate a stray coat hanging in the surgeons' locker room. She knew it was Guy Santini's, just by the coffee stains on the front. The size 46 label only confirmed it.

"I didn't know King Kong was on your staff," David grunted, thrusting his arms into the huge sleeves. He buttoned up and stood straight. "What do you think? Are they going to fall down laughing?"

Stepping back, she gave him a critical look. The coat sagged on his shoulders. One side of the collar was turned up. But the truth was, he looked absolutely irresistible. And perversely untouchable. She smoothed down his collar. Just that brief contact, that brushing of her fingers against his neck, seemed to flood her whole arm with warmth.

"You'll do," she said.

"I look that bad?" He glanced down at the coffee stains. "I feel like a slob."

She laughed. "The owner of that particular coat *is* a slob. So don't worry about it. You'll fit right in." As they walked to the elevators, she added, "Just remember to think *doctor*. Get into the right mind-set. You know—brilliant, dedicated, compassionate."

"Don't forget *modest*."

She gave him a slap on the back. "Go get 'em, Dr. Kildare."

He stepped into the elevator. "Look, don't vanish on me, okay? If they get suspicious, I'll need you to back me up."

"I'll be waiting in the O.R. Oh, David…one last bit of advice."

"What's that?"

"Don't commit malpractice, Doctor. You might have to sue yourself."

He let out a groan as the doors snapped shut between them. The elevator whined faintly as it descended to the third floor. Then there was silence.

It was a simple test. Even if David was stopped by Security, it would take only a word from Kate to set him free. Nothing could possibly go wrong. But as she headed up the hallway, her uneasiness grew.

Back in O.R. 5, she settled into her usual seat near the head of the table and thought of all the hours she'd spent anchored to this one spot. A very small world. A very safe world.

The sound of a door slapping shut made her glance up. Why was David back so soon? Had there been trouble? She hopped off the stool and pushed into the corridor. There she halted.

Just down the hall, a faint crack of light shone through the door to O.R. 7. She listened for a moment and heard the rattle of cabinets, the squeal of a drawer sliding open.

Someone was rummaging through the supplies. A nurse? Or someone else—someone who didn't belong?

She glanced toward the far end of the corridor—her only route of escape. The reception desk lay around that corner. If she could just get safely past O.R. 7, she could slip out and call Security. She had to decide now; whoever was going through O.R. 7 might proceed to the other rooms. If she didn't move now, she'd be trapped.

Noiselessly she headed down the hall. The slam of a cabinet told her she wouldn't make it. O.R. 7's door suddenly swung open. Panicked, she reeled backward to see Dr. Clarence Avery freeze in the doorway. Something slid out of his hand and the sound of shattering glass seemed to reverberate endlessly in the hall. She took one look at his bloodlessly white face, and her fear instantly turned to concern. For a terrifying moment she thought he'd keel over right then and there of a heart attack.

"Dr.—Dr. Chesne," he stammered weakly. "I—I didn't expect— I mean, I..." Slowly he stared down at his feet; that's when she noticed, through the shadows, the sparkle of glass lying on the floor. He shook his head helplessly. "What...what a mess I've made...."

"It's not that bad," she responded quickly. "Here, I'll help you clean it up."

She flicked on the corridor lights. He didn't move. He just stood there, blinking in the sudden glare. She had never seen him look so old, so frail; the white hair seemed to tremble on his head. She grabbed a handful of paper towels from the scrub sink dispenser and offered him a few sheets, but he still didn't move. So she crouched at his feet and began gathering up the broken glass. He was wearing one blue sock and one white sock. As she reached for one of the shards, she noticed a label was still affixed.

"It's for my dog," he said weakly.

"Excuse me?"

"The potassium chloride. It's for my dog. She's very sick."

Kate looked up at him blankly. "I'm sorry" was all she could think of saying.

He lowered his head. "She needs to be put to sleep. All morning, she's been whimpering. I can't stand listening to it anymore. And she's old, you know. Over ninety in dog years. But it—it seems cruel, taking her to the vet for that. A total stranger. It would terrify her."

Kate rose to her feet. Avery just stood there, clutching the paper towels as if not quite sure what to do with them.

"I'm sure the vet would be gentle," she replied. "You don't have to do it yourself."

"But it's so much better if I do, don't you think? If I'm the one to tell her goodbye?"

She nodded. Then she turned to the anesthesia cart and took out a vial of potassium chloride. "Here—" She offered quietly, placing it in his hand. "This should be enough, don't you think?"

He nodded. "She's not a very…big dog." He let out a shaky breath and turned to leave. Then he stopped and looked back at her. "I've always liked you, Kate. You're the only one who never seemed to be laughing behind my back. Or dropping hints that I'm too old, that I ought to retire." He sighed and shook his head. "But maybe they're right, after all." As he turned to leave, she heard him say, "I'll do what I can at your hearing."

His footsteps creaked off into the corridor. As the sound faded away, her gaze settled on the bits of broken glass in the trash can. The label KCL stared up at her. Potassium chloride, she thought with a frown. When pushed intravenously, it was a deadly poison, resulting in sudden cardiac arrest. And it occurred to her that the same poison that would kill a dog could just as easily be used to kill a human being.

THE CLERK ON WARD 3B was hunched at her desk, clutching a paperback book. On the cover, a half-naked couple grappled beneath the blazing scarlet title: *His Wanton Bride*. She flipped a page. Her eyes widened. She didn't even notice David walk by. Only when he was standing right beside her in the nurses' station did she bother to glance up. Instantly flushing, she slapped down the book.

"Oh! Can I help you, Doctor…uh…"

"Smith," finished David and flashed her such a dazzling smile that she sank like melted jelly into her chair. *Wow,* he thought as he gazed into a pair of rapturous violet eyes. *This white coat really does the trick.* "I need to see one of your charts," he said.

"Which one?" she asked breathlessly.

"Room…er…" He glanced over at the chart rack. "Eight."

"A or B?"

"B."

"Mrs. Loomis?"

"Yes, that's the name. Loomis."

She seemed to float out of her chair. Swaying over to the chart rack, she struck a pose of slinky indifference. It took her an inordinately long time to locate Room 8B's chart, despite the fact it was staring her right in the face. David glanced down at the book cover and suddenly felt like laughing.

"Here it is," she chirped, holding it out to him in both hands, like some sort of sacred offering.

"Why, thank you, Ms…."

"Mann. Janet. Miss."

"Yes." He cleared his throat. Then, turning, he fled to a chair as far away as possible from Miss Janet Mann. He could almost hear her sigh of disappointment as she turned to answer a ringing telephone.

"Oh, all right." She sighed. "I'll bring them down right now." She grabbed a handful of red-stoppered blood tubes from the pickup tray and hurried out, leaving David alone in the station.

So that's all there is to it, he thought, flipping open the metal chart cover. The unfortunate Mrs. Loomis in room 8B was obviously a complicated case, judging by the thickness of her record and the interminable list of doctors on her case. Not only did she have a surgeon and anesthesiologist, there were numerous consultation notes by an internist, psychiatrist, dermatologist and gynecologist. He was reminded of the old saying about too many cooks. Like the proverbial broth, this poor lady didn't have a chance.

A nurse walked past, wheeling a medication cart. Another nurse slipped in for a moment to answer the ringing telephone then hurried out again. Neither woman paid him the slightest attention.

He flipped to the EKG, which was filed at the back of the chart. It would take maybe ten seconds to remove that one page and replace it with another. And with so many doctors passing through the ward—six for Mrs. Loomis alone—no one would notice a thing.

Murder, he decided, couldn't be easier. All it took was a white coat.

Chapter Nine

"I GUESS YOU PROVED YOUR point tonight," said David as he set two glasses of hot milk on the kitchen table. "About murder in the O.R."

"No, we didn't." Kate looked down bleakly at the steaming glass. "We didn't prove a thing, David. Except that the chief of anesthesia's got a sick dog." She sighed. "Poor old Avery. I must have scared the wits out of him."

"Sounds like you scared the wits out of each other. By the way, does he have a dog?"

"He wouldn't lie to me."

"I'm just asking. I don't know the man." He took a sip of milk and it left a faint white mustache on his stubbled lip. He seemed dark and out of place in his gleaming kitchen. A faint beard shadowed his jaw, and his shirt, which had started out so crisp this morning, was now mapped with wrinkles. He'd undone his top button and she felt a peculiar sense of weightlessness as she caught a glimpse of dark gold hair matting his chest.

She looked down fiercely at her milk. "I'm pretty sure he does have a dog," she continued. "In fact, I remember seeing a picture on his desk."

"He keeps a picture of a dog on his desk?"

"It's of his wife, really. She's holding this sort of brownish terrier. She was really very beautiful."

"I take it you mean his wife."

"Yes. She had a stroke a few months ago. It devastated that poor man, to put her in a nursing home. He's been shuffling through his duties ever since." Mournfully she took a sip. "I bet he couldn't do it."

"Do what?"

"Kill his dog. Some people are incapable of hurting a fly."

"While others are perfectly capable of murder."

She looked at him. "You still think it *was* murder?"

He didn't answer for a moment, and his silence frightened her. Was her only ally slipping away? "I don't know what I think." He sighed. "So far I've been going on instinct, not facts. And that won't hold up in a courtroom."

"Or a committee hearing," she added morosely.

"Your hearing's on Tuesday?"

"And I still haven't the faintest idea what to tell them."

"Can't you get a delay? I'll cancel my appointments tomorrow. Maybe we can pull together some evidence."

"I've already asked for a delay. It was turned down. Anyway, there doesn't seem to *be* any evidence. All we have is a pair of murders, with no obvious connection to Ellen's death."

He sat back, frowning at the table. "What if the police are barking up the wrong tree? What if Charlie Decker's just a wild card?"

"They found his fingerprints, David. And I saw him there."

"But you didn't actually see him kill anyone."

"No. But who else had a motive?"

"Let's think about this for a minute." Idly, David reached for the saltshaker and set it in the center of the table. "We know Henry Tanaka was a very busy man. And I'm not talking about his practice. He was having an affair—" David moved the pepper shaker next to the salt "—probably with Ann Richter."

"Okay. But where does Ellen fit in?"

"That's the million-dollar question." He reached over and tapped the sugar jar. "Where does Ellen O'Brien fit in?"

Kate frowned. "A love triangle?"

"Possible. But a man doesn't have to stop at one mistress. He could've had a dozen. And they each in turn could have had jealous lovers."

"Triangles within triangles? This sounds wilder by the minute. All this romping around in bedrooms! Doctors having affairs left and right! I just can't picture it."

"It happens. And not just in hospitals."

"Law offices, too, hmm?"

"I'm not saying *I've* done it. But we're all human."

She couldn't help smiling. "It's funny. When we first met, I didn't think of you as being particularly human."

"No?"

"You were a threat. The enemy. Just another damn lawyer."

"Oh. Scum of the earth, you mean."

"You did play the part well."

He winced. "Thanks a lot."

"But it's not that way anymore," she said quickly. "I can't think of you as just another lawyer. Not since…"

Her voice faded as their eyes suddenly locked.

"Not since I kissed you," he finished softly.

Warmth flooded her cheeks. Abruptly she rose to her feet and carried the glass to the sink, all the time aware of his gaze on her back. "It's all gotten so complicated," she commented with a sigh.

"What? The fact I'm human?"

"The fact we're *both* human," she blurted out. Even without looking at him, she could sense the attraction, the electricity, crackling between them.

She washed the glass. Twice. Then, calmly, deliberately, she sat back down at the table. He was watching her, a wry look of amusement on his face.

"I'll be the first to admit it," he said, his eyes twinkling. "It *is* a hell of an inconvenience, being human. A slave to all those pesky biological urges."

Biological urges. What a hopelessly pale description of the hormonal storm now raging inside her. Avoiding his gaze, she focused on the saltshaker, sitting at the center of the table. She thought suddenly of Henry Tanaka. Of triangles within triangles. Had all those deaths been a consequence of nothing more than lust and jealousy gone berserk?

"You're right," she agreed, thoughtfully touching the saltshaker. "Being human leads to all sorts of complications. Even murder."

She sensed his tension before he even spoke a word. His gaze fell on the table and all at once he went completely still. "I can't believe we didn't think of it."

"Of what?" she asked.

He shoved his empty glass toward the sugar jar. It gave the diagram a fourth corner. "We're not dealing with a triangle. It's a *square*."

There was a pause. "Your grasp of geometry is really quite amazing," she said politely.

"What if Tanaka *did* have a second girlfriend—Ellen O'Brien?"

"That's our old triangle."

"But we've left someone out. Someone very important." He tapped the empty milk glass.

Kate frowned at the four objects on the table. "My God," she whispered. "Mrs. Tanaka."

"Exactly."

"I never even thought of his wife."

He looked up. "Maybe it's time we did."

THE JAPANESE WOMAN WHO opened the clinic door was wearing fire-engine-red lipstick and face powder that was several shades too pale for her complexion. She looked like a fugitive from a geisha house. "Then you're not with the police?" she asked.

"Not exactly," replied David. "But we do have a few questions—"

"I'm not talking to any more reporters." She started to shut the door.

"We're not reporters, Mrs. Tanaka. I'm an attorney. And this is Dr. Kate Chesne."

"Well, what do you want, then?"

"We're trying to get information about another murder. It's related to your husband's death."

Sudden interest flickered in the woman's eyes. "You're talking about that nurse, aren't you? That Richter woman."

"Yes."

"What do you know about her?"

"We'll be glad to tell you everything we know. If you'll just let us come in."

She hesitated, curiosity and caution waging a battle in her eyes. Curiosity won. She opened the door and gestured for them to come into the waiting room. She was tall for a Japanese; taller, even, than Kate. She was wearing a simple blue dress and high heels and gold seashell earrings. Her hair was so black it might have looked artificial had there not been the single white strand tracing her right temple. Mari Tanaka was a remarkably beautiful woman.

"You'll have to excuse the mess," she apologized, pausing in the impeccably neat waiting room. "But there's been so much confusion. So many things to take care of." She gazed around at the deserted couches, as though wondering where all the patients had gone. Magazines were still arrayed on the coffee table and a box of children's toys sat in the corner, waiting to be played with. The only hint that tragedy had struck this office was the sympathy card and a vase of white lilies, sent by a grieving patient. Through a glass partition in front of the reception desk, two women could be seen in the adjoining office, surrounded by stacks of files.

"There are so many patients to be referred," said Mrs. Tanaka with a sigh. "And all those outstanding bills. I had no idea things would be so chaotic. I always let Henry take care of everything. And now that he's gone…" She sank tiredly onto the couch. "I take it you know about my husband and that—that woman."

David nodded. "Did you?"

"Yes. I mean, I didn't know her name. But I knew there had to be someone. Funny, isn't it? How they say the wife is always the last to know." She gazed at the two women behind the glass partition. "I'm sure *they* knew about her. And people at the hospital, they must have known, as well. I was the only one who didn't. The *stupid* wife." She looked up. "You said you'd tell me about this woman. Ann Richter. What do you know about her?"

"I worked with her," Kate began.

"Did you?" Mrs. Tanaka shifted her gaze to Kate. "I never even met her. What was she like? Was she pretty?"

Kate hesitated, knowing instinctively that the other woman was only searching for more information with which to torture herself. Mari Tanaka seemed consumed by some bizarre need for self-punishment. "Ann was…attractive, I suppose," she said.

"Intelligent?"

Kate nodded. "She was a good nurse."

"So was I." Mrs. Tanaka bit her lip and looked away. "She was a blonde, I hear. Henry liked blondes. Isn't that ironic? He liked the one thing I couldn't be." She glanced at David with sudden feminine hostility. "And I suppose *you* like Oriental women."

"A beautiful woman is a beautiful woman," he replied, unruffled. "I don't discriminate."

She blinked back a veil of tears. "Henry did."

"Have there been other women?" Kate asked gently.

"I suppose." She shrugged. "He was a man, wasn't he?"

"Did you ever hear the name Ellen O'Brien?"

"Did she have some—connection with my husband?"

"We were hoping you could tell us."

Mrs. Tanaka shook her head. "He never mentioned any names. But then, I never asked any questions."

Kate frowned. "Why not?"

"I didn't want him to lie to me." Somehow, by the way she said it, it made perfect sense.

"Have the police told you there's a suspect?" David asked.

"You mean Charles Decker?" Mrs. Tanaka's gaze shifted back to David. "Sergeant Brophy came to see me yesterday afternoon. He showed me the man's photograph."

"Did you recognize the face?"

"I never saw the man, Mr. Ransom. I didn't even know his name. All I knew was that my husband was attacked by some psychotic five years ago. And that the stupid police let the man go the very next day."

"But your husband refused to press charges," said David.

"He what?"

"That's why Decker was released so quickly. It seems your husband wanted the matter dropped."

"He never told me that."

"What did he tell you?"

"Almost nothing. But there were lots of things we never talked about. That's how we managed to stay together all these years. By not talking about certain things. It was almost an agreement. He didn't ask how I spent the money. I didn't ask about his women."

"Then you don't know anything more about Decker?"

"No. But maybe Peggy can help you."

"Peggy?"

She nodded toward the office. "Our receptionist. She was here when it happened."

Peggy was a blond, fortyish Amazon wearing white stretch pants. Though invited to sit, she preferred to stand. Or maybe she simply preferred not to occupy the same couch as Mari Tanaka.

"Remember the man?" Peggy repeated. "I'll never forget him. I was cleaning up one of the exam rooms when I heard all this yelling. I came right out and that psychotic was here, in the waiting room. He had his hands around Henry's—the doctor's—neck and he kept screaming at him."

"You mean cursing him?"

"No, not cursing. He said something like 'What did you do with her?'"

"Those were his words? You're sure?"

"Pretty sure."

"And who was this 'her' he was referring to? One of the patients?"

"Yes. And the doctor felt just awful about that case. She was such a nice woman, and to have both her and the baby die. Well…"

"What was her name?"

"Jenny… Let me think. Jenny something. Brook. I think that was it. Jennifer Brook."

"What did you do after you saw the doctor being attacked?"

"Well, I pulled the man away, of course. What do you think I did? He was holding on tight, but I got him off. Women aren't completely helpless, you know."

"Yes, I'm quite aware of that."

"Anyway, he sort of collapsed then."

"The doctor?"

"No, the man. He crumpled in this little heap over there, by the coffee table and he just sat there, crying. He was still there when the police arrived. A few days later, we heard he'd shot himself. In the mouth." She paused and stared at the floor, as though seeing some ghostlike remnant of the man, still sitting there. "It's weird, but I couldn't help feeling sorry for him. He was crying like a baby. I think even Henry felt sorry...."

"Mrs. Tanaka?" The other clerk poked her head into the waiting room. "You have a phone call. It's your accountant. I'll transfer it to the back office."

Mrs. Tanaka rose. "There's really nothing more we can tell you," she said. "And we do have to get back to work." She shot Peggy a meaningful glance. Then, with only the barest nod of goodbye, she walked sleekly out of the waiting room.

"Two weeks' notice," Peggy muttered sullenly. "That's what she gave us. And then she expects us to get the whole damn office in order. No wonder Henry didn't want that witch hanging around." She turned to go back to her desk.

"Peggy?" asked Kate. "Just one more question, if you don't mind. When your patients die, how long do you keep the medical records?"

"Five years. Longer if it's an obstetrical death. You know, in case some malpractice suit gets filed."

"Then you still have Jenny Brook's chart?"

"I'm sure we do." She went into the office and pulled open the filing cabinet. She went through the B drawer twice. Then she checked the J's. In frustration, she slammed the drawer closed. "I can't understand it. It should be here."

David and Kate glanced at each other. "It's missing?" said Kate.

"Well, it's not here. And I'm very careful about these things. Let me tell you, I do not run a sloppy office." She turned and glared at the other clerk as though expecting a dissenting opinion. There was none.

"What are you saying?" said David. "That someone's removed it?"

"He must have," replied Peggy. "But I can't see why he would. It's barely been five years."

"Why *who* would?"

Peggy looked at him as if he was dim-witted. "Dr. Tanaka, of course."

"JENNIFER BROOK," SAID the hospital records clerk in a flat voice as she typed the name into the computer. "Is that with or without an *e* at the end?"

"I don't know," answered Kate.

"Middle initial?"

"I don't know."

"Date of birth?"

Kate and David looked at each other. "We don't know," replied Kate.

The clerk turned and peered at them over her horn-rimmed glasses. "I don't suppose you'd know the medical-record number?" she asked in a weary monotone.

They shook their heads.

"That's what I was afraid of." The clerk swiveled back to her terminal and punched in another command. After a few seconds, two names appeared on the screen, a Brooke and a Brook, both with the first name Jennifer. "Is it one of these?" she questioned.

A glance at the dates of birth told them one was fifty-seven years old, the other fifteen.

"No," said Kate.

"It figures." The clerk sighed and cleared the screen. "Dr. Chesne," she continued with excruciating patience, "why, exactly, do you need this particular record?"

"It's a research project," Kate said. "Dr. Jones and I—"

"Dr. Jones?" The clerk looked at David. "I don't remember a Dr. Jones on our staff."

Kate said quickly, "He's with the University—"

"Of Arizona," David finished with a smile.

"It's all been cleared through Avery's office. It's a paper on maternal death and—"

"Death?" The clerk blinked. "You mean this patient is deceased?"

"Yes."

"Well, no wonder. We keep those files in a totally different place." From her tone, their other file room might have been on Mars. She rose reluctantly from her chair. "This will take a while. You'll have to wait." Turning, she headed at a snail's pace toward a back door and vanished into what was no doubt the room for deceased persons' files.

"Why do I get the feeling we'll never see her again?" muttered David.

Kate sagged weakly against the counter. "Just be glad she

didn't ask for your credentials. I could get in big trouble for this, you know. Showing hospital records to the enemy."

"Who, me?"

"You're a lawyer, aren't you?"

"I'm just poor old Dr. Jones from Arizona." He turned and glanced around the room. At a corner table, a doctor was yawning as he turned a page. An obviously bored clerk wheeled a cart up the aisle, collecting charts and slapping them onto an already precarious stack. "Lively place," he remarked. "When does the dancing start?"

They both turned at the sound of footsteps. The clerk with the horn-rimmed glasses reappeared, empty-handed.

"The chart's not there," she announced.

Kate and David stared at her in stunned silence.

"What do you mean, it's not there?" asked Kate.

"It should be. But it's not."

"Was it released from the hospital?" David snapped.

The clerk looked aridly over her glasses. "We don't release originals, Dr. Jones. People always lose them."

"Oh. Well, of course."

The clerk sank down in front of the computer and typed in a command. "See? There's the listing. It's supposed to be in the file room. All I can say is it must've been misplaced." She added, under her breath, "Which means we'll probably never see it again." She was about to clear the screen when David stopped her.

"Wait. What's that notation there?" he asked, pointing to a cryptic code.

"That's a chart copy request."

"You mean someone requested a copy?"

"Yes," the clerk sighed wearily. "That is what it means, Doctor."

"Who asked for it?"

She shifted the cursor and punched another button. A name and address appeared magically on the screen. "Joseph Kahanu, Attorney at Law, Alakea Street. Date of request: March 2."

David frowned. "That's only a month ago."

"Yes, Doctor, I do believe it is."

"An attorney. Why the hell would he be interested in a death that happened five years ago?"

The clerk turned and looked at him dryly over her horn-rimmed glasses. “You tell me.”

THE PAINT IN THE HALL WAS chipping and thousands of footsteps had worn a path down the center of the threadbare carpet. Outside the office hung a sign:

Joseph Kahanu, Attorney at Law

Specialist in Divorce, Child Custody, Wills, Accidents, Insurance, Drunk Driving, and Personal Injury

“Great address,” whispered David. “Rats must outnumber the clients.” He knocked on the door.

It was answered by a huge Hawaiian man dressed in an ill-fitting suit. “You’re David Ransom?” he asked gruffly.

David nodded. “And this is Dr. Chesne.”

The man’s silent gaze shifted for a moment to Kate’s face. Then he stepped aside and gestured sullenly toward a pair of rickety chairs. “Yeah, come in.”

The office was suffocating. A table fan creaked back and forth, churning the heat. A half-open window, opaque with dirt, looked out over an alley. In one glance, Kate recognized all the signs of a struggling law practice: the ancient typewriter, the cardboard boxes stuffed with client files, the secondhand furniture. There was scarcely enough room for the lone desk. Kahanu looked unbearably hot in his suit jacket; he’d probably pulled it on at the last minute, just for the benefit of his visitors.

“I haven’t called the police yet,” said Kahanu, settling into an unreliable-looking swivel chair.

“Why not?” asked David.

“I don’t know how you run *your* practice, but I make it a point not to squeal on my clients.”

“You’re aware Decker’s wanted for murder.”

Kahanu shook his head. “It’s a mistake.”

“Did Decker tell you that?”

“I haven’t been able to reach him.”

“Maybe it’s time the police found him for you.”

“Look,” Kahanu shot back. “We both know I’m not in your

league, Ransom. I hear you got some big-shot office over on Bishop Street. Couple of dozen lapdog associates. Probably spend your weekends on the golf course, cozying up to some judge or other. Me?" He waved around at his office and laughed. "I got just a few clients. Most times they don't even remember to pay me. But they're my clients. And I don't like to go against 'em."

"You know two people have been murdered."

"They got no proof he did it."

"The police say they do. They say Charlie Decker's a dangerous man. A sick man. He needs help."

"That what they call a jail cell these days? Help?" Disgusted, he fished out a handkerchief and mopped his brow, as though buying time to think. "Guess I got no choice now," he muttered. "One way or the other, police'll be banging on my door." Slowly he folded the handkerchief and tucked it back in his pocket. Then, reaching into his drawer, he pulled out a folder and tossed it on the battered desk. "There's the copy you asked for. Seems you're not the only who one wants it."

David frowned as he reached for the folder. "Has someone else asked for it?"

"No. But someone broke into my office."

David looked up sharply. "When?"

"Last week. Tore apart all my files. Didn't steal anything, and I even had fifty bucks in the cash box. I couldn't figure it out at the time. But this morning, after you told me about those missing records, I got to thinking. Wondering if that file's what he was after."

"But he didn't get it."

"The night he broke in, I had the papers at home."

"Is this your only copy?"

"No. I ran off a few just now. Just to be safe."

"May I take a look?" Kate asked.

David hesitated, then handed her the chart. "You're the doctor. Go ahead."

She stared for a moment at the name on the cover: Jennifer Brook. Then, flipping it open, she began to read.

Recorded on the first few pages was a routine obstetrical admission. The patient, a healthy twenty-eight-year-old woman at thirty-six weeks of pregnancy, had entered Mid Pac Hospital in the early stages of labor. The initial history and physical exam, performed by Dr. Tanaka, were unremarkable. The fetal heart tones were normal, as were all the blood tests. Kate turned to the delivery-room record.

Here things began to go wrong. Terribly wrong. The nurse's painstakingly neat handwriting broadened into a frantic scrawl. The entries became terse, erratic. A young woman's death was distilled down to a few coldly clinical phrases.

> Generalized seizures… No response to Valium and Dilantin… Stat page to E.R. for assistance… Respirations now irregular… Respirations ceased… No pulse… Cardiac massage started… Fetal heart tones audible but slowing… Still no pulse… Dr. Vaughn from E.R. to assist with stat C-section… Live infant…

The record became a short series of blotted-out sentences, totally unreadable.

On the next page was the last entry, written in a calm hand.

> Resuscitation stopped. Patient pronounced dead at 01:30.

"She died of a cerebral hemorrhage," Kahanu said. "She was only twenty-eight."

"And the baby?" Kate asked.

"A girl. She died an hour after the mother."

"Kate," David murmured, nudging her arm. "Look at the bottom of the page. The names of the personnel in attendance."

Kate's gaze dropped to the three names. As she took them in one by one, her hands went icy.

Henry Tanaka, M.D.
Ann Richter, RN
Ellen O'Brien, RN

"They left out a name," Kate pointed out. She looked up. "There was a Dr. Vaughn, from the E.R. He might be able to tell us—"

"He can't," said Kahanu. "You see, Dr. Vaughn had an accident a short time after Jennifer Brook died. His car was hit head-on."

"You mean he's dead?"

Kahanu nodded. "They're all dead."

The chart slid from her frozen fingers onto the desk. There was something dangerous about this document, something evil. She stared down, unwilling to touch it, for fear the contagion would rub off.

Kahanu turned his troubled gaze to the window. "Four weeks ago Charlie Decker came to my office. Who knows why he chose me? Maybe I was convenient. Maybe he couldn't afford anyone else. He wanted a legal opinion about a possible malpractice suit."

"On this case?" said David. "But Jenny Brook died five years ago. And Decker wasn't even a relative. You know as well as I do the lawsuit would've been tossed right out."

"He paid for my services, Mr. Ransom. In cash."

In cash. Those were magic words for a lawyer who was barely surviving.

"I did what he asked. I subpoenaed the chart for him. I contacted the doctor and the two nurses who'd cared for Jenny Brook. But they never answered my letters."

"They didn't live long enough," explained David. "Decker got to them first."

"Why should he?"

"Vengeance. They killed the woman he loved. So he killed them."

"My client didn't kill anyone."

"Your client had the motive, Kahanu. And you provided him with their names and addresses."

"You've never met Decker. I have. And he's not a violent man."

"You'd be surprised how ordinary a killer can seem. I used to face them in court—"

"And I *defend* them! I take on the scum no one else'll touch. I *know* a killer when I see one. There's something different about them, about their eyes. Something's missing. I don't know what it is. A soul, maybe. I tell you, Charlie Decker wasn't like that."

Kate leaned forward. "What was he like, Mr. Kahanu?" she asked quietly.

The Hawaiian paused, his gaze wandering out the dirty window to the alley below. "He was—he was real… ordinary. Not tall, but not too short, either. Mostly skin and bones, like he wasn't eating right. I felt sorry for him. He looked like a man who's had his insides kicked out. He didn't say much. But he wrote things down for me. I think it hurt him to use his voice. He's got something wrong with his throat and he couldn't talk much louder than a whisper. He was sitting right there in that chair where you are now, Dr. Chesne. Said he didn't have much money. Then he took out his wallet and counted out these twenty-dollar bills, one at a time. I could see, just by the way he handled them, real slow and careful, that it was everything he had." Kahanu shook his head. "I still don't see why he even bothered, you know? The woman's dead. The baby's dead. All this digging around in the past, it won't bring 'em back."

"Do you know where to find him?" asked David.

"He has a P.O. box," said Kahanu. "I already checked. He hasn't picked up his mail in three days."

"Do you have his address? Phone number?"

"Never gave me one. Look, I don't know where he is. I'll leave it to the police to find him. That's their job, isn't it?" He pushed away from the desk. "That's all I know. If you want anything else, you'll have to get it from Decker."

"Who happens to be missing," said David.

To which Kahanu added darkly: "Or dead."

Chapter Ten

IN HIS FORTY-EIGHT YEARS as cemetery groundskeeper, Ben Hoomalu had seen his share of peculiar happenings. His friends liked to say it was because he was tramping around dead people all day, but in fact it wasn't the dead who caused all the mischief but the living: the randy teenagers groping in the darkness among the gravestones; the widow scrawling obscenities on her husband's nice new marble tombstone; the old man caught trying to bury his beloved poodle next to his beloved wife. Strange goings-on—that's what a fellow saw around cemeteries.

And now here was that car, back again.

Every day for the past week Ben had seen the same gray Ford with the darkly tinted windows drive through the gates. Sometimes it'd show up early in the morning, other times late in the afternoon. It would park over by the Arch of Eternal Comfort and just sit there for an hour or two. The driver never got out; that was odd, too. If a person came all this way to visit a loved one, wouldn't you think he'd at least get out and take a look at the grave?

There was no figuring out some folks.

Ben picked up the hedge clippers and started trimming the hibiscus bush. He liked hearing the clack, clack of the blades in the afternoon stillness. He looked up as a beat-up old Chevy drove through the gate and parked. A spindly man emerged from the car and waved at Ben. Smiling, Ben waved back. The man was carrying a bunch of daisies as he headed toward the woman's grave. Ben paused and watched the man go about his ritual. First, he gathered up the wilted flowers left behind on his previous visit and meticulously collected all the dead leaves and twigs. Then, after laying his new offering beside the stone, he settled reverentially on the grass. Ben knew the man would sit there a long time; he always did. Every visit was exactly the same. That was part of the comfort.

By the time the man got up to leave, Ben had finished with the hibiscus and was working on the bougainvillea. He watched the man walk slowly back to the car and felt a twinge of sadness as the old Chevy wound along the road toward the cemetery gates. He didn't even know the man's name; he only knew that whoever lay buried in that grave was still very much loved. He dropped his hedge clippers and wandered over to where the fresh daisies lay bundled together in a pink ribbon. There was still a dent in the grass where the man had knelt.

The purr of another car starting up caught his attention and he saw the gray Ford pull away from the curb and slowly follow the Chevy out the cemetery gates.

And what did *that* mean? Funny goings-on, all right.

He looked down at the name on the stone: Jennifer Brook, 28 years old. Already a dead leaf had blown onto the grave and now lay trembling in the wind. He shook his head.

Such a young woman. Such a shame.

"YOU GOT A HAM ON RYE, hold the mayo, and a call on line four," said Sergeant Brophy, dropping a brown bag on the desk.

Pokie, faced with the choice between a sandwich and a blinking telephone, reached for the sandwich. After all, a man had to set his priorities, and he figured a growling stomach ranked somewhere near the top of anyone's priority list. He nodded at the phone. "Who's calling?"

"Ransom."

"Not again."

"He's demanding we open a file on the O'Brien case."

"Why the hell's he keep bugging us about that case, anyway?"

"I think he's got a thing for that—that—" Brophy's face suddenly screwed up as he teetered on the brink of a sneeze and he whipped out a handkerchief just in time to muffle the explosion "—doctor lady. You know. Hearts 'n' flowers."

"Davy?" Pokie laughed out a clump of ham sandwich. "Men like Davy don't go for hearts 'n' flowers. Think they're too damn smart for all that romantic crap."

"No man's that smart," Brophy said glumly.

There was a knock on the door and a uniformed officer poked his head into the office. "Lieutenant? You got a summons from on high."

"Chief?"

"He's stuck with an office full of reporters. They're askin' about that missing Sasaki girl. Wants ya up there like ten minutes ago."

Pokie looked down regretfully at his sandwich. Unfortunately, on that cosmic list of priorities, a summons from the chief ranked somewhere on a par with breathing. Sighing, he left the sandwich on his desk and pulled on his jacket.

"What about Ransom?" reminded Brophy, nodding at the blinking telephone.

"Tell him I'll call him back."

"When?"

"Next year," Pokie grunted as he headed for the door. He added under his breath, "If he's lucky."

DAVID MUTTERED AN OATH as he slid into the driver's seat and slammed the car door. "We just got the brush-off."

Kate stared at him. "But they've seen Jenny Brook's file. They've talked to Kahanu—"

"They say there's not enough evidence to open a murder investigation. As far as they're concerned, Ellen O'Brien died of malpractice. End of subject."

"Then we're on our own."

"Wrong. We're pulling out." Suddenly agitated, he started the engine and drove away from the curb. "Things are getting too dangerous."

"They've been dangerous from the start. Why are you getting cold feet now?"

"Okay, I admit it. Up till now I wasn't sure I believed you—"

"You thought I was *lying*?"

"There was always this—this nagging doubt in the back of my mind. But now we're hearing about stolen hospital charts. People breaking into lawyer's offices. There's something weird going on here, Kate. This isn't the work of a raging psychopath. It's too reasoned. Too methodical." He frowned at the road ahead. "And it all has to do with Jenny Brook. There's something dangerous about her hospital chart, something our killer wants to keep hidden."

"But we've gone over that thing a dozen times, David! It's just a medical record."

"Then we're overlooking something. And I'm counting on Charlie Decker to tell us what it is. I say we sit tight and wait for the police to find him."

Charlie Decker, she thought. Her doom or her salvation? She stared out at the late-afternoon traffic and tried to remember his face. Up till now, the image had been jelled in fear; every time she'd thought of his face in the mirror, she'd felt an automatic surge of terror. Now she tried to ignore the sweat forming on her palms, the racing of her pulse. She forced herself to think of that face with its tired, hollow eyes. Killer's eyes? She didn't know anymore. She looked down at Jenny Brook's chart, lying on her lap. Did it contain some vital clue to Decker's madness?

"I'll corner Pokie tomorrow," said David, weaving impatiently through traffic. "See if I can't change his mind about the O'Brien case."

"And if you can't convince him?"

"I'm very convincing."

"He'll want more evidence."

"Then let *him* find it. I think we've gone as far as we can on this. It's time for us to back off."

"I can't, David. I have a career at stake—"

"What about your life?"

"My career is my life."

"There's one helluva big difference."

She turned away. "I can't really expect you to understand. It's not your fight."

But he did understand. And it worried him, that note of stubbornness in her voice. She reminded him of one of those ancient warriors who'd rather fall on their swords than accept defeat.

"You're wrong," he told her. "About it not being my fight."

"You don't have anything at stake."

"Don't forget I pulled out of the case—a potentially lucrative case, I might add."

"Oh. Well, I'm sorry I cost you such a nice fee."

"You think I care about the money? I don't give a damn about the money. It's my reputation I put on the line. And all because I happened to believe that crazy story of yours. Murder on the operating table! I'm going to look like a fool if it can't be proved. So don't tell me I have nothing to lose!" By now he was yelling. He couldn't help it. She could accuse him of any number of things and he wouldn't bat an eye. But accusing him of not giving a damn was something he couldn't stand.

Gripping the steering wheel, he forced his gaze back to the road. "The worst part is," he muttered, "I'm a lousy liar. And I think the O'Briens can tell."

"You mean you didn't tell them the truth?"

"That I think their daughter was murdered? Hell, no. I took the easy way out. I told them I had a conflict of interest. A nice, noncommittal excuse. I figured they couldn't get too upset since I'm referring the case to a good firm."

"You're doing *what*?" She stared at him.

"I was their attorney, Kate. I have to protect their interests."

"Naturally."

"This hasn't been easy, you know," he went on. "I don't like to shortchange my clients. Any of them. They're dealing with enough tragedy in their lives. The least I can do is see they get a decent shot at justice. It bothers the hell out of me when I can't deliver what I promise. You understand that, don't you?"

"Yes. I understand perfectly well."

He knew by the hurt tone of her voice that she really didn't. And that annoyed him because he thought she should understand.

She sat motionless as he pulled into the driveway. He parked the car and turned off the engine but she made no move to get out. They lingered there in the shadowy heat of the garage as the silence between them stretched into minutes. When she finally spoke again, it was in the flat tones of a stranger.

"I've put you in a compromising position, haven't I?"

His answer was a curt nod.

"I'm sorry."

"Look, forget about it, okay?" He got out and opened her door. She was still sitting there, rigid as a statue. "Well?" he asked. "Are you coming inside?"

"Only to pack."

He felt an odd little thump of dismay in his chest, which he tried to ignore. "You're leaving?"

"I appreciate what you've done for me," she answered tightly. "You went out on a limb and you didn't have to. Maybe, at the start, we needed each other. But it's obvious this…arrangement is no longer in your best interests. Or mine, for that matter."

"I see," he said, though he didn't. In fact he thought she was acting childishly. "And just where do you plan to go?"

"I'll stay with friends."

"Oh, great. Spread the danger to them."

"Then I'll check into a hotel."

"Your purse was stolen, remember? You don't have any money, credit cards." He paused for dramatic effect. "No nothing."

"Not at the moment, but—"

"Or are you planning to ask me for a loan?"

"I don't need your help," she snapped. "I've never needed any man's help!"

He briefly considered the old-fashioned method of brute force, but knowing her sense of pride, he didn't think it would work. So he simply retorted, "Suit yourself," and stalked off to the house.

While she was packing, he paced back and forth in the kitchen, trying to ignore his growing sense of uneasiness. He grabbed a carton of milk out of the refrigerator and took a gulp straight from the container. *I should order her to stay,* he thought. *Yes, that's exactly what I should do.* He shoved the milk back in the refrigerator, slammed the door and stormed toward her bedroom.

But just as he got there, he pulled himself up short. Bad idea.

He knew exactly how she'd react if he started shouting out orders. You just didn't push a woman like Kate Chesne around. Not if you were smart.

He hulked in the doorway and watched as she folded a dress and tucked it neatly into a suitcase. The fading daylight was glimmering behind her in the window. She swept back a stray lock of hair and a lead weight seemed to lodge in his throat as he glimpsed the bruised cheek. It reminded him how vulnerable she really was. Despite her pride and her so-called independence, she was really just a woman. And like any woman, she could be hurt.

She noticed him in the doorway and she paused, nightgown in hand. "I'm almost finished," she said, matter-of-factly tossing the nightgown on top of the other clothes. He couldn't help glancing twice at the mound of peach-colored silk. He felt that lead weight drop into his belly. "Have you called a cab yet?" she asked, turning back to the dresser.

"No, I haven't."

"Well, I shouldn't be a minute. Could you call one now?"

"I'm not going to."

She turned and frowned at him. "What?"

"I said I'm not going to call a cab."

His announcement seemed to leave her momentarily stunned. "Fine," she said calmly. "Then I'll call one myself." She started for the door. But as she walked past him, he caught her by the arm.

"Kate, don't." He pulled her around to face him. "I think you should stay."

"Why?"

"Because it's not safe out there."

"The world's never been safe. I've managed."

"Oh, yeah. What a tough broad you are. And what happens when Decker catches up?"

She yanked her arm away. "Don't you have better things to worry about?"

"Like what?"

"Your sense of ethics? After all, I wouldn't want to ruin your precious reputation."

"I can take care of my own reputation, thank you."

She threw her head back and glared straight up at him. "Then maybe it's time I took better care of mine!"

They were standing so close he could almost feel the heat mounting in waves between them. What happened next was as unexpected as a case of spontaneous combustion. Their gazes locked. Her eyes suddenly went wide with surprise. And need. Despite all her false bravado, he could see it brimming there in those deep, green pools.

"What the hell," he growled, his voice rough with desire. "I think both our reputations are already shot."

And then he gave in to the impulse that had been battering at his willpower all day. He hauled her close into his arms and kissed her. It was a long and savagely hungry kiss. She gave a weak murmur of protest, just before she sagged backward against the doorway. Almost immediately he felt her respond, her body molding itself against his. It was a perfect fit. Absolutely perfect. Her arms twined around his neck and as he urged her lips apart with his, the kiss became desperately urgent. Her moan sent a sweet agony of desire knifing through to his belly.

The same sweet fire was now engulfing Kate. She felt him fumbling for the buttons of her dress but his fingers seemed as clumsy as a teenager's exploring the unfamiliar territory of a woman's body. With a groan of frustration, he tugged the dress off her shoulders; it seemed to fall in slow motion, hissing down her hips to the floor. The lace bra magically melted away and his hand closed around her breast, branding her flesh with his fingers. Under his pleasuring stroke, her nipple hardened instantly and they both knew that this time there would be no retreat; only surrender.

Already she was groping at his shirt, her breath coming in hot, frantic little whimpers as she tried to work the buttons free. Damn. Damn. Now they were both yanking at the shirt. Together they stripped it off his shoulders and she immediately sought his chest, burying her fingers in the bristling gold hairs.

By the time they'd stumbled down the hall and into the evening glow of his bedroom, his shoes and socks were tossed to the four corners of the room, his pants were unzipped and his arousal was plainly evident.

The bed creaked in protest as he fell on top of her, his hands trapping her face beneath his. There were no preludes, no formalities. They couldn't wait. With his mouth covering hers and his hands buried in her hair, he thrust into her, so deeply that she cried out against his lips.

He froze, his whole body suddenly tense. "Did I hurt you?" he whispered.

"No…oh, no…."

It took only one look at her face to tell him it wasn't pain that had made her cry out, but pleasure—in him, in what he was doing to her. She tried to move; he held her still, his face taut as he struggled for control. Somehow, she'd always known he would claim her. Even when the voice of common sense had told her it was impossible, she'd known he would be the one.

She couldn't wait. She was moving in spite of him, matching agony for agony.

He let her take him to the very brink and then, when he knew it was inevitable, he surrendered himself to the fall. In a frenzy he took control and plunged them both over the cliff.

The drop was dizzying.

The landing left them weak and exhausted. An eternity passed, filled with the sounds of their breathing. Sweat trickled over his back and onto her naked belly. Outside, the waves roared against the seawall.

"Now I know what it's like to be devoured," she whispered as the glow of sunset faded in the window.

"Is that what I did?"

She sighed. "Completely."

He chuckled and his mouth glided warmly to her earlobe. "No, I think there's still something here to eat."

She closed her eyes, surrendering to the lovely ripples of pleasure his mouth inspired. "I never dreamed you'd be like this."

"Like what?"

"So…consuming."

"Just what did you expect?"

"Ice." She laughed. "Was I ever wrong!"

He took a strand of her hair and watched it drift like a cloud of silk through his fingers. "I guess I can seem pretty icy. It runs in my family. My father's side, anyway. Stern old New England stock. It must've been terrifying to face him in court."

"He was a lawyer, too?"

"Circuit-court judge. He died four years ago. Keeled over on the bench, right in the middle of sentencing. Just the way he would've wanted to go." He smiled. "Run-'em-in Ransom, they used to call him."

"Oh. The law-and-order type?"

"Absolutely. Unlike my mother, who thrives on anarchy."

She giggled. "It must have been an explosive combination."

"Oh, it was." He stroked his finger across her lips. "Almost as explosive as we are. I never did figure out their relationship. It didn't make sense to me. But you could almost see the chemistry working between them. The sparks. That's what I remember about my parents, all those sparks, flying around the house."

"So they were happy?"

"Oh, yeah. Exhausted, maybe. Frustrated, a lot. But they were definitely happy."

Twilight glowed dimly through the window. In silent awe, he ran his hand along the peaks and valleys of her body, a slow and leisurely exploration that left her skin tingling. "You're beautiful," he whispered. "I never thought…"

"What?"

"That I'd end up in bed with a lawyer-hating doctor. Talk about strange bedfellows."

She laughed softly. "And I feel like a mouse cozying up to the cat."

"Does that mean you're still afraid of me?"

"A little. A lot."

"Why?"

"I can't quite get over the feeling you're the enemy."

"If I'm the enemy," he said, his lips grazing her ear, "then I think one of us has just surrendered."

"Is this all you ever think about, counselor?"

"Since I met you, it is."

"And before you met me?"

"Life was very, very dull."

"I find that hard to believe."

"I'm not saying I've been celibate. But I'm a careful man. Maybe too careful. I find it hard to…get close to people."

"You seem to be doing a pretty good job tonight."

"I mean, emotionally close. It's just the way I am. Too many things can go wrong and I'm not very good at dealing with them."

By the evening glow, she studied his face hovering just above hers. "What did go wrong with your marriage, David?"

"Oh. My marriage." He rolled over on his back and sighed. "Nothing, really. Nothing I can put my finger on. I guess that just goes to show you what an insensitive clod I am. Linda used to complain I was lousy at expressing my feelings. That I was cold, just like my father. I told her that was a lot of bull. Now I think she was right."

"And I think it's just an act of yours. An icy mask you like to hide behind." She rolled onto her side, to look at him. "People show affection in different ways."

"Since when did you go into psychiatry?"

"Since I got involved with a very complex man."

Gently he tucked a strand of hair behind her ear. His gaze lingered on her cheek. "That bruise of yours is already fading. Every time I see it I get angry."

"You told me once it turned you on."

"What it really does is make me feel protective. Must be some ancient male instinct. From the days when we had to keep the other cavemen from roughing up our personal property."

"Oh, my. We're talking *that* ancient, are we?"

"As ancient as—" his hand slid possessively down the curve of her hip "—this."

"I'm not so sure 'protective' is what you're feeling right now," she murmured.

"You're right. It's not." He laughed and gave her an affectionate pat on the rump. "What I'm feeling is starved—for food. Why don't we heat up some of Mrs. Feldman's spaghetti sauce. Open a bottle of wine. And then…" He drew her toward him and his skin seemed to sear right into hers.

"And then?" she whispered.

"And then…" His lips lingered maddeningly close. "I'll do to you what lawyers have been doing to doctors for decades."

"David!" she squealed.

"Hey, just kidding!" He threw his arms up in self-defense as she swung at him. "But I think you get the general idea." He pulled her out of bed and into his arms. "Come on. And stop looking so luscious, or we'll never get out of the room. They'll find us sprawled on the bed, starved to death."

She gave him a slow, naughty look. "Oh," she murmured, "but what a way to go."

IT WAS THE SOUND OF THE waves slapping the seawall that finally tugged Kate awake. Drowsily she reached out for David but her hand met only an empty pillow, warmed by the morning sun. She opened her eyes and felt a sharp sense of abandonment when she discovered that she was alone in the wide, rumpled bed.

"David?" she called out. There was no answer. The house was achingly silent.

She swung her legs around and sat up on the side of the bed. Naked and dazed, she peered slowly around the sunlit room and felt the color rise in her cheeks as the night's events came back to her. The bottle of wine. The wicked whispers. The hopelessly twisted sheets. She noticed that the clothes they'd both tossed aside so recklessly had all been picked up from the floor. His pants were hanging on the closet door; her bra and underwear were now draped neatly across a chair. It made her flush even hotter to think of him gathering up all her intimate apparel. Giggling, she hugged the sheets and found they still bore his scent. But where was he?

"David?"

She rose and went into the bathroom; it was empty. A damp towel hung on the rack. Next she wandered out into the living room and marveled at the morning sun, slanting in gloriously through the windows. The empty wine bottle was still sitting on the coffee table, mute evidence of the night's intoxication. She still felt intoxicated. She poked her head into the kitchen; he wasn't there, either. Back in the living room, she paused in that brilliant flood of sunlight and called out his name. The whole house seemed to echo with loneliness.

Her sense of desolation grew as she headed back up the hall, searching, opening doors, peeking into rooms. She had the strange feeling that she was exploring an abandoned house, that this wasn't the home of a living, breathing human being, but a shell, a cave. An inexplicable impulse sent her to his closet where she stood and touched each one of those forbidding suits hanging inside. It brought him no closer to her. Back in the hallway, she opened the door to a book-lined office. The furniture was oak, the lamps brass, and everything was as neat as a pin. A room without a soul.

Kate moved down the hall, to the very last room. She was prying, she knew it. But she missed him and she longed for some palpable clue to his personality. As she opened the door, stale air puffed out, carrying the smell of a space shut away too long from the rest of the world. She saw it was a bedroom. A child's room.

A mobile of prisms trembled near the window, scattering tiny rainbows around the room. She stood there, transfixed, watching the lights dance across the wallpaper with its blue Swedish horses, across the sadly gaping toy shelves, across the tiny bed with the flowered coverlet. Almost against her will, she felt herself moving forward, as though some small, invisible hand were tugging her inside. Then, just as suddenly, the hand was gone and she was alone, so alone, in a room that ached with emptiness.

For a long time she stood there among the dancing rainbows, ashamed that she had disturbed the sanctity of this room. At last she wandered over to the dresser where a stack of books lay awaiting their owner's return. She opened one of the covers and stared at the name on the inside flap. Noah Ransom.

"I'm sorry," she whispered, tears stinging her eyes. "I'm sorry…."

She turned and fled the room, closing the door behind her.

Back in the kitchen, she huddled over a cup of coffee and read and reread the terse note she'd finally discovered, along with a set of keys, on the white-tiled counter.

Catching a ride with Glickman. The car's yours today. See you tonight.

Hardly a lover's note, she thought. No little words of endearment, not even a signature. It was cold and matter-of-fact, just like this kitchen, just like everything else about this house. So that was David. Man of ice, master of a soulless house. They had just shared a night of passionate lovemaking. She'd been swept off her feet. He left impersonal little notes on the kitchen counter.

She had to marvel at how he'd compartmentalized his life. He had walled off his emotions into nice, neat spaces, the way he'd walled off his son's room. But she couldn't do that. Already she missed him. Maybe she even loved him. It was crazy and illogical; and she wasn't used to doing crazy, illogical things.

Suddenly annoyed at herself, she stood up and furiously rinsed her coffee cup in the sink. Dammit, she had more important things to worry about. Her committee hearing was this afternoon; her career hung in the balance. It was a stupid time to be fretting over a man.

She turned and picked up Jenny Brook's hospital chart, which had been lying on the breakfast table. This sad, mysterious document. Slowly she flipped through it, wondering what could possibly be so dangerous about a few pages of medical notes. But something terrible had happened the night Jenny Brook gave birth—something that had reached like a claw through time to destroy every name mentioned on these pages. Mother and child. Doctors and nurses. They were all dead. Only Charlie Decker knew why. And he was a puzzle in himself, a puzzle with pieces that didn't fit.

A maniac, the police had called him. A monster who slashed throats.

A harmless man, Kahanu had said. A lost soul with his insides kicked out.

A man with two faces.

She closed the chart and found herself staring at the back cover. A chart with two sides.

A man with two faces.

She sat up straight, suddenly comprehending. Of course.

Jekyll and Hyde.

"THE MULTIPLE PERSONALITY IS a rare phenomenon. But it's well described in psychiatric literature." Susan Santini swiveled around and reached for a book from the shelf behind her. Turning back to her desk, she perused the index for the relevant pages. Her red hair, usually so unruly, was tied back in a neat little knot. On the wall behind her hung an impressive collection of medical and psychiatric degrees, testimony to the fact Susan Santini was more than just Guy's wife; she was also a professional in her own right, and a well-respected one.

"Here it is," she said, leaning forward. "'From Eve to Sybil. A collection of case histories.' It's really a fascinating topic."

"Have you had any cases in your practice?" asked Kate.

"Wish I had. Oh, I thought I had one, when I was working with the courts. But that creep turned out to be just a great actor trying to beat a murder rap. I tell you, he could go from Caspar Milquetoast to Hulk Hogan in the blink of an eye. What a performance!"

"It is possible, though? For a man to have two completely different personalities?"

"The human psyche is made up of so many clashing parts. Call it id versus ego, impulse versus control. Look at violence, for example. Most of us manage to bury our savage tendencies. But some people can't. Who knows why? Childhood abuse? Some abnormality in brain chemistry? Whatever the reason, these people are walking time bombs. Push them too far and they lose all control. The scary part is, they're all around us. But we don't recognize them until something inside them, some inner dam, bursts. And then the violent side shows itself."

"Do you think Charlie Decker could be one of these walking time bombs?"

Susan leaned back in her leather chair and considered the possibility. "That's a hard question, Kate. You say he came from a broken home. And he was arrested for assault and battery five years ago. But there's no lifelong pattern of violence. And the one time he used a gun, he turned it on himself." She looked doubtful. "I suppose, if he had some precipitating stress, some crisis…"

"He did."

"You mean this?" Susan gestured to the copy of Jenny Brook's medical chart.

"The death of his fiancée. The police think it triggered some sort of homicidal rage. That he's been killing the people he thought were responsible."

"It sounds weird, but the most compelling reason for violence does seem to be love. Think of all those crimes of passion. All those jealous spouses. Spurned lovers."

"Love and violence," said Kate. "Two sides of the same coin."

"Exactly." Susan handed the medical record back to Kate. "But I'm just speculating. I'd have to talk to this man Decker before I can pass judgment. Are the police getting close?"

"I don't know. They won't tell me a thing. A lot of this information I had to dig up myself."

"You're kidding. Isn't it their job?"

Kate sighed. "That's the problem. For them it's nothing but a job, another file to be closed."

The intercom buzzed. "Dr. Santini?" said the receptionist. "Your three-o'clock appointment's waiting."

Kate glanced at her watch. "Oh, I'm sorry. I've been keeping you from your patients."

"You know I'm always glad to help out." Susan rose and walked with her to the door. There she touched Kate's arm. "This place you're staying—you're absolutely sure it's safe?"

Kate turned and saw the worry in Susan's eyes. "I think so. Why?"

Susan hesitated. "I hate to frighten you, but I think you ought to know. If you're correct, if Decker is a multiple personality, then you're dealing with a very unstable mind. Someone totally unpredictable. In the blink of an eye, he could change from a man to a monster. So, please, be very, very careful."

Kate's throat went dry. "You—you really think he's that dangerous?"

Susan nodded. "Extremely dangerous."

Chapter Eleven

IT LOOKED LIKE A FIRING SQUAD and she was the one who'd been handed the blindfold.

She was sitting before a long conference table. Arranged in a grim row in front of her were six men and a woman, all physicians, none of them smiling. Though he'd promised to attend, Dr. Clarence Avery, the chief of anesthesia, was not present. The one friendly face in the entire room was Guy Santini's, but he'd been called only as a witness. He was sitting off to the side and he looked every bit as nervous as she felt.

The committee members asked their questions politely but doggedly. They responded to her answers with impassive stares. Though the room was air-conditioned, her cheeks were on fire.

"And you personally examined the EKG, Dr. Chesne?"

"Yes, Dr. Newhouse."

"And then you filed it in the chart."

"That's correct."

"Did you show the tracing to any other physician?"

"No, sir."

"Not even to Dr. Santini?"

She glanced at Guy, who was hunched down in his chair, staring off unhappily. "Screening the EKG was my responsibility, not Dr. Santini's," she said evenly. "He trusted my judgment."

How many times do I have to repeat this story? she asked herself wearily. *How many times do I have to answer the same damn questions?*

"Dr. Santini? Any comment?"

Guy looked up reluctantly. "What Dr. Chesne says is true. I trusted her judgment." He paused, then added emphatically, "I still trust her judgment."

Thank you, Guy, she thought. Their eyes met and he gave her a faint smile.

"Let's return to the events during surgery, Dr. Chesne," continued Dr. Newhouse. "You say you performed routine induction with IV Pentothal...."

The nightmare was relived. Ellen O'Brien's death was dissected as thoroughly as a cadaver on the autopsy table.

When the questions were over, she was allowed a final statement. She delivered it in a quiet voice. "I know my story sounds bizarre. I also know I can't prove any of it—at least, not yet. But I know this much: I gave Ellen O'Brien the very best care I could. The record shows I made a mistake, a terrible one. And my patient died. But did I kill her? I don't think so. I really don't think so...." Her voice trailed off. There was nothing else to say. So she simply murmured, "Thank you." And then she left the room.

It took them twenty minutes to reach a decision. She was called back to her chair. As her gaze moved along the table, she noticed with distinct uneasiness that two new faces had joined the group. George Bettencourt and the hospital attorney were sitting at one end of the table. Bettencourt looked coldly satisfied. She knew, before a word was even spoken, what the decision would be.

Dr. Newhouse, the committee chairman, delivered the verdict. "We know your recall of the case is at odds with the record, Dr. Chesne. But I'm afraid the record is what we must go on. And the record shows, unquestionably, that your care of patient Ellen O'Brien was substandard." Kate winced at the last word, as though the worst insult imaginable had just been hurled at her. Dr. Newhouse sighed and removed his glasses—a tired gesture that seemed to carry all the weight of the world. "You're new to the staff, Dr. Chesne. You've been with us for less than a year. This sort of…mishap, after so short a time on the staff, concerns us very much. We regret this. We really do. But based on what we've heard, we're forced to refer the case to the Disciplinary Committee. They'll decide what action to take in regards to your position here at Mid Pac. Until then—" he glanced at Bettencourt "—we have no objection to the measures already taken by the hospital administration regarding your suspension."

So it's over, she thought. *I was stupid to hope for anything else.*

They allowed her a chance to respond but she'd lost her voice; it was all she could manage to remain calm and dry-eyed in front of these seven people who'd just torn her life apart.

As the committee filed out, she remained in her chair, unable to move or even to raise her head. "I'm sorry, Kate," Guy said softly. He lingered beside her for a moment, as though hunting for something else to say. Then he, too, drifted out of the room.

Her name was called twice before she finally looked up to see Bettencourt and the attorney standing in front of her.

"We think it's time to talk, Dr. Chesne," announced the attorney.

She frowned at them in bewilderment. "Talk? About what?"

"A settlement."

Her back stiffened. "Isn't this a little premature?"

"If anything, it's too late."

"I don't understand."

"A reporter was in my office a few hours ago. It appears the whole case is out in the open. Obviously the O'Briens took their story to the newspapers. I'm afraid you'll be tried—and convicted—in print."

"But the case was filed only last week."

"We have to get this out of the public eye. Now. And the best way to do it is a very fast, very quiet settlement. All we need is your agreement. I plan to start negotiations at around half a million, though we fully expect they'll push for more."

Half a million dollars, she thought. It struck her as obscene, placing a monetary value on a human life. "No," she said.

The attorney blinked. "Excuse me?"

"The evidence is still coming in. By the time this goes to trial, I'm sure I'll be able to prove—"

"It won't go to trial. This case *will* be settled, Doctor. With or without your permission."

Her mouth tightened. "Then I'll pay for my own attorney. One who'll represent me and not the hospital."

The two men glanced at each other. When the attorney spoke again, his tone was distinctly unpleasant. "I don't think you fully understand what it means to go to trial. Dr. Santini will, in all probability, be dropped from the case. Which means *you* will be the principal defendant. *You'll* be the one sweating on that stand. And it'll be *your* name in the newspapers. I know their attorney, David Ransom. I've seen him rip a defendant to shreds in the courtroom. Believe me, you don't want to go through that."

"Mr. Ransom is no longer on the case," she said.

"What?"

"He's withdrawn."

He snorted. "Where on earth did you hear that rumor?"

"He told me."

"Are you saying you talked to him?"

Not to mention went to bed with him, she reflected, flushing. "It happened last week. I went to his office. I told him about the EKGs—"

"Dear God." The attorney turned and threw his pencil in his briefcase. "Well, that's it, folks. We're in big trouble."

"Why?"

"He'll use that crazy story of yours to push for a higher settlement."

"But he believed me! That's why he's withdrawing—"

"He couldn't possibly believe you. I know the man."

I know him too! she wanted to yell.

But there was no point; she'd never be able to convince them. So she simply shook her head. "I won't settle."

The attorney snapped his briefcase shut and turned in frustration to Bettencourt. "George?"

Kate shifted her attention to the chief administrator. Bettencourt was watching her with an utterly smooth expression. No hostility. No anger. Just that quintessential poker player's gaze.

"I'm concerned about your future, Dr. Chesne," he said.

So am I, she felt like snapping back.

"There's a good chance, unfortunately, that the Disciplinary Committee will view your case harshly. If so, they'll probably recommend you be terminated. And that would be a shame, having that on your record. It would make it almost impossible for you to find another job. Anywhere." He paused, to let his words sink in. "That's why I'm offering you this alternative, Doctor. I think it's far preferable to an out-and-out firing."

She stared down at the sheet of paper he was holding out to her. It was a typed resignation, already dated, with a blank space awaiting her signature.

"That's all that'd appear in your file. A resignation. There'd be no damning conclusions from the Disciplinary Committee. No record of termination. Even with this lawsuit, you could probably find another job, though not in this town." He took out a pen and held it out to her. "Why don't you sign it? It really is for the best."

She kept staring at the paper. The whole process was so neat, so efficient. Here was this ready-made document. All it needed was her signature. Her capitulation.

"We're waiting, Dr. Chesne," challenged Bettencourt. "Sign it."

She rose to her feet. She took the resignation sheet. Looking him straight in the eye, she ripped the paper in half. "There's my resignation," she declared. Then she turned and walked out the door.

Only as she stalked away past the administrative suite did it occur to her what she'd just done. She'd burned her bridges. There was no going back now; her only course was to slog it out to the very end.

Halfway down the hall, her footsteps slowed and finally stopped. She wanted to cry but couldn't. She stood there, staring down the corridor, watching the last secretary straggle away toward the elevators. It was five-fifteen and only a janitor remained at the far end of the hall, listlessly shoving a vacuum cleaner across the carpet. He rounded the corner and the sound of the machine faded away, leaving only a heavy stillness. Farther down the hall, a light was shining through the open door of Clarence Avery's office. It didn't surprise her that he was still at work; he often stayed late. But she wondered why he hadn't attended the hearing as he'd promised. Now, more than ever, she needed his support.

She went to the office. Glancing inside, she was disappointed to find only his secretary, tidying up papers on the desk.

The woman glanced up. "Oh. Dr. Chesne."

"Is Dr. Avery still in the hospital?" Kate asked.

"Haven't you heard?"

"Heard what?"

The secretary looked down sadly at the photograph on the desk. "His wife died last night, at the nursing home. He hasn't been in the hospital all day."

Kate felt herself sag against the doorway. "His…wife?"

"Yes. It was all rather unexpected. A heart attack, they think, but— Are you all right?"

"What?"

"Are you all right? You don't look well."

"No, I'm—I'm fine." Kate backed into the hall. "I'm fine," she repeated, walking in a daze toward the elevators. As she rode down to the lobby, a memory came back to her, an image of shattered glass sparkling at the feet of Clarence Avery.

She needs to be put to sleep…. It's so much better if I do it, if I'm there to say goodbye. Don't you think?

The elevator doors hissed open. The instant she stepped out into the bright lights of the lobby, a sudden impulse seized her, the need to flee, to find safety. To find David. She walked outside into the parking lot and the urge became compelling. She couldn't wait; she had to see him now. If she hurried, she might catch him at his office.

Just the thought of seeing his face filled her with such irrational longing that she began to run. She ran all the way to the car.

Her route took her into the very heart of downtown. Late-afternoon sunlight slanted in through the picket shadows of steel-and-glass high rises. Rush-hour traffic clogged the streets; she felt like a fish struggling upstream. With every minute that passed, her hunger to see him grew. And with it grew a panic that she would be too late, that she'd find his office empty, his door locked. At that moment, as she fought through the traffic, it seemed that nothing in her life had ever been as important as reaching the safety of his arms.

Please be there, she prayed. *Please be there....*

"AN EXPLANATION, MR. RANSOM. That's all I'm asking for. A week ago you said our chances of winning were excellent. Now you've withdrawn from the case. I want to know why."

David gazed uneasily into Mary O'Brien's silver-gray eyes and wondered how to answer her. He wasn't about to tell her the truth—that he was having an affair with the opposition. But he did owe her some sort of explanation and he knew, from the look in her eye, that it had better be a good one.

He heard the agitated creaking of wood and leather and he glanced in irritation at Phil Glickman, who was squirming nervously in his chair. David shot him a warning look to cool it. If that was possible. Glickman already knew the truth. And damned if he didn't look ready to blurt it all out.

Mary O'Brien was still waiting.

David's answer was evasive but not entirely dishonest. "As I said earlier, Mrs. O'Brien, I've discovered a conflict of interest."

"I don't understand what that means," Mary O'Brien said impatiently. "This conflict of interest. Are you telling me you work for the hospital?"

"Not exactly."

"Then what does it mean?"

"It's...confidential. I really can't discuss it." Smoothly changing the subject, he continued, "I'm referring your case to Sullivan and March. It's an excellent firm. They'll be happy to take it from here, assuming you have no objections."

"You haven't answered my question." She leaned forward, her eyes glinting, her bony hands bunched tightly on his desk. Claws of vengeance, he thought.

"I'm sorry, Mrs. O'Brien. I just can't serve your needs objectively. I have no choice but to withdraw."

It was a very different parting from the last visit. A cold and businesslike handshake, a nod of the head. Then he and Glickman escorted her out of his office.

"I expect there'll be no delays because of this," she said.

"There shouldn't be. All the groundwork's been laid." He frowned as he saw the frantic expression of his secretary at the far end of the hall.

"You still think they'll try to settle?"

"It's impossible to second-guess…." He paused, distracted. His secretary now looked absolutely panicked.

"You told us before they'd want to settle."

"Hmm? Oh." Suddenly anxious to get rid of her, he guided her purposefully toward the reception room. "Look, don't worry about it, Mrs. O'Brien," he practically snapped out. "I can almost guarantee the other side's discussing a settlement right—" His feet froze in their tracks. He felt as though he were mired in concrete and would never move again.

Kate was standing in front of him. Slowly, her disbelieving gaze shifted to Mary O'Brien.

"Oh, my God," Glickman groaned.

It was a tableau taken straight out of some soap opera: the shocked parties, all staring at one another.

"I can explain everything," David blurted out.

"I doubt it," retorted Mary O'Brien.

Wordlessly Kate spun around and walked out of the suite. The slam of the door shook David out of his paralysis. Just before he rushed out into the hall he heard Mary O'Brien's outraged voice say: "Conflict of interest? Now I know what he meant by *interest*!"

Kate was stepping into an elevator.

He scrambled after her but before he could yank her out, the door snapped shut between them. "Dammit!" he yelled, slamming his fist against the wall.

The next elevator took forever to arrive. All the way down, twenty floors, he paced back and forth like a caged animal, muttering oaths he hadn't used in years. By the time he emerged on the ground floor, Kate was nowhere to be seen.

He ran out of the building and down the steps to the sidewalk. Scanning the street, he spotted, half a block away, a bus idling near the curb. Kate was walking toward it.

Shoving frantically through a knot of pedestrians, he managed to grab her arm and haul her back as she was about to step aboard the bus.

"Let me go!" she snapped.

"Where the hell do you think you're going?"

"Oh, sorry. I almost forgot!" Thrusting her hand in her skirt pocket, she pulled out his car keys and practically threw them at him. "I wouldn't want to be accused of stealing your precious BMW!"

She looked around in frustration as the bus roared off without her. Yanking her arm free, she stormed away. He was right behind her.

"Just give me a chance to explain."

"What did you tell your client, David? That she'll get her settlement now that you've got the dumb doctor eating out of your hand?"

"What happened between you and me has nothing to do with the case."

"It has everything to do with the case! You were hoping all along I'd settle."

"I only asked you to think about it."

"Ha!" She whirled on him. "Is this something they teach you in law school? When all else fails, get the opposition into bed?"

That was the last straw. He grabbed her arm and practically dragged her off the sidewalk and into a nearby pub. Inside, he plunged straight through the boisterous crowd that had gathered around the bar and hauled her through the swirling cigarette smoke to an empty booth at the back. There he plopped her down unceremoniously onto the wooden bench. Sliding into the seat across from her, he shot her a look that said she was damn well going to hear him out.

"First of all—" he started.

"Good evening," said a cheery voice.

"Now what?" he barked at the startled waitress who'd arrived to take their order.

The woman seemed to shrink back into her forest-green costume. "Did you…uh, want anything—"

"Just bring us a couple of beers," he snapped.

"Of course, sir." With a pitying look at Kate, the waitress turned ruffled skirts and fled.

For a solid minute, David and Kate stared at each other with unveiled hostility. Then David let out a sigh and clawed his fingers through his already unruly hair. "Okay," he said. "Let's try it again."

"Where do we start? Before or after your client popped out of your office?"

"Did anyone ever tell you you've got a lousy sense of timing?"

"Oh, you're wrong there, mister. My sense of timing happens to be just dandy. What did I hear you say to her? 'Don't worry, there's a settlement in the works'?"

"I was trying to get her out of my office!"

"So how did she react to your straddling both sides of the lawsuit?"

"I wasn't—" he looked pained "—straddling."

"Working for her and going to bed with me? I'd call that straddling."

"For an intelligent woman, you seem to have a little trouble comprehending one little fact: I'm off the case. Permanently. And voluntarily. Mary O'Brien came to my office demanding to know why I withdrew."

"Did you—did you tell her about us?"

"You think I'm nuts? You think I'd come out and announce I had a roll in the hay with the opposition?"

His words hit her like a slap across her face. Was that all it had meant to him? She'd imagined their lovemaking meant far more than just the simple clash of hormones. A joining of souls, perhaps. But for David, the affair had only meant complications. An angry client, a forced withdrawal from a case. And now the humiliation of having to confess an illicit romance. That he'd tried so hard to conceal their affair gave it all a lurid glow. People only hid what they were ashamed of.

"A weekend fling," she said. "Is that what I was?"

"I didn't mean it that way!"

"Well, don't worry about it, David," she assured him with regal composure as she rose to her feet. "I won't embarrass you any more. This is one skeleton who'll gladly step back into the closet."

"*Sit down.*" It was nothing more than a low growl but it held enough threat to make her pause. "Please," he added. Then, in a whisper, he said it again. "Please."

Slowly, she sat back down.

They fell silent as the waitress returned and set down their beers. Only when they were alone again did David say, quietly, "You're not just a fling, Kate. And as for the O'Briens, it's none of their business what I do on my weekends. Or weekdays." He shook his head in amazement. "You know, I've withdrawn from other cases, but it was always for perfectly logical reasons. Reasons I could defend without getting red in the face. This time, though…" He let out a brittle laugh. "At my age, getting red in the face isn't supposed to happen anymore."

Kate stared down at her glass. She hated beer. She hated arguing. Most of all, she hated this chasm between them. "If I jumped to conclusions," she admitted grudgingly, "I'm sorry. I guess I never did trust lawyers."

He grunted. "Then we're even. I never did trust doctors."

"So we're an unlikely pair. What else is new?"

They suffered through another one of those terrible loaded silences.

"We really don't know each other very well, do we?" she finally said.

"Except in bed. Which isn't the best place to get acquainted." He paused. "Though we certainly tried."

She looked up and saw an odd little tilt to his mouth, the beginnings of a smile. A lock of hair had slipped down over his brow. His shirt collar gaped open and his tie had been yanked into a limp version of a hangman's noose. She'd never seen him look so wrenchingly attractive.

"Are you going to get in trouble, David? What if the O'Briens complain to the state bar?" she asked softly.

He shrugged. "I'm not worried. Hell, the worst they can do is disbar me. Throw me in jail. Maybe send me to the electric chair."

"David."

"Oh, you're right, I forgot. Hawaii doesn't have an electric chair." He noticed she wasn't laughing. "Okay, so it's a lousy joke." He lifted his mug and was about to take a gulp of beer when he focused on her morose expression. "Oh, I completely forgot. What happened at your hearing?"

"There were no surprises."

"It went against you?"

"To say the least." Miserable, she stared down at the table. "They said my work was substandard. I guess that's a polite way of calling me a lousy doctor."

His silence, more than anything he could have said, told her how much the news disturbed him. With a sense of wonder she watched his hand close gently around hers.

"It's funny," she remarked with an ironic laugh. "I never planned on being anything but a doctor. Now that I'm losing my job, I see how poorly qualified I am for anything else. I can't type. I can't take dictation. For God's sake, I can't even *cook*."

"Uh-oh. Now that's a serious deficiency. You may have to beg on street corners."

It was another lousy joke, but this time she managed a smile. A meager one. "Promise to drop a few quarters in my hat?"

"I'll do better than that. I'll buy you dinner."

She shook her head. "Thanks. But I'm not hungry."

"Better take me up on the offer," he urged, squeezing her hand. "You never know where you next meal's coming from."

She lifted her head and their gazes met across the table. The eyes she'd once thought so icy now held all the warmth of a summer's day. "All I want is to go home with you, David. I want you to hold me. And not necessarily in that order."

Slowly he moved around the table and slid next to her. Then he pulled her into his arms and held her long and close. It was what she needed, this silent embrace, not of a lover but a friend.

They both stiffened at the sound of the waitress clearing her throat. "I don't believe this woman's timing," David muttered as he pulled away.

"Anything else?" asked the waitress.

"Yes," David replied, smiling politely through clenched teeth. "*If* you don't mind."

"What's that, sir?"

"A little privacy."

KATE LET HIM TALK HER INTO dinner. A full stomach and a few glasses of wine left her flushed and giddy as they walked the dark streets to the parking garage. The lamps spilled a hazy glow across their faces. She clung to his arm and felt like singing, like laughing.

She was going home with David.

She slid onto the leather seat of the BMW and the familiar feeling of security wrapped around her like a blanket. She was in a capsule where no one, nothing, could hurt her. The feeling lasted all the way down the Pali Highway, clung to her as they slipped into the tunnel through the Koolau Mountains, kept her warm on the steep and winding road down the other side of the ridge.

It shattered when David glanced in the rearview mirror and swore softly.

She glanced sideways and saw the faint glow of a car's headlights reflected on his face. "David?"

He didn't answer. She felt the rising hum of the engine as they accelerated.

"David, is something wrong?"

"That car. Behind us."

"What?"

He frowned at the mirror. "I think we're being followed."

Chapter Twelve

KATE WHIPPED HER HEAD AROUND and stared at the pair of headlights twinkling in the distance. "Are you sure?"

"I only noticed because it has a dead left parking light. I know it pulled out behind us when we left the garage. It's been on our tail ever since. All the way down the mountain."

"That doesn't mean he's following us!"

"Let's try a little experiment." He took his foot off the gas pedal.

She went rigid in alarm. "Why are you slowing down?"

"To see what he does."

As her heart accelerated wildly, Kate felt the BMW drift down to forty-five, then forty. Below the speed limit. She waited for the headlights to overtake them but they seemed to hang in the distance, as though some invisible force kept the cars apart.

"Smart guy," said David. "He's staying just far enough behind so I can't read his license."

"There's a turnoff! Oh, please, let's take it!"

He veered off the highway and shot onto a two-lane road cut through dense jungle. Vine-smothered trees whipped past, their overhanging branches splattering the windshield with water. She twisted around and saw, through the backdrop of jungle, the same pair of headlights, twinkling in the darkness. Phantom lights that refused to vanish.

"It's him," she whispered. She couldn't bring herself to say the name, as if, just by uttering it, she would unleash some terrible force.

"I should have known," he muttered. "Dammit, I should've known!"

"What?"

"He was watching the hospital. That's the only way he could've followed you—"

He must have been right behind me, she thought, suddenly sick with the realization of what could have happened. *And I never even knew he was there.*

"I'm going to lose him. Hold on."

She was thrown sideways by the violent lurch of the car. It was all she could do to hang on for dear life. The situation was out of her hands; this show was entirely David's.

Houses leaped past, a succession of brightly lit windows punctuated by the silhouettes of trees and shrubbery. The BMW weaved like a slalom skier through the darkness, rounding corners at a speed that made her claw the dashboard in terror.

Without warning, he swerved into a driveway. The seat belt sliced into her chest as they jerked to a sudden standstill in a pitch-dark garage. Instantly, David cut off the engine. The next thing she knew, he was pulling her down into his arms. There she lay, wedged between the gearshift and David's chest, listening, waiting. She could feel his heart hammering against her, could hear his harsh, uneven breaths. At least he was still able to breathe; she scarcely dared to.

With mounting terror, she watched a flicker of light slowly grow brighter and brighter in the rearview mirror. From the road came the faint growl of an engine. David's arms tensed around her. Already he had shifted his weight and now lay on top of her, shielding her body with his. For an eternity she lay crushed in his embrace, listening, waiting, as the sound of the engine faded away. Only when there was total silence did they finally creep up and peer through the rear window.

The road was dark. The car had vanished.

"What now?" she whispered.

"We get the hell out of here. While we still can." He turned the key; the engine's purr seemed deafening. With his headlights killed, he let the car creep slowly out of the garage.

As they wound their way out of the neighborhood, she kept glancing back, searching for the twin lights dancing beyond the trees. Only when they'd reached the highway did she allow herself a breath of relief. But to her alarm, David turned the car back toward Honolulu.

"Where are we going?"

"We can't go home. Not now."

"But we've lost him!"

"If he followed you from the hospital, then he trailed you straight to my office. To me. Unfortunately, I'm in the phone book. Address and all."

She sank back in shock and struggled to absorb this latest blow. They entered the Pali Tunnel. The succession of lights passing overhead was wildly disorienting, flash after flash that shocked her eyes.

Where do I go now? she wondered. *How long before he finds me? Will I have time to run? Time to scream?* She shuddered as they emerged from the tunnel and were plunged into sudden darkness.

"It's my last resort," David said. "But it's the only place I can think of. You won't be alone. And you'll be perfectly safe." He paused and added with an odd note of humor, "Just don't drink the coffee."

She turned and stared at him in bewilderment. "Where are we going?"

His answer had a distinctly apologetic ring. "My mother's."

THE TINY GRAY-HAIRED WOMAN who opened the door was wearing a ratty bathrobe and pink bunny slippers. For a moment she stood there, blinking like a surprised mouse at the unexpected visitors. Then she clapped her hands and squeaked: "My goodness, David! How nice you've come for a visit! Oh, but this is naughty of you, not to call. You've caught us in our pajamas, like two ol—"

"You're gorgeous, Gracie," cut in David as he tugged Kate into the house. Quickly he locked and bolted the door. Then, glancing out the curtained window, he demanded, "Is Mother awake?"

"Why, yes, she's…uh…" Gracie gestured vaguely at the foyer.

From another room, a querulous voice called out: "For heaven's sake, get rid of whoever it is and get in here! It's your turn! And you'd better come up with something good. I just got a triple word score!"

"She's beating me again." Gracie sighed mournfully.

"Then she's in a good mood?"

"I wouldn't know. I've never seen her in one."

"Get ready," David muttered to Kate as he guided her across the foyer. "Mother?" he called out pleasantly. *Too* pleasantly.

In a mauve and mahogany living room, a regal woman with blue-gray hair was sitting with her back turned to them. Her wrapped foot was propped up on a crushed velvet ottoman. On the tea table beside her lay a Scrabble board, crisscrossed with tiles. "I don't believe it," she announced to the wall. "It must be an auditory hallucination." She turned and squinted at him. "Why, my son has actually come for a visit! Is the world at an end?"

"Nice to see you, too, Mother," he responded dryly. He took a deep breath, like a man gathering up the nerve to yank out his own teeth. "We need your help."

The woman's eyes, as glitteringly sharp as crystals, suddenly focused on Kate. Then she noticed David's arm, which was wrapped protectively around Kate's shoulder. Slowly, knowingly, she smiled. With a grateful glance at the heavens she murmured fervently: "Glory hallelujah!"

"YOU NEVER TELL ME ANYTHING, David," Jinx Ransom complained as she sat with her son in the fern-infested kitchen an hour later.

They were huddled over cups of cocoa, a ritual they hadn't shared since he was a boy. *How little it takes to be transported back to childhood,* he reflected. One sip of chocolate, one disapproving look from his mother, and the pangs of filial guilt returned. Good old Jinx; she really knew how to make a guy feel young again. In fact, she made him feel about six years old.

"Here you have a woman in your life," said Jinx, "and you hide her from me. As if you're ashamed of her. Or ashamed of me. Or maybe you're ashamed of us both."

"There's nothing to talk about. I haven't known her that long."

"You're just ashamed to admit you're human, aren't you?"

"Don't psychoanalyze me, Mother."

"I'm the one who diapered you. I'm the one who watched you skin your knees. I even saw you break your arm on that blasted skateboard. You almost never cried, David. You still don't cry. I don't think you can. It's some gene you inherited from your father. The Plymouth Rock curse. Oh, the emotions are in there somewhere, but you're not about to let them show. Even when Noah died—"

"I don't want to talk about Noah."

"You see? The boy's been gone eight years now and you still can't hear his name without getting all tight in the face."

"Get to the point, Mother."

"Kate."

"What about her?"

"You were holding her hand."

He shrugged. "She has a very nice hand."

"Have you gone to bed with her yet?"

David sputtered hot chocolate all over the table. "Mother!"

"Well it's nothing to be ashamed of. People do it all the time. It's what nature intended, though I sometimes think you imagine yourself immune to the whole blasted process. But tonight, I saw that look in your eye."

Swatting away a stray fern, he went to the sink for a paper towel and began dabbing the cocoa from his shirt.

"Am I right?" asked Jinx.

"Looks like I'll need a clean shirt for tomorrow," he muttered. "This one's shot."

"Use one of your father's shirts. So am I right?"

He looked up. "About what, Mother?" he asked blankly.

She raised her arm and made a throttling motion at the heavens. "I knew it was a mistake to have only one child!"

Upstairs there was a loud thud. David glanced up at the ceiling. "What the hell is Gracie doing up there, anyway?"

"Digging up some clothes for Kate."

David shuddered. Knowing Gracie's incomparable taste in clothes, Kate would come down swathed from head to toe in some nauseating shade of pink. With bunny slippers to match. The truth was, he didn't give a damn what she was wearing, if only she'd hurry downstairs. They'd been apart only fifteen minutes and already he missed her. It annoyed him, all these inconvenient emotions churning around inside him. It made him feel weak and helpless and all too…human.

He turned eagerly at hearing a creak on the stairs and saw it was only Gracie.

"Is that hot chocolate, Jinx?" Gracie demanded. "You know the milk upsets your stomach. You really should have tea instead."

"I don't want tea."

"Yes, you do."

"No, I don't."

"Where's Kate?" David called out bleakly.

"Oh, she's coming," said Gracie. "She's up in your room, looking at your old model airplanes." Giggling, she confided to Jinx, "I told her they were proof that David was once a child."

"He was never a child," grumbled Jinx. "He sprang from the womb a fully mature adult. Though smaller, of course. Perhaps he'll do it backward. Perhaps he'll get younger as the years go by. We'll see him loosen up and become a real child."

"Like you, Mother?"

Gracie put on the teakettle and sighed happily. "It's so nice to have company, isn't it?" She glanced around, startled, as the phone rang. "My goodness, it's after ten. Who on earth—"

David shot to his feet. "I'll get it." He grabbed the receiver and barked out: "Hello?"

Pokie's voice boomed triumphantly across the wires. "Have I got news for you."

"You've tracked down that car?"

"Forget the car. We got the man."

"Decker?"

"I'll need Dr. Chesne down here to identify him. Half an hour, okay?"

David glanced up to see Kate standing in the kitchen doorway. Her eyes were filled with questions. Grinning, he snapped her a victorious thumbs-up sign. "We'll be right over," he told Pokie. "Where you holding him? Downtown station?"

There was a pause. "No, not the station."
"Where, then?"
"The morgue."

"HOPE YOU HAVE STRONG stomachs." The medical examiner, a grotesquely chirpy woman named M.J., pulled open the stainless-steel drawer. It glided out noiselessly. Kate cringed against David as M.J. casually reached in and unzipped the plastic shroud.

Under the harsh morgue lights, the corpse's face looked artificial. This wasn't a man; it was some sort of waxen image, a mockery of life.

"Some yachtie found him this evening, floating facedown in the harbor," explained Pokie.

Kate felt David's arm tighten around her waist as she forced herself to study the dead man's bloated features. Distorted as he was, the open eyes were recognizable. Even in death they seemed haunted.

Nodding, Kate whispered, "That's him."

Pokie grinned, a response that struck her as surreal in that nightmarish room. "Bingo," he grunted.

M.J. ran her gloved hand over the dead man's scalp. "Feels like we got a depressed skull fracture here…." She whisked off the shroud, revealing the naked torso. "Looks like he's been in the water quite a while."

Suddenly nauseated, Kate turned and buried her face against David's shoulder. The scent of his aftershave muted the stench of formalin.

"For God's sake, M.J.," David muttered. "Cover him up, will you?"

M.J. zipped up the shroud and slid the drawer closed. "You've lost the old ironclad stomach, hey, Davy boy? If I remember right, you used to shrug off a lot worse."

"I don't hang around stiffs the way I used to." He guided Kate away from the body drawers. "Come on. Let's get the hell out of here."

The medical examiner's office was a purposefully cheerful room, complete with hanging plants and old movie posters, a bizarre setting for the gruesome business at hand. Pokie poured coffee from the automatic brewer and handed two cups to David and Kate. Then, sighing with satisfaction, he settled into a chair across from them. "So that's how it wraps up," he said. "No trial. No hassles. Just a convenient corpse. Too bad justice ain't always this easy."

Kate stared down at her coffee. "How did he die, Lieutenant?" she whispered.

Pokie shrugged. "Happens now and then. Get some guy who's had a little too much to drink. Falls off a pier, bashes his head on the rocks. Hell, we find floaters all the time. Boat bums, mostly." He glanced at M.J. "What do you think?"

"Can't rule out anything yet," mumbled M.J. She was hunched at her desk and wolfing down a late supper. A meat-loaf sandwich dripping with ketchup, Kate noted, her stomach threatening to turn inside out. "When a body's been in the water that long, anatomy gets distorted. I'll tell you after the autopsy."

"Just how long was he in the water?" asked David.

"A day. More or less."

"A *day*?" He looked at Pokie. "Then who the hell was following us tonight?"

Pokie grinned. "You just got yourself an active imagination."

"I'm telling you, there was a car!"

"Lot of cars out on the road. Lot of headlights look the same."

"Well, it sure wasn't my guy in the drawer," said M.J., crumpling up her sandwich wrappings. She chomped enthusiastically into a bright red apple. "Far as I know, dead men don't drive."

"When are you going to know the cause of death?" David snapped.

"Still need skull X rays. I'll open him up tonight, check the lungs for water. That'll tell us if he drowned." She took another bite of apple. "But that's *after* I finish my dinner. In the meantime—" swiveling around, she grabbed a cardboard box from a shelf and tossed it down on the desk "—his personal effects."

Methodically she took out the items, each one sealed in its own plastic bag. "Plastic comb, black, pocket-size…cigarettes, Winston, half empty…matchbook, unlabeled…man's wallet, brown vinyl, containing fourteen dollars…various ID cards…"

She reached in for the last item. "And these." The set of keys clattered on the desk. Attached was a plastic tag with gaudy red lettering: The Victory Hotel.

Kate picked up the key ring. "The Victory Hotel," she murmured. "Is that where he was living?"

Pokie nodded. "We checked it out. What a dive. Rats crawling all over the place. We know he was there Saturday night. But that's the last time he was seen. Alive, anyway."

Slowly Kate lay the keys down and stared at the mockingly bright lettering. She thought about the face in the mirror, about the torment in those eyes. And as she gazed at the sad and meager pile of belongings, an unexpected wave of sorrow welled up in her, sorrow for a man's shattered dreams. *Who were you, Charlie Decker?* she wondered. *Madman? Murderer?* Here were the bits and pieces of his life, and they were all so ordinary.

Pokie gave her a grin. "Well, it's over, Doc. Our man's dead. Looks like you can go home."

She glanced at David, but he was staring off in another direction. "Yes," she said in a weary voice. "Now I can go home."

Who were you, Charlie Decker?

That refrain played over and over in her head as she sat in the darkness of David's car and watched the streetlights flash by. *Who were you?* She thought of all the ways he'd suffered, all the pain he'd felt, that man without a voice. Like everyone else, he'd been a victim.

And now he was a convenient corpse.

"It's too easy, David," she said softly.

He glanced at her through the gloom of the car. "What is?"

"The way it's all turned out. Too simple, too neat..." She stared off into the darkness, remembering the reflection of Charlie Decker's face in the mirror. "My God. I saw it in his eyes," she whispered. "It was right there, staring at me, only I was too panicked to recognize it."

"What?"

"The fear. He was terrified. He must have known something, something awful. And it killed him. Just like it killed the others...."

"You're saying he was a victim? Then why did he threaten you? Why did he make that call to the cottage?"

"Maybe it wasn't a threat...." She looked up with sudden comprehension. "Maybe he was warning me. About someone else."

"But the evidence—"

"What evidence? A few fingerprints on a doorknob? A corpse with a psychiatric record?"

"And a witness. You saw him in Ann's apartment."

"What if he was the real witness? A man in the wrong place at the wrong time." She watched their headlights slash the darkness. "Four people, David. And the only thing that linked them together was a dead woman. If I only knew why Jenny Brook was so important."

"Unfortunately, dead men don't talk."

Maybe they do. "The Victory Hotel," she said suddenly. "Where is it?"

"Kate, the man's dead. The answers died with him. Let's just forget it."

"But there's still a chance—"

"You heard Pokie. The case is closed."

"Not for me, it isn't."

"Oh, for God's sake, Kate! Don't turn this into an obsession!" Gripping the steering wheel, he forced out an agitated breath. When he spoke again, his voice was quiet. "Look, I know how much it means to you, clearing your name. But in the long run, it may not be worth the fight. If vindication's what you're after, I'm afraid you won't get it. Not in the courtroom, anyway."

"You can't be sure what a jury will think."

"Second-guessing juries is part of my job. I've made a good living, cashing in on doctors' mistakes. And I've done it in a town where a lot of lawyers can barely pay their rent. I'm not any smarter than the other guy, I just pick my cases well. And when I do, I'm not afraid to get down and get dirty. By the time I'm finished, the defendant's scarred for life."

"Lovely profession you're in."

"I'm telling you this because I don't want it to happen to you. That's why I think you should settle out of court. Let the matter die quietly. Discreetly. Before your name gets dragged through the mud."

"Is that how they do it in the prosecutor's office? 'Plead guilty and we'll make you a *deal*'?"

"There's nothing wrong with a settlement."

"Would you settle? If you were me?"

There was a long pause. "Yes. I would."

"Then we must be very different." Stubbornly she gazed ahead at the highway. "Because I can't let this die. Not without a fight."

"Then you're going to lose." It was more than an opinion; it was a pronouncement, as final as the thud of a judge's gavel in the courtroom.

"And I suppose lawyers don't take on losing battles, do they?"

"Not this lawyer."

"Funny. Doctors take them on all the time. Try arguing with a stroke. Or cancer. We don't make bargains with the enemy."

"And that's exactly how I make my living," he retorted. "On the arrogance of doctors!"

It was a vicious blow; he regretted it the instant he said it. But she was headed for trouble, and he had to stop her before she got hurt. Still, he hadn't expected such brutal words to pop out. It was one more reminder of how high the barriers were between them.

They drove the rest of the way in silence. A cloud of gloom filled the space of the car. They both seemed to sense that things were coming to an end; he guessed it had been inevitable from the start. Already he could feel her pulling away.

Back at his house, they drifted toward the bedroom like a pair of strangers. When she pulled down her suitcase and started to pack, he said simply, "Leave it for the morning," and shoved it back in the closet. That was all. He couldn't bring himself to say he wanted her to stay, needed her to stay. He just shut the closet door.

Then he turned to her. Slowly he removed his jacket and tossed it on the chair. He went to her, took her face in his hands and kissed her. Her lips felt chilled. He took her in his arms and held her, warmed her.

They made love, of course. One last time. He was there and she was there and the bed was there. Love among the ruins. No, not love. Desire. Need. Something entirely different, all-consuming yet wholly unsatisfying.

And afterward he lay beside her in the darkness, listening to her breathing. She slept deeply, the unarousable slumber of exhaustion. He should be sleeping, too. But he couldn't. He was too busy thinking about all the reasons he shouldn't fall in love.

He didn't like being in love. It left him far too vulnerable. Since Noah's death, he'd avoided feeling much of anything. At times he'd felt like a robot. He'd functioned on automatic pilot, breathing and eating out of necessity, smiling only when it was expected. When Linda finally left him, he'd hardly noticed; their divorce was a mere drop in an ocean of pain. He guessed he'd loved her, but it wasn't the same total, unconditional love he'd felt for his son. For David, love was quantified by how much he suffered by its loss.

And now here was this woman, lying beside him. He studied the dark pool of her hair against the pillow, the glow of her face. He tried to think of the last time there'd been a woman in his bed. It had been a long time ago, a blonde. But he couldn't even dredge up her name. That's how little she'd meant to him.

But Kate? He'd remember her name, all right. He'd remember this moment, the way she slept, curled up like a tired kitten, the way her very presence seemed to warm the darkness. He'd remember.

He rose from the bed and wandered into the hall. Some strange yearning pulled him toward Noah's room. He went inside and stood for a moment, bathed in the window's moonlight. For so long he'd avoided this room. He'd hated the sight of that unoccupied bed. He'd always remembered how it used to be, tiptoeing in to watch his son sleep. Noah, by some strange instinct, always seemed to choose that moment to awaken. And in the darkness, they'd murmur their ritual conversation.

Is that you, Daddy?

Yes, Noah, it's me. Go back to sleep.

Hug first. Please.

Good night. Don't let the bedbugs bite.

David sat down on the bed, listening to the echoes of the past, remembering how much it had hurt to love.

At last he went back to Kate's bed, crawled in beside her and fell asleep.

He woke up before dawn. In the shower he purposefully washed off all traces of their lovemaking. He felt renewed. He dressed for work, donning each item of clothing as if it was a piece of armor to shield him from the world. Alone in the kitchen, he had a cup of coffee.

Now that Decker was dead, there was no reason for Kate to stay. David had done his moral duty; he'd played the white knight and kept her safe. It had been clear from the start that none of this was for keeps. He'd never led her on. His conscience was clear. Now it was time for her to go home; and they both knew it. Perhaps her leaving was all for the better. A few days, a few weeks apart, might give him a saner perspective. Maybe he'd decide this was all a case of temporary, hormonal madness.

Or maybe he was only kidding himself.

He worried about all the things that could happen to her if she kept on digging into Charlie Decker's past. He also knew she would keep on digging. Last night he hadn't told her the truth: that he thought she was right, that there was more to this case than a madman's vengeance. Four people were dead; he didn't want her to be the fifth.

He got up and rinsed his cup. Then he went back to the bedroom. There he sat at the foot of the bed—a safe distance—and watched her sleep. Such a beautiful, stubborn, maddeningly independent woman. He used to think he liked independent women. Now he wasn't so sure. He almost wished Decker was still alive, just so Kate would go on needing him. How incredibly selfish.

Then he decided she did still need him. They'd shared two nights of passion. For that he owed her one last favor.

He nudged her gently. "Kate?"

Slowly she opened her eyes and looked at him. Those sleepy green eyes. He wanted so badly to kiss her but decided it was better if he didn't.

"The Victory Hotel," he said. "Do you still want to go?"

Chapter Thirteen

MRS. TUBBS, THE MANAGER OF the Victory Hotel, was a toadlike woman with two pale slits for eyes. Despite the heat, she was wearing a ratty gray sweater over her flowered dress. Through a hole in her sock poked an enormously swollen big toe. "Charlie?" she asked, cautiously peering at David and Kate through her half-open door. "Yeah, he lived here."

In the room behind her, a TV game show blared and a man yelled, "You retard! I coulda guessed that one!"

The woman turned and yelled: "Ebbie! Turn that thing down! Can't you see I'm talkin' to someone?" She looked back at David and Kate. "Charlie don't live here no more. Got hisself killed. Police already come by."

"If it's all right, we'd like to see his room," said Kate.

"What for?"

"We're looking for information."

"You from the po-lice?"

"No, but—"

"Can't let you up there without a warrant. Po-lice give me too much trouble already. Gettin' everyone in the building all nervous. 'Sides, I got orders. No one goes up." Her tone implied that someone very high, perhaps even God Himself, had issued those orders. To emphasize the point, she started to close the door. She looked outraged when David stopped it with a well-placed hand.

"Seems to me you could use a new sweater, Mrs. Tubbs," David remarked quietly.

The door swung open a fraction of an inch. Mrs. Tubbs's pale eyes peered at him through the crack. "I could use a lot of new things," she grunted. From the apartment came a man's loud and enthusiastic burp. "New husband, mostly."

"Afraid I can't help you there."

"No one can, 'cept maybe the good Lord."

"Who works His magic in unexpected ways." David's smile was dazzling; Mrs. Tubbs stared, waiting for the proffered miracle to occur.

David produced it in the form of two twenty-dollar bills, which he slipped discreetly into her fat hands.

She looked down at the money. "Hotel owner'll kill me if he finds out."

"He won't."

"Don't pay me nearly enough to manage this here trash heap. Plus I'm s'posed to pay off the city inspector." David slipped her another twenty. "But you ain't no inspector, right?" She wadded up the bills and stuffed them into the dark and bottomless recess of her bosom. "No inspector I seen ever come dressed like you." Shuffling out into the hall, she closed the door on Ebbie and the TV. In her stockinged feet, she led David and Kate toward the staircase. It was a climb of only one flight, but for her each step seemed to be agony. By the time she reached the top, she was wheezing like an accordion. A brown carpet—or had it once been mustard yellow?—stretched out into the dim hallway. She stopped before room 203 and fumbled for the keys.

"Charlie was here 'bout a month," she gasped out, a few words at a time. "Real quiet. Caused no—no trouble, not like some—some of them others...."

At the other end of the hall, a door suddenly opened and two small faces peered out.

"Charlie come back?" the little girl called.

"I already told you," Mrs. Tubbs said. "Charlie gone and left for good."

"But when's he comin' back?"

"You kids deaf or somethin'? How come you ain't in school?"

"Gabe's sick," explained the girl. As if to confirm the fact, little Gabe swiped his hand across his snotty nose.

"Where's your ma?"

The girl shrugged. "Out workin'."

"Yeah. Leaves you two brats here to burn down the place."

The children shook their heads solemnly. "She took away our matches," replied Gabe.

Mrs. Tubbs got the door unlocked. "There y'are," she said and pushed it open.

As the room swung into view, something small and brown rustled across the floor and into the shadows. The mingled odors of cigarette smoke and grease hung in the gloom. Pinpoints of light glittered through a tattered curtain. Mrs. Tubbs went over and shoved the curtain aside. Sunshine splashed in through the grimy window.

"Go 'head, have a look 'round," she said, planting herself in a corner. "But don't take nothin'."

It was easy to see why a visit by the city inspector might cause her alarm. A baited rattrap, temporarily unoccupied, lay poised near a trash can. A single lightbulb hung from the ceiling, its wires nakedly exposed. On a one-burner hot plate sat a frying pan coated with a thick layer of congealed fat. Except for the one window, there was no ventilation and any cooking would have made the air swirl with grease.

Kate's gaze took in the miserable surroundings: the rumpled bed, the ashtray overflowing with cigarette butts, the card table littered with loose scraps of paper. She frowned at one of the pages, covered with scribblings.

Eight was great
Nine was fine,
And now you're ten years old.
Happy Birthday, Jocelyn,
The best will yet unfold!

"Who's Jocelyn?" she asked.

"That brat in 210. Mother's never around to watch 'em. Always out workin'. Or so she calls it. Kids just 'bout burned the place down last month. Woulda throwed 'em all out, 'cept they always pay me in cash."

"Just how much is the rent?" David asked.

"Four hundred bucks."

"You've got to be kidding."

"Hey, we got us a good location. Close to the bus lines. Free water 'n 'lectricity." At that instant, a cockroach chose to scuttle across the floor. "And we take pets."

Kate looked up from the pile of papers. "What was he like, Mrs. Tubbs?"

"Charlie?" She shrugged. "What's to say? Kept to hisself. Never made no noise. Never blasted the radio like some of these no-accounts. Never complained 'bout nothin' far as I remember. Hell, we hardly knew he was here. Yeah, a real good tenant."

By those standards, the ideal tenant would have been a corpse.

Mrs. Tubbs settled into a chair and watched as they searched the room. Their inspection revealed a few wrinkled shirts hanging in the closet, a dozen cans of Campbell's soup neatly stacked in the cabinet under the sink, some laundered socks and men's underwear in the dresser drawer. It was a meager collection of belongings; they held few clues to the personality of their owner.

At last Kate wandered to the window and looked down at a glass-littered street. Beyond a chain-link fence there was a condemned building with walls that sagged outward, as though a giant had stepped on it. A grim view of the world, this panorama of broken bottles and abandoned cars and drunks lolling on the sidewalk. This was a dead end, the sort of place you landed when you could fall no farther.

No, that wasn't quite right. There was one place lower you could fall: the grave.

"Kate?" said David. He'd been rummaging in the nightstand. "Prescription pills," he said, holding up a bottle. "Haldol, prescribed by Dr. Nemechek. State hospital."

"That's his psychiatrist."

"And look. I also found this." He held out a small, framed photograph.

The instant Kate saw the face, she knew who the woman was. She took the picture and studied it by the window's light. It was only a snapshot in time, a single image captured on a sheet of photographic paper, but the young woman who'd smiled into the camera's lens had the glow of eternity in her eyes. They were rich brown eyes, full of laughter, narrowed slightly in the sunlight. Behind her, a brassy sky met the turquoise blue of the sea. A strand of dark hair had blown across her face and clung almost wistfully to the curve of her cheek. She was wearing a simple white bathing suit; and though she'd struck a purposely sexy pose, kneeling there in the sand, there was a sweet gawkiness about her, like a child playing grown-up in her mother's clothes.

Kate slipped the photo out of its frame. The edges were tattered, lovingly worn by years of handling. On the other side was a handwritten message: "Till you come back to me. Jenny."

"Jenny," Kate said softly.

For a long time she stood there, staring at those words, written by a woman long since dead. She thought about the emptiness of this room, about the soup cans, so carefully stacked, about the pile of socks and underwear in the drawer. Charlie Decker had owned so very little. The one possession he'd guarded through the years, the one thing he'd treasured, had been this fading photograph of a woman with eternity in her eyes. It was hard to believe that such a glow could ever be extinguished, even in the depths of a grave.

She turned to Mrs. Tubbs. "What will happen to his things? Now that he's dead?"

"Guess I'll have to sell it all off," replied Mrs. Tubbs. "Owed me a week's rent. Gotta get it somehow. Though there ain't much of value in here. 'Cept maybe what you're holding."

Kate looked down at the smiling face of Jenny Brook. "Yes. She's beautiful, isn't she?"

"Naw, I don't mean the picture."

Kate frowned. "What?"

"The frame." Mrs. Tubbs went to the window and snapped the curtain closed. "It's silver."

JOCELYN AND HER BROTHER were hanging like monkeys on the chain-link fence. As David and Kate came out of the Victory Hotel, the children dropped to the ground and watched expectantly as though something extraordinary was about to happen. The girl—if she was indeed ten—was small for her age. Toothpick legs stuck out from under her baggy dress. Her bare feet were filthy. The little boy, about six and equally filthy, held a clump of his sister's skirt in his fist.

"He's dead, isn't he?" Jocelyn blurted out. Seeing Kate's sad nod, the girl slouched back against the fence and addressed one of the smudges on her bodice. "You see, I knew it. Stupid grown-ups. Don't ever tell us the truth, any of 'em."

"What did they tell you about Charlie?" asked Kate.

"They just said he went away. But he never even gave me my present."

"For your birthday?"

Jocelyn stared down at her nonexistent breasts. "I'm ten."

"And I'm seven," her brother said automatically, as if it was called for in the script.

"You and Charlie must have been good friends," David remarked.

The girl looked up, and seeing his smile—a smile that could melt the heart of any woman, much less that of a ten-year-old—immediately blushed. Looking back down, she coyly traced one brown toe along a crack in the sidewalk. "Charlie didn't have any friends. I don't, either. 'Cept Gabe here, but he's just my brother."

Little Gabe smiled and rubbed his slimy nose on his sister's dress.

"Did anyone else know Charlie very well?" David asked. "I mean, besides you."

Jocelyn chewed her lip thoughtfully. "Well—you could try over at Maloney's. Up the street."

"Who's Maloney?"

"Oh, he's nobody."

"If he's nobody, then how does he know Charlie?"

"He's not a him. He's a place. I mean, *it's* a place."

"Oh, of course," said David, looking down into Jocelyn's dazzled eyes. "How stupid of me."

"WHAT'RE YOU KIDS doing in here again? Go on. Get out before I lose my license!"

Jocelyn and Gabe skipped through the air-conditioned gloom, past the cocktail tables and up to the bar. They clambered onto two counter stools. "Some people here to see you, Sam," announced Jocelyn.

"There's a sign out there says you gotta be twenty-one to come in here. You kids twenty-one yet?"

"I'm seven," answered Gabe. "Can I have an olive?"

Grumbling, the bartender dipped his soapy hand in a glass jar and plopped half a dozen green olives on the counter. "Okay, now get going before someone sees you in—" His head jerked up as he noticed David and Kate approaching through the shadows. From his wary look, it was obvious Maloney's was seldom frequented by such well-heeled clientele. He blurted out: "It's not my doing! These brats come runnin' in off the street. I was just gonna throw 'em out."

"They're not liquor inspectors," said Jocelyn with obvious disdain as she popped an olive in her mouth.

Apparently everyone in this part of town lived in fear of some dreaded inspector or another.

"We need information," said David. "About one of your customers. Charlie Decker."

Sam took a long and careful look at David's clothes, and his train of thought was clearly mirrored in his eyes. *Nice suit. Silk tie. Yessir, all very expensive.* "He's dead," the bartender grunted.

"We know that."

"I don't speak ill of the dead." There was a long, significant pause. "You gonna order something?"

David sighed and finally settled onto a bar stool. "Okay. Two beers."

"That's all?"

"And two pineapple juices," added Jocelyn.

"That'll be twelve bucks."

"Cheap drinks," said David, sliding a twenty-dollar bill across the counter.

"Plus tax."

The children dumped the remaining olives in their drinks and began slurping down the juice.

"Tell us about Charlie," Kate prodded.

"Well, he used to sit right over there." Sam nodded at a dark corner table.

David and Kate leaned forward, waiting for the next pearl of information. Silence. "And?" prompted David.

"So that's where he sat."

"Doing what?"

"Drinking. Whiskey, mostly. He liked it neat. Then sometimes, I'd make him up a Sour Sam. That's if the mood hit him for somethin' different. That's my invention, the Sour Sam. Yeah, he'd drink one of those 'bout once a week. But mostly it was whiskey. Neat."

There was another silence. The talking machine had run out of money and needed a refill.

"I'll try a Sour Sam," said Kate.

"Don't you want your beer?"

"You can have it."

"Thanks. But I never touch the stuff." He turned his attention to mixing up a bizarre concoction of gin, club soda, and the juice of half a lemon, which undoubtedly accounted for the drink's name.

"Five bucks," he announced, passing it to Kate. "So how do you like it?"

She took a sip and gasped. "Interesting."

"Yeah, that's what everyone tells me."

"We were talking about Charlie," David reminded him.

"Oh, yeah, Charlie." The talking machine was back in order. "Let's see, he came around just 'bout every night. Think he liked the company, though he couldn't talk much, what with that bad throat of his. He'd sit there and drink, oh, one or two."

"Whiskeys. Neat," David supplied.

"Yeah, that's right. Real moderate, you know. Never got out-and-out drunk. He was a regular for 'bout a month. Then, few days ago, he stopped comin'. Too bad, you know? Hate to lose a steady one like that."

"You have any idea why he stopped?"

"They say police were looking for him. Word was out he killed some people."

"What do you think?"

"Charlie?" Sam laughed. "Not a chance."

Jocelyn handed Sam her empty glass. "Can I have another pineapple juice?"

Sam poured out two more pineapple juices and slid them over to the kids. "Eight bucks." He looked at David, who resignedly reached for his wallet.

"You forgot the olives," said Gabe.

"Those are free." The man wasn't entirely heartless.

"Did Charlie ever mention the name Jenny Brook?" Kate asked.

"Like I said, he never talked much. Yeah, ol' Charlie, he'd just sit over at that table and write those ol' poems. He'd scribble and scribble for hours just to get one right. Then he'd get mad and toss it. There'd be all these wadded-up papers on the floor whenever he left."

Kate shook her head in wonder. "I never imagined he'd be a poet."

"Everyone's a poet these days. That Charlie, though, he was real serious about it. That last day he was here, didn't have no money to pay for his drink. So he tears out one of his poems and gives it to me. Says it'll be worth somethin' some day. Ha! I'm such a sucker." He picked up a dirty rag and began to give the counter an almost sensuous rubdown.

"Do you still have the poem?" asked Kate.

"That's it, tacked over on the wall there."

The cheap, lined paper hung by a few strips of Scotch tape. By the dim light of the bar, the words were barely readable.

This is what I told them:
That healing lies not in forgetfulness
But in remembrance
Of you.
The smell of the sea on your skin.
The small and perfect footprints you leave in the sand.
In remembrance there are no endings.
And so you lie there, now and always, by the sea.
You open your eyes. You touch me.
The sun is in your fingertips.

And I am healed.
I am healed.

"So," said Sam, "think it's any good?"
"Gotta be," said Jocelyn. "If Charlie wrote it."
Sam shrugged. "Don't mean nothin'."

"SEEMS LIKE WE'VE HIT a dead end," David commented as they walked out into the blinding sunshine.

He might as well have said it of their relationship. He was standing with his hands thrust deep in his pockets as he gazed down the street at a drunk slouched in a doorway. Shattered glass sparkled in the gutter. Across the street, lurid red letters spelled out the title *Victorian Secrets* on an X-rated movie marquee.

If only he'd give her a smile, a look, anything to indicate that things weren't drawing to a close between them. But he didn't. He just kept his hands in his pockets. And she knew, without him saying a word, that more than Charlie Decker had died.

They passed an alley, scattering shards of broken beer bottles as they walked.

"So many loose ends," she remarked. "I don't see how the police can close the case."

"When it comes to police work, there are always loose ends, nagging doubts."

"It's sad, isn't it?" She gazed back at the Victory Hotel. "When a man dies and he leaves nothing behind. No trace of who or what he was."

"You could say the same about all of us. Unless we write great books or put up buildings, what's left of us after we're gone? Nothing."

"Only children."

For a moment he was silent. Then he said, "That's if we're lucky."

"We do know one thing about him," she concluded softly. "He loved her. Jenny." Staring down at the cracked sidewalk, she thought of the face in the photograph. An unforgettable woman. Even five years after her death, Jenny Brook's magic had somehow affected the lives of four people: the one who had loved her and the three who'd watched her die. She was the one tragic thread weaving through the tapestry of their deaths.

What would it be like, she wondered, to be loved as fiercely as Jenny had been? What enchantment had she possessed? *Whatever it was, I certainly don't have it.*

She said, without conviction, "It'll be good to get home again."

"Will it?"

"I'm used to being on my own."

He shrugged. "So am I."

They'd both retreated to their separate emotional corners. So little time left, she thought with a sense of desolation. And here they were, mouthing words like a pair of strangers. This morning, she'd awakened to find him showered and shaved and dressed in his most forbidding suit. Over breakfast they'd discussed everything but the subject that was uppermost in her mind. He could have made the first move. The whole time she was packing, he'd had the chance to ask her to stay. And she would have.

But he didn't say a thing.

Thank God she'd always been so good at holding on to her dignity. Never any tears, any hysterics. Even Eric had said as much. You've always been so sensible about things, he'd told her as he'd walked out the door.

Well, she'd be sensible this time, too.

The drive was far too short. Glancing at his profile she remembered the day they'd met. An eternity ago. He looked just as forbidding, just as untouchable.

They pulled up at her house. He carried her suitcase briskly up the walkway; he had the stride of a man in a hurry.

"Would you like to come in for a cup of coffee?" she asked, already knowing what his answer would be.

"I can't. Not right now. But I'll call you."

Famous last words. She understood perfectly, of course. It was all part of the ritual.

He cast a furtive glance at his watch. *Time to move on,* she reflected. *For both of us.*

Automatically she thrust the key in the lock and gave the door a shove. It swung open. As the room came into view, she halted on the threshold, unable to believe what she was seeing.

Dear God, she thought. *Why is this happening? Why now?*

She felt David's steadying hand close around her arm as she swayed backward in horror. The room swam, just for an instant, and then her eyes refocused on the opposite wall.

On the flowered wallpaper the letters "MYOB" had been spray painted in bloodred. And below them was the hollow-eyed figure of a skull and crossbones.

Chapter Fourteen

"NO DICE, DAVY. THE CASE IS CLOSED."

Pokie Ah Ching splashed coffee from his foam cup as he weaved through the crammed police station, past the desk sergeant arguing into the phone, past clerks hurrying back and forth with files, past a foul-smelling drunk shouting epithets at two weary-looking officers. Through it all, he moved as serenely as a battleship gliding through stormy waters.

"Don't you see, it was a warning!"

"Probably left by Charlie Decker."

"Kate's neighbor checked the house Tuesday morning. That message was left sometime later, when Decker was already dead."

"So it's a kid's prank."

"Yeah? Why would some kid write MYOB? Mind your own business?"

"You understand kids? I don't. Hell, I can't even figure out my own kids." Pokie headed into his office and scooted around to his chair. "Like I said, Davy, I'm busy."

David leaned across the desk. "Last night I told you we were followed. You said it was all in my head."

"I still say so."

"Then Decker turns up in the morgue. A nice, convenient little accident."

"I'm starting to smell a conspiracy theory."

"Your sense of smell is amazing."

Pokie set his cup down, slopping coffee on his papers. "Okay." He sighed. "You got one minute to tell me your theory. Then I'm throwing you out."

David grabbed a chair and sat down. "Four deaths. Tanaka. Richter. Decker. And Ellen O'Brien—"

"Death on the operating table isn't in my jurisdiction."

"But murder is. There's a hidden player in this game, Pokie. Someone who's managed to get rid of four people in a matter of two weeks. Someone smart and quiet and medically sophisticated. And very, very scared."

"Of what?"

"Kate Chesne. Maybe Kate's been asking too many questions. Maybe she knows something and just doesn't realize it. She's made our killer nervous. Nervous enough to scrawl warnings all over that wall."

"Unseen player, huh? I suppose you already got me a list of suspects."

"Starting with the chief of anesthesia. You check out that story on his wife yet?"

"She died Tuesday night in the nursing home. Natural causes."

"Oh, sure. The night after he walks off with a bunch of lethal drugs, she kicks the bucket."

"Coincidence."

"The man lives alone. There's no one to track his comings and goings—"

"I can just see the old geezer now." Pokie laughed. "Geriatric Jack the Ripper."

"It doesn't take much strength to slit someone's throat."

"But what's the old guy's motive, huh? Why would he go after members of his own staff?"

David let out a frustrated sigh. "I don't know," he admitted. "But it's got something to do with Jenny Brook."

Ever since he'd laid eyes on her photograph, he'd been unable to get the woman out of his mind. Something about her death, about the cold details recorded in her medical chart kept coming back to him, like a piece of music being played over and over in his head.

Uncontrollable seizures.

An infant girl, born alive.

Mother and child, two soft sparks of humanity, extinguished in the glare of the operating room.

Why, after five years, did their deaths threaten Kate Chesne?

There was a knock on the door. Sergeant Brophy, red-eyed and sniffling, dropped some papers on Pokie's desk. "Here's that report you been waiting for. Oh, and we got us another sighting of that Sasaki girl."

Pokie snorted. "Again? What does that make it? Forty three?"

"Forty-four. This one's at Burger King."

"Geez. Why do they always spot 'em at fast-food chains?"

"Maybe she's sittin' there with Jimmy Hoffa and—and—" Brophy sneezed. "Elvis." He blew his nose three times. They were great loud honks that, in the wild, could have attracted geese. "Allergies," he said, as if that was a far more acceptable excuse than the common cold. He aimed a spiteful glance out the window at his nemesis: a mango tree, seething with blossoms. "Too many damn trees around here," he muttered, retreating from the office.

Pokie laughed. "Brophy's idea of paradise is an air-conditioned concrete box." Reaching for the report, he sighed. "That's it, Davy. I got work to do."

"You going to reopen the case?"

"I'll think about it."

"What about Avery? If I were you, I'd—"

"I said I'll think about it." He flipped open the report, a rude gesture that said the meeting was definitely over.

David saw he might as well bang his head against a brick wall. He rose to leave. He was almost to the door when Pokie suddenly snapped out: "Hold it, Davy."

David halted, startled by the sharpness of Pokie's voice. "What?"

"Where's Kate right now?"

"I took her to my mother's. I didn't want to leave her alone."

"Then she is in a safe place."

"If you can call being around my mother safe. Why?"

Pokie waved the report he was holding. "This just came in from M.J.'s office. It's the autopsy on Decker. He didn't drown."

"What?" David moved over to the desk and snatched up the report. His gaze shot straight to the conclusions.

> Skull X rays show compression fracture, probably caused by lethal blow to the head. Cause of death: epidural hematoma.

Pokie sank back wearily and spat out an epithet. "The man was dead hours before he hit the water."

"VENGEANCE?" SAID Jinx Ransom, biting neatly into a freshly baked gingersnap. "It's a perfectly reasonable motive for murder. If, that is, one accepts there is such a thing as a reasonable motive for murder."

She and Kate were sitting on the back porch, overlooking the cemetery. It was a windless afternoon. Nothing moved—not the leaves on the trees, not the low-lying clouds, not even the air, which hung listless over the valley. The only creature stirring was Gracie, who shuffled out of the kitchen with a tray of rattling coffee cups and teaspoons. Pausing outside, Gracie cocked her head up at the sky.

"It's going to rain," she announced with absolute confidence.

"Charlie Decker was a poet," said Kate. "He loved children. Even more important, children loved him. Don't you think they'd know? They'd sense it if he was dangerous?"

"Nonsense. Children are as stupid as all the rest of us. And as for his being a mild-mannered poet, that doesn't mean a thing. He had five years to brood about his loss. That's certainly long enough to turn an obsession into violence."

"But the people who knew him all agree he wasn't a violent man."

"We're all violent. Especially when it concerns the ones we love. They're intimately connected, love and hate."

"That's a pretty grim view of human nature."

"But a realistic one. My husband was a circuit-court judge. My son was once a prosecutor. Oh, I've heard all their stories and believe me, reality's much grimmer than we could ever imagine."

Kate gazed out at the gently sloping lawn, at the flat bronze plaques marching out like footsteps across the grass. "Why did David leave the prosecutor's office?"

"Hasn't he told you?"

"He said something about slave wages. But I get the feeling money doesn't really mean much to him."

"Money doesn't mean diddly squat to David," Gracie interjected. She was looking down at a broken gingersnap, as if she wasn't quite sure whether to eat it or toss it to the birds.

"Then why did he leave?"

Jinx gave her one of those crystal-blue looks. "You were a surprise to me, Kate. It's rare enough for David to bring any woman to meet me. And then, when I heard you were a doctor…Well," She shook her head in amazement.

"David doesn't like doctors much," Gracie explained helpfully.

"It's a bit more than just dislike, dear."

"You're right," agreed Gracie after a few seconds' thought. "I suppose *loathe* is a better word."

Jinx reached for her cane and stood up. "Come, Kate," she beckoned. "There's something I think you should see."

It was a slow and solemn walk, through the feathery gap in the mock orange hedge, to a shady spot beneath the monkeypod tree. Insects drifted like motes in the windless air. At their feet, a small bunch of flowers lay wilting on a grave.

Noah Ransom
Seven Years Old.

"My grandson," said Jinx.

A leaf fluttered down from the tree and lay trembling on the grass.

"It must have been terrible for David," Kate murmured. "To lose his only child."

"Terrible for anyone. But especially for David." Jinx nudged the leaf aside with her cane. "Let me tell you about my son. He's very much like his father in one way: he doesn't love easily. He's like a miser, holding on to some priceless hoard of gold. But then, when he does release it, he gives it all and that's it. There's no turning back. That's why it was so hard on him, losing Noah. That boy was the most precious thing in his life and he still can't accept the fact he's gone. Maybe that's why he has so much trouble with you." She turned to Kate. "Do you know how the boy died?"

"He said it was a case of meningitis."

"Bacterial meningitis. Curable illness, right?"

"If it's caught early enough."

"*If*. That's the word that haunts David." She looked down sadly at the wilted flowers. "He was out of town—some convention in Chicago—when Noah got sick. At first, Linda didn't think much of it. You know how kids are, always coming down with colds. But the boy's fever wouldn't go away. And then Noah said he had a headache. His usual pediatrician was on vacation so Linda took the boy to another doctor, in the same building. For two hours they sat in the waiting room. After all that, the doctor spent only five minutes with Noah. And then he sent him home."

Kate stared down at the grave, knowing, fearing, what would come next.

"Linda called the doctor three times that night. She must have known something was wrong. But all she got from him was a scolding. He told her she was just an anxious mother. That she ought to know better than to turn a cold into a crisis. When she finally brought Noah into Emergency, he was delirious. He just kept mumbling, asking for his Daddy. The hospital doctors did what they could, but..." Jinx gave a little shrug. "It wasn't easy for either of them. Linda blamed herself. And David...he just withdrew. He shrank into his tight little shell and refused to come out, even for her. I'm not surprised she left him." Jinx looked off, toward the house. "It came out later, about the doctor. That he was an alcoholic. That he'd lost his license in California. That's when David turned it into his personal crusade. Oh, he ruined the man, all right. He did a very thorough job of it. But it took over his life, wrecked his marriage. That's when he left the prosecutor's office. He's made a lot of money since then, destroying doctors. But the money's not why he does it. Somewhere, in the back of his mind, he'll always be crucifying that one doctor. The one who killed Noah."

That's why we never had a chance, Kate thought. *I was always the enemy. The one he wanted to destroy.*

Jinx wandered slowly back to the house. For a long time, Kate stood alone in the shadow of the old tree, thinking about Noah Ransom, seven years old. About how powerful a force it was, this love for a child; as cruelly obsessive as anything between a man and a woman. Could she ever compete with the memory of a son? Or ever escape the blame for his death?

All these years, David had held on to that pain. He'd used it as some mystical source of power to fight the same battle over and over again. The way Charlie Decker had used his pain to sustain him through five long years in a mental hospital.

Five years in a hospital.

She frowned, suddenly remembering the bottle of pills in Decker's nightstand. Haldol. Pills for psychotics. Was he, in fact, crazy?

Turning, she looked back at the porch and saw it was empty. Jinx and Gracie had gone into the house. The air was so heavy she could feel it weighing oppressively on her shoulders. A storm on the way, she thought.

If she left now, she might make it to the state hospital before the rain started.

DR. NEMECHEK WAS a thin, slouching man with tired eyes and a puckered mouth. His shirt was rumpled and his white coat hung in folds on his frail shoulders. He looked like a man who'd slept all night in his clothes.

They walked together on the hospital grounds. All around them, white-gowned patients wandered aimlessly like dandelion fluffs drifting about the lawn. Every so often, Dr. Nemechek would stop to pat a shoulder or murmur a few words of greeting. *How are you, Mrs. Solti? Just fine, Doctor. Why didn't you come to group therapy? Oh, it's my old trouble, you know. All those mealyworms in my feet. I see. I see. Well, good afternoon, Mrs. Solti. Good afternoon, Doctor.*

Dr. Nemechek paused on the grass and gazed around sadly at his kingdom of shattered minds. "Charlie Decker never belonged here," he remarked. "I told them from the beginning that he wasn't criminally insane. But the court had their so-called expert from the mainland. So he was committed." He shook his head. "That's the trouble with courts. All they look at is their evidence, whatever that means. I look at the man."

"And what did you see when you looked at Charlie?"

"He was withdrawn. Very depressed. At times, maybe, delusional."

"Then he was insane."

"But not criminally so." Nemechek turned to her as if he wanted to be absolutely certain she understood his point. "Insanity can be dangerous. Or it can be nothing more than a gentle affliction. A merciful shield against pain. That's what it was for Charlie: a shield. His delusion kept him alive. That's why I never tried to tamper with it. I felt that if I ever took away that shield, it would kill him."

"The police say he was a murderer."

"Ridiculous."

"Why?"

"He was a perfectly benign creature. He'd go out of his way to avoid stepping on a cricket."

"Maybe killing people was easier."

Nemechek gave a dismissive wave. "He had no reason to kill anyone."

"What about Jenny Brook? Wasn't she his reason?"

"Charlie's delusion wasn't about Jenny. He'd accepted her death as inevitable."

Kate frowned. "Then what was his delusion?"

"It was about their child. It was something one of the doctors told him, about the baby being born alive. Only Charlie got it twisted around in his head. That was his obsession, this missing daughter of his. Every August, he'd hold a little birthday celebration. He'd tell us, 'My girl's five years old today.' He wanted to find her. Wanted to raise her like a little princess, give her dresses and dolls and all the things girls are supposed to like. But I knew he'd never really try to find her. He was terrified of learning the truth: that the baby really was dead."

A sprinkling of rain made them both glance up at the sky. Wind was gusting the clouds and on the lawn, nurses hurried about, coaxing patients out of the coming storm.

"Is there any possibility he was right?" she asked. "That the girl's still alive?"

"Not a chance." A curtain of drizzle had drifted between them, blotting out his gray face. "The baby's dead, Dr. Chesne. For the last five years, the only place that child existed was in Charlie Decker's mind."

THE BABY'S DEAD.

As Kate drove the mist-shrouded highway back to Jinx's house, Dr. Nemechek's words kept repeating in her head.

The baby's dead. The only place that child existed was in Charlie Decker's mind.

If the girl had lived, what would she be like now? Kate wondered. Would she have her father's dark hair? Would she have her mother's glow of eternity in her five-year-old eyes?

The face of Jenny Brook took shape in her mind, an impish smile framed by the blue sky of a summer day. At that instant, fog puffed across the road and Kate strained to see through the mist. As she did, the image of Jenny Brook wavered, dissolved; in its place was another face, a small one, framed by ironwood trees. There was a break in the clouds; suddenly, the mist vanished from the road. And as the sunlight broke through, so did the revelation. She almost slammed on the brakes.

Why the hell didn't I see it before?

Jenny Brook's child was still alive.

And he was five years old.

"WHERE THE HELL is she?" muttered David, slamming the telephone down. "Nemechek says she left the state hospital at five. She should be home by now." He glanced irritably across his desk at Phil Glickman, who was poking a pair of chopsticks into a carton of chow mein.

"You know," Glickman mumbled as he expertly shuttled noodles into his mouth, "this case gets more confusing every time I hear about it. You start off with a simple act of malpractice and you end up with murder. In plural. Where's it gonna lead next?"

"I wish I knew." David sighed. Swiveling around toward the window, he tried to ignore the tempting smells of Glickman's take-out supper. Outside, the clouds were darkening to a gunmetal gray. It reminded him of just how late it was. Ordinarily, he'd be packing up his briefcase for home. But he'd needed a chance to think, and this was where his mind seemed to work best—right here at this window.

"What a way to commit murder, slashing someone's throat," Glickman said. "I mean, think of all that blood! Takes a lot of nerve."

"Or desperation."

"And it can't be that easy. You'd have to get up pretty close to slice that neck artery." He slashed a chopstick through the air. "There are so many easier ways to do the job."

"Sounds like you've put some thought into the matter."

"Don't we all? Everyone has some dark fantasy. Cornering your wife's lover in the alley. Getting back at the punk who mugged you. We can all think of someone we'd really like to put away. And it can't be that hard, you know? Murder. If a guy's smart, he does it with subtlety." He slurped up a mouthful of noodles. "Poison, for instance. Something that kills fast and can't be traced. Now there's the perfect murder."

"Except for one thing."

"What's that?"

"Where's the satisfaction if your victim doesn't suffer?"

"A problem," Glickman conceded. "So you make 'em suffer through terror. Warnings. Threats."

David shifted uneasily, remembering the bloodred skull on Kate's wall. Through narrowed eyes, he watched the clouds hanging low on the horizon. With every passing minute, his sense of impending disaster grew stronger.

He rose to his feet and began throwing papers into his briefcase. It was useless, hanging around here; he could worry just as effectively at his mother's house.

"You know, there's one thing about this case that still bothers me," remarked Glickman, gulping the last of his supper.

"What's that?"

"That EKG. Tanaka and Richter were killed in just about the bloodiest way possible. Why should the murderer go out of his way to make Ellen O'Brien's death look like a heart attack?"

"The one thing I learned in the prosecutor's office," said David, snapping his briefcase shut, "is that murder doesn't have to make sense."

"Well, it seems to me our killer went to a lot of trouble just to shift the blame to Kate Chesne."

David was already at the door when he suddenly halted. "What did you say?"

"That he went to a lot of trouble to pin the blame—"

"No, the word you used was *shift*. He *shifted* the blame!"

"Maybe I did. So?"

"So who gets sued when a patient dies unexpectedly on the operating table?"

"The blame's usually shared by..." Glickman stopped. "Oh, my God. Why the hell didn't I think of that before?"

David was already reaching for the telephone. As he dialed the police, he cursed himself for being so blind. The killer had been there all along. Watching. Waiting. He must have known that Kate was hunting for answers, and that she was getting close. Now he was scared. Scared enough to scrawl a warning on Kate's wall. Scared enough to tail a car down a dark highway.

Maybe even scared enough to kill one more time.

IT WAS FIVE-THIRTY AND most of the clerks in Medical Records had gone for the day. The lone clerk who remained grudgingly took Kate's request slip and went to the computer terminal to call up the chart location. As the data appeared, she frowned.

"This patient's deceased," she noted, pointing to the screen.

"I know," said Kate, wearily remembering the last time she'd tried to retrieve a chart from the Deceased Persons' room.

"So it's in the inactive files."

"I understand that. Could you please get me the chart?"

"It may take a while to track it down. Why don't you come back tomorrow?"

Kate resisted the urge to reach over and grab the clerk by her frilly dress. "I need the chart *now*." She felt like adding: *It's a matter of life and death.*

The clerk looked at her watch and tapped her pencil on the desk. With agonizing slowness, she rose to her feet and vanished into the file room.

Fifteen minutes passed before she returned with the record. Kate retreated to a corner table and stared down at the name on the cover: Brook, Baby Girl.

The child had never even had a name.

The chart contained pitifully few pages, only the hospital face sheet, death certificate, and a scrawled summary of the infant's short existence. Death had been pronounced August 17 at 2:00 a.m., an hour after birth. The cause of death was cerebral anoxia: the tiny brain had been starved of oxygen. The death certificate was signed by Dr. Henry Tanaka.

Kate next turned her attention to the copy of Jenny Brook's chart, which she'd brought with her. She'd read these pages so many times before; now she studied it line by line, pondering the significance of each sentence.

"...28-year-old female, G1PO, 36 weeks' gestation, admitted via E.R. in early labor..."

A routine report, she thought. There were no surprises, no warnings of the disaster to come. But at the bottom of the first page she stopped, her gaze focusing on a single statement: "Because of maternal family history of spina bifida, amniocentesis was performed at eighteen weeks of pregnancy and revealed no abnormalities."

Amniocentesis. Early in her pregnancy, fluid had been withdrawn from Jenny Brook's womb for analysis. This would have identified any fetal malformations. It also would have identified the baby's sex.

The amniocentesis report was not included in the hospital chart. That didn't surprise her; the report had probably been filed away in Jenny Brook's outpatient record.

Which had conveniently vanished from Dr. Tanaka's office, she realized with a start.

Kate closed the chart. Suddenly feverish, she rose and returned to the file clerk. "I need another record," she said.

"Not another deceased patient, I hope."

"No, this one's still alive."

"Name?"

"William Santini."

It took only a minute for the clerk to find it. When Kate finally held it in her hands, she was almost afraid to open it, afraid to see what she already knew lay inside. She stood there beside the clerk's desk, wondering if she really wanted to know.

She opened the cover.

A copy of the birth certificate stared up at her.

Name: William Santini.
Date of Birth: August 17.
Time: 03:00.

August 17, the same day. But not quite the same time. Exactly one hour after Baby Girl Brook had left the world, William Santini had entered it.

Two infants; one living, one dead. Had there ever been a better motive for murder?

"Don't tell me you still have charts to finish," remarked a shockingly familiar voice.

Kate's head whipped around. Guy Santini had just walked in the door. She slapped the chart closed but instantly realized the name was scrawled in bold black ink across the cover. In a panic, she hugged the chart to her chest as an automatic smile congealed on her face.

"I'm just…cleaning up some last paperwork." She swallowed and managed to add, conversationally, "You're here late."

"Stranded again. Car's back in the shop so Susan's picking me up." He glanced across the counter, searching for the clerk, who'd temporarily vanished. "Where's the help around here, anyway?"

"She was, uh, here just a minute ago," said Kate, inching toward the exit.

"I guess you heard the news. About Avery's wife. A blessing, really, considering her—" He looked at her and she froze, just two feet from the door.

He frowned. "Is something wrong?"

"No. I've just— Look, I've really got to go." She turned and was about to flee out the door when the file clerk yelled: "Dr. Chesne!"

"What?" Kate spun around to see the woman peering at her reproachfully from behind a shelf.

"The chart. You can't take it out of the department."

Kate looked down at the folder she was still holding to her chest and frantically debated her next move. She didn't dare return the chart while Guy was standing right beside the counter; he'd see the name. But she couldn't stand here like a half-wit, either.

They were both frowning at her, waiting for her to say something.

"Look, if you're not finished with it, I can hold it right here," the clerk offered, moving to the counter.

"No. I mean…"

Guy laughed. "What's in that thing, anyway? State secrets?"

Kate realized she was clutching the chart as though terrified it would be forcibly pried from her grasp. With her heart hammering, she willed her feet to move forward. Her hand was barely steady as she placed the chart facedown on the counter. "I'm not finished with it."

"Then I'll hold it for you." The clerk reached over and for one terrifying second seemed poised to expose the patient's name. Instead she merely scooped up the request list that Guy had just laid on the counter. "Why don't you sit down, Dr. Santini?" she suggested. "I'll bring your records over to you." Then she turned and vanished into the file room.

Time to get the hell out of here, thought Kate.

It took all her self-control not to bolt out the door. She felt Guy's eyes on her back as she moved slowly and deliberately toward the exit. Only when she'd actually made it into the hall, only when she heard the door thud shut behind her, did the impact of what she'd discovered hit her full force. Guy Santini was her colleague. Her friend.

He was also a murderer. And she was the only one who knew.

GUY STARED AT THE door through which Kate had just retreated. He'd known Kate Chesne for almost a year now and he'd never seen her so jittery. Puzzled, he turned and headed to the corner table to wait. It was his favorite spot, this little nook; it gave him a sense of privacy in this vast, impersonal room. Someone else obviously favored it, as well. There were two charts still lying there, waiting to be refiled. He grabbed a chair and was about to nudge the folders aside when his gaze suddenly froze on the top cover. He felt his legs give away. Slowly he sank into the chair and stared at the name.

Brook, Baby Girl. Deceased.

Dear God, he thought. *It can't be the same Brook.*

He flipped it open and hunted for the mother's name on the death certificate. What he saw sent panic knifing through him.

Mother: Brook, Jennifer.

The same woman. The same baby. He had to think; he had to stay calm. Yes, he would stay calm. There was nothing to worry about. No one could connect him to Jenny Brook or the child. The four people involved with that tragedy of five years ago were now dead. There was no reason for anyone to be curious.

Or was there?

He shot to his feet and hurried back to the counter. The chart that Kate had so reluctantly parted with was still lying there, face down. He flipped it over. His own son's name stared up at him.

Kate Chesne knew. She *had* to know. And she had to be stopped.

"Here you are," said the file clerk, emerging from the shelves with an armload of charts. "I think I've got all—" She halted in amazement. "Where are you going? Dr. Santini!"

Guy didn't answer; he was too busy running out the door.

THE HOSPITAL LOBBY WAS reassuringly bright when Kate stepped off the elevator. A few visitors still lingered by the lobby doors, staring out at the storm. A security guard lounged at the information desk, chatting with a pretty volunteer. Kate hurried over to the public telephones. An out-of-order sign was taped to the first phone; a man was feeding a quarter into the other. She planted herself right behind him and waited. Wind rattled the lobby windows; outside, the parking lot was obscured by a heavy curtain of rain. She prayed that Lieutenant Ah Ching would be at his desk.

But at that moment it wasn't Ah Ching's voice she longed to hear most of all; it was David's.

The man was still talking on the phone. Glancing around, she was alarmed to see the security guard had vanished. The volunteer was already closing down the information desk. The place was emptying out too fast. She didn't want to be left alone—not here, not with what she knew.

She fled the hospital and headed out into the downpour.

She'd parked Jinx's car at the far end of the lot. The storm had become a fierce, tropical battering of wind and rain. By the time she'd dashed across to the car, her clothes were soaked. It took a few seconds to fumble through the unfamiliar set of keys, another few seconds to unlock the door. She was so intent on escaping the storm that she scarcely noticed the shadow moving toward her through the gloom. Just as she slid onto the driver's seat, the shadow closed in. A hand seized her arm.

She stared up to see Guy Santini towering over her.

Chapter Fifteen

"MOVE OVER," HE SAID.

"Guy, my arm—"

"I said move over."

Desperate, she glanced around for some passerby who might hear her screams. But the lot was deserted and the only sound was the thudding of rain on the car's roof.

Escape was impossible. Guy was blocking the driver's exit and she'd never be able to scramble out the passenger door in time.

Before she could even plan her next move, Guy shoved her aside and slid onto the driver's seat. The door slammed shut. Through the window, the gray light of evening cast a watery glow on his face.

"Your keys, Kate," he demanded.

The keys had dropped beside her on the seat; she made no move to retrieve them.

"Give me the damn keys!" He suddenly spotted them in the dim light. Snatching them up, he shoved the key into the ignition. The second he did, she lashed out. Like a trapped animal, she clawed at his face but at the last instant, some inner revulsion at the viciousness of her attack made her hesitate. It was only a split second, but it was enough time for him to react.

Flinching aside, he seized her wrist and wrenched her sideways so hard she was thrown back against the seat.

"If I have to," he said in a deadly quiet voice, "I swear I'll break your arm." He threw the gear in reverse and the car jerked backward. Then, hitting the gas, he spun the car out of the parking lot and into the street.

"Where are you taking me?" she asked.

"Somewhere. Anywhere. I'm going to talk and you're going to listen."

"About—about what?"

"You know what the hell about!"

Her chin snapped up expectantly as they approached an intersection. If she could throw herself out—

But he'd already anticipated her move. Seizing her arm, he yanked her toward him and sped through the intersection just as the signal turned red.

That was the last stoplight before the freeway. The car accelerated. She watched in despair as the speedometer climbed to sixty. She'd missed her chance. If she tried to leap out now, she'd almost certainly break her neck.

He knew as well as she did that she'd never be so reckless. He released her arm. "It was none of your business, Kate," he said, his eyes shifting back to the road. "You had no right to pry. No right at all."

"Ellen was my patient—*our* patient—"

"That doesn't mean you can tear my life apart!"

"What about her life? And Ann's? They're dead, Guy!"

"And the past died with them! I say let it stay dead."

"My God, I thought I knew you. I thought we were friends—"

"I have to protect my son. And Susan. You think I'd stand back and let them be destroyed?"

"They'd never take the boy away from you! Not after five years! The courts are bound to give you custody—"

"You think all I'm worried about is custody? Oh, we'd keep William all right. There's no judge on earth who'd be able to take him away from me! Who'd hand him over to some lunatic like Decker! No. It's Susan I'm thinking of."

The highway was slick with rain, the road treacherous. Both

his hands were fully occupied on the steering wheel. If she lunged at him now, the car would surely spin out of control, killing them both. She had to wait for another time, another chance to escape.

"I don't understand," she persisted, scanning the road ahead for a stalled car, a traffic jam, anything to slow them down. "What do you mean, it's Susan you're worried about?"

"She doesn't know." At Kate's incredulous look, he nodded. "She thinks William is hers."

"How can she not know?"

"I've kept it from her. For five years, it's been my little secret. She was under anesthesia when our baby was born. It was a nightmare, all that rush, all that panic to do an emergency C-section. That was our third baby, Kate. Our last chance. And she was born dead...." He paused and cleared his throat; when he spoke again, his voice was still thick with pain. "I didn't know what to do. What to tell Susan. There she was, sleeping. So peaceful, so happy. And there I was, holding our dead baby girl."

"You took Jenny Brook's baby as your own."

He hastily scraped the back of his hand across his face. "It was—it was an act of God. Can't you see that? *An act of God.* That's how it seemed to me at the time. The woman had just died. And there was her baby boy, this absolutely *perfect* baby boy, crying in the next room. No one to hold him. Or love him. No one knew a thing about the child's father. There didn't seem to be any relatives, anyone who cared. And there was Susan, already starting to wake up. Can't you understand? It would have killed her to find out. God *gave* us that boy! It was as if—as if He had planned it that way. We all felt it. Ann. Ellen. Only Tanaka—"

"He didn't agree?"

"Not at first. I argued with him. I practically begged him. It was only when Susan opened her eyes and asked for her baby that he finally gave in. So Ellen brought the boy to the room. She put him in Susan's arms. And my Susan—she just looked at him and then she—she started to cry...." Guy wiped his sleeve across his face. "That's when we knew we'd done the right thing."

Yes, Kate could see the perfection of that moment. A decision as wise as Solomon's. What better proof of its rightness than the sight of a newborn baby curled up in his mother's arms?

But that same decision had led to the murder of four people.

Soon it would be five.

The car suddenly slowed; with a new burst of hope, she looked up. Traffic was growing heavier. Far ahead lay the Pali tunnel, curtained off by rain. She knew there was an emergency telephone somewhere near the entrance. If he would just slow down a little more, if she could shove the car door open, she might be able to fling herself out before he could stop her.

The chance never came. Instead of heading into the tunnel, Guy veered off onto a thickly wooded side road and roared past a sign labeled: Pali Lookout. The last stop, she thought. Set on a cliff high above the valley, this was the overhang where suicidal lovers sealed their pacts, where ancient warriors once were flung to their deaths. It was the perfect spot for murder.

A last flood of desperation made her claw for the door. Before she could get it open, he yanked her back. She turned and flew at him with both fists. Guy struggled to fight her off and lost control of the wheel. The car swerved off the road. By the erratic beams of their headlights, she caught glimpses of trees looming ahead. Branches thudded against the windshield but she was beyond caring whether they crashed; her only goal was escape.

It was Guy's overwhelming strength that decided the battle. He threw all his weight into shoving her back. Then, cursing, he grabbed the wheel and spun it wildly to the left. The right fender scraped trees as the car veered back onto the road. Kate, sprawled against the seat, could only watch in defeat as they weaved up the last hundred yards to the lookout.

Guy stopped the car and killed the engine. For a long time he sat in silence, as though summoning up the courage to get the job done. Outside, the rain had slowed to a drizzle and beyond the cliff's edge, mist swirled past, shrouding the fatal plunge from view.

"That was a damned crazy stunt you pulled," he said quietly. "Why the hell did you do it?"

Slowly she bowed her head; she felt a profound sense of weariness. Of inevitability. "Because you're going to kill me," she whispered. "The way you killed the others."

"I'm going to *what*?"

She looked up, searching his eyes for some trace of remorse. If only she could reach inside him and drag out some last scrap of humanity! "Was it easy?" she asked softly. "Cutting Ann's throat? Watching her bleed to death?"

"You mean— You really think I— Dear God!" He dropped his head in his hands. Suddenly he began to laugh. It was soft at first, then it grew louder and wilder until his whole body was racked by what sounded more like sobs than laughter. He didn't notice the new set of headlights, flickering like a beacon through the mist. She glanced around and saw that another car had wandered up the road. This was her chance to throw open the door, to run for help. But she didn't. In that instant she knew that Guy had never really meant to hurt her. That he was incapable of murder.

Without warning, he shoved his door open and stumbled out into the fog. At the edge of the lookout, he halted, his head and shoulders bowed as if in prayer.

Kate got out of the car and followed him. She didn't say a thing. She simply reached out and touched his arm. She could almost feel the pain, the confusion, coursing through his body.

"Then you didn't kill them," she said.

He looked up and slowly took in a deep breath of air. "I'd do almost anything to keep my son. But murder?" He shook his head. "No. God, no. Oh, I thought about killing Decker. Who would have missed him? He was nothing, just a—a scrap of human garbage. And it seemed like such an easy way out. Maybe the only way out. He wouldn't give up. He kept hounding people for answers. Demanding to know where the baby was."

"How did he know the baby was alive?"

"There was another doctor in the delivery room that night—"

"You mean Dr. Vaughn?"

"Decker talked to him. Learned just enough."

"And then Vaughn died in a car accident."

Guy nodded. "I thought it'd all be okay, then. I thought it was over. But then Decker got out of the state hospital. Sooner or later, someone would've talked. Tanaka was ready to. And Ann was scared out of her mind. I gave her some money, to leave the islands. But she never made it. Decker got to her first."

"That doesn't make sense, Guy. Why would he kill the only people who could give him the answers?"

"He was psychotic."

"Even psychotics have some sort of logic."

"He must have done it. There was no one else who—"

From somewhere in the mist came the hard click of metal. Kate and Guy froze as footsteps rapped slowly across the pavement. Out of the gathering darkness, a figure emerged, like vapor taking on substance until it stood before them. Even in the somber light of dusk, Susan Santini's red hair seemed to sparkle with fire. But it was the dull gray of the gun that held Kate's gaze.

"Move out of the way, Guy," Susan ordered softly.

Guy was too stunned to move or speak; he could only stare mutely at his wife.

"It was you," Kate murmured in astonishment. "All the time *you* were the one. Not Decker."

Slowly, Susan turned her unfocused gaze on Kate. Through the veil of mist drifting between them, her face was as vague and formless as a ghost's. "You don't understand, do you? But you've never had a baby, Kate. You've never been afraid of someone hurting it or taking it away. That's all a mother ever thinks about. Worries about. It's all *I* ever worried about."

A low groan escaped Guy's throat. "My God, Susan. Do you understand what you've done?"

"You wouldn't do it. So I had to. All those years, I never knew about William. You should have told me, Guy. You should have told me. I had to hear it from Tanaka."

"You killed four people, Susan!"

"Not four. Only three. I didn't kill Ellen." Susan looked at Kate. "She did."

Kate stared at her. "What do you mean?"

"That wasn't succinylcholine in the vial. It was potassium chloride. You gave Ellen a lethal dose." Her gaze shifted back to her husband. "I didn't want you to be blamed, darling. I couldn't stand to see you hurt, the way you were hurt by the last lawsuit. So I changed the EKG. I put *her* initials on it."

"And I got the blame," finished Kate.

Nodding, Susan raised the gun. "Yes, Kate. You got the blame.

I'm sorry. Now please, Guy. Move away. It has to be done, for William's sake."

"No, Susan."

She frowned at him in disbelief. "They'll take him away from me. Don't you see? They'll take my baby away."

"I won't let them. I promise."

Susan shook her head. "It's too late, Guy. I've killed the others. She's the only one who knows."

"But *I* know!" Guy blurted out. "Are you going to kill me, too?"

"You won't tell. You're my husband."

"Susan, give me the gun." Guy moved slowly forward, his hand held out to her. His voice dropped, became gentle, intimate. "Please, darling. Nothing will happen. I'll take care of everything. Just give it to me."

She retreated a step and almost lost her balance on the uneven terrain. Guy froze as the barrel of the gun swayed for an instant in his direction.

"You're not going to hurt me, Susan."

"Please, Guy…"

He took a step forward. "Are you?"

"I love you," she moaned.

"Then give me the gun. Yes, darling. Give it to me…."

The distance between them slowly evaporated. Guy's hand stretched out to her, coaxing her with the promise of warmth and safety. She stared at it with longing, as though knowing in some deep part of her mind that it was forever beyond her reach. The gun was only inches from Guy's fingers and still she didn't move; she was paralyzed by the inevitability of defeat.

Guy, at last sensing he had won, quickly closed the gap between them. Seizing the gun by the barrel, he tried to tug it from her hands.

But she didn't surrender it. At that instant, something inside her, some last spark of resistance, seemed to flare up and she tried to wrench it back.

"Let go!" she screamed.

"Give it to me," Guy demanded, wrestling for control of the weapon. "Susan, give it to me!"

The gun's blast seemed to trap them in freeze-frame. They

stared at each other in astonishment, neither of them willing to believe what had just happened. Then Guy stumbled backward, clutching his leg.

"*No!*" Susan's wail rose up and drifted, ghostlike, through the mist. Slowly she turned toward Kate. The glow of desperation was in her eyes. And she was still clutching the gun.

That's when Kate ran. Blindly, desperately, into the mist. She heard a pistol shot. A bullet whistled past and thudded into the dirt near her feet. There was no time to get her bearings, to circle back toward the road. She just kept running and prayed that the fog would shroud her from Susan.

The ground suddenly rose upward. Through fingers of mist, she saw the sheer face of the ridge, sparsely stubbled with brush. She spun around and realized instantly that the way back to the main road was blocked by Susan's approach. Her only escape route lay to the left, down the crumbling remains of the old Pali road. It was the original cliff pass. The road had long ago been abandoned to the elements. She had no idea how far it would take her; parts of it, she knew, had collapsed down the sheer slope.

The sound of footsteps closing in left her no choice. She scrambled over a low concrete wall and at once found herself sliding helplessly down a muddy bank. Clawing at branches and vines, she managed to break her fall until she landed, scratched and breathless, on a slab of pavement. The old Pali road.

Somewhere above, hidden among the clouds, bushes rustled. "There's nowhere to run, Kate!" Susan's disembodied voice seemed to come from everywhere at once. "The old road doesn't go very far. One wrong step and you'll be over the cliff. So you'd better be careful…."

Careful…careful… The shouted warning echoed off the ridge and shattered into terrifying fragments of sound. The rustling of bushes moved closer. Susan was closing in. She was taking her time, advancing slowly, steadily. Her victim was trapped. And she knew it.

But trapped wasn't the same as helpless.

Kate leaped to her feet and began to run. The old road was full of cracks and potholes. In places it had crumbled away entirely and young trees poked through, their roots rippling the asphalt. She strained to see through the fog but could make out no more than a few feet ahead. Darkness was falling fast; it would cut off the last of her visibility. But it would also be a cloak in which to hide.

But where could she hide? On her right, the ridge loomed steeply upward; on her left, the pavement broke off sharply at the cliff's edge. She had no choice; she had to keep running.

She stumbled over a loose boulder and sprawled onto the brutal asphalt. At once she was back on her feet, mindless of the pain searing her knees. Even as she ran, she forced herself to think ahead. Would there be a barrier at the road's end? Or would there simply be a straight drop to oblivion? In either case, there'd be no escape. There would only be a bullet, and then a plunge over the cliff. How long would it be before they found her body?

A gust of wind swept the road. For an instant, the mist cleared. She saw looming to her right the face of the ridge, covered by dense brush. Halfway up, almost hidden by the overgrowth, was the mouth of a cave. If she could reach it, if she could scramble up those bushes before Susan passed this way, she could hide until help arrived. If it arrived.

She threaded her way into the shrubbery and began clambering up the mountainside. Rain had muddied the slope; she had to claw for roots and branches to pull herself up. All the time, there was the danger of dislodging a boulder, of sending it thundering to the road. The crash would certainly alert Susan. And here she'd be, poised like a fly on the wall. One well-placed bullet would end it all.

The sound of footsteps made her freeze. Susan was approaching. Desperately, Kate hugged the mountain, willing herself to blend into the bushes.

The footsteps slowed, stopped. At that instant, the wind nudged the clouds against the ridge, draping Kate in silvery mist. The footsteps moved on, slowly clipping across the pavement. Only when the sound had faded did Kate dare continue her climb.

By the time she reached the cave's mouth, her hands had cramped into claws. In took her last ounce of strength to drag herself up into the muddy hollow. There she collapsed, fighting to catch her breath. Dampness trickled from the tree roots above and dripped onto her face. She heard, deep in the shadows, the rustle of movement and something scuttled across her arm. A beetle. She didn't have the energy to brush it off. Exhausted and shivering, she curled up like a tired puppy in the mud. The wind rose, sweeping the clouds from the pass. Already the mist was fading. If she could just hold out until nightfall. That was the most she could hope for: darkness.

Closing her eyes, she focused on a mental image of David. If only he could hear her silent plea for help. But he couldn't help her. No one could. She wondered how he'd react to her death. Would he feel any grief? Or would he simply shrug it off as a tragic end to a fading love affair? That was what hurt most—the thought of his indifference.

She cradled her face in her arms, and warm tears mingled with the icy water on her cheeks. She'd never felt so alone, so abandoned. Suddenly it didn't matter whether she lived or died; only that someone cared.

But I'm the only one who really cares.

A desperate new strength stirred inside her. Slowly she unfolded her limbs and looked out at the thin wisps of fog drifting past the cave. And she felt a new sense of fury that her life might be stolen from her and that the man she loved wasn't even here to help.

If I want to be saved, I have to do it myself.

It was the footsteps, moving slowly back along the road, that told her darkness would come too late to save her. Through the tangle of branches fringing the cave mouth, she saw against the sky's fading light the velvety green of a distant ridge. The mist had vanished; so had her invisibility.

"You're up there, aren't you?" Susan's voice floated up from the road, a sound so chilling Kate trembled. "I almost missed it. But there's one unfortunate thing about caves. Something I'm sure you've realized by now. They're dead ends."

Rocks rattled down the slope and slammed onto the road, their impact echoing like gunshot. *She's climbing the ridge,* Kate thought frantically. *She's coming for me....*

Her only escape route was back out through the cave mouth. Right into Susan's line of fire.

A twig snapped and more rocks slithered down the mountain.

Susan was closing in. Kate had no choice left; either she bolted now or she'd be trapped like a rat.

Swiftly she groped around in the mud and came up with a fist-size rock. It wasn't much against a gun, but it was all she had. Cautiously, she eased her head out. To her horror, she saw that Susan was already halfway up the slope.

Their eyes met. In that instant, each recognized the other's desperation. One was fighting for her life, the other for her child. There could be no compromise, no surrender, except in death.

Susan took aim; the barrel swung up toward her prey's head.

Kate hurled the rock.

It skimmed the bushes and thudded against Susan's shoulder. Crying out, Susan slid a few feet down the mountainside before she managed to grab hold of a branch. There she clung for a moment, stunned.

Kate scrambled out of the cave and began clawing her way up the ridge. Even as she pulled herself up, branch by branch, some rational part of her brain was screaming that the ascent was impossible, that the cliff face was too steep, the bushes too straggly to support her weight. But her arms and legs seemed to move on their own, guided not by logic but by the instinct to survive. Her sleeves were shredded by thorns and her hands and arms were already scraped raw but she was too numbed by terror to feel pain.

A bullet ricocheted off a boulder. Kate cringed as shattered rock and earth spat out and stung her face. Susan's aim was wide; she couldn't cling to the mountain and shoot accurately at the same time.

Kate looked up to find herself staring at an overhanging rock, laced with vines. Was she strong enough to drag herself over the top? Would the vines hold her weight? The surface was impossibly steep and she was so tired, so very tired….

Another shot rang out; the bullet came so close she could feel it whistle past her cheek. Kate frantically grabbed a vine and began to drag herself up the rock face. Her shoes slid uselessly downward, then found a toe hold. She shimmied up a few precious inches, then a few more, her knees scraping the harsh volcanic boulder. High above, clouds raced across the sky, taunting her with the promise of freedom. How many bullets were left?

It only takes one....

Every inch became an agony. Her muscles screamed for rest. Even if a bullet found its mark, she doubted she'd feel the pain.

When at last she cleared the overhang, she was too exhausted to feel any sense of triumph. She hauled herself over the top and rolled onto a narrow ledge. It was nothing more than a flat boulder, turned slick with rain and lichen, but no bed had ever felt so wonderful. If only she could lie here forever. If she could close her eyes and sleep! But there was no time to rest, no time to allow the agony to ease from her body; Susan was right behind her.

She staggered to her feet, her legs trembling with exhaustion, her body buffeted by the whistling wind. One of her shoes had dropped off during the climb and with every step, thorns bit into her bare foot. But here the ascent was easier and she had only a few yards to go until she reached the top of the ridge.

She never made it.

A final gunshot rang out. What she felt wasn't pain, but surprise. There was the dull punch of the bullet slamming into her shoulder. The sky spun above her. For a moment she swayed, as unsteady as a reed in the wind. Then she felt herself fall backward. She was rolling, over and over, tumbling toward oblivion.

It was a halekoa bush—one of those tough stubborn weeds that clamp their roots deep into Hawaiian soil—that saved her life. It snagged her by the legs, slowing her fall just enough to keep her from plunging over the edge of the boulder. As she lay there, fighting to make sense of where she was, she became aware of a strange shrieking in the distance; to her confused brain, it sounded like an infant's wail, and it grew steadily louder.

The hallucination dragged her into consciousness. Groggily she opened her eyes to the dull monochrome of a cloudy sky. The infant's cry suddenly turned into the rhythmic wail of police sirens. The sound of help. Of salvation.

Then, across her field of vision, a shadow moved. She struggled to make out the figure standing over her. Against the sky's fading light, Susan Santini's face was nothing more than a black cutout with wind-lashed hair.

Susan said nothing as she slowly pointed her gun at Kate's head. For a moment she stood there, her skirt flapping in the wind, the pistol clutched in both hands. A gust whipped the narrow ledge, making her sway uneasily on the slippery rock.

The siren's cry suddenly cut off; men's shouts rose up from the valley.

Kate struggled to sit up. The barrel was staring her in the face. She managed to say, quietly, "There's no reason to kill me now, Susan. Is there?"

"You know about William."

"So will they." Kate nodded feebly toward the distant voices, which were already moving closer.

"They won't. Not unless you tell them."

"How do you know I haven't?"

The gun wavered. "No!" Susan cried, her voice tinged with the first trace of panic. "You couldn't have told them! You weren't certain—"

"You need help, Susan. I'll see you get it. All the help you need."

The barrel still hovered at her head. It would take only a twitch of the finger, the clap of the pistol hammer, to make Kate's whole world disintegrate. She gazed up into that black circle, wondering if she would feel the bullet. How strange, that she could face her own death with such calmness. She had fought to stay alive and she had lost. Now all she could do was wait for the end.

Then, through the wind's scream, she heard a voice calling her name. *Another hallucination,* she thought. *It must be….*

But there it was again: David's voice, shouting her name, over and over.

Suddenly she wanted to live! She wanted to tell him all the things she'd been too proud to say. That life was too precious to waste on hurts of the past. That if he just gave her the chance, she could help him forget all the pain he'd ever suffered.

"Please, Susan," she whispered. "Put it down."

Susan shifted but her hands were still gripping the pistol. She seemed to be listening to the voices, moving closer along the old Pali road.

"Can't you see?" cried Kate. "If you kill me, you'll destroy your only chance of keeping your son!"

Her words seemed to drain all the strength from Susan's arms. Slowly, almost imperceptibly, she let the gun drop. For a moment she stood motionless, her head bent in a silent gesture of mourning. Then she turned and gazed over the ledge, at the road far below. "It's too late now," she said in a voice so soft it was almost drowned in the wind. "I've already lost him."

A chorus of shouts from below told them they'd been spotted.

Susan, her hair whipping like flames, stared down at the gathering of men. "It's better this way," she insisted. "He'll have only good memories of me. That's the way childhood should be, you know. Only good memories..."

Perhaps it was a sudden gust that threw Susan off balance; Kate could never be certain. All she knew was that one instant Susan was poised on the edge of the rock and then, in the next instant, she was gone.

She fell soundlessly, without uttering a cry.

It was Kate who sobbed. She collapsed back against the cold and unforgiving bed of stone. As the world spun around her she cried, silently, for the woman who had just died, and for the four others who had lost their lives. So many deaths, so much suffering. And all in the name of love.

Chapter Sixteen

DAVID WAS THE FIRST TO REACH HER.

He found her seventy-five feet up the mountainside, unconscious and shivering on a bloodstained boulder. What he did next had nothing to do with logic; it was pure panic. He ripped off his jacket and threw it over her body, only one thought in his mind. *You can't die. I won't let you. Do you hear me, Kate? You can't die!*

He cradled her in his arms and as the warmth of her blood seeped through his shirt, he said her name over and over, as though he could somehow keep her soul from drifting forever beyond his reach. He scarcely heard the shouts of the rescue workers or the ambulance sirens; his attention was focused on the rhythm of her breathing and the beating of her heart against his chest.

She was so cold, so still. If only he could give her his warmth. He had made just such a wish once before, when his only child had lain dying in his arms. *Not this time,* he prayed, pulling her tightly against him. *Don't take her from me, too….*

That plea rang over and over in his head as they carried her down the mountain. The descent ended in mass confusion as ambulance workers crowded in to help. David was shunted to the sidelines, a helpless observer of a battle he wasn't trained to fight.

He watched the ambulance scream off into the darkness. He

imagined the emergency room, the lights, the people in white. He couldn't bear to think of Kate, lying helplessly in all that chaos. But that's where she would be soon. It was her only chance.

A hand clapped him gently on the shoulder. "You okay, Davy?" Pokie asked.

"Yeah." He sighed deeply. "Yeah."

"She'll be all right. I got a crystal ball on these things." He turned at the sound of a sneeze.

Sergeant Brophy approached, his face half-buried in a handkerchief. "They've brought the body up," said Brophy. "Got tangled up in all that—that—" he blew his nose "—shrubbery. Broken neck. Wanna take a look before it goes to the morgue?"

"Never mind," Pokie grunted. "I'll take your word for it." As they walked to the car, he asked, "How did Dr. Santini handle the news?"

"That's the weird thing," replied Brophy. "When I told him about his wife, he sort of acted like—well, he'd expected it."

Pokie frowned at the covered body of Susan Santini, now being loaded into the ambulance. He sighed. "Maybe he did. Maybe he knew all along what was happening. But he didn't want to admit it. Even to himself."

Brophy opened the car door. "Where to, Lieutenant?"

"The hospital. And move it." Pokie nodded toward David. "This man's got some serious waiting to do."

IT WAS FOUR HOURS BEFORE David was allowed to see her. Four hours of pacing the fourth-floor waiting room. Four hours of walking back and forth past the same *National Enquirer* headline on the coffee table: Woman's Head Joined To Baboon's Body.

There was only one other person in the room, a mule-faced man who slouched beneath a No Smoking sign, puffing desperately on a cigarette. He stubbed out the butt and reached for another. "Getting late," the man commented. That was the extent of their conversation. Two words, uttered in a monotone. The man never said who he was waiting for. He never spoke of fear. It was there, plain in his eyes.

At eleven o'clock, the mule-faced man was called into the recovery room and David was left alone. He stood at the window, listening to the wail of an approaching ambulance. For the hundredth time, he looked at his watch. She'd been in surgery three hours. How long did it take to remove a bullet? Had something gone wrong?

At midnight, a nurse at last poked her head into the room. "Are you Mr. Ransom?"

He spun around, his heart instantly racing. "Yes!"

"I thought you'd want to know. Dr. Chesne's out of surgery."

"Then… She's all right?"

"Everything went just fine."

He let out a breath so heavy its release left him floating. *Thank you,* he thought. *Thank you.*

"If you'd like to go home, we'll call you when she—"

"I have to see her."

"She's still unconscious."

"I have to see her."

"I'm sorry, but we only allow immediate family into…" Her voice trailed off as she saw the dangerous look in his eyes. She cleared her throat. "Five minutes, Mr. Ransom. That's all. You understand?"

Oh, he understood, all right. And he didn't give a damn. He pushed past her, through the recovery-room doors.

He found her lying on the last gurney, her small, pale form drowning in bright lights and plastic tubes. There was only a limp white curtain separating her from the next patient. David hovered at the foot of her stretcher, afraid to move close, afraid to touch her for fear he might break one of those fragile limbs. He was reminded of a princess in a glass bell, lying in some deep forest: untouchable, unreachable. A cardiac monitor chirped overhead, marking the rhythm of her heart. Beautiful music. Good and strong and steady. Kate's heart. He stood there, immobile, as the nurses fussed with tubes, adjusted IV fluids and oxygen. A doctor came to examine Kate's lungs. David felt useless. He was like a great big boulder in everyone's path. He knew he should leave and let them do their job, but something kept him rooted to his spot. One of the nurses pointed to her watch and said sternly, "We really can't work around you. You'll have to leave now."

But he didn't. He wouldn't. Not until he knew everything would be all right.

"SHE'S WAKING UP."

The light of a dozen suns seemed to burn through her closed eyelids. She heard voices, vaguely familiar, murmuring in the void above her. Slowly, painfully, she opened her eyes.

What she saw first was the light, brilliant and inescapable, glaring down at her. Bit by bit, she made out the smiling face of a woman, someone she knew from some dim and distant past, though she couldn't quite remember why. She focused on the name tag: Julie Sanders, RN. Julie. Now she remembered.

"Can you hear me, Dr. Chesne?" Julie asked.

Kate made a feeble attempt to nod.

"You're in the recovery room. Are you in pain?"

Kate didn't know. Her senses were returning one by one, and pain had yet to reawaken. It took her a moment to register all the signals her brain was receiving. She felt the hiss of oxygen in her nostrils and heard the soft beep of a cardiac monitor somewhere over the bed. But pain? No. She felt only a terrible sense of emptiness. And exhaustion. She wanted to sleep….

More faces had gathered around the bed. Another nurse, a stethoscope draped around her neck. Dr. Tam, dour as always. And then she heard a voice, calling softly to her.

"Kate?"

She turned. Framed against the glare of lights, David's face was blackly haggard. In wonder, she reached up to touch him but found that her wrist was hopelessly tangled in what seemed like a multitude of plastic tubes. Too weak to struggle, she let her hand drop back to the bed.

That's when he took it. Gently, as if he were afraid he might break her.

"You're all right," he whispered, pressing his lips to her palm. "Thank God you're all right…."

"I don't remember…."

"You've been in surgery." He gave her a small, tense smile. "Three hours. It seemed like forever. But the bullet's out."

She remembered, then. The wind. The ridge. And Susan, quietly slipping away like a phantom. "She's dead?"

He nodded. "There was nothing anyone could do."

"And Guy?"

"He won't be able to walk for a while. I don't know how he made it to that phone. But he did."

For a moment she lay in silence, thinking of Guy, whose life was now as shattered as his leg. "He saved my life. And now he's lost everything…."

"Not everything. He still has his son."

Yes, she thought. *William will always be Guy's son.* Not by blood, but by something much stronger: by love. Out of all this tragedy, at least one thing would remain intact and good.

"Mr Ransom, you really will have to leave," insisted Dr. Tam.

David nodded. Then he bent over and dutifully gave Kate a gruff and awkward kiss. If he had told her he loved her, if he had said anything at all, she might have found some joy in that dry touch of lips. But too quickly his hand melted away from hers.

Things seemed to move in a blur. Dr. Tam began asking questions she was too dazed to answer. The nurses bustled around her bed, changing IV bottles, disconnecting wires, tucking in sheets. She was given a pain shot. Within minutes, she felt herself sliding irresistibly toward sleep.

As they moved her out of the recovery room, she fought to stay awake. There was something important she had to say to David, something that couldn't wait. But there were so many people around and she lost track of his voice in the confusing buzz of conversation. She felt a burst of panic that this was her last chance to tell him she loved him. But even to the very edge of consciousness, some last wretched scrap of pride kept her silent. And so, in silence, she let herself be dragged once again into darkness.

DAVID STAYED IN HER hospital room until almost dawn. He sat by her bed, holding her hand, brushing the hair off her face. Every so often he would say her name, half hoping she would awaken. But whatever pain shot they'd given her was industrial strength; she scarcely stirred all night. If only once she'd called for him in her sleep, if she'd said even the first syllable of his name, it would have been enough. He would have known she needed him and then he would have told her he needed her. It wasn't the sort of thing a man could just come out and say to anyone. At least, *he* couldn't. In truth, he was worse off than poor mute Charlie

Decker. At least Decker could express himself in a few lines of wretched poetry.

It was a long drive home.

As soon as he walked in the door, he called the hospital to check on her condition. "Stable." That was all they'd say but it was enough. He called a florist and ordered flowers delivered to Kate's room. Roses. Since he couldn't think of a message, he told the clerk to simply write "David." He fixed himself some coffee and toast and ate like a starved man, which he was, since he'd missed supper the night before. Then, dirty, unshaven, exhausted, he went into the living room and threw himself on the couch.

He thought about all the reasons he couldn't be in love. He'd carved out a nice, comfortable existence for himself. He looked around at the polished floor, the curtains, the books lined up in the glass cabinet. Then it struck him how sterile it all was. This wasn't the home of a living, breathing man. It was a shell, the way he was a shell.

What the hell, he thought. She probably wouldn't want him anyway. Their affair had been rooted in need. She'd been terrified and he, conveniently, had been there. Soon she'd be back on her feet, her career on track. You couldn't keep a woman like Kate down for long.

He admired her and he wanted her. But did he love her? He hoped not.

Because he, better than anyone else, knew that love was nothing more than a setup for grief.

DR. CLARENCE AVERY stood awkwardly in the doorway of Kate's hospital room and asked if he could come in. He was carrying a half dozen hideously tinted green carnations, which he waved at her as though he had no idea what one did with flowers. Tinted green ones, anyway. The stems were still wrapped in supermarket cellophane, price tag and all.

"These are for you," he said, just in case she wasn't quite certain about that point. "I hope… I hope you're not allergic to carnations. Or anything."

"I'm not. Thank you, Dr. Avery."

"It's nothing, really. I just..." His gaze wandered to the dozen long-stemmed red roses set in a porcelain vase on the nightstand. "Oh. But I see you've already gotten flowers. Roses." Sadly, he looked down at his green carnations the way one might study a dead animal.

"I prefer carnations," she replied. "Could you put them in water for me? I think I saw a vase under the sink."

"Certainly." He took the flowers over to the sink and as he bent down, she saw that, as usual, his pants were wrinkled and his socks didn't match. The carnations looked somehow touching, flopping about in the huge, watery vase. What mattered most was that they'd been delivered in person, which was more than could be said about the roses.

They had arrived while she was still sleeping. The card said simply, "David." He hadn't called or visited. She thought maybe he'd decided this was the time to make the break. All morning she'd alternated between wanting to tear the flowers to bits and wanting to gather them up and hug them. Now that was an apt analogy—hugging thorns to one's breast.

"Here," she said. "Put the carnations right next to me. Where I can smell them." She brusquely shoved the roses aside, an act that made her wince. The surgical incision had left her with dozens of stitches and it had taken a hefty dose of narcotics just to dull the pain. Carefully she eased back against the pillows.

Pleased that his offering was given such a place of honor, Dr. Avery took a moment of silence to admire the limp blossoms. Then he cleared his throat. "Dr. Chesne," he began, "I should tell you this isn't just a—a social visit."

"It's not?"

"No. It has to do with your position here at Mid Pac."

"Then there's been a decision," she said quietly.

"With all the new evidence that's come out, well..." He gave a little shrug. "I suppose I should have taken your side earlier. I'm sorry I didn't. I suppose I was... I'm just sorry." Shuffling, he looked down at his ink-stained lab coat. "I don't know why I've held on to this blasted chairmanship. It's never given me anything but ulcers. Anyway, I'm here to tell you we're offering you your old job back. There'll be nothing on your record. Just a notation that a lawsuit was filed against you and later dropped. Which it will be. At least, that's what I'm told."

"My old job," she murmured. "I don't know." Sighing, she turned and looked out the window. "I'm not even sure I want it back. You know, Dr. Avery, I've been thinking. About other places."

"You mean another hospital?"

"Another town." She smiled at him. "It's not so surprising, is it? I've had a lot of time to think these last few days. I've been wondering if I don't belong somewhere else. Away from all this—this ocean." *Away from David.*

"Oh, dear."

"You'll find a replacement. There must be hundreds of doctors begging to come to paradise."

"No, it's not that. I'm just surprised. After all the work Mr. Ransom put into this, I thought certainly you'd—"

"Mr. Ransom? What do you mean?"

"All those calls he made. To every member of the hospital board."

A parting gesture, she thought. *At least I should be grateful for that.*

"It was quite a turnaround, I must say. A plaintiff's attorney asking—demanding—we reinstate a doctor! But this morning, when he presented the police evidence and we heard Dr. Santini's statement, well, it took the board a full five minutes to make a decision." He frowned. "Mr. Ransom gave us the idea you wanted your job back."

"Maybe I did once," she replied, staring at the roses and wondering why she felt no sense of triumph. "But things change. Don't they?"

"I suppose they do." Avery cleared his throat and shuffled a little more. "Your job is there if you want it. And we'll certainly be needing you on staff. Especially with my retirement coming up."

She looked up in surprise. "You're retiring?"

"I'm sixty-four, you know. That's getting along. I've never seen much of the country. Never had the time. My wife and I, we used to talk about traveling after my retirement. Barb would've wanted me to enjoy myself. Don't you think?"

Kate smiled. "I'm sure she would have."

"Anyway..." He shot another glance at the drooping carnations. "They are rather pretty, aren't they?" He walked out of the room, chuckling. "Yes. Yes, much better than roses, I think. Much better."

Kate turned once again to the flowers. Red roses. Green carnations. What an absurd combination. Just like her and David.

IT WAS RAINING HARD when David came to see her late that afternoon. She was sitting alone in the solarium, gazing through the watery window at the courtyard below. The nurse had just washed and brushed her hair and it was drying as usual into those frizzy, little girl waves she'd always hated. She didn't hear him as he walked into the room. Only when he said her name did she turn and see him standing there, his hair damp and windblown, his suit beaded with rain. He looked tired. Almost as tired as she felt. She wanted him to pull her close, to take her in his arms, but he didn't. He simply bent over and gave her an automatic kiss on the forehead and then he straightened again.

"Out of bed, I see. You must be feeling better," he remarked.

She managed a wan smile. "I guess I never was one for lying around all day."

"Oh. I brought you these." Almost as an afterthought, he handed her a small foil-wrapped box of chocolates. "I wasn't sure they'd let you eat anything yet. Maybe later."

She looked down at the box resting in her lap. "Thank you," she murmured. "And thank you for the roses." Then she turned and stared out at the rain.

There was a long silence, as if both of them had run out of things to say. The rain slid down the solarium windows, casting a watery rainbow of light on her folded hands.

"I just spoke with Avery," he finally said. "I hear you're getting your old job back."

"Yes. He told me. I guess that's something else I have to thank you for."

"What's that?"

"My job. Avery said you made a lot of phone calls."

"Just a few. Nothing, really." He took a deep breath and continued with forced cheerfulness, "So. You should be back at work in the O.R. in no time. With a big raise in pay, I hope. It must feel pretty good."

"I'm not sure I'm taking it—the job."

"What? Why on earth wouldn't you?"

She shrugged. "You know, I've been thinking about other possibilities. Other places."

"You mean besides Mid Pac?"

"I mean…besides Hawaii." He didn't say a thing, so she added, "There's really nothing keeping me here."

There was another long silence. Softly he said, "Isn't there?"

She didn't answer. He watched her, sitting so quiet, so still in her chair. And he knew he could wait around till doomsday and there she'd still be. *A fine pair we are,* he thought in disgust. They were two so-called intelligent people, and they couldn't hunt up a single word between them.

"Dr. Chesne?" A nurse appeared in the doorway. "Are you ready to go back to your room?"

"Yes," Kate answered. "I think I'd like to sleep."

"You do look tired." The nurse glanced at David. "Maybe it's time you left, sir."

"No," said David, suddenly drawing himself to his full height.

"Excuse me?"

"I'm not going to leave. Not yet." He looked long and hard at Kate. "Not until I've finished making a fool of myself. So could you leave us alone?"

"But, sir—"

"Please."

The nurse hesitated. Then, sensing that something momentous was looming in the balance, she retreated from the solarium.

Kate was watching him, her green eyes filled with uncertainty. And maybe fear. He reached down and gently touched her face.

"Tell me again what you just said," he murmured. "That you have nothing to keep you here."

"I don't. What I mean is—"

"Now tell me the real reason you want to leave."

She was silent. But he saw the answer in her eyes, those soft and needy eyes. What he read there made him suddenly shake his head in wonder. "My God," he muttered. "You're a bigger coward than I am."

"A coward?"

"That's right. So am I." He turned away and with his hands in his pockets began to wander restlessly around the room. "I didn't plan to say this. Not yet, anyway. But here you're talking about leaving. And it seems I don't have much of a choice." He stopped and looked out the window. Outside, the world had gone silvery. "Okay." He sighed. "Since you're not going to say it, I guess I will. It's not easy for me. It's never been easy. After Noah died, I thought I'd taught myself not to feel. I've managed it up till now. Then I met you and..." He shook his head and laughed. "God, I wish I had one of Charlie Decker's poems handy. Maybe I could quote a few lines. Anything to sound halfway intelligible. Poor old Charlie had that much over me: his eloquence. For that I envy him." He looked at her and a half smile was on his lips. "I still haven't said it, have I? But you get the general idea."

"Coward," she whispered.

Laughing, he went to her and tilted her face up to his. "All right, then. I love you. I love your stubbornness and your pride. And your independence. I didn't want to. I thought I was going along just fine on my own. But now that it's happened, I can't imagine ever not loving you." He pulled away, offering her a chance to retreat.

She didn't. She remained perfectly still. Her throat seemed to have swollen shut. She was still clutching the little box of candy, trying to convince herself it was real. That he was real.

"It won't be easy, you know," he said.

"What won't?"

"Living with me. There'll be days you'll want to wring my neck or scream at me, anything to make me say 'I love you.' But just because I don't say it doesn't mean I don't feel it. Because I do." He let out a long sigh. "So. I guess that's about it. I hope you were listening. Because I'm not sure I could come up with a repeat performance. And damned if this time I forgot to bring my tape recorder."

"I've been listening," she replied softly.

"And?" he asked, not daring to let his gaze leave her face. "Do I hear the verdict? Or is the jury still out?"

"The jury," she whispered, "is in a state of shock. And badly in need of mouth-to-mouth—"

If resuscitation was what he'd intended, his kiss did quite the opposite. He lowered his face to hers and she felt the room spin. Every muscle of her neck seemed to go limp at once and her head sagged back against the chair.

"Now, fellow coward," he murmured, his lips hovering close to hers. "Your turn."

"I love you," she said weakly.

"That's the verdict I was hoping for."

She thought he would kiss her again but he suddenly pulled away and frowned. "You're looking awfully pale. I think I should call the nurse. Maybe a little oxygen—"

She reached up and wound her arms around his neck. "Who needs oxygen?" she whispered, just before his mouth settled warmly on hers.

Epilogue

THERE WAS A BRAND-NEW BABY visiting the house, a fact made apparent by the indignant squalls coming from the upstairs bedroom.

Jinx poked her head through the doorway. “What in heaven’s name is the matter with Emma now?”

Gracie, her mouth clamped around a pale pink safety pin, looked up helplessly from the screaming infant. “It’s all so new to me, Jinx. I’m afraid I’ve lost my touch.”

“Your touch? When were you ever around babies?”

“Oh, you’re right.” Gracie sighed, tugging the pin out of her mouth. “I suppose I never did have the touch, did I? That explains why I’m doing such a shoddy job of it.”

“Now, dear. Babies take practice, that’s all. It’s like the piano. All those scales, up and down, every day.”

Gracie shook her head. “The piano’s much easier.” Resignedly, she stuffed the safety pin back between her lips. “And look at these impossible diapers! I just don’t see how anyone could poke a pin through all that paper and plastic.”

Jinx burst out in hoots of laughter, so loud that Gracie turned bright red with indignation. “And exactly what did I say that was so funny?” Gracie demanded.

“Darling, haven’t you figured it out?” Jinx reached out and

peeled open the adhesive flap. "You don't use pins. That's the whole *point* of disposable diapers." She looked down in astonishment as baby Emma suddenly let out a lusty howl.

"You see?" sniffed Gracie. "She didn't like your pun, either."

A LEAF DRIFTED DOWN from the monkeypod tree and settled beside the fresh gathering of daisies. Chips of sunlight dappled the grass and danced on David's fair hair. How many times had he grieved alone in the shade of this tree? How many times had he stood in silent communion with his son? All the other visits seemed to blend together in a gray and dismal remembrance of mourning.

But today he was smiling. And in his mind, he could hear the smile in Noah's voice, as well.

Is that you, Daddy?

Yes, Noah. It's me. You have a sister.

I've always wanted a sister.

She sucks the same two fingers you did....

Does she?

And she always smiles when I walk in her room.

So did I. Remember?

Yes, I remember.

And you'll never forget, will you, Daddy? Promise me, you'll never forget.

No, I'll never forget. I swear to you, Noah, I will never, ever forget....

David turned and through his tears he saw Kate, standing a few feet away. No words were needed between them. Only a look. And an outstretched hand.

Together they walked away from that sad little patch of grass. As they emerged from the shade of the tree, David suddenly stopped and pulled her into his arms.

She touched his face. He felt the warmth of the sun in her fingertips. And he was healed.

He was healed.

CALL AFTER MIDNIGHT

To Jacob, who is always there

Prologue

Berlin

IT TAKES TWENTY SECONDS OF PRESSURE on the carotid arteries to render a man unconscious. Two minutes longer, and death is inevitable. Simon Dance didn't need a medical textbook to tell him these facts—he knew them from experience. He also knew there could be no slack in the garrote. If the cord wasn't taut, if it allowed just a short spurt of precious blood to reach the victim's brain, the struggle would be prolonged. It made the whole process sloppy, even dangerous. There was nothing as savage as a dying man.

As he crouched in the darkness, Dance wound the garrote twice around his hands and glanced at the luminous dial of his watch. Two hours had passed since he'd turned off the lights. His assassin was obviously a cautious man who wanted to be sure Dance was deeply asleep. If the man was a professional, he would know that the first two hours of sleep are the heaviest. Now was the time to strike.

In the hallway outside, a footstep creaked. Dance stiffened, then rose slowly and waited in the darkness beside the door. He ignored the pounding of his own heart. He felt the familiar spurt of adrenaline as it kicked his reflexes into high gear. He stretched the garrote between his hands.

A key was easing into the lock. Dance heard the metallic click of the teeth grating softly across metal. The key turned, and the lock opened with a soft clunk. Slowly the door swung in, and light from the hall spilled into the room. A shadow moved through the doorway and turned toward the bed, where a man appeared to be sleeping. The shadow raised its arm. Three bullets from a silencer thudded into the pillows. As the third bullet struck, so did Dance.

He whipped the garrote around the intruder's neck and snapped the cord up and back. It tightened precisely around the most exposed portion of the carotid artery, by the angle of the jaw. The gun fell to the floor. The man thrashed as if he were a hooked fish and tore frantically at the garrote. He reached back and tried to claw Dance's face. His arms and legs went out of control, wildly jerking and thrusting in all directions. Then gradually the legs crumpled, and the arms reached out one last time before going limp. As Dance counted the minutes, he felt the body's last spasms, the seizures of starved and dying brain cells. He held on.

When three minutes had passed, Dance released the garrote, and the body dropped to the floor. Dance turned on the lights and gazed down at the man he'd just killed.

The mottled face was vaguely familiar. Perhaps he'd seen the man on a street or on a train somewhere, but he didn't know his name. Quickly he went through the man's clothes but found only money, car keys and a few tools of the trade: extra ammunition clips, a switchblade, a lock pick. A nameless professional, thought Dance, wondering offhandedly how much the man had been paid.

He dragged the body onto the bed and tossed aside the three pillows that had been fluffed up beneath the covers. He estimated the body's size to be six feet plus or minus an inch. The same height. Good. Dance exchanged clothes with the corpse; it was probably unnecessary, but he was a thorough man. Then he took off his wedding ring and tried to slip it onto the corpse's finger, but it wouldn't quite fit over the knuckle. He went to the bathroom, soaped the ring and finally managed to jam it on the dead man's finger. Then he sat down and smoked a few cigarettes. He tried to think of any details he might have missed.

The three bullets, of course. Hunting around in the pillows and ticking, Dance managed to retrieve two of the bullets. The third was probably embedded somewhere in the mattress. Before he could probe any deeper, he heard footsteps in the hallway. Did the assassin have an accomplice? Dance swept up the gun, aimed at the door and waited. The footsteps moved on and faded down the corridor. A false alarm. Still, he should leave now; to stay any longer would be foolish.

From the dresser drawer, he pulled out a bottle of methanol. It would burn rapidly and leave no residue. He poured it over the body, the bed and the surrounding rug. The room contained no smoke alarms or automatic sprinklers—Dance had chosen the old hotel for just that reason. He set the ashtray beside the bed and gathered the dead man's belongings, along with the empty methanol bottle, and put them in a trash bag. Then he set the bed on fire.

With a whoosh the flames took off, and in seconds the body was engulfed. Dance waited just long enough to be certain there'd be nothing recognizable left.

Carrying the trash bag, he left the room, locked the door and walked down the hall to the fire alarm. He didn't see the point of killing innocent people, so he broke the glass and pulled the alarm lever. Then he took the stairs down to the ground floor.

From an alley across the street, he watched the flames shoot from his window. The hotel was evacuated, and the street filled with sleepy-eyed people wrapped in blankets. Three fire trucks responded within ten minutes. By that time his room was a blazing inferno.

It took an hour to extinguish the fire. A crowd of curious onlookers joined the shivering hotel guests, and Dance studied their faces, filing them away in his memory. If he saw any of them again, he would be warned.

Then, through the knot of people, he spotted a black limousine crawling slowly down the street. He recognized the man sitting in the back seat. So the CIA was here. Interesting.

He had seen enough. It was late, and he needed to be on his way, back to Amsterdam.

Three blocks away, he threw the trash bag with the empty methanol bottle into a dumpster. With that the last detail was taken care of. He'd done what he had come to Berlin to do. He'd killed off Geoffrey Fontaine. Now it was time to vanish. He walked off whistling into the darkness.

Amsterdam

THE OLD MAN was awakened at three in the morning with the news. "Geoffrey Fontaine is dead."

"How?" asked the old man.

"A hotel fire. They say he was smoking in bed."

"An accident? Impossible! Where is the body?"

"Berlin morgue. Very badly burned."

Of course, thought the old man. He should have known the body would not be recognizable. Simon Dance, as usual, had done a superb job of covering his tracks. So they had lost him again.

But the old man still had one card to play. "You told me there was an American wife," he said. "Where does she live?"

"Washington."

"I will have her followed."

"But why? I just told you the man's dead."

"He's *not* dead. He's alive. I'm sure of it. And this woman may know where he is. I want her watched."

"I'll have my men—"

"No. I will send my own man. Someone I can count on."

There was a pause. "I will get you her address."

After he'd hung up, the old man could not go back to sleep. For five years he'd waited. For five years he'd been searching. To have come so close, only to fail again! Now everything depended on what this woman in Washington knew.

He had to be patient and wait for her to betray herself. He would send Kronen, a man who'd never failed him. Kronen had his own methods to extract information—methods difficult to resist. But then, that was Kronen's special talent. Persuasion.

Chapter One

Washington

IT WAS AFTER MIDNIGHT WHEN THE telephone rang.

Through a heavy curtain of sleep, Sarah heard it ring. The sound seemed impossibly far away, as if it were a distant alarm going off in a room beyond her reach. She struggled to wake up, but she was trapped somewhere in a world between sleep and wakefulness. She had to answer the phone; she knew her husband, Geoffrey, was calling.

All evening she'd waited to hear Geoffrey's voice. It was Wednesday night, and on his monthly trips to London, Geoffrey always called home on Wednesday. Tonight, however, she'd crawled into bed early, sniffling and coughing, a victim of the latest flu virus to hit Washington. It was influenza A-63 from Hong Kong, a particularly miserable strain that she now shared with half her colleagues in the microbiology lab. For an hour she'd sat up reading in bed, fighting valiantly to stay awake. But the combination of a cold capsule plus the most recent *Journal of Microbiology* had worked faster than any sleeping pill. Within minutes she'd fallen back on the pillows with her glasses still perched on her nose. It would be just a short rest, she had promised herself, just a catnap.... In the end, sleep had crept up and ambushed her.

She woke with a start to find that the bedside lamp was on, *Journal of Microbiology* still draped across her chest. The room was slightly out of focus. Pushing her glasses back in place, Sarah glanced at the clock on the nightstand. Twelve-thirty. The telephone was dead silent. Had she been dreaming?

She jumped as the phone rang again. Eagerly she grabbed the receiver.

"Mrs. Sarah Fontaine?" asked a man's voice.

It wasn't Geoffrey. Sudden alarm shot through her like a jolt of electricity. Something was terribly wrong. She sat up at once, fully awake. "Yes. Speaking," she said.

"Mrs. Fontaine, this is Nicholas O'Hara, U.S. State Department. I'm sorry to call you at this hour, but..." He paused. It was the silence that terrified her most, for it was too deliberate, too practiced, a strategically placed buffer to ready her for a blow. "I'm afraid I have some bad news," he finished.

Her throat tightened. She felt like shouting, *Just tell me! Tell me what's happened!* But all she could manage was a whisper. "Yes. I'm listening."

"It's about your husband, Geoffrey," he said. "There's been an accident."

This isn't real, she thought, closing her eyes. *If Geoffrey were hurt, I would have felt it. Somehow I would have known....*

"It happened about six hours ago," he continued. "There was a fire in your husband's hotel." Another pause. Then, with concern in his voice, he asked, "Mrs. Fontaine? Are you still there?"

"Yes. Please go on."

The man cleared his throat. "I'm sorry to tell you this, Mrs. Fontaine. Your husband...he didn't make it."

He allowed her a moment of silence, a moment in which she struggled to contain her grief. It was a stupid, irrational act of pride that made her press her hand over her mouth to stifle the sob. This pain was too private to share with any stranger.

"Mrs. Fontaine?" he asked gently. "Are you all right?"

At last she managed to take a shaky breath. "Yes," she whispered.

"You don't have to worry about the…arrangements. I'll coordinate all the details with our consulate in Berlin. There'll be a delay, of course, but once the German authorities clear the body's release, there should be no—"

"Berlin?" she broke in.

"It's in their jurisdiction, you see. There'll be a full report as soon as the Berlin police—"

"But this isn't possible!"

Nicholas O'Hara was struggling to be patient. "I'm sorry, Mrs. Fontaine. His identity's been confirmed. Really, there's no question about—"

"Geoffrey was in *London*," she cried.

A long silence followed. "Mrs. Fontaine," he said at last in an irritatingly calm voice, "the accident occurred in Berlin."

"Then they've made a mistake. Geoffrey was in London. He couldn't have been in Germany!"

Again there was a pause, longer this time. Now she could tell he was puzzled. The receiver was pressed so tightly to her ear that all she heard for a few seconds was the pounding of her heart. There had to be a mistake. Some crazy, stupid misunderstanding. Geoffrey had to be alive. She pictured him, laughing at the absurd reports of his own death. Yes, they would laugh about it together when he came home. If he came home.

"Mrs. Fontaine," the man said at last, "which hotel was he staying at in London?"

"The—the Savoy. I have the phone number somewhere here—I have to look it up—"

"That's all right, I'll find it. Let me do some calling around. Perhaps I should see you in the morning." His words were measured and cautious, spoken in the unemotional monotone of a bureaucrat who'd learned how to reveal nothing. "Can you come by my office?"

"How—how do I find it?"

"You'll be driving?"

"No. I don't have a car."

"I'll have one sent by."

"It's a mistake, isn't it? I mean…you do make mistakes, don't you?" A bit of hope, that was all she was asking him for. Some small thread to cling to. At least he could have given her that much. He could have shown her a little kindness.

But all he said was "I'll see you in the morning, Mrs. Fontaine. Around eleven."

"Wait, please! I'm sorry, I can't even think. Your name—what was it again?"

"Nicholas O'Hara."

"Where was your office?"

"Don't worry about it," he said. "The driver will see you get here. Good night."

"Mr. O'Hara?"

Sarah heard the dial tone and knew that he had already hung up. She immediately dialed the number of the Savoy Hotel in London. One phone call, and the matter would be settled. *Please,* she prayed as the phone connection went through, *let me hear your voice....*

"Savoy Hotel," answered a woman from halfway around the world.

Sarah's hand was shaking so hard she could barely hold the receiver. "Hello. Mr. Geoffrey Fontaine's room, please," she blurted out.

"I'm sorry, ma'am," the voice said. "Mr. Fontaine checked out two days ago."

"Checked *out*?" she cried. "But where did he go?"

"He gave us no destination. However, if you wish to send a message, we'd be happy to forward it to his permanent address...."

She never remembered saying goodbye. She found herself staring down at the telephone as if it were something alien, something she'd never seen before. Slowly her gaze wandered to Geoffrey's pillow. The king-sized bed seemed to stretch forever. Sarah had always curled herself into one small part of it. Even when Geoffrey was away from home and she had the bed to herself, she still never moved from her spot.

Now Geoffrey might never come home.

Sarah was left alone in a bed that was too large, in an apartment that was too quiet. She shuddered as a silent wave of pain rose and caught in her throat. She wanted desperately to cry, but the tears refused to fall.

She collapsed onto the bed with her face against the pillows. They smelled of Geoffrey. They smelled of his skin and his hair and his laughter. She clutched one of the pillows in her arms and curled up in the very center of the bed, in the spot where Geoffrey always lay. The sheets were ice-cold.

Geoffrey might never come home. They had been married only two months.

NICK O'HARA DRAINED his third cup of coffee and jerked his tie loose. After a two week vacation wearing nothing but bathing trunks, his tie felt like a hangman's noose. He'd been back in Washington only three days, and already he was edgy. Vacations were supposed to recharge the old batteries. That's why he'd gone to the Bahamas. He'd spent two glorious weeks doing absolutely nothing except lie around half-naked in the sun. He'd needed the time to be alone, to ask himself some hard questions and come to some conclusions.

But the only conclusion he'd reached was that he was unhappy.

After eight years with the State Department, Nick O'Hara was fed up with his job. He was headed in circles, a ship without a rudder. His career was at a standstill, but the fault was not entirely his. Bit by bit he'd lost his patience for political games of state—he wasn't in the mood to play. He'd hung in there, though, because he'd believed in his job, in its intrinsic worth. From peace marches in his youth to peace tables in his prime.

But ideals, he had discovered, got people nowhere. Hell, diplomacy didn't run on ideals. It ran, like everything else, on protocol and party-line politics. While he'd perfected his protocol, he hadn't gotten the politics quite right. It wasn't that he couldn't. He wouldn't.

In that regard Nick knew he was a lousy diplomat. Unfortunately those in authority apparently agreed with him. So he had been banished to this bottom-of-the-barrel consular post in D.C., calling bad news to new widows. It was a not-so-subtle slap in the face. Sure, he could have refused the assignment. He could've gone back to teaching, to his comfortable old niche at American University. He had needed to think about it. Yes, he'd needed those two weeks alone in the Bahamas.

What he didn't need was to come home to this.

With a sigh, he flipped open the file labeled Fontaine, Geoffrey H. One small item had bothered him all morning. Since 1:00 a.m. he'd been staring at a computer terminal, digging out everything he could get from the vast government files. He'd also spent half an hour on the phone with his buddy Wes Corrigan in the Berlin consulate. In frustration he'd finally turned to a few unusual sources. What had started off as a routine call to the widow to give her his regrets was turning into something a bit more complicated, a puzzle for which Nick didn't have all the pieces.

In fact, except for the well-established details of Geoffrey Fontaine's death, there were hardly any pieces at all to play with. Nick didn't like incomplete puzzles. They drove him crazy. When it came to poking around for more information, more facts, he could be insatiable. But now, as he lifted the thin Fontaine file, he felt as if he were holding a bagful of air: nothing of substance but a name.

And a death.

Nick's eyes were burning; he leaned back in his chair and yawned. When he was twenty and in college, staying up half the night used to give him a high. Now that he was thirty-eight, it only made him crotchety. And hungry. At 6:00 a.m. he'd wolfed down three doughnuts. The surge of sugar into his system, plus the coffee, had been enough to keep him going. And now he was too curious to stop. Puzzles always did that to him. He wasn't sure he liked it.

He looked up as the door opened. His pal Tim Greenstein strode in.

"Bingo! I found it!" said Tim. He dropped a file on the desk and gave Nick one of those big, dumb grins he was so famous for. Most of the time, that grin was directed at a computer screen. Tim was a troubleshooter, the man everyone called when the data weren't where they should be. Heavy glasses distorted his eyes, the consequence of infantile cataracts. A bushy black beard obscured much of the rest of his face, except for a pale forehead and nose.

"Told you I'd get it," said Tim, plopping into the leather chair across from Nick. "I had my buddy at the FBI do a little fishing. He came up with zilch, so I did a little poking around on my own.

Not easy, I'll tell ya, getting this out of classified. They've got some new idiot up there who insists on doing his job."

Nick frowned. "You had to get this through security?"

"Yep. There's more, but I couldn't access it. Found out central intelligence has a file on your man."

Nick flipped the folder open and stared in amazement. What he saw raised more questions than ever, questions for which there seemed to be no answers. "What the hell does this mean?" he muttered.

"That's why you couldn't find anything about Geoffrey H. Fontaine," said Tim. "Until a year ago, the guy didn't exist."

Nick's jaw snapped up. "Can you get me more?"

"Hey, Nick, I think we're trespassing on someone else's turf. Those Company boys might get hot under the collar."

"So let 'em sue me." Nick wasn't in the least intimidated by the CIA. Not after all the incompetent Company men he'd met. "Anyway," he said with a shrug, "I'm just doing my job. I've got a grieving widow, remember?"

"But this Fontaine stuff goes pretty deep."

"So do you, Tim."

Tim grinned. "What is it, Nick? Turning detective?"

"No. Just curious." He scowled at the day's pile of work on his desk. It was all bureaucratic crap—the bane of his existence—but it had to be done. This Fontaine case was distracting him. He should just give the grieving widow a pat on the shoulder, murmur a kind word and send her out the door. Then he should forget the whole thing. Geoffrey Fontaine, whatever his real name, was dead.

But Tim had set Nick's curiosity on fire. He glanced at his friend. "Say, how about hunting up a few things about the guy's wife? Sarah Fontaine. That might get us somewhere."

"Why don't you get it yourself?"

"You're the one with all that hot computer access."

"Yeah, but you've got the woman herself." Tim nodded toward the door. "I heard the secretary take down her name. Sarah Fontaine's sitting in your waiting room right now."

THE SECRETARY WAS a graying, middle-aged woman with china-blue eyes and a mouth that seemed permanently etched in two straight lines. She glanced up from her typewriter just long enough to take Sarah's name and direct her toward a nearby couch.

Stacked neatly on a coffee table by the couch were the usual waiting room magazines, as well as a few issues of *Foreign Affairs* and *World Press Review*, to which the address labels were still attached: Dr. Nicholas O'Hara.

As the secretary turned back to her typewriter, Sarah sank into the cushions of the couch and stared dully at her hands, which were now folded in her lap. She hadn't yet shaken the flu, and she was still cold and miserable. But in the past ten hours, a layer of numbness had built up around her, a protective shell that made sights and sounds seem distant. Even physical pain bore a strange dullness. When she'd stubbed her toe in the shower this morning, she'd felt the throb, but somehow she hadn't cared.

Last night, after the phone call, the pain had overwhelmed her. Now she was only numb. Gazing down, she saw for the first time what a mess she'd made of getting dressed. None of her clothes quite matched. Yet on a subconscious level, she'd chosen to wear things that gave her solace: a favorite gray wool skirt, an old pullover, brown walking shoes. Life had suddenly turned frightening for Sarah; she needed to be comforted by the familiar.

The secretary's intercom buzzed, and a voice said, "Angie? Can you send Mrs. Fontaine in?"

"Yes, Mr. O'Hara." Angie nodded at Sarah. "You can go in now," she said.

Sarah slipped on her glasses, rose to her feet and entered the office marked N. O'Hara. Just inside the door, she paused on the thick carpet and looked calmly at the man on the other side of the desk.

He stood before the window. The sun shone in through pencil-sketch trees, blinding her. At first she saw only the man's silhouette. He was tall and slender, and his shoulders slouched a little—he looked tired. Moving from the window, he came around the desk to meet her. His blue shirt was wrinkled; a nondescript tie hung loosely around his neck, as if he'd been tugging at it.

"Mrs. Fontaine," he said, "I'm Nick O'Hara." Instantly she recognized the voice from the telephone, the same voice that had shattered her world just ten hours earlier.

He held his hand out to her, a gesture that struck Sarah as too automatic, a mere formality that he no doubt extended to all widows. But his grip was firm. As he shifted toward the window, the light fell fully on his face. She saw long, thin features, an angular jaw, a sober mouth. She judged him to be in his late thirties, perhaps older. His dark brown hair was woven with gray at the temples. Beneath the slate-colored eyes were dark circles.

He motioned her to a chair. As she sat down, she noticed for the first time that a third person was in the room, a man with glasses and a bushy black beard who was sitting quietly in a corner chair. She'd seen him when he'd passed through the reception room earlier.

Nick settled on the edge of the desk and looked at her. "I'm very sorry about your husband, Mrs. Fontaine," he said gently. "It's a terrible shock, I know. Most people don't want to believe us when they get that phone call. I felt I had to meet you face-to-face. I have questions. I'm sure you have, too." He nodded at the man with the beard. "You don't mind Mr. Greenstein listening in, do you?"

She shrugged, wondering vaguely why Mr. Greenstein was there.

"We're both with state," Nick continued. "I'm with consular affairs in the foreign service. Mr. Greenstein's with our technical support division."

"I see." Shivering, she pulled her sweater tighter. The chills were starting again, and her throat was sore. Why were government offices always so cold? she wondered.

"Are you all right, Mrs. Fontaine?" Nick asked.

She looked up miserably at him. "Your office is chilly."

"Can I get you a cup of coffee?"

"No, thank you. Please, I just want to know about my husband. I still can't believe it, Mr. O'Hara. I keep thinking something's wrong. That there's been a mistake."

He nodded sympathetically. "That's a common reaction, to think it's all a mistake."

"Is it?"

"Denial. Everyone goes through it. That's what you're feeling now."

"But you don't ask every widow to your office, do you? There must be something different about Geoffrey."

"Yes," he admitted. "There is."

He turned and swept up a file folder from his desk. After flipping through it, he pulled out a page covered with notes. The handwriting was an illegible scrawl; it had to be his writing, she thought. No one but the writer himself would ever be able to decipher it.

"After I called you, Mrs. Fontaine, I got in touch with our consulate in Berlin. What you said last night bothered me. Enough to make me recheck the facts." His pause made her gaze up at him expectantly. She found two steady eyes, tired and troubled, watching her. "I talked to Wes Corrigan, our consul in Berlin. Here's what he told me." He glanced down at his notes. "Yesterday, about 8:00 p.m. Berlin time, a man named Geoffrey Fontaine checked into Hotel Regina. He paid with a traveler's check. The signature matched. For identification he used his passport. About four hours later, at midnight, the fire department answered a call at the hotel. Your husband's room was in flames. By the time they got it under control, the room was totally destroyed. The official explanation was that he'd fallen asleep while smoking in bed. Your husband, I'm afraid, was burned beyond recognition."

"Then how can they be sure it was him?" Sarah blurted. Until that instant she'd been listening with growing despair. But Nick O'Hara had just introduced too many other possibilities. "Someone could have stolen his passport," she pointed out.

"Mrs. Fontaine, let me finish."

"But you just said they couldn't even identify the body."

"Let's try and be logical, here."

"I *am* being logical!"

"You're being emotional. Look, it's normal for widows to clutch at straws like this, but—"

"I'm not yet convinced I *am* a widow."

He held up his hands in frustration. "Okay, okay, look at the evidence, then. The hard evidence. First, they found his briefcase in the room. It was aluminum, fire resistant."

"Geoffrey never owned anything like that."

"The contents survived the fire. Your husband's passport was inside."

"But—"

"Then there's the coroner's report. A Berlin pathologist briefly examined the body—what was left of it. While there weren't any dental records for comparison, the body's height was the same as your husband's."

"That doesn't mean a thing."

"Finally—"

"Mr. O'Hara—"

"Finally," he said with sudden force, "we have one last bit of evidence, something found on the body itself. I'm sorry, Mrs. Fontaine, but I think it'll convince you."

All at once she wanted to clap her hands over her ears, to shout at him to stop. Until now she'd withstood the evidence. But she couldn't listen any longer. She couldn't stand having all her hopes collapse.

"It was a wedding ring. The inscription was still readable. Sarah. 2-14." He looked up from his notes. "That *is* your wedding date, isn't it?"

Everything blurred as her eyes filled with tears. In silence she bowed her head. The glasses slipped off her nose and fell to her lap. Blindly she hunted in her purse for a tissue, only to find that Nick O'Hara had somehow produced a whole box of Kleenex out of thin air.

"Take what you need," he said softly.

He watched as she wiped away her tears and tried, somehow, to blow her nose gracefully. Under his scrutiny she felt so clumsy and stupid. Even her fingers refused to work properly. Her glasses slid from her lap to the floor. Her purse wouldn't snap shut. Desperate to leave, she fumbled for her things and rose from the chair.

"Please, Mrs. Fontaine, sit down. I'm not quite finished," he said.

As if she were an obedient child, Sarah returned to her seat and stared at the floor. "If it's about the burial arrangements..."

"No, you can take care of that later, after we fly the body back. There's something else I need to ask you. It's about your husband's trip. Why was he in Europe?"

"Business."

"What kind of business?"

"He was a—a representative for the Bank of London."

"So he traveled a lot?"

"Yes. Every month or so he was in London."

"Only London?"

"Yes."

"Tell me why he was in Germany, Mrs. Fontaine."

"I don't know."

"You must have an idea."

"I don't know."

"Was it his habit not to tell you where he was going?"

"No."

"Then why was he in Germany? There must have been a reason. Other business, perhaps? Other…"

She looked up sharply. "Other women? That's what you want to ask, isn't it?"

He didn't answer.

"Isn't it?"

"It's a reasonable suspicion."

"Not about Geoffrey!"

"About anyone." His eyes met hers head-on. She refused to turn away. "You were married a total of two months," he said. "How well did you know your husband?"

"Know him? I loved him, Mr. O'Hara."

"I'm not talking about love, whatever that means. I'm asking how well you *knew* the man. Who he was, what he did. How long ago did you meet?"

"It was…I guess six months ago. I met him at a coffee shop, near where I work."

"Where do you work?"

"NIH. I'm a research microbiologist."

His eyes narrowed. "What kind of research?"

"Bacterial genomes…. We splice DNA…. Why are you asking these questions?"

"Is it classified research?"

"I still don't understand why—"

"Is it *classified*, Mrs. Fontaine?"

She stared at him, shocked into silence by the sharp tone of his voice. Softly she said, "Yes. Some of it."

He nodded and pulled another sheet from the folder. Calmly

he continued. "I had Mr. Corrigan in Berlin check your husband's passport. Whenever you fly into a new country, a page is stamped with an entry date. Your husband's passport had several stamps. London. Schiphol, near Amsterdam. And last, Berlin. All were dated within the last week. Any explanation why he'd visit those particular cities?"

She shook her head, bewildered.

"When did he call you last?"

"A week ago. From London."

"Can you be sure he was in London?"

"No. It was direct dial. There was no operator involved."

"Did your husband have a life-insurance policy?"

"No. I mean, I don't know. He never mentioned it."

"Did anyone stand to benefit from his death? Financially, I mean."

"I don't think so."

He took this in with a frown. Settling back onto the desk, he crossed his arms and looked away for a moment. She could almost see his mind churning over the facts, juggling the puzzle pieces. She was just as confused as he was. None of this made sense; none of it seemed possible. Geoffrey had been her husband, and now she was beginning to wonder if Nick O'Hara was right. That she'd never really known him. That all she and Geoffrey had shared was a bed and a home, but never their hearts.

No, this was all wrong; it was a betrayal of his memory. She believed in Geoffrey. Why should she believe this stranger? Why was this man telling her these things? Was there another purpose to all this? Suddenly she disliked Nick O'Hara. Intensely. He was flinging these questions at her for some unspoken reason.

"If you're finished…" she said, starting to rise again.

He glanced at her with a start, as if he'd forgotten she was still there. "No. I'm not."

"I'm not feeling well. I'd like to go home."

"Do you have a picture of your husband?" he asked abruptly.

Taken aback by his sudden request, Sarah opened her purse and pulled a photograph from her wallet. It was a good likeness of Geoffrey, taken on a Florida beach during their three-day honeymoon. His brilliant blue eyes stared directly at the camera. His hair was bright gold, and the sunlight fell at an angle across his face, throwing shadows on his uncommonly handsome features. He was smiling. From the start she'd been drawn to that face—not by just the good looks, but by the strength and intelligence she'd seen in the eyes.

Nick O'Hara took the picture and studied it without comment. Watching him, she thought, *He's so unlike Geoffrey. Not golden haired but dark, not smiling but very, very sober.* A troubled cloud seemed to hang over Nick O'Hara, a cloud of unhappiness. She wondered what he was thinking as he gazed at the picture. He showed little emotion, and except for the lines of fatigue, Sarah could read very little in his face. His eyes were a flat, impenetrable gray. He passed the photo briefly to Mr. Greenstein, then silently handed Geoffrey's picture back to her.

She closed her purse and looked at him. "Why are you asking all these questions?"

"I have to. I'm sorry, but it really is necessary."

"For whom?" she asked tightly. "For you?"

"For you, too. And maybe even for Geoffrey."

"That doesn't make sense."

"It will when you've heard the Berlin police report."

"Is there something else?"

"Yes. It's about the circumstances of your husband's death."

"But you said it was an accident."

"I said it *looked* like an accident." He watched her carefully while he spoke, as if afraid to miss any change in her face, any flicker of her eye. "When I spoke to Mr. Corrigan a few hours ago, there had been a new development. During a routine investigation of the fire, the debris from the room was examined. When they sifted through the mattress remains, they found a bullet."

She stared at him in disbelief. "A bullet?" she said. "You mean…"

He nodded. "They think it was murder."

Chapter Two

SARAH STARTED TO SPEAK, BUT HER voice refused to work. Like a statue, she sat frozen in her chair, unable to move, unable to do anything but stare at him.

"I thought you should know," said Nick. "I had to tell you in any event, because now we'll need your help. The Berlin police want information about your husband's activities, his enemies…why he might have been killed."

She shook her head numbly. "I can't think of… I mean I just don't know…. My God!" she whispered.

The gentle touch of his hand on her shoulder made Sarah flinch. She looked up and saw the concern in his eyes. *He's worried I'll faint,* she thought. *He's worried I'll get sick all over his nice thick carpet and embarrass us both.* With sudden irritation she shook off his hand. She didn't need anyone's rehearsed sympathy. She needed to be alone—away from bureaucrats and their impersonal file folders. She rose unsteadily to her feet. No, she was not going to faint, not in front of this man.

Nick reached for her arm and nudged her gently back into the chair. "Please, Mrs. Fontaine. Another minute, that's all I need."

"Let me go."

"Mrs. Fontaine—"

"Let me go."

The sharpness of her voice seemed to shock him. He released her but did not back away. As she sat there, she was acutely aware of various aspects of his presence—the faint smell of after-shave and fatigue, the dull gleam of his belt buckle, the wrinkled shirt sleeves.

"I'm sorry," he said. "I didn't mean to crowd you. I was just worried that…well…"

"Yes?" She looked up into those slate eyes. Something she saw there—a steadiness, a strength—made her suddenly, and against all instinct, want to trust him. "I'm not going to faint, if that's what you mean," she said. "Please, I'd like to go home now."

"Yes, of course. But I have just a few more questions."

"I don't have any answers. Don't you understand?"

He was silent for a moment. "Then I'll contact you later," he said at last. "We have to talk about the arrangements for the body."

"Oh. Yes, the body." She stood up, blinking back a new wave of tears.

"I'll have the car take you home now, Mrs. Fontaine." He moved toward her slowly, as if afraid of scaring her. "I'm sorry about your husband. Truly sorry. Feel free to call me if you have any questions."

She knew none of those words came from the heart, that none of them held any genuine sympathy. Nicholas O'Hara was a diplomat, saying what he'd been taught to say. Whatever the catastrophe, the U.S. State Department always had the right words ready. He'd probably said the same thing to a hundred other widows.

Now he was waiting for her response, so she did what was expected of any widow. She pulled herself together. Reaching out, she shook his hand and thanked him. Then she turned and walked out the door.

"DO YOU THINK she knows?"

Nick stared at the door that had just closed behind Sarah Fontaine's retreating figure. He turned and glanced at Tim Greenstein. "Knows what?"

"That her husband was a spook?"

"Hell, *we* don't even know that."

"Nick my man, this whole thing reeks of espionage. Geoffrey

Fontaine was a total nonentity till a year ago. Then his name shows up on a wedding license, he has a brand new Social Security number, a passport and what have you. The FBI doesn't seem to know a damn thing. But intelligence—they've got the guy's file under classified! Am I dumb or what?"

"Maybe I'm the dumb one," grunted Nick. He walked to his desk and dropped into the chair. Then he scowled at the Fontaine file. Tim was right, of course. The case stank to high heaven of funny business. Espionage? International crime? An ex-federal witness, hiding from the mob?

Who the hell *was* Geoffrey Fontaine?

Nick slouched down and threw his head back against the chair. Damn, he was tired. But he couldn't get Geoffrey Fontaine out of his head. Or Sarah Fontaine, for that matter.

He'd been surprised when she walked into the office; he'd been expecting someone with a little more sophistication. Her husband had been a world-class traveler, a guy who'd whisked through London and Berlin and Amsterdam. A man like that should have a wife who was sleek and elegant. Instead, in had walked this skinny, awkward creature who was almost, but not quite, pretty. Her face had been too full of angles: high, sharp cheeks, a narrow nose, a square forehead softened only by a gentle widow's peak. Her long hair had been a rich, coppery color; even tied back in a ponytail, it had been beautiful. Her horn-rimmed glasses had somehow amused him. They had framed two wide, amber-colored eyes—her best feature. With no makeup and with that pale, delicate complexion, she'd seemed much younger than the thirty or so years she must be.

No, she was not quite pretty. But throughout the interview Nick had found himself staring at her face and wondering about her marriage. And about her.

Tim rose. "Hey, all this grief is making me hungry. Let's hit the cafeteria."

"Not the cafeteria. Let's go out. I've been sitting in this building all morning, and I'm going stir-crazy." Nick pulled on his jacket, and together they walked out past Angie's desk and headed for the stairs.

Outside a brisk spring wind blew in their faces as they strode down the sidewalk. The buds were just starting to swell on the cherry trees. In another week the whole city would be awash in pink and white flowers. It was Nick's first D.C. springtime in eight years—he'd forgotten how pretty it could be, walking through the trees. He thrust his hands in his pockets and hunched over a little as the wind bit through his wool jacket.

Vaguely he wondered whether Sarah Fontaine had reached her apartment yet, whether she was lying across her bed now, sobbing her eyes out. He knew he'd been rough on her. It had bothered him, hounding her like that, but someone had to break through all of her denial. She had to understand the facts. It was the only way she'd ever really recover from her grief.

"Where we going, Nick?" asked Tim.

"How about Mary Jo's?"

"That salad place? What, are you on a diet or something?"

"No, but it's quiet there. I'm not into loud conversation right now."

After two more blocks, they turned into the restaurant and sat down at a table. Fifteen minutes later the waitress brought their salads, which were cloaked in homemade mayonnaise and tarragon. Tim looked at the lettuce and arugula on his fork and sighed.

"This is rabbit food. Give me a greasy burger any day." He stuffed a forkful of the salad into his mouth and looked across the table at Nick. "So what's bugging you? The new post got you down already?"

"It's a damned slap in the face, that's what it is," said Nick. He drained his cup of coffee and motioned to the waitress for another. "To go straight from being number two man in London to shuffling papers in D.C."

"So why didn't you resign?"

"I just might. Since that fiasco in London, my career's been shot. And now I've got to put up with this bastard, Ambrose."

"Is he still out of town?"

"One more week. Till then I can do the job my way. Without all that bureaucratic nonsense. Hell, if he rewrites any more of my reports to make 'em 'conform to administration policy,' I'm going to puke." Nick put his fork down and scowled at the salad. The mention of his boss had just ruined his appetite.

From the very first day, Nick and Ambrose had rubbed each other the wrong way. Charles Ambrose reveled in the bureaucratic merry-go-round, whereas Nick always insisted on getting straight to the point, however unpleasant. The clash had been inevitable.

"Your trouble, Nick, is that even though you're an egghead, you don't talk gobbledegook like all the others. You've got 'em all confused. They don't like guys they can understand. Plus you're a bleeding-heart liberal."

"So? You are, too."

"But I'm also a certified nerd. They make allowances for nerds. If they don't, I shut down their computers."

Nick laughed, suddenly glad for the company of his old buddy, Tim. Four years of being college roommates had left strong bonds. Even after eight years abroad, Nick had come home to find Tim Greenstein just as bushy and likable as ever.

He picked up his fork and finished off the salad.

"So what're you going to do with this Fontaine case?" Tim asked over dessert.

"I'm going to do my job and look into it."

"You gonna tell Ambrose? He'll want to hear about it. So will the guys at the Company, if they don't already know."

"Let 'em find out on their own. It's my case."

"It sounds like espionage to me, Nick. That's not exactly a consular affair."

But Nick didn't like the idea of turning Sarah Fontaine over to some CIA case officer. She seemed too fragile, too vulnerable. "It's my case," he repeated.

Tim grinned. "Ah, the widow Fontaine. Could it be she's your type? Though I can't quite see the attraction. What I really can't see is how she hooked that husband. Blond Adonis, wasn't he? Not the kind of guy to go for a woman in horn-rimmed glasses. My deduction is that he married her for reasons other than the usual."

"The usual? You mean love?"

"Naw. Sex."

"Just what the hell are you getting at?"

"Hmm. Touchy. You liked her, didn't you?"

"No comment."

"Seems to me the old love life's been pretty barren since your divorce."

Nick set his coffee cup down with a clatter. "What's with all these questions?"

"Just trying to see where your head's at, Nick. Haven't you heard? It's the latest thing. Men opening up to each other."

Nick sighed. "Don't tell me. You've been to another one of those sensitivity training sessions."

"Yeah. Great place to meet women. You should try it."

"No, thanks. The last thing I need is to join some big cry-in with a bunch of neurotic females."

Tim gave his friend a sympathetic look. "Let me tell you, Nick. You need to do something. You can't just sit around and be celibate the rest of your life."

"Why not?"

Tim laughed. "Because, dammit, we both know you're not the priestly type!"

Tim was right. In the four years since his split-up with Lauren, Nick had avoided any close relationships with women, sexual or otherwise, and it was starting to show. He was irritable. He'd thrown himself into salvaging what was left of his career, but work, he'd discovered, was a poor substitute for what he really wanted—a warm, soft body to hold; laughter in the night; thoughts shared in bed. To avoid being hurt again, he'd learned to live without these things. It was the only way to stay sane. But those old male instincts didn't die easily. No, Nick was not the priestly type.

"Heard from Lauren lately?" asked Tim.

Nick looked up with a scowl. "Yeah. Last month. Told me she misses me. What she really misses, I think, is the embassy life."

"So she called you. Sounds promising. Sounds like a reconciliation in the works."

"Yeah? It sounded more to me like her latest romance wasn't going so well."

"Either way, it's obvious she regrets the divorce. Did you follow up on it?"

Nick pushed away what remained of his chocolate mousse cake. "No."

"Why not?"

"Didn't feel like it."

Tim leaned back and laughed. "He didn't feel like it." He sighed to no one in particular. "Four years of moaning and groaning about being divorced, and now he tells me this."

"Look, every time things go bad for her, she decides to call good old Nick, her ever-loyal chump. I can't handle that anymore. I told her I was no longer available. For her or anyone else."

Tim shook his head. "You've sworn off women. That's a very bad sign."

"Nobody's ever died of it." Nick grunted as he threw a few bills on the table and rose. He wasn't going to think about women right now. He had too many other things on his mind, and he sure as hell didn't need another bad love affair.

But outside, as they walked back through the cherry trees, he found himself thinking about Sarah Fontaine. Not about Sarah, the grieving widow, but about Sarah, the woman. The name fit her. Sarah with the amber eyes.

Nick quickly shook off the thoughts. Of all the women in Washington, she was the last one he should be thinking about. In his line of work, objectivity was the key to doing the job right. Whether it was issuing visas or arguing a jailed American's case before a magistrate, getting personally involved was almost always a mistake. No, Sarah Fontaine was nothing more to him than a name in a file.

She would have to remain that way.

Amsterdam

THE OLD MAN loved roses. He loved the dusky smell of the petals, which he often plucked and rubbed between his fingers. So cool, so fragrant, not like those insipid tulips that his gardener had planted on the banks of the duck pond. Tulips were all color, no character. They threw up stalks, bloomed and vanished. But roses! Even through winter they persisted, bare and thorny, like angry old women crouched in the cold.

He paused among the rosebushes and breathed in deeply, enjoying the smell of damp earth. In a few weeks, there'd be flowers. How his wife would have loved this garden! He could picture her standing on this very spot, smiling at the roses. She would have worn her old straw hat and a housedress with four pockets, and she would have carried her plastic bucket. *My uniform,* she'd have said. *I'm just an old soldier, going out to fight the snails and beetles.* He remembered how the rose clippers used to clunk against the bucket when she walked down the steps of their old house—the house he'd left behind. *Nienke, my sweet Nienke,* he thought. *How I miss you.*

"It is a cold day," said a voice in Dutch.

The old man turned and looked at the pale-haired young man walking toward him through the bushes. "Kronen," he said. "At last you've come."

"I am sorry, *meneer*. A day late, but it couldn't be helped." Kronen took off his sunglasses and peered up at the sky. As usual, he avoided looking directly at the old man's face. Since the accident, everyone avoided looking at his face, and it never failed to annoy him. It had been five years since anyone had stared him boldly in the eye, five years since he'd been able to meet another person's gaze without detecting the invariable flinching. Even Kronen, whom he'd come to regard almost as a son, made it a point to look anywhere else. But then, young men of Kronen's generation always fussed too much about appearances.

"I take it things went well in Basra," said the old man.

"Yes. Minor delays, that's all. And there were problems with the last shipment…the computer chips in the aiming mechanism…. One of the missiles failed to lock in."

"Embarrassing."

"Yes. I have already spoken to the manufacturer."

They followed a path from the rosebushes toward the duck pond. The cold air made the old man's throat sore. He wrapped his scarf a little tighter around his neck and forced out a thin, dry cough. "I have a new assignment for you," he said. "A woman."

Kronen paused, sudden interest in his eyes. His hair looked almost white in the sunshine. "Who is she?"

"The name is Sarah Fontaine. Geoffrey Fontaine's wife. I want you to see where she leads you."

Kronen frowned. "I don't understand, sir. I was told Fontaine was dead."

"Follow her anyway. My American source tells me she has a modest apartment in Georgetown. She is a microbiologist, thirty-two years old. Except for her marriage, she has no apparent intelligence connections. But one can never be certain."

"May I contact this source?"

"No. His position is too…delicate."

Kronen nodded, at once dropping the subject. He'd worked for the old man long enough to know the way things were done. Each man had his own territory, his own small box in which to operate. Never must one try to break out. Even Kronen, trusted as he was, saw only a part of the picture. Only the old man saw it all.

They walked together along the banks of the pond. The old man reached into his coat pocket and pulled out the bag of bread he'd brought from the house. Silently he flung a handful into the water and watched the crumbs swell. The ducks splashed among the reeds. When Nienke was alive, she had walked to the park every morning, just to feed the ducks her breakfast toast. She had worried that the weak ones would not get enough to eat. Look there, Frans, she would say. The little ones grow so fat! All on our breakfast crumbs!

Now, here he was, throwing bread on the water to the ducks he cared nothing about, except that Nienke would have loved them. He carefully folded the wrapper and stuffed it back into his pocket. As he did this, it struck him what a very sad and very feeble gesture it was, trying to preserve an old bread wrapper, and for what?

The pond had turned a sullen gray. Where had the sun gone? he wondered. Without looking at Kronen, he said, "I want to know about this woman. Leave soon."

"Of course."

"Be careful in Washington. I understand the crime there has become abominable."

Kronen laughed as he turned to leave. "*Tot ziens, meneer.*"

The old man nodded. "Till then."

THE LAB WHERE Sarah worked was spotless. The microscopes were polished, the counters and sinks were repeatedly disinfected, the incubation chambers were wiped clean twice daily. Sarah's job required strict attention to asepsis; by habit she insisted on cleanliness. But as she sat at her lab bench, flipping through the last box of microscope slides, it seemed to Sarah that the sterility of the room had somehow extended to the rest of her life.

She took off her glasses and blinked tiredly. Everywhere she looked, stainless steel seemed to gleam back at her. The lights were harsh and fluorescent. There were no windows, and therefore, no sunshine. It could be noon or midnight outside; in here she'd never know the difference. Except for the hum of the refrigerator, the lab was silent.

She put her glasses on again and began to stack the slides back into the box. From the hallway came the clip of a woman's heels on the floor. The door swung open.

"Sarah? What're you doing here?"

Sarah glanced around at her good friend, Abby Hicks. In her size forty lab coat, Abby filled most of the doorway.

"I'm just catching up on a few things," said Sarah. "So much work's piled up since I've been gone…."

"Oh, for heaven's sake, Sarah! The lab can manage without you for a few weeks. It's already eight o'clock. I'll check the cultures. Go on home."

Sarah closed the box of slides. "I'm not sure I want to go home," she murmured. "It's too quiet there. I'd almost rather be here."

"Well, this place isn't exactly jumping. It's about as lively as a tomb—" At once Abby bit her lip and reddened. Even at age fifty-five, Abby could blush as deeply as a schoolgirl. "Bad choice of words," she mumbled.

Sarah smiled. "It's all right, Abby."

For a moment the two women said nothing. Sarah rose and opened the incubator to deposit the specimen plate she'd been working on. The foul smell of agar drifted out from the warm petri dishes and permeated the room.

"How are you doing, Sarah?" Abby asked gently.

Sarah shut the incubator after setting the plate inside. With a sigh she turned and looked at her friend. "I'm managing, I guess."

"We've all missed you. Even old Grubb says it's not the same without you and your silly bottle of disinfectant. I think everyone's just a little afraid to call you. None of them really knows what to do with grief, I suppose. But we do care, Sarah."

Sarah nodded gratefully. "Oh, Abby, I know you care. And I appreciate everything you've done for me. All the casseroles and cards and flowers. Now I just have to get back on my feet." She gazed sadly around the room. "I thought that coming back to work was what I needed."

"Some people need the old routine. Others need to get away for a while."

"Maybe that's what I should do. Get away from Washington for a while. Away from all the places that remind me of him…." She swallowed back the familiar ache in her throat and tried to smile. "My sister has asked me to visit her in Oregon. You know, I haven't seen my nephew and nieces in years. They must be getting huge."

"Then go. Sarah, it hasn't even been two weeks! You need to give it some time. Go see your sister. Have yourself a few more cries."

"I've spent too many days crying. I've been sitting at home, wondering how to get through this. I still can't bear to see his clothes hanging in the closet." Sarah shook her head. "It's not just losing him that hurts so much. It's the rest…."

"You mean the part about Berlin."

Sarah nodded. "I'll go crazy if I think about it much longer. That's why I came in tonight—to get my mind off the whole thing. I thought it was time to get back to work." She stared at the stack of lab books by her microscope. "But it's strange, Abby. I used to love this place. Now I wonder how I've stood it these past six years. All these cold cabinets and steel sinks. Everything so closed in. I feel as if I can't breathe."

"It's got to be more than the lab. You've always liked this job, Sarah. You're the one who stands humming by the centrifuge."

"I can't picture myself working here the rest of my life. Geoffrey and I had so little time together! Three days for a honeymoon. That's all. Then I had to rush back to finish that damned grant proposal. We were always so busy, no time for vacations. Now we'll never have another chance." Sighing, she went back to her bench and flicked off the microscope lamp. Softly she added, "And I'll never really know why he…" She sat down without finishing the sentence.

"Have you heard anything else from the State Department?"

"That man called again yesterday. The police in Berlin have

finally released the—the body. It's coming home tomorrow." Her eyes suddenly filmed with tears. She gazed down, struggling not to cry. "The service will be Friday. You'll be there?"

"Of course I'll be there. We'll all be there. I'll drive you, okay?" Abby came over and laid a hand on her friend's shoulder. "It's still so recent, Sarah. You've got every right to cry."

"There's so much I'll never understand about his death, Abby. That man in the State Department—he kept hounding me for answers, and I couldn't give him a single one! Oh, I know it was just his job, but he brought up these…possibilities that have bothered me ever since. I've started wondering about Geoffrey. More and more."

"You weren't married that long, Sarah. Heck, my husband and I were married thirty years before we split up, and I never did figure out the jerk. It's not surprising you didn't know everything there was to know about Geoffrey."

"But he was my husband!"

Abby fell silent for a moment. Then, with some hesitation, she said, "You know, Sarah, there was always something about him…. I mean, I never felt I could get to *know* him very well."

"He was shy, Abby."

"No, it wasn't just shyness. It was as if—as if he didn't want to give anything away. As if—" She looked at Sarah. "Oh, it's not important."

But Sarah was already thinking about what Abby had said. There was some truth to her observation. Geoffrey had been an aloof man, not given to lengthy or revealing conversations. He'd never talked much about himself. He had always seemed more interested in her—her work, her friends. When they first met, that interest had been flattering; of all the men she'd known, he was the only one who'd ever really *listened.*

Then for some reason, another face sprang to mind. Nick O'Hara. Yes, that was his name. She had a sudden, vivid memory of the way Nick O'Hara had studied her, the way his gray eyes had focused on her every expression. Yes, he'd listened, too; but then, it had been his job. Had it also been his job to torment new widows? She didn't want to think about him. She never wanted to speak to the man again.

Sarah put the plastic cover over the microscope. She thought about taking her data book home. But as she scanned the open page, it occurred to her that the column of entries symbolized the way she was living her life. Neatly, carefully and precisely within the printed boundaries.

She closed the book and put it back on the shelf.

"I think I'm going home," she said.

Abby nodded her approval. "Good. No sense burying yourself in here. Forget about work for a while."

"Are you sure you can handle the extra load?"

"Of course."

Sarah took off her lab coat and hung it by the door. Like everything else in the room, her coat looked too neat, too clean. "Maybe I will take some time off, after the funeral. Another week. Maybe a month."

"Don't stay away too long," said Abby. "We do want you back."

Sarah glanced around one last time to make sure things were tidy. They were. "I'll be back," she said. "I just don't know when."

THE COFFIN SLID down the ramp and landed with a soft thud on the platform. The sound made Nick shudder. Years of packing off dead Americans hadn't dulled his sense of horror. But like everyone else in the consular corps, he'd found his own way to handle the pain. Later today he'd take a long walk, go home and pour himself a drink. Then he'd sit in his old leather chair, turn on the radio and read the newspaper; find out how many earthquakes there'd been, how many plane and train and bus crashes, how many bombs had been dropped. The big picture. It would make this one death seem insignificant. Almost.

"Mr. O'Hara? Sign here, please."

A man in an airline uniform held out a clipboard with the shipment papers. Nick glanced over the documents, quickly noting the deceased's name: Geoffrey Fontaine. He scrawled his signature and handed back the clipboard. Then he turned and watched as the coffin was loaded into a waiting hearse. He didn't want to think about its contents, but all at once an image rose up in his mind, something he'd seen in a magazine, a picture of dead Vietnamese villagers after a bombing. They had all burned to death. Is that what lay inside Geoffrey Fontaine's coffin? A man charred beyond recognition?

He shook off the image. Damn, he needed a drink. It was time to go home. The hearse was headed off safely to a designated mortuary; as previously arranged, Sarah Fontaine would take charge from there. He wondered if he should call her just one more time. But for what? More condolences, more regrets? He'd done his part. She'd already paid the bill. There was nothing else to say.

By the time he got to his apartment, Nick had shoved the whole grisly affair out of his mind. He threw his briefcase onto the couch and went straight to the kitchen, where he poured out a generous glass of whiskey and slid a TV dinner into the oven. Good old Swanson, the bachelor's friend. He leaned back against the counter and sipped his drink. The refrigerator began to growl, and the oven light clicked off. He thought of turning on the radio, but he couldn't quite force himself to move. So ended another day as a public servant. And to think it was only Tuesday.

He wondered how long it had been since he'd been happy. Months? Years? Trying to recall a different state of mind was futile. Sights and sounds were what he remembered—the blue of a sky, the smile on a face. His last distinct image of happiness was of riding a bus in London, a bus with torn seats and dirty windows. He'd just left the embassy for the day and was on his way home to Lauren....

The apartment buzzer made him jump. Suddenly he felt starved for company, any company, even the paperboy's. He went to the intercom. "Hello?"

"Hey, Nick? It's Tim. Let me in."

"Okay. Come on up."

Nick released the front lock. Would Tim want supper? Dumb question. He always wanted supper. Nick poked in the freezer and was relieved to find two more TV dinners. He put one in the oven.

He went to the front doorway and waited for the elevator to open.

Tim bounded out. "Okay, are you ready for this? Guess what my FBI friend found out?"

Nick sighed. "I'm afraid to ask."

"You know that guy, Geoffrey Fontaine? Well, he's dead all right."

"So what's new?"

"No, I'm talking about the *real* Geoffrey Fontaine."

"Look," said Nick. "I've pretty much closed my file on this case. But if you want to stay for dinner…"

Tim followed him into the apartment. "See, the real Geoffrey Fontaine died—"

"Right," said Nick.

"Forty-two years ago."

The door slammed shut. Nick turned and stared at him.

"Ha!" said Tim. "I thought that'd get your attention."

Chapter Three

THE DAY SMELLED OF FLOWERS. On the grass at Sarah's feet lay a mound of carnations and gladioli and lilies. For the rest of her life, the smell would sicken her. It would bring back this hilltop and the marble plaques dotting the shorn grass and the mist hanging in the valley below. Most of all, it would bring back the pain. Everything else—the minister's words, the squeeze of her good friend Abby's hand around her arm, even the first cold drops of rain against her face—she scarcely felt, for it was peripheral to the pain.

She forced herself not to concentrate on the gash of earth at her feet. Instead she stared at the hill across the valley. Through the mist she could see a faint dappling of pink. The cherry trees were blooming. But the view only saddened her; it was a springtime Geoffrey would not see.

The minister's voice receded to a faintly irritating drone. A cold drizzle stung Sarah's cheeks and clouded her glasses; fog moved in, closing off the world. Abby's sudden nudge brought her back to reality. The casket had been lowered. She saw faces, all watching her, all waiting. These were her friends, but in her pain she scarcely recognized them. Even Abby, dear Abby, was a stranger to her now.

Automatically Sarah bent down and took a handful of earth. It was damp and rich and it smelled of rain. She tossed it into the grave. The thud of the casket made her wince.

Faces passed by as if they were ghosts in the mist. Her friends were gentle. They spoke softly. Through it all she stood dry-eyed and numb. The smell of flowers and the mist against her face overpowered her senses, and she was aware of nothing else until she looked around and saw that the others had gone. Only she and Abby were standing beside the grave.

"It's starting to rain," said Abby.

Sarah looked up and saw the clouds descending on them like a cold, silvery blanket. Abby draped her stout arm around Sarah's shoulders and nudged her toward the parking lot.

"A cup of tea, that's what we both need," said Abby. It was her remedy for everything. She had survived a nasty divorce and the departure of her college-bound sons on nothing more potent than Earl Grey. "A cup of tea, and then let's talk."

"A cup of tea does sound nice," admitted Sarah.

Arm in arm, they slowly walked across the lawn. "I know it means nothing to you now," said Abby, "but the pain will pass, Sarah. It really will. We women are strong that way. We have to be."

"What if I'm not?"

"You are. Don't you doubt it."

Sarah shook her head. "I question everything now. And everyone."

"You don't doubt me, do you?"

Sarah looked at Abby's broad, damp face and smiled. "No. Not you."

"Good. When you get to be my age, you'll see that it's all—" Suddenly Abby stopped in her tracks. Her breathing was loud and husky. Sarah followed the direction of her gaze.

A man was walking toward them through the mist.

Sarah took in the windblown dark hair and the gray overcoat, now sparkling with water droplets. She could tell he had been standing outside a long time, probably through the whole funeral. The cold had turned his face ruddy.

"Mrs. Fontaine?" he asked.

"Hello, Mr. O'Hara."

"Look, I realize this is a bad moment, but I've been trying to get hold of you for two days. You haven't returned my calls."

"No," she admitted, "I haven't."

"I need to talk to you. There've been some new developments. I think you should hear about them."

"Sarah, who is this man?" broke in Abby.

Nick turned to the older woman. "Nick O'Hara. I'm with the State Department. If it would be all right, ma'am, I'd like a moment alone with Mrs. Fontaine."

"Maybe she doesn't want to talk to you."

He looked back at Sarah. "It's important."

Something about the way he looked at her, the stubborn angle of his jaw, made Sarah consider his request. She hadn't planned to speak to him again. For the past two days, her answering machine had recorded his half dozen calls, all of which she'd ignored. Geoffrey was dead and buried; that was pain enough. Nick O'Hara would only make things worse by asking his unanswerable questions.

"Please, Mrs. Fontaine."

At last she nodded. With a glance at Abby, she said, "I'll be all right."

"Well, you can't stand around chatting out here. It'll be pouring in a minute!"

"I can drive her home," said Nick. At Abby's dubious look, he smiled. "Really, I'm okay. I'll take care of her."

Abby gave Sarah one last hug and kiss. "I'll call you tonight, sweetheart. Let's have breakfast in the morning." Then, with obvious reluctance, she turned and headed toward her car.

"A good friend, I take it," he said, watching Abby's retreat.

"We've worked together for years."

"At NIH?"

"Yes. The same lab."

He glanced up at the sky, which was now dark with storm clouds. A chill had fallen over them. "Your friend's right. It'll be pouring in a minute. Come on. My car's this way."

Gently he touched her sleeve. She moved ahead mechanically, allowing him to guide her into the front seat of his car. He slid in beside her and pulled his door shut. For a moment they sat in silence. The car was an old Volvo, practical, without frills, a model one chose purely for transportation. It fit him, somehow. A trace of warmth still clung to the interior, and Sarah's glasses clouded over. Pulling them off, she turned and looked at him and saw that his hair was wet.

"You must be cold," he said. "Let's get you home."

The engine roared to life. A blast of air erupted from the heater, gradually warming them as they drove along the winding road from the cemetery. The windshield wiper squeaked back and forth.

"It started out so beautiful this morning," she said, watching the rain fall.

"Unpredictable. Just like everything else."

He smoothly turned the car onto the highway bound for D.C. He was a calm driver, with steady hands. The kind who probably never took risks. Savoring the heater's warmth, Sarah settled back in her seat.

"Why didn't you return my calls?" he asked.

"It was rude of me. I'm sorry."

"You didn't answer my question. Why didn't you call me back?"

"I guess I didn't want to hear any more speculation about Geoffrey. Or about his death."

"Even if they're facts?"

"You weren't giving me facts, Mr. O'Hara. You were guessing."

He stared ahead grimly at the road. "I'm not guessing anymore, Mrs. Fontaine. I've got the facts. All I need is a name."

"What are you talking about?"

"Your husband. You said that six months ago you met Geoffrey Fontaine at a coffee shop. He must have swept you clean off your feet. Four months later you were married. Correct?"

"Yes."

"I don't know how to say this, but Geoffrey Fontaine—the real Geoffrey Fontaine—died forty-two years ago. As an infant."

She couldn't believe what she was hearing. "I don't understand…"

He didn't look at her; he kept his eyes on the road as he talked. "The man you married took the name of a dead infant. It's easy enough to do. You hunt around for the name of a baby who died around the year you were born. Then you get a copy of the birth certificate. With that you apply for a Social Security number, a driver's license, a marriage license. You *become* that infant, grown up. A new identity. A new life. With all the records to prove it."

"But—but how do you know all this?"

"Everything's on computer these days. From a few cross-checks, I found out that Geoffrey Fontaine never registered for the draft. He never attended school. He never held a bank account—until a year ago, when his name suddenly appeared in a dozen different places."

The breath went out of her. "Then who was he?" she whispered at last. "Who did I marry?"

"I don't know," Nick answered.

"Why? Why would he do it? Why would he start a new life?"

"I can think of lots of reasons. My first thought was that he was wanted for some crime. His thumbprints were on record with the driver's license bureau, so I had them run through the FBI computer. He's not on any of their lists."

"Then he wasn't a criminal."

"There's no proof that he was. Another possibility is that he was in some kind of federal witness program, that he was given a new name for protection. It's hard for me to check on that. The data are locked up tight. It would, however, give us a motive for his murder."

"You mean—the people he testified against—they found him."

"That's right."

"But he would have told me about something like that, he would have shared it with me…."

"That's what makes me think of one more possibility. Maybe you can confirm it."

"Go on."

"What if your husband's new name and new life were just part of his job? He might not have been running from anything. He might have been sent here."

"You mean he was a spy," she said softly.

He looked at her and nodded. His eyes were as gray as the storm clouds outside.

"I don't believe this," she said. "None of it!"

"It's real. I assure you."

"Then why are you telling *me*? How do you know I'm not an accomplice or something?"

"I think you're clean, Mrs. Fontaine. I've seen your file—"

"Oh. I have a file, too?" she shot back.

"You got security clearance some years ago, remember? For the research you were working on. Naturally a file was generated."

"Naturally."

"But it's not just your file that makes me think you're clean. It's my own gut feeling. Now convince me I'm right."

"How? Should I hook myself up to a polygraph?"

"Start off by telling me about you and Geoffrey. Were you in love?"

"Of course we were!"

"So it was a real marriage? You had…relations?"

She flushed. "Yes. Like any normal couple. Do you want to know how often? When?"

"I'm not playing games. I'm sticking my neck out for you. If you don't like my approach, perhaps you'd prefer the way the Company handles it."

"Then you haven't told the CIA?"

"No." His chin came up in an unintended gesture of stubbornness. "I don't care much for the way they do things. I may get slapped down for this, but then again, I may not."

"So why are you putting yourself on the line?"

He shrugged. "Curiosity. Maybe a chance to see what I can do on my own."

"Ambition?"

"That's part of it, I guess. Plus…" He glanced at her, and their eyes met. Suddenly he fell silent.

"Plus what?" she asked.

"Nothing."

The rain was coming down in sheets and streamed across the windshield. Nick left the freeway and edged into city-bound traffic. Driving through D.C. rush hour usually made Sarah nervous; today, though, she took it calmly. Something about the way Nick O'Hara drove made her feel safe. In fact, everything about him spoke of safety—the steadiness of his hands on the wheel, the warmth of his car, the low timbre of his voice. Just sitting beside him, she felt secure. She could imagine how safe a woman might feel in his arms.

"Anyway," he continued, "you can see we've got a lot of unanswered questions. You might have some of the answers, whether you know it or not."

"I don't have any answers."

"Let's start off with what you do know."

She shook her head, bewildered. "I was married to him and I can't even tell you his real name!"

"Everyone, Sarah, even the best spy, slips up. He must've let his guard down for a moment. Maybe he talked in his sleep. Maybe he said things you can't explain. *Think.*"

She bit her lip, suddenly thinking not about Geoffrey, but about Nick. He'd called her by her first name. Sarah. "Even if there were things," she said, "little things—I might not have considered them significant."

"Such as?"

"Oh, he might have—he might have called me Evie once or twice. But he always apologized right away. He said she was an old girlfriend."

"What about family? Friends? Didn't he talk about them?"

"He said he was born in Vermont, then raised in London. His parents were theater people. They're dead. He never talked about any other relatives. He always seemed so…self-sufficient. He didn't have any close friends, not even from work. At least, none he introduced me to."

"Oh, yes. His work. I've been checking on that. It seems he *was* listed on the Bank of London payroll. He had a desk in some back office. But no one remembers quite what he did."

"Then even that part wasn't real."

"So it seems."

Sarah sank deeper into the seat. Each thing this man told her left another slash in the fabric of her life. Her marriage was dissolving away to nothing. It had been all shadow and no substance. Reality was here and now, the rain hitting the car, the windshield wipers beating back and forth. Most of all, reality was the man sitting silently beside her. He was not an illusion. She scarcely knew him, and yet he'd become the only reality she could cling to.

She wondered about Nick O'Hara. She didn't think he was married. Despite his aloofness she found him attractive enough; any woman would have. But there was more than just the physical attraction. She sensed his need. Something told her he was lonely, troubled. Vague shadows of unhappiness surrounded his eyes, creating a feeling of restlessness; it was the look of a man without a home. He probably had none. The foreign service was a career for nomads, not for people who craved a house in the suburbs. Nick O'Hara was definitely not the suburban type.

Shivering, she longed desperately to be back in her apartment, drinking that cup of tea with Abby. *It won't be long,* she thought as the streets became more and more familiar. Connecticut Avenue glistened in the rain. The downpour had already stripped the cherry trees of half their blossoms; the first rush of spring had been short-lived.

They pulled up in front of her apartment, and Nick dashed around the car to open her door. It was a funny little gesture, the sort of thing Geoffrey used to do, gallant and sweetly impractical. By the time they stamped into the lobby they were both soaked. The rain had plastered his hair in dark curls against his forehead.

"I suppose you have more questions." She sighed as they headed toward the stairs leading to the second floor.

"If you mean do I want to come up, the answer is yes."

"For tea or interrogation?"

He smiled and brushed away the water dripping down his cheek. "A little of both. I've had so much trouble getting hold of you, I'd better ask all my questions now."

They reached the top of the stairs. She was just about to say something when the hallway came into view. What she saw made her freeze.

The door to her apartment was hanging open. Someone had broken in.

Instinctively Sarah retreated, terrified of whatever lay beyond the door. She fell back against Nick and found herself wordlessly clutching his arm. He stared at the open door, his face suddenly tense. Except for the pounding of her own heart, she heard nothing. The apartment was absolutely silent.

Light spilled into the hall through the open doorway. Nick motioned her to stay where she was, then cautiously approached the door. Sarah started to follow him, but he gave her such a dark look of warning that she shrank back at once.

He nudged the door open, and the arc of light widened and spilled across his face. For a few seconds, he stood in the doorway, staring at the room beyond. Then he entered the apartment.

In the hall Sarah waited, frightened by the absolute silence. What was happening inside? A shadow flickered in the doorway, and panic began to overtake her as she watched the outline grow larger. Then, to her relief, Nick poked his head out.

"It's all right, Sarah," he said. "There's no one here."

She ran past him into the apartment. In the living room, she paused, surprised by what she saw. She had expected to find her possessions gone, to find only empty shelves where her TV and stereo had always sat. But nothing had been touched. Even the antique clock was in its place, ticking softly on the bookshelf.

She turned and ran into the bedroom with Nick close behind. He watched from the doorway as she went directly to the jewelry box on her dresser. There, on red velvet, was her string of pearls, right where it should be. Slamming the box shut, she turned and quickly surveyed the room, taking in the king-size bed, the nightstand with its china lamp, the closet. In confusion she looked back at Nick.

"What's missing?" he asked.

She shook her head. "Nothing. Could I have just left the door unlocked?"

He stalked out of her bedroom, back to the hall. She found him crouched in the doorway. "Look," he said, pointing down at the wood splinters and fragments of antique-white paint littering the gray carpet. "It's definitely been forced open."

"But it doesn't make sense! Why break into an apartment and then not take anything?"

"Maybe he didn't have time. Maybe he was interrupted...."

Rising, he turned and looked at her. "You look shook up. Are you all right?"

"I'm just—just bewildered."

He touched her hand; his fingers felt hot against hers. "You're also freezing. You'd better get out of those wet clothes."

"I'm fine, Mr. O'Hara. Really."

"Come on. Off with the coat." He insisted. "And sit down while I make a few calls."

Something about his tone seemed to leave Sarah no choice but to obey. She let him tug off her coat, then sat on the couch and watched numbly as he reached for the telephone. Suddenly she felt as though she'd lost control of her actions. As though, just by walking into her apartment, Nick O'Hara had taken over her life. Almost as an act of protest, she rose and headed for the kitchen.

"Sarah?"

"I'm going to make a pot of tea."

"Look, don't go to any trouble—"

"It's no trouble. We could both use a cup, I think."

From the kitchen doorway, she saw him dial his call. As she put the kettle on, she heard him say, "Hello? Tim Greenstein, please. This is Nick O'Hara calling.... Yes, I'll hold."

The next pause seemed to last forever. Nick began to pace back and forth, like an animal in a cage, first pulling off his overcoat, then loosening his tie. His agitation made him entirely out of place in her small, tidy living room.

"Shouldn't you call the police?" she asked.

"That's next on the list. First I'd like an informal chat with the bureau. If I can just get through the damned lines."

"The bureau? You mean the FBI? But why?"

"There's something about all this that bugs me...."

His words were lost when the kettle abruptly whistled. Sarah filled the teapot and carried the tray out to the living room, where Nick was still waiting on the phone.

"Dammit," he muttered to himself. "Where the hell are you, Greenstein?"

"Tea, Mr. O'Hara?"

"Hmm?" He turned and saw the cup she held out to him. "Yeah. Thanks."

She sat down, holding a cup and saucer on her lap. “Does Mr. Greenstein work for the FBI?”

“No. But he has a friend who—hello? Tim? It’s about time! Don’t you answer your calls anymore?”

In the silence that followed, Nick’s face and the way he stood, with his shoulders squared and his back rigid, told Sarah that something was wrong. He was livid. The loud clatter of his teacup on the saucer made her jump.

“How the hell did Ambrose get wind of it?” he snapped into the receiver, turning away from Sarah.

Another silence. She stared at his back, wondering what kind of catastrophe had made Nick O’Hara so angry. Up until now she’d thought of him as a man completely in control of his emotions. No longer. His anger surprised her, yet somehow it also reassured her that he was human.

“Okay,” he said into the phone. “I’ll be there in half an hour. Look, Tim, something else has come up. Someone’s broken into Sarah’s apartment. No, nothing’s been touched. Can you get me the number of this FBI friend? I want to—Yeah, I’m sorry I got you into this, but…” He turned and gave Sarah a harassed look. “Okay! Half an hour. My trip to the woodshed. Meet you in Ambrose’s office.” He hung up with a scowl.

“What’s wrong?” she asked.

“So end eight glorious years with the State Department,” he muttered, furiously snatching up his overcoat and walking toward the door. “I’ve gotta go. Look, you’ve still got the chain. Use it. Better yet, stay with your friend tonight. And call the police. I’ll get back to you as soon as I can.”

She followed him into the hallway. “But Mr. O’Hara—”

“Later!” he called over his shoulder as he stalked away. She heard his footsteps echo in the stairwell, and moments later the lobby door slammed shut.

She closed the door and slid the chain in place, then slowly gazed around the room. Her stack of *Advances in Microbiology* lay on the coffee table. A vase of peonies dropped petals onto the bookshelf. Everything was as it should be.

No, not quite. Something was different. If she could just put her finger on it…

She was halfway across the room when it suddenly struck her—there was an empty space on the bookshelf. Her wedding picture was gone.

A cry of anger welled up in her throat. For the first time since she'd returned to the apartment, she felt a sense of violation, of fury that someone had invaded her house. It had only been a photograph, a pair of happy faces beaming at a camera, yet it meant more to her than anything else she owned. The picture had been all she had left of Geoffrey. Even if her marriage had been mere illusion, she never wanted to forget how she had loved him. Of all the things in her apartment, why would anyone steal a photograph?

Her heart skipped a beat as the phone rang. It was probably Abby, calling as promised. She picked up the receiver.

The first sound she heard was the hiss of a long-distance connection. Sarah froze. For some reason she found herself staring at the empty shelf, at the spot where the photograph should have been.

"Hello?" she said.

"Come to me, Sarah. I love you."

A scream caught in her throat. The room was spinning wildly, and she reached out for support. The receiver slipped from her fingers and thudded on the carpet. *This is impossible!* she thought. *Geoffrey is dead....*

She scrambled on the floor for the receiver, scrambled to hear the voice of what could only be a ghost.

"Hello? *Hello? Geoffrey!*" she screamed.

The long-distance hiss was gone. There was only silence and then, a few seconds later, the hum of the dial tone.

But she had heard enough. Everything that had happened in the past two weeks faded away as if it were a nightmare remembered in the light of day. None of it had been real. The voice she'd just heard, the voice she knew so well—*that* was real.

Geoffrey was alive.

Chapter Four

"YOU'VE HAD IT, O'HARA!" Charles Ambrose stood outside the closed door of his office and looked pointedly at his watch. "And you're twenty minutes late!"

Unperturbed, Nick hung up his coat and said, "Sorry. I couldn't help it. The rain had us backed up for—"

"Do you know who just happens to be waiting in my office right now? I mean, do you have any idea?"

"No. Who?"

"Some son of a—" Ambrose abruptly lowered his voice. "The *CIA*, that's who! A guy named Van Dam. This morning he calls me up wanting to know about the Fontaine case. What's the Fontaine case, I ask. He had to tell me what's going on in my own department! For God's sake, O'Hara! What the hell do you think you're doing?"

Nick gazed back calmly. "My job, as a matter of fact."

"Your job was to tell the widow you were sorry and to fly the damned body back. That was it, period. Instead, Van Dam tells me you've been out playing James Bond with Sarah Fontaine."

"I'll admit that I went to the funeral. And I did drive Mrs. Fontaine home. I wouldn't call that playing James Bond."

In reply, Ambrose turned and flung the office door open. "Get in there, O'Hara!"

Without blinking, Nick walked into the office. The blinds were open and the last drab light of day fell on the shoulders of a man sitting at Ambrose's desk. He was in his midforties, tall, silent, and like the day outside, totally without color. His hands were folded in a gesture of prayer. There was no sign of Tim Greenstein. Ambrose closed the door, stalked past Nick and seated himself off to the side. The fact that Ambrose had been evicted from his own desk spoke volumes about his usurper's prestige. *This guy,* thought Nick, *must be hot stuff in the CIA.*

"Please sit down, Mr. O'Hara," said the man. "I'm Jonathan Van Dam." That was the only label he gave himself: a name.

Nick took a chair, but obedience had nothing to do with it. He was simply not going to stand at attention while he was put through the wringer.

For a moment Van Dam silently regarded him with those colorless eyes. Then he picked up a manila folder. It was Nick's employment record. "I hope you're not nervous. It's just a minor thing, really." Van Dam glanced through the folder. "Let's see. You've been with state for eight years."

"Eight years, two months."

"Two years in Honduras, two in Cairo and four years in London. All in the consular service. A good record, with the exception of two adverse personnel memos. It says here that in Honduras you were too—er, sympathetic to native concerns."

"That's because our policy there stinks."

Van Dam smiled. "Believe me, you're not the first person to say that."

The smile threw Nick off guard. He glanced suspiciously at Ambrose, who'd obviously been hoping for an execution and now looked sorely disappointed.

Van Dam sat back. "Mr. O'Hara, this is a country of diverse opinions. I respect men who think for themselves, men like you. Unfortunately, independent thinking is often discouraged in government service. Is that what led to this second memo?"

"I assume it's about that incident in London."

"Yes. Could you elaborate?"

"I'm sure Roy Potter filed a report with your office. His version of the story, anyway."

"Tell me yours."

Nick sat back, the memory of the incident at once reawakening his anger. "It happened the week our consular chief, Dan Lieberman, was out of town. I was filling in for him. A man named Vladimir Sokolov approached me one night, in confidence. He was an attaché with the Russian embassy in London. Oh, I'd met him before, you know, at the usual round of receptions. He'd always struck me as a little nervous. Worried. Well, he took me aside at one of their—I don't know, I guess it was a reception for the ambassador. He wanted to talk asylum. He had information to trade—good information, to my mind. I immediately brought the matter to Roy Potter." Nick glanced at Ambrose. "Potter was chief of intelligence in our London mission." He looked back at Van Dam. "Anyway, Potter was skeptical. He wanted to try using Sokolov as a double agent first. Maybe get some hard intelligence from the Soviets. I tried to convince him the man was in real danger. And he had a family in London, a wife and two kids. But Potter decided to wait before taking him in."

"I can see his point. Sokolov had strong links to the KGB. I would've questioned his motives, too."

"Yeah? If he was a KGB plant, why did his kids find him dead a few days later? Even the Soviets don't dispose of their own operatives without good reason. Your people left him to the wolves."

"It's a dangerous business, Mr. O'Hara. These things do happen."

"I'm sure they do. But I felt personally responsible in this case. And I wasn't going to let Roy Potter off the hook."

"It says here you two had a shouting match in the embassy stairwell." Van Dam shook his head and laughed as he scanned the report. "You called Mr. Potter a large variety of—er, colorful names. My goodness, here's one I've never heard before. And all within public hearing."

"To that I plead guilty."

"Mr. Potter also claims you were…let me quote: 'incensed, out of control and close to violence,' unquote."

"I was not close to violence."

Van Dam closed the file and smiled sympathetically. "I know how it feels, Mr. O'Hara, to be surrounded by incompetents. God knows, not a day goes by that I don't wonder how this country stays afloat. I'm not talking about just the intelligence business. Everything. I'm a widower, you see, and my wife left me with a rather large house to keep up. I can't even find a decent housekeeper, or a gardener who can keep my azaleas alive. Sometimes, at work, I want to throw my hands up and just say, 'Forget it! I'm doing things my own way and the rules be damned!' Haven't you felt that way, too? Of course you have. I can see you're a nonconformist, like me."

Nick began to feel he'd been trapped in the wrong conversation. Housekeepers? Azaleas? What was the guy leading up to?

"I see you were with American University before you joined the State Department," said Van Dam.

"I was an associate professor. Linguistics."

"Oh, I'm sorry. It's really *Dr.* O'Hara, isn't it?"

"A minor point."

"Even at the university, you were the independent sort. Traits like that don't change. Mr. Ambrose says you don't quite fit into this department. You're an outsider. I imagine that gets a bit lonely."

"Just what are you trying to say, Mr. Van Dam?"

"That a lonely man might find it…tempting, shall we say, to associate with other nonconformists. That, in anger, you might be persuaded to cooperate with outside interests."

Nick stiffened. "I'm not a traitor, if that's what you're implying."

"No, no. I'm not saying that at all! I dislike that word, traitor. It's so imprecise. After all, the definition of traitor varies with one's political orientation."

"I know what a traitor is, Mr. Van Dam! It so happens I don't agree with a lot of our policies, but that doesn't make me disloyal!"

"Well, then. Perhaps you can explain your involvement in the Fontaine case."

Nick forced himself to take a deep breath. They'd finally gotten to the real issue. "I was just doing my job. Two weeks ago Geoffrey Fontaine died in Germany. I got the routine task of calling the widow. Certain things she said bothered me. I ran Fontaine's name through the computer—just checking, you understand. I came up with a lot of blanks. So I called a friend…"

"Mr. Greenstein," offered Van Dam.

"Look, leave him out of this. He was just doing me a favor. He has a buddy in the FBI who looked up Fontaine's name. Not much turned up. I had more questions than answers. So I went straight to the widow."

"Why didn't you come to us?"

"I wasn't aware your authority extended to American soil. Legally speaking, that is."

For the first time, a faint look of irritation flashed in Van Dam's eyes. "You realize, don't you, that you may have done irreparable damage?"

"I don't understand."

"We had things under tight control. Now I'm afraid you've warned her."

"Warned her? But Sarah's as much in the dark as I am."

"Is that an amateur spy's conclusion?"

"It's my gut feeling."

"You don't know all the implications—"

"What *are* the implications?"

"That Geoffrey Fontaine's death is still in question. That his wife may know more about it than you think. And that a lot rides on this case—more than you'll ever know."

Nick stared at him, stunned. What was the man talking about? Was Geoffrey Fontaine dead or alive? Could Sarah possibly be such a good actress that she'd totally fooled Nick?

"Just what does ride on this case?" Nick asked.

"Let's just say the repercussions will be international."

"Was Geoffrey Fontaine a spy?"

Van Dam's mouth tightened. He said nothing.

"Look," said Nick. "I've had enough of this. Why am I being grilled on a routine consular matter?"

"Mr. O'Hara, I'm here to ask the questions, not answer them."

"Pardon me for interfering with your standard operating procedures."

"For a diplomat, you're damned undiplomatic." Van Dam turned to Ambrose. "I can't tell if he's clean. But I agree with your plan of action."

Nick frowned. "What plan of action?"

Ambrose cleared his throat. Nick knew exactly what that meant. It was a sure sign of impending unpleasantness. "Upon review of your personnel record," said Ambrose, "and based on this latest act of—uh, indiscretion, we feel it best you take an extended leave of absence from the department. Your security clearance will need reevaluation. Until we confirm your noninvolvement in anything subversive, you will be on leave. If we find evidence of something more serious than indiscretion, you will be hearing from Mr. Van Dam again. Not to mention the Justice Department."

Nick didn't need a translation—he'd just been labeled a traitor. The logical response would be to protest his innocence and resign, here and now. But damned if he would do it in front of Jonathan Van Dam.

Instead he rose stiffly and said, "I understand. Is that all, *sir*?"

"That's all, O'Hara."

With that brusque dismissal, Nick turned and strode out of the office. *So that's it,* he thought as he walked down the hall to what had been, up to a moment ago, his own office. After eight years with the State Department, a little curiosity had gotten him canned.

The funny part was that except for being called a traitor, he wasn't at all bothered about losing the job. In fact, as he turned the key to unlock his door, he felt strangely buoyant, as though a terrible weight had just been lifted from his shoulders. He was free. The decision he'd struggled so hard to make had just been made for him. In a way it had been inevitable.

Now he could start a new life. He had saved enough money to keep him going another six months or so. Perhaps he'd consider returning to the university. The last eight years had given him a big dose of reality; it would make him a better teacher than he ever could have been.

As he turned to the task of cleaning out his desk, he was actually grinning. One by one he emptied out his drawers, throwing the year's accumulated junk into a cardboard box. Next he threw in his dozens of journals, just part of the huge library of a man addicted to facts. To his surprise he found himself whistling. It would be a great night to go out and get roaring drunk. On second thought, he'd rather skip the hangover. He had too many things to do, too many answers to find. Losing his job he could handle, but he wasn't going to exit with his loyalty in question. He had to set the record straight, to get to the truth. And for that he had to see Sarah Fontaine again.

The prospect was not at all unpleasant. In fact, he looked forward to sharing a little civilized conversation, maybe over dinner.

The urge to see her became instantly compelling. Nick dropped the box on his desk and dialed her number. As usual, he was greeted by her answering machine. With an oath he hung up, suddenly remembering his suggestion that she stay with her friend. If only he knew the friend's number…

Leaning back in his chair, he found himself engaging in a rare moment of fantasy. Sarah. Of all the women in the world, to be thinking of her! This afternoon, at the cemetery, she'd looked so helpless, so thin, walking toward him through the mist. Not beautiful, but very, very vulnerable. In the car she'd huddled beside him like a cold, wet sparrow. Then she'd taken off her glasses and looked at him. And at that moment, as he'd looked into those huge amber eyes, he'd been awestruck. *I'm wrong,* he'd thought. *Dead wrong. In her own quiet way, Sarah Fontaine is the most beautiful woman I have ever seen.*

He was attracted to her, which wasn't very smart. With all of these unanswered questions about her husband—and about Sarah herself—Nick had plenty of reasons to keep his emotional distance. But now, as he leaned back in his chair and propped his feet up on the desk, he couldn't help painting all those mental pictures lonely men like to paint. He saw her standing in his apartment—in his bedroom—with her copper-colored hair loose about her shoulders. He saw the look in her eyes—shy and awkward, yet at the same time somehow eager. Her hands would be cold. He'd warm them against his skin. Then she—

"Nick!"

The fantasy shattered as Tim Greenstein walked into the room. "What're you still doing here?"

Nick looked up, startled. "What does it look like I'm doing? I'm cleaning out my desk."

"Cleaning out your—you mean you got sacked?"

"The moral equivalent. I've been asked to take an 'extended leave of absence,' as Ambrose so politely put it."

"Geez, that's tough!" Tim dropped into a chair. He was looking unusually pale, as if he'd just been shaken up badly.

"Where were you?" asked Nick. "I thought you were meeting me in Ambrose's office."

"I got sidetracked by my supervisor. And the FBI. *And* the CIA. Not pleasant. They even threatened to take away my computer pass card. I mean—that's cruel!"

Nick shook his head and sighed. "It's my fault, isn't it? Sorry, Tim. Looks like we were on forbidden turf. Did your FBI friend get slapped down, too?"

"No. Funny thing is, he may come out of this smelling like a rose. See, all his digging around just happened to embarrass the CIA. Over at the bureau, you get bonus points for making the Company look bad." Tim laughed, but something about the sound made Nick uneasy. His friend's laughter faded.

"What's going on, Tim?"

"It's a bad scene, Nick. We've been poking around in a hornet's nest."

"So it involves a little espionage. We've dealt with spooks before. What's so special about Geoffrey Fontaine?"

"I don't know. And I don't want to know any more than I already do."

"Lost your curiosity?"

"Damn right. So should you."

"I've got a personal interest in this case."

"Back off, Nick. For your own good. It'll blow your career apart."

"My career's already blown. I'm a private citizen now, remember? And I just might spend a little more time with Sarah Fontaine."

"Nick, as a friend I'm telling you to forget her. You're wrong about her. She's no Little Miss Innocent."

"That's what everyone keeps telling me. But I'm the only one who's spent any time with her."

"Look, you're *wrong*, okay?"

Tim's sharp tone puzzled Nick. *What's going on?* he thought. *What's happened?* Leaning forward, he looked his friend straight in the eye. "What are you trying to tell me, Tim?" he asked evenly.

Tim looked miserable. "She pulled one over on you, Nick. My

FBI buddy's been keeping tabs on her. Her movements. Her contacts. And he just called and told me…"

"Told you what?"

"She knows something. It's the only explanation for what she did—"

"Dammit, Tim! What happened?"

"Soon after you left her apartment, she took a taxi to the airport. She boarded a plane."

Nick froze in disbelief. Sarah had left town? Why?

"Where did she go?" he snapped.

Tim gave him a sympathetic look. "London."

LONDON. It was the logical place to start. Or so it seemed to Sarah. London had been Geoffrey's favorite city, a town of green parks and cobblestoned alleys, of streets where men in stiff black suits and bowler hats rubbed elbows with turbaned Sikhs. He'd told her of St. Paul's Cathedral, soaring high above the rooftops; of red and yellow tulips blanketing Regent's Park; of Soho, where both the laughter and music were always loud. She'd heard all of these things and now, as she stared out the taxi window, she felt the same stirring that Geoffrey must have felt whenever he came to London. She saw broad, clean streets, and black umbrellas bobbing along the sidewalks. Over the skyline hung a gentle mist, and in the parks the first spring flowers were bursting open. This was Geoffrey's city. He knew it and loved it. If he were in trouble, this is where he would hide.

The cab dropped her off on the Strand, in front of the Savoy Hotel. At the front desk the clerk, a sweet-faced young woman neatly dressed in a blazer, looked up and smiled at her. Yes, she told Sarah, a room was available. The tourist rush hadn't started yet.

Sarah was filling out the registration form when she said casually, "By the way, my husband was here about two weeks ago."

"Was he, now?" The clerk glanced across the ledger at her name. "Oh! You're Mrs. Fontaine? Is your husband Geoffrey Fontaine?"

"Yes. Do you remember him?"

"Of course we do, ma'am! Your husband's been a regular here. Such a nice man. Queer, though, I never imagined you were American. I always thought…" Her voice trailed off as she turned her attention to Sarah's registration card. "Will your husband be joining you in London?"

"No, not—not yet." Sarah paused. "Actually I was expecting a message of some sort. Could you check for me?"

The clerk glanced over at the mail slots. "I don't see anything."

"Then there haven't been any calls? For either of us?"

"They'd be here in the slot. Sorry." The clerk turned back to her paperwork.

Sarah fell silent for a moment. What next? Search his hotel room? But of course it would have been cleaned weeks ago.

"Anyway," said the clerk, "if there had been a message, we would have forwarded it to your house in Margate. That's what he always had us do."

Sarah blinked in bewilderment. "Margate?"

The clerk was too busy writing to look up. "Yes."

What house in Margate? Sarah wondered. Did Geoffrey own a residence here in England that he'd never told her about?

The clerk was still writing. Sarah steadied her hands on the counter and prayed she could lie convincingly. "I hope—I hope you don't have the wrong address," she said. "We're still in Margate, but we—we moved last month."

"Oh, dear," sighed the clerk, heading toward the back office. "Let me see if the address has been updated…." A moment later, she emerged with a registration card. "Twenty-five Whitstable Lane. Is that the old address or the new?"

Sarah didn't answer. She was too busy committing the address to memory.

"Mrs. Fontaine?" asked the clerk.

"I'm sure it's all right," said Sarah, quickly sweeping up her suitcase and turning for the elevator.

"Mrs. Fontaine, you needn't carry that up! I'll call the boy…."

But Sarah was already stepping into the elevator. "Twenty-five Whitstable Lane," she murmured as the door closed. "Twenty-five Whitstable Lane…"

Was that where she'd find Geoffrey?

THE SEA POUNDED against the white chalk cliffs. From the dirt path where Sarah walked, she could see the waves crashing on the rocks below. Their violence frightened her. The sun had already burned through the morning fog, and in a dozen cottage gardens, flowers bloomed and thrived despite the salt air and chalk soil.

At the end of Whitstable Lane, Sarah found the house she'd been seeking. It was only a cottage, tucked behind a white picket fence. In the tiny front garden, stately rosebushes mingled with riotous marigolds and cornflowers. The soft clip of garden shears drew her attention to the side of the cottage, where an elderly man was trimming a hedge.

"Hello?" she called across the fence.

The old man stood up and looked at her.

"I'm looking for Geoffrey Fontaine," she said.

"Isn't 't 'ome, miss."

Sarah's hands started to shake. Then Geoffrey *had* been here. But why? she wondered. Why keep a cottage so far from his work in London?

"Where can I find him?" she asked.

"Don't rightly know."

"Do you know when he'll be coming home?"

The old man shrugged. "Neither he nor the missus tells me 'bout their comin's 'n goin's."

"Missus?" she repeated stupidly.

"Aye. Mrs. Fontaine."

"You don't mean—his wife?"

The old man looked at her as if she were an idiot. "Aye," he said slowly. "It would seem that way. 'Course, with a little imagination, one could always figure on 'er bein' 'is mother, but I'd say she's a bit young for that." He suddenly burst out laughing, as if the whole thing was quite absurd.

Sarah was clutching the picket fence so hard that the wooden points were biting into her palms. A strange roar rose in her ears, as if a wave had swept over her and was dragging her to the ground. With fumbling hands she dug in her purse and pulled out Geoffrey's photograph. "Is this Mr. Fontaine?" she asked hoarsely.

"That's 'im, all right. I've got a good eye for faces, you know."

She was trembling so hard she could barely stuff the picture back into her purse. She held on to the fence, trying to absorb what the man had said. The knowledge came as a shock, and the pain was more than she could bear.

Another woman. Hadn't someone asked her about that? She couldn't remember. Oh yes, it had been Nick O'Hara. He'd wondered about another woman. He'd called it a logical assumption, and she'd been angry with him.

Nick O'Hara had been right. She was the blind one, the stupid one.

She didn't know how long she had been standing there among the marigolds; she had lost track of time and place. Everything—her hands, her feet, even her face—had gone mercifully numb. Her mind refused to take in any more pain. If it did, she thought she'd go crazy.

Only when the old man called to her a third time did she hear him.

"Miss? Miss? Do you need some 'elp?"

Still in a daze, Sarah looked at him. "No. No, I'll be all right."

"You're sure, now?"

"Yes, I…please, I need to find the Fontaines."

"I don't rightly know 'ow, miss. The lady packed 'er bags and took off 'bout two weeks ago."

"Where did she go?"

"She weren't in the 'abit of leavin' a forwardin' address."

Sarah hunted in her purse for a piece of paper, then scribbled down her name and hotel. "If she—if either of them—shows up, please tell them to call me immediately. Please."

"Aye, miss." The old man folded up the paper without looking at it and slipped it into his pocket.

Like a drunken woman, she stumbled toward the road. At the beginning of Whitstable Lane, she saw a row of mailboxes. Glancing back, she saw that the old man was once more at work, clipping his hedge. She looked inside the box labeled 25 and found only a mail-order catalog from a London department store. It was addressed to Mrs. Eve Fontaine.

Evie.

More than once, Geoffrey had called Sarah by that name.

She shoved the catalog back into the mailbox. As she walked down the cliff road to the Margate train station, she was crying.

Six hours later, tired, empty and hungry, Sarah walked into her room at the Savoy. The phone was ringing.

"Hello?" she said.

"Sarah Fontaine?" It was a woman. Her voice was low and husky.

"Yes."

"Geoffrey had a birthmark, left shoulder. What shape?"

"But—"

"What shape?"

"It was—it was a half-moon. Is this Eve?"

"The Lamb and Rose. Dorset Street. Nine o'clock."

"Wait—Eve?"

Click.

Sarah looked at her watch. She had half an hour to get to Dorset Street.

Chapter Five

Fog swirled around the door of the Lamb and Rose. The cab-driver took Sarah's bills, grunted something unintelligible and sped off. Sarah was left standing alone in the dark street.

From the pub came the muffled sounds of laughter and the clink of glassware. Through the haze the window glowed a soft, welcoming yellow. She crossed the cobblestoned street and pushed open the door.

Inside, a fire crackled in the hearth. At the gleaming mahogany bar, two men hunched over glasses of ale. They looked up as she walked in, then just as quickly stared down at their glasses. Sarah paused to warm herself by the fire, all the time searching the room with her eyes. Only a serving girl, standing by the tap, met her gaze. Without a word the girl nodded toward the back of the room.

Sarah returned the nod and walked in the direction the girl had indicated. Several wooden booths lined the wall. In the first booth sat a couple, staring intently into each other's eyes. In the second an old man in tweeds quietly nursed a whiskey. There was only one booth left. Even before she reached it, she knew Eve would be sitting there. A wisp of cigarette smoke drifted from the shadows. The woman looked up as Sarah approached. Their eyes met, and in that one glance, they both understood. Even in the pub's dimly lighted interior, each could see the other's pain.

Sarah slid onto the bench across from the other woman. Eve nervously took a puff from her cigarette and flicked off the ashes, all the while studying Sarah. She was slender—almost too slender—and fair haired, with greenish eyes that looked tired and pinched. Her hands moved constantly. Every few seconds she glanced toward the pub door, as if expecting someone else to walk inside. The cigarette smoke curled like a serpent between them.

"You're not what I expected," said Eve. Sarah recognized the husky voice from the telephone. The accent was faintly Continental, not English. "You're not as plain as I expected. And you're younger than he said. How old are you? Twenty-seven? Twenty-eight?"

"I'm thirty-two," said Sarah.

"Ah. So he wasn't lying."

"Geoffrey told you about me?"

Eve took another puff and nodded. "Of course. He had to. It was my idea."

Sarah's eyes widened in astonishment. "*Your* idea? You mean—but *why*?"

"You don't know anything at all about Geoffrey, do you?" The green eyes stabbed cruelly into Sarah's. "No," said Eve with a trace of satisfaction. "Obviously you don't. And I suppose I'm scotching it all up now, telling you this. But you seem to have found out about me on your own. And I wanted to see you for myself."

"Why?"

"Call it morbid curiosity. Masochism. I hated to think of you two together. I loved him too much." Her chin came up, a poor attempt at nonchalance. "Tell me. Were you happy with him?"

Sarah nodded, her eyes suddenly stinging. "Yes," she whispered. "We—at least *I* was happy. As for Geoffrey…I don't know anymore. I don't know anything anymore."

"How often did you make love? Every night? Once a week?"

Sarah's mouth tightened. "Why should it matter to you? It was all part of your plan, wasn't it?"

The eyes softened, but only for an instant. "You loved him, too, didn't you?" asked Eve. She glanced down as she flicked off another ash. When she looked up, her eyes were once more as hard as emeralds. "So we both lost out, didn't we? It had to happen some day. It's the nature of the business."

"*What* business?"

Eve leaned back. "You're better off not knowing. But you want to hear it, don't you? If I were you, I'd forget all this. I'd forget it and go home. While you still can."

"Who *is* Geoffrey?"

Eve inhaled the smoke deeply and gazed into the distance, conjuring up the memories. "I met him ten years ago, in Amsterdam. He was a different man then." She smiled wanly, as if amused by some private joke. "By different, I mean both literally and figuratively. His name was Simon Dance. At the time, we were both working for Mossad—the Israeli Secret Service. We were quite a team then, the three of us. Simon and I and another woman, our chief. Mossad's best. And then Simon and I fell in love."

"You were spies?"

"I suppose you could call us that. Yes, let's leave it at that." She stared thoughtfully at the patterns her cigarette smoke was weaving in the air. "We'd been together only a year when one of our assignments went badly. We worried too much about each other, you see. That can't happen, not in our business. The work must be everything. Otherwise, things go wrong. And they did. The old man escaped."

"Escaped? Was that your assignment, to arrest someone?"

Eve laughed. "Arrest? In our business, we do not bother to arrest. We terminate."

Sarah's hands went ice-cold. Surely this wasn't the same Geoffrey they were talking about? No, she reminded herself. He wasn't Geoffrey then. He was *Simon*.

"So the old man lived. Magus, we called him. A holy name for an unholy man. Magus, the magician. To us it was more than just a code name. In a way he was a magician. That case finished us." She stubbed out her cigarette and lighted another, ruining three matches in the process. Her hands were shaking too much. She sighed, gratefully inhaling the smoke. "After that, we all dropped out of the business. Simon and I were married, and for a while we lived in Germany, then France. We changed our names twice.

But we kept feeling as though things were closing in. We knew there was a contract out on all of us. Ordered by Magus, of course. We decided to leave Europe."

"So you chose America."

Eve nodded. "Yes. It's all so simple, really. He found a new name. And a plastic surgeon. His cheeks were brought in, the nose narrowed. The difference was dramatic—no one could've recognized him. My face was changed, too. He went first, to America. It takes time to establish a new base, a new identity. I was to going to follow."

"Why did he marry me?"

"He needed an American wife. He needed your home, your bank account, the cover you could provide. I could not pass as an American. My accent, my voice—I could not change them. But Simon—ah, he could sound like a dozen different people!"

"Why did he choose me?"

Eve shrugged. "Convenience. You were lonely, not so pretty. You had no boyfriends. Yes, you were very vulnerable. You fell in love quickly, didn't you?"

Choking back a sob, Sarah nodded. Yes, she had been vulnerable. Before Geoffrey, her days had been spent at work, her nights mostly at home alone. She'd longed for a relationship with a man, for the closeness and caring her parents had had. But her career had been demanding and she'd been single too long; with each year that passed, marriage had seemed less and less likely.

Then Geoffrey had appeared. Geoffrey, who had filled the void. She'd fallen in love at once. Yet all this time, he had thought of her as nothing more than a convenience. She looked up in anger. "You didn't care, did you?" she asked. "Either of you. You didn't care who got hurt."

"We had no choice. We had our own lives—"

"*Your* lives? What about *my* life?"

"Lower your voice."

"My life, Eve. I loved him. And you can sit there, so smug, and justify what you both did!"

"Please lower your voice. They can hear you."

"I don't care."

Eve started to rise. "I think I've said all I care to."

"No, wait!" Sarah grabbed her hand. "Please," she said softly. "Sit down. I have to hear the rest. I have to know."

Slowly Eve sank into the booth. She was silent for a moment, then said, "The truth is, he didn't love you. I was the one he loved. His trips here to London—they were only to see me. He'd check into the Savoy before taking the train to Margate. Every few days he'd return to London to call you or post you a letter. I hated it, these last two months, sharing him with you. But it was necessary and only temporary. We were both surviving. Until..." She looked away. Her eyes suddenly glistened with tears.

"What happened, Eve?"

Eve cleared her throat and lifted her head bravely. "I don't know. All I know is, he left London two weeks ago. He had joined an operation against Magus. Then things went wrong. He was being followed. Someone left explosives, set to go off in his hotel room. He called from Berlin and told me he'd decided to vanish. I was to go into hiding. When the time was right, he'd come for me. But the night before I left Margate, I had a—a premonition. I tried to call him in Berlin. That's when I learned he was dead."

"But he's not dead!" Sarah blurted. "He's alive!"

Eve's hands jerked, almost causing her to drop the cigarette. "What?"

"He called me two days ago. That's why I'm here. He told me to come to him—that he loved me—"

"You're lying."

"It's true!" cried Sarah. "I know his voice."

"A recording, perhaps—some kind of trick. It's easy to imitate a voice. No, it couldn't have been him. He wouldn't call *you*," Eve said coldly.

Sarah fell silent. Why would someone use Geoffrey's voice to draw her to Europe? Then she remembered something else, another piece of the puzzle that made no sense. She looked across the table at Eve. "The day I left Washington, someone broke into my apartment. All they took was a photograph—that's all, just a photograph—and I still don't underst—"

"A photograph?" Eve asked sharply. "Of Geoffrey?"

"Yes. It was our wedding picture."

The woman's face went chalk white. She stubbed out her cigarette and snapped up her purse and sweater.

"Where are you going?" asked Sarah.

"I have to get back—he'll be searching for me."

"Who?"

"Geoffrey."

"But you said he was dead!"

Eve's eyes were suddenly as bright and sparkling as jewels. "No. No, he's alive. He must be! Don't you see? They don't know his face so they've stolen his photograph. It means they're looking for him, too." She threw on her sweater and ran for the door.

"Eve!" Sarah scrambled from the booth and chased after her. But when she stepped outside, the street was empty. She saw only fog, great thick clouds of it, creeping at her feet. "Eve?" she called. There was no answer.

Eve had disappeared.

EVE DIDN'T GET far. Wild and reckless with hope, she ran through the fog of Dorset Street toward the underground station. She didn't stop to listen for footsteps; she didn't take all the usual precautions she'd learned to take during her years as a Mossad operative. Simon was alive—that was all that mattered. He was alive, and he'd be waiting for her. She didn't have the patience to zigzag through the neighborhood, to pause in doorways and see if she was alone. Instead, her path took her in a straight line for the subway station.

After only two blocks of running, her breathing became hard and heavy. It was the cigarettes, she thought. Too many years of smoking had left her easy to tire and short of breath. But she forced herself to keep moving, until the ache started in her chest and she knew she'd have to rest, just for a moment. The pain was an old problem, one she'd lived with since she was a child. It meant nothing. It would ease up a bit and she could keep going.

She paused to lean against a lamppost. Little by little the ache subsided. Her breathing came easier. The roaring in her ears faded. She closed her eyes and took a deep breath.

Then another sound penetrated her awareness, a sound so soft she almost missed it. She stiffened, and her eyes shot open. There it was again, a few yards away. A footstep. But in which direction?

Staring desperately through the mist she tried to make out a face, a figure, but she saw nothing. Reaching into her purse, she withdrew the pistol she always carried. The cold steel felt instantly reassuring in her palm. She realized that the lamplight was a beacon, and she was standing right beneath it. She fled into the shadows. Darkness had always been her ally.

Another sound made her swing the pistol around. *Where is he?* she thought. *Why can't I see him?*

She realized too late that the last sound had been nothing more than a decoy, a trick meant to draw her aim. From behind, something rushed at her. Before she could twist around and fire, she was flung to the ground. The pistol flew from her hand, and then, in the next instant, she felt a blade press firmly against her throat.

A face was smiling down at her, a face she recognized. Even in the darkness, his pale hair gleamed like silver.

"Kronen," she whispered.

She felt the blade slide across her skin, as gentle as a caress. She wanted to scream, but terror had clamped off her throat.

"Little Eva," Kronen murmured. Then he laughed softly, and that was when Eve knew she would not live through the night.

THE WORLD LOOKED different from thirty-five thousand feet. No neon lights, no traffic, no concrete, just an endless black sky glittering with stars.

Nick leaned his head back tiredly and wished he could sleep. Almost everyone else on Flight 201 to London seemed to be snoring blissfully across the Atlantic. On the other side of the dim cabin, he saw a stewardess gently tuck in a child and tiptoe away down the aisle. It was 1:00 a.m., D.C. time, yet Nick was wide awake, with an airline blanket still folded neatly on his lap.

He was too disgusted to sleep. He kept remembering Sarah and how innocent she'd looked, how grief stricken and vulnerable. What a great actress. She'd given an Oscar-winning performance. She'd also stirred up a whole host of male instincts he'd forgotten he had. He'd wanted to protect her, to hold her.

Now he wasn't sure *what* he wanted to do to her. Whatever it was, protection had nothing to do with it.

Because of Sarah Fontaine he was out of a job, his patriotism was in question and worst of all, he felt like a damned fool. Van Dam had been right. As a spy Nick was nothing but a rank amateur.

The more he thought about how she'd fooled him, the angrier he got. He slapped the armrest and stared out the window at the stars.

By God, when he got to London, he'd get the truth out of her. He owed it to himself; he couldn't leave the foreign service without clearing his record.

She wouldn't be expecting him in London. He already knew where to find her; a phone call confirmed that she'd checked into the Savoy, her husband's usual hotel. He looked forward to seeing the look on her face when she opened her door to find him standing there. Surprise, surprise! Nick O'Hara was in town to set the record straight. And this time he wouldn't settle for lies.

But mingled with his anger was another emotion, much deeper and infinitely more disturbing. He kept coming back to that old fantasy, the vision of her standing in his bedroom, gazing at him with those soft amber eyes. The confusion of what he really felt was driving him nuts. He didn't know if he wanted to kiss her or strangle her. Maybe both.

He did know one thing. Boarding this flight to London had surely been the craziest stunt he'd ever pulled. All his life he'd made decisions thoughtfully. He was not, by nature, a careless man. But tonight he'd thrown his clothes into a suitcase, caught a taxi to Dulles and slapped a credit card down on the British Airways ticket counter. It was totally unlike him to do something so impulsive, so emotional. So stupid. He hoped it wasn't the start of a new trend.

THE OLD MAN would not be happy.

As Kronen wiped the woman's blood from his knife, he considered putting off the inevitable phone call for another hour, another day. At least until he'd eaten a stout breakfast or perhaps put away a few pints. But the old man would be hungry for news, and Kronen didn't want to keep him waiting too long. The old man didn't tolerate frustrations very well these days. Ever since the tragedy, he had been impatient and easily irritated. One did not irritate him if one wanted to remain in good health.

Not that Kronen was afraid. He knew the old man needed him too much.

At the age of eight, Kronen had been plucked from the trash heaps of Dublin and adopted by the old man. Perhaps it was the boy's fair, almost white hair that caught his attention; perhaps it was the utter emptiness in the boy's eyes, the sign of a soulless vacuum within a shell of human flesh and bone. The old man recognized, even then, that the boy could someday be dangerous. A boy without a soul had no use for love, and as a man he might someday turn on his guardian.

But a boy without a soul could also be very useful. So the old man took the boy in, fed him, taught him, maybe even loved him a little, but he never quite trusted him.

Kronen, even at a young age, had sensed the old man's distrust. Instead of resenting it, he had worked hard to overcome it. Anything the old man wanted done, Kronen would do. After thirty years of doing his bidding, it had become automatic. Kronen was well compensated. More important, he enjoyed his work. It gave him a sense of pleasure and satisfaction. Especially when it involved women.

Like tonight.

Unfortunately the woman had not talked. She'd been stronger that way than any man he'd ever met. Even an hour of his most persuasive techniques had been to no avail. She'd done a lot of screaming, which had both annoyed and excited him, but she'd given him absolutely no information. And then, when he'd least expected it, she'd died.

That had bothered him most of all. He hadn't meant to kill her. At least not yet. What bad luck to discover too late that his victim had a weak heart. She'd looked healthy enough.

He finished wiping his blade. He believed in cleanliness, especially when it came to his favorite knife. A sharp edge required care. He put the knife in its sheath and stared at the telephone. There was no point in delaying the matter any longer. He decided to call Amsterdam.

The old man answered.

"Eva did not talk," said Kronen.

The silence was enough. He could sense the disappointment through the receiver. "Then she is dead?"

"Yes," said Kronen.

"What about the other?"

"I am still watching her. Dance has not come near."

The old man made a sound of impatience. "I cannot wait forever. We have to force his hand."

"How?"

"Abduct her."

"But she has the CIA following her."

"I'll see they're taken care of. By tomorrow. Then you take the woman."

"And then?"

"See if she knows anything. If she does not, we can still use her. We will broadcast an ultimatum. If Dance is alive, he'll respond."

Kronen was not so sure. Unlike the old man, he held no faith in something as ridiculous as love. Besides, he'd seen Sarah Fontaine, and he didn't think any man—certainly not Simon Dance—would come to her rescue. No, to risk one's life for a woman was absurd. He didn't think Dance would be so stupid.

Nevertheless, it would be an interesting experiment. And when it was over the old man would let Kronen take care of the woman. Her heart would certainly be stronger than Eva Fontaine's. She would last much longer. Yes, it would be an interesting experiment. It gave him something to look forward to.

IN A DREAM it came back to Sarah. But everything was distorted and strange and swirling with mist. She was running through the streets, running after Geoffrey, crying out his name. She heard his footsteps ahead of her, but he was always out of sight, always beyond her reach. Then the footsteps changed. They were behind her. She was no longer the pursuer, but the pursued. She was running through the fog, and the footsteps were growing closer. Her heart was pounding. Her legs refused to work. She struggled to move forward.

Her path was blocked by a woman with green eyes, a woman who was standing in the middle of the street, laughing at her. The footsteps closed in. Sarah whirled around.

The man who came toward her was someone she knew, someone with tired gray eyes. Slowly he emerged from the mist. And as he did, her fears dissolved. Here was safety, here was warmth. His footsteps echoed on the cobblestoned streets....

Sarah woke up, drenched in sweat. Someone was knocking at her door. She turned on the light. It was 4:00 a.m.

The knock came again, louder. "Mrs. Fontaine?" said a man's voice. "Please open up, ma'am."

"Who is it?" she called.

"The police."

She stumbled out of bed, struggled into a robe and opened the door. Two uniformed policemen stood outside, accompanied by a sleepy-eyed hotel clerk.

"Mrs. Sarah Fontaine?"

"Yes. What is it?"

"Sorry for the intrusion, ma'am, but it will be necessary for you to accompany us to the station headquarters."

"I don't understand. Why?"

"We're obliged to place you under detention."

She clutched the door with both hands and stared at them in amazement. "Do you mean I'm under *arrest*? But for what?"

"For murder. The murder of Mrs. Eve Fontaine."

Chapter Six

THIS CANNOT BE HAPPENING, THOUGHT SARAH.

Surely it was a nightmare, a scenario pulled from the darkest reaches of her subconscious. She was sitting in a hard chair, staring at a bare wooden table. Glaring fluorescent lights shone down on her from the ceiling and illuminated her every movement, like a spotlight waiting for guilt to appear. The room was cold and she felt half-naked, dressed only in her nightgown and robe. A detective with ice-blue eyes brusquely fired question after question, without letting her finish a single sentence. Only after she'd asked him half a dozen times did he let her use the bathroom, and then only with a matron standing outside the stall.

Once back in the interrogation room, she was left shivering and alone for a moment to ponder her situation. *I am going to jail,* she thought. *I am going to be locked up forever, for murdering a woman I met only last night….*

Dropping her head in her hands, she felt another wave of tears threaten to flood her eyes. She was trying so hard to keep from crying that she scarcely heard the door open and close.

But she did hear the voice calling her name. That one word was like a burst of warm sunshine. She looked up.

Nick O'Hara was standing in front of her. By some miracle he'd been transported across an ocean, and here he was, her only friend in London, looking down at her.

Or was he a friend?

Immediately she saw that something was wrong. His mouth was set in two hard lines. His eyes showed no expression. Desperately she searched for some warmth, some comforting look in his face, but what she saw was rage. Little by little she took in the other details: his wrinkled shirt, the slack tie, the British Airways sticker on his briefcase. He had just come off a plane.

He turned and pushed the door shut. The loud slam made her flinch. Then he practically threw his briefcase on the table and glowered at her.

"Lady, you are in one *helluva* mess!" he grunted.

She sniffed pitifully. "I know."

"Is that all you can say? I *know*?"

"Are you going to get me out of here?" she asked in a small voice.

"It all depends."

"On what?"

"On whether or not you did it."

"Of course I didn't do it!" she cried.

He seemed taken aback by her violent outburst. For a moment he was silent. Then he crossed his arms and settled irritably on the edge of the table.

She was afraid to look at him, afraid to see the accusing look in his eyes. The man she'd thought was her friend had suddenly turned into someone she scarcely knew. So he thought she was guilty, too. What hope did she have of convincing complete strangers of her innocence when even Nick O'Hara didn't believe her? Bitterly she told herself how wrong she'd been about him. As for why he was here, the reason was now obvious. The man was just doing his job.

She clenched her hands in a hard knot on the table. She was furious with him for seeing her in this helpless position, for betraying her trust in him as a friend.

"Why are you in London, anyway?" she muttered.

"I could ask you the same question. This time, though, I expect the truth."

"The truth?" She looked up. "I've never lied to you! You were the one—"

"Oh, come *on*!" he roared. Agitated, he shot to his feet and began to pace the floor. "Don't give me that innocent look, Mrs. Fontaine. You must think I'm pretty damned stupid. First you insist you don't know a thing, and then you take off for London. I just finished talking to the inspector. Now I want to hear your side. You knew about Eve, didn't you?"

"I didn't know! At least, not until yesterday. And you were the one who lied, Mr. O'Hara."

"About what?"

"About Geoffrey. You told me he was dead. Oh, you gave me all that nice evidence, you laid it out so neatly, so perfectly. And I believed you! All this time you knew, didn't you? You *must* have known."

"What are you talking about?"

"Geoffrey's alive!"

The incredulous look on his face was too real. She stared at him, wondering if it was possible that Nick really didn't know Geoffrey was alive.

"I think you'd better explain," he said. "And I want it all, Sarah. Right down to what you ate for breakfast. Because, as you no doubt know, you're in deep trouble. The evidence—"

"The *evidence* is all circumstantial."

"The evidence is this: Eve Fontaine's body was found about midnight in a deserted alley a few blocks from the Lamb and Rose. I won't go into the body's condition; let's just say someone obviously didn't like her. The barmaid in the Lamb and Rose remembered seeing Eve with a woman—an American. That was you. She also remembered that you two had an argument. Eve ran out, you followed. And that's the last anyone saw of Eve Fontaine."

"I lost her outside the Lamb and Rose!"

"Do you have any witnesses?"

"No."

"Too bad. The police called Eve's house in Margate and spoke with the groundskeeper. The old man remembered you, all right. He said he gave Eve your message over the phone. And he just happened to have that slip of paper with your name and hotel."

"I gave it to him so she could call me."

"Well, to the police you've got an obvious motive. Revenge.

You found out Geoffrey Fontaine was a bigamist. You decided to get even. That's the evidence. Good, hard and undeniable."

"It doesn't mean I killed her!"

"No?"

"You have to believe me!"

"Why should I?"

"Because no one else does." Without warning, all the fear and weariness seemed to sweep through her in one overpowering wave. Lowering her head, she repeated softly, "No one else does...."

Nick watched her with a disturbing mix of emotions. She looked so drained, so terrified, as she huddled against the table. Her robe sagged open, and he caught a glimpse of her flimsy blue nightgown. A long strand of reddish-brown hair fell across her face, across that smooth, pale cheek. It was the first time he'd seen her hair loose, and it reminded him once again of that fantasy he'd tried so hard to suppress. But the image came back to him now, warm and compelling. He forced it out of his mind, trying instead to concentrate on why he was here. A woman had been murdered, and Sarah was in very bad trouble. Yet all he could think about was how she would feel in his arms.

Suddenly all his anger toward her evaporated. He'd hurt her, and now he felt like a monster. Gently he touched her head. "Sarah. Sarah, it'll be all right," he murmured. "You'll be all right." He crouched down and clumsily laid her face against his shoulder. Her hair felt so soft, so silky; the warm, feminine scent of her skin was intoxicating. He knew the emotions coursing through him now were dangerous, but he couldn't control them. He wanted to take her from this room, to keep her safe and warm and protected. He was most definitely not being objective.

Reluctantly he pulled away. "Sarah, talk to me. Tell me why you think your husband's alive."

She took a deep breath and looked at him. Her eyes were like a fawn's, soft and moist. He knew then how much courage it had taken for her to meet his gaze. To keep the tears at bay. He'd been wrong about Sarah. She wasn't broken at all. She had reserves of strength that he'd never suspected.

"He called me," she said. "Two days ago, in Washington—the afternoon of the funeral—"

"Wait. He *called* you?"

"He told me to come to him. It ended so quickly—he never told me where he was—"

"Was it long-distance?"

"I'm sure of it."

"That's why you jumped on a plane? But why to London?"

"It—it was just a feeling. This was his home. This is where he should have been."

"And when did you find out about Eve?"

"After I got here. The hotel clerk showed me an address on Geoffrey's registration card. It was Eve's cottage in Margate."

He absorbed this torrent of new facts with a feeling of growing confusion. Pulling up a chair, he sat down and focused intently on her face.

"You've just thrown me a wild card," he said. "That call from Geoffrey—it's so crazy, I'm beginning to think you must be telling the truth."

"I *am* telling the truth! When are you going to believe me?"

"All right. I'll give you the benefit of the doubt. For now."

He was beginning to believe her. That was all she needed, that tiny kernel of trust. It meant more to her at this moment than anything else in the world. *This is crazy,* she thought. After all she'd been through this morning, only now were the tears beginning to fall. She shook her head and laughed sheepishly. "What is it about you, Mr. O'Hara?" she asked. "I always seem to be crying when you're around."

"It's okay," he said. "Crying, I mean. Women are always doing that to me. I guess it comes with the job."

She looked up and found him smiling. What a startling transformation, from stranger to friend. Somehow she'd forgotten how attractive he was. Not just physically. There was a new gentleness, an intimacy in his voice, as though he really cared. Did he? Or was she reading too much into all of this? Certainly she could recognize her own response, could feel the blood rising in her face.

He seemed hesitant, almost clumsy, as he leaned toward her. She shivered. Immediately he pulled off his jacket and draped it around her shoulders. It smelled like him; it felt so warm and safe, like a blanket. She pulled it close and a calmness came over her, a feeling that nothing could harm her while Nick O'Hara's jacket was around her shoulders.

"As soon as our man from the consulate shows up, we'll get you out of here," he said.

"But aren't you handling this?"

"Afraid not. This isn't my territory."

"But then, why are you here?"

Before he could answer, the door flew open.

"Nick O'Hara," said a short fireplug of a man. "What the hell *are you* doing here?"

Nick turned to face the man in the doorway. "Hello, Potter," he said after a distinctly uncomfortable pause. "It's been a long time."

"Not long enough." Potter stalked into the room, his critical gaze examining Sarah from head to toe. He tossed his damp hat deliberately on Nick's briefcase. "So you're Sarah Fontaine."

She shot a puzzled glance at Nick.

"Sarah, this is Mr. Roy Potter," Nick said tightly. "The embassy's—er, what is it they call you these days? Political officer?"

"Third secretary," snapped Potter.

"Charming euphemism. So where's Dan Lieberman? I thought he was coming."

"I'm afraid our consul couldn't make it. I'm here instead." Potter gave Sarah a perfunctory handshake. "I hope you've been treated well, Mrs. Fontaine. Sorry you had to go through all this. But I think we'll have it cleared up in no time."

"Cleared up?" Nick asked suspiciously. "How?"

Potter turned grudgingly back to Nick. "Maybe you should leave, O'Hara. Get on with your—uh, vacation, is it?"

"No. I think I'll stick around."

"This is official business. And if I've heard right, you're no longer with us, are you?"

"I don't understand," said Sarah, frowning. "What do you mean he's no longer with you?"

"What he means," Nick said calmly, "is that I've been placed on indefinite leave of absence. News gets around fast, I see."

"It does when it's a matter of national security."

Nick snorted. "I didn't know I was so dangerous."

"Let's just say your name's on a most unflattering list, O'Hara.

If I were you, I'd make sure I kept my nose clean. That is, if you expect to keep your job."

"Look, let's get down to business. Sarah's case, remember?"

Potter looked at Sarah. "I've discussed it with Inspector Appleby. He tells me the evidence against you isn't as solid as he'd like. He's willing to release you—provided I take responsibility for your conduct."

Sarah was astonished. "You mean I'm free?"

"That's right."

"And there's nothing—I'm not—"

"The charges have been dropped." He extended his hand. "Congratulations, Mrs. Fontaine. You're a free woman."

She leaped up and grabbed his pudgy hand. "Mr. Potter, thank you! Thank you so much!"

"No problem. Just stay out of trouble, okay?"

"Oh, I will. I will!" She looked joyously at Nick, expecting to see a smile on his face. But he wasn't smiling. Instead he looked completely baffled. And suspicious. Something was bothering him, and she felt instantly uneasy. She turned to Potter. "Is there anything else? Anything I should know?"

"No, Mrs. Fontaine. You can leave right now. In fact, I'll drive you back to the Savoy myself."

"Don't bother," said Nick. "I'll take her back."

Sarah drew closer to Nick. "Thank you, Mr. Potter," she said, "but I'll go with Mr. O'Hara. We're—we're sort of old friends."

Potter frowned. "Friends?"

"He's been so helpful since Geoffrey died."

Scowling, Potter turned and swept his hat off the table. "Okay. Good luck, Mrs. Fontaine." He glanced at Nick. "Say, O'Hara, I'll be sending a report to Mr. Van Dam in Washington. I'm sure he'll be interested to hear you're in London. Will you be returning Stateside soon?"

"I might," said Nick. "Then again, I might not."

Potter headed for the door, then turned one last time and gave Nick a long, hard look. "You know, you've had a decent career with the foreign service. Don't screw it up now. If I were you, I'd watch my step."

Nick dipped his head. "I always do."

"WHAT DOES THAT mean—indefinite leave of absence?" Sarah asked as Nick drove her back to the hotel.

He smiled humorlessly. "Let's just say it's not a promotion."

"Have you been fired?"

"In a word—yes."

"But why?"

He didn't answer. Pausing at the next stoplight, he leaned back and sighed. It was a sound of utter weariness and defeat.

"Nick?" she asked quietly. "Was it because of me?"

He nodded. "You were part of it. Because of you, it seems my patriotism's been called into question. Eight years of good, solid work don't mean a thing to them. But don't let it bother you. I guess, on a subconscious level, I've been working my way out of the job for some time. You were just the last straw."

"I'm sorry."

"Don't be. Getting canned might be the best thing that ever happened to me."

The light changed, and they merged with the morning traffic. It was ten o'clock and the cars were bumper-to-bumper. An oncoming bus roared by on their right, and Sarah felt a momentary flash of panic. The left-sided driving unsettled her. Even Nick seemed uneasy as he frowned at the rearview mirror.

She forced herself to sit back and ignore the road. "I can't believe everything that's happened," she said. "It's all so crazy. And the more I try to figure it out, the more confused I get…." Glancing sideways at Nick, she saw that his frown was deepening. "Nick?"

"The plot has just thickened," he said softly.

"What are you talking about?"

"Keep your eyes straight ahead. Don't look back. We're being followed."

The urge to turn her head was overwhelming, but Sarah managed to focus her attention on the wet road in front of them. *Why is this happening?* she asked herself, as fear made her heart beat faster. "What are you going to do, Nick?"

"Nothing."

"Nothing?"

He ignored the dismay in her voice. "That's right. We're going to act like nothing at all is wrong. We're going to stop at your hotel, where you'll change, pack your bags and check out. Then we're going to have some breakfast. I'm starved."

"Breakfast? But you just said we're being followed!"

"Look, if those guys were out for blood, they could've grabbed you last night."

"Like they grabbed Eve?" she asked in a whisper.

"No. That's not going to happen." He looked in his mirror. "Hang on, Sarah. We're gonna see just how good these guys are…."

He swerved into a narrow street, zipped past a row of small shops and cafés, then hit the brakes. The car behind them skidded to a stop, missing their rear bumper by inches. Unexpectedly Nick laughed. Glancing at Sarah, he saw that she was gripping the dashboard. "You all right?"

She nodded, too frightened to say a word.

"We're okay, Sarah. I think I know these guys. I've seen 'em before." He stuck his hand out and flashed an unmistakably obscene gesture at the car behind them. An instant later he grunted with satisfaction at their response, which was equally obscene. "I was right. Those are Company boys. The driver just flipped me the sign of the eagle."

"You mean they're CIA?" she asked with sudden relief.

"Don't go celebrating yet. I don't trust them. Neither should you."

But her panic was already fading. Why should she be afraid of the CIA? Weren't they on the same side? But then why were they following her? She wondered how long she'd been tailed. If it had been since her arrival in London, they might have seen who killed Eve….

She turned to Nick. "What did happen to Eve?" she asked.

"You mean besides murder?"

"You said something about—the way she died. They did more than just kill her, didn't they?"

The look he gave her made Sarah shudder. "Yes," he said. "They did more than just kill her."

The stoplight was red. Nick pulled up behind a long line of cars and let the engine idle. Rain began to fall, big, fat droplets that slid down the windshield. The ubiquitous black umbrellas filled the intersection. Nick sat motionless as he gazed at the street.

"They found her in an alley," he said at last. "Her hands were tied to an iron fence post. Her mouth was gagged. She must have screamed like hell, but no one heard her. Whoever did the job took his time. An hour, maybe longer. He knew how to use a knife. It was not a…good death."

His flint eyes turned and locked on hers. She was aware of his closeness, of the warmth and the smell of his wool coat around her shoulders. A woman had been tortured to death. A car was following them. And yet, at this moment, with this man sitting beside her, she felt infinitely safe. She knew Nick O'Hara was hardly a savior. He was just an ordinary man, someone who'd probably spent his life behind a desk. She didn't even know why he was here, but he was, and for that she was grateful.

The car behind them honked its horn. The light had changed to green. Nick turned his attention reluctantly to the traffic.

"Why did they kill her that way?" murmured Sarah. "Why—why torture her?"

"The police say it looked like the work of a maniac. Someone who gets his thrills from causing pain."

"Or someone out for vengeance," Sarah added. Eve had been playing a deadly game. Perhaps it had caught up with her. "Magus," she said, suddenly remembering the name. At Nick's quizzical glance, she explained, "It's a code name. For a man they called the Magician. Eve told me about him."

"We'll get to all that," he said, glancing at the mirror again. "The Savoy's right up this block. And we're still being followed."

AN HOUR AND a half later, they sat in a booth at the back of a Strand café and finished off a breakfast of eggs and bacon and grilled tomatoes. At last Sarah was starting to feel human again. Her stomach was full, and a cup of hot tea warmed her hands. Most important, she was dressed in a skirt and a shetland gray sweater. She realized now what good police strategy it had been to keep her in her nightclothes. She'd felt so naked and helpless, the right frame of mind to be forced into a confession.

And the ordeal still wasn't over; her troubles were really just beginning.

Nick had eaten quickly, all the while watching the door as he listened to Sarah's story. By the time she'd finished talking, the dishes were cleared and they were working on their second pot of tea.

"So Eve agreed with you that Geoffrey's alive?" he asked.

"Yes. The stolen photograph convinced her."

"Okay," he said, reviewing what she'd just told him. "So according to Eve, someone's out to kill Geoffrey. Someone who doesn't know his face but does know his new name's Fontaine. Geoffrey discovers he's being followed. He goes to Berlin, calls Eve and tells her to vanish. Then he stages his own death."

"That doesn't explain why she was tortured."

"It doesn't explain a lot of things. There are too many holes. Whose body was buried, for one. But at least we've got an explanation for that stolen photograph. If Simon Dance had plastic surgery to change his appearance, then whoever's after him may not recognize his face."

"And why are we being followed? Do they think I'll lead them to Geoffrey?"

He nodded. "And that brings up the detail that really bothers me: your release. I don't buy that story about the police not having enough evidence against you. When I talked to Inspector Appleby, he seemed ready to shut you away for life. Then Potter showed up and—poof! Everything's hunky-dory. Just like that, you're out. I think someone put a little pressure on the good inspector. The order must have come from above—way above. Someone wants you free to move around, and he's waiting for your next move."

Fatigue had drawn new shadows on Nick's face. She wondered how much sleep he'd had. Probably not much, not on a trans-Atlantic flight. She had an impulse to reach out and tenderly stroke his haggard face, to run her fingers across the harsh stubble on his jaw. Instead, hesitantly she reached out and brushed her fingers across his hand. He seemed startled by her touch, by the mingling of their hands on the table. *I've embarrassed him*, she thought as the blood rose to her cheeks. *I've em-*

barrassed us both. But as she started to pull away, his fingers closed tightly around hers. The warmth of his skin seemed to creep up her arm and invade every part of her body.

"You believe Geoffrey's alive, don't you?" she murmured.

He nodded. "I think he's alive."

She stared down at their hands woven together on the table. "I never believed he was dead," she whispered.

"Now that you've heard the facts, how do you feel about him?"

"I don't know. I don't know anymore...." With sudden intensity, she looked at Nick. "All this time I trusted him. I *believed* in him. Oh, you probably think I was naive, don't you? Maybe I was. But we all have dreams, Nick. Dreams we want to come true. And when you're like me, thirty-two and lonely and not very pretty, when a man says he loves you, you want so much to believe him."

"You're wrong, Sarah," he said gently. "You're very pretty."

She knew he was only being kind. She looked down at the table and wondered what he really thought of her. That only a plain woman could be so gullible? She pulled her hand away and reached for the teacup. Of course she knew what he was thinking—that Geoffrey had picked his target well; that Sarah, foolish woman, had fallen hard and fast. She saw it just as clearly. As clearly as if she were holding up a mirror and could coldly, critically, see herself as a man might see her: not beautiful, but shy and awkward. Not the kind of woman to attract a man like Geoffrey.

"It was a marriage of lies," she said. "Strange, how I feel as though I dreamed the whole thing. As though I was never married at all..."

He nodded. "I've felt that way myself, sometimes."

"You were married, then?"

"Not long. Three years. I've been divorced for four."

"I'm sorry."

His eyes focused on hers. "You really mean that, don't you?"

She nodded. Up till this moment, she hadn't seen the sadness in his eyes. She recognized it now, the same pain she was feeling. His marriage had failed; Sarah's had never existed. They both had their wounds.

But hers wouldn't heal. Not until her questions were answered. Not until she knew why Geoffrey had called her.

"Whatever your feelings about Geoffrey," said Nick, "you know, don't you, that it's a big risk, staying here in London. If someone's after him, you're the one they'll watch. Obviously you've been followed, at least since yesterday. You've already led them to Eve."

She looked up sharply. "Eve?"

"I'm afraid so. Eve was a professional. An ex-Mossad agent, on the run for years. She knew how to drop out of sight, and she did it well. But curiosity—maybe jealousy—made her careless. Against her better judgment, she agreed to meet you. It's no coincidence that the night you two met was the same night she was killed."

"Then I caused her death?" Sarah asked in what was barely a whisper.

"Yes, in a way. They must have tailed you to the Lamb and Rose. Right to Eve."

"Oh, God!" She shook her head miserably. "I almost hated her, Nick. When I thought about her and Geoffrey, I couldn't help it. But to be responsible for her death… I didn't want that!"

"She was the professional, Sarah, not you. You can't blame yourself."

She began to tremble and pulled her sweater tight. "Vengeance," she said softly, remembering the way Eve had died. "That's why they killed her."

"I'm not so sure."

"What else could it be?"

"Consider all the possible motives for torture. Granted, vengeance is one. People like to get even. But let's suppose there were more practical reasons…."

She suddenly understood his point. "You mean interrogation? They thought Eve knew something?"

"Maybe they saw through Geoffrey's faked death. Maybe they think he's still alive, too. So they put the knife to Eve, hoping for information. The question is, did she give them any?"

Sarah thought of Eve, remembering the green eyes, windows to a tough soul that did what was necessary to survive. Eve would have killed without a second thought. The business she was in required that ruthlessness. Tough as she was, though, Eve had also been in love. Last night in the Lamb and Rose, Sarah had sensed, even through her heartache, that Eve loved Geoffrey just as deeply, perhaps even more deeply, than Sarah ever had. Eve must have known where to find him. But whatever the torture, she would have held fast. She never would have betrayed Geoffrey. She had died with her secret.

Would Sarah have been as brave? She thought of the knife, of the pain that a blade could inflict on naked flesh, and she shuddered. There was no way to judge one's own courage, she thought. Courage surfaced only when it was needed, when one was forced to meet one's darkest terrors.

Sarah hoped hers would never be tested.

Chapter Seven

"I WANT ANSWERS, DAN. Starting with who ordered Sarah Fontaine's release and why."

Dan Lieberman, chief of consular affairs, regarded Nick with the passive face of a career man long attached to the State Department. Years of giving nothing away but a smile had left their mark; since the day they had met four years ago, Nick had not seen a single strong emotion emerge on Lieberman's face. The foreign service had turned the man into one hell of a poker player.

Yet Nick's instincts told him that somewhere beneath that polite facade was a voice of integrity trying to scream through the politics. Unlike Nick, Lieberman had learned to live with his demons. At least he still had a job and an enviable post here in London. He hadn't held on to it by rocking the boat. No, he'd kept his opinions to himself, had stayed out of trouble, and he'd survived.

But a little trouble was just what Nick was bringing him today.

"What's going on with her case?" asked Nick. "It seems to me it's being handled in a damned peculiar way."

"There have been irregularities," admitted Lieberman.

"Yeah. Starting with that son of a bitch Potter showing up at the police station."

At this remark Lieberman did crack a faint grin. "I'd forgotten you and Roy Potter knew each other so well. What was it between you guys again?"

"Sokolov. Don't tell me you've forgotten that, too."

"Oh, yeah. The Sokolov case. I remember now. You and Potter had it out in the stairwell. I hear your vocabulary would've made a sailor blush." He shook his head. "Bad move, Nick. Generated a very nasty personnel memo."

"You never met Sokolov, did you?"

"No."

"They say his kids found him New Year's day. He had two sons, ten years old or so. They went down to the basement looking for Daddy. They found him with a bullet in his head. Nice New Year's surprise, don't you think?"

"These things happen, Nick. You shouldn't ruin a career over it."

"Two kids, for God's sake! If Potter had listened to me, those two little boys would be safe in Montana or somewhere. Now they're probably freezing in Siberia, hauled back by the KGB."

"He was a defector. He took a risk and lost. Hey, this is all history. You didn't really come here to grouse about Potter, did you?"

"No. I'm here about Sarah Fontaine. I want to know why Potter's involved."

Lieberman shook his head. "Nick, I shouldn't even be talking to you. I hear from the grapevine that you're as popular as a dead fish. So before I say a thing, tell me why you're interested in the Fontaine case."

"Let's call it a sense of moral outrage."

"What're you outraged about?"

"Right now, Sarah Fontaine's sitting in my hotel room, wondering whether she's a widow. I happen to think her husband's alive. But all I've been hearing from our people is that he's dead. That I should give the widow my condolences and forget about it."

"So why not take the easy way out and do what you're told?"

"I don't like being lied to. And I really don't like being ordered to pass those same lies along. If there's a reason for keeping her in the dark, then I want to hear it. If it's valid, okay, I'll back off. But she's going through hell, and I think she has a right to know the truth."

Lieberman sighed. "Back tilting at windmills, aren't you?

Know what we used to call you around here? Don Quixote. Nick, why don't you save yourself an ulcer and just go home?"

"Then you won't help me."

"No, it's not that I don't want to. I just don't have any answers."

"Can you tell me why Potter showed up at the station in your place?"

"Okay, I can tell you that much. I got a call this morning from above that Potter would be handling the case, that I wasn't to get involved."

"A call from above? How far above?"

"Let's just say very far above."

"How was her release arranged?"

"Through the British chain of command, I assume. Someone must've whispered in their ear."

"The Brits?" Nick frowned. "Then it's a cooperative effort?"

"Draw your own conclusions." Lieberman's smile revealed he did not disagree.

"What's Roy Potter's involvement?"

"Who knows? Obviously the Company's very interested in your widow. Enough to spring her from jail. Since Potter himself is doing the footwork, I imagine there must be high stakes involved."

"Have you looked over the Fontaine case?" asked Nick.

"Briefly. Before they called me off of it."

"What did you think?"

"I thought the murder charge had a few major holes. A good barrister could've knocked it to pieces."

"And what did you think about Geoffrey Fontaine's death?"

"Irregular."

"An understatement if ever I've heard one. Did you know anything about Eve Fontaine?"

"Not really. I was told she bought the cottage a year ago. They say she was a recluse. Spent all her time out at Margate. But I'm sure you know a lot more about that than I do. Did you say the widow's staying in your room?"

"That's right. At my old bed and breakfast on Baker Street."

"Oh, the Kenmore." Lieberman filed away this information without a change in expression. "What sort of woman is she?"

Nick thought a moment. "Quiet," he said at last. "Intelligent. At the moment, very bewildered."

"I saw her passport photo. She struck me as rather, well… unremarkable."

"She strikes a lot of people that way."

"May I ask what your involvement is?"

"No."

Lieberman smiled. "Blunt as ever! Look, Nick, that really is all I know." He made a gesture that implied he had more pressing business. "If I have more information, I'll give you a call. How long will you be at the Kenmore?"

Nick rose. "For a few days, probably. After that, I'm not sure."

"And Sarah Fontaine? Will she be staying with you?"

Nick didn't have an answer. If it were up to him, Sarah would be on a plane back to Washington. Just the fact she was sitting alone in his room right now made him nervous. The Kenmore's proprietress, an old acquaintance of Nick's, had assured him that her two beefy sons would handle any trouble. Still, Nick was anxious to get back. Eve Fontaine's gruesome death still weighed on his mind.

"If Sarah decides to stay in London," Nick said, "then I'll be around."

They shook hands. Lieberman's grip was the same as always, firm and connected. It made Nick want to trust him. "By the way," Nick said as they walked to the door, "have you ever heard of someone called Magus?"

Lieberman's brow remained absolutely smooth. Not a ripple passed through his blue eyes. "Magus?" he repeated. "In biblical terms, it refers to a wise man. Or a magician."

"No. I'm referring to a code name."

"Doesn't ring a bell."

Nick paused in the doorway. "One last thing. Could you relay a message to Roy Potter for me?"

"Sure. Just keep the language decent."

"Tell him to call off his bloodhounds. Or at least have them follow us at a more discreet distance."

For the first time, a frown appeared on Lieberman's face. "I'll tell him," he said. "But if I were you, I'd make damn sure it really is the Company on your tail. Because if it isn't, let's just say the alternative might be a lot less pleasant."

"Less pleasant than the Company?" asked Nick. "I doubt it."

WHEN NICK RETURNED to his room at the Kenmore Bed and Breakfast, Sarah was fast asleep. She was sprawled, fully dressed, on the bed by the window, her face nestled against the pillow, her arm trailing over the side. Her glasses had fallen to the floor, as if she'd drifted to sleep still clutching them. The sun shone in brightly and illuminated her coppery hair.

For a moment he stood over the bed and gazed down at her, taking in the baggy sweater and the plain gray skirt. Lieberman had called her unremarkable. *Maybe to everyone else she is,* thought Nick. *Maybe I'm not seeing straight. Maybe I'm too lonely to care about looks anymore.* Whatever the reason, as he watched her now, he was starting to think she was really quite beautiful.

Not in the classical sense. Not like Lauren, the woman he'd once been married to. Black-haired, green-eyed Lauren could walk into a room and make a dozen heads turn. Nick had gotten a kick out of that—for a while. When Lauren was on his arm, other men would glance enviously in his direction, and he'd marvel at his own good luck. She'd been the perfect embassy wife: charming, witty, always ready with the repartee. And she'd been beautiful, in a way any man could appreciate. She'd known it, too. Maybe that had been the problem.

The woman sleeping on this bed was nothing like Lauren. Sarah had called herself plain. She'd felt a sense of wonder that a man like Geoffrey had married her. It must have been painful to learn that her marriage had been nothing but a sham. Nick knew all about pain; he'd lived through it himself four years ago. In a way, he'd never recovered. After his divorce he'd promised himself he'd never be hurt again. So here he was, stubbornly single. At least the bitterness had faded. At least he was still human enough to look at Sarah and think of the possibilities.

The possibilities? Who was he kidding? There were none. Not until they learned the truth about Geoffrey.

Sarah wasn't ready to abandon what for her had been a happy marriage. It was obvious she still loved her husband. She wanted to believe in him. The perverse part about it all was that this very loyalty to Geoffrey was what made Sarah so appealing. Loyalty.

Nick turned and gazed out the window. In the street below, the same black car was parked. The Company was still watching them. He waved, wondering what in God's name had happened to the quality of spies these days. Then he closed the curtain and went to lie down on the other bed.

The daylight was disconcerting. He couldn't sleep. Tired as he was, he could only lie there with his eyes closed and think.

What exactly am I doing here? he wondered. Boarding the plane last night had been an impulse of pure anger. He'd thought Sarah had lied to him; she had hammered the last nail in the coffin of his career, and he had meant to find her and get to the truth. Instead, here he was, not ten feet away from her, daydreaming about the possibilities.

He glanced over at her bed. She was sleeping so soundly, so peacefully, like a tired child. Yet she wasn't a child, and he was too aware of that fact. He remembered how it had felt this morning to touch her hair, to feel her face against his shoulder. Something began to stir in his belly, something very, very dangerous. It had been a long time since he'd had a woman, and Sarah looked so soft, so near….

He closed his eyes, suddenly angry at his own lack of control. Why was he putting himself through this unnecessary agony? The smart thing to do would be to go home and let the CIA handle the whole affair. But if they let anything happen to her, he'd never forgive himself.

Gradually, fitfully, Nick drifted toward sleep. A vision intruded: a woman with amber eyes. He wanted to reach out and touch her, but his hands became tangled in the long strands of her hair. Sarah, Sarah. How could anyone not think you beautiful? His hands moved leadenly, caught in a web too thick to penetrate. Beyond his grasp, Sarah faded away. He was alone. As always, he was alone.

IN ONE OF Roy Potter's back rooms, a radio report came over the receiver. "O'Hara left Lieberman's office forty minutes ago," the agent called in. "Now he's back at the Kenmore. Haven't seen the woman for an hour. Curtains are drawn. Looks like they're hitting the sack."

"And I'll bet ya two bangers it's not to sleep," Potter muttered to his assistant. Agent Tarasoff barely smiled. Tarasoff had no sense of humor, no sense of fun. His style of dressing was absolutely correct: a conservative gray suit, a tie in dull blues and silvers, a plain white shirt, and all of it spotless. Even the way Tarasoff ate his roast-beef sandwich was boring. He took neat little nibbles, wiping his fingers between bites. Now Potter, on the other hand, ate like a normal person. No pussyfooting around. He just ate and got it over with. Potter gulped down his last bite of corned-beef sandwich and reached for the transmitter.

"Okay, guys, just stick it out. See who wanders by."

"Yes, sir. Have you got anything on the Kenmore folks?"

"Clean Brits. Plain old B and B types, widow and two sons."

"Check. We've seen 'em."

"How're you guys situated?"

"Can't complain. Got a pub right across the street."

"Has he spotted you yet?"

"Afraid so, sir. He flipped us a bird some time back."

Tarasoff made a sound that might have been a chuckle. But when Potter glanced over at him, all he saw was the same impassive face.

"Geez, he's on to you already? What'd you guys do? Go up and introduce yourselves?"

"No, sir. He saw us way back, after we left the station."

"Okay. It's one-thirty. You can clock yourselves out in two hours. Keep alive."

Potter hung up, crumpled the waxed paper from his lunch and tossed it at the trash can. It missed by a mile, but he didn't feel like getting up.

Tarasoff rose and retrieved the crumpled paper. "What do you make of all this, Mr. Potter?" he asked, neatly dropping the trash into the can.

Potter shrugged. "Wild-goose chase? I hope not."

"Should we be looking at this Nick O'Hara in a different light?"

"What do you mean?"

"Is it possible there's something more complex involved? Could he be under deep cover for someone?"

Potter burst out laughing. "O'Hara? Let me tell you something about him. He's not the deep-cover type. Too damned honest. Thinks he's on a quest for the Holy Grail or something. You know, the kind of guy who spends all day worrying about dead whales." Potter eyed Tarasoff's half-eaten roast-beef sandwich. His stomach was still growling. "You gonna finish that thing?"

"No, sir. You can have it."

Potter took a bite and almost choked. Horseradish. Why did folks have to go and ruin perfectly good roast beef? But there was no point wasting it. "O'Hara's smart enough, I guess," he said between bites. "I mean, in an intellectual sort of way—all theory, no practice. Speaks about four languages. Not a bad consular officer. But he just doesn't operate in the real world."

"It's strange, though," said Tarasoff. "Why should he get mixed up in this affair? He's jeopardized his career. It doesn't make sense to me."

"Tarasoff, have you ever been in love?"

"I'm married."

"No, I mean *in love*?"

"Well, yes, I suppose so."

"You suppose so. Hell, that's not love. By love, I mean something red-hot, something that'll make you go crazy, risk your life. Maybe even get married."

"He's in love? With Sarah Fontaine?"

"Why not?"

Tarasoff shook his head gravely. "I think he's under deep cover."

Potter laughed. "Never underestimate the power of hormones."

"That's what my wife always says." Tarasoff suddenly frowned at Potter's arm. "Sir, you'd better wipe up that mustard. It'll ruin your jacket."

Potter glanced down at the yellow blob on his sleeve. Another day, another stain. He looked around for a napkin, then gave up and reached for a scrap of memo paper. It was a note he'd scrawled to himself earlier in the week: *"Mail alimony checks!"* Dammit, late again. If he got over to the post office right now, the checks might arrive by Tuesday....

He tossed the memo at the trash can. It missed. With a groan he forced himself out of his chair. He was reaching down for the scrap of paper when the door opened. "Yeah?" he asked. Then he fell silent.

Puzzled, Tarasoff turned and looked at the man standing in the doorway. It was Jonathan Van Dam.

Potter cleared his throat. "Mr. Van Dam. I didn't know you were in London. Is there new business?"

"No. Actually it's old business." Van Dam settled into Potter's chair and carelessly brushed aside the mound of crumpled waxed paper and Styrofoam cups before sliding his briefcase on the desk. "An odd bit of information has come to my attention, and I really can't account for it. Perhaps you can shed some light."

"Uh—information?"

"Yes. I've had a tap on Sarah Fontaine's phone. To my surprise I learned she had a call from her husband a few days ago. Rather amazing feat, don't you think? Or has long-distance service improved that much?"

Potter and Tarasoff looked at each other. "Mr. Van Dam," said Potter, "I can explain…."

"Yes," said Van Dam. He wasn't smiling. "I think you should."

ON THE HIGH cliffs above Margate, Nick and Sarah stood with their faces against the wind. Gulls dove from the teal-blue sky, and their cries pierced the air like a hundred voices raised in mourning. The sun was shining brightly, and the sea sparkled like broken glass. Even Sarah was stirring to life under the healing touch.

Since starting out from London that morning, she'd shed her sweater and scarf. Now, dressed in a white cotton shirt and the old gray skirt, she paused in the sunshine and drank in its warmth. She was alive. For the past two weeks, she'd somehow forgotten that fact. She'd wanted to bury herself along with Geoffrey—or who she'd thought was Geoffrey. Only now, as she felt the salt wind in her face, did life seem to creep back into her body. She'd survived Geoffrey's death; now she would survive his resurrection. To think how deeply she'd loved him! Now she could barely recall the feeling. All she had left were images, freeze-frame memories of a man she'd hardly known.

"Sarah?" Nick touched her arm and nodded toward the path.

His hair was wild and windblown, his face ruddy in the sunshine. In his faded shirt and trousers, he looked more like a fisherman than a bureaucrat. "How much farther?" he asked.

"Not far. It's at the top of the hill."

As they walked up the path to Whitstable Lane, she found herself watching him. He strode easily, without effort, as though he'd spent all his life scaling cliffs. Once again, she wondered about Nick O'Hara. Whatever his reasons for being here, she knew this much: she trusted him. There was no point questioning his motives. He was a friend; that was all that mattered.

Nick turned and squinted down the path. The town of Margate was nestled below at the foot of the cliff. There was no sign of pursuit. They were alone.

"I wonder why they're not following us," said Nick.

"Maybe they're tired."

"Well, let's keep moving. At least we've got some breathing room now."

They turned and continued walking.

"You don't like the CIA, do you?" she asked.

"No."

"Why not?"

"They're a different breed. I don't trust them. And I especially don't trust Roy Potter."

"What did Mr. Potter do to you?"

"To me? Nothing. Except maybe get me shipped back to Washington."

"Is Washington that bad?"

"It's not the place foreign service careers are made."

"Where are they made?"

"Hot spots. Africa. South America."

"Yet you were in London."

"London wasn't my first choice. They offered me Cameroon, but I had to turn it down."

"Why?"

"Lauren. My ex-wife."

"Oh." So that was her name, Lauren. Sarah wondered what had gone wrong between them. Had it been like so many other failed marriages, in which there was a gradual drifting apart?

Boredom? She couldn't imagine ever being bored of Nick. He was a man of many layers, each one more complex than the last, each waiting to be discovered. Could a woman ever really know him?

They walked in silence, past the row of mailboxes and around the curve leading to Whitstable Lane. The cottage came into view, a small white house behind a low picket fence. The old grounds keeper was nowhere in sight.

"This is the house," she said.

"Then let's find out who's home," said Nick. He walked up to the front door and rang the bell. There was no answer. The door was locked. "Sounds like it's empty," he said. "All the better."

"Nick?" she called, following him around to the back door. She found him jiggling the knob. It was unlocked.

Slowly the door swung open. The shaft of daylight swept across a polished stone floor. At their feet lay a single shattered china plate. Nothing else appeared out of place. The kitchen drawers were closed. Copper pots hung in rows on an overhead rack. On the window sill sat two wilted plants. Except for the soft drip of a leaky faucet, the house was eerily silent.

Sarah jumped when Nick touched her arm. "Wait here," he whispered. His footsteps crunched loudly on the broken china as he walked through the kitchen and disappeared into the next room. As she waited for him, her eyes slowly explored the strange surroundings. She was standing in the very heart and soul of the house. Here was where Eve had cooked, where she and Geoffrey had laughed and eaten together. Even now, the room seemed to resonate with their presence. Sarah didn't belong here. She was the intruder.

"Sarah?" Nick was calling from the doorway. "Come take a look."

She followed him into a sitting room. Leather-bound books lined the wall shelves; china figurines sat in a row on the mantelpiece. In the fireplace were the ashes from Eve's last fire. Only a desk had been disturbed. Its drawers had been pulled out and dumped. A pile of correspondence—mostly bills and advertisements—had been ripped open and tossed on the floor.

"Robbery wasn't the motive," he said, nodding at an obviously antique pewter goblet on the mantelpiece. "I think someone was after information. An address book, maybe. Or a phone number."

She gazed around the room. It would have been a cozy place, with the flames crackling and the lights burning low. She could picture Eve sitting quietly in the leather chair, smoke trailing from her cigarette. Would there be music? Yes, of course, Mozart and Chopin. There were the records, stacked by an old phonograph. The ashtray was still full of butts. Fear must have made her light one cigarette after another. Here, alone in the shadows, Eve must have jumped every time the windows rattled or the floor creaked.

A few feet away, Sarah saw an open door. She felt herself drawn toward it by an inexplicable and painful fascination. She knew what lay beyond, yet she couldn't stop herself from going in.

It was the bedroom. With gathering tears she stood at the foot of the double bed and looked at the flowered coverlet. This was another woman's bed. In her mind she saw Geoffrey lying here, with his arms around Eve. The vision filled her with such pain she could barely refrain from screaming. How many nights had he slept here? How many times had they made love? As he lay in this bed, hadn't he ever missed Sarah, just a little?

These were questions only he could answer. She had to find him. She had to know, or she'd never be free.

In tears she bolted from the room. A moment later she was standing alone near the edge of the cliff, staring out to sea. She scarcely heard Nick's footsteps as he walked up behind her.

But she did feel his hands settle gently on her shoulders. He said nothing; he merely stood there, a warm, solid presence. It was precisely what she needed from him: the silence. And the touch. As the waves churned below, she closed her eyes and felt his breath in her hair.

She'd been married to Geoffrey and she'd never really known him. Here was Nick, a man she'd met just two weeks ago. Already their lives had mingled inextricably. And now she desperately wanted him to pull her closer, to gather her into his arms.

How did things get so crazy? she wondered. Was it just the loneliness? The grief? She wanted to turn to him, to be held by him, but she knew it was more than simple desire. It was also need. She was afraid and vulnerable, and Nick was the only safe anchor in her world. It was the wrong reason to fall in love.

Pulling away, she turned and faced him. He stood very still and erect. His eyes were the color of smoke. The wind whipped his shirt. In the sky above, gulls soared and circled like a silver cloud.

"I have to find Geoffrey," she said, her words almost lost in the gulls' cries. "And you can't come with me."

"You can't go off on your own. Look what happened to Eve—"

"They don't want *me*! They want Geoffrey. And I'm their only link. They won't hurt me."

"How are you going to find him?"

"He'll find *me*."

Nick shook his head, and his hair danced wildly in the wind. "This is crazy! You don't know what you're up against."

"Do you? If you know, Nick, you have to tell me."

He didn't answer. He only stared at her with eyes that had darkened to tarnished silver. *What does he know?* she wondered. *Is he somehow part of all this?*

She turned and kept walking. Nick followed her, his hands jammed deeply into his pockets. They stopped at the row of mailboxes, where Whitstable Lane curved into the cliff path. An old man in a postal uniform tipped his hat and rode away on his bike, down the path to Margate. He had just delivered the mail. Sarah reached into the slot marked 25. Inside were another catalog and three bills, all addressed to Eve.

"She won't be needing them," Nick pointed out.

"No. I guess not." Sarah stuffed the bills into her purse. "I was hoping there'd be something…."

"What did you expect? That he'd write you a letter? You don't even know where to start, do you?"

"No," she admitted. Then she added stubbornly, "But I'll find him."

"How? Don't forget, you've got the CIA down there, waiting for you."

"I'll lose them. Somehow."

"And then what? What happens if Eve's killer decides to come after you? You think you can handle him on your own?"

She broke away and headed down the path. He seized her arm and pulled her around.

"Sarah! Don't be stupid!"

"I'm going to find Geoffrey!"

"Then let me come with you."

"*Why?*" she cried, her word lost in the wind.

His answer caught her completely off guard. In one swift motion, he pulled her into his arms. Before she could react, before she could even comprehend what was happening, his mouth came down on hers. The force of his embrace crushed the very breath from her lungs. The cry of the gulls faded, and the wind seemed to carry her up and away, until she lost all sense of where she was. As if by their own accord, her arms found their way around him, to clutch at the hard curve of his back. Willingly her lips parted; at once he was exploring her mouth, devouring her with an animal's hunger. Nothing mattered anymore, nothing but Nick, the taste of his mouth, the smell of the sea on his skin.

The gull cries turned into screams as reality rushed in. Sarah wrenched herself free. His expression mirrored her own look of surprise, as though he, too, had been swept up by something he couldn't explain.

"I guess that's why," he said softly.

She shook her head in confusion. He had kissed her. It had happened so fast, so unexpectedly, that she could barely take in what it all meant. She did know this much: she had wanted him. She still wanted him. With every second that passed, her hunger grew.

"Why did you do that?"

"It just happened. Sarah, I didn't mean to—" Suddenly agitated, he turned away. "No, dammit!" he blurted out, wheeling around to look at her again. "I take it back! I sure as hell *did* mean to do that!"

She retreated, more confused than ever. What was wrong with her? Only days ago, she'd thought herself desperately in love with Geoffrey. Now, at this moment, Nick O'Hara was the only man she wanted. She could still taste him on her lips, could still feel his hands pulling her against him, and all she could think of was how good it would feel to kiss him again. No, she couldn't have him near her. Not now, not after this.

"Please, Nick," she said. "Go back to Washington. I have to find Geoffrey, and you can't be with me."

"Wait. Sarah!"

But she was already walking away.

They were quiet as they approached the village. She didn't know what to say to him anymore. It had been easier when they were simply friends, when they were only two people searching for answers. Now just looking at him ignited fires deep inside her, fires she'd never known existed.

Last night she'd been so tired and afraid, she'd been almost glad to share his room. Today everything had changed. She had to leave him. As soon as they reached London, she would pack her bags and walk out of the Kenmore. Finding Geoffrey was something she could only do alone.

By the time they entered Margate, she'd hardened her resolve. Nothing he could say would change her mind. But by God, he'd try; she could see it in his face, in the stubborn set of his jaw. He wasn't through with her yet. It would be a long drive back to London.

Like two strangers walking side by side, they headed for Nick's rented M.G., which was parked on a street lined by tiny shops. Just behind the M.G. was the same black Ford that had tailed them all the way from London. The CIA. So they'd given up all pretenses of subtlety. They were operating in the open now. That would make it easier for Sarah to lose them.

One of the agents was silhouetted against the tinted window. As they walked past, she glanced through the windshield; there was absolutely no movement inside the car. Nick noticed it, too. He paused and tapped on the window. The agent didn't move, didn't speak. Was he sleeping? It was hard to tell through the dark glass.

"Nick?" she whispered. "Is something wrong with him?"

"Keep moving," he said softly, nudging her toward the M.G. "I want you to get inside the car." Calmly he unlocked her door. "Get inside and stay there."

"Nick—"

He was cautiously approaching the Ford. Burning curiosity drew her to follow him; she stood right behind him on the sidewalk as slowly, carefully, he took hold of the passenger door. The agent still hadn't moved. Nick hesitated only a second, then jerked the door open.

The agent's shoulder slumped sideways. A face slid past the window, a face with wide, staring eyes. An arm flopped out of the car and dangled into the street. Nick reeled away in horror as bright red droplets spattered the sidewalk.

Chapter Eight

SARAH SCREAMED. IN THE NEXT INSTANT, gunfire spat out the windows of the Ford, sending both Nick and Sarah diving for cover. Nick's body landed squarely on hers as they hit the concrete. She couldn't move. She couldn't even speak; all the breath had been slammed out of her by the impact.

Nick rolled aside and shoved her forward. "The car—get in!" he barked.

His harsh command jarred her into action. Like a terrified animal, she scrambled into the M.G. Gunfire shattered store windows, and all around them, people were screaming. Nick dove in behind Sarah, crawling over her and landing in a heap under the steering wheel. His keys were already out as he slid onto the seat.

The engine roared to life. Sarah struggled to close her door, but Nick yelled, "Get down! Get the hell down!" She sank to the floor.

Blindly he sent the car in reverse. It thudded into the Ford. Nick shifted to first, jammed the wheel to the right, and floored the gas pedal. They jerked forward. Sarah was thrown back helplessly against the seat. The car swerved wildly into the street. They were hurtling aimlessly, toward an inevitable collision. She braced herself.

But the crash never came. There was only the rumble of the engine and Nick's coarse oath as he shifted into third gear.

"Close your door!" he ordered.

She looked over at him. He had both hands on the steering wheel and his eyes on the road. They were safe. Nick was in control. Outside, the narrow streets of Margate hurtled by.

She tugged the door shut. "Why are they trying to kill us?"

"Good question!" A lorry appeared from nowhere. Nick swerved aside. From behind came the screech of tires and the other driver's angry shout.

"That agent—"

"His throat was slit."

"Oh, God...."

A sign marked Westgate loomed ahead. Nick shifted into fourth. They had left Margate behind them. Empty fields now whipped past the windows.

"But who, Nick? Who's trying to kill us?"

Nick shot a glance in the rearview mirror. "Let's hope we're not about to find out."

She snapped her head around in horror. A blue Peugeot was closing in fast. She caught only a glimpse of the driver, a flash of reflective sunglasses.

"Hold on," said Nick. "We're going for a ride...." He floored the pedal, and the M.G. cut recklessly through traffic. The Peugeot shot off after them. It was a larger, clumsier car; it pulled into the wrong lane and almost clipped a van. The error cost it a split second of speed; the Peugeot fell behind. But traffic was getting thin. On the open stretch, there'd be no contest. The Peugeot was too fast.

"I can't lose him, Sarah!"

She heard the desperation in his voice. They were doomed, and there was nothing he could do about it. *It's all my fault,* she thought, *all my fault that Nick's going to die.*

"Put on your seat belt," he instructed. "We've run out of options."

Out of options. A nice way of saying they'd reached the end. She watched as the Peugeot hurtled relentlessly toward them. Through the windshield she saw the driver, a glare of sunlight on his silvered glasses. There was something monstrous, something inhuman, about a man whose eyes you couldn't see.

She buckled the seat belt and glanced at Nick. His profile was hard and cool, his gaze fixed ahead on the road. He was too busy to look terrified. Only his hands betrayed him. His knuckles were white.

The road forked. To the left a sign pointed to Canterbury. Nick veered left, throwing her hard against the seat belt. The Peugeot almost missed the turnoff. It skidded onto the shoulder, then zoomed after them onto the Canterbury highway.

Nick's voice, low and steady, penetrated the cloud of fear that had formed in her brain. "The bullets'll be flying any second. Get your head down. I'll keep us on the road as long as I can. If we crack up, get out and run like hell. The gas tank could blow."

"I won't leave you!"

"Yes, you will."

"No, Nick!"

"Dammit!" he shouted. *"Just do what I say!"*

The Peugeot was right behind them, so close Sarah could see the driver's teeth, bared in a smile. "Why aren't they shooting?" she cried. "They're close enough to hit us!"

The Peugeot nudged their back bumper. Sarah clung to the door as Nick jammed the wheel right, then left. The Peugeot skidded and fell behind a few yards.

"That's why." Nick answered. "They want to run us off the road."

Again there was a thump, this time against the left bumper. Nick swerved again. The Peugeot roared up beside them. The cars were neck and neck. Paralyzed by terror, Sarah found herself staring through the window at the face of a killer. His blond hair—so pale it was almost white—fell jaggedly above the mirrored sunglasses. His cheeks were sunken, his skin was dull as wax. He was grinning at her.

Only vaguely did her mind register the obstacle ahead. She was hypnotized by the man's face, by the death's-head grin. Then she heard Nick's sharp intake of breath. Her eyes snapped ahead to the curve, to the car stalled in the road.

Nick spun the wheel right, flinging them into a lane of oncoming traffic. Tires shrieked. They pitched wildly out of control as cars swerved to avoid them. Green fields spun past

Sarah's eyes, and then she focused on Nick's hands as he fought the steering wheel. She scarcely registered the metallic thud, the shattering of glass, somewhere behind them.

Then the world came abruptly to a halt. They found themselves staring wide-eyed at a field of astonished cows. Sarah's heart began to beat again. Only then did she remember to take another breath. In that same instant, Nick hit the gas pedal and turned the M.G. back onto the highway.

"That'll slow 'em down," he said. His understatement struck her as somehow hilarious.

She looked back. The Peugeot was lying on its side in the field. Standing in the mud beside it was the blond driver, the man with the death's-head grin. Even from that distance, she could see the fury in his face. Then he and the Peugeot shrank into the distance and vanished.

"You okay?" asked Nick.

"Yes. Yes…" She tried to swallow but her mouth felt drier than sand.

Nick grunted. "One thing's obvious. You sure as hell can't go off alone."

Alone? The very thought terrified her. No, she didn't want to be alone. Never again! But how much could she count on Nick? He was no soldier; he was a diplomat, a man behind a desk. Right now he was operating on pure instinct, not training. Yet he was all that stood between her and a killer.

The road forked again. Canterbury and London lay to the west. Nick turned east, onto the road marked Dover.

"What are you doing?" asked Sarah, turning in dismay as they bypassed the London exit.

"We're not going to London," he said.

"But we need help—"

"We *had* help. Didn't do us a lot of good, did it? So much for protective surveillance."

"London will be safer!"

He shook his head. "No, it won't. They'll be waiting for us there. This whole fiasco proves we can't count on our own people. Maybe they're just incompetent. Maybe it's something worse…."

Something worse? Did he mean betrayal? She thought the

nightmare was over, that they'd simply knock on the embassy door in London and be swept into the protective arms of the CIA. She'd never considered the possibility that the very people she trusted would want her dead. It didn't make sense!

"The CIA wouldn't kill its own man!" she pointed out.

"Maybe not the Company itself. But someone inside. Someone with other connections."

"What if you're wrong?"

"Dammit, think about it! The agent didn't just sit back while someone cut his throat! He was taken by surprise. By someone he knew, someone he trusted. There's got to be an insider involved. Someone who wants us out of the way."

"But I don't know anything!"

"Maybe you do. Maybe you just don't realize it."

She shook her head frantically. "No, this is crazy. *It's crazy!* Nick, I'm just an average woman. I go to work, I go shopping, I cook dinner—I'm not a spy! I'm not like—like Eve...."

"Then it's time we started thinking like her. Both of us. I'm new to this game, too. And it looks like I'm in just as deep."

"We could fly home—to Washington—"

"You really think it's safer there?"

No, she thought with mounting despair. He was right. Home would be no safer. They had nowhere to run.

"Then where do we go?" she asked desperately.

He glanced at his watch. "It's twelve o'clock," he said. "We'll ditch the car and get the Hovercraft in Dover. It'll be a quick ride to Calais. We'll take the train to Brussels. And then you and I are going to vanish. For a while, at least."

She stared numbly at the road. *A while?* she wondered. *How long is a while? Forever? Will I be like Eve, always running, always looking over my shoulder?*

Just an hour ago, on the cliffs of Margate, it had been so clear what she needed to do—she had to find Geoffrey and get to the truth of her marriage. Now it was down to something more elemental, a goal so stark that nothing else mattered.

She had to stay alive.

She'd think about Geoffrey later. She'd take the time to wonder where he was and how she'd find him. She *had* to find him; he was the only one who had the answers. But now she couldn't look that far ahead.

She saw how tightly Nick gripped the steering wheel. He was afraid, too. That was what terrified her most—the fact that even Nick O'Hara was afraid.

"I guess I have to trust you," she said.

"It looks that way."

"Who else can we trust, Nick?"

He looked at her. The answer he gave had an awful ring of finality. "No one."

ROY POTTER GRABBED the receiver on the first ring. What he heard next made him hit the recording button. Through the crackle of a trans-Channel connection came the voice of Nick O'Hara. "I've got one thing to say."

"O'Hara?" shouted Potter. "Where the hell—"

"We're dropping out, Potter. Stay off our tails."

"You can't go off in the cold! O'Hara, listen! You need us!"

"Like hell."

"You think you're gonna stay alive out there without our help?"

"Yeah. I do. And you listen good, Potter. Take a close hard look at your people. Because something's rotten in the State of Denmark. And if I find out you're responsible, I'm going to see they nail your ass to the wall."

"Wait, O'Hara—"

The line went dead. Muttering a curse, Potter hung up. Then he looked reluctantly across the desk at Jonathan Van Dam. "They're alive," he said.

"Where are they?"

"He wouldn't say. We're tracing the call right now."

"Are they coming in?"

"No. They're going under."

Van Dam leaned across the desk. "I want them, Mr. Potter. I want them soon. Before someone else gets to them."

"Sir, he's afraid. He doesn't trust us—"

"I'm not surprised, considering this latest foul-up. Find them!"

Potter grabbed the phone, silently hurling every oath he knew at Nick O'Hara. This was all his fault. "Tarasoff?" he barked. "Did you get that number?... What the hell does that mean, *somewhere* in Brussels? I already know he's in Brussels! I want the damned address!" He slammed the receiver down.

"Simple surveillance," said Van Dam. "That was your plan, wasn't it? So what happened?"

"I had two good agents on the Fontaine woman. I don't know what went wrong. One of my men's still missing, and the other's in the morgue—"

"I can't be bothered with dead agents. I want Sarah Fontaine. What about those train stations and airports?"

"The Brussels office is already on it. I'm flying out tonight. There's been activity in their bank accounts—big withdrawals. Looks as if they plan to stay under a long time."

"Watch those accounts. Circulate their photographs. To local police, Interpol, everyone who'll cooperate. Don't arrest her, just locate her. And we need a psychological profile on O'Hara. I want to know that man's motives."

"O'Hara?" Potter snorted. "I can tell you all you need to know."

"What do you think the man'll do next?"

"He's new to the game. Wouldn't know the ropes of picking up a new identity. But he speaks fluent French. He could move around Belgium without raising an eyebrow. And he's smart. We might have trouble."

"What about the woman? Could she blend in as well?"

"Doesn't know any foreign languages, to my knowledge. Totally inexperienced. She'd be helpless on her own."

Tarasoff entered the office. "Got the address. It's a pay phone, center of town. No chance of tracking him down now."

"Who does O'Hara know in Belgium?" asked Van Dam. "Any friends he'd trust?"

Potter frowned. "I'd have to check his file...."

"What about Mr. Lieberman in the consular division?" suggested Tarasoff. "He'd know about O'Hara's friends."

Van Dam gave Tarasoff a look of appraisal. "Good start. I'm glad someone's thinking. What else?"

"Well, sir, I wonder if we should look at other angles, other themes running this man's life...." Tarasoff suddenly noticed the dark look Potter was flashing at him. He added quickly, "But of course, Mr. Potter knows O'Hara inside and out."

"What themes are you referring to, Mr. Tarasoff?" prodded Van Dam.

"I keep wondering if he's—well, working for someone."

"No way," said Potter. "O'Hara's an independent."

"But your man makes a good point," said Van Dam. "Did we miss something when we vetted O'Hara?"

"He spent four years in London," said Tarasoff. "He could have made numerous contacts."

"Look, I know the guy," insisted Potter. "He's his own man." Van Dam didn't seem to hear him. Potter felt as if he was shouting from the wrong side of a soundproof window. Why did he always feel like the outsider, the slob with mustard on his ten-year-old suit? He'd worked like hell to be a good agent, but it wasn't enough, not in the eyes of men like Van Dam. What Potter lacked was *style*.

Tarasoff had it. And Van Dam—why, his suit was definitely Savile Row, his watch a Rolex. He'd been smart to marry money. That, of course, was what Potter should have done. He should have married rich women. Then they'd be paying *him* alimony.

"I'll expect results soon, Mr. Potter," Van Dam said as he pulled on his overcoat. "Let me know the minute something turns up. How you handle O'Hara after that point is your affair."

Potter frowned. "Uh—what does that mean?"

"I'll leave it up to you. Just make it discreet." Van Dam left the room.

Potter stared in puzzlement at the closed door. What exactly had he meant by "I'll leave it up to you?" Oh, he knew what he'd *like* to do to Nick O'Hara. O'Hara was just another high-minded career diplomat. Potter knew the breed all too well. They looked down their noses at spooks. None of them appreciated the dirty work Potter had to do. Hell, *someone* had to do it! When things went well, he got no credit. But when things went wrong, guess who got the blame?

Those invectives he and O'Hara had hurled at each other a year ago still rankled. Mainly because he knew, deep down, that O'Hara had been right. Sokolov's death had been his fault.

This time he couldn't afford any mistakes. He'd already lost two agents. Even worse, he'd lost track of the Fontaine woman. By God, there'd be no more screwups. Even if he had to search every hotel in Brussels, he'd find them.

FOR REASONS OF his own, Jonathan Van Dam was just as determined to find them. Somehow O'Hara had managed to foul up what should have been a simple operation. He was the unexpected factor, the one little detail that no one had predicted, just the sort of thing that gives an operative nightmares. What really troubled Van Dam was something Tarasoff had suggested, that O'Hara could be more than just a man in love. Was he working for someone else?

Van Dam stared down at his plate of mixed grill and considered this last disturbing possibility. He was sitting alone in his favorite London restaurant. The food wasn't bad here. The lamb chops were tender and pink, the sausages homemade. The chips were dry, true, but he never ate them anyway. He liked the candlelight and the soft hum of conversation. He liked seeing other people around him, if only anonymously. It helped him focus on the problem at hand.

He finished his chop and, sitting back, slowly sipped a glass of fine port. Yes, that young Tarasoff had brought up a good point. It was dangerous to assume anything was as it seemed. Van Dam, better than most people, knew that. For two years he'd endured what outsiders had called a happy marriage. For two years he'd shared a bed with a woman he could barely stand to touch. He had dutifully nursed her out of her gin binges, put up with her rages and, afterward, her remorse. Through it all he'd laughed in silence at the inane comments her friends had made. "You know, Jonathan, you've made Claudia so happy!" or "You're so good for her!" or "You're both so lucky!" Claudia's death had stunned everyone—most of all, perhaps, Claudia herself. The bitch had thought she'd live forever.

Yes, the port *was* excellent. He ordered another. A woman two tables away was staring at him but he ignored her, knowing, by some strange and certain instinct, that she had a fondness for spirits. Like Claudia.

The matter of Sarah Fontaine and Nick O'Hara returned to

mind. He knew that finding a man like O'Hara, a man who spoke fluent French, would be impossible in a city as big as Brussels. Sarah Fontaine was a different matter. All she had to do was open her mouth at the wrong time, and the game would be up. Yes, better to concentrate on finding her, not O'Hara. She was the easier quarry. And after all, she was the one they really wanted.

HUGGING HER LEGS to her chest, Sarah sat on the hard mattress and checked her watch again. Nick had been gone two hours and all that time she'd been sitting like a zombie, listening for his footsteps. And thinking. Thinking about fear, wondering if she'd ever feel safe again.

On the train from Calais, she had struggled against panic, against the premonition that something terrible was about to happen. All of her senses had become acutely raw. She'd registered every sound, every sight, right down to the loose threads on the ticket taker's jacket. Details took on new importance. Their lives might hang on something as trivial as the look in a stranger's eye.

The trip had gone smoothly—they'd made it to Brussels without a hitch. Hours had passed, dulling the sharp edges of fear until terror gave way to mere gnawing anxiety. For the moment she was safe.

But where was Nick? Surely he would come back for her? She didn't want to think of the other possibilities. That he'd been caught. Or that he'd come to his senses and bailed out of a hopeless situation. She wouldn't blame him if he had bailed out. What man in his right mind would stick around waiting for death?

She rose and went to the window. Dusk was blotting out the city. Through a gray drizzle, the rooftops of Brussels hovered unanchored, like ghosts.

She flicked on the one bare lightbulb. The room was small and shabby, a mere box on the second floor of a run-down hotel. Everything smelled of dust and mildew. The double mattress was lumpy. The wood floor was covered only by a single small throw rug, which was worn and stained. A few hours ago, she hadn't cared what the room looked like. Now the four walls were driving her mad. She felt trapped. She craved fresh air, and even more than that, food. Their last meal had been breakfast, and her body was screaming to eat. But she had to wait until Nick returned.

If he returned.

Downstairs a door slammed. She spun around and listened as footsteps thumped up the stairs, then creaked heavily along the hall. A key jiggled in the lock. The knob turned. Slowly the door squealed open. She froze. A stranger loomed on the threshold.

Nothing about him seemed familiar. He wore a black fisherman's cap, pulled low over his eyes. A cigarette butt, trailing smoke, dangled carelessly from his mouth. He brought with him the reek of fish and wine, a smell he wore as distinctly as the tattered jacket on his shoulders. But when he looked up, Sarah suddenly found herself laughing with relief. "Nick! It's you!"

He frowned. "Who else would it be?"

"It's your clothes—"

He regarded his jacket with distaste. "Isn't this gross? Smells like the original owner died in it." He stubbed out the cigarette and tossed her a brown-paper package.

"Your new identity, madame. I guarantee no one'll recognize you."

"Oh, brother. I'm afraid to look." She opened the package and removed a short black wig, a packet of hairpins and a singularly hideous wool dress. "I think it looked better on the sheep," she sighed.

"Look, no fair grousing about the dress. Just be glad I didn't put you in a miniskirt with fishnet stockings. Believe me, I thought about it."

She looked dubiously at the wig. "Black?"

"It was on sale."

"I've never worn one of these before. Which way does it go? Like this?"

His hoot of laughter made her flush. "No, you've got it backward. Here, let me do it."

She wrenched it off her head. "This isn't going to work."

"Sure it'll work. Hey, I'm sorry I laughed. You just have to get the thing on right." He grabbed the pins from the bed. "Come on, turn around. Let's get your hair out of the way first."

Obediently she turned and let him pin up her hair. He was

terribly awkward; she could have done the task more efficiently by herself. But at the first touch of his hands, a warmth, a contentment, seemed to melt through her body; she never wanted the feeling to end. It was so soothing, so incredibly sensuous, having a man stroke her hair, especially a man with hands as warm and gentle as Nick's.

As the tension eased from Sarah's shoulders, Nick felt the tension in his own body mounting to unbearable heights. Even while he struggled with the hairpins, he found himself staring at the smooth skin on the back of her neck. His gaze slipped down, tracing the delicate bones of her spine to the collar of her blouse. The strand of hair felt like liquid fire in his hand. The heat surged like a current up his fingers, straight to his gut. The old fantasy rose to mind: Sarah standing before him in his bedroom, her breasts bared, her hair loose about her shoulders.

He forced himself to concentrate on what he was doing. What *was* he doing? Oh yes. The wig. With clumsy fingers he began slipping in hairpins.

"I never knew you smoked," she murmured drowsily.

"I don't anymore. Gave it up years ago. Tonight's just for show."

"Geoffrey used to smoke. I couldn't get him to quit. That's the only thing we ever fought about."

He swallowed thickly as a strand tumbled loose and fell softly on his arm.

"Ouch. That pin hurts, Nick."

"Sorry." He placed the wig on her head and turned her toward him. The expression on her face—a mingling of doubt and resignation—made him smile.

"I look stupid, don't I?" she sighed.

"No. You look different, which was the whole idea."

She nodded. "I look stupid."

"Come on, try the dress."

"What is this?" she asked, holding up the garment. "One size fits all?"

"I know it's big, but I couldn't pass it up. It was—"

"Don't tell me. On sale, right?" She laughed. "Well, if we're a pair, we ought to fit together." She glanced at his tattered clothes. "What are you supposed to be, anyway? A bum?"

"From the odor of this jacket, I'd say I'm a drunk fisherman. Let's call you my wife. Only a wife would put up with a slob like me."

"All right, I'm your wife. Your very hungry wife. Can we eat now?"

He went to the window and looked down at the street. "I think it's dark enough. Why don't you change?"

She began to undress. Nick gazed steadily out at the night and struggled feverishly to ignore the tempting sounds behind him: the rustle of the blouse as it slid from her shoulders, the whisper of the skirt as it fell past her hips.

And it suddenly occurred to him what a ridiculous situation he was in.

For four years Nick O'Hara had managed to stay sanely independent. For those same four years, he'd kept his emotional doors tightly closed against women. And then, quite unexpectedly, Sarah Fontaine, of all people, had slipped in a back entrance. Sarah, who was obviously still in love with Geoffrey. Sarah, who in the course of two and a half weeks had managed to get him fired from his job, shot at and nearly run off the road. It was a spectacular beginning.

He couldn't wait to see what came next.

Chapter Nine

IN A TAVERN THICK WITH LAUGHTER and smoke, they sat at a wobbly table and split a bottle of burgundy. The wine was rough and undisciplined; farmer's wine, thought Sarah, as she downed her third glass. The room had grown too warm and too bright. At the next table, old men swapped tales over bread and ale and their laughter rang in her ears. A cat strolled through the chairs and quietly lapped at a saucer of milk by the bar. Hungrily Sarah took in every sight, every sound. It was so good to be out of hiding. So good to be out in the world again, if only for a night! Even the flecks of red wax on the tablecloth struck her as strangely beautiful.

Through the haze of cigarette smoke, she saw Nick smiling at her. His shoulders drooped in the tired slouch of a man who has labored long and hard all his life. Day-old stubble darkened his jaw. She could hardly believe he was the same man she'd met in a sleek government office only two weeks ago. But then, she was not the same woman. Fear and circumstances had changed them both.

"You did justice to your meal," he said, nodding at the empty plate. "Feeling better?"

"Much better. I was starved."

"Coffee?"

"In a bit. Let me finish my wine."

Shaking his head, he reached across the table and pushed her glass aside. "Maybe you'd better stop. We can't afford to get careless."

She regarded the displaced wineglass with irritation. As usual, Nick O'Hara was trying to run her life. It was time to fight back. Deliberately she slid the glass in front of her. "I've never been drunk in my life," she said.

"It's a very bad time to start."

Gazing at him steadily, she took a sip. "Is that a hobby of yours? Ordering people around?"

"What do you mean?"

"Since the day we met, you've been in total control, haven't you?"

"Over you? Or the situation?"

"Both."

"Hardly. Skipping off to London was your bright idea. Remember?"

"You never did say why you followed me. You were angry, weren't you?"

"I was mad as hell."

"Is that why you came? To wring my neck?"

"To be perfectly honest, I considered it." He raised the glass of wine to his lips and stared at her over the rim. "But I changed my mind."

"Why?"

"It was the way you looked at the police station. So exposed. Defenseless."

"I may be stronger than you think."

"Is that so?"

"I'm not a kid, Nick. I'm thirty-two years old. I've always taken care of myself."

"I'm not calling you incompetent. You're a very bright woman. A well-respected researcher."

"How do you know?"

"I've seen your security file."

"Oh, yes. That mysterious file. So what did you learn?"

He sat back. "Let's see. Sarah Gillian Fontaine, graduated University of Chicago. Co-researcher on half a dozen papers in the field of microbiology. Successful grant applicant for the last two years—not bad in this era of tight federal budgets. Oh, you're obviously bright." He paused. Quietly he added, "I also think you need my help."

They fell silent as the waiter came by to collect the bill. When the man was once more out of earshot, Nick said with dead seriousness, "I know you can take care of yourself, Sarah. Under ordinary circumstances. But these aren't ordinary circumstances."

She couldn't argue that point. "Okay," she sighed. "I'll admit it, Nick. I'm scared. And I'm tired. Tired of having to be careful all the time. Tired of checking the street before I walk. Wondering who's a friend and who isn't." She returned his steady gaze. "But don't underestimate me, Nick. I'll do anything to stay alive."

"Good. Because before this is over, you may have to turn into a dozen different women. Remember, you're not Sarah Fontaine anymore. You can't be, not in public. So leave her behind."

"How?"

"Make someone up. Down to the very last detail. *Become* that person. Now describe yourself. Who are you?"

She thought it over for a moment. "I'm—I'm a fisherman's wife…struggling to make ends meet…."

"Keep going."

"My life isn't easy. I'm tired a lot. And I have children—six of them—screaming all the time."

"Good. Go on."

"My husband, he…" She suddenly focused on Nick. "I mean you…you're not home very much."

"Often enough to give you six children," he pointed out with a smile.

"It's a crowded flat. All of us screaming at each other."

"Are we happy?"

"I don't know. Are we?"

He cocked his head thoughtfully. "Since I'm one half of this fabricated couple, I'll put in my two cents' worth. Yes, we're happy. I love my children, all five girls and a boy. I also love my wife. But I'm drunk a lot and I'm not very gentle."

"Do you beat me?"

"When you deserve it." Then he added softly, "But afterward I'm very, very sorry."

All at once they were staring at each other, the way two strangers do when they realize, for the first time, that they know each other well. His eyes softened. She suddenly found herself wondering how it would feel to lie beneath him in their hard bed. To feel the crushing weight of his body on hers. Though Geoffrey had been a gentle lover, there had been something cool and passionless about him. She sensed that Nick would be very different. He would take her like a starved man.

With an unsteady hand, she reached for her wineglass. "How long have we been married?" she asked.

"Fourteen years. I was twenty-four. You were…only eighteen."

"Then I'm sure my mama didn't approve."

"Neither did mine. But it didn't matter." He brushed his hand across hers. The touch of his fingers left her tingling. "We were crazy about each other."

Something about the tone of his voice made her stop speaking. This game of make-believe, so lighthearted a moment ago, had somehow changed. She heard the blood roaring in her ears, and everything melted away—the roomful of strangers, the laughter, the smoke. There was only Nick's face and his eyes, bright as silver, staring at her.

"Yes," he said again, so softly she barely heard him. "We were crazy about each other."

The sound of her glass hitting the table jerked her back to reality. She watched, bewildered, as a river of burgundy trickled across the tablecloth. The noise of the tavern suddenly swelled and burst over her.

Nick was already out of his chair, a napkin in hand. She sat mutely as he blotted up the wine. *I'm drunk,* she thought. *I must be drunk to be acting like this….*

"Sarah? What's wrong?"

Her chair flew backward as she bolted from the table and out of the tavern. The night air was like a cold slap in the face. Halfway down the alley she heard Nick's footsteps; he was running after her. She didn't stop until he grabbed her from behind and whirled her around. They were standing in the middle of a square. The buildings shone like gold in the lamplight. Around the shuttered flower carts, bruised petals lay scattered and fragrant on the cobblestones.

"Sarah. Listen to me."

"It's make-believe, Nick!" she said, trying desperately to pull free. "That's all it is! Just a silly game we're playing!"

"No. It's not a game anymore. Not for me."

He pulled her against him, pulled her so abruptly that she didn't have time to fight or even to feel surprised. She was only aware of the dizzy sensation of falling through darkness and of the jolt as she landed against his chest. She had no time to recover, no time to even draw the next breath.

Nick tasted of wine, of that rough farmer's burgundy, and she reeled like a drunken woman. She tried to make sense of what she felt, but there was no logic in this moment. Her lips parted. Her hands found their way to the back of his neck, and she felt the dampness of his hair.

"Sarah. Oh, Sarah," he groaned, pulling away to look at her. "It's not a game. It's real. More real than anything I've ever known."

"I'm afraid, Nick. Afraid of making another mistake. The way I did with Geoffrey—"

"I'm not Geoffrey. Hell, I'm just an ordinary guy, pushing middle age, not very rich. Probably not even very bright. I haven't got a hidden agenda. I just—Sarah, I'm *lonely*. I have been, for so long. I want you. Enough to get myself into one hell of a lot of hot water…."

With a sigh he drew her against him. She buried her face in the reeking wool jacket, but she no longer cared how it smelled; she only cared that Nick was wearing it, that it was his shoulder she was resting against, his arms that were holding her so tightly.

The drizzle turned to rain, and the drops splattered on the cobblestones. Laughing, Nick and Sarah dashed across the windows, past lovers huddled beneath an umbrella, past a bakery that smelled of coffee and bread.

By the time they'd climbed the stairway to their room, they were soaked. She stood beside the bed, rainwater dripping from her clothes, as Nick bolted the door. He turned and watched silently as she pulled the wig off and shook her hair free. Damp copper waves fell to her shoulders. The light above cast strange shadows on his face. Water trickled from his wet hair and down his cheek.

He came toward her, his eyes burning. At the touch of his

hands on her face, she shivered. Gently he covered her mouth with his. She tasted the wine again and then the rain, trickling down his cheek to her lips. His hands slid down her neck, to the top button of her dress. One by one the buttons came undone, and then the dress sagged open. As their mouths drank each other in, his fingers slid beneath the fabric of her dress. He took her breast in his hand.

They were both shivering now, but beneath their rain-soaked clothes, fires were raging out of control.

He shrugged off his jacket, letting it fall heavily to the floor. His wet shirt was like ice against her naked breasts. The light bulb above seemed to sway and recede. They sank to the mattress and the bedsprings creaked as his weight came down beside her. With eager hands he peeled off his shirt and threw it onto the floor. She remembered what she'd thought earlier that night, that Nick would not take her gently; he'd take her like a starved man.

But did she want him to? She was just as starved as he was; surely he sensed it! He also sensed her confusion. Frowning, he drew back and gazed at her. "You're shaking, Sarah," he whispered. "Why?"

"I'm afraid, Nick."

"Of what? Me?"

"I don't know. Of myself, I think.... I'm afraid of feeling guilty."

"About making love?"

She closed her eyes tightly. "Oh, God, what am I doing? He's alive, Nick! My husband's alive...."

Slowly his hand slid away from her breast and moved to her face, willing her to look at him. He was studying her, trying to see through her eyes, into her mind. His gaze stripped away all her defenses; never had she felt so naked. "What husband, Sarah? Simon Dance? Geoffrey? Some ghost who never existed?"

"Not a ghost. A man."

"And you'd call what you had a marriage?"

She shook her head. "No. I'm not stupid."

"Then let him go, Sarah!" He pressed his lips to her forehead and his breath warmed her hair. "Let the memories go. They weren't real. Get on with your life."

"But there's a part of me that still wonders...." She sighed. "I've learned something about myself, Nick, something I don't like. I loved an illusion. That's what he was, nothing but a dream. But I wanted him to be real. I made him real because I needed him." She shook her head sadly. "Need. That's what destroys us, you know. It makes us blind to everything else. And now I need you."

"Is that so bad?"

"I'm not sure of my motives anymore. Am I falling in love with you? Or am I just talking myself into it because I need you so much?"

Slowly, reluctantly, Nick began to button up her dress. "You won't know the answer to that one," he said, "until you're safe. Not till you're free to walk away from me. That's when you'll know."

She touched his lips. "It's not that I don't want you, Nick. It's just that…" Her voice faded.

He could see the inner struggle in her eyes, those utterly trusting, open windows that concealed no secrets. He wanted her. So badly, in fact, that just looking at her now was enough to awaken that familiar ache. He wanted her, but the time and circumstances were all wrong. She was still in a state of shock. And even if there'd never been a husband, Nick didn't think Sarah was a woman who gave herself easily to any man.

"You're disappointed," she said softly.

He forced a smile to his lips. "I'll admit it."

"It's just that—"

"Don't, Sarah." He hushed her. "There's no need to explain. Just lie here with me. Let me hold you."

She buried her face against the naked warmth of his shoulder. "Nick, my guardian angel."

His laughter was quick and gentle. "And here I was all set to tarnish the old halo!"

In silence they lay together, and the flames that had raged so brightly between them were slowly beaten back to a warm glow. If only they could find a cottage on a moor where they'd never be found! But those were wild, unreasonable dreams. Even if they came true, she wouldn't be content. Not while the past remained unresolved. Not while she still wondered about Geoffrey.

"What are we going to do, Nick?" she whispered.

"I'm working on it."

"We can't keep running."

"No. We could stretch the money out a few months, maybe. But even if it lasted forever, this cloud would always be hanging over our heads. You'd always wonder. You'd never really be free...." He looked at her with new intensity. "You have to close that part of your life," he said. "To do that, you have to find him."

He might as well have said they had to fly to the moon. It was just as impossible. How could they search all of Europe for one man? Even worse, how could they find him and not be caught themselves? They were innocents, forced into a game they didn't understand, a game with unseen players and unknown stakes, except one—their lives.

"We haven't got much to go on," said Nick. "I had to take a gamble today. I called Roy Potter."

She jerked out of his arms and stared at him. "You *called* him?"

"From a pay phone across town. Look, he already knows we're in Brussels. He's probably got an eye on our bank accounts. I guarantee that withdrawal we made this afternoon is now blinking on a CIA computer somewhere."

"Why did you call? I thought you didn't trust him!"

"I don't. But what if I'm wrong? What if he's really okay? Then at least I've got him thinking. Now he'll take a closer look at his people, if he hasn't already."

"He'll be searching for us...."

"Brussels is a big city. And we can always move on." His gaze turned insistent. "Sarah, I could have all the contacts in the world, but the rest is up to you. You were married to Geoffrey. Think, Sarah. Where would he go?"

"I've thought about it so long. I just don't know."

"Could he have left you a message? Somewhere you haven't looked?"

"I've only got my purse."

"Then let's start with that."

She grabbed the purse from the nightstand and emptied the contents onto the bed. There was only the usual clutter of a woman's handbag, plus the unopened bills they'd taken from Eve's mailbox.

Nick picked up the wallet and gave her a questioning glance.

"Go ahead," she said. "I don't have any secrets. Not from you."

One by one he slipped out the credit cards, then the photographs. For a few seconds, he paused at Geoffrey's picture before laying it on the bed. Over the years, snapshots of nieces and nephews had found their way into her wallet, and now they all spilled out.

"You've practically got a whole photo album in here," he observed.

"I don't have the heart to throw them away. Don't you carry any pictures?"

"Only my driver's license."

As he went through the scraps of paper she'd tucked away in various pockets—the phone numbers, the business cards, the little reminders—she found herself wondering why he carried no photographs. Had his divorce been that unfriendly? And why had there been no other women in his life since then? It reminded her how much she had to learn about him.

She put on her glasses and began to open Eve's mail.

There were three bills. After scanning the electricity statement, she flipped to the credit-card bill. Eve had used it only twice last month. Both items were purchases made at Harrod's, and both were listed as women's apparel.

She slit open the third bill. It was for the telephone. Quickly she glanced over the list of charges and was about to set it aside with the other two bills when one word leaped out at her from the bottom of the page: *Berlin.* It was a long-distance call, made on an evening two weeks earlier.

She clutched Nick's arm. "Look at this! The last entry."

His eyes widened, and he snatched the bill from her fingers. "This call was made the day of the fire!"

"She told me she tried to call him, remember? She must have known where he'd be in Berlin—"

"But to be so careless—to leave a trail like this—"

"Maybe it wasn't to him directly. Maybe this is a go-between. A contact. She didn't know what had happened to him or where he was. Nick, she must have been at wit's end…so she called Berlin. I wonder what this number is."

"We can't try it. Not yet."

"Why not?"

"A long-distance call at this point might scare off any contact. Let's wait till we hit Berlin." He began to throw things back into her purse. "Tomorrow we'll catch the commuter line out of the city. From Düsseldorf we can get the express. I'll buy all the tickets. I think it's better if we board separately and meet inside the train."

"What happens when we get to Berlin?"

"We'll call the number and see who answers. I've got an old friend in the Berlin consulate, Wes Corrigan. He might be able to do our legwork."

"Can we trust him?"

"I think so. We were posted together in Honduras. He was okay…."

"You said we couldn't trust anyone."

He nodded soberly. "We've got no choice, Sarah. It's a risk we have to take. I'm gambling on friendship…." He suddenly saw the worry in her eyes. Without a word he took her in his arms and pulled her down with him onto the pillows. It was a feeble attempt to banish the fear they both felt.

"What an awful feeling, to be caught without a future," she whispered. "If I look too far ahead, all I see is Eve."

"You're not Eve."

"That's what scares me. Eve knew what she was doing. She knew how to survive. Now she's dead. What chance do I have?"

"If it's any small comfort, you have me."

She touched his face and smiled. "Yes. I have you. Why am I so lucky?"

"Windmills, I guess."

"I don't understand."

"Lieberman said they used to call me Don Quixote, for all my tilting at windmills. Funny. I never knew I cut such a ridiculous figure."

"Am I another one of your windmills?"

"No. Not you." His lips brushed her hair. "You're more than that, now."

"You don't have to stay with me, Nick. I'm the one they want. You could go home—"

"Shh, Sarah."

"If you left me, I'd understand. Really I would."

"And what would you do on your own? You can't speak a word of German. Your French is—well, it's…quaint. No, you need me."

There it was again. *Need.* Yes, he was right. She needed him.

"Besides," he said, "I can't leave you now."

"Why not?"

He laughed softly. "Because I'm now an unemployed bum. And when this is all over, I plan to live off your income."

She rose up on her elbow and gazed at him. He was squinting up drowsily, and the bare lightbulb cast strange shadows over his face. "Nick. My sweet Don Quixote." Gently she lowered her mouth to his and placed a kiss on his lips. "Here's to Berlin," she whispered.

"Yes," he murmured, pulling her against him. "To Berlin."

DAWN, BRIGHT AND BEAUTIFUL. The train tracks, which a moment before had been a wet, dismal gray, suddenly gleamed like gold in the morning light. Wisps of steam curled from the rails. On the platform where Sarah now stood, commuters were already shedding raincoats and scarves. It would be warm today, and as bright as an April day should be. Schoolgirls dressed in uniforms lingered in the sunshine with their eyes closed and their faces turned like flowers to the sky. It had been a long, wet winter for Belgium, and the country was yearning for spring.

Nick and Sarah stood a dozen yards apart on the platform, exchanging only the briefest of glances. Nick was unrecognizable. With his cap pulled low and a cigarette hanging precariously from his mouth, he slouched against a platform post and scowled at the world.

From the distance came the clackity-clack of an approaching train. It was a signal that drew people from their benches. Like a wave, they flowed to the platform's edge as the train to Antwerp rolled gently to a stop. A stream of departing passengers emerged: businessmen in wool suits, students in regimental blue jeans and backpacks, smartly dressed women who would soon return home with their shopping bags full.

From her position near the end of the queue, Sarah saw Nick

crush his cigarette under his heel and board the train. Seconds later, his face appeared at a window. They did not look at each other.

The line grew shorter. Only a few yards more, and she would be safely on board. Then, from her peripheral vision, came a strange flash of light. A sudden premonition of fear made her turn slowly toward its source. It was sunshine, reflected off a pair of silvered glasses.

She froze. By the ticket window stood a man with pale hair, a man whose gaze was fixed on the train door. Though he was partly hidden behind the platform post, Sarah saw enough of his face to recognize him. Her blood ran cold. It was the same man who'd stared at her through the window of the blue Peugeot. The man with the death's-head grin.

And she was headed straight for his line of vision.

Chapter Ten

HER FIRST IMPULSE WAS TO TURN and run, to lose herself in the vast crowd of commuters. But any sudden movement now would surely draw his attention. She couldn't turn back. The man would see her break away and he would wonder. She had to keep moving forward, hoping against hope that he wouldn't recognize her.

Frantically she searched the train for the window where she'd seen Nick's face. If only she could signal for help! But the window was too far behind; she couldn't see him.

At the head of the line, an elderly passenger had dropped his ticket on the ground. Slowly he bent down to retrieve it. *Dear God, please hurry!* she prayed. The longer she stood here, the longer she could be studied. Swallowing her panic, she struggled to assume the role she'd chosen, that of a sickly Belgian wife. Keeping her eyes lowered, she clutched her purse tightly in her arms. Beneath her breast her heart was thudding. The black wig felt like a blessed shield against the man's eyes. Perhaps the wig would be enough. The man was looking for a woman with reddish-brown hair. Perhaps he wouldn't notice her.

"Madame?"

She flinched at the hand on her arm. An old man was tugging at her sleeve. Stupidly she stared at him as he spoke to her in loud, rapid French. She tried to jerk her arm away, but he trailed after her, waving a woman's scarf. Again he repeated his question and pointed to the ground. With sudden comprehension she shook her head and gestured that no, she had not dropped the scarf. The old man shrugged and walked away.

Almost in tears, she turned to climb aboard. But someone stood in her way.

She raised her head and saw her own terrified face reflected in a pair of mirrored sunglasses.

The blond man smiled. "Madame?" he said softly. "Come..."

"No. No!" she whispered, backing away.

He moved toward her and something in his hand glinted, an object whose image burned its way like a hot iron into her brain. She thought of the arc the four-inch blade would follow; she anticipated the pain of its thrust. She felt herself falling dizzily backward and then realized it wasn't her own movement, but the train's. It was leaving her behind.

She caught a glimpse of the train door receding slowly down the final fifty yards of the platform. Her last chance to escape.

Sarah sensed the man moving closer. His momentum carried him forward, toward a prey he thought would turn and run.

And she did run. But in the opposite direction. Instead of turning to flee, she dashed past him, after the departing train.

The unexpected move bought her a precious split second. He was caught totally off balance.

The train was picking up speed. Only a dozen yards of platform were left before it would move beyond her reach. Her feet seemed weighted with lead; she heard his footsteps behind her, and they were gaining. With her heart close to exploding, she sprinted the last few yards. The grab bar hovered only inches away. Then her fingers touched cold steel. She fought to hold on, to pull herself aboard.

She scrambled onto the steps and collapsed, gasping for air. Buildings and gardens flashed by, fast-moving images of light and color. The ache in her throat dissolved into an incomprehensible sob of relief. *I made it,* she thought. *I made it....*

A shadow swung across the sunlight. The step creaked with a terrible new weight, and a chill settled like frost on her shoulders, a foreshadowing of her own death. She had no strength left to fight and nowhere left to retreat. She could do nothing but huddle there as the man towered above her.

The pace of the train quickened. It pounded in her head and drowned out everything else, even the thudding of her heart. *You can't be real,* she thought. *You're not a man, you're a nightmare!*

Paralyzed, she watched as he bent toward her, blotting out the last bits of sunshine. She waited to be swallowed up in his shadow.

Then, from somewhere behind her, came a low sound of rage. She sensed the movement more than saw it, a savage thrust of a foot as it connected with flesh. The shadow looming before her toppled backward with a groan.

The blond man seemed to hang forever, suspended in an endless fall. Sunlight flickered on the sallow face; the glasses slid away. Almost as if by magic, he dropped from the steps, and his parting curse was lost in the train's clatter. She caught one last glimpse of him, scrambling to his knees in the gravel below, and then he disappeared from view. Somehow she was still living, breathing; the nightmare had been shaken free.

"Sarah! My God...."

Rough hands wrenched her upward, away from the edge, away from death. With a shudder she fell into Nick's arms. There he held her so tightly she could feel the drumbeat of his heart.

"It's all right," he murmured over and over. "It's all right."

"Who is he?" she cried. "Why won't he leave us alone!"

"Sarah, listen to me. *Listen!* We've got to get off this train. We've got to change course before he intercepts us—"

And then what? she wanted to scream. Where did they go next?

He glanced at the scenery hurtling past. They were moving too fast to jump off. "The next stop," he said. "We'll have to travel some other way. Walk. Hitchhike. Once we cross the Dutch border, we can catch another train east."

She clung to him, not really hearing his words. The danger had taken on wild, irrational proportions. The man in the sunglasses had turned into something more than human. He was supernatural, beyond any horror that existed in the real world. She closed her eyes, and in her mind she saw him waiting for her at the next train station, and the next. Even Nick could not hold him off forever.

She stared ahead at the train tracks and prayed that the next stop would come soon. They had to get off before they were trapped. Blending into the countryside was their only chance.

But as far as she could see, the tracks stretched on without end. And it seemed to her that the train had turned into a steel coffin, bearing them straight into the arms of a killer.

KRONEN EXAMINED HIS bruised face in the mirror, and a wave of unspeakable anger rose inside him like hot magma. For the second time, the woman had escaped. He had had her in his grasp, there on the platform, but she had startled him by dashing off in an unexpected direction. Then, to be kicked like an animal off the train just as he'd caught up with her—that was the part that enraged him most.

Kronen slammed his fist into the mirror. Twice, this man, Nick O'Hara, had gotten in his way. Who was he, anyway? CIA? A friend of Simon Dance? Whoever he was, he'd be a dead man when Kronen found him and Sarah again.

Finding them, however, was going to be a difficult matter.

They had disappeared. By the time Kronen's associates had intercepted the train at Antwerp, the woman and her companion had vanished. They could be anywhere. He had no idea where they were headed or why.

He'd have to call the old man again for help. The prospect made Kronen at first apprehensive and then angry—at the woman, for escaping, at her companion, for interfering. She'd pay dearly for all the trouble she'd caused him.

Kronen put on his sunglasses. The bruise was plainly visible over his right cheekbone. It was a humiliating reminder that he'd been bested by such an unassuming creature as Sarah Fontaine.

But this was only a temporary setback. The old man would be looking for her, and his eyes were everywhere, even in the most unexpected places. Yes, they would find her again.

She couldn't hide forever.

IT WAS THE pigeons flapping overhead that awakened Sarah. She opened her eyes. By the gentle light of dusk, she saw smooth stone walls, the fluttering of wings and the mill's wooden shaft revolving slowly. A pigeon settled on a window ledge high above and began to coo. The gears of the windmill creaked and groaned, like the timbers of an old ship. As she lay there in the straw, she was filled with a strange sense of wonder, and a fear that she had few such moments left to live. Oh, but she was so hungry for life! She'd never *known* such hunger. Only now, as the pigeons flapped and the sunlight faded, did she realize how precious each moment had become. And she owed them all to Nick.

She turned and smiled at him. He was sleeping beside her in the straw, his hands clasped behind his neck, his chest rising and falling. Poor, exhausted Nick. They had hitched a ride across the Dutch border; then they had walked, miles and miles it seemed. Now they were less than a mile from the next train station. But Sarah had balked at the thought of boarding another train. We'll wait until dark, he'd said. They'd found a place to rest, a windmill in the fields, and in their stone tower they'd both dropped immediately to sleep.

Berlin, she thought. *Will we ever make it?*

She curled up against Nick and listened to his steady breathing. With a shudder he awakened, and his arm came around and encircled her.

"It'll be dark soon," she whispered.

"Mmm-hmm."

"I wish we never had to leave this place."

He sighed deeply. "So do I."

For a moment they lay together, listening to the creak of the gears, to the sails flapping in the wind. Suddenly he laughed.

"How ironic," he said. "Brave Don Quixote, hiding out in a windmill. I can hear 'em now, laughing in London."

"Laughing? Why?"

"Because dumb O'Hara's back in trouble."

She smiled. "In trouble, maybe. But not dumb. Never dumb."

"Thanks for the vote."

She studied him curiously. "You sound so bitter, Nick. Is the foreign service that bad?"

"No. It's a great job. If you can smother your conscience. When you join up, they make you sign this paper. It says, essentially, 'When in public, I swear to always toe the party line.' I signed it."

"Big mistake, huh?"

"When I think of all the asinine policies I had to uphold. And then there were the cocktail parties. Night after night of standing around, trying not to get drunk on the sherry. The games we used to play with the Russians! Baiting Ivan, we called it. We were like little kids, trying to learn each other's secrets."

"Ah. Diplomacy is hell."

He smiled. "But not as bad as war."

"I used to think you were just another bureaucrat."

"Yep, that's me, shuffling papers all day."

"Oh, Nick, you're the most unbureaucratic man I know! And believe me, I've known quite a few!"

"Men?"

"No, silly. Bureaucrats. Those guys in Washington who dole out my grant money. You're not like them. You're...*involved*."

"Damn right I'm involved," he said with a laugh.

"Not just with me. With the world. Most people can't be bothered with anything outside their immediate existence. But you go out and fight for strangers."

"No, I don't. I used to. When I was in college, all those issues mattered to me. Believe it or not, Tim Greenstein and I once spent a very cold night in jail. We got arrested for illegal assembly on the chancellor's doorstep. But you know, these days, people don't seem to care about the world anymore. Maybe we all got older." He touched her face. "Or maybe we all found more important things to care about."

The pigeons suddenly flapped their wings, and straw fluttered down like bits of gold raining in from the window. They both sat up, and he began picking the pieces of straw from her hair.

"And what were you like in college?" he asked. "Very well-behaved, I'd imagine."

"Diligent."

"Of course."

"Up until now I was very good at ignoring distractions."

"Such as men?"

She tapped his nose lightly and grinned. "Such as men."

For a long time they looked at each other. Her ears were filled with the sound of her own heartbeat and the creak of the mill as it turned in the wind.

"Now I wonder what I missed," she whispered.

"You did what was important to you. That's what matters. You liked your work, didn't you?"

She nodded. Rising, she went to the doorway and looked at the newly plowed fields. "Yes. There's something nice about having the big picture right there, in my microscope. Being able to move it closer or farther away with just the flick of a lens. It's all so safe, so under my control. But you know, it never struck me till now. There are no windows in my laboratory. No windows to look out of..." She shook her head and sighed. "Now it seems like nothing's under my control anymore. But I've never felt more alive. Or more afraid of dying."

"Don't talk about it, Sarah. Don't even think about it." He came up behind her and turned her around so that she was facing him. "We'll just take one day, one moment, at a time. That's all we can do."

"I know."

"You're strong, Sarah. In some ways you're stronger than I am. Only now do I realize that...."

He kissed her then, kissed her hard and long, like a man hungry for the taste of her. In the stone tower above, the birds cooed, and the last light of day faded. Blessed night, the safety of darkness, fell over the fields.

With a groan Nick drew back, breathing heavily. "If we keep this up, we'll sure as hell miss the train. Not that I'd mind, but..." He pressed his lips once more against hers. "Now's the time to move. Are you ready?"

She took a deep breath and nodded. "I'm ready."

THE OLD MAN had a dream.

Nienke was standing before him with her long hair tied in a delft-blue kerchief. Her wide, plain face was streaked with garden dirt, and she was smiling. "Frans," she said, "you must build a stone path through the rosebushes so our friends can walk among the flowers. Now they have to walk around the bushes, never through the center, where all the pretty lavenders and yellows are. They miss them completely. I have to lead them through, and then their shoes get muddy. A stone path, Frans, like the one we had in our cottage in Dordrecht."

"Of course," he said. "I'll ask the gardener to build it."

Nienke smiled. She came toward him. But when he reached out to touch her, her blue kerchief suddenly vanished. What had once been Nienke's hair was now a bright halo of fire. He tried to tear it off before it engulfed her face, but great clumps of hair came off in his hands. The more he tried to tear the flames away, the more hair and flesh he pulled off. Bit by bit, trying to save her, he tore his wife apart. He looked down and saw that his arms were on fire, but he felt no pain, nothing at all, except a silent scream exploding in his throat, as he watched Nienke leave him forever.

IT TOOK WES CORRIGAN a good five minutes to answer the pounding on his back door. When he finally opened it, he could only stand there in his pajamas and bathrobe, blinking in surprise at his nocturnal visitors. Two people stood outside. At first glance he thought them strangers. The man was tall, white-haired, unshaven. The woman was dressed in a nondescript sweater and a gray cap. Their breath steamed in the cool night air.

"What's happened to the old sense of hospitality?" asked Nick.

Wes gaped. "What the—Nick? Is that *you*?"

"Can we come in?"

"Uh, yeah! Sure!" Still dazed, Corrigan gestured them into his kitchen and closed the door. He was a short, compact man in his midthirties. Beneath the harsh kitchen light, his skin was sallow and his eyes were puffy with sleep. He looked at his two visitors and shook his head in bewilderment. Then his gaze settled on Nick's white hair. "My God. Has it been that long?"

Nick shook his head and laughed. "Talcum powder. But any wrinkles you see are mine. Is anyone else in the house?"

"Just my cat. Nick, what the hell is going on?"

Nick strode past him, out of the kitchen and into the living room.

"Was I supposed to know about all this?" called Wes. There was no answer from Nick. He turned to Sarah just as she pulled off her cap. "Uh, hello. I'm Wes Corrigan. And who're you?"

"Sarah."

"Yeah, nice to meet you. Is this Nick's idea of a cheap date?"

"The street looks clean," said Nick, stalking into the kitchen.

"Sure, it's clean. They sweep it every Thursday."

"What I meant was, you're not under surveillance."

Corrigan looked sheepish. "Well, actually I live kind of a dull life. Hey, come *on*, buddy. What gives?"

Nick sighed. "We're in a little trouble, Wes."

Corrigan nodded. "I was starting to come to that conclusion. Who's after you?"

"The Company. Plus or minus a few others."

Wes stared at him incredulously. Quickly he went to the kitchen door, glanced outside and slid the bolt shut. He turned back to Nick. "You've got the *CIA* after you? What'd you do? Sell a few national secrets?"

"It's a long story. We're going to need your help."

Wes nodded tiredly. "I was afraid of that. Look, sit down, sit down. God, the kitchen's a mess. I don't usually entertain at two in the morning. I'll make us up a fresh pot of coffee. You hungry?"

Nick and Sarah looked at each other and smiled. "Famished," said Sarah.

Corrigan went to the refrigerator, "Bacon and eggs, coming up."

It took them an hour to tell him everything. By that time the coffeepot was empty, Nick and Sarah had polished off half a dozen eggs between them, and Corrigan was wide-awake and worried.

"Why do you think this guy Potter's involved?" asked Wes.

"He's obviously the case officer. It was his word that got Sarah released. He must've ordered those agents to tail us to Margate. But in Margate things all went wrong. While the Company isn't exactly a tight outfit, they don't usually screw up this royally without a little help. Someone had that agent killed. Someone who then proceeded to fire on us."

"The man with the sunglasses. Whoever he is." Wes shook his head. "I don't like what you're up against."

"Neither do I."

Corrigan looked thoughtful. "So you want me to check out the file on Magus. Could be tough, Nick. If they've got it super-classified, I'm not going to be able to touch it."

"Get us what you can. We can't do it alone. Until Sarah finds Geoffrey and gets some answers, we're out in the cold."

"Yeah. That's a mighty uncomfortable place to be."

He walked them to the back door. Outside, the stars were burning in a crisp clear sky.

"Where are you two sleeping?" asked Wes.

"We have a room near the Ku-damm."

"You could sack out on my floor."

"Too risky. We were lucky to get through the East German checkpoint. By now they know we're in the city. If they're smart they'll be watching your house soon."

"So how do I get hold of you?"

"I'll phone you. The name'll be Barnes. Get back to me from an outside line. It's better if you don't know where we are."

"Don't you trust me?"

Nick hesitated on the doorstep. "You know it's not that, Wes," he said, nudging Sarah into the darkness.

"Then what is it?"

"This is nasty business. It's better if you don't get too deeply involved."

Nick and Sarah turned and headed into the night. But as they left, they heard Wes say behind them, softly, "Buddy, you just got me involved."

AS DAWN BRIGHTENED outside their window, Sarah lay snuggled in Nick's arms. Despite their exhaustion, neither of them could sleep; too much depended on what happened today. At least they were no longer alone. Wes Corrigan was on their side.

Nick stirred, his breath suddenly warming her hair. "When this is over," he whispered, "I want us to be just like we are now. Just like this."

"When this is over…" She sighed and stared up at the bare white ceiling. "I wonder if it'll ever be over. If I'll ever go home again."

"We'll go home. Together."

She looked at him with longing. "Will we?"

"I promise. And Nick O'Hara always keeps his promises."

She turned her face into the hollow of his shoulder. "Oh,

Nick. I want you so much. I don't know anymore if I'm blind or scared or in love. I'm so mixed up."

"No, you aren't."

"Aren't you confused? Just a little?"

"About you? No. It sounds crazy, Sarah, but I really think I know you. You're the first woman I can say that about."

"What about your wife? Didn't you know her?"

"Lauren?" His voice, so warm and gentle a moment before, all at once sounded hollow. "Yeah, I guess I did know her. When it was over."

"What went wrong, Nick?"

He lay back against the pillows. "You know the old saying? That there are two sides to every story? Our marriage was a perfect example. If you asked Lauren what went wrong, she'd say it was my fault. She'd say I didn't understand her needs."

"And if I asked you?"

He shrugged. "As time passes you get a sense of perspective. I guess I'd have to say it was no one's fault, really. But I can't forget what she did." He turned to Sarah with such a look of sadness that she could almost reach out and touch his pain. "We were married—oh, three years. She liked Cairo. She liked the embassy whirl. She was an outstanding foreign service wife. I think that's one reason she married me. She thought I could show her the world. Unfortunately my career required going to places she didn't quite consider civilized."

"Like Cameroon?"

"That's right. I wanted that post. It would only have been for a year or two. But she refused flat out to go. Then I got offered London, which made her happy. It might have all worked out eventually. Except…" His voice trailed off. Sarah felt his arm stiffen beneath her shoulder.

"You don't have to tell me, Nick. Not if you don't want to."

"People always say time heals all wounds. But sometimes it doesn't. You see, she got pregnant. I found out in London. She didn't tell me—the embassy doctor had to come up and slap me on the back with the news. Told me I was going to be a father. I was—hell, Sarah, for about six short hours I was so high they had to peel me off the ceiling. Then I got home. I found out she didn't want it."

There was nothing Sarah could say to ease his pain. She could only hope that when he'd finished talking, he'd find some comfort in her arms.

"Sometimes I wonder," he said. "I wonder what it would have looked like. Whether it would have been a boy or a girl. What color its hair would've been. I catch myself counting the years, thinking of all the birthdays it never had. I don't have much family. I wanted that baby. I practically begged her for it. But Lauren called it an inconvenience." He looked at Sarah with bewilderment in his eyes. "An *inconvenience*. What was I supposed to say to that?"

"There's no answer you can give."

"No. There isn't. That's when I realized I didn't know her. We had all kinds of fights then. She flew home and…took care of the problem. She never came back. I got the divorce papers a month later. Special delivery. It's been four years now."

"Do you ever miss her?"

"No. I was almost relieved when the papers came. I've been on my own ever since. It's easier that way. No pain. Nothing." He touched her face and a smile formed on his lips. "Then you walked into my office. You with your funny glasses. The first day I saw you, I wasn't paying attention to your looks. But you took off those glasses and then all I saw were your eyes. That's when I wanted you."

"I'm going to throw those old glasses away."

"Never. I love them."

She laughed, grateful for the kind and funny things lovers say. For the first time in her life, she almost felt beautiful.

A breeze blew in the open window, carrying with it the faint smell of exhaust from the street below. Berlin was waking up. Sounds of traffic drifted in: the honk of a horn, a bus roaring by. The night was over. It was time to make that phone call.

"Sarah? Have you thought about what happens when we find him?"

"I can't think that far ahead."

"You still love him."

She shook her head. "I don't know who I loved anymore. Not

Simon Dance. Maybe the man I loved never existed. He was never real."

"But I am," whispered Nick. "I'm real. And unlike Geoffrey Fontaine, I've got nothing to hide."

Chapter Eleven

IS THIS WHERE I'LL FIND HIM?

The thought played over and over in Sarah's mind as they rode the bus north, past broad, clean streets, past avenues where shopkeepers were out in the early morning sunshine, sweeping the sidewalks.

A half hour earlier, they had called the number on Eve's phone bill and learned it was a flower shop. The woman on the other end had been courteous and helpful. Yes, the shop was easy to find. It was several miles north of the Ku-damm. The bus stop was only a block away.

It was not a good part of town. Sarah watched as the broad streets gave way to alleys littered with glass and a neighborhood of squat, shabby houses. Here, children played in the streets, and old men sat dully on their porch steps. Was Geoffrey hiding in the back room of one of these houses? Was he waiting for her in the basement of a flower shop?

At a street corner, they stepped off the bus. A block away they found the address. The shop was small, with dirty windows. On the sidewalk just outside sat plastic buckets overflowing with roses. A tiny brass bell tinkled as they opened the door.

The smell of flowers overwhelmed them. Inside, a plump

woman of about fifty smiled at them across a counter piled high with satin ribbons and roses and baby's breath. She was making bouquets. For a few seconds, her gaze lingered on Sarah, then it settled on Nick. "*Guten tag,*" she said.

Nick nodded. "*Guten tag.*" Casually he wandered about the shop, noting the refrigerators with their sweating glass doors and the shelves of vases and china figurines and plastic flowers. Near the door was a funeral wreath, packed in cellophane and ready for delivery. The shop woman clipped the thorns from the roses and began to wind wire ribbon around the stems. It was a bride's bouquet. She hummed as she worked, not at all perturbed by the silence of her two visitors. At last she put the bouquet down and her eyes met Sarah's.

"*Ja?*" she asked softly.

Sarah pulled out Geoffrey's picture and placed it on the counter. The woman stared at it but said nothing.

Nodding at the photograph, Nick asked her a question in German. She shook her head. "Geoffrey Fontaine," he said. The woman didn't react. "Simon Dance," he said. Again the woman only stared at him blankly.

"But you must know him!" Sarah blurted. "He's my husband—I have to find him."

"Sarah, let me—"

"He's waiting for me. If you know where he is, call him. Tell him I'm here!"

"Sarah, she doesn't understand you."

"She has to understand! Nick, ask her about Eve. Maybe she knows Eve."

At Nick's questions the woman shrugged again. She knew nothing at all about Geoffrey. Or if she did know, she wasn't talking.

To have all their hopes end like this! After traveling halfway across Europe, they had reached nothing but a dead end. Sick with disappointment, Sarah slipped the picture back into her purse. The German woman calmly turned her attention to wrapping the bouquets in green tissue paper.

Sarah turned miserably to Nick. "What do we do now?"

He was staring off in frustration at the funeral wreath. "I don't know," he muttered. "I just don't know."

The shop woman began tearing off sheets of tissue paper. The soft ripping noise made Sarah shudder.

"Why here?" she murmured. "Why would she call this place? There had to be a reason."

Sarah wandered to the refrigerator and stared through the glass at the buckets of carnations and roses. The smell of flowers was beginning to sicken her. It reminded her too vividly of a painful day on a cemetery hilltop just two weeks ago. "Please, Nick," she said quietly. "Let's leave."

Nick dipped his head at the shop woman. *"Danke schön."*

The woman smiled and beckoned to Sarah. Puzzled, Sarah went to the counter. The woman held out a single rose with a tissue-wrapped stem and murmured, *"Auf wiedersehen."* Then, gazing steadily, the woman gave the rose to Sarah. Their eyes met. It was only the briefest of looks, but in that instant Sarah understood its significance; something had just been passed to her. Something for her eyes only.

Nodding, she accepted the rose. *"Auf wiedersehen!"* she said. Then she turned and followed Nick out of the shop.

Outside, Sarah clutched the rose tightly in her fist. Her mind was racing; the stem felt like a hot poker. It took all her willpower not to tear away the tissue paper and read the message she knew was written inside. But something about the woman's eyes had conveyed another message, a warning. A look that said, *You are in danger, from someone nearby.*

But the only person nearby was Nick.

Nick, the man she trusted, the man she loved.

Since Geoffrey's disappearance, Nick had been her friend, her protector. Whenever she'd needed him, he'd been there. Had it been mere coincidence? Or had it all been planned? If so, it had worked brilliantly. They had picked the right man for the job. They had known she'd be frightened and lonely, that she'd be desperate for a friend, for someone to trust. Then, like magic, Nick had appeared in London. Since then he'd been with her almost twenty-four hours a day. Why?

She didn't want to believe it, but the answer was staring her right in the face. Surveillance.

No, she couldn't be sure. And she loved him.

But the woman's look of warning had burned into her memory; she couldn't forget it.

The bus ride seemed to take forever. All the way back, Nick's hand rested on her knee. His touch burned like a brand into her skin. She wanted to meet his eyes, but she was afraid of what she might see. Afraid that he would read her fear.

As soon as they reached the *pension*, she fled into the bathroom at the end of the hall and bolted the door. With shaking hands she peeled the tissue paper from the rose's stem. Beneath the naked light bulb by the sink, she read the message. It was in English and had been scrawled hurriedly in pencil.

Potsdamer Platz, one o'clock tomorrow.

Trust no one.

She stared at the last three words. *Trust no one.* Its meaning was unmistakable. She had been careless. She could afford to make no more mistakes. Geoffrey's life depended on her.

Savagely she ripped the note into a dozen pieces and flushed it down the toilet. Then she headed back to the room, to Nick.

She couldn't leave him yet. First she had to be certain. She loved Nick O'Hara, and in her heart she knew he would never hurt her. But she had to know: for whom was he working?

Tomorrow, in Potsdamer Platz, she'd find her answers.

"WE WERE BEGINNING to think you wouldn't make it," said Nick.

Wes Corrigan looked uneasy as he took a chair across from Nick and Sarah. "So was I," he muttered, glancing over his shoulder.

"Trouble?" said Nick.

"I'm not sure. That's what bothers me. It's like one of those old horror flicks. You're never sure when the monster's going to leap at you." He slouched down, in a vain attempt to hide in the chair's depths.

In search of a discreet meeting place, they had come to this dark café. Their table was dimly lighted by a single candle; around them were people who spoke in whispers, people who purposefully minded their own business. No one looked twice at the two men and a woman sitting at the corner table.

Almost by instinct, Sarah's eyes searched the room for a back entrance. If things went wrong, she'd need an easy escape. The door was clearly marked, but it would require a dash across the room. She picked out her route through the tables and chairs. Three seconds, that's all it should take. If it came to that, she'd be on her own. She could no longer count on Nick.

It struck her then how much her existence had changed. A few weeks ago, she'd been an ordinary woman, living an ordinary life. Now she was scouting out escape routes.

"I tell you, Nick," said Wes, after he'd ordered a beer. "This whole thing has got me spooked."

"What's happened?"

"Well, to begin with, you were right. I'm being watched. Not long after you left last night, a van showed up across the street from my house. It's been there ever since. I had to sneak out the back door, through the alley. I'm not used to this kind of life. Makes me nervous."

"Have you got anything for us?"

Wes looked around again, then lowered his voice. "First of all, I went back to review my file on Geoffrey Fontaine's death. When I called you a few weeks ago, I had all the data in front of me. The pathology report, the police report. I had a whole file of notes, the photocopy of his passport…"

"And?"

"They're missing." He glanced at Sarah. "Everything. It's *all* gone. Not just my file. It's disappeared from the computer."

"What *have* you got, then?"

"On Geoffrey Fontaine? Nothing. It's as if I never filed that report."

"They can't erase a man's existence," Sarah pointed out.

Wes shrugged. "Someone's trying to. I can't be sure who did it. We've got a big staff in our mission. It could have been any of a dozen."

They stopped talking as the waitress served their suppers: warm, crusty bread; escargots sizzling in garlic and butter; wedges of Gouda cheese.

"What about Magus?" asked Nick.

Wes dabbed a drop of butter from his chin. "I was getting to that. Okay, after I found out Geoffrey Fontaine had been dropped from the records, I hunted around for info on Magus. Except for the obvious biblical references, there's nothing under that name."

"Doesn't surprise me," said Nick.

"I'm not cleared for the top secret stuff. And I think this Magus fellow falls into that category."

"So we're left with nothing," said Sarah.

"Not exactly."

Nick frowned. "What did you find?"

Wes reached into his jacket and pulled out an envelope, which he tossed on the table. "I found Simon Dance."

Nick grabbed the envelope. Inside were two pages. "My God. Look at this!" He passed the pages to Sarah.

It was a photocopy of a six-year-old visa application. Included was a poor-quality reproduction of a passport photo. The eyes were strangely familiar. But had Sarah seen this man on the street, she would have passed him by without a second glance.

Sarah's heart was beating fast. "This is Geoffrey," she said softly.

Wes nodded. "At least that's how he looked six years ago. When his name was Dance."

"How did you get this stuff?" asked Nick.

"Whoever cleaned out Geoffrey Fontaine's file didn't bother to dispose of Dance's. Maybe the file's too old. Maybe they figured the face and name have changed, so why bother?"

Sarah flipped to the next page. Simon Dance, she saw, had had a German passport, with an address in Berlin. His occupation had been architect. He was married.

"Why did he apply for this visa?" she asked.

"It was a tourist visa," Wes pointed out.

"No, I mean *why*?"

"Maybe he wanted to see the sights."

"Or scout out the possibilities," added Nick.

"Have you checked this old Berlin address?" asked Sarah.

Wes nodded. "It's gone. Got demolished last year to make way for a high rise."

"Then we're left with no leads," said Nick.

"I've got one last source," offered Wes. "An old friend, who used to work for the Company. He retired last year. Got disgusted with the practice of spying. He just might know about Simon Dance. And Magus."

"I hope so," said Nick.

Wes rose. "Look, I can't hang around too long. That van's waiting outside my house. Call me tomorrow around noon. I should have something by then."

"Same procedure?"

"Yeah. Give me fifteen minutes after you call. I can't always get to a pay phone right away." He looked at Sarah. "Let's hope this thing's resolved soon. You must be tired of running."

She nodded. And as she gazed across the table at the two men, she thought that it wasn't the lack of sleep or the irregular meals or even the minute-to-minute fear that was wearing her down. It was the anxiety of not knowing whom to trust.

"YOU'VE BEEN AWFULLY quiet," Nick said. "Is something wrong?"

They were walking the streets back to their *pension*. Night had turned the city garish; darkness was what Sarah longed for, a place away from the traffic and the neon billboards. She gazed up at the sky, but there were no stars; there was only the gray haze of reflected city lights.

"I don't know, Nick," she sighed. She stopped and turned to him. Beneath a flashing billboard, they stared at each other as the neon lights glowed red and white and red on their faces. His eyes were impenetrably dark, the eyes of a stranger. "Can I really trust you, Nick?"

"Oh, Sarah. What a ridiculous question."

"If only we'd met some other way! If only we were like everyone else—"

He touched her face, a quiet gesture of reassurance. "What happened, happened. We take it from here. You just have to trust me."

"I trusted Geoffrey," she whispered.

"I'm Nick, remember?"

"Who *is* Nick O'Hara? I wonder, sometimes. I wonder if you're real, if you're flesh and blood. I worry that someday you'll just dissolve before my eyes."

"No, Sarah." He drew her into his arms. "After a while you'll stop wondering. You'll know I'm real. It might take a year, two years, maybe even a dozen years. But you'll learn to trust me."

Trust? she thought bitterly. Trust was something you learned as a baby, something that was supposed to keep you wrapped up and warm, like a blanket. It was one of life's cruel illusions. She'd outgrown the concept. She'd discovered how alone everyone really was.

But she hadn't outgrown desire. Or need.

A short time later, as they stood holding each other in their room, she found herself hungrily storing up what might be her last memories of Nick: his smile, his laughter, the smell of his skin. From somewhere in the building came the scratchy music of a phonograph, a German ballad, sung by a woman with a sad, throaty voice. It was a song meant for a cabaret, a song for a room of darkness and smoke. The music drifted lazily through the night, into their open window.

Nick turned off the light. The music swelled with sadness; it was a song of parting, a woman's farewell. As long as she lived, Sarah would carry that song in her heart. Then, through the shadows, Nick came to her. The music rose, note upon note of sorrow, as she buried herself in his arms. She sensed him struggling to understand. How she wanted to tell him everything! She loved him. Only now, with her trust in him stretched to a mere thread, did she recognize it. She loved him.

The music faded and died. The only sound left was their breathing.

"Make love to me," she whispered. "Please. Now. Make love to me."

His fingers slid down her face and lingered on her cheek. "Sarah, I don't understand.... There's something wrong...."

"Don't ask me anything. Just make love to me. Make me forget. I want to forget."

"Oh, God," he groaned, trapping her face in his hands. "I'll make you forget...."

All at once she was drowning in the taste of his mouth. The hunger that had always burned just beneath Nick's cool surface suddenly burst free. His fingers slid down her neck to her blouse. Slowly the fabric parted, and she felt his hand and then his mouth close eagerly over her breast. She was barely conscious of the skirt falling from her hips; all her awareness centered on what his mouth was doing to her.

She sank down into the bed. He toppled like a tree over her, crushing the breath from her lungs.

"I've wanted you," he murmured, raking his fingers through her hair, "from the very first day. It's all I've thought about, seeing you like this. Having you, tasting you." With sudden recklessness he began to tug at his shirt, and in his clumsiness a button tore loose and fell on her naked belly. He pushed the button aside and, bending down, he reverently kissed the flesh where it had lain. Then he rose up and shed the last of his clothes.

Through the window the faint city lights shone in on his bare shoulders. She could see only a faint outline of his face; he was just a shadow hovering above her, a shadow that took on fire and substance as their bodies met. Their mouths found each other. It was a frantic kiss, too passionate to be gentle; he was invading her mouth, devouring her. With both body and soul, she welcomed him in.

His entry was slow, hesitant, as though he was afraid he might hurt her. But in his fever he soon lost all restraint. He was no longer Nick O'Hara; he was something wild, something untamed. Yet even as the end came, even as he threw himself against her, there was a tenderness between them, a caring that went beyond need.

Only when he had fallen exhausted beside her and their hearts had slowed did Nick wonder again about her silence. He knew she had wanted him; she had responded in a way that had exceeded any fantasy. Just lying beside her now, feeling her head against his chest, stirred his hunger again. But something was wrong. He touched her cheek and felt the dampness. Something had changed.

Later he would ask her. After they'd spent all their passion on each other, he would make her tell him why she was crying. Not now. She wasn't ready. And he wanted her again; he couldn't wait any longer.

As he slid into her a second time, he forgot all those questions. He forgot everything. There was only Sarah, so soft and warm. Tomorrow he would remember what it was he had to ask.

Tomorrow.

"GOOD MORNING, MR. CORRIGAN. May we have a word with you?"

From the tone of his voice, Wes knew at once this was not a social visit. He glanced up from the stack of papers on his desk and saw two men standing inside the doorway. One was rumpled and on the heavy side; the other was tall and a little too sleek, even for a Company man. They were not smiling.

Wes cleared his throat. "Hello, gentlemen. How can I help you?"

The tall man sat down and looked Wes straight in the eye. "Nick O'Hara. Where is he?"

Wes felt his voice freeze up. It took him a few seconds to regain his poise, but by then it was too late. He'd given himself away. Shoving aside the stack of papers, he said, "Uh—Nick O'Hara… Isn't he still in Washington?"

The chubby man snorted. "Don't play games with us, Corrigan!"

"Who's playing games? Who are you guys, anyway?"

The tall man said, "The name's Van Dam. And this is Mr. Potter."

The Company, thought Wes. *Oh, boy, am I in trouble. Now what do I do?* He rose from his chair, trying hard to look indignant. "Look, it's Saturday. I've got other things to do. Maybe you could book an appointment for a weekday like everyone else?"

"Sit down, Corrigan."

Wes reached for the phone to call a security officer, but Potter intercepted his hand before he could hit the button. Fear shot through Wes for the first time. Verbal aggression was one thing; actually manhandling him was another. These guys were playing rough. Wes didn't like violence. Especially when it involved his own body.

"We want O'Hara," said Potter.

"I can't help you."

"Where is he?"

"I told you. Washington. As a matter of fact, I called him just two weeks ago, on a consular matter." Wes looked down at his trapped hand. "Now if you'll kindly let me go?" Potter released him.

Van Dam sighed. "Let's not prolong this nonsense any longer. We know the man's in Berlin. We also know that yesterday, you started making odd little computer searches on his behalf. Obviously he's contacted you."

"This is all pure specul—"

"Someone with your access code has been busily ferreting out data." He opened a small notebook. "Let me see. Yesterday, seven a.m., you did a search on the name Geoffrey Fontaine...."

"Yes, well, I filed a report on Fontaine's death a few weeks back. I wanted to review the facts."

"At seven-thirty you keyed in the name Simon Dance. Curious name. Any reason for that search?"

Wes was silent.

"Finally, twelve noon—your lunch hour, I presume—you requested data on someone or something called Magus. Have you, perhaps, an interest in the Old Testament?"

Wes didn't answer.

"Come, Mr. Corrigan. We both know why you're making these searches. You're doing it for O'Hara, aren't you?"

"Why do you want to know?"

Potter snapped impatiently, "We want him!"

"Why?"

"We're concerned about his safety," said Van Dam. "As well as the safety of the woman traveling with him."

"Oh, sure."

"Look, Corrigan," said Potter. "His life depends on our finding him in time."

"Tell me another fairy tale."

Van Dam leaned forward, his eyes locked on Wes. "They're in on deadly business. They need protection."

"Why should I believe you?"

"If you don't help us, you'll have their blood on your hands."

Wes shook his head. "Like I said, I can't help you."

"Can't or won't?"

"Can't. I don't know where he is. And that's the honest-to-God truth."

Van Dam and Potter exchanged glances. "Okay," said Van Dam. "Get your men set up. We'll simply have to wait it out."

Potter nodded and whisked out of the office.

Wes started to rise again. "Look, I don't know what the hell you think you're doing, but—"

Van Dam motioned him back to his chair. "I'm afraid you

won't be leaving the building for a while. If you need to use the head, just let us know, and we'll send an escort with you."

"Dammit, what's going on here?"

Van Dam smiled. "A waiting game, Mr. Corrigan. We're going to sit back and see how long it takes for your phone to ring."

Chapter Twelve

IT WAS 12:50 THAT AFTERNOON WHEN the taxi let Sarah off on the edge of Potsdamer Platz. She was alone. Losing Nick had been easier than she'd thought. Thirty seconds after he'd left the room to call Wes Corrigan, she had grabbed her purse and headed out the door.

She forced herself not to think of Nick as she walked deliberately across the square. From the map she had seen that Potsdamer Platz was a point of intersection between the British, American and Soviet sectors. Cutting like a knife across the square was the Berlin Wall, which now loomed before her. No matter where one stood in the square, it was the wall that held one's gaze. People paused in the weak spring sunshine and stared at it, as if trying to see through the concrete to a different Germany beyond. Here, even in the presence of barbed wire, were ice-cream stands and laughing children and wanderers out to enjoy the light blue day.

She paused near a busload of students and pretended to listen as the teacher lectured in very precise German. But all the time, Sarah was searching for a face. Where was the woman? The beating of her heart became faster. The teacher's voice faded. Even the laughter of the children receded from her ears.

Then, despite the pounding of her heart, she heard a woman's voice; it spoke softly in passing.

"Follow me. Keep your distance."

Turning, she spotted the woman from the flower shop walking away with a net shopping bag dangling from her arm. She could be mistaken for any housewife out on her daily errands. At a leisurely pace, the woman headed northwest, toward Bellevuestrasse. Sarah followed at a discreet distance.

After three blocks, the woman disappeared into a candle shop. For a moment Sarah hesitated outside on the sidewalk. Curtains hung across the shop windows; she could see nothing beyond. At last she stepped inside.

The woman was nowhere to be seen. The smell of burning candles, bayberry and pine and lavender, filled the dimly lighted room. On display tables sat strange little creatures shaped from wax. A flame burned brightly on the figure of a twisted old gnome, slowly melting away his face. On the counter sat a candle in the shape of a woman. Melted wax had streamed down her breasts, like strands of hair.

Sarah started with surprise when an old man popped up on the other side of the counter. He nodded at her. "*Geradeaus,*" he murmured. She gave him a quizzical look. He pointed to the back of the shop. "*Geradeaus,*" he repeated, and she understood. He wanted her to move on.

With her heart in her throat, she walked past him, through a small storage room and out the back door.

Sunlight blinded her. The door slammed shut, locking immediately. She was now standing in an alley. Somewhere to her right lay Potsdamer Platz. She could hear the distant sounds of traffic. Where was the woman?

The roar of a car engine made her whirl around. From nowhere a black Citroën had appeared and was barreling down the alley, straight at her. She had no way to escape. The shop door was locked. The alley was an endless tunnel of buildings set tightly side by side. In terror she fell back, her hands pressed flat against the wall, her eyes fixed on the gleaming black hood of the Citroën, looming closer and closer.

The car skidded to a halt. The door flew open. "Get in!" hissed the woman from the back seat. "Hurry!"

Sarah peeled herself from the wall and scrambled inside.

"*Schnell!*" the woman snapped at the driver.

Sarah was thrown backward as the car jerked ahead. One block up, it turned left, then right, then left again. Sarah lost her bearings. The woman kept staring over her shoulder. At last, satisfied that no one was following them, she turned to Sarah.

"Now we can talk," she said. At Sarah's questioning glance toward the driver, the woman nodded. "He's all right. Say what you want."

"Who are you?" asked Sarah.

"I'm a friend of Geoffrey's."

"Then you know where he is?"

The woman didn't answer. Instead she said something in German to the driver. He responded by turning off the main street and heading onto a quiet park road. A short distance beyond, they stopped among the trees.

The woman tugged on Sarah's arm. "Come. We'll walk here."

Together they crossed the grass. A fine haze seemed to hang over the city, dulling the sky to a silvery blue.

"How did you know my husband?" asked Sarah.

"Years ago we worked together. His name was Simon, then." She nodded, remembering. "He was most promising, Simon was. One of my best."

"Then you're also…in the business?"

"I was. Until five years ago."

It was hard to imagine this woman as anything but a plump housewife. Her hair was already streaked with gray; her face was round and moist. Perhaps that was her strength, the fact that she looked so ordinary.

"No, I do not look the part," said the woman, reading Sarah's mind. "The best ones never do."

They walked a few paces in silence. Even here, in the midst of trees and grass, the smell of the city hung in the air. "Like Simon, I was one of the best," the woman confided. "And now even I am afraid."

They stopped and looked at each other. The woman's eyes were like two brown raisins pressed into a face of bread dough.

"Where is he?" asked Sarah.

"I don't know."

"Then why did you ask me here?"

"To warn you. As a favor to an old friend."

"You mean Geoffrey?"

"Yes. In this business we have few friends, but the ones we do have mean everything to us."

They began to walk again. Sarah looked back and saw the black Citroën, waiting for them by the road.

"I last saw him a little over two weeks ago," the woman continued. "What a shock, to meet after all this time! I knew Simon had left the business. Yet here he was in Berlin, carrying his tools once again. He was worried. He thought he had been betrayed by the people he was working for. He was going to drop out of sight."

"Betrayed? By whom?"

"The CIA."

Sarah halted, an expression of amazement on her face. "He was working for the *CIA*?"

"They forced him into it. He had skills—he knew things that made him vital to their operation. But too many things were going wrong. Simon wanted out. He came to me for a few essentials. I provided him with a new passport, identity cards. Things he'd need to leave Berlin, once he'd disposed of his old identity. For a few hours, we visited." She shook her head sadly. "The turns our lives have taken! I saw your photograph in his wallet. That's how I recognized you yesterday. He told me you were a very…delicate person. That he was sorry you'd been hurt. When he left he promised I'd see him again someday. But that night I learned about the fire. I heard a body had been found."

"Do you think he's dead?"

"No."

"Why not?"

"If he's dead, then why are they still following *you*?"

"You mentioned a CIA operation. Does it have anything to do with a man called Magus?"

The woman's eyes showed only a faint trace of surprise. "He should not have told you about Magus."

"He didn't. Eve did."

"Ah. Then you know about Eva." The woman gave her a searching look. "I hope you aren't jealous. We can't be jealous in this work." She smiled. "Little Eva! She must be close to forty now. And still beautiful, I imagine."

"You mean—you haven't heard?"

"Heard what?"

"Eve is dead."

The woman froze, all color drained from her face. "How did it happen?" she whispered.

"A back alley in London…just a few days ago."

"She was tortured?"

Sarah nodded, feeling sick at the memory.

Swiftly the woman scanned the park. Except for the driver in the Citroën, there was no one else in sight. "Then we've no time to waste," she said, turning to Sarah. "They'll be coming for me. Listen to what I'm going to say. After we part you will not see me again. Two weeks ago, when your husband came to me, it was on business. Deadly business."

"Magus?"

"Yes. What's left of him. Five years ago the three of us were given an assignment. It was—how should I put it—to terminate with extreme prejudice. Our target was Magus. Simon planted the explosives in his car. The old man always drove himself to work. But on that one morning, he stayed home. His wife took the car instead."

The woman's voice held Sarah in a trance. She was afraid to hear the rest; she could already guess what had happened.

"The woman died instantly, of course. After the explosion the old man ran out of the house and tried to pull her from the car. The flames were terrible. But somehow he survived. And now he wants us."

"Vengeance," murmured Sarah. "That's what he's after, then."

"Yes. Against us all. Me. Eva. And most of all, Simon. He has already found Eva."

"What do I have to do with all of this?"

"You're his wife. You're their link to Simon."

"What should I do? Should I go home—"

"You can't go home. Not now; perhaps never." She looked toward the Citroën.

"But I can't run forever! I'm not like you—I don't know how to live this way. I need help. If you can just tell me how to find him…."

The woman studied Sarah for a moment, sizing up her chances of survival. "If Simon is still alive, then he is in Amsterdam."

"In Amsterdam? Why?"

"Because that is where Magus is."

THE PHONE SEEMED to ring forever. Nick's fingers tapped nervously against the booth. Where the hell was the operator? he wondered.

"American Consulate."

Instantly Nick snapped to attention. "Mr. Wes Corrigan," he said.

"One moment, please." There was a pause. Then another voice came on. "You're calling for Mr. Corrigan? I believe he's somewhere in the building having lunch. I'll page him. Please hold."

Before he could protest, she cut him off. For five minutes he waited on the line. Then, just as he was about to hang up, she returned.

"I'm sorry. He's not answering. But he's due back any minute for a meeting. Can I take a message?"

"Yes. Tell him Steve Barnes called. It's about my passport trouble."

"Your number?"

"He knows it." Nick hung up.

By their arrangement, Wes would leave the embassy grounds and use an outside line to call Nick's pay phone. Nick would give Wes fifteen minutes to get back to him. If there was no call, he'd try again later. But something told him he was taking a risk, waiting around for the phone to ring. This last exchange with the operator worried him. Especially that pause at the beginning. He glanced at his watch. It was 1:14 p.m. He'd wait until one-thirty.

Someone tapped on the booth. A young woman was standing outside, waving a coin. She wanted to use the phone. With a silent oath, he left the booth and waited as she made her call. The conversation seemed to last for hours. At 1:25 she was still talking. He held up his watch and pointed at the time, but the woman merely turned her back on him.

Cursing, he started up the street. But he had already waited too long.

Out of a crowd of pedestrians standing on the corner emerged a man in a charcoal-gray suit. He was walking toward Nick. Something about the way the man reached into his jacket told

Nick he was in trouble. In one smooth motion, the man crouched and brought up his hands. Nick found himself staring into the barrel of a gun.

"Freeze, O'Hara!" shouted Roy Potter from somewhere behind him.

Nick spun to his right, poised to bolt into the busy street. Instantly two more guns appeared. A cold steel barrel was pressed against his jugular. He heard the resounding click of a pistol hammer being cocked. For a few seconds, no one moved, no one breathed. A few feet away in the street, a limousine screeched to a halt and the door flew open.

Slowly Nick turned to look at Potter, who was now cautiously edging forward, his gun aimed squarely at Nick's head. "Put the damn thing away, Potter," said Nick. "You're making me nervous."

"Get in the car," Potter commanded.

"Where are we going?"

"To a little debriefing with Jonathan Van Dam."

"Then what happens?"

Potter's grin was distinctly unpleasant. "That all depends on you."

"WHERE IS SARAH FONTAINE?"

Nick slouched down in the leather chair and gave Van Dam his best go-to-hell look. He was surprised to find himself in such comfortable surroundings. He'd expected glaring lights and a hard bench, certainly not the expensive armchair in which he was now sitting. He had no doubt things would soon get less pleasant.

"Mr. O'Hara, I'm getting impatient," said Van Dam. "I asked you a question. Where is she?"

Nick merely shrugged.

"If you care at all about her, you'll tell us where she is, and you'll tell us fast."

"I do care," said Nick. "That's why I'm not telling you anything."

"She won't last a week out there. She's inexperienced. Frightened. We've got to bring her in—now!"

"Why? You need her for target practice?"

"You're a royal pain in the ass, O'Hara," muttered Potter, who stood sulking a few feet away. "Always have been, always will be."

"I'm crazy about you, too," Nick grunted.

Van Dam pointedly ignored the interchange. "Mr. O'Hara, the woman needs our help. She's better off under our wing. Tell us where she is. You may be saving her life."

"She was under your wing at Margate. What kind of protection did you give her then? What the hell is going on?"

"I can't tell you."

"You want Geoffrey Fontaine, don't you?"

"No."

"You arranged her release in London. Then you followed her. You thought she'd lead you right to Fontaine, didn't you?"

"We already know she can't."

"What's that supposed to mean?"

"We're not after Fontaine."

"So tell me another story."

Potter couldn't stay silent any longer. "Dammit!" he blurted out, his palms slapping the desk. "Don't you get it, O'Hara? Fontaine was one of *ours*!"

The revelation stunned Nick into a momentary silence. He stared at Potter. "You mean—he's with the *Company*?"

"That's right."

"Then where is he?"

Potter sighed, looking suddenly tired. "He's dead."

Nick sat back, floored by the new information. All the running, all the searching, had been for nothing. They'd crossed half of Europe in pursuit of a dead man. "I—I seem to have a major gap of knowledge here. Enlighten me. Who's after Sarah?"

Van Dam broke in, "I'm not sure we can—"

"We've got no choice," said Potter. "We've gotta tell him."

After a pause Van Dam nodded. "Very well, then. Go ahead, Mr. Potter."

Potter paced as he talked, moving like an old bulldog between the chairs. "Five years ago, one of Mossad's top agents was a man named Simon Dance. He was part of a team of three. The other two were women: Eva Saint-Clair and Helga Steinberg. They were assigned a routine termination job, but the operation got fouled up. Their target survived. Instead the man's wife was killed."

"Dance was a hired assassin?"

Potter halted and scowled at Nick. "Sometimes, O'Hara, you've gotta fight fire with fire. The target in this case was the head of a worldwide terror cartel. These guys don't operate on ideology; they do it for hard cash. A hundred big ones gets you a bombing. Three hundred will sink you a small ship. If you're a do-it-yourselfer, they'll get you the equipment. A crate of Uzis. A surface-to-air missile. Anything your little heart desires, for a price. There's no way to deal with a club like that, except on terms they understand. The job had to be done, and Dance's team was the best."

"But the target got away."

"Unfortunately, yes. Within a year a contract was out on all three Mossad agents, with the biggest price on Dance's head. By that time they had wisely dropped out of sight. Helga Steinberg, we think, is still in Germany. Dance and Eva Saint-Clair vanished. For five years no one knew where they were. Then, three weeks ago one of our London agents was sitting in his favorite pub when he just happened to overhear a voice he recognized. He'd worked with Dance some years ago so he knew that voice. That's how we found out about Dance's new identity: Geoffrey Fontaine."

"How did he come to work for the Company?"

"I persuaded him."

"With what?"

"I tried the usual. Money. A new life. He didn't want any of it. But he did want one thing: to be able to live without any more fear. I pointed out to him that the only way was to go back and finish the job on Magus, the man he should have terminated. For years I'd been trying to track Magus myself, without luck. I traced him only as far as Amsterdam and I needed Dance's help. He agreed."

Magus, thought Nick. The old man, the magician. At last he was beginning to understand. "Couldn't do the job yourself," he said. "So you hired a hit man for the good old U.S.A."

"Oh, yeah. Yeah, tell me your old-fashioned diplomacy's any damned good in this situation. A bullet, at least, gets results."

"The easy answer to everything. Just blow off their heads. So what went wrong? Why didn't your hit man deliver?"

Potter shook his head. "I don't know. In Amsterdam Dance got…nervous. He took off like a scared rabbit. For some weird reason, he flew to Berlin and checked into that old hotel. That night there was a fire. But you know about that. And that's the last we heard of Simon Dance."

"It was his body in the hotel?"

"We've got no dental records to prove it, but I'm inclined to think it was. No one else from Berlin has been reported missing. Dance hasn't surfaced anywhere. How it happened is anyone's guess. Murder? Suicide? Both are possibilities. He was depressed. Tired."

Nick frowned. "But if he died in that hotel—then who called Sarah?"

"I did."

"You?"

"It was a composite message, spliced together from recordings of his voice. You see, we'd tapped his London hotel room."

Nick's fingers tightened around the armrest as he fought to keep his voice steady. "You wanted her here in Europe? You're telling me you set her up as a target?"

"Not a target, O'Hara. Bait. I heard Magus still had the contract out on Dance. Obviously he didn't believe Dance was dead. If we could make him think Sarah knew something, he might make a move on her. So we drew her to Europe. We were hoping Magus would show his hand. The whole time, we had our eyes on her. That is, until you pulled her underground."

"You *bastards*," cried Nick. "She was nothing more to you than a—a goat tied to a stake!"

"There are deeper issues here—"

Nick shot to his feet. "*To hell* with your issues!"

Van Dam shifted uncomfortably in his chair. "Mr. O'Hara, please sit down. Try and see the broader situation…."

Nick turned on Van Dam. "Was this your bright idea?"

"No, it was mine," Potter admitted. "Mr. Van Dam had nothing to do with it. He found out about it later, when he showed up in London."

Nick looked at Potter. "You? I should've known. It smells like your kind of job. So what've you got planned next? Shall we tie her up in the town square with a big sign saying Fair Game?"

Potter shook his head and said quietly, "No. The operation's over. Van Dam wants to bring her in."

"Then what happens?"

"It will soon be plain to everyone involved that Fontaine's really dead. They'll leave her alone. We'll have to find Magus some other day."

"What about Wes Corrigan? I want him let off the hook."

"Already done. There'll be no harm to his career. Not a mark'll show up on his personnel file."

Slowly Nick sat down. He gave Potter a long, hard look. His decision and its consequences rested on only one thing: Could he trust these men? Even if he couldn't, what choice did he have? Sarah was alone out there, hiding from a killer. She'd never survive on her own. "If this is some kind of scam—"

"There's no need to threaten me, O'Hara. I know what you're capable of."

"No," said Nick. "I don't think you do. And let's hope you never find out."

"WHERE WILL I FIND HIM in Amsterdam?" Sarah asked the woman.

They were walking through the trees to the Citroën. The ground was damp, and Sarah's heels sank deeply into the young grass.

"Are you certain you wish to find him?" asked the woman.

"I have to. He's the only one I can turn to for help. And he's waiting for me."

"You may not survive this search. You know that, don't you?"

Sarah shivered. "I'm barely surviving now. Every moment I'm afraid. I keep wondering when and how it'll end. If it will be painful." She shuddered. "They used a knife on Eve."

The woman's eyes darkened. "A knife? Kronen's trademark."

"Kronen?"

"Son of the Devil, we used to call him. He is Magus's favorite."

"He wears sunglasses? And he has blond, almost white hair?"

The woman nodded. "You've seen him, then. He'll be looking for you. In Amsterdam. In Berlin. Wherever you go, he'll be waiting."

"What would you do if you were me?"

The woman looked at Sarah thoughtfully. "In your place? With your youth? Yes, I would do what you're doing. I would try to find Simon."

"Then help me. Tell me how I can find him."

"What I tell you could kill him."

"I'll be careful."

The woman searched Sarah's face, once more weighing her chances. "In Amsterdam," she said, "there is a club, the Casa Morro. On the street Oude Zijds Voorburgwal. It is owned by a woman named Corrie. She was once a friend to Mossad. To all of us. If Simon is in Amsterdam, she will know how to find him."

"And if she doesn't?"

"Then no one will know."

The Citroën's door was already open. They climbed in and the driver headed toward the Ku-damm.

"When you see the Casa Morro, don't be shocked," the woman said.

"Why would I be shocked?"

The woman laughed softly. "You'll find out." She leaned forward and spoke to the driver in German. "We can drop you off near your *pension*," she told Sarah. "Is that what you wish?"

Sarah nodded. To reach Amsterdam she would need money, and Nick was carrying most of their cash. Tonight, when he was asleep, she could lift it from his wallet and leave Berlin. By morning she'd be miles away. "I'm staying just south of—"

"We know where it is," said the woman. She muttered a few more words to the driver. Then she turned to Sarah. "There is one last thing. Be careful whom you trust. That man you were with yesterday—what is his name?"

"Nick O'Hara."

The woman frowned, as if trying to place the name. "Whoever he is," she said, "he could be dangerous. How long have you known him?"

"A few weeks."

The woman nodded. "Don't trust him. Go alone. It's safest."

"Whom can I trust?"

"Only Simon. Tell no one what I've told you. Magus has eyes and ears everywhere."

They were nearing the *pension*. The street outside looked so exposed, so dangerous. Sarah felt safer in the car; she didn't want to get out. But the Citroën had already slowed down. She was reaching for the door handle when the driver suddenly cursed and floored the gas pedal. Sarah's shoulder slammed against the door as they swerved away from the curb and shot back into the traffic.

"*Nach rechts!*" the woman shouted, her face instantly taut with fear.

"What is it?" cried Sarah.

"CIA! They're all over this street!"

"*CIA?*"

"Look for yourself!"

They were coming up fast on the *pension*. Like all the other buildings on this street, it was a featureless box of gray concrete, distinguished only by a splash of shocking red graffiti scrawled on its front wall. On the sidewalk next to the graffiti stood two men. Sarah recognized them both. Planted solidly on his two short legs was Roy Potter, who squinted up the street in their direction. And standing close by, his face frozen in disbelief, was Nick.

He seemed unable to move, unable to react. As the Citroën roared past, he could only stand and stare. Just for an instant, his eyes met Sarah's through the car window. He grabbed Potter's arm. Both men dashed into the street after the Citroën in a futile attempt to grab the car door. That's when she understood. At last it was clear.

Nick had been working with Potter all along. Together they'd engineered a plan so intricate, so well acted, that she'd been totally taken in. Nick was with the Company. She'd just seen the proof, there on the sidewalk. He must have returned to the room and found her missing. Then he'd sounded the alarm.

Sarah collapsed against the seat in shock. She heard Nick's voice one last time as he shouted her name. Then the sound faded away, drowned out by the engine's roar. All of Sarah's strength was gone. She huddled against the car door like a hunted animal. She *was* a hunted animal. The CIA was after her. Magus was after her. No matter which way she fled, someone's net would be closing in.

"We'll have to leave you at the airport," said the woman. "If you board a plane immediately, you may have time to get out of Berlin before they can stop you."

"But where are you going?" cried Sarah.

"Away. We take a different route."

"What if I need you? How can I find you—"

"You can't."

"But I don't even know your name!"

"If you find your husband, tell him Helga sent you."

The sign for Tegel Airport came up too quickly. There was so little time to gather her courage, so little time to think. Before she was ready, the Citroën stopped at the curb. She had to climb out. She didn't have a chance to say goodbye to Helga. As soon as Sarah's feet hit the pavement, the door slammed and the car sped off.

Sarah was alone.

On the way to the ticket counter, she glanced through the cash in her wallet. There was barely enough for a meal, much less a plane ticket. She had no choice. She'd have to use her credit card.

Twenty minutes later a flight took off for Amsterdam. Sarah was on it.

Chapter Thirteen

AFTER IT LEFT TEGEL AIRPORT, THE BLACK Citroën headed south toward the Ku-damm. Helga had to make one last stop before she left Berlin. She knew she was taking a big chance. The CIA had seen her license plate; they could trace her address. Death was closing in fast. Already Eva was gone. She would have to call Corrie, tell her to warn Simon. And she would ask her about this man, Nick O'Hara. Helga wondered who he was. She didn't like new faces. The most dangerous enemy in the world is the one you do not recognize.

She would have to abandon the car and board the train to Frankfurt. From there she could move south to Switzerland and Italy, or west to Spain. It didn't matter where she went; what mattered was that she left Berlin. Before Eva's fate caught up with her, too.

But even spies can be sentimental. Helga couldn't leave the city without her few precious possessions. To anyone else they were worthless things, but to Helga they were bits and pieces of a life she'd left behind: photographs of her sister and her parents, all of whom had died in the war; a half dozen love letters from a boy she would never forget; her mother's silver locket. These things reminded her of her humanity, and she would never leave without them, even under threat of death.

Her driver understood why they were stopping at the house. He knew it was useless to argue. He took her home one last time and sat in the car while she ran inside to collect her belongings.

From all the secret places in her bedroom came those few treasured items. They were packed, along with her pistol, in the false bottom of a satchel. Then clothes were thrown on top, the old skirts and housedresses she favored for their lack of distinction. She glanced out the window and saw the Citroën parked in the street below. What a pity to abandon such a fine car, she thought, but she had no choice.

She closed the window and headed downstairs. Outside, the sunlight made her blink. For a few seconds, she stood on the porch and let her eyes adjust before she locked the door. Those few seconds saved her life.

From the street came the screech of tires. Almost simultaneously, gunfire ripped the afternoon silence. Bullets spattered the Citroën. Helga threw herself to the porch, behind a row of clay tulip pots. Gunfire burst out again, and shards of glass rained down from the windows above her head.

Desperately she rolled beneath the railing and threw herself into the flower bed behind the porch, dragging the satchel with her. She had only a few seconds to act, a few seconds before the assassin would move in to finish the job. Already she heard his car door slam. He was coming.

She reached in the satchel. The false bottom slid open. Her hand closed around cold steel.

The footsteps moved closer. He was climbing the steps now; for him it would be a straight shot into the flower bed.

But she beat him to it. She raised the pistol, aimed and fired. The man's head was flung backward as a bright blotch of scarlet sprang out above his right eye. He fell, smashing through the far railing, and toppled like a disjointed doll among the garden tools.

Helga didn't bother to check his condition. She knew he was dead. The man's companion didn't wait around to confirm her marksmanship, either. He was already back in the driver's seat. Before she could aim and fire again, the car had roared off and disappeared.

One look at the Citroën told her her driver could not have

survived. She had time for only a twinge of regret, but no tears. She had trusted the man. While they hadn't been lovers, they had been colleagues and they had worked well together these past five years. Now he was dead.

She grabbed the satchel and walked briskly down the street. A block away she broke into a run. To remain in Berlin any longer would be foolish. She had made one costly mistake, and she had survived; next time she might not be so lucky.

BLOOD WAS EVERYWHERE.

Nick shoved through the crowd of onlookers, across a street littered with broken glass, toward the black Citroën. Voices were shouting around him in German; on the sidewalk ahead, ambulance attendants crouched next to a body. Nick fought to get through, only to find himself blocked by a policeman. But he was close enough to see the dead man lying on the sidewalk, face exposed, eyes wide and staring.

"Potter!" he shouted. But there were too many other voices, too many sirens. His cry was lost in the noise. He was utterly paralyzed, unable to move or think, just another stunned body in a crowd of onlookers, all staring at the blood. The man beside him suddenly sank to his knees and began to retch.

"O'Hara!" It was Potter, calling to him from across the street. "She's not here! There're only two men, the driver and another guy, over by the porch. Both dead."

Nick shouted back, "Then where is she?"

Potter shrugged and turned as Tarasoff approached.

Enraged by his own helplessness, Nick pushed through the crowd and walked aimlessly down the street. He didn't know or care where he was headed; the sight of blood was more than he could bear. It could just as easily have been Sarah's body lying in the street, Sarah's blood splattered all over that Citroën.

A few yards away, he sank to the curb and dropped his head in his hands. There was nothing he could do. All his hopes rested on the skills of a man he'd never trusted and an organization he'd always despised. Roy Potter and the good old CIA. Potter had never been bothered by moral questions of right or wrong; he just did what he had to, and the rules be damned. For the first time in his life, Nick could appreciate such amoral practicality. With Sarah's life at stake, he didn't care how Potter did his job, either, as long as he got her back alive.

"O'Hara?" Potter was waving at him. "Let's move it! We've got a lead!"

"What?" Nick scrambled to his feet and followed Potter and Tarasoff to the car.

"KLM Airlines," said Potter. "She used her credit card."

"You mean she's leaving Berlin? Roy, you've gotta stop that plane!"

Potter shook his head. "We're too late for that."

"What do you mean?"

"The plane landed ten minutes ago. In Amsterdam."

THE DUTCH, it is said, never close their curtains. To do so would imply that one has something to hide. At night, when the houses are lighted, anyone who walks down an Amsterdam street can look through the windows, straight into the soul of a Dutch home, and see supper tables where well-scrubbed children sit watching as their mothers spoon out applesauce and potatoes. The hours will pass, and the children will disappear to their beds. Mother and father will go to their accustomed chairs. There they will watch TV or read, all in plain view of the world.

This open-curtain policy extends even to the Wallen district of Amsterdam, where members of the world's oldest profession display their charms. In the brothel windows, ladies knit or read novels, or they look out the windows and smile at the men gawking from the street. To them it is only a business, and they have nothing to hide.

It was in this neighborhood that Sarah found the Casa Morro. The afternoon had already slipped toward dusk by the time she crossed the small canal bridge to Oude Zijds Voorburgwal. In the sunlight the city had glowed with the gentle patina of age. But with the darkness came neon lights and throbbing music and all the strange and restless people who do not sleep at night. Sarah was just one more in a street of wanderers.

In the shadows by the low stone bridge, she stood and watched the passersby. The dark waters of the canal gently slapped the boats behind her. A young man shambled by with the bent shuffle of a street addict. In the window across from her, four women in various stages of undress were displayed, the human offerings of Casa Morro. They looked like altogether ordinary women. The tallest one glanced around as someone called her name. Then, putting down her book, she rose and disappeared through the blue curtains. The other three women did not even look up. *Don't be shocked,* Helga had said. This is what she had meant. After living on the edge of death, something as commonplace as a brothel could hardly shock Sarah.

For half an hour, she observed the steady flow of men in and out the door. The three women in the window eventually departed through the curtain; two others emerged in their place. Casa Morro appeared to be a thriving business.

At last Sarah went inside.

Even the scent of perfume could not hide the building's smell of age. The odor hung like a heavy curtain over what had once been an elegant seventeenth century home. Narrow wooden stairs led to a dim hallway above. Persian carpets, worn from years of traffic, muffled Sarah's footsteps as she walked from the foyer into a sitting room.

A woman looked up from a desk. She was in her forties, black-haired, elegantly tall and rawboned. Her gaze swept across Sarah in a swift look of assessment. *"Kan ik u helpen?"*

"I am looking for Corrie."

After a pause the woman nodded. "You are American, aren't you?" she asked in perfect English.

Sarah didn't answer. Slowly she circled the room, taking in the low couch, the fireplace with its brightly polished grate, the bookcase with its shelves of obscenely humorous knickknacks. At last she turned back to the woman. "Helga sent me," she said.

The woman's face remained absolutely expressionless.

"I want to find Simon. Where is he?"

The woman was silent for a moment. "Perhaps Simon does not wish to be found," she said softly.

"Please. It's important."

The woman shrugged. "With Simon everything is important."

"Is he in the city?"

"Perhaps."

"He'll want to see me."

"Why?"

"I'm his wife. Sarah."

For the first time, the woman looked perturbed. She went to her desk and sat down. Tapping a pencil nervously, she studied Sarah. "Leave me your wedding ring," she said. "Then come back tonight. Midnight."

"Will he be here?"

"Simon is a cautious man. He'll want proof before he comes anywhere near you."

Sarah removed her ring and gave it to the woman. Her hand felt naked without it. "I'll be back at midnight," she said.

"Madame!" the woman called as Sarah turned to leave. "There are no guarantees."

Sarah nodded. "I know." The woman's warning had not been necessary; Sarah had learned that nothing was guaranteed. Not even her next heartbeat.

CORRIE WAITED ONLY a moment after Sarah left. Then she walked outside and down the block, to a pay telephone where she dialed an Amsterdam number. It was answered immediately.

"The woman Helga called about was just here," said Corrie. "Long hair, brown eyes, early thirties. I have her wedding ring. It is gold, inscribed Geoffrey, 2-14. She will be back at midnight."

"She's alone?"

"I saw no one else."

"And that man Helga mentioned—O'Hara—what did your friends find out?"

"He's not CIA. His involvement appears to be purely… personal."

There was a pause. Corrie listened carefully to the instructions that followed. Then she hung up and returned to the Casa Morro, where she placed the wedding ring on a pedestal in the front window where it would be easily visible from the street.

Corrie smiled when she thought of what would happen when the woman returned. Sarah looked like all the other straitlaced types who so despised working women like Corrie. All of her life, Corrie had sensed the disdain of those "virtuous women." She'd wanted to fight back, but how can one spar with cold silence? Tonight the tables would be turned. It was a brazen way to do things, putting this woman Sarah on display, but Corrie didn't question her instructions.

In fact, she rather relished them.

IN A QUIET coffeehouse a mile away, Sarah sat on a hard wooden bench and stared at the candle on the table. Her life—what there was of it—had somehow come to this strange and lonely point in time. Outside, the world went about its business. Cars honked on the street, young men and women laughed and shouted as they walked in the night. But Sarah's universe was made up of this table and this room. Had she ever existed before this moment? She could hardly remember. *Was I ever a child?* she wondered. *Did I ever laugh and dance and sing? Was there ever a time when I wasn't afraid?*

She didn't ask these questions out of self-pity. She felt only bewilderment. In two weeks she'd lost touch with everything she'd once called familiar. Closing her eyes, she hungrily pictured her old bedroom, the mahogany nightstand, the brass alarm clock, the chipped china lamp. She went over every detail, the way one goes over a favorite photograph. Her old life, before fear had swept it away forever.

Strange, she thought, how one learns to keep going. Now her money was running low. She was alone. She didn't know where she was headed or how she would get there. But she had learned one thing about herself: She was a survivor.

Today had proved it. The pain of Nick's betrayal still cut like a knife; she would never recover from a wound that deep. Yet somehow she'd found the strength to move on. Surviving had turned into something automatic, something one did by way of instinct. All those false, pretty dreams of love had been left behind. Now she had only one clear goal in mind: to live long enough to end this nightmare.

In a few hours, she'd be with Geoffrey again. He would see to her safety. Moving in this world of shadows was second nature to him. And even if there was no love between them, she did believe he cared, just a little. It was the one hope she had left.

She dropped her head as a profound weariness settled on her shoulders. She'd walked for miles through the streets of Amsterdam. Both body and soul had been battered, and she longed to sleep, to forget. But as she closed her eyes, the memories returned: the taste of Nick's mouth, the way he laughed so gently when they made love. Angrily she forced the images from her mind. What had once been love was now turning to cold fury. At Nick for betraying her. At herself for being unable to give up the memories. Or the longing.

He had used her, and she'd never forget that. Never.

"THERE'S NO WORD on Sarah," said Potter as he walked into Nick's Amsterdam hotel room. He was carrying two cups of coffee. He closed the door with his foot and handed a cup to Nick.

Nick watched Potter flop into a chair and wearily rub his eyes. They were both dead beat. And hungry. Somehow they'd forgotten about supper; probably a first for Potter, judging by his girth. Since leaving Berlin they'd consumed nothing more substantial than black coffee. A quick shot of caffeine was what they both needed, thought Nick as he downed his cup and tossed it into the wastebasket. It was going to be a sleepless night.

"Slow down, O'Hara," said Potter. "You're gonna eat up your stomach, gulping it fast like that!"

Nick grunted. "You don't know my stomach."

"Yeah, well, the last thing I need is to get blamed for your bleeding ulcer, too." Potter glanced at his watch. "Damn. That deli down the street just closed. I could've used a sandwich." He fished a package of broken crackers from his pocket. "Saltines. Want some?" Nick shook his head. Potter tossed the broken crackers into his mouth and crumpled the cellophane. "Bad for my blood pressure. Too much sodium but, what the hell, when you're hungry, you're hungry." He brushed the crumbs off his suit and watched Nick pace the floor. "Look, things are moving fine without you having a nervous breakdown. Why don't you just turn in?"

"I can't." Nick stopped at the window. The city of Amsterdam stretched out in an endless sea of light. "She's out there somewhere. If I only knew where…"

Potter lighted a cigarette and strode across the room for an ashtray. After sixteen hours on the job, he was looking a little frayed. His suit was rumpled and his face was pastier than usual. But if he was discouraged by the recent turn of events, he didn't show it. Potter, the bulldog. No style, no charm, just a thick body with a thick head, all dressed up in a polyester suit. "For God's sake, O'Hara." He sighed. "Turn in! Finding her is our job."

Nick said nothing.

"Still don't trust us," said Potter.

"No. Why should I?"

Potter sat down and blew out a mouthful of smoke. "Something's always eating you, isn't it? What is it about you career guys in the foreign service? You go around the world nursing your ulcers, whining about the idiots in Washington. Then you turn around in public and put on that patriotic face. Hell, no wonder our foreign policy's so screwed up. It's administered by schizophrenics."

"Unlike central intelligence, which is run by sociopaths."

Potter laughed. "Yeah? At least we get things done. Matter of fact, you might be interested to hear I just got off the line to Berlin. We've turned up some info on those two dead men."

"Who were they?"

"The driver of the Citroën was German, once connected to Mossad. The neighbors had a notion he and Helga Steinberg were brother and sister, but it's obvious now they were just associates."

"Helga," Nick murmured thoughtfully. "She's the link we need. If we could find her..."

"Not a chance. Helga Steinberg's too good. She knows every trick in the book."

"What about that hit man?"

Potter sat back down and blew out a cloud of smoke. "The hit man was Dutch."

"Any connection to Helga?"

"None. Obviously he was just carrying out a contract. But she got him first." He grinned. "What a shot! I'd like to meet the broad someday. Hopefully not in a dark alley."

"The man had no record at all?"

"Nothing. His papers indicated he was a sales rep for some legitimate company, here in Amsterdam. Did a lot of traveling. But there's one interesting thing. It may be just the slipup we've been waiting for. Two days ago there was a transfer of funds to the man's account. A big transfer. We traced the source to another firm, the F. Berkman company, also here in Amsterdam. They import and export coffee. F. Berkman has been in business ten years. It has offices in a dozen countries. Yet it barely shows a profit. Funny, don't you think?"

"Who's this F. Berkman?"

"No one knows. The company's run by a board of directors. None of them have ever met the man."

Nick stared at Potter. The same thought had occurred to them both. "Magus," said Nick softly.

"That's what I wondered."

"Sarah's right smack in his territory! If I were her, I'd be running like hell in the other direction!"

"Seems to me she's done a lot of unexpected things. She's sure not behaving like your everyday scared broad."

"No," said Nick, sinking tiredly onto the bed. "She's not your everyday scared broad. She's smarter."

"You're in love with her."

"I suppose I am."

Potter regarded him in wonderment. "She's some change from Lauren."

"You remember Lauren?"

"Yeah. Who could forget her? You were the envy of every guy in the embassy. Tough luck, about your divorce."

"That was one hell of a mistake."

"The divorce?"

"No. The marriage."

Potter laughed. "I'll let you in on a secret, O'Hara. After two divorces I've finally figured it out. Men don't need love. They need their meals cooked and their shirts ironed and maybe a little action three times a week. But they don't need love."

Nick shook his head. "That's what I thought, too. Until a few weeks ago…"

The phone by the bed suddenly rang.

"Probably for me," said Potter, stubbing out his cigarette. He started across the room, but Nick had already grabbed the receiver.

For a moment there was only silence. Then a man's voice asked, "Mr. Nick O'Hara?"

"Yes."

"You'll find her at the Casa Morro. Midnight. Come alone."

"Who is this?" demanded Nick.

"Get her out of Amsterdam, O'Hara. I'm counting on you."

"Wait!"

The line went dead. Cursing, Nick slammed the receiver down and ran for the door.

"What—where you going?" called Potter.

"Some place called Casa Morro! She'll be there!"

"Hold on!" Potter grabbed the phone. "Let me call Van Dam. We need backup—"

"I'm on my own on this one!"

"O'Hara!"

But Nick was already gone.

FIVE MINUTES AFTER Nick left his hotel, the old man received a call. It was his informant.

"She's at the Casa Morro."

"How do you know this?" asked the old man.

"O'Hara was called. We don't know by whom. He's already left. The Company will be following shortly—you haven't got much time."

"I'll send Kronen for her now."

"What about O'Hara? He'll be in the way."

The old man made a sound of dismissal. "O'Hara? A minor detail," he said. "Kronen can deal with him."

JONATHAN VAN DAM hung up and walked briskly from the phone booth. It had started out as a mild spring evening, but now a chill had crept in with the mist and he found himself buttoning his overcoat. The thought of returning immediately to the warmth of his hotel room was tempting. First, though, he had to stop at a drugstore. A simple excuse was all he needed, a bottle of antacid for an upset stomach, or perhaps some milk of magnesia for sluggish digestion. Should anyone ask, he would have a reason for his short absence from the hotel.

He stopped at an all-night pharmacy. The clerk barely looked up from his magazine as Van Dam walked in and surveyed the shelves of medicine. There was something comforting about seeing all those good American brands. It made him feel close to home. The doorbell tinkled and another customer wandered in, a man in a black overcoat. The man was hacking loudly as he paused by the cold remedies and rubbed his hands together. Van Dam selected a bottle of Maalox, for which he paid eight guilders, and walked out into the mist.

It took him ten minutes to reach the hotel. He opened the Maalox, poured a therapeutic dose down the drain and changed into his pajamas. Then he waited in bed by the phone.

In a short while, things would be happening at Casa Morro. He didn't like to think about it. In all his years with the Company, he'd never once felt bullets whistle past his cheek, never once engaged in violence. He'd certainly never killed a man—in person, that is. When violence was necessary, he'd done it secondhand. Even his wife Claudia's death had been arranged at a comfortable distance. Van Dam disliked the sight of blood. He had been a continent away when Claudia was shot by the prowler. By the time he returned home, the blood had been cleaned up and the floor waxed. It was as if nothing at all had changed, except that he was free, and also extremely wealthy.

But a month later he'd received a note. "The Viking has talked to me," was all it said. The Viking. The man who'd pulled the trigger.

Van Dam had been paralyzed by fear. He'd thought of disappearing, to Mexico perhaps, or South America. But every morning he'd awakened in the bright sunshine of his bedroom and thought, *No, I can't leave my home, my comforts....* So he'd waited. And when the old man at last made contact, Van Dam had been ready to deal.

Information was all that was asked of him. It was minor data at first, the budget of a particular consular office, the takeoff schedule of transport planes. He suffered only a few pangs of guilt. After all, it wasn't the KGB he was dealing with. The old man was merely an entrepreneur, unconcerned with global politics. He could not be considered the enemy. Van Dam could not be considered a traitor.

Before long, though, the demands grew serious. They always arrived without warning. Two rings on the telephone, then silence, and Van Dam would find a package left in the woods or a note stuffed in a tree hollow. He'd never laid eyes on the old man. He didn't even know his real name. He was given a phone number, to be used only in emergencies. The few times he'd used it, the calls had been brief and mediated by a series of clicks and pauses—obviously a string of radio patches, designed to make tracing the calls impossible. Van Dam had found himself trapped by a captor who had no name and no face. But it was not a disagreeable arrangement. He was still safe. He had his house and his fine suits and his brandy. In truth, the old man was a most benign master.

"IT'S MIDNIGHT," SAID SARAH. "Where is he?"

Corrie swept a strand of long black hair off her face and looked up from her desk. "Simon wants proof."

"He's seen my wedding ring."

"Now he wants to see you. But from a safe distance. You'll have to look the part. Go upstairs, second room on your right. Look in the closet. I think the green satin will suit you."

"I don't understand."

The woman sat back and smiled. The lamplight fell fully on her face, and for the first time, Sarah saw the wrinkles around her eyes and mouth. Life hadn't been kind to this woman. "Just put on the dress," she said. "There's no other way."

Sarah climbed the stairs to a hall lighted dimly by a single Tiffany lamp. The room was unlocked. Inside she found a wide brass bed and a closet full of gowns. She changed into the green satin dress and glanced at herself in the mirror. The thin fabric clung to her breasts, and her nipples stood out plainly. But modesty meant nothing to her now. Staying alive was all that mattered. For that she'd wear anything.

Downstairs, Corrie eyed her critically. "You're so thin," she sniffed. "And take off your glasses. You can see without them, can't you?"

"Well enough."

Corrie gestured toward the front window. "Go, then. I'll watch your purse. Take a book if you like, but sit with your face toward the street, so he can see you. It will not take long."

The heavy velvet curtains parted. Sarah stepped through into a cloud of perfumed air. What struck her first were the faces, staring at her from the street, all of them strangers'. Was Geoffrey's among them?

"Sit," said one of the whores, nodding toward a chair. Sarah sat down and was handed a book. She opened the cover and looked intently at the first page. The book was written in Dutch. Even though she couldn't read a word, it was still a shield between her and the men outside. She clung to it until her fingers ached.

For what seemed like forever, Sarah sat as still as a statue. She heard laughter drifting in from the street. Footsteps rained on the cobblestones. From the disco a block away came the steady beat of music. Time slowed down and stopped. Her nerves were stretched to the breaking point. Where was he? Why was it taking so long?

Then, through the noise surrounding her, she heard her name. The book slid from her nerveless fingers and thudded to the floor. She felt the blood drain from her face as she looked up.

Nick was staring incredulously through the window. "*Sarah?*"

Her reaction was instantaneous. She ran. She bolted through the velvet curtains and dashed up the stairs to the room where she'd found the dress. It was mindless flight, the instinct of a desperate woman fleeing from pain. She was afraid of him. He was out to hurt her, to hurt Geoffrey.

If she could just reach the room and lock him out...

But as she scrambled through the door, Nick grabbed her arm. She jerked herself free and flung the door in his face, but he'd already forced his way in. Stumbling backward, she retreated as far as she could, until the backs of her legs collided with the bed. She was trapped.

Shaking uncontrollably, she screamed at him, "Get out!"

He moved forward, his hands held out to her. "Sarah, listen to me—"

"You bastard, I hate you!"

He kept moving closer. The distance between them inexorably melted away. She swung at him. The blow struck him so hard her fingers left red welts on his cheek. She would have hit him again, but he grabbed her wrists and hauled her toward him.

"No," he said, "listen to me. Dammit, will you listen!"

"You *used* me!"

"Sarah—"

"Was it fun? Or was it a chore, bedding the widow for the good old CIA?"

"Stop it!"

"Damn you, Nick!" she cried, flailing helplessly against his grasp. "I loved you! I loved you…." Somehow she found the strength to wrench free again, but her momentum carried her backward and she toppled across the bed. He came down on top of her, his hands closing over her wrists, his body covering hers. He was too heavy to push away. She couldn't fight him any longer. All she could do was lie beneath him, sobbing and struggling vainly, until her strength was gone and she was limp and exhausted.

At last, when he knew all the fight had left her, he released her hands. Slowly, tenderly, he pressed his lips against her mouth.

"I still hate you," she said weakly.

"And I love you," he said.

"Don't lie to me."

He kissed her again, and this time his lips lingered, unwilling to part from hers. "I'm not lying, Sarah. I never have."

"You were working for them all along—"

"No. You're wrong. I'm not with them. They cornered me. Then they told me everything. Sarah, it's over. You can stop running."

"Not until I find him."

"You can't find him."

"What do you mean?"

The look he gave her said everything. Even before he spoke, she knew what his answer would be. "I'm sorry, Sarah. He's dead."

His words hit her like a physical blow. She stared at him, stunned. "He can't be dead. He called me…."

"It wasn't him. It was a Company trick. A recording."

"Then what happened to him?"

"The fire. That was his body they found in the hotel."

She closed her eyes in pain as his words sank in. "I don't understand. I don't understand any of this," she cried.

"The Company set you up, Sarah. They wanted Magus to make a move on you. They hoped he'd get careless. Reveal his whereabouts. But then they lost us. That is, until Berlin."

"And now?"

"It's over. They've called off the operation. We can go home."

Home. It had a magical sound, like a fairy-tale place she no longer believed existed. And Nick was somehow magical, too. But the arms wrapped around her now were made of flesh, not dreams. Nick was real. He'd always been real.

He rose and pulled her from the bed, tugging her in an arc that ended in his arms. "Let's go home, Sarah," he whispered. "First thing in the morning, let's fly the hell out of here."

"I can't believe it's over," she murmured. "I can't believe you're really here...."

In answer he turned her face to meet his. It was the gentlest of kisses, not one of hunger, but of tenderness; it told her she was safe, that she'd always be safe, as long as Nick O'Hara was around.

Tucked under his arm, she walked with him down the hall, toward the stairs. It would be cold outside. But he would keep her warm, the way his jacket had kept her warm on that rainy day in London. They reached the top of the stairs. The foyer came into view, right below them. And Nick stopped dead in his tracks.

At first she didn't understand. All she saw was his shocked face. Then her eyes followed the direction of his gaze.

Below them, at the foot of the steps, a dark pool of blood was soaking into a blue Persian rug. And flung out across the wood floor, her hair mingling with her own blood, was Corrie.

Chapter Fourteen

A SHADOW FELL ACROSS THE FOYER WALL. Someone was walking in the sitting room, just out of sight. The shadow grew larger; it was approaching the stairs. Nick and Sarah couldn't flee through the street exit without passing through the foyer, crossing the killer's line of view. There was only one other way to run, and that was up the hallway.

Nick grabbed Sarah's hand and hauled her toward a far staircase. From the sitting room came a woman's cry, running footsteps, then two sharp thuds—bullets muffled by a silencer. The hall seemed to stretch on forever. If the killer started up the stairs now, he'd spot them.

Panic sent Sarah scrambling up the narrow staircase to the room above. They had reached the attic. Nick softly closed the door, but there was no lock. They left the lights off. Through a tiny window came the faint glow of a city night. Scattered in the darkness about their feet were vague shapes and shadows: boxes, old furniture, a rack of clothes. Nick ducked behind a trunk, pulling Sarah into his arms. She pressed her face against his chest and felt the pounding of his heart.

From downstairs came the crack of splintering wood. Someone was kicking the doors open. Methodically, he made his way down the hall, toward their staircase. *Please stop,* she prayed. *Please don't search the attic....*

Nick pushed her to the floor. "Stay down," he hissed.

"Where are you going?"

"When the chance comes, *move.*"

"But Nick..." He'd already slipped away into the darkness.

The footsteps were coming up the attic staircase.

Sarah hugged the floor, afraid to move, afraid to even breathe. The steps creaked closer and closer. With no time left, she searched frantically in the darkness for a weapon, for something with which to defend herself. The floor around her was bare.

The door flew open, slamming into the wall. Light flooded in from the stairway.

In that same instant, she heard the unmistakable sound of a fist colliding with flesh, then a heavy thud shook the floor. She leaped up to find Nick grappling with the killer, a man she'd never seen before. They rolled across the floor, over and over. Nick threw a second punch, but the blow glanced off the killer's cheek. Nick's advantage had been surprise—he wasn't a trained fighter. The killer, bloodied as he was, managed to break free and slam his fist upward into Nick's stomach. Nick grunted and rolled away. The killer dove across the floor toward a pistol lying a few feet away.

Still stunned by the last blow, Nick couldn't move fast enough. The killer's fingers closed around the gun. Desperately Nick lunged for the other man's wrist, but he could only reach his forearm. Slowly, inexorably, the barrel turned toward Nick's face.

Sarah didn't have time to think, only to react. Nick's death was inches away. She sprang from the trunk. Her foot shot up in a clumsy arc and connected with the killer's hand. The pistol flew up and clattered somewhere beyond a pile of boxes. The killer, thrown off balance, couldn't fend off the next blow.

Nick's fist caught him squarely on the jaw. With a look of total surprise, the killer fell backward. His head slammed against a trunk. He slumped to the floor, knocked out cold.

Nick staggered to his feet. "Get going!" he gasped.

She led the way down the attic staircase to the second-floor hallway. Nick was a few paces behind her. Shattered stained glass from the Tiffany lamp littered the carpet. As she sprinted toward the stairs, she suddenly thought of Corrie's body in the foyer. It made her sick to think of running through the blood, but she'd have to do it to reach the front door.

She headed down the stairs, forcing her feet to keep moving. It would take only a few steps to cross the floor, then she'd be out. She'd be safe.

She didn't see the man waiting in the foyer until it was too late. His movement was only a flash, like a snake striking from the shadows. Pain clawed her arm. She was wrenched sideways, into an embrace so tight she couldn't scream. A gloved hand and the heartless gleam of a gun swept past her field of vision. The weapon was not aimed at her; it was aimed at the top of the stairs, where Nick was standing.

The gun went off.

Nick jerked backward, as if punched in the chest. Blood blossomed across his shirt. Sarah screamed. Again and again she screamed Nick's name as she was dragged toward the door. The cold night air hit her face. Bright lights blurred past, and then she was thrust into the back seat of a car. The door slammed shut. She looked up; a gun was pointed at her head.

Only then did she see Kronen's face, the pale blond hair, the waxy smile. In a thousand train stations, in a thousand cities, he had waited for her. It was the face of her nightmares.

It was a face from hell.

VAN DAM WAS still sitting by the phone when Tarasoff called him with word of the bloody fiasco. O'Hara was in the emergency room. The Fontaine woman hadn't been found. Shaken by the news, Van Dam managed to sound appropriately upset.

After the call he rose and began to pace the room. He was uneasy. He worried about this newfound link to the F. Berkman company. That transfer of funds to a contract killer had been incredibly careless. Now Potter sniffed blood, and the persistent little bastard would never let up. Roy Potter was like a dog with his teeth sunk in too deep to let go. Somehow he had to be thrown off track; Van Dam's future depended on it. If the old man were captured, he was likely to be a pragmatist. He would use whatever chips he had to bargain for freedom. And what he had was information: specifically, names. Van Dam's would be among the first revealed.

Events were piling up too fast. If the worst happened, would he have time enough to escape?

Prison. Van Dam shuddered. Soon after Claudia's death, he'd thought about prison, about being shut away in a small, dark room. He'd thought of the four walls, pressing in around him. He'd thought of unwashed bodies and rough hands and things that happened between men who were trapped together. He'd been terrified by those thoughts, and now the terror returned.

He decided to pack, just in case. In minutes the suitcase was ready. He considered his sequence of action. Lock the door. Take the stairs. Hail a taxi. He'd go straight to the Russian embassy. It was a move he'd reserved for only the most desperate of situations, a move he'd hoped to avoid. He'd never cared for the Russians. He wondered how it would be, spending all the years of his life in a dreary Moscow flat. God, no. Was that what lay ahead?

But surely the Russians would treat him well! They made special arrangements for defectors, gave them large flats and abundant privileges. He wouldn't be left to starve. He would be taken care of.

When he was a boy in West Virginia, he and his mother had lived in a two-room shack owned by the mining company. His mother would dump their trash in the woods out back, and when he went to use the outhouse at night, he'd hear the rats, hundreds of them, an army watching from the darkness. He'd do anything to avoid that walk to the outhouse. He would huddle in his bed, fighting the cramps, the urgency. For Van Dam poverty had been more than uncomfortable; it had been horrifying.

He was too deep in thought to notice the footsteps in the hallway. The sudden knock on his door made him jerk around in fright.

"Yes?"

"Status report, sir. May I come in?"

Shaking with relief, Van Dam called through the door: "Look, Tarasoff just called me. Unless there's something new…"

"There is, sir."

Some instinct made Van Dam slide the chain in place. He opened the door a crack.

Just as he did, the door flew open and slammed into his face. Wood splinters rained on the carpet. Van Dam staggered backward, almost knocked senseless by the pain.

He tried to focus. A man was standing in the doorway, a man dressed entirely in black, a man who should be dead. Van Dam's gaze slowly took in something else, something the man was holding. *Why?* he wanted to scream. His whole universe shrank to the size of a small deadly circle, the mouth of a gun.

"This is for Eva," said the man.

He pulled the trigger three times. Three bullets ripped into Van Dam's chest and exploded.

The impact hurled Van Dam to the floor. His scream of pain dribbled to a gurgle, then faded to silence. He had one last, brief image of light as he lay there, a few short seconds that filled him with wonder. It was only the glow of a hotel lamp. Then, bit by bit, the light was blotted out, like dusk falling gently into night.

SARAH HUDDLED ON the wood floor and hugged her knees to her chest. Her teeth were chattering. The room was unheated, and the green satin dress provided little warmth. She had been thrust into darkness. The only light came through a small window high above; it was moonlight, glowing through the clouds. She wondered what time it was. Three o'clock? Four? She'd lost track of the hours. Terror had turned this night into an eternity.

She closed her eyes tightly, but all she could see was Nick's face, his look of surprise and pain, and then the blood, spreading magically across his shirt. A terrible ache rose in her chest, an ache that flooded her throat and spilled out into tears that ran down her cheeks. She dropped her face against her knees, and the tears soaked the satin dress, turning it cold and wet. *Please be alive!* she prayed. *Dear God, please let him be alive!*

But even if he was alive, she was beyond his help. She was beyond anyone's help. In the darkness it had come to her: She was going to die. With this certainty had come a strange peace, a final acknowledgment that her fate was inevitable and that struggling against it was hopeless. She was too cold and tired to care. After days of terror, she at last saw her own death drawing near, and she was calm.

This new peace brought everything sharply into focus. Without panic clouding her every perception, she could study the situation coolly, clinically, the way she once had studied bacteria beneath the lens of her microscope. She concluded that the situation was hopeless.

She was being held in a large storeroom on the fourth floor of an old building. The only way out was through the door, which was now bolted solidly. The window was for ventilation; it was small and too high to reach. The smell of coffee permeated the air and she remembered the roasting ovens she'd seen on the ground floor, and the loading platform, covered with burlap bags stamped F. Berkman, Koffie, Hele Bonen. At the time she'd shuddered, thinking that one of those burlap bags could easily conceal her body.

There might be some small hope from the fact this building was not a residence, but a business. Workers would have to show up sometime. If she screamed, someone would hear her.

Then she remembered that it was Sunday morning. No one would be coming to work today. No one except Kronen.

She stiffened at the creak of footsteps. Someone was climbing the stairs. A door opened and banged shut. Through the cracks she saw light shining from the room next door. Two men were speaking in Dutch. One was Kronen. The other voice was low and hoarse, almost inaudible. The footsteps crossed the room and headed toward her door. She froze as the bolt squealed open.

Light burst in brightly from the next room. She fought to see the faces of the two men standing in the doorway, but at first all she could make out were silhouettes. Kronen flicked on the wall switch. What she saw in that initial flood of fluorescent light made her cringe.

The man towering above her had no face.

The eyes were pale and lashless and as lifeless as cold stones. But as the man took in her appearance, his eyes moved; it was his first sign of life. She realized she was staring at a mask. The face was covered by a featureless shield of flesh-toned rubber. Only the eyes and mouth were visible. What hair he had left grew in wispy white patches on a naked scalp. With a macabre touch of fashion, he had swathed his neck in a bright red silk scarf.

The lashless eyes settled on her face. Before he spoke she

knew who he was. This was the man called Magus. The man Geoffrey should have killed.

"Mrs. Simon Dance," he said. The voice came out in a whisper. His vocal cords, like his face, must have been scarred in the fire. "Stand up, so I may see you better."

She cowered as he grabbed her wrist. "Please," she begged. "Don't hurt me. I don't know anything—really, I don't."

"But you do know something. Why did you leave Washington?"

"It was the CIA. They tricked me…."

"Whom are you working for?"

"No one!"

"Then why did you come to Amsterdam?"

"I thought I'd find Geoffrey—I mean Simon—please, let me go!"

"Let you go? Why should I?"

Her voice stopped working. She stared at him, unable to think of a single good reason why he should let her live. He would kill her, of course. All the pleading in the world wouldn't change things.

Magus turned to Kronen, who was looking profoundly amused. "This is the woman you spoke of?" he asked Kronen incredulously. "This stupid creature? It took you two weeks to find *her*?"

Kronen's smile vanished. "She had help," he pointed out.

"She found Eva without help."

"She is smarter than she looks."

"Undoubtedly." The mask turned back to Sarah. "Where is your husband?"

"I don't know."

"You found Eva. And Helga. Surely you must know how to find your own husband."

She bent her head and stared down at the floor. "He's dead," she whispered.

"You're lying."

"He died in Berlin. The fire."

"Who says this? The CIA?"

"Yes."

"And you believe them?" At her silent nod, the man turned to Kronen in fury. "This woman is worthless! We've wasted our time! If Dance shows up for her, he's a fool."

The contempt in his voice made Sarah stiffen. To Magus her

life was worth nothing more than an insect's. Killing her would be as easy for him as rubbing his heel in the dirt. There would be no regret, no pity; all he'd feel would be distaste. A knot of anger tightened in her belly. With sudden violence her chin came up. If she had to die, it wouldn't be as an insect. Swallowing hard, she lashed out at him defiantly.

"And if my husband does show up," she said, "I hope he sends you straight to hell."

The pale eyes in the mask registered a faint flicker of surprise. "Hell? We'll meet down there in any event. An eternity together, your husband and I. I've already felt the flames. I know what it's like to burn alive."

"I had nothing to do with it."

"But your husband did."

"He's dead! Killing *me* won't make him suffer!"

"I don't kill for the dead. I kill for the living. Dance is alive."

"I'm just an innocent—"

"In this business," he said slowly, "there are no innocents."

"And your wife? What was she?"

"My wife?" He stared off, as though suddenly hypnotized by something on the wall. "My wife…yes. Yes, she was an innocent. I never thought she would be the one…" He turned to her. "Do you know how she died?"

"I'm sorry. I'm sorry for what happened. But can't you see it had nothing to do with me?"

"I saw it. I watched her die."

"Please, won't you listen—"

"From my bedroom window, I saw her walk through the garden to the car. She stopped beside the roses and waved. I have never forgotten that moment. How she waved. And smiled." He tapped his forehead. "It is like a photograph, here, in my mind. The last time I saw her alive…"

He fell silent. Then he turned to Kronen and said, "Before morning move her to a safer place. Where she cannot be heard. If Dance does not come for her in two days, kill her. Make it slow. You know how."

Kronen was smiling. Sarah shuddered as he reached down and playfully ran a strand of her hair through his fingers. "Yes," he said softly. "I know how…." Suddenly his body went rigid, and his jaw snapped up.

Somewhere in the building, an alarm had gone off. Over the door a red light blinked on the warning panel.

"Someone is inside!" said Kronen.

Magus's eyes were bright as diamonds. "It's Dance," he said. "It must be Dance…."

Kronen already had his gun drawn as they ran from the room. The door slammed shut. The bolt squealed into place. Sarah was left alone, her eyes fixed on the red warning light flashing on and off.

The effect was hypnotic. Red, the universal color of alarm, the color of blood, the color of fear, went on blinking. You are going to die, it screamed at her. In two days you are going to die.

Just moments ago she had accepted her own death calmly. Now fear was pumping adrenaline by the quart into her veins. She wanted to live! In panic she lunged at the door, but it was made of solid oak and impossibly strong. Two days, her brain kept repeating. Two days, and then she'd feel Kronen's knife. The way Eve had felt it. But Sarah couldn't let herself think that far ahead. If she did she'd go mad with terror.

The light was still flashing. It seemed to blink faster and faster, accelerating with the pounding of her heart.

She fell back against the door and stared around the room. In their haste to leave, Kronen and Magus had left the lights on. For the first time, she examined her surroundings.

The storeroom was not empty. Cardboard boxes, stamped with F. Berkman, were piled in a corner. She turned first to the boxes and found only a wrinkled invoice, made out in Dutch. Then she spotted a band of strapping tape around the largest box. She tore off the tape and pulled it taut a few times, testing its strength. Used right, it could easily strangle a man. She didn't know if she had the power—or the nerve—to do it. But in her current situation, any weapon—even four feet of old tape—was a gift from heaven.

Next she examined the window. Immediately she discarded it as an escape route. She'd never fit through.

There was only one way out of the room: the door. But how was she to get out?

The stacking chairs gave her an idea. A single chair was light enough to lift and swing. Good. One more weapon. Stacked together, the chairs were so heavy she could barely drag them across the floor. Her plan just might work.

She tugged the stack of chairs to one side of the doorway and tied the strapping tape to a leg of the bottom chair. She strung out the tape and crouched on the opposite side of the doorway. She pulled her end of the tape. It rose a few inches off the floor. If her timing was right, it would work as a trip wire. It would buy her a few seconds, enough time to get through the door.

Over and over she rehearsed her moves. Then she ran through everything with her eyes closed, until she could do it blind. It had to work; it was her only chance.

She was ready. She climbed onto one of the chairs and disconnected the fluorescent light tubes in the ceiling. The room was plunged into darkness. It would be to her advantage; she now knew her way around the room in the darkness. As she was jumping off the chair, she heard what sounded like thunder. It was gunfire echoing off the buildings. Outside there were shouts, then more gunfire. The building was in an uproar. In all the confusion, her escape would be easier.

First she had to draw someone's attention. She took a chair to the window. At the count of three, she swung. The chair shattered the glass.

She heard another shout, then footsteps pounding up the stairs. She brought the chair to the doorway and groped in the darkness for her end of the tape. Where was it?

The footsteps had reached the next room and were crossing to her door. The bolt squealed. Desperately her fingers swept across the floor and came up with the tape just as the door swung open. A man lunged into the room, moving so fast she barely had time to react. She jerked on the tape. It snagged the man by the foot. His momentum almost wrenched the tape out of her hand. Something clattered across the floor. The man pitched forward and fell flat on his belly. At once he scrambled to his knees and started to rise.

Sarah didn't let him. She swung the chair, slamming it on his head. She felt, more than heard, the heavy thud against his skull, and the horror of what she'd done made her drop the chair.

He wasn't moving. But as she rummaged through his pockets, he began to moan, a low, terrible sound of agony. So she hadn't killed him. She found no gun in his pockets. Had he dropped it? There was no time to search the dark room on her hands and knees. Better to run while she could.

She fled the storeroom and bolted the door behind her. One down, she thought with a raw sense of satisfaction. How many more to go?

Now to find her way out of the building. Three flights of stairs and then a front entrance. Could she slip through it all without being seen? No time to think, no time to plan. Every nerve, every muscle, was focused on this last dash for freedom. She was nothing but reflexes now, an animal, moving on instinct.

She dashed through the office and started down the stairs. But a few steps into her descent, she froze. Voices rose from below. They were growing louder. Kronen was climbing the steps—her only escape route was cut off.

She scrambled into the office and closed and bolted the door. Unlike the other door, it was not solid wood. It would hold them off for only a few minutes, no longer. She had to find another way out.

The storeroom was a dead end. But in the office, above the desk, there was a window….

She climbed up on the desk and peered out. All she could see was mist, swirling in the darkness. She tugged at the sash, but it wouldn't budge. Only then did she see that the window had been nailed shut. For security, no doubt. She'd have to break the glass.

Clutching the sash for support, she kicked. The first three tries were worthless; her heel bounced harmlessly off the glass. But on the fourth kick, the window shattered. Shards flew out and rained onto the tiles below. Cold air hit her face. Peering outside, she saw she was at a gable window. A few feet down was a steeply tiled roof that dropped off into darkness. What lay below? It could be a deadly three story fall to the street, or it could slope down to an adjacent roof. In the older blocks of Amsterdam, she'd seen how the buildings were crammed side by side, the roofs running in an almost continuous line. In this mist she had no way of knowing what the darkness hid. Only a fall would tell her….

The tiles would be slippery. She'd be better off barefoot. She bent down and pulled off her shoes. With sudden alarm she noticed the blood on her ankle. Her brain registered no pain; all it noted was the brightness of the blood as it oozed steadily down her foot. Even as she stared at it, mesmerized, she was aware of new noises: Kronen's pounding on the office door, and from the storeroom the loud moans of the man she'd knocked unconscious.

Time was running out.

She stepped through the window, onto the sill. Her dress caught on a shard of broken glass; with a desperate jerk, she ripped the fabric free. For a few seconds she clung by one hand to the sash and groped for another handhold, for some way to pull herself up over the gable. But the roof was too high, and the eaves hung too far out. She was trapped.

The sound of splintering wood forced her to act. Her choice was simple now. A quick death or a painful one. To fall into the darkness, to feel a split second of terror and then to feel nothing at all, would be infinitely better than to die at Kronen's hands. She could stand the thought of dying. Pain was another matter.

She heard the door give way, followed by Kronen's shout of rage. With that shout ringing in her ears, she dropped from the window.

She landed on a roof a few feet below and began sliding helplessly down the tiles. There was nothing to grab on to, nothing to stop her descent. The tiles were too wet; she felt them slipping away beneath her clawing fingers. Her legs dropped over the edge. For an instant she clung to the roof gutter, her feet dangling uselessly. The night sky swirled with mist above her, a sky more beautiful than any she had seen, because it was her last. Her numb fingers could hold on no longer. The gutter slipped from her grasp. Eternity rushed toward her from the darkness.

Chapter Fifteen

"It's only a flesh wound."

"Get back in that bed, O'Hara!" barked Potter.

Nick stalked across his hospital room and flung the closet door open. It was empty. "Where's my damn shirt?"

"You can't walk out of here—you've lost too much blood."

"My shirt, Potter."

"In the garbage. You bled all over it, remember?"

Cursing, Nick wriggled out of his hospital top and glanced down at the bandages on his left shoulder. The pain shot they'd given him in the emergency room was wearing off. He was starting to feel as if someone had taken a sledgehammer to his upper torso. But he couldn't lie around here waiting for something to happen. Too many precious hours had already slipped away.

"Look," said Potter, "why don't you just lie down and let me handle things?"

Nick turned on him in fury. "You mean like you've handled everything else?"

"And what the hell good are *you* gonna do her out there? Tell me that."

Nick turned away, grief suddenly replacing his anger. He

slammed his fist against the wall. "I had her, Roy! I had her in my arms...."

"We'll find her."

"Like you found Eve Fontaine?" Nick shot back.

Potter's face tightened. "No. No, I hope not."

"Then what are you doing about it?" cried Nick.

"We're still waiting for that guy you knocked out to start talking. All we've gotten out of him so far is gibberish. And we're tracking down that other lead, the Berkman Company."

"Search the building!"

"Can't. We need Van Dam's go-ahead and we can't reach him. We also need more evidence—"

"Screw the evidence," muttered Nick, turning toward the door.

"Where you going?"

"To do some breaking and entering."

"O'Hara, you can't go there without backup!" He followed Nick into the corridor.

"I've seen your backup. I think I'd rather have a gun."

"You know how to shoot one?"

"I learn real fast."

"Look, let me clear this through Van Dam—"

"Van Dam?" Nick snorted. "That guy wouldn't clear a trip to the john!" He punched the elevator button, then glanced at Potter's clothes. "Give me your shirt."

"What?"

"Breaking and entering's bad enough. I don't need a charge of indecent exposure."

"You're nuts! I'm not giving you my shirt. I'll get it back full of bullet holes."

Nick hit the elevator button again. "Thanks for the vote of confidence."

The elevator doors suddenly whished open. Potter looked up in annoyance as agent Tarasoff stepped out. "Sir?" said Tarasoff. "We've got a new development."

"Now what?"

"Just came over the police radio. There's been a report of gunfire. The Berkman building."

Nick and Potter stared at each other.

"Gunfire!" said Nick. "My God. Sarah…"

"Where's Van Dam?" Potter snapped.

"I don't know, sir. He still doesn't answer his hotel phone."

"That's it. Let's go, O'Hara!" As the three men rode the elevator down to street level, Potter muttered to Nick, "I don't know why I should put my career on the line for you. I don't even like you. But you're right. We've gotta move in now. By the time Van Dam gives the okay, we'll all be in a damned nursing home." He glanced sharply at Tarasoff. "And that comment's off the record. You got that?"

"Yes, sir."

Potter suddenly eyed Tarasoff's build. "What size are you?"

"Excuse me, sir?"

"Shirt size."

"Uh…sixteen."

"That'll do. Lend your shirt to Mr. O'Hara here. I'm sick of looking at his hairy chest. Don't worry, I'll see he doesn't get blood all over it."

Tarasoff immediately complied, but he looked distinctly ill at ease in his undershirt and jacket. They headed for the parking garage.

"Get on the radio and have the team meet us at the Berkman building."

"Shall I keep trying to get hold of Van Dam?"

Potter hesitated as he caught Nick's glance of warning. "No," he said at last. "For now, let's keep this our own little secret."

Tarasoff gave him a puzzled look as he opened the car door. "Yes, sir."

Nick slid into the back seat. "You know, Potter," he said, easing into Tarasoff's shirt, "maybe you're not as dumb as I thought."

Potter shook his head grimly. "On the other hand, O'Hara, maybe I am," he said. "Maybe I am."

WITH A HOLLOW thud, Sarah landed on her back.

The first thing she felt was wonderment. She was alive. By God, she was alive! For what seemed like hours, she lay there in the darkness, the breath knocked out of her, the sky spinning. Then she saw the gable window, not more than fifteen feet above her, and she realized she had fallen only a short distance. She was lying on an adjacent rooftop.

Kronen's shouts jolted her into action. He was standing above at the window, barking out commands. From somewhere in the darkness below, other voices responded. His men were searching the ground for her body. They wouldn't find it. Soon they'd turn their attention to the rooftop.

She scrambled to her feet. Already her eyes had adjusted to the darkness. She could discern the faint outline of roof against sky. Then it suddenly struck her that it wasn't just her eyes; the sky had lightened. The difference was almost imperceptible; the significance was frightening. Dawn was coming. In minutes she'd be an easy target, scurrying across the tiles. Before the sun rose, she had to make her way to safety.

Flashlight beams streaked below. Footsteps circled the building, and then the men shouted again. They had not found her body.

Sarah was already crawling up the next slope of tiles. The angle was shallow, and she easily reached the apex. She slipped over the top and eased her way down toward the next roof. The mist seemed to close around her in a thick, protective veil. Her dress was soaked from the wet tiles, and the satin clung to her like a freezing second skin. Her bare feet scraped across mortar, which rubbed them raw, but the cold had numbed them so completely she felt no pain. Terror had robbed her of every distraction; the unrelenting awareness of her own death blocked everything else from her mind.

She slid off the tiles onto a flat gravel surface and ran through the lifting darkness to a rooftop door. The knob was ice-cold. The door was locked. She beat it with her fists, beat it until her hands were bruised and she was weak and sobbing. The door did not open. Whirling around, she looked for another escape route—another door, a stairway. With every second the sky brightened. She had to get off this roof! Then a man's far-off shout told her she'd already been spotted.

The next roof loomed before her, a sheer wall of slate. Except for a gable window far above and an antenna at the top, the surface was smooth as ice. She could never climb it.

The shouts came again, closer. A loose tile clattered from the roof and smashed to the sidewalk. She spun around and saw Kronen lowering himself out the broken gable window. He was coming after her.

Like a trapped bird, she circled her rooftop cage, searching desperately for a way off. At the rear of the building, there was only a sheer drop to an alley. She dashed to the other side and stared down. Far below, through fingers of mist, she saw the street. There were no balconies, no stairways, to break her fall if she jumped. There was only the wet pavement, waiting to receive her body.

She heard something clatter across the tiles. Kronen cursed; his gun had fallen to the street. He was already over the top of the second roof. In seconds he'd be on her.

Her eyes darted back to the smooth slate roof, an impassable barrier between her and safety. Staring up, she felt a cold drizzle descend on her face and mingle with her tears. *If only I could fly!* she thought. *If only I could soar away!* Then, through her tears, she sighted a black wire running down the roof from the antenna. Was it strong enough to support her weight? If it broke she might tumble over the edge to the street.

The sound of Kronen's feet hitting the gravel rooftop tore away her last threads of hesitation. Reaching for the wire, she dragged herself up the slate roof. Her toes slid down a few inches, then held. As footsteps crunched across the gravel toward her, she clambered up the roof, out of Kronen's reach.

His curse echoed off the buildings. She didn't dare look back to see if he was following. Every ounce of her concentration was focused ahead, on the soaring surface of gray slate. Her fingers ached. Her feet were raw and swollen. The roof seemed to rise forever; at any moment she expected to hear gunfire from Kronen's men on the ground below, to feel a bullet slam into her back. All she heard was the wind and Kronen's angry shouts. Even without his gun, he could easily kill her. A toss of his knife would send her hurtling to the street. But she knew that Magus wanted her alive. For now.

She kept moving, unable to see her goal, unable to judge how much farther she had to climb. Surely it couldn't be far! she thought desperately. She couldn't hold on much longer.

Her feet gave way beneath her. With a cry she felt her legs swing free. Gravity was pulling her relentlessly downward, an unshakable force she couldn't fight. Her arms were exhausted. As she struggled for a foothold, her right calf twisted into a cramp. She felt the wire slipping through her hands. Then, nudged aside by a sudden breath of wind, the mist faded and she saw, only inches away, the top of the roof.

Somehow she found the strength to drag herself upward. At last her fingers closed around the antenna. The metal felt so solid, so strong! She pulled herself those last few inches to the top. There she collapsed against the hard angle of slate, her arms hugging the sides of the roof. She had to rest, just for a few seconds. She had to let the cramp ease from her calf.

But when she raised her head and looked down at the other side, she saw there was nowhere else to go. She had reached the end of the line. No other rooftop lay below to catch her. There was only a drop to the street.

Tears of despair streamed down her face. She lowered her head and sobbed into the slate, sobbed like a terrified child at what she could not escape. The sound of her own cries drowned out everything else.

Then gradually she was aware of another sound, faint at first, but growing louder: two notes piercing the dawn, over and over. A siren.

Kronen heard it, too. He stared up at her like a man possessed. Pacing back and forth, he searched for some other way up. There was none. Cursing, he grabbed the wire and started up the roof. He was coming after her.

In disbelief she watched him climb. He was long and wiry; he moved like a monkey up the slate roof. Frantically she worked at the wire, trying in vain to disconnect it from the antenna. She'd never get it loose in time. With nowhere else to go, she backed away from the edge. She could already hear his breathing, loud and harsh, as he neared the top. She tried to stand. Tottering on bruised feet, she waited for him. The siren grew louder. Just a few moments more! That's all she needed!

Kronen's fingers closed over the top. Frozen, she watched as his head rose above the peak. His eyes locked on hers. She saw no anger or hatred; what she saw was infinitely more terrifying: anticipation. He was looking forward to her death.

"No!" she screamed, her voice piercing the mist. *"No!"*

She lashed out at him. Her fingers clawed at his eyes, forcing him backward, toward the edge. He grabbed her wrist, twisting it so hard she cried out. Wrenching free, she stumbled and almost lost her balance. He scrambled onto the top. Slowly he came toward her.

For a moment they stood staring at each other, the wind making them sway uneasily on the wet slate. It had come to this—the two of them alone on a rooftop. One of them would not survive. She would not let him take her alive.

His hand slid into his jacket. A knife appeared. Even in the dull gray dawn, the blade seemed to glitter. He held it easily, almost casually, as if it were nothing more than a toy.

She took another step backward. How far did she have left? How far until retreat took her to the other edge? The blade moved closer. Taking her alive was no longer his goal. He was going to kill her. Through a curtain of mist, she saw him coil for the spring. She saw the blade, thrusting toward her. Her arms crossed in front of her, an automatic gesture of protection. Pain shot through her forearm as the blade came down on naked flesh. She crumpled to her knees. His shoes creaked as he came to stand over her. His heel planted itself heavily on a fold of her dress, trapping her against the roof. She could not escape now. She couldn't even stand. In silent dread she watched the blade rise again in a deadly arc.

All her feral instincts rose to a last, desperate act of survival. With a cry she hurled herself at his knees. He staggered backward, tottering on one leg, struggling for balance. She didn't let him regain it. She lunged at his foot.

The blow swept his ankle out from under him. He twisted, clawing to hold on. The knife clattered down the slate. As he started to drop toward the street, he caught the top of the roof, but only for a second. His eyes met Sarah's; it was a look of infinite surprise. He slid away, his eyes still staring upward, his arms reaching toward the sky. She shut her eyes. Long after he hit the street below, his scream was still echoing in her ears.

She was going to be sick. The world seemed to spin around her. Dropping her head, she pressed her cheek against the cold, wet slate and fought off the nausea. There she huddled, shivering, as the sound of sirens and voices rose up from the street. She was too cold, too exhausted, to move. Only when she heard Nick's shout did she stir.

It's not possible, she thought. *I'm imagining things. I saw him die....*

Yet there he was, standing on the street, waving wildly at her. Tears sprang to her eyes. She wanted to shout that she loved him, that she would always love him, but she was crying too hard for anything sensible to come out.

"Don't move, Sarah!" shouted Nick. "We're calling for a fire truck to get you down!"

She wiped the tears away and nodded. *It's all over,* she thought, watching three more police cars pull up with sirens blaring. *It's all over....*

But she had forgotten about Magus.

A loud slam made her turn and look down. A door had opened and closed. Magus emerged on the graveled roof just below. He carried a rifle. Only she could see him. From the street where Nick and the police stood, Magus was invisible. He was a lone man, trapped on a rooftop. A man about to make one last gesture in the name of vengeance. For a moment he stood staring at her, like a man longing for the one thing he cannot have. Then slowly he raised his rifle. She watched the barrel point up at her and waited for the fatal blast.

The rifle's crack thundered over the rooftops. *Where is the pain?* she thought, *Why don't I feel the pain...?*

Then, in wonderment, she saw Magus stagger backward, his shirt splattered brightly with blood. The rifle thudded to the gravel. He made a sound, a death cry that might have been only a name. With his eyes wide open, he collapsed on his back. He didn't move.

On another rooftop something glittered. It drew Sarah's attention away from the bloodied body, beckoning her gaze with the brightness of spun gold. The sun burst through the last veil of mist. It fell in a brilliant beam upon the head and shoulders of a man standing on a high roof two buildings away. The man lowered his rifle. The wind whipped his shirt and hair. He was looking at her. She could not see his face, but she knew, in that instant, who he was. In a trance she tried to stand up. As he faded from view, she tried to reach out to him, to call him back, to thank him before he disappeared forever.

"Geoffrey!" she screamed.

The wind swept her voice up and carried it away. "No, come back! Come back!" she screamed, over and over. But all she saw was a last glimpse of golden hair, and then there was only a wet, empty roof, sparkling beneath the morning sun.

ON THE STREET below Sarah, the rifle crack echoed like thunder over the rooftops. A half dozen cops immediately dived for cover. Nick froze in alarm. "What's going on?" he cried.

Potter turned and barked to Tarasoff, "Who the hell's shooting up there?"

"Not one of ours, sir. Maybe the cops—"

"That was a rifle, dammit!"

"It was not my men," said a Dutch police officer, peering out from the safety of a nearby doorway.

Nick looked up and saw immediately that Sarah was still alive. Frantically his eyes searched the surrounding windows. Who had fired the shot? Was Sarah the target? Down here, on the street, he was totally helpless to save her. Panicking, he shouted at Potter, "For God's sake, *do something*!"

"Tarasoff!" yelled Potter. "Get your men up there! Find out where the hell that shot came from!" He turned to the Dutch cop. "How long till the ladder gets here?"

"Five, ten minutes."

"She'll be dead by then!" said Nick, taking off toward the buildings. He didn't look twice as he passed the dead body lying on the blood-spattered sidewalk. He had to get to Sarah.

"O'Hara!" shouted Potter. "We've got to clear the building first!"

But Nick was already across the street and heading for the door. The building was unlocked. Inside, he took the stairway two steps at a time. All the way up, he was terrified he would hear a second rifle shot, terrified that he'd emerge on the roof and find Sarah dead. But all he heard were his own footsteps pounding up the stairs.

Somewhere below, a door slammed shut. Potter's voice shouted, "O'Hara?"

Nick kept going.

The wide steps led to a small staircase that spiraled to the roof. He dashed up the last steps and scrambled through the door at the top.

Outside, the sun was shining. Nick halted, stunned by the sudden burst of light and by the horror of what lay in the gravel at his feet. The dead eyes of a faceless man stared up at him. A red silk scarf fluttered in the wind, as bright and alarming as the blood seeping slowly from the man's chest. Beside him lay a rifle.

The roof door flew open. Potter rushed through and almost collided with Nick.

"My God!" said Potter, staring at the body. "It's Magus! Did he shoot himself?"

From a roof above them came a sudden wail, a ghostly sound of despair. Nick looked up in alarm.

Sarah was reaching out helplessly, as though pleading with the wind. She didn't notice Nick or Potter; she was gazing into the distance, at something only she could see. What she screamed next made Nick shudder. It didn't make sense; it was the cry of a terrified woman, driven to hysteria. He turned and looked in the direction of her gaze. He saw only rooftops, wet and sparkling in the sunlight. And echoing off the buildings, he heard Sarah's voice, over and over, screaming to a man who did not exist.

When they finally brought her down from the roof, she was quiet and composed. Nick was right beside her as they lowered her onto the stretcher. She looked so small and weak and cold. There was so much blood on her arms. He was scarcely aware of what he said or did at that moment; he only knew he wanted to be near her.

Down on the street, the ambulance was waiting. "Let me ride with her," Nick muttered, brushing off Potter's restraining hand. "She needs me."

"Just keep out of their way, O'Hara."

Nick climbed in beside Sarah's stretcher. She was awake. "Sarah?"

She turned her head and gazed at him in wonder. "I thought I'd never see you again," she whispered.

"Sarah, I love you."

Potter stuck his head in the ambulance. "For God's sake, O'Hara! Give 'em some room to work in!"

Nick glanced around and saw the two attendants scowling at him.

"No, please!" Sarah pleaded. "Let him stay. I want him to stay."

Potter gave the attendants a shrug of helplessness. Grumbling, they went on with their work. From the looks they exchanged, it was obvious what they thought of this extra passenger. But they decided it was better to leave Nick alone. From experience they knew that frantic husbands could be stubborn, unreasonable creatures. And this one, obviously, was very, very frantic.

Chapter Sixteen

WITH AN OVERWHELMING SENSE OF RELIEF, Roy Potter watched the ambulance pull away from the curb. Even after it had turned the corner, he could still hear the siren's two notes piercing the quiet Sunday morning. As the sound faded into the maze of Amsterdam streets, Potter stifled a yawn and walked toward the other ambulance, which was parked a few yards away. For the first time in twenty-four hours, he could allow himself to feel tired. No, exhausted was a better word. Exhausted and triumphant. The operation was over.

Mentally he tabulated their gains. Magus and his key associate were dead. Four other men were in custody. And last, but not least, Sarah Fontaine was alive.

She would need hospitalization, of course. She had sustained nasty lacerations on her arms and feet; they'd probably require a surgeon's skill. More important, she would need immediate psychiatric attention. She'd been hallucinating, seeing ghosts on rooftops. Under the circumstances, hysteria was perfectly understandable. It might take weeks, even months, to recover from the ordeal she'd just survived. But she would recover. He had no doubt about it. Sarah Fontaine, he'd decided, was made of sterner stuff than anyone had suspected.

Potter watched as the next stretcher was loaded into the waiting ambulance. The siren would be silent this time; both men were dead. He shuddered, remembering the sight of Kronen's body on the sidewalk. Thank God the ambulance crew had cleared it away so quickly. After a night of nothing but black coffee, Potter's stomach was just waiting for an excuse to puke. Would have been damned undignified, to say the least, especially with a dozen Dutch cops standing around as witnesses.

The second stretcher was now being placed in the vehicle. It was Magus. Potter frowned, wondering at the irony of the old man's suicide. After all these years of evading capture, Magus had chosen to take his own life. Or had he? The ballistics lab would surely confirm it. Suicide was the only explanation. There had been no other gunman. None, that is, except for the one seen by Sarah Fontaine, and she'd seen nothing but a ghost.

"Mr. Potter?"

He turned. A Dutch policeman was coming toward him through the knot of bystanders.

"What is it?"

"There is a man inside who wishes to see you. An American, I think."

"Have him talk to Mr. Tarasoff."

"He said he'd only talk to you."

Potter stifled a curse. What he really wanted to do right now was crawl into bed. But he grudgingly followed the officer through the police line, into the F. Berkman building. The smell of coffee was everywhere; it reminded him he'd hardly eaten since the previous afternoon. Breakfast would taste good right now. Bacon and eggs and then an honest-to-God hot shower. Hell, he deserved it. They all deserved it. He made a mental note to put in a commendation for Tarasoff and the others. They'd held up well.

The officer nodded toward the front office. "There he is."

Potter glanced through the doorway and frowned. The man standing at the window had his back turned. He was dressed completely in black. There was something disturbingly familiar about the golden color of his hair, which was sparkling in the window's light.

Potter went in and closed the door. "I'm Roy Potter," he said. "Did you want to see me?"

The man turned and smiled. "Hello, Mr. Potter."

Potter's jaw dropped. He couldn't speak. He could only stare like a dumb animal. *What the hell is going on?* he thought. *Am I seeing ghosts, too?*

It was Simon Dance.

AN HOUR LATER Simon Dance—the man once known as Geoffrey Fontaine—finally turned and wandered back to the window. For a moment he stood there motionless, his face silhouetted against the sunlight. "So that, Mr. Potter, is what happened," he said softly. "Rather more complicated than you suspected. I thought you might appreciate hearing the facts. In return I ask only that one favor."

"If I'd only known—why the hell didn't you tell me all this before?"

"It was instinct at first. Then the explosives appeared in my hotel room. That's when I was certain. I knew I couldn't trust you. Any of you. There'd been a leak all along. High level, I'm afraid."

Potter said nothing. Somehow he'd already guessed who it might be.

"Van Dam," said Dance.

"How can you be sure?"

Dance shrugged. "Why does a man leave his warm hotel at midnight to use a phone booth?"

"When was this?"

"Last night, right after I tipped O'Hara."

"That was your call?" Cursing softly, Potter shook his head. "Then it's partly my fault. I told Van Dam about the tip. I had to."

Dance nodded. "I didn't understand his little walk to the phone booth. At first. Then I heard that Kronen and his men appeared at Casa Morro shortly afterward. That's when I knew who Van Dam had called. Magus."

"Look, I need more evidence. You don't expect me to proceed on the basis of one phone call?"

"No, no. The matter has already been taken care of."

"What do you mean?"

"You'll understand. Shortly."

"What about his motive? A man doesn't go bad without a good reason!"

Calmly Dance lighted a cigarette and shook out the match. "Motives are funny things. We all have them. We all have our secrets, our hidden agendas. Van Dam was a wealthy man, I understand."

"His wife left him millions."

"Was she old when she died?"

"In her forties. There was some kind of crime involved. A burglary, I think. Van Dam was out of the country at the time."

"Of course he was."

Potter fell silent. There it was. Motive. Yes, if you looked deep enough, you might find it, hidden in the shadows of a man's life. "I'll begin an internal investigation," he said. "Immediately."

Dance smiled. "No hurry. I doubt he'll be vanishing any time soon."

"What about you?" asked Potter. "Now that it's over, will you surface?"

Dance slowly blew out a cloud of smoke. "I don't know what I'll do yet," he said, staring off sadly. "Eva was the only thing that ever mattered to me. And I've lost her."

"There's still Sarah."

Dance shook his head. "I've caused her enough pain." He turned and looked out the window again. "Your ballistics report will reveal that Magus was killed not by his own rifle, but by a bullet fired from a distance. Promise me Sarah will never learn this fact."

"If that's what you want."

"It's what I want."

"You won't even say goodbye to her?"

"It's kinder if I don't." Dance squinted out at the street. The last police car had just driven off. The bystanders were gone. Except for the bloodstains on the curb, it looked like any Amsterdam street on a Sunday morning. "Mr. O'Hara seems like a good man," he said softly. "I think they'll be happy together."

Potter nodded. Yes, he had to admit, Nick O'Hara wasn't so bad after all. "Tell me, Dance," he said. "Did you ever love Sarah?"

Dance shook his head. "In this business love is always a mistake. No, I didn't love her. But I did not want her harmed." He gave Potter a hard look. "Next time, avoid the use of innocents in your operations. We cause enough misery in this world without making those who are blameless suffer."

Potter was suddenly uncomfortable. The whole operation had been his idea; if Sarah had been killed, he'd be the one responsible. Thank God she'd survived.

"Someday," said Dance, "I'll tell you how the operation should have been run. You're still amateurs. But you'll learn. You'll learn." He took one last puff and stubbed out his cigarette. "Now I think it's time I be on my way. I have a great deal to do."

"Will you be going back to the States? If so, I'll see what I can do to get you a new identity—"

"That won't be necessary. I've always managed best on my own."

Potter couldn't argue that point. Dance's one brief affiliation with the Company had almost proved fatal for him.

"I think perhaps a change in climate will suit me," said Dance as he walked to the door. "I have never liked the dampness. Or the cold."

"What if I need to get hold of you?"

"I'm afraid I won't be available, Mr. Potter."

"But—but how do I find you?"

Dance paused in the doorway. For a moment he was thoughtful. Then, with a smile, he said, "You can't."

IT WAS LATE afternoon when Sarah woke up. The first thing she saw was the white curtains, blowing gently beside the open window. Slowly her unfocused gazed took in the pots of red and yellow tulips, sitting in a row on the table. And then, in a chair beside her bed, she saw Nick clutching a tulip pot in his lap. He was fast asleep. His shirt was a map of wrinkles and sweat. His hair was streaked with more gray than she'd remembered. But he was smiling.

She reached over and touched his hand. With a start he woke up and looked at her with bloodshot eyes.

"Sarah," he murmured.

"My poor, poor Nick. I think you need this bed more than I do."

"How are you feeling?"

“Strange. Safe.”

“You are safe, Sarah.” He put the tulip pot down and took her hands. “You really are.”

She gazed at the table. “Oh, look at all the flowers!”

“I guess I overdid it. I didn’t know two dozen pots would go so far.”

They both laughed then, a tentative laugh that quickly faded. Neither of them was ready to let go of the fear. Not yet. Too much had happened. In silence he watched her and waited.

“I did see him, Nick,” she said softly. “I know I did.”

“It doesn’t matter, Sarah….”

“But it *does* matter. To me. Whether he was real or imagined—I saw him….” She sank back on the pillows and stared up at the ceiling. “And I’ll always wonder.”

“When you’re scared, your mind can do funny things.”

“Perhaps.”

“I don’t believe in ghosts.”

“Neither did I. Until today.”

He took her hand and pressed it to his lips. “If he was a ghost, then I owe him one. For letting me keep you.” Nick looked so rumpled, so tired, as his dark head bent down to her palm. A sudden, overwhelming wave of tenderness swept through her. He raised his head and she saw, in his tired gray eyes, the love she’d never really seen in Geoffrey’s.

“I love you, Nick,” she said. “And you’re right. Maybe, just for a moment, I *was* seeing things. I was so scared. And there was no one else to help me. No one but a ghost.”

“He’s dead, Sarah. Your seeing him then—at that moment—it was just your way of saying goodbye.”

There was a knock at the door. They looked up as Roy Potter stuck his head in the room. “Both awake, I see,” he said cheerily. “Can I come in?”

Sarah smiled. “Of course, Mr. Potter.”

Potter stared at the tulip pots and whistled. “Wow. What’d you do, O’Hara? Go into the flower business?”

“Just being romantic.”

“Romantic? A slob like you?” Potter winked at Sarah. “Better tell this guy to shave. Before he’s arrested for vagrancy.”

She stroked the stubble on Nick's jaw. "I think he looks just wonderful."

Potter shook his head in wonderment. "Just goes to prove love really is blind." He gave Sarah a thoughtful look. "The doc says you'll be released in the morning. You feeling up to it?"

"I think so." She nodded at her bandaged arm. "It's sore. They had to put in a dozen or so stitches." Nick's arm came around her shoulder and she glanced up at him. "But I'm sure I'll be all right."

For a few seconds, Potter regarded them in silence. "Yeah," he said at last. "I think you'll be all right."

"So your operation's wrapped up?" asked Nick.

"Just about. We've still got a few…details to clean up. A few things we hadn't expected. But you know how it is in this business. For every gain you take a few losses. Those dead agents in Margate. Eve Fontaine."

"And Geoffrey," said Sarah softly.

Potter fell silent again. "Anyway," he said after a pause, "what's next for you two?"

"Home," said Nick, taking Sarah's hand. "We've got a flight back to D.C. day after tomorrow."

"And then what?"

Nick's eyes turned to Sarah. "I'll let you know," he said softly.

The room fell silent. Potter got the message, loud and clear. It was time to leave these two alone. Rising, he patted Nick on the back. "Well, good luck to both of you. I'll put in a good word with your boss, Nick. That is, if you want your job back."

Nick didn't answer. His eyes were still locked with Sarah's.

"Okay," muttered Potter as he walked unnoticed to the door. "Then I'll just tell old Ambrose that Nick O'Hara says go to hell." In the doorway he turned and glanced back one last time to see Nick pulling Sarah into his arms. They didn't say a word, but the way they held each other said everything. Potter shook his head and grinned. Yes, Simon Dance was right. Nick and Sarah would be happy together.

Suddenly the afternoon sun burst through the clouds and flooded the room so brightly Potter had to squint. At that instant, Nick took Sarah's face in his hands and kissed her. And as he watched their lips meet, it seemed to Roy Potter that all the world's shadows had suddenly vanished, taking with them forever the ghost of Geoffrey Fontaine.